THE DRAGON LEGACY

COMPLETE SERIES

BROADFEATHER BOOKS
www.AuthorNicoleConway.com

Ma
LUN
LAPILOQUE'S TREE

CLARAX
CERNHEIST
BARROWTON

BOWFIN

AUSTLEN
Brine's
WESTWATCH
Brinto
FARCHASE

CANRACK
ISLANDS
MARSH
Blybrig
Academy
M
IVANGOL
SALTM
WO

...RDA

LUNSURAI

AVLAR

NORTHWATCH

HIGHLAND COUNTRY

DAYRISE

OSBRAN

Port Murlowe

Breaker's Cliffs

LDOBAR

EASTWATCH

Solhelm

FARROW ESTATE

HALFAX

PRISON CAMP RUINS

TWO RIVERS

...VATCH

...AILSPOT

N W E S

THE DRAGONRIDER LEGACY COMPLETE SERIES

NICOLE CONWAY

BROADFEATHER
BOOKS

THE PANTHEON OF MALDOBAR

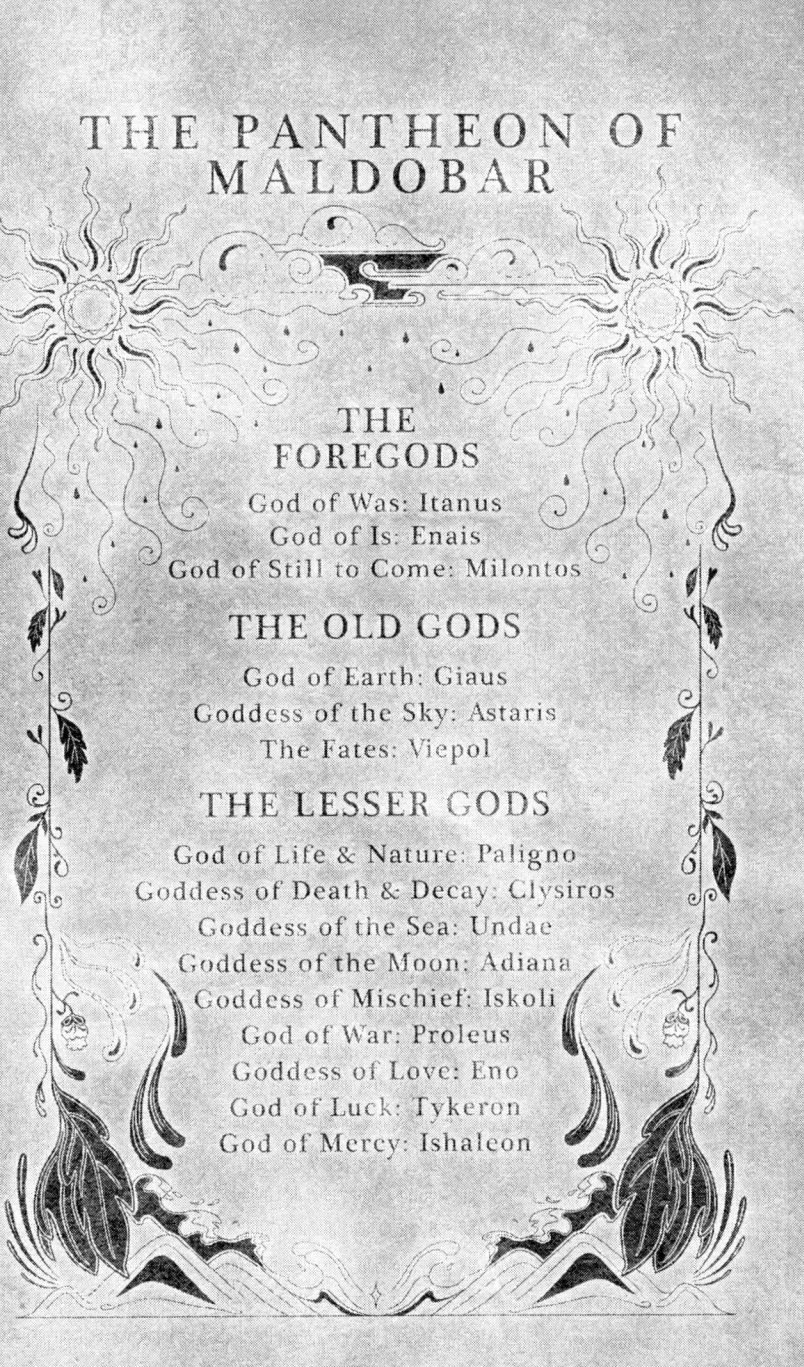

THE FOREGODS

God of Was: Itanus
God of Is: Enais
God of Still to Come: Milontos

THE OLD GODS

God of Earth: Giaus
Goddess of the Sky: Astaris
The Fates: Viepol

THE LESSER GODS

God of Life & Nature: Paligno
Goddess of Death & Decay: Clysiros
Goddess of the Sea: Undae
Goddess of the Moon: Adiana
Goddess of Mischief: Iskoli
God of War: Proleus
Goddess of Love: Eno
God of Luck: Tykeron
God of Mercy: Ishaleon

REIGH'S ORIGINS

A Dragonrider Bonus Short Story

Reigh's Origins
A Dragonrider Short Story

CHAPTER ONE

I winced as the baby let out a shrill cry. His tiny face scrunched, going almost as red as his fiery-hued hair for a moment as he screamed. For his size, he had an impressive capability for volume—something my people took as a sign of strength in babies, be they elf or human. He'd also grown a bit in the two weeks since I'd last seen him. Another good sign. He was healthy, despite his bizarre entrance into the world.

"You must remember to keep him warm, but not too hot. That shouldn't be so troublesome in Luntharda. I hear it's quite warm there." The old woman smiled, deepening the creases around her eyes and mouth. Hers was a face I knew well enough. She'd served in the royal household for quite sometime, as I had. We'd seen one another in passing. Now, she too was moving on, looking for a change of scenery elsewhere.

But first, there was this small matter to attend to.

"You can give him goat's milk, but human or elf would be best. Reach out to a midwife, they usually know a wet nurse or someone who can help." Miss Harriet continued to prattle while the infant wriggled and wailed. "Are you sure you can manage on your own?"

No. I absolutely was not sure about any of this. Even as she passed the squirming bundle of cloth to me, my chest grew tight. Every breath was a struggle. The baby let out another high-pitched shriek. My hands shook as I moved to cradle him in my arms. I nestled his head right into the crux of my elbow to support his fragile neck.

"My, my." Miss Harriet had a strange, wistful smile on her lips. "You seem to know what you're doing."

I frowned. "It is not the first time I have held a child."

She nodded; probably assuming I was talking about Aubren and Jenna. True, I had held both of them a few times as infants. But my experience with babies hadn't begun with them, either.

Just the mere thought put a hard knot in the center of my chest, as though someone were slowly pressing a cold blade into it. This was insanity. By all the gods, what was I doing? I must have lost my mind entirely. This was doomed to fail—*I* was doomed to fail.

"Is that so? Then I don't have to warn you that they don't sleep through the night," she laughed softly. "Or at least, this one doesn't. He's as ravenous as a little dragonlet. Hardly makes it two hours before he's howling for more."

"I can manage," I insisted stiffly.

The baby screamed louder, his tiny mouth opening wide as he cried and squirmed in my arms. His tiny hands clenched into fists, tucked up around his face as he wobbled his head, searching for something to suckle. He was hungry, indeed.

"Here, this should make him happier." The old woman shuffled away, disappearing into the small farmhouse's kitchen. She came back with a glass feeder bottle shaped like a fist-sized egg. One end had a short spout tipped with a soft leather nipple with a small hole pricked—just enough to let milk through if the baby were to nurse against it. I'd seen this sort of contraption before while working as a medic's apprentice. The Maldobarians used them to feed infants in the absence of a mother or if the mother's milk proved insufficient. There were a variety of reasons it might be used, and so long as all the pieces were kept clean, it was perfectly safe to use.

Miss Harriet handed me bottle with a knowing smile. "I've never seen a newborn eat like this one. He's an insatiable little thing."

As soon as he was presented with the leather nipple, the baby in my arms practically lunged for it. The smell of the milk was all the encouragement he needed. Latched on and suckling fiercely, he finally went silent and lay still in my arms. His big eyes blinked up at me with a moment of what almost seemed like clarity. I could have sworn our gazes met.

I knew better, of course. At this age, babies orientated primarily by scent. Their instincts were to seek out the smell of nourishment and the comfort of body warmth. Armed with a bottle of warm goat's milk, he was bound to be as content with me as anyone else.

"Well you certainly seem to have the magic touch, Kiran." Miss Harriet stepped around me, holding up a long piece of soft linen cloth. "This will make carrying him easier. I know you've a long way to go," she explained as she began to wrap the fabric around the child and me. She positioned the baby so that he was tied against my chest with his head at my shoulder. "They like this, you see—

the closeness, the sound of your heart, and the motion of your movement. It's soothing to them."

Nostalgia made my stomach swim. "Yes, I ... I remember my mother doing this with—" I stopped short, biting back against the words. The memory was still too near. A wound that would never heal. Now, with yet another child now depending on me for survival, fear like an earthquake tremored violently in my soul. This was a mistake. I was unfit. Gods and Fates—why? Why had I volunteered to do this?

Miss Harriet didn't seem to notice my uneasiness. "Indeed. It was a Gray elf that showed me this method, years ago. Long before the war." She checked the wrapping and then gave the child an affectionate pet on the back. "Good of you to take him in. I didn't know Gray elf men did such things."

Normally, they didn't. Especially not men in my situation. To become a father was the highest honor a Gray elf man could achieve. It was not something to be taken on lightly, or by a man without any family here or in Luntharda. My people had long believed that the children you sired would carry your legacy, your teachings, with them forever and pass them on to future generations. To have that tiny piece of yourself preserved for all of time was, undeniably, the most precious thing any man could ask for.

But this child was not mine—not by blood. His ears were round and his skin as pale as cream. The fine layer of fuzzy, downy hair on his head was as red as flame. His blood was purely human and yet the Fates had apparently schemed to entwine our lives. For how long, I had no idea. All I did know was that I, a former slave, scout, and ambassador for the royal court, was now his only chance at survival. An utterly terrifying truth that froze me down to the very marrow of my bones. It took every ounce of my willpower to keep my expression collected. I didn't want to appear fazed or unequal to the task.

"He seems to like you," the old woman crooned. "Have you decided on a name?"

My body tensed as that piercing tightness rose in my chest again. Memories like drops of acid sizzled over my brain. "He already has a name," I replied as I turned for the door. "He will be called Reigh."

She arched one of her eyebrows. "But isn't that a human name?"

I didn't answer. What good would it do to give him an elf name? There was no mistaking him for one. Besides, it was not my place to change the one thing his parents had given him.

"You should get going," Miss Harriet sighed. "The sun is rising. Won't the caravan be leaving soon?"

I nodded. It was time.

Gathering my cloak, bag, bow, and quiver on the way, I slung them over my shoulder and started toward the door. Having the baby tied to my chest threw my balance off. My movements were limited, and I struggled to keep a grip on my gear and hold the bottle at the same time. I couldn't run. Even walking was awkward. I wouldn't be able to fight or defend myself. We were utterly vulnerable.

That realization brought me to an abrupt halt in the doorway, staring out at the sleeping city of Halfax. It stood, cold and silent, only a few miles away. From the steps of the small farmhouse, I could barely see the faint glimmering of lights dotting the buildings and even glowing through the windows of the castle. Beyond the city, the first rays of morning light burned the horizon deep purple and scarlet.

It was just enough light to see the silhouettes of large winged beasts approaching from the south. I knew exactly what they were—dragonriders from Southwatch. I'd seen more than my share of those mighty, flame-spitting creatures while living here. And yet, the sight of dragons soaring high, the rising sun shimmering across their scaly hides, never ceased to amaze and terrify me. Their broad, bat-like wings caught the gusting winds that howled across the open plains. From miles away, I could hear their roar like a faint roll of thunder. They were the masters of the sky—Maldboar's champions and greatest defenders. I had once called them enemies. Then they became my allies and friends. Now, they were just a memory. My time in Maldobar had come to an end.

There was nothing left for me here.

The icy wind stung my eyes and bit at my cheeks and nose. I wrapped my cloak around us tighter, turned to shield the baby from the brunt of it.

"Take care of yourself, Kiran," Miss Harriet murmured quietly. She stood right behind me, her weary eyes panning the sky. "Beautiful, aren't they?"

"What?"

"The stars." She was looking up, beyond the reach of the sun's light, to where the dark night sky still boasted millions of sparkling pinpricks.

My skin prickled, though not because of the cold. Worry seized my throat. I couldn't answer. After this, I might never be able to simply look at the stars anymore.

For me, their majesty was forever tainted.

CHAPTER TWO

Five days—five grueling, utterly exhausting days. That's how long it took to get from Halfax to Dayrise by horse-drawn wagon.

It might as well have been an eternity.

My eardrums throbbed and my brain seemed to pulse with sharp agony as Reigh began to wail from the wicker basket where I'd placed him to try and steal a moment to eat. Just a few bites of food, maybe a short nap, that's all I needed— and exactly what I couldn't seem to get. With his back arching and fists clenched in tiny rage, he gave one shrill cry after another. He hardly even stopped to take a breath, sometimes screaming until his whole face turned purple.

I buried my face in my hands.

His crying seemed ceaseless. He cried when he soiled a diaper, and then screamed even louder when I changed him. He cried when he was hungry, which was nearly all the time. He cried when he was tired, every time the wagon bounced too hard, or if something startled him.

After five days and only a few hours sleep, my sanity was beginning to slip. I hadn't so much as stopped to eat a full meal in that time. Keeping the bottles cleaned, the diapers washed, and making sure he was fed—it was all I could take. At last, the wife of one of the merchants in our company offered to try holding and nursing him. She had her own infant, a girl who was apparently used to the commotion of a fourteen-wagon caravan constantly moving along Maldobar's rugged coastline.

"It's no trouble," the young woman insisted as she took my screaming baby into her arms. "Go and have a nap. You look like you could use a rest."

In that moment, I wondered if she might be a goddess in disguise—sent to save me in this moment of utter desperation. I couldn't help but stare in total envy as she nursed Reigh, humming to him a tune that seemed to mimic the rumble and roll of the moving wagons. My eyes got heavy. Reigh was already asleep, lulled into a deep slumber almost immediately.

I barely made it back to the cramped space I had bought for us in the back of the very last wagon before I collapsed. All the wagons were styled the same with tall, square metal frames over the top that protected the contents from the elements thanks to a thick tarp made of heavily oiled leather. Some even had small metal chimneys poking up through them from travel-sized stoves inside. Each wagon was drawn by four large horses who lurched along doggedly day after day, stopping only a few hours to eat and drink. Food would have been nice for me, too. A bath would have been utter bliss. But sleep trumped all other needs, and I was unconscious as soon as collapsed onto my bedroll.

It was past dark when I awoke. There was a large puddle of drool on my bedroll, making my face cold and sticky. I sat up, rubbing my forehead and raking my hair from my face. It was matted with dirt and knots, and I could smell the stench of my own sweat. Gods, how could I have ever thought I could do this alone? Stupid ... idiotic ... completely insane.

Flexing against the soreness in my back and shoulders, I grabbed the linen wrap, a clean diaper, and jumped out of the back of our wagon. I reached the middle of the caravan at a jog, easily finding the place where I'd left Reigh with the merchant's wife. Peering through the door flap in the tarp, I spied her still sitting on the floor of their rolling homestead. She had Reigh stretched out on a wool blanket in front of her, propped up on his stomach.

Panic shot through my body to see him that way. He could smother! He wasn't strong enough for this yet.

Or was he?

As I bolted through the doorway into the back of the wagon, Reigh's head bobbed up and he lifted up onto his elbows for a second or two. He let out a gurgle and flopped back down again, his head coming to rest safely on its side.

My heart still pounded and my body shivered with adrenaline as I looked to the merchant's wife for an explanation. Why would she put him down that way?

"It's all right," she consoled with a calm smile. "They need to be on their bellies a little. It helps them grow stronger. Think of it as play."

"Play?" I barked in disbelief. Was she serious? He couldn't even sit up on his own. How could he possibly play?

"It all begins simply. Eventually he will crawl, sit up, and fidget with toys. But for now, this is all he needs," she explained as she patted the spot beside her. "Have a seat. Would you like something to drink?"

I tried not to let my eyes water with gratitude as I nodded. Sitting down beside her, I watched Reigh continue to squirm and kick on his stomach. Every now and then, he would lift his head shakily and look around while trying to get his elbows underneath him while giving little grunts of effort. It only lasted a few seconds each time, but I had to admit, he did seem amused. At least he wasn't crying.

"You can call me Leila." The merchant's wife flashed me a quick glance. Perhaps she didn't see many gray elf men. "Do you like cider?"

"Yes, thank you." Honestly, I would have taken anything she offered at that point—wine, ale, or a cup of drool—as long as it was hot enough to chase the chill out of my body and the weariness from my soul.

Leila passed me a ceramic cup filled with something that smelled faintly of apples and cinnamon. Just the feel of the warm mug in my hands made me feel a little less haggard. I took a sip of the spicy drink and let out a deep, involuntary sigh.

She giggled. "If it's any consolation, the first 6 weeks are always the hardest. It's like a trial by fire. You're doing just fine."

My mouth scrunched as I stared down into the mug. "It doesn't seem that way. He has spent nearly every waking minute crying."

"It will pass," she assured me and patted my shoulder. "But maybe there's a few things you can do to help. Are you burping him after feedings?"

I arched a brow. "Burping?"

"Yes. You're having to use the feeder bottles, right? They tend to take more air in with those as they nurse. It fills their belly and causes a bit of pain. So you'll need to burp him at least once, preferably twice. That should ease some discomfort."

I suddenly wondered if I should be taking notes. "H-How do I ...?"

Leila scooped Reigh up, balancing him on her lap in a sitting position so that he was leaning forward with his chin resting in her hand. She jostled him gently up and down and patted his back, rubbing along his spine.

He let out a loud, man-sized belch.

"Gods and Fates," I muttered, my eyes wide.

"See?" She beamed and carefully passed him over to me. "Now you try."

We worked with the burping exercise and eventually, I got it right. Another monstrous belch. I couldn't comprehend how a noise like that could come from such a tiny human.

While we sat, sipping mugs of warm cider, Leila began talking me through other parenting exercises. She showed me how to stroke his face lightly with my fingers a certain way in order to calm him, and how to roll up a blanket and position it so that he could be propped into a crawling position. She demonstrated how to massage the muscles in his neck and work his legs to make sure the muscles developed properly.

"Remember not to leave him in any one position for too long. Think of his head like a ball of soft clay. If you leave it on one side for too long, it will go flat. So you want to rotate it—front, back, one side, then the other. Once he's able to hold his head up steadily and sit up on his own, you won't have to worry with that as much."

"When does that happen?"

"Oh, it varies from child to child. Usually about seven months or so. But you've got quite a little fighter there. I wouldn't be surprised if he crawls early." Leila gave a gentle shrug as she sat, holding her own daughter in one arm and her mug in the other. For her, a young woman who probably wasn't a day over twenty, she looked utterly natural and at peace. Her long black hair was woven into a smooth braid over one shoulder and her skin was a healthy, deep bronze.

"I see." Seven months? I had yet to survive seven days.

"Don't look so glum," she giggled. "Like I said—six weeks. After that, things get easier. You get used to their rhythm."

"How old is yours? Your daughter, that is."

Leila's smile dimmed slightly. She glanced down to the little girl in her lap, who was cooing and gnawing happily on her pudgy little hands. "Nine months. Her sister would have been three, though." Something twanged in her voice, like an instrument with one string out of tune.

My stomach soured. I knew that tone—that look—as plainly as I knew my own face. "How did she pass?"

"Dry fever," she answered softly without ever looking up. "Not even a year ago. I was still pregnant, so I couldn't even be with her at the end. They were afraid I might catch it and lose the baby."

Lowering my head, I bit down hard and steeled myself against words that threatened to tear past my lips. "I am sorry for your loss."

When I dared to glance at her again, Leila was staring straight at me. There was a haunting sense of knowing in her gaze. Loss knew loss. "Who did you lose? Your wife?"

I swallowed hard several times, waiting until I was sure I could speak without my voice wavering to answer, "No. First, my sister. She was four years old. We were slaves in Maldobar. Our parents perished in one of the prison camps. I was supposed to look after her. It was … a very long time ago."

"I see." Leila's voice was so quiet I could hardly hear her over the rumble of the wagon wheels. "Time doesn't make it any better, does it? The hurt never fades. There's always that empty place—that silence where their sound used to be."

My eyes welled and I bowed my head, turning my face away so she wouldn't see. Her words cut through me, piercing my soul with such brutal exactness that left me breathless. I clenched my jaw and took in tight, controlled breaths. It would pass.

"This boy isn't a halfbreed," she spoke again. "Meaning, he's not your son."

"No."

"So he was an orphan, then? Why take him in?"

Pulling Reigh's squirming tiny body closer, I wrapped the linen cloth around us to hold him against my chest. "I don't know," I admitted.

Leila didn't seem satisfied with that answer. Her lips thinned and she sank back a little. "Is it restitution, then? For your sister? You blame yourself for her passing?"

I couldn't answer that. I wouldn't. I didn't know this woman, and she did not know me. It was best to keep it that way. Getting to know people, getting close, was generally where things went wrong in my life. My presence attracted all manner of ill fortune, as though the Fates enjoyed mocking all my efforts to find some single shred of happiness. As much as I despised blaming things on divinities, so many things had gone catastrophically wrong, I could no longer come up with a different reason for it. What could I have done to deserve this?

Standing quickly, I gathered the rest of my belongings and thanked her with a quick bow. Then I ducked out of the wagon to return to the back of the caravan without another word.

CHAPTER THREE

Mau Kakuri was more than just a welcomed sight. My blood rushed and my pulse raced at the mere sight of it. I got a swell of energy as we crossed the threshold into the city. Two weeks spent in a slow, agonizing journey had brought me here—all the way to Luntharda, the kingdom of the gray elves. Here, my people had thrived for centuries. We'd carved a life of perfect balance into the wild heart of this jungle.

Although I'd spent more years in the human kingdom of Maldobar than I ever had in the land of my forefathers, just one breath of that sweet, humid, warm jungle air brought me back to life. I took it in, drinking in every flavor of fragrant trees, damp soil, wild fruit, flowers, and fresh dew. The markets were bustling. They smelled of drying spices and the healthy musk of animals. People filled the streets with noise, footsteps, laughter, and the calls of merchants from their selling stalls. Above it all, an ambient rumble like a low clap of thunder boomed from the curtain of waterfalls that dwarfed the entire city. They fell, plummeting from a broad mossy cliff face, down into the river that split and wound through the city.

Mau Kakuri had been built like a living work of art, with its many elegant bridges, crystal clear pools filled with brightly scaled fish, flourishing markets, and the royal palace rising up like a cluster of white alabaster stalagmites. This would be our home now. Tied securely against my chest, Reigh let out a burbling noise. He'd be hungry soon. I had to get settled quickly.

So far, acquiring a new place to live had been the simplest part of this transition. At least, it was one of the only things that didn't involve feces or vomit.

Thanks to my connections in the royal court, and my moderate skill in medicine, getting appointed as a healer in Luntharda was easy. Being a city healer meant I would be given a place to live by the royal family. I was not expecting anything fancy, of course. I could manage a small clinic with modest living quarters for Reigh and myself. Nothing more was required.

"Master Kiran?" A tentative voice called my name.

I turned, nearly smacking into a young man who'd been standing right next to me. He was dressed out in the light leather armor of a scout and his silver hair was wound into an intricate series of braids. Despite those marks of accomplishment, and the bow and sword belted to his small frame, I doubted he was a day over seventeen—young, even for a new scout.

He stumbled back, bowing deeply and apologizing. "Forgive me, sir! I just received notice you would be arriving today. I hope I haven't kept you waiting long."

I shook my head, jostling Reigh a little to rebalance his weight where the wrap was making my back sore. "No. It's fine."

"I was sent to show you to the clinic and make sure everything was set up according to your tastes," the young man spoke quickly, his voice still tinged with nervousness. "Right this way."

It was an easy route to find the building. Perched at the end of a quiet market avenue, on the crest of a small hill, the outside of the clinic had suffered some neglect. Vines and undergrowth had taken over the front garden and were climbing the windows. It needed to be repainted—something I would likely have to do myself until I could afford to hire out for that sort of thing. There was no sign above the door or any indication that this was a healing house. I'd have to remedy that, as well.

The scout hastily unlocked the door before dashing in ahead to begin lighting lamps along the hall. Straight through was a small foyer with a stone floor. It was set lower than the wood flooring of the rest of the house, an indication for guests to stop and remove their shoes before continuing on.

I didn't bother with that now. Until this place had been scrubbed to my satisfaction, there was no point.

Past the foyer was a long narrow hall. On the left were three rooms for seeing to patients. On the right was a homier looking main room that would be solely for our use, complete with a tiled, bowl-shaped fire pit in the floor with an iron cooking grate and pot hook. Boxes and crates were stacked around, crowding every corner. I sighed in relief at the sight of them. Inside were all the items I had shipped ahead; the few things in this world I owned. Most were medical journals and tools, things I would need to run the clinic, as well as a few herbs that couldn't be found here in Luntharda.

"I went ahead and brought everything inside," the scout announced, fidgeting with another oil lamp. "I hope that's all right. Some of them weren't marked, though, so I just left them down here."

I nodded, pacing the room and peering into the tiny kitchen. It would be cramped, but I could manage.

"There's two bedrooms upstairs," the scout added, gesturing to a staircase tucked in the far corner of the room. "There's also a small washroom, since you'll need a place to wash bandaging and sheets, I made sure the plumbing is good. There's a public bathhouse right down the street, so you won't have to walk far. Oh, and the roof is pretty spacious. You could do gardening up there, if you wanted." He gave a thin, anxious smile. "Is this to your liking, sir?"

Reigh gave an impatient squeal and wriggled in his wrapping. I patted his back, jostling him a little more. Patience, boy.

"It will do," I mumbled and rubbed the back of my neck with my only free hand. "What about upstairs? The beds?"

"Ah! Yes, of course." The scout nodded enthusiastically. "All as you requested. A bed for you and a crib for the child. I made sure they already have the appropriate bedding—you know, sheets, blankets, pillows—put in place for you. I thought it might save you some trouble since you might be tired from your journey."

The mention of a bed made my eyes want to droop. "Very good," I replied. "You've done well."

The young scout straightened, his chest swelling a bit. "If there's anything else I can do for y—"

"Milk," I said.

"S-Sir?"

"I need milk from the market. Two jugs worth will suffice for now. Goat only."

He blinked, and then gave a slow nod. "Okay."

"And make an inquiry to the city midwife. I need to know if there are any wet nurses on hire."

"Yes, sir." The scout spun on a heel and darted for the door. I waited until I heard his footsteps retreat and the front door of the clinic shut with a *thud*.

Then I all but dropped to my rear in the sitting room. I had no cushions or rugs, but the wooden floor wasn't moving or bouncing. That was a welcomed change. My shoulders and back creaked with exhaustion, so tender I could hardly bear to move them as I untied Reigh from my chest, spread the cloth out before me, and laid him out on the floor. I dropped all my other bags and let out a heavy sigh. We'd made it at last.

Sitting alone in the near dark of the clinic, I stared around at the small, round colored glass windows, the bare beams on the ceiling, the plain plaster walls, and the stacks of crates waiting to be emptied. It was quiet. Something about this place felt calm, close, and familiar. Home—this could be home.

Reigh let out another grumpy coo.

"Not impressed?" I asked, smiling as I leaned over to pull back the edge of his diaper. A foul stench from inside made my eyes water. I shuddered. That smell never got any easier to stomach.

Rummaging through my belongings, I pulled out another square of cloth—the last clean diaper from my stash. I'd need to wash them all again soon. There was a sealed leather bag full of foulness that could have choked a dragon.

Unbuckling my cloak, I made myself comfortable before I dared to pull back the diaper from Reigh's small bottom and assess the damage. My throat spasmed and fought not to gag as I cleaned him up, adding the soiled diaper to the bag of hate. It grew more and more tempting to simply burn the thing rather than washing the contents over and over.

As soon as I turned back around to apply the clean one, a spray of something warm and wet hit my face.

Pee.

Reigh was *peeing* on me.

"Stop that!" I cringed back, grabbing the first thing I could to cover him—my cloak.

He didn't respond. Lying there with pudgy arms and legs spread wide, Reigh just blinked up at me indifferently. Still, this felt personal.

"That is why I have the diapers. You see? That is why I wash them over and over again, just so you can soil them." I held up the clean one and waved it in front of his eyes. "You pee in this. Not on me. Understood?"

He gave me a broad, toothless smile that put dimples in his cheeks and waggled his chunky arms.

Pulling my cloak away, I sighed at the big wet stain and tossed it over the bag of foulness. I'd deal with both later. Right now, I needed to cover the source of all my current problems.

Taking him by his ankles, I lifted Reigh's rear just enough to slide the clean diaper under him. I muttered under my breath, again wondering how anyone survived this sort of torment. Having two parents would have made it easier, of course. We could have taken turns or drawn straws. But that was a luxury I doubted I would ever know.

Reigh gave another coo, wriggling his ankles in my grasp.

"Almost done." I coaxed with a sigh. For now, anyway. Fates willing, he wouldn't soil this one too badly before I had a chance to wash the others and hang them to dry.

Reigh's expression skewed, brows rumpling together and mouth flattening. His face flushed. His stomach made a loud, gurgling sound.

Oh no.

I looked down an instant before it hit—too late.

Fresh, warm, runny, vileness hit me like the spray from an uncorked champagne bottle. It splattered the front of my tunic, my neck, even my chin.

Fates, why? Why me?

For a few seconds, all I could do was sit there, paralyzed in quiet horror while I came to terms with my situation.

Reigh cackled and waggled his arms again.

Okay, so this *was* personal.

CHAPTER FOUR

"I stuck!"

"Yes, you are. We've been over this many times, Reigh," I grunted as I attempted to wrestle my tiny ward into a full body hold so I could carefully extract his head from where he'd wedged it between the wooden railing of the stairs ... *again*.

He fought me, exerting a startling amount of strength for a two-year-old. "All done! All done," he let out a panicked whimper.

"No. Not all done," I grumbled as I finally got a good hold. "This is why you don't play on the stairs."

With one last twist, his head popped free. Immediately, Reigh let out a yelp. His cheeks were splotched almost as red as the unruly mop of hair on his head and he blinked up at me, tears welling in his eyes. "Hurts."

I picked him up, checking his head over one more time, just in case. A few more months and maybe he wouldn't be able to poke it through the bars like that anymore. One could hope, however futile that hope might be. In my opinion, parental hope might be the most desperate and futile of all.

"You're fine," I assured him. "But remember this, okay? You play on the stairs and your head gets hurt. So don't do it again."

He bobbed his head as though he understood while sheepishly hiding his eyes with his hands. His bottom lip puckered, chin trembling as he gradually came closer to hide his face against my leg.

I squatted down in front of him and patted his head, ruffling his hair a little.

We'd made it a little over two years, and by all accounts, Reigh was as normal as any other human child. He walked, talked a little, and still ate as voraciously as ever. He'd crawled and weaned right on schedule. Now he was even sleeping through the night—which was a welcomed miracle I'd thought would never happen. The gods could be merciful, after all.

But with mobility and tiny fragments of independent thought came a whole new challenge in the form of toddler mischief. It was a phase I was beginning to suspect might kill us both. Or at the very least, I'd wind up having to cut apart the stair railings to free his head the next time he got stuck.

"Come on, then. If you can't stay off the stairs, you have to come work with me," I reasoned. "We have patients."

"Kiran, no! No!" Reigh wailed and threw himself backwards, feigning total distress.

Ignoring his theatrics, I pulled a long strip of cloth from my pocket and tied one end around his waist before fastening the other to my belt. As humiliating as it was to leash him like that, there really was no other choice. Left to his own devices, he'd already brushed death twice today—before sticking his head through the bannisters for the fifth time this week. It was this, or I would have to attempt to scrape together enough money to hire a nanny that could watch him. Knowing what I did about him, I wasn't entirely comfortable with that idea. I needed to have him in my sights at all times. I had to be ready in case certain ... issues arose.

Reigh pitched and bucked like a wild faundra being saddled for the first time as I dragged him into the first exam room where my last patient of the day was waiting. The elderly elf woman sitting on the examination table frowned as my tiny human continued to fight his restraint and cry. Her mouth pinched up and her eyes narrowed.

"Don't you have a wife that looks after him?" The old woman wrinkled her nose with obvious distaste. "Human children are rotten from the start, I take it?"

I tightened my grip on my patient logbook, careful not to look up and meet her gaze. My pulse thrashed wildly, but I had to remain calm. She was a patient, after all.

Besides, we'd gotten that reaction before. It happened from time to time, although generally only from someone of the older generation who hadn't quite forgotten the crimes of the Gray War that had nearly driven our race to extinction. Forgiving humanity for that genocide was an unspeakable impossibility for some. I tried not to fault my elderly kin for their anger. I'd lived through that same war. Lost family to it, as well. I knew that pain firsthand.

Still, she had a lot of nerve to speak that way about Reigh. I wasn't his father. But he was *my* child.

"Had to go with a human bride, eh?" the old woman jibed again. "And where is she now? Not helping you at all, it would seem. Typical. Couldn't find some elven girl to please you, then?"

"No," I snapped, already pressed for patience. "I've met not one that came close to meeting my standards. And I'm no longer looking." Rummaging through my cabinets, I took out a bag of mild herbal tea and dropped it into her hand. "You have a cold, for which there is no cure apart from divine intervention. Since I am a mere mortal, I suggest you drink this tea and rest. You should recover in a few days."

The old woman gaped in surprise. "T-That's all?" she sputtered over the sound of my crying toddler.

I narrowed my eyes at her. "If I receive an unexpected shipment of miracles, you'll be the first to know. Now if you'll excuse me, I have other patients for which I might actually be of some service. Good day."

The rest of the day didn't go much better. Reigh was irate to be tethered to my hip, literally. I wasn't necessarily elated with that arrangement, either, but it was the best I could do to ensure we both survived to see dinnertime. He cried until he was exhausted, then he sat down on the floor and whimpered. It was only after I'd fed him, bathed him, and put him down for the night that I got any real work done. That always felt like borrowed time, and I cringed at any loud or sudden sound that might wake him and I'd be forced to start the whole process again from the beginning.

After eating my cold dinner alone at the fireside, I finished the last of the day's paperwork and translated a few pages from my medical texts. It was one of the few things in the day I looked forward to, apart from sleeping. I'd brought quite a few books with me from Maldobar, many of which contained recipes for new medicines that had shown promising results. I was eager to try them here, but being able to read the human language was not common this deep in Luntharda.

The longer I worked, the more my eyes burned and itched. My head drooped lower and lower. A sudden smack to the face gave me a jolt and I sat up, realizing I'd nodded off and hit myself in the face with my book. Time to surrender.

Giving up the fight, I put everything away and covered the fire with the grate for the night. I left the embers to smolder down and went upstairs. I took my time washing my face and hands before changing into my bedclothes—a long light tunic and cotton pants cut off at the knee—that I always left hanging by the washroom.

On my way down the hall, I stopped in the doorway to Reigh's bedroom and pushed the door open, just a crack, so I could see that he was all right. It was a habit leftover from his infancy. I couldn't sleep unless I was sure he was still breathing.

Moonlight was pouring through his window. His toys were scattered across the floor.

But his bed was empty.

My heart jumped to the back of my throat.

I ran without thinking, searching the downstairs and all the exam rooms one by one. The door—Gods, could he reach the handle now? What if he had let himself out? No, surely I would have heard that. Darting back up the stairs, I burst into his room and searched everywhere, throwing back the blankets on his bed before looking underneath it.

Reigh wasn't there.

"Reigh?" I finally remembered to yell. "Reigh? Where are you?"

No reply.

Bolting to my room, I dashed to my armoire and grabbed for my scout's attire. I had to go to the city guard immediately. They could start a search and go door to door.

A soft little sigh came from behind me.

I turned slowly, my whole body shaking as I looked back. Reigh was on my bed, curled up with his head on my pillow. His eyes were shut and his face serene, as though he had never done anything the least bit mischievous that day.

But he wasn't alone.

A creature like a living shadow moved along beside the bed, slinking silently along the wall and suddenly halting.

My heart stopped. My breath seemed to freeze in my lungs.

Gods and Fates. That was …

The creature seemed to hesitate, standing on four long legs with its gaunt, almost wolfish-looking body flickering as though it were made of black flame. Its tall ears perked in my direction, head moving as it stared straight back at me with two red eyes that glowed in the dim light like smoldering embers.

Dread pierced my gut like a red-hot poker. Had it come for him? Already? No … this couldn't happen. Not yet. He was still so young. Too young. Reigh wasn't ready for this yet.

I swallowed hard. My hands drew tightly into fists at my sides. I shook my head slightly, never breaking eye contact.

The creature's maw opened, revealing a hauntingly wide, smiling mouth filled with jagged dripping white teeth. Dark laughter crackled in the air like the biting crack of a whip, sending a flourish of chills up my spine.

I cringed and set my jaw, drawing on every shred of my nerve to hold my position.

The beast dissolved away into the shadows of the bedroom without another sound.

"R-Reigh," I managed to gasp his name hoarsely.

I ran to the bedside.

Lying peacefully amidst all my blankets, Reigh slept soundly. He didn't even twitch, even when I sank to my knees at the bedside and buried my face in my hands.

Relief and adrenaline still made my body tremble as I sat there, listening to him breathing softly. Gods and Fates. This child … he would be the death of me.

Or of a great many other people. Perhaps both.

Scooping him up, I carefully moved him over far enough that I could climb into bed next to him. I told myself it was only because of that scare, the idea that I'd almost lost him, that I wanted to keep him close tonight. I didn't want to ever feel that again. I didn't want him out of my sight.

As soon as I lay down, Reigh scooted in as close as he could, tucking his tiny body right up against mine with his head nestled into the crux of my shoulder. He gave another faint, murmuring sigh as I combed my fingers through his wild red hair, brushing it away from his forehead. It fell in ringlets around his ears and the base of his neck, although it wasn't quite long enough yet to braid. His face was beginning to change. I saw less of that tiny, crying baby every day, and more and more of a strong-willed, determined little boy who was going to make every last strand of my hair fall out at this rate.

I'd be completely bald before he turned ten.

Then, I'd have to do more than simply tie him to my belt to get through the day. I'd have to start teaching him how to work, how to hold a blade, fire a bow, and walk the tree paths. I'd have to teach him how to survive in Luntharda, as my father had taught me.

My chest constricted at the thought. Until this human child had been placed in my arms, I had been completely alone in the world.

Now ...

Somehow, at some time I couldn't even place, this little boy had become important to me—and not just because I'd been charged with ensuring his survival. This was no longer just a chore. It was beyond him simply being a ward temporarily in my care, the fulfillment of a promise, or potential protection against an unknown threat. Where he came from and why he was here with me instead of with his true family—none of that mattered now.

Reigh mattered. That was it, nothing more.

Our relationship wouldn't be simple. I wasn't foolish enough to think he wouldn't question his presence here, or my reason for adopting him as my own. Maybe he would never understand it or why I'd brought him to Luntharda. He might even come to resent me for it.

I was prepared to live with that, if it meant he would be safe. I would do whatever was necessary to guide him to finding the happiness that had long eluded me.

Hopefully, he'd be able to forgive my many mistakes. He could never call me "father." Not while his real family still lived. I could not take that right away from a man I respected—even if I didn't fully understand why he'd sent this child away. Perhaps, someday, Reigh and I would both learn the complete truth about that matter.

Until then, I would never be Reigh's father.

But he would always be my son.

SAVAGE

The Dragonrider Legacy Book One

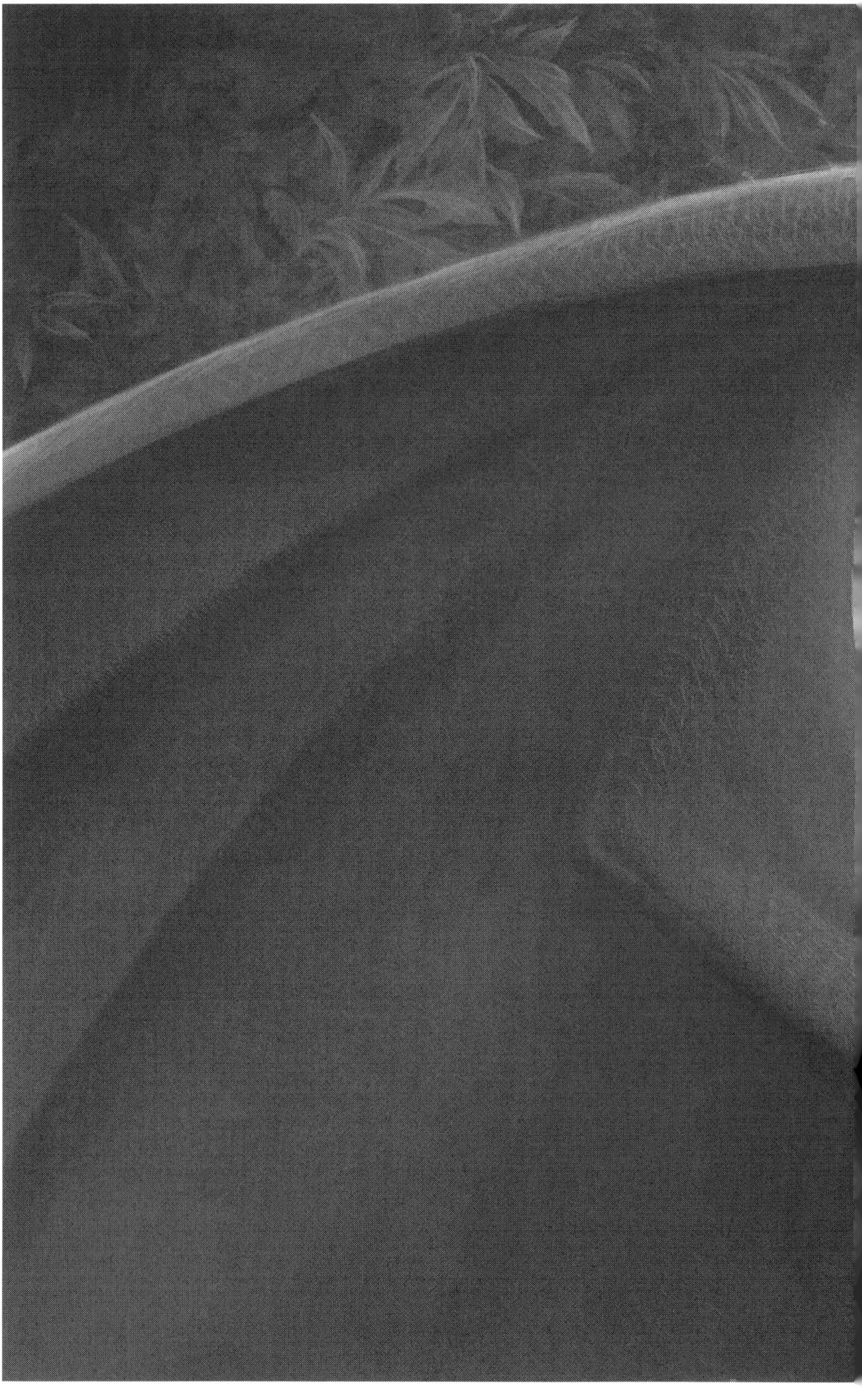

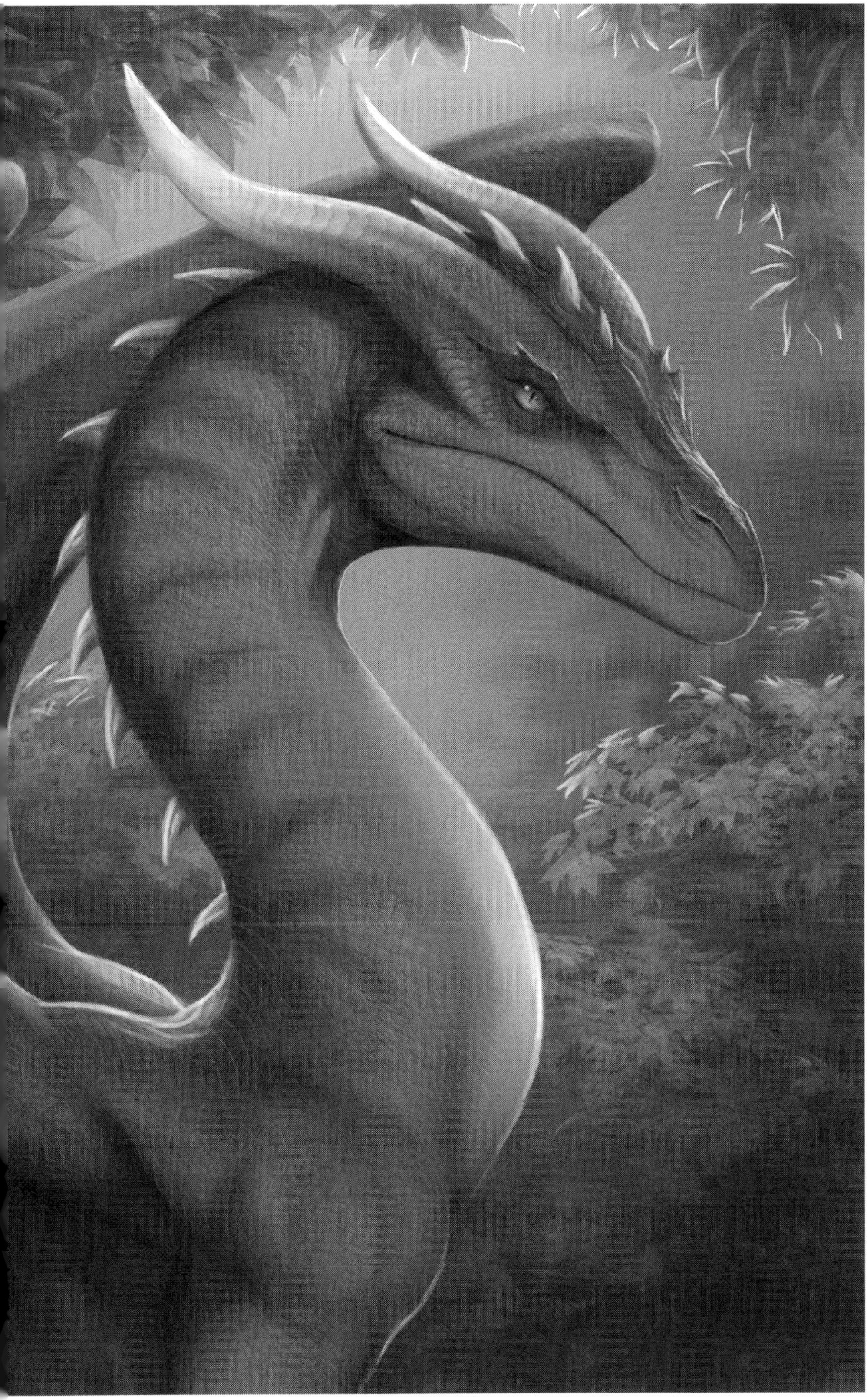

CHAPTER ONE

The jungle was quiet. Every fern frond, leaf, and flower petal dripped with cold dew. The first rays of morning sunlight bled through the canopy overhead, turning everything a surreal shade of green and sparkling through the clouds of mist that drifted between the tree trunks. The thick air smelled of rich, damp soil and the faintly sweet fragrance of the vividly colored flowers.

My bare feet squished on the damp moss as I crept along the tree limbs. I squeezed my bow tightly in my fist. My heartbeat throbbed in my ears and my palms were already slick with sweat. I clenched my teeth to stop them from chattering. Now was not the time to lose my nerve.

Out of nowhere, a brightly-colored parrot burst from the foliage and fluttered across my path. I slipped, losing my footing and rocking back on my heels as I flailed to get away. My stomach lurched. I opened my mouth to yell.

Someone grabbed my belt from behind.

Enyo dragged me down into a squat, hiding amidst the leaves. Together we watched the bird disappear into the distance while I struggled to catch my breath. So much for being stealthy.

Enyo's eyes sparkled like aquamarines in the dim light and the brightly painted beads woven into her dark hair clattered as she turned and shot me a hard look. I scowled back at her. It wasn't *my* fault. That stupid bird had come out of nowhere.

I wrenched out of her grip and slung my bow over my shoulder, crawling down a steep turn in the limb and leaping over into the next tree. That was how you moved in Luntharda—scurrying from tree to tree like a squirrel. The ground wasn't impassable, but it was extremely difficult terrain. Not to mention it was practically writhing with things that would have been happy to make breakfast out of a pair of novice scouts.

Technically, we weren't supposed to be this far away from the city without a senior scout to escort us. But today was different—today I had a mission. And it didn't include falling to my death from fifty feet in the air.

"This isn't going to work, you know," Enyo muttered as we scaled a network of thick vines that snaked up a tree trunk.

I ignored her, but couldn't outrun her. Even if I was taller, she was much faster. Together, we ran along the boughs, leaping, dodging, and climbing until I knew we had to be within earshot. I stopped first, and Enyo skidded to a halt beside me with a broad grin on her lips.

I glanced around for the perfect spot right above the narrow, well-beaten trail that zigzagged through the underbrush below. Faundra left those trails when they moved between their favorite grazing spots. My father had spent years teaching me how to track them, hunt them, and kill them. I could do this—by myself.

I smirked when I found it; the ideal spot where an overgrowth of giant lichen made a great place to hide and watch the trail below. I slipped my bow off my shoulder and took out an arrow, making sure to check the fletching and the shaft for damage before setting it in the string.

"Say you do actually kill one this time. Say we even manage to field dress it and get it back to the city. Do you really think Kiran is going to be okay with you running off without him?" Enyo whispered as she tucked herself into the lichen beside me. I could feel the heat off her skin when her arm brushed mine.

"Well obviously, if I did it without him, then I don't need him in the first place, right? I'm not a kid anymore," I growled under my breath. "He's holding me back on purpose."

Okay, so that was debatable. Gray elves went through puberty around fifteen. Their hair turned from black to as white as frost and their bodies matured to look more adult. After that, they were considered adults and could choose a profession, get married, and basically do whatever they wanted. I was sixteen. I *should* have been treated like an adult, too.

There was just one problem—I wasn't a Gray elf.

To make matters worse, my adoptive father, Kiran, didn't want me trying to make my first kill yet. He didn't want me going anywhere without his permission. He still treated me like a little kid.

"Maybe because you never listen," Enyo muttered under her breath.

I narrowed my eyes at her. "Just shut up. Why did you even come?"

She glared back. "Well if you die, someone should at least be able to explain what happened."

"Pfft" I snorted and looked away. "Just keep out of my way."

Enyo pushed some of her long, coal-black hair behind one of her pointed ears. "And stay here—I know, I know."

A twig snapped.

We both fell silent. My heart raced, making my fingers throb and my body flush. This was it, the chance I'd been waiting for.

One-by-one they emerged from the morning mist. The herd of faundra traveled quickly with their littlest fawns grouped in the center to shield them from predators. The does were as big as horses, some even seven feet tall, with their white pelts flecked with soft gray markings. They had long, powerful legs and one kick to the face would crush your skull like an egg. But they weren't the ones you really had to watch out for.

The stags were even bigger. Their shaggy pelts had stark black swirls and a blaze right down the front of their snout. Their heads were crowned with sweeping white antlers with ten razor sharp points. You definitely did not want to be on the wrong end of those.

"Beautiful," Enyo whispered faintly.

I smirked.

Then I saw him—the alpha male. He stepped from the shadows, an impressive beast much larger than the other members of his herd by far. He had a single black stripe that ran from the end of his snout, down his back, and all the way to his tail. He was older, so his pelt was thicker around his neck like a mane, and all the other black marks along his hide had faded away. His horns sloped back to almost touch ends with four extra points on each side.

My stomach fluttered and swirled with excitement. I could barely breathe. When I drew my bow back, my hands shook. It made my arrow point bounce all over the place.

Enyo placed one of her palms on my back.

I closed my eyes for a moment and tried to remember everything Kiran had taught me. I took a deep breath. I listened to the jungle. Then, slowly, I opened my eyes again and took aim straight for the alpha male's heart. My hand was steady and my bowstring taut.

All I had to do was let go.

Something caught my eye. It was fast, like a flickering shadow darting through the underbrush.

I hesitated. My eyes searched, tracking through the underbrush for more movement. A snagwolf? Or maybe a wild shrike?

A sinking sensation rose in the pit of my stomach. It made all the tiny hairs on my arms and neck stand on end.

Oh no. Not this—not now.

Clenching my teeth, I tried to ignore it, to push it out of my mind, to fight it.

A cold chill hit me suddenly, making my body jerk beyond my control. The bowstring slipped, and my arrow went flying. It zipped through the moist air, grazing leaves and lodging deep into the side of a doe. She bucked and bleated, sending the rest of the herd into a frenzy. They bolted in every direction, disappearing like ghosts into the jungle.

But the doe I'd shot was badly wounded. She couldn't run far. Without thinking, I ran for the trunk of the tree and started my descent, jumping down from branch-to-branch.

"Reigh! Stop!" Enyo screamed.

No. There was no stopping now. When my feet finally struck the forest floor, I went to the spot where I'd shot her. There was blood on the ground and more droplets speckling the leaves and ferns, leading away into the undergrowth. She wouldn't last long. Running would make her bleed out faster.

Enyo seized my wrist suddenly. Her face was pale and her eyes as round as two moons. "We can't be down here. It's too dangerous." Her voice trembled.

"I can't just leave a kill lying out there. Stag or not it's still a—"

"Reigh! Don't be stupid. Something will have heard them," she pleaded and pulled on my arm. "Something will smell the blood!"

"Go back to the tree and wait for me, then." I snatched away from her and pointed. "I'm finishing this, with or without you."

Her expression faltered. She looked back at the tree, then to me, with her eyebrows crinkled and her mouth mashed into a desperate line.

"I said go!" I yelled.

Startled, Enyo backed away a few steps. She blinked at me, lips parted as she took in a few quick breaths. Then she turned and ran.

I tried not to think about all the rules I was breaking as I dove into the foliage, alone, to track down my kill.

Leaving the city without telling Kiran—that's one. Going into the jungle unsupervised was another. Taking Enyo with me was worth at least two more because we hadn't told her parents about it, either. And then there was the whole "hunting alone before I'd been officially marked a scout" thing. So yeah—basically, Kiran was going to be furious.

My only salvation was finding this doe. At least then, when I returned, he wouldn't be able to argue that I wasn't ready. The stag would have been much more impressive, but a kill was a kill. This was proof I could handle myself. I deserved to get my scout's mark.

The blood trail wasn't hard to find even among all the towering fronds and enormous leaves of the plants. I'd never stood on the jungle floor alone like this before. I felt insignificant, like a tiny insect, as I looked up at the giant trees. Everything seemed bigger now that I was this close to it. The air seemed cooler, too. The canopy was so far away, like a distant sky of endless green leaves. It gave me chills.

Or maybe that was just my *problem* acting up again.

I crept through the undergrowth, traveling fast and trying to stay out of sight as I followed the blood trail. The drops were getting bigger and closer together. She was slowing down. It wouldn't be long.

And then I saw her.

The doe was lying in the middle of a small clearing between two big ferns. She was motionless, but I could see her side rising and falling with the shaft of my arrow sticking straight out. She was still alive.

I quickly shouldered my bow and drew my hunting knife. As I got close to the edge of the clearing, I paused. I did a quick glance around, waiting to see if anything or anyone else was nearby. Enyo was right—the smell of blood might draw the attention of other predators.

Everything was quiet and still.

The doe bleated loudly when she saw me. Her legs kicked, eyes looking around with wild anxiety. Standing over her, I could feel my hand begin to shake again. I had to kill her, end her suffering—preferably before she gave away my position to every dangerous creature in a five-mile radius.

I put my knee over her snout to hold her head still. She was too weak from blood loss to fight me off. Her milky brown eyes stared straight ahead as I drew back, ready to plunge my dagger into her heart.

A deep, heavy snort broke the silence.

I froze, slowly raising my gaze just in time to see him stride free of the underbrush, his white horns gleaming in the morning light. The alpha male had come back for her.

Our eyes locked. His ears flicked back and he stamped a hoof. I tightened my grip on my knife, and tried to think of what to do—any fragment of a lesson Kiran had given that would help me right now.

There wasn't one.

The stag lowered his head, pointing those deadly horns straight at me, and charged.

I scrambled to my feet and ran for the nearest tree. His thundering hooves on the ground got closer and closer. I wasn't going to make it. I was fast, but he was faster.

The second before I could grab onto the lowest handhold, I heard a bowstring snap. The alpha bellowed. I dared to look back, just in time to see him fall and begin rolling. An arrow was sticking out of his haunches. He tumbled toward me, rolling like a giant furry boulder.

The massive stag smashed right into me.

The impact knocked the wind out of my lungs. Something popped and one of my arms went numb. Not good.

When everything stopped, I realized I couldn't move at all. Was I ... dead? Dying? No—I was pinned. Crushed between a tree and a very angry faundra stag, I couldn't escape. Something sharp, probably one of the stag's horns, sliced right across my face. Warm blood began running down my face.

"Reigh!" Enyo's voice was calling my name, but I couldn't see her.

The stag staggered back to his feet, shifting his weight off me. I sucked in a desperate, wheezing breath as I crumpled to the forest floor in a daze.

"Don't just sit there! Climb!" Enyo yelled again.

What?

I looked up, my vision still spotting, to see the stag charging straight for her.

Even with the arrow sticking out of his flank, he galloped at full speed. She clumsily drew back another, eyes stuck on the shaggy monster thundering straight for her. Her whole body trembled with terror. She was hesitating, trying to decide if she should fire or flee.

She wasn't going to make it either way.

Something inside me burst, like the last raindrop before the dam broke.

I screamed her name at the top of my lungs. The chill came over me again, a coldness that rushed through every vein, making my body jerk and my eyes tear up. This time I didn't fight it. I clenched my fists and let it take me.

Time seemed to slow down and stop altogether. My pulse got slower. My skin went cold. I could see my own breaths turning to white fog in the air. Before me, darkness pooled, amassing into one dark, inky puddle on the ground. It rose like a flickering column of black flames, and took the form of *him* ...

The black wolf I called Noh.

He looked at me with a smiling canine mouth and red, wavering bog fire eyes.

"Kill it," I commanded.

"*With pleasure*," his hissing voice replied.

CHAPTER TWO

I couldn't remember a time in my life when Noh hadn't been there. Ever since I was a little kid, he'd always been hiding in the back of my mind, like a memory from a former life that refused to fade. Almost as soon as I'd noticed his presence, Noh had absolutely terrified me.

Nothing about that had changed.

It wasn't that he'd ever tried to hurt me. Somehow, I didn't think he could even if he wanted to. But I could feel his presence just as clearly as I could sense his intentions—and they weren't good. He thrived on my anger, sadness, and confusion. Whenever Kiran and I had an argument, he would start creeping around the corners of the room, slipping soundlessly from shadow to shadow, almost like he was waiting for me to finally lose it.

I didn't know what he would do. Frankly, I didn't want to know. Kiran had warned me over and over that I had to keep myself under control, and make sure not to go too far. The repercussions could be severe. Noh might hurt someone, and it would be my fault. I was the only one who could see and hear Noh, and the only person he listened to. I could control him—for now. But who knew how long that would last. There was always a chance that one day, when I let him off the chain, I might not be able to get control of him again.

Then no one would be able to stop him from doing whatever he wanted.

The worst part was knowing that eventually it was going to happen. Somehow, someway, I was going to mess up. I always did. That's me—Reigh—Luntharda's number one screw up.

I couldn't move. Lying on my back with my arms and legs spread wide, my whole body was numb except for the cold pinpricks on my skin. The dull, constant sound of my heartbeat droned in my ears. Maybe that meant I wasn't dead.

Suddenly, there was a voice. Someone was shouting above me. "Reigh? Reigh!"

A strong hand smacked my face.

My eyes popped open. I bolted upright and choked, sucking in a deep breath.

"It's all right. Breathe. You'll be fine." Kiran knelt next to me, studying me with a concerned furrow in his brow.

"E-Enyo ... " I tried to speak, but I was barely able to catch my breath. My head wouldn't stop spinning.

"She's fine." Kiran put a hand on the back of my head and leaned in close, poking experimentally at the open wound on my face. Pain shot through my nose, making my eyes water.

"You'll need stitches," he decided aloud. "One of the stag's horns had blood on it. I feared the worst."

That's right. The stag had nicked me.

I looked past Kiran to the place where the doe should have been lying, but she was gone. There was no trace of her or the stag anywhere. Across the clearing, a few other Gray elf scouts were checking Enyo. She was unconscious, but her cheeks were still flushed with color. She was alive.

My body sagged with relief. I met Kiran's knowing gaze. The hard lines in the corners of his mouth grew deeper as he frowned.

"Is he still here?" he asked quietly so that no one would hear.

I glanced around. There were no dark shapes or creeping shadows anywhere that I could see. Noh was gone, for now.

I shook my head slightly and winced. My arm—no, my whole shoulder—felt like it was on fire. I couldn't even stand to move it.

"Good. Now get up." He patted the top of my head; a gesture that passed as his gruff, awkward effort at parental affection.

I struggled to stand, and Kiran had to help me to my feet. He dusted the leaves, moss, and twigs off my clothes and picked up my bow. Across the clearing, one of the other scouts picked up Enyo and carried her back with the others toward the nearest tree-path.

I followed with Kiran walking right behind me. I could feel his gaze burning at my back. Anyone else would have thought he was just lurking back there to make sure I didn't stumble and fall to my death because of my injured arm. I guess that could have been part of the reason, but that wasn't all of it. He was worried about Noh showing up again. I was worried about that, too. Worried—and confused about what had happened to the doe and the stag.

Kiran managed to keep his temper in check as we made our way back into the city. We split off from the group when we reached the first market square. I craned my neck, watching them carry Enyo off toward her house. She still wasn't awake yet. My stomach soured and guilt squeezed at my chest like a cold fist around my heart.

I wanted to know she'd be okay.

With Kiran still right on my heels, I made my way back to the small medical clinic where we lived and worked. Kiran was a healer by trade—something he'd also been teaching me since I was a little kid. He ran the best Healing House in the whole city, caring for the sick and wounded while I served as his apprentice.

The clinic wasn't a fancy place by any stretch. Kiran wasn't big on decorating. But it was home—where I'd spent my entire life. The house stood at the end of a street lined with other shops, on crest of a small hill. It was a narrow, plain looking building with three levels—most of which were rooms for patients. A general clinic room where Kiran treated minor illnesses and injuries took up most of the first floor. There was also a kitchen and a living room with a fire pit that was just for us. The rooftop garden was where Kiran grew the herbs and plants he used to make medicines, and where Enyo and I sometimes practiced sparring.

My heart was hammering as we climbed the steps to the front door. Not even the familiar smell of the drying herbs comforted me. This was going to be bad. Like an angry specter, Kiran haunted my steps as I went inside.

Then he let me have it.

"Have I taught you nothing? Did you ever hear a single word I said?" Kiran stared me down, expecting an answer.

I couldn't decide what was more terrifying, that he was about to pop my dislocated arm back into its socket or that he was using the human language to scold me. He only did that when he didn't want anyone to overhear what we were saying—usually when we were talking about Noh.

Kiran hadn't said much while he cleaned the wound on my nose. The gash was deep, and it took fifteen stitches to close it. I was going to have a brutal looking scar from one cheek to the other, right across the bridge of my nose. Painful? You bet. And I had a feeling Kiran had intentionally taken longer than usual to close it. That was part one of my punishment.

Now it was time for part two.

I swallowed, my entire body tense as his fingers probed my shoulder. Whenever he poked too hard, my vision swam and a whimper tore past my clenched teeth.

"And this time you took Enyo with you," he went on. "You risked her life, as well. She is not yet fifteen, Reigh. A *child!*"

I looked away. "I told her to go back. She didn't listen."

He gave my shoulder a sudden, violent jerk. It snapped, and I screamed. But the tingling numbness in my joints was gone. I could move my arm again.

"You do not listen, either. You are a reckless, thoughtless boy," he growled as he began to rotate my arm, testing to see if it was set properly. Then he sternly wrapped my whole shoulder in a bandage. "Everything you do, every decision you make, has consequences. Why don't you understand this? You only think of yourself. And that is exactly why I do not let you take your place as a scout."

I glared at the woven grass mats on the floor. "So, is that why you're ashamed of me? Or is it because I'm human?"

Kiran stopped. "I am not ashamed of you."

"Then it's because I'm a monster?"

"You aren't a monster, Reigh."

I raised my burning gaze up to him. "Then what am I? Do you know anyone else who can feel when someone is dying? Who else has a bad spirit living in their head? Noh killed the faundra didn't he?"

When I started to shout, Kiran raised a hand. I closed my mouth and glowered back down at the floor. Right. I wasn't supposed to get angry. We wouldn't want my dark friend showing up again.

"Is that why you won't let me call you 'father?'" I asked.

He didn't answer. He never did. We'd had this argument before—lots of times already. And that was where it always stopped.

Kiran wasn't my father—not my biological one, anyway. He was a full-blooded Gray elf who had taken me in when I was a baby. According to him, I'd been abandoned, left lying on a rock just inside the boundary of the jungle, alone and vulnerable. Luckily, he heard me crying before a hungry tigrex or snagwolf could make an easy meal of me. Kiran took me in and raised me like a son, although I wasn't sure why. Clearly parenting wasn't his thing. He avoided people like others avoided the plague. And while he did try to be warm to me sometimes, it was like he didn't know what to say, so instead, he didn't say much at all.

And never once allowed me to call him father.

He was plenty old enough to be my father. He'd earned his scars almost forty years ago, fighting in the Gray War. Of course, he never talked about any of that. He was strange, even by Gray elf standards. He'd never married, never had any biological children of his own, and he didn't have many friends. Not that he wasn't well thought of in our community—his reputation from the war made him a local legend. He was regarded as a hero. But that didn't seem to matter much. He seldom smiled, rarely laughed, and he never talked about his past.

But sometimes I overheard others telling stories during the great feast. They talked about how he'd ridden on the back of a dragon, fought to end the war, and stood alongside the King of Maldobar. Some said he'd even called the lapiloque by name.

I didn't know if any of that was true, although sometimes Kiran would sit for hours in front of the fire pit, completely silent, watching the flames slowly die. Those were the nights when I saw the darkness in his eyes.

And sometimes, when he didn't think I was paying attention, I would catch him staring at me that way, too.

"Drink this," he muttered, pushing a cup of strong smelling tea into my hands. It was an herbal remedy to treat swelling and pain, and it tasted so bitter I could barely swallow it. But every awful sip made the soreness in my shoulder subside.

"Enyo's okay, isn't she?" I dared ask once his back was turned. "I didn't hurt her, too, did I?"

Kiran paused. He let his hands rest on top of the chest where he stored all of our medicines. When he turned around, his expression was wrinkled with a sour frown. "She was unharmed," he replied. "But her mother will break her bow for this. She will have to start her training over to earn another one."

My head sagged toward my chest. Great. She was alive, but she was going to hate my guts from now on.

"Did she see what I did?" I couldn't make my chin stop trembling so I bowed my head lower, hoping Kiran wouldn't see. "It's just, you know, I don't have a lot of friends and Enyo is the only one who ... " I couldn't finish.

"No. I don't think she knows what happened."

A sniffle escaped before I could choke it back in. With a sigh, Kiran sat down next to me and put his arm around my shoulders, pulling me over to lean against him. "I found you before the others did. You were right. Noh did kill the doe and stag. But I disposed of the carcasses. No one will find them. No one will know what happened. You'll be fine, but this *cannot* happen again. We were very fortunate."

I nodded shakily. Yeah, we'd been insanely lucky. Noh had never killed before. I'd always been able to stop him. "I just couldn't control it. I just—I didn't know what else to do. I had to save her."

He patted my head. "I understand."

"It's getting stronger. I see him almost every day. He won't leave me alone."

Kiran didn't answer.

"What's wrong with me?" I asked quietly. "What am I?"

His answer was barely a whisper. "I don't know."

IT WAS CLOSE TO MIDNIGHT WHEN I GAVE UP TRYING TO SLEEP.

My mind spun over the memories of what had happened in the jungle. I couldn't stop thinking about the faundra, the feeling of letting Noh go, and how the wound on my face was making my whole face throb. Kiran had smeared it with a thick salve that would keep it from getting infected, but it still made my eyes tear up if I touched it.

Finally, I couldn't stand it anymore. Between my aching face and overwhelmed brain, sleep was not going to happen. I got up and peeled the bandage off my shoulder to stretch and flex my arm. It hurt, too, but the herbal remedy helped a lot. By tomorrow it would be as good as new.

Pulling on a long, silk tunic with baggy sleeves, I buckled my belt and dagger around my waist. I carried my sandals downstairs, careful to hold my breath when I crept past Kiran's room. He had ears like a fox, and I shuddered to think of what he'd do if he caught me sneaking out again.

I grabbed my bow and quiver off the hook and slipped out the door of the clinic. Above me, hung a wooden sign with the words HEALING HOUSE painted in green elven letters. It was a little faded, and if I wasn't careful it would rattle when I shut the door and wake Kiran up.

Outside, the market square was dark and quiet. Up and down the street, all the shops were closed and the streets were empty. From where I stood on our doorstep, I could see a long way because of where our clinic was perched on the crest of that small hill. All around the lights of the city twinkled in the night. Oil lamps flickered against colored glass windows and towering buildings made of cool alabaster stone. It was a sight I knew well.

Mau Kakuri was the largest Gray elf city rebuilt after the war. Some called it the "City of Mist" because it stood against a steep mountainside where a curtain of waterfalls poured down into a shallow river that ran through the middle of the garden district. The falls provided a constant haze of cool, crisp mist that hung in the air, trapped beneath the dense jungle canopy. Sometimes, if the sunlight broke through the trees just right, it made dozens of shimmering rainbows. And on nights like tonight, when the moon was full and bright, its silver light managed to bleed through the canopy and make the mist shine like a floating sea of diamonds.

With a deep breath, I started down the steps and out into the street. Nothing and no one stirred this late at night. The streets, arched bridges, tall stone buildings, and elegantly spiraling palace towers were all built atop the mossy boulders surrounding the plummeting water. The water from the falls made canals, pools, and streams that filled the air with the sound of running water. It also divided the city into districts along the canals—the market district where craftsmen ran their shops, the garden district where the orchards and vegetable gardens were kept for public use, and a few residential districts where most everyone lived. Kiran and I were one of a few exceptions because being the prominent city healer meant sometimes he had late night emergencies. It made more sense for us to live where we could be on call all the time.

Mau Kakuri was where the royal family had chosen to live, where the ancient archives were kept in caverns behind the falls, and where I had lived my entire life. I was one of only two humans living there, and we were so far from the boundary of Luntharda and Maldobar, so deep within the dense jungle, that odds were I'd never see another human ... ever. Not that the Gray elves were hostile to them, but making the journey through the dangerous jungle to reach it wasn't for the faint of heart. According to Kiran, humans didn't spend much time learning to climb and walk along the tree paths. This jungle—our world—terrified them.

I took the quiet back road to the edge of the city. I wasn't sure she'd be there. After all, Enyo was probably furious with me. She might never want to speak to me again. But I was willing to take that chance.

At the end of a long, narrow path that zigzagged treacherously up the side of the cliff face behind a few of the falls, I found her. She was sitting in our usual spot, her bare feet dangling over the edge of the mossy rocks. The water poured over the edge before her, a constant veil from the city below.

It was tricky to get to her. The boulders were slick and the edge was steep. But I'd come this way so many times I could have done it with my eyes closed.

"Did you come here to apologize?" Enyo wouldn't look at me as I sat down beside her.

"Would it help?" I hesitated and studied her profile. She didn't look thrilled to see me.

"No. And I'm not sure I would believe it, anyway."

I chewed on my lip.

"Your nose looks awful."

I poked at the fresh stitches gingerly. "Hurts, too."

"Good."

We sat in uncomfortable silence for what seemed like hours. Then, I took my bow off my back and placed it gently on her lap.

She stared and ran her fingers over it, then slowly raised her eyes to meet my gaze. "You're giving it to me?"

I nodded.

"But you'll lose your place to become a warrior and scout. You'll have to start all your training over."

"Yeah, well, I'll probably have to do that anyway." I shrugged. "Kiran doesn't think I'm ready. He thinks I'm selfish and probably stupid, too."

Enyo smirked and nudged me playfully with her elbow. "I kind of agree."

"As long as you don't hate me, that's all I care about." I sighed and sat back, resting my weight on my hands. "But I am sorry, you know. I shouldn't have brought you along."

She snorted sarcastically. "I saved your life! You'd be dead without me."

"As if."

"You're such an idiot, Reigh." She socked me in my sore shoulder.

I whimpered and rubbed my arm.

After a few seconds of sitting there, watching the falls and listening to the constant rumbling of the water, she looked my way again. She was still rubbing her hand along the bow I'd given her as though she were anxious about something.

"Do you remember what happened? After the stag charged for me?" she asked at last.

I tried to avoid her probing stare. "Do you?"

"No," she said quietly. "Everything got hazy. I was so afraid I must have fainted. I just remember feeling so cold. When I woke up, I was home. No one would tell me where you were. I thought you were dead, Reigh."

I swallowed hard.

"Was Kiran angry with you?"

"No more than usual."

She nibbled on her bottom lip. "My mother was furious. She said that we both should have died. It doesn't make any sense, does it? Why would the stag just decide to let us go? And what happened to the doe?"

I didn't want to answer any of her questions. Lying had never been one of my finer skills.

"My mother said it was a miracle," she said softly, like it was some kind of secret. "The spirit of the lapiloque saved us."

I stared at her. Seriously? I couldn't help it. I laughed out loud. "You think the ghost of some dead god saved us?"

Enyo pursed her lips, her cheeks flushed and her eyes narrowed. "Don't say it like that. He's real."

"Right." I rolled my eyes.

"He's not dead, Reigh. I know it."

"How? How can you possibly know that?"

Her expression became dreamy, like she was lost in her own private fantasy. "I can't explain it. I just do."

"That's ridiculous, even by your standards."

She glared at me. "Haven't you ever just believed in something, Reigh? Even though you couldn't see it or touch it?"

I thought about Noh and my body instantly got chilled.

"He's not just a myth. He *is* real." She spoke with such conviction; I almost wanted to believe her. "And he's coming back, just like he promised."

I cleared my throat. Maybe it wasn't such a bad thing to let lapiloque take the credit this time. After all, I didn't want Enyo to find out about Noh. "Right. Well, be sure to thank him when you meet him."

She socked me again. "You better thank him, too! We both should have died. My parents were furious. Father won't even speak to me."

"You think it would help if I apologized to them?"

"No." Her shoulders sagged some and she looked back down at my bow resting in her palms. "Besides, I ... I'm not even sure I want to be a scout anymore."

My jaw dropped. "What? Because of today?"

Some of her wavy black hair fell from where she'd tucked it behind her pointed ear, blocking my view of her face. "That's not the reason. I've been thinking about it for a while now. I know Mother will be upset. She's spent a lot of time training me. But there's something else—something I've wanted to try for a long time."

I leaned in closer, a little afraid she wouldn't tell me. Enyo hadn't hit the Gray elf version of puberty yet, so by their standards she was still a child. Even so, I could tell she was starting to change. Things were different. Growing up, she'd always told me what she thought about everything. Now she was keeping secrets, even from me. I tried not to let it faze me. It was bound to happen, sooner or later.

Still, I didn't like feeling like I was losing her trust.

Enyo turned a thin, forced smile back at me. "It's not a big deal. I haven't made up my mind yet, anyway."

"Don't lie. You're just trying to make me feel better," I grumbled and crossed my arms.

"No I'm not!" She giggled and tugged playfully at the rounded top part of my ear. "If I wanted to do that, then I'd say something like 'having a big scar on your nose will look so good!'"

I scowled. "Maybe it will."

That only made her laugh harder.

CHAPTER THREE

Things were quiet for a while and life got back to its normal rhythm for Kiran and me. I kept a low profile, following his orders to stay in the city and out of trouble. He didn't want me out of his sight. This was part three of my punishment, I guess. Part four was when he took the stitches out of my nose.

I spent long days working the clinic with him, tending to patients, washing linens, making medicines, and treating some of the minor injuries. It was easy work that kept me indoors and my mind occupied. But at the same time, it was smothering. Being trapped behind the walls of the clinic day in and day out was beginning to drive me crazy. I was safer, and yet I was aching for something more.

It didn't help that our little mishap had the city buzzing. Rumors swirled through the crowded markets and bustling public baths about how Enyo and I had miraculously escaped being mauled to death by a faundra stag. Some of our local friends even came by the clinic to ask me about it and check out my battle scar, although Kiran forbade me to tell them any details. Most people agreed with Enyo's theory that the spirit of the lapiloque had somehow intervened and protected us.

Only Kiran and I knew differently, and that was how it had to stay.

But Kiran didn't act like anything had happened. He went on running the clinic, treating patients for snake bites, broken bones, cuts, and all the usual daily ailments. He must have sensed my restlessness because he doubled my load of chores—probably to make sure I didn't have any spare time to do anything else stupid. After that, I didn't even have time to visit Enyo.

Early in the mornings, I ran errands on foot through the city squares, buying ingredients so I could spend the evenings grinding herbs and making medicines. Then I changed bed sheets, washed bandages, scrubbed Kiran's surgical tools, and helped him make the delivery kits for the midwives. Kiran was the best healer in the city, so his schedule was always packed and there was rarely a day when we didn't have a line of patients going out the door. We worked till sundown, ate our last meal of the day in awkward silence, and then I dragged myself upstairs to collapse into bed. That was it—my life in a nutshell.

On rare occasions, before the sun rose, Kiran left me in charge while he went out with the other warriors to lead scouting parties that kept a close watch on the city's outer perimeter. Every able-bodied warrior had to take a turn doing that. Well, everyone except for me.

For extra money, Kiran tutored some of the younger warriors, too. He taught them to fight and to shoot a bow, throw a dagger, or wield a scimitar with deadly accuracy. And all I got to do was watch him leave from the clinic doorway.

Being left at the clinic was beyond unfair. Before the incident, he'd at least let me be a sparring partner. I was his best student with a blade. But without a bow, I was going to have to wait until he decided I was trustworthy enough to be trained again.

Never, basically.

"Everyone else my age has already gone on their first hunt or done a patrol. They've brought down graulers, battled tigrex, and I'm just sitting here," I moaned.

Kiran was ignoring me, crouched at our fire pit stoking the coals so he could cook our dinner of roasted fish and potatoes.

"It's embarrassing. They're making fun of me, you know. All those warriors you're training call me names sometimes."

"I'll ask them to stop," he answered calmly.

"Right. Because getting my father to tell them off is really going to make them not treat me like a little kid," I scoffed.

Then I realized what I'd said.

Kiran pointed a harrowing glare in my direction. "I am *not* your father."

I cringed and bowed my head slightly. "I know."

My jaw clenched and I swallowed against the hard knot in my throat. Didn't he know how that made me feel? Or did he even care? Sure, I knew the Gray elf culture and traditions. Bloodlines were traced through the mothers, so being a father was considered an immense honor and privilege. It's not a word they used lightly. It was basically the pinnacle of any man's entire life to earn that title.

But Kiran refused it—even if I had no one else to call father.

He went on working quietly, almost as though he were trying to ignore me. At last, he got up to shove a few small silver coins into my hand. "Go and buy bread. No wandering. Come straight back."

I managed to keep it together until I got outside.

As soon as I was a safe distance from the door, I kicked the crap out of the first small tree I came across. I wailed at it hard, breaking the trunk and stomping it into the ground over and over until I was out of breath.

When I stopped, my face was flushed and my heart was racing. I raked my long, dark red hair out of my eyes and sat down a step to cool off. I squeezed the coins in my fist and thought about all the things I could do with them instead of buying bread.

Maybe I could pay a seer to tell me who I really was. But as enticing as that seemed, I was terrified of what a mystic might see if they looked at me too closely. Nothing good, that's for sure. Good people didn't have bad spirits following them around.

Besides, Kiran didn't have to say it. I already knew why he didn't want me calling him father. I was the kid no one wanted. My own parents had left me to die—probably because someone had tipped them off about the monster I was destined to become. It was bad enough Kiran was stuck with me now, if he claimed me as his son, then every stupid, horrible thing I ever did would reflect badly on him. He didn't want a monster as his only progeny.

"*A spider is only a monster to a fly,*" a familiar, whispering voice echoed through my mind. It sent shivers over my skin.

"Go away, Noh," I muttered. "Leave me alone."

I saw his red, glowing eyes smoldering in the shadows nearby. He materialized from the gloom and began to approach me, the edges of his pitch-black body wavering like licking black flames. He always appeared as a wolf-like creature with tall pointed ears and a long bushy tail, but I knew Noh wasn't an animal at all. He was something else entirely.

"*I cannot leave.*" He padded over to lurk cautiously nearby.

"Why not?"

"*Because we are one, you and I.*"

"What is that supposed to mean?"

His toothy maw curled into a menacing smile, before he vanished into a puff of black mist without answering.

"Reigh?"

I looked up and saw Enyo climbing the steps toward me. She had a confused frown on her face.

"Who are you talking to?"

I shook my head and grumbled, "Myself."

Her expression became sympathetic. "You had another fight with Kiran?" she guessed.

I nodded.

Enyo stood over me, tapping my foot with hers. "Come on. I want to show you something." There was an excited edge to her voice I couldn't resist.

I got to my feet, cramming Kiran's coins into my pocket, and followed Enyo into the sleeping city. Moonlight broke the canopy, casting eerie shadows over our path as we ran along the narrow passes between buildings, scaling garden walls, darting over bridges, and climbing terraces to get to the rooftops. Enyo was light on her feet, springing the gaps from one roof to another like a cat. It was fun, and I couldn't keep from grinning as I landed and kicked into a roll, leaping immediately to my feet to keep running.

For an instant, I truly felt free.

Enyo darted ahead, her legs pumping faster and faster until she sprang, arms up to grasp a low hanging limb. She whirled over, using the branch like an acrobat to flip herself over and land on top of it. My attempt at the same trick wasn't as graceful and she giggled as I flailed to get my balance again.

"You're still so clumsy," she laughed as she crouched next to me. "Maybe that's why Kiran won't make you a scout."

I pretended to sulk—right up until she grabbed one of my ears to pull me in closer so she could plant a kiss on my cheek.

"Aw, Reigh, don't pull that face. You know I'm just teasing."

I blushed, unable to come up with a good comeback.

We lingered there for a minute or two, watching the moonlit mist sparkling like a swirling shower of diamonds over the city. Well, that's what she was looking at. I was looking at her. I wondered what she'd be like after she went through that Gray elf change. Her hair would turn white and she'd look more mature, sure. But would she still like going running with me? Would she even want me around?

Before I could come up with the nerve to ask, Enyo took off again. I sprang down to chase after her, gulping in deep breaths of the cool, earthy jungle air. We dodged through the nearly empty market district. A few merchants were still closing down their shops. The blacksmith's forge still glowed in the gloom, his hammer making a rhythmic *clang-ping-clang ping* sound and sending up a spray of sparks as he worked. A few shepherds shouted us as we startled the flock of faundra yearlings they were carefully herding through the street. Oops.

I followed Enyo up the side of another building, through someone's rooftop courtyard. Happy sounds of laughing and lively conversation came from inside the house—along with the smell of something delicious. The farther we ran, the brighter the air seemed. Skidding to a halt at the edge of the last residential rooftop, the palace loomed before us with its slender spires bathed in silver light. Behind it, the waterfalls made a constant roaring sound.

Enyo sat down and began taking off her sandals.

"What are you doing?" I squatted down next to her.

"Shh! We have to be quiet. Now hurry and take yours off, too," she whispered.

I left my shoes next to hers and followed as she started climbing down the side of the building. There was a high, white stone wall separating the palace from the rest of the city. It only had one gate, and I didn't think we were going to just go waltzing through it.

Enyo had found her own way inside.

Between two young trees was a place where the roots had cracked the stone, breaking it just enough for a small person to slip through. She'd obviously been here before, because she'd taken the time to dig out the ground around the hole so I might be able to squeeze through.

"You first," she whispered, grinning from one pointed ear to the other, as the moonlight shimmered brightly in her multicolored eyes.

Okay; I had a bad feeling about this.

As I wriggled and squirmed my way through the hole, I prayed to whatever god might be listening that I wouldn't get stuck.

My body came to a screeching halt.

Yep. Definitely stuck. The gods hated me.

I tried to turn and flail, but it wasn't any good. My shoulders were wedged in tight. I could imagine the look on Kiran's face as he dragged me out by the ankles. I'd never hold another bow as long as I lived. Behind me, I could feel Enyo trying to help. She was pushing on my rear as hard as she could. This was a new low.

Suddenly, with one great push from behind, my shoulders popped free and I launched out of the hole and onto the soft grass right on my face.

I sat up sputtering and brushing my hair out of my eyes. Then I got a good look around. I was sitting in what appeared to be a garden. Before me was a small pond surrounded by willow trees. Through the wavering fronds, I could see stone archways and open hallways leading away into the palace. There were statues everywhere carved into the shapes of different animals, and beautiful flowering water plants grew in the still water.

Voices echoed from across the pond. I saw a fluttering of white fabric. And then Enyo grabbed me from behind, dragging me into a hiding place behind one of the statues. She pressed a finger to my mouth as a warning. We had to stay quiet.

"She is so fragile, Jace. We must do something. She won't survive on her own," an old woman's voice pleaded. "If we take her to the temple, perhaps he will hear our prayers. I can't just sit back and do nothing."

"Araxie ... I'm just as worried about her as you are," a man's deep voice answered. "But it's been so long. Nothing has changed. I think we need to look to our own medicines and methods—the things your people have relied on all these years. Or perhaps Kiran learned something about this when he studied in Maldobar."

"You don't believe, then?" The woman stepped into view, her long white gown billowing around her, a golden crown nestled in her snowy white hair. Her features were crinkled with age, and yet she stood with her shoulders back and her head held high.

The man moved in closer and took her hand. He wore dark green and silver robes with a circlet of silver on his head. He was an older man, too—but he was no Gray elf. His features were rugged and his ears were like mine ... round and undeniably human.

I sucked in a sharp breath.

I'd never seen the king and queen this close before. They didn't make many public appearances and were much older than I expected. The king had a stubborn looking cut to his jaw as he considered his wife. Age hadn't bent him or made him frail, probably because he'd been a dragonrider before leaving the human kingdom of Maldobar. At least, that's what everyone said whenever they told the old stories.

With a square-cut white beard and long hair that was salt-and-pepper colored, he walked like a warrior as he moved to put his arms around the queen. The way his eyes sagged at the corners made him look exhausted, though.

"I can't lose another one. She is my only grandchild, Jace. The last of our bloodline. I can't bear it." The queen's voice weakened. She started to cry as the king held her close at his side, slowly walking with her back into the palace.

Once they were gone, Enyo and I exchanged a glance.

"Is that what this was all about? Eavesdropping on the royal family?" I whispered.

Enyo scowled. "Of course not. I want to show you something." She grabbed my wrist and dragged me out of our hiding place.

Across the garden, on the other side of the pond, stood a large, flat stone tablet made of bone white marble. It had been polished until it was completely smooth and engraved with an intricate picture. It was a scene depicting a young man in strange armor holding a round object in the air over his head. I'd never seen him before, but I immediately knew who he was.

I'd heard the stories, after all. Everyone had. With his distinctly-human stature and pointed ears, wearing a carved pendant around his neck and the cloak of a dragonrider—it could only be one person.

Jaevid Broadfeather. The lapiloque.

The rest of the scene carved into the stone was just as detailed. There was an elven maiden on one side of him, and a human king on the other. Both were kneeling in great respect while their armies placed their weapons on the ground.

"It's from the end of the Gray War. When the lapiloque took up the god stone and destroyed it so it could never fall into evil hands again." Enyo was smiling again, her expression that of dreamy-eyed wonder. "You see? He was real."

"Just because someone carved it on a piece of rock doesn't make it true."

"And just because you don't believe in him doesn't mean it's not," she countered.

I pursed my lips. "What is it with girls and falling for these hero types, anyway?"

Enyo's cheeks turned as red as ripe apples. "I never said I liked him like *that*!"

"You didn't have to," I teased. "Just look at those rippling arms he's got, eh? I bet you dream about him."

"I do not!" She started after me with her fists tight.

I backed up and laughed, darting out of the way as she took a swing at my face. "I bet you can't stop thinking about what it would be like to get whisked away on the back of his dragon."

Enyo dove at me again, rearing back and trying to land a punch wherever she could. Then suddenly, she stopped short. I saw her face go pale and her eyes grew wide, focusing on something—or someone—behind me.

I felt the chill a second too late. My breath turned to white fog in the air. Slowly, I began to turn around.

Noh was standing right behind me, his red eyes smoldering like coals against the night. Only, this time he didn't look like a wolf. He looked like a human teenager with long, unruly hair, a squared jaw, thin frowning mouth, and the same long scar across the bridge of his nose that I now had.

He looked *exactly* like me.

Only, instead of dark, muddy red hair his was black. His skin was a strange ashen gray color, and his eyes had no center—just bottomless pools of vivid red light.

For an instant, I was captivated. I stood there marveling at the sight of him, totally unafraid. Why did he look like me? Was this something he'd always been able to do? I resisted the urge to reach out and offer him my hand, just to see what he would do.

Then I saw his attention shift. He stared at Enyo, and I could sense the change in his mood before a wicked smirk curled across his features. He licked his lips hungrily.

"No," I shouted and stumbled away from him. "You can't have her. Leave now!"

Noh tilted his head to the side slightly. He studied Enyo for a second longer and then looked back to me. His smile widened, showing slightly pointed canine teeth.

"I mean it! *Leave!*" I shouted louder, throwing my arms out as I planted myself between him and Enyo. "I won't let you touch her. You don't get to hurt anyone unless I say so!"

"*As you wish, my master.*" He chuckled, his whispering voice sending chills over my skin. With a flourish of his hands, he bowed at the waist and swiftly began to dissolve, vanishing into fine black mist.

The sound of his laugh was still hanging in the air even after he was gone. I tried forcing myself to calm down, but I was angry and panicked. I couldn't think straight. Enyo had seen him. No one else had *ever* been able to see him before—not even Kiran.

The situation was changing from my private problem with one random bad spirit to something I didn't even have a name for.

"R-Reigh?" Enyo's voice trembled.

"It's fine! It's nothing!"

"Nothing? Are you insane?"

I bit down hard on the inside of my cheek.

"Reigh, who was that?" She grabbed onto my arm so I would look at her. "What's going on?"

I jerked away and started for the hole in the garden wall. "Nothing! You didn't see anything! Just forget it ever happened!"

Enyo darted in front of me, planting her hands on my shoulders and forcing me to stop. "No! Tell me what's going on!"

I wanted to. I really did. But as often as we argued, there was one thing Kiran and I both agreed on: no one could ever know about the things I could do. I was dangerous. And while he called me master, Noh was becoming more and more difficult to control.

I couldn't risk it—I couldn't let him hurt Enyo. I'd let this thing, whatever it was, tear me apart before I ever let anything happen to her.

"No," I growled at her fiercely. "Get away from me. Never come near me again."

Her eyes widened and her mouth opened, but no sound came out. Slowly, she took her hands off me. "You don't mean that. I know you, Reigh. You're my best friend. Please, just talk to me. You can trust—"

I shoved her out of my way hard enough she fell back onto the grass. "You're wrong. You don't know anything about me. I'm not your friend. You're annoying and ... a waste of my time. I can't even stand the sight of you. Stay away from me, Enyo. I mean it."

When she didn't answer, I started running.

I dove for the hole in the wall and crammed myself back through it as fast as I could. I staggered to my feet on the other side and began sprinting through the city streets, past the empty market squares with gurgling fountains and down dark alleys crowded with wooden crates. I didn't bother going back for my shoes.

I ran for home.

CHAPTER FOUR

He knew. As soon as I burst through the door, barefooted and without any bread, Kiran knew something bad had happened. In an instant, he was on his feet and racing to shut and bolt the front door to our clinic. He grabbed the collar of my shirt, dragging me into the living room before he went around dousing all the lamps in the house. The glow from the embers smoldering in the fire pit gave off just enough light that I could see him blur around me, his expression grim as he shut all the windows and closed the drapes.

Our home became as dark as a tomb. Long shadows climbed the walls, taunting my frazzled nerves as I stood, wringing the hem of my tunic between my sweaty fingers. I was too afraid to look at them closely—afraid they might begin to move or take the shape of *him* again. My heart drummed in my ears and my whole body was numb. Whether it was because of Noh or just pure terror, I wasn't sure.

"Tell me what happened," Kiran commanded in a quiet, eerily calm voice. He was standing in front of me, holding my shoulders so I couldn't turn away.

I tried. But when I opened my mouth, nothing would come out. Questions whirled through my brain. Was I losing control? What if I couldn't get Noh to leave? What if he hurt someone? Would Kiran abandon me, too? Where would I go? What would I do? Would I ever find a home again?

My throat grew tight. I squeezed my eyes shut and bowed my head, trying to silence the whispering doubts.

Suddenly, Kiran pulled me in and wrapped his arms around me tightly, holding me like I was a small child.

"It's all right, Reigh," he said. "Whatever happened, I'll fix it. You're going to be okay."

I buried my face against his shoulder. Regardless of what he said, he couldn't fix it—not this time. And when I told him what had happened, I think he began to realize that, too.

Whatever I was becoming, I wouldn't be able to hide it for much longer. Noh was getting stronger, and for better or worse, he and I were bound somehow. I didn't know how or why, but he was here because of me. I couldn't get rid of him.

Kiran sat across the hearth from me, quiet despair creeping into his features as he stared at the flames. For a few minutes, he didn't say a word. We sat in heavy silence, watching the flames hiss and dance in the darkness. Dinner was finished and while it smelled good, neither of us had touched it.

A sound echoed through the house.

Knock, knock, knock.

Someone was at the door. My stomach did a frantic backflip and my heart hit the back of my throat. Kiran jumped up and snatched his scimitar off the hook by the door. I started to get up, too, but he snapped his fingers and gestured for me to stay put. I did—at least, until I heard him open the front door. Then I crept to the doorway. It was a long way down the hall, past the examination room to the front door, but sound bounced off the stone walls of our home like a cave.

"W-we apologize for the late hour, master. We bring word, an urgent request from Her Majesty the Queen," a young man's voice stammered with nervousness as he addressed Kiran.

My stomach did another backflip. Had Enyo been caught on the castle grounds?

"What is it?" Kiran demanded.

There was a rattling commotion and the sound of the door shutting. Whoever it was, Kiran had let them inside.

"News from the border. Maldobar is under siege. Northwatch burns and a company of human soldiers has retreated into the jungle. They are headed this way, but they travel with many wounded and no supplies. It is doubtful they will survive to reach the city," the young man reported. "Her Majesty would like you to lead a rescue mission to intercept them with supplies and guide them safely here. Your knowledge of the human language and customs would be essential."

"Leaving when? I have responsibilities to my patients here," Kiran spoke sharply.

"Immediately. The errand is most urgent. It's believed that one of these men is a member of Maldobar's royal family."

There was a tense silence. I waited, holding my breath, until at last I heard Kiran let out a growling, frustrated sigh.

"Very well. I'll need some time to arrange for my boy to stay with someone. Bring shrikes. We leave at dawn," he answered.

There were a few mutterings of gratitude and the retreating sound of footsteps. The front door snapped shut and I heard Kiran coming back down the hall. Quickly, I slipped away, up the stairs, and into my bedroom. I left the door cracked and flopped down onto my bed, jerking the blankets up to my chin.

I pretended to be asleep when I heard Kiran push the door open in a bit further. He sighed again, whispering something under his breath that I couldn't make out. Then he pulled the door closed and I heard his footsteps fading away down the hallway toward his own room.

Minutes passed and I waited until the house was quiet. Kiran hadn't come back out of his room. I figured he was either busy packing or stealing a few hours of sleep before he had to leave.

I got up and opened my closet, digging through my stuff until I unearthed a backpack made from soft, tanned leather. It was stocked with a few basic supplies, two days' worth of rations, and something else—something Kiran didn't know I had.

I pulled the long, curved blades out of the bag and held them firmly in my hands. The soft leather grips felt at home there, as though they'd been made especially for me. They hadn't, of course. These blades were a lot older than I was. Each pommel was plated with silver and set with chips of mica to make the shape of a snarling snagwolf's head.

The Gray elves called these weapons "kafki," and only the finest fighters for the royal family had wielded them. Each blade was twelve inches long and curved, like a pair of small shotels or scythes. But that wasn't what made them unique.

The blades weren't made of metal. They were made of wood that was as white as bone and harder than iron—wood from the most dangerous predator in all Luntharda. Greevwood trees were legendary, even among the Gray elves. They were subtle monsters, not something you'd think twice about until one had its roots around your neck and was slowly digesting you.

Gruesome? Oh yeah. But their wood was as prized as it was hard to gather. Once you cut away the bark and exposed the white meat of the tree beneath, you only had a short time to cut and mold it. After that, it became harder than iron. The elves liked making knives, swords, and scimitars from it because they couldn't be broken and they never went dull.

I'd come across these purely by chance, and Kiran didn't know anything about them. I was afraid that if he ever saw them, he'd take them from me and insist on giving them back to their rightful owner—whoever that was.

I'd found them during one of my many outings with Enyo, several years ago. After all, that encounter with the stag wasn't the first time we'd been out in the jungle alone. That day, we'd ventured farther than either of us had ever been before, out to one of the burial groves. That was where Gray elves traditionally buried their dead and planted a new tree atop the gravesite—something else they'd begun doing in honor of the lapiloque. We were exploring when I'd gotten one of those familiar, harrowing chills. Only, this one hadn't involved Noh. As soon as I stopped to look back ... I saw these. They were lying in a clear area between two of the trees, placed carefully on a patch of green moss like someone had left them there especially for me.

Only, there was no one else in sight.

Enyo thought they were a gift from the lapiloque or maybe even the foundling spirits. Whoever left them there, I wasn't about to turn down a free pair of Greevewood blades. All I had to do was keep them out of sight until I became an official scout—then it wouldn't matter where they came from.

It wasn't that weapons were forbidden to me. After all, Kiran had given me my first bow and taught me everything I knew about how to handle a blade. He'd trained me to wield a spear, a scimitar, fire a bow, how to throw daggers with lethal proficiency, and even how to fight with a human-styled sword. But I doubted if even he had any experience with kafki. They were considered an ancient weapon, used more for decoration now than anything else.

Maybe I'd bring them back into style.

I dug through my wardrobe for my scouting clothes—the best thing for traveling in Luntharda when you didn't want to be spotted. Since I wasn't a scout, I'd never worn them before, so they were still new and creased. They'd been waiting for me at the bottom of the drawer for a year.

Quickly and quietly, I took off my casual clothes and put on the black undergarments. I tucked the sleeveless black silk shirt into the matching long black pants, and bound each of my legs from my ankle to my knee with a strip of thick, black canvas, making sure to tuck my pants down into it snuggly. It was padding for running, skidding, rolling, leaping, and climbing through the trees. Then I did the same with my arms, binding from my wrists to my elbows with several layers.

The outer tunic was made of something thicker, and it was midnight blue with a silver border stitched into the elbow-length sleeves and around the base. It came down to my knees and was split up the sides so I could move easily. Over it, I buckled a light, black leather jerkin and a belt with sheaths for the two Greevwood kafki. I laced up my nicest pair of sandals, the ones with soles made especially for gripping even the slickest of tree limbs, and threw my pack over my shoulders.

The night air rushed in when I opened my bedroom window. Cool, sweet, humid, and delicious—I breathed it in deeply and climbed out onto the ledge.

A twinge of pain pinched in my chest. Crouched on the windowsill, I looked behind me at my childhood bedroom.

I had two choices.

Kiran was going to leave at dawn. He was going to strike out into the jungle, leading a group of warriors to help those human soldiers. And once again, I was going to get left behind. No way he'd take me with him, especially after what happened with Noh today. So, either I could stay here, hiding in the clinic like a coward and trying to keep my dark companion at bay while pretending there wasn't something seriously wrong with me.

Or I could do what Kiran didn't have the guts to do:

I could kick myself out.

He was probably hoping this would all blow over, that I'd regain control of Noh, or that he might even leave altogether and I'd get to finish out my life as a normal person. But deep down, the truth wasn't something either of us could change. Noh had killed once. He would do it again, and whether I liked it or not —whether it was fair or not—I would be the one to blame.

No one here would be safe from Noh unless I was gone.

Clenching my teeth, I looked out across the sleeping city of Mau Kakuri and knew I couldn't stay here anymore.

It was time to break free.

THIS WAS MY ONLY CHANCE. I HAD A FEW HOURS TO GET A HEAD START BEFORE Kiran figured out I was gone. He wouldn't be able to look for me, not right away. He'd gotten orders from the Queen, so he was obligated. I had to be long gone by the time he wrestled with his better sense and decided to ignore it and come looking for me.

First challenge—leaving the city. At least that was one I knew I could pull off. Enyo and I had done it dozens of times already. Despite having fairly tight security protecting the city perimeter, I was confident I could slip out without having to work too hard. The scouts on the ground rode on trained faundra, patrolling every five minutes to make sure no ground-based predators wandered in. The scouts navigating the tree paths above came by less frequently. After all, it wasn't as though no one could leave the city if they wanted to. But the fact that I was, you know, still known as a *kid* might give them reason to stop me to figure out where I was going at this hour.

I moved hastily down the stone paved streets to the edge of the city, slipping from shadow to shadow until I got to the boundary. There, the jungle rose before me like a swelling tidal wave, ready to drag me under. Dense, dark, deep, and dangerous, you had to be a special kind of stupid to go out there alone at night.

No one had ever accused me of being all that smart.

I waited, hiding behind a cluster of ferns, until I saw a scout pass by, riding in the saddle of a large faundra doe. As soon as she was gone, I raced for the nearest trunk and started to climb, scaling the side of the giant tree and clambering onto the first low limb almost twenty feet off the jungle floor. My pulse raced and my senses were honed, listening for the faint footsteps of man or beast.

There was nothing—just the eerie, humming songs of the frogs and insects. I took a deep breath, my insides buzzing with a panicked sort of excitement as I got moving again. My breathing hitched as I crossed the border into the wild, leaving the city behind me. There were no scouts anywhere in sight. I was free. Wherever I wanted to go, whatever I wanted to do—no one could stop me now. I was my own man.

I ran for the trees and struck out toward Maldobar. That's where I had to go. I wanted to see it for myself, the land where I was born. A kingdom filled with people with round ears like mine, and where dragons ruled the wide, open skies. It would take days to get to the boundary line, and that was if I didn't stop or get eaten by something first.

It sounded good at the time.

I kept up a fierce pace, sprinting along the tree-paths until my lungs burned and there were miles between Mau Kakuri and me. The rising sun was just beginning to break through the cracks in the canopy overhead, casting long beams of ethereal golden light all the way to the ground below. Fresh dew dripped off every petal and leaf. Colorful little birds squabbled and chased one another through the limbs.

And right about now, Kiran would be figuring out that I was gone.

Clenching my teeth, I pushed those thoughts from my mind and listened to the jungle instead. I couldn't hear the rumble of the falls or smell their moisture in the air anymore. Instead, I heard the ambient sounds of life all around me—the dripping of dewdrops pattering from the leaves, the rustle of bird wings, the chattering of insects, and the distant calls of sarbien monkeys. I spooked a young shrike that was napping in a sunny spot out on an open branch, warming his translucent wings. He hissed at me as I darted by, but didn't give chase.

Finally, I stopped to catch my breath and check my bearings. The jungle was a tangled mass of dense greenery and entwined tree branches. Getting lost would have been easy, but the first thing Kiran had ever taught me was how to navigate. It's the first thing all Gray elves learned because if you couldn't find your way back home, you were guaranteed to get eaten by something.

The elves had their own system of roadways along the broad limbs of the trees, far above the jungle floor. They marked them with symbols engraved into certain places on the trees. A circle meant a road leading north. A circle with a horizontal line through it meant east, one with a vertical line meant west, and one with a single dot in the center meant south. Easy, right?

But those were just the main pathways that led between major cities. There were plenty of other destinations in the jungle like temples, mineral springs, hunting grounds, burial sites, and things like that. There were also warnings of things to avoid—like a grove of Greevwood trees that had sprung up too close to a city or village.

Novice warriors and scouts weren't supposed to leave those marked paths.

But if you ever found yourself lost in an unknown part of the jungle, far from a city where someone might not hear you calling for help, there was always *the* tree.

Kiran told me that the humans navigated using the stars. Because of the dense jungle canopy, we didn't get to see the stars often. Or the moon, either, for that matter. However, if you climbed high enough to peek out of the canopy, you could see the tree from almost anywhere. Day or night, winter or summer, the tree was there. It never changed—never dropped its leaves in fall or grew an inch in springtime.

Paligno had planted that tree when the lapiloque had died—or at least, that's what everyone believed. They said it had just sprung up, willed to being by the ancient god of life to cover the lapiloque's burial place and guard the entrance to his tomb. That was the reason the Gray elves had adopted the custom of planting trees over the gravesites of their own loved ones. Regardless of how it had gotten there, the lapiloque's tree had grown to a size that towered over all the others in Luntharda. It loomed over the canopy, and could be seen for miles and miles. It was a fixed point, which is all you needed to navigate.

I'd only seen the tree once. When I was ten, Kiran had taught me how to climb up to the very top of the canopy and hoist myself through the barrier of leaves and brambles. Up there, the air blew freely, the sky was endless, and the sun was like a warm caress on my skin. I could see the tree from Mau Kakuri. It wasn't that far away, though it was closer to the boundary line with Maldobar than the city. Kiran said few people went to see it now. It was out of great respect for lapiloque that they let him sleep in peace, leaving the temple grounds untouched and the area around it free of civilization. They believed sincerely that one day he would rise again.

A load of crap, really. If there was one thing I knew for certain, it's that dead people stayed dead.

CHAPTER FIVE

After two days, I was exhausted.

I ran until my feet were so sore and blistered from my shoes I could barely stand to take them off. I didn't dare stop for more than a few minutes; just long enough to eat, drink, and catch my breath. I knew every second that passed meant Kiran was gaining on me.

I wasn't going to make it easy on him. I doubled back on my own steps occasionally, avoided leaving as much trace evidence as possible, but I knew Kiran was a keen hunter—arguably one of the best in Mau Kakuri. He would find my trail and he would be relentless in following it. My only chance was to get to the boundary first.

I stood out in Luntharda. My red hair, thicker human build, height, even my voice was a dead giveaway that I wasn't one of them. But if I could cross over into Maldobar, I could vanish into the tapestry of other humans without a trace. He'd never be able to find me.

At least, that's what I was hoping.

I limped along a narrow branch, surveying the ground, searching for a good, secluded place to hide and rest. The rushing roar of water drowned out the other jungle sounds. I could smell it close by like a crisp sweetness in the air.

Generally, this wouldn't be a good place to stop and make camp. Water meant lots of foot traffic—both from elves and from prey animals. Prey meant predators, which was something I didn't particularly want to contend with when I didn't have a bow.

But my water skin was empty. I was parched, my feet were aching, and I was far enough from any village or city that I felt confident I wouldn't see anyone else who might be able to tell my very angry parental guardian which direction I'd gone.

I began the steep climb down out of the trees. Either I was going to die or get something to drink, it was as simple as that. Slowly, step-by-step, I made my way across the damp soil to the edge of the water. I gave one last long look around and then cupped my hands into the water.

I drank until I could feel my stomach sloshing, and then I slung my bag off my shoulders. I refilled my water skin and slipped it back into my bag before I started taking off my shoes. I had angry blisters between my toes and my heels were bruised. Soaking them made it a little better, though.

After catching a few small fish by hand, I packed up my things and retreated to the safety of the trees. I chose a dark place on a smaller, narrower limb to curl up and eat my dinner—raw. Gross, but I couldn't risk lighting a fire. Fire drew curious creatures from the depth of the jungle and that was exactly the kind of attention I was trying to avoid.

With my back against the trunk and my knees pulled to my chest, I gazed up at the interwoven branches of the trees overhead. It wasn't exactly comfortable. I was cold and sore. Sitting that way made my neck cramp. I couldn't help but think about how, miles from here, there was a soft, warm bed in a safe house where I could have been sleeping. Kiran wasn't a great cook, but at least whatever he made for us wasn't raw. I wondered where he was. For all I knew, he could be just a few feet away, watching me right this second, waiting to see if I would give up and go back home.

I sort of hoped he was.

I thought about Enyo, too. I hadn't even said goodbye. Our last words hadn't been nice ones. I'd said horrible things just so she would stay away from me. Kiran was right; she was just a child, too naïve to see that nothing good would ever come from being close to me.

Sure, I had gotten her into trouble plenty of times over the years. But this situation wasn't anything like those. This wasn't some prank, and I'd never set out to intentionally hurt her. If I let her get close to me now, knowing what Noh might do, I was intentionally putting her life at risk. And that wasn't so different from murder. Not in my mind, anyway.

For her sake, I hoped she would just forget about me.

I started nodding off as I listened to the sound of the water and imagined myself being carried away on it, weightless in the cool current.

I wondered if that's what it felt like to fly.

There were voices in the dark.

Someone was shouting.

I bolted to my feet out of a sound sleep, my mind hazy and my hands immediately going to my weapons. I looked around in a daze. But I was alone—nothing but the sound of the rushing water below.

At first, I thought it had been a dream. Or maybe Noh was playing tricks on me. He did that sometimes, the jerk.

Then I heard it again—the voices of men shouting echoed through the trees. My pulse raced. I squeezed my blades tighter.

Kiran? No. I knew he wouldn't be that stupid. Making that kind of noise in the wild at night was essentially a death wish.

Besides the voices sounded foreign. I couldn't understand them, at first, but then I recognized their language.

They were speaking the human tongue.

The noise carried through the darkness, making it hard to pinpoint where it was coming from. Then, out of the corner of my eye, I saw a flicker of light. Fire winked in the gloom.

Fire *and* noise? Seriously, how stupid could they be?

I crept closer, stalking carefully through the shadows along the overhanging limbs. A high-pitched yipping and guttural snarling made me freeze in place.

There they were—a company of men crowded together with torches and swords raised, pinned at the edge of the river by a snarling pack of snagwolves. The men wore thick armor made of metal and long cloaks of red and blue. Their hair was cut short and their ears were rounded. They were human—just like me.

Two of them were badly wounded and bound to makeshift stretchers made from limbs and vines. Their comrades gathered around them to stand guard against their attackers. Meanwhile, the snagwolves circled, their noses twitching at the smell of blood and fresh meat.

Suddenly, two of the men stepped off into the water. They tried to swim for the opposite bank, but the current was swift and their heavy metal armor weighed them down. They sank like stones, disappearing beneath the depths. There was nothing anyone could do.

The snagwolves closed in, their bright green eyes shining wickedly under the orange glow of the torches. They were spooked by the fire, although not enough to be discouraged. They hunted as a unit, and were as cautious as they were cunning. Their gnarled, green-tinted pelts mimicked the texture of roots and plants so they blended in perfectly with the jungle. They could hide in plain sight, and their powerful jaws could crush your bones to splinters. Once one got his teeth into you, there was little chance you'd ever be able to pry him off.

It was bad news for the soldiers.

The men tried to muster. One of them kept shouting over all the noise, calling to the others. He wore a different cloak than the rest, more intricate with a golden eagle embroidered onto the back.

The sight of that emblem struck a chord in my brain. That was the mark of Maldobar's king—so these had to be the men Kiran had been asked to find.

It was a miracle they'd made it this far. But at the rate things were going, they were all going to die long before Kiran or anyone else found them.

That is, unless *someone* was willing to get their hands dirty.

A snagwolf lunged at the leader of the soldiers, locking its powerful jaws around his calf. The man shouted and raised his sword to strike. Suddenly, a second snagwolf got a mouthful of his cloak and dragged him to the ground. His comrades stepped in to help, and were immediately attacked by the rest of the pack.

It was total chaos.

I clenched my teeth and coiled my legs beneath me; gripping my blades so tightly my fingers went numb. I took a breath and leapt out of the tree, hurling myself into the air with my arms spread wide. As soon as I felt my feet touch the ground, I kicked into a roll to ease the impact. It still knocked the wind out of me, and I was seeing stars when I sprang to my feet again.

But there was no time to recover. The fight was on.

I plunged both of my blades into the side of the nearest snagwolf. The creature shrieked in pain, drawing the attention of the rest of the pack. Their wicked green eyes turned to me, recognizing me as the greatest threat to their dinner plans.

Ripping my kafki free of the dead snagwolf, I sank into a crouch as the pack converged, attacking me in waves of snapping vice grip jaws and razor-sharp teeth. I whirled my weapons, spinning through maneuvers and slicing through the monsters one after another. I could hear Kiran's voice in my head, chiseling his training methods into my brain. *Don't think. Feel the rhythm of your enemy. Good. Now, react. Counter. Faster. Move with him. Never drop your arms. Watch your footing. Keep your breathing steady. Good.*

I kicked one snagwolf square across the snout, sending it rolling while I rammed my weapon through another's chest. My white blades were stained pink with blood. I was more focused than I'd ever been. My blood ran hot through my veins. I ducked as a snagwolf leapt at me, kicking into a roll and thrusting both kafki upwards into the belly of the animal as it sailed past me.

Out of nowhere, my shoulder exploded with pain. I yelled. One of the snagwolves had jumped me from behind. Now I was in its grip. Its jaws clamped down on my collarbone with crushing force, threating to snap it in half.

I flailed, tried to writhe free, but the more I fought, the harder the animal squeezed. My arm started to go numb. I felt my weapon slip out of my hand. Not good.

Suddenly, the snagwolf let me go.

I dropped to the earth, reeling from the pain and the sensation of my own hot blood soaking through my clothes. When I looked back, I saw the leader of the human soldiers standing over me. He had rammed his sword up to the hilt through the snagwolf's neck. One wrenching flip of his wrist twisted the blade and cut the monster's head clean off.

He looked down at me, breathless and pasty with terror. He asked me something in the human language, but I was too delirious to understand.

Then I saw it. Another one of the creatures stalking him from behind, green eyes winking in the dark, shoulders pumping in preparation for the attack.

I didn't think. There wasn't time. I still had one blade in my hand when I sprang up, shoved the human leader out of the way, and met the snagwolf in mid-air. I howled like a maniac and swung, jamming my kafki into the open mouth of the beast.

We fell together. The snagwolf landed on top of me, my blade still lodged in its open mouth—rammed straight through to the back of its head. The full weight of the beast bore down on me, crushing my lungs so I couldn't get a good breath until I managed to wrench myself out from under it.

I didn't have either of my weapons anymore when I staggered to my feet. My head was swimming with pain. Blood ran down my back. My vision started to spot and tunnel and I had to clench my teeth and flex my legs to force blood back up into my head.

Then I saw them—four angry snagwolves prowling toward me from all sides.

I was going to die.

I bent down to snatch up the nearest object I could use for a weapon: a big rock.

I raised the rock and shouted at the snagwolves, daring them to come at me.

The monsters recoiled, hesitating. They winced, tucked their tails, and bolted away from me. I stood in stunned silence, watching as the rest of the snagwolves retreated into the jungle, yelping and shrieking in panic like they couldn't get away fast enough.

A cold blast of breath tickled the back of my neck. I dropped the rock and slowly turned around.

Noh was lurking behind me, his form boiling like a menacing black cloud. He looked like a large, shadowy wolf again, which was kind of a relief. But that didn't mean I was happy to see him—even if he had saved my life.

His red eyes glowed in the dark and his mouth was twisted into a smug, wolfish grin. *"Death. Blood. Carnage. Slaughter. Such a glorious smell!"*

I frowned. "I won't thank you."

"You don't need to. I am eager to serve you, my master."

My gaze followed the trail the snagwolves had taken back into the jungle. "Go, then," I said at last. "Make sure they don't return."

"Yes, as you command." Noh's outline shivered with enthusiasm and he vanished without a sound or trace.

When I turned around again, I was met with a crowd of bloodied, wide-eyed human soldiers. They were gathering around me cautiously, and I could sense the tension in the air as they looked me over. I was a strange sight for them, a human dressed like a Gray elf accompanied by a weird-black-misty-demon-thing. Not something you come across every day, even in Luntharda. They were eyeing me up as though they weren't sure whose side I was on.

Unfortunately, I didn't get a chance to argue my case. I smiled, managed a small wave of greeting ... and passed out cold.

CHAPTER SIX

My body refused to respond. My lungs wouldn't work. I couldn't even get my eyes to open. Everything spun, like I was being whipped around in a churning whirlpool. I couldn't tell up from down. There was nothing—nothing but darkness, confusion, and that aching, squeezing sensation in my chest as I ran out of air.

Was this what dying felt like?

"*There you are.*" A woman's whispering voice echoed through the dark, chilling me to the marrow. "*I was wondering when you would find your way.*"

W-what? I couldn't even take in enough air to reply.

"*It's time. You must awaken he who sleeps. You need his blood—pure blood—to complete the ritual.*"

Ritual? He who sleeps? Nothing about that made sense. I didn't recognize that voice; I couldn't even concentrate on it because I was spinning faster and faster. Air—I needed air!

Something or someone smacked me across the face. Instantly, the spinning stopped. There was cold, moist earth underneath me. Strange voices muttered in the human language, seeming to come from all around. At first, it was just garbled and confusing. But as my head started to clear, I understood what they were saying.

"Wake up, boy!"

"Maybe he's dead?"

"He's not dead. Look there, he's breathing."

I was? Then why did it feel like I was still drowning? If I could just move a little, maybe I could break this trance before it crushed the life out of me.

"I think I saw his eye twitch!"

"Shh! Stand back! You're too close."

"He's not moving."

"Maybe if we poured a bit of water over his head? I've seen that work before."

Someone smacked my face a little harder. "Come on, boy! You're not dead. A reckless fool, maybe, but not a dead one."

Suddenly, my eyes popped open and I gulped in a deep, frantic breath of the cool night air. I wheezed and wheezed as my vision slowly cleared. Lying on my back, I stared up into the glare of torchlight. The human soldiers were crowded around me, peering down at where I was sprawled out on the ground. Their expressions were mixture of fear and bewilderment. When I stirred, a few of them jumped back.

I recognized their leader. He was kneeling next to me, and was apparently the one who'd been smacking me into consciousness. When he saw me moving, he let out a heavy sigh of relief. "Welcome back to the realm of the living."

"L-lumori," I rasped in elven.

"What?"

I struggled to remember the human word. I hadn't spoken that language to anyone but Kiran before, and even then, only on special occasions—like when I was being lectured. "L-lights. Douse the lights."

The soldiers exchanged confused glances.

"The lights will bring them," I said. "More ... from the darkness."

They didn't stop to ask who, what, or why. Immediately, all the soldiers began extinguishing their torches, either by stamping out the flames or running over to dip them in the water. Darkness swallowed us, and the soldiers gathered in close again. I guess they were warier of what might be hiding in the dark than me. Maybe that was because they'd also seen Noh.

The human leader helped me sit up. The pain in my shoulder from the snagwolf's bite made my vision spot and blur again. I clenched my teeth, unable to stop myself from shaking. The wound had been crudely bandaged, but I was going to need some real medical attention soon.

The air was tense. Everyone was looking at me, like they were expecting me to suddenly attack them, too. Really, though, I was in shock. I stared wordlessly at all the human men. I'd never seen so many.

"We'd all be dead if you hadn't showed up," the leader said. He gave me a broad, friendly smile and patted my back reassuringly. "You're quite a fighter for such a young man. What's your name?"

I hesitated. I didn't have a reason not to trust this guy—after all, he'd prevented that snagwolf from tearing my arm off. But it was kind of intense to answer questions with everyone gawking at me like that. I glanced around at my captive audience and lowered my head in embarrassment.

The leader seemed to get it. His expression softened and he gave me a sympathetic smile before commanding his men to prepare to move out. No one questioned him. They all scurried around, gathering their belongings and tending to their injuries, leaving us alone for the time being. There were considerably fewer of them now. The snagwolves had dragged more than a couple of them off into the jungle. Judging by the two smashed wooden stretchers, they'd taken the easiest prey first.

I shuddered to think I'd almost joined them in that fate.

"Just when I thought I'd seen everything this jungle could possibly surprise me with, a human teenager pops out of the trees and saves my life by fighting like a Gray elf."

The leader chuckled as he sat down next to me. He wasn't very old, but he wasn't anywhere close to my age, either. It was hard for me to tell with humans. They wore their age more harshly than elves did. But the shaggy golden hair that fell around his neck didn't have any traces of white in it, and his tanned, sun-bronzed skin wasn't all that wrinkled. He did have a few tired-looking lines in the corners of his dark blue eyes, but the squared cut to his jaw still made him seem fiercely capable.

"Reigh," I answered at last. "My name is Reigh."

"Well met, Reigh. You can call me Aubren." He offered to shake my hand. Kiran had told me about that human gesture—it was a sign of friendship and trust.

I awkwardly shook it. Learning to be human was going to be harder and stranger than I'd anticipated.

"We need to move soon," I said. "We can't stay here. The smell of blood will bring other predators."

He looked worried. "Are you willing to go with us?"

It wasn't like I had a choice. They weren't going to last long otherwise.

"We need to make our way to the royal city of the Gray elves as soon as possible. I am seeking an audience with Queen Araxie. Can you take us there?" His expression became earnest, almost desperate.

I couldn't hold eye contact for long. Talking to him, sitting next to him—it was bizarre to suddenly be this close to another human.

"What's the matter?" Aubren looked worried, like he was afraid I might refuse. "You don't know where it is?"

I scratched nervously at the back of my neck with my good arm. "N-no, I mean, it's just ... I've never met another human before."

He raised his eyebrows in surprise. "Never?"

"Well, I've seen King Jace before. He's human, too. But I've never actually met or talked to him before."

"I see." I could tell by his tone he thought that was strange.

Poor guy. He had no clue just how strange I actually was.

"You're a long way from Mau Kakuri. But the Queen knows you're here. She's already dispatched a scouting party to find you and help bring you back safely."

Aubren's broad shoulders went slack. He slowly closed his eyes and bowed his head. For a moment, I thought he was upset. But then I heard him chuckle. "That's the first good news I've heard in months."

I started to get up, wincing and cursing under my breath at the pain in my shoulder. I was going to have to do something more permanent to fix the wound. Or rather, I was going to have to get someone to *help* me do it. But first, we had to get away from here—away from the water and the smell of fresh blood.

"I know a place we can take refuge for the night." I nodded for him to follow. "But we need to leave. Now. It's not safe on the jungle floor. Too many big hungry bad things are looking for food, and I can't fight them like this."

"Of course. Lead on, Reigh." Aubren shakily got to his feet, giving me an earnest, hopeful smile.

I took one look at his leg, which was still bleeding through the sloppy bandage he had wrapped around it, and realized this wasn't going to be easy. He wouldn't be walking very far. At least, not without leaving a rather obvious trail of blood for any hungry predator to follow.

We were going to have to find somewhere close to hide, tend our wounds, and wait for help.

While Aubren limped around, checking on his men and getting them ready to move out, I searched around for one of their discarded torches. I broke off a piece of the charred end and found a smooth, flat stone. If Kiran was out here somewhere, looking for these guys or me, odds were, he'd be able to track us this far. So, I left him a message etched into the stone and positioned it carefully on top of a stack of more rocks, right in the middle of the clearing. It would be obvious, especially to a seasoned warrior and scout.

"Leaving breadcrumbs?" Aubren was standing over me, watching with a bemused grin.

"They might be a few hours away, or a few days. Either way, eventually they will find this. Then they'll know where to find us."

"Smart boy." He had a strange, almost impish smirk on his face when I turned to face him. He held something out to me—my two kafki.

I took the blades and slipped them back into my belt. "Not really. But if we are going to survive, I need you and your men to do as I say. No noise. No talking. And no fire or light. Follow in a straight line, right behind me. No one goes anywhere alone. And if you see any pink fruit lying on the ground, *do not* touch it."

Aubren didn't say anything else as we finished gathering the group and finally struck out into the jungle. I took the lead and immediately began looking for a good place to ascend into the safety of the trees. After all, the place I had in mind for us was a few miles away and the less time we spent on the ground, the better.

We crossed the river at a shallow place and kept going, making a zigzag trail through the towering undergrowth. The men clumped together. They were afraid, not that I blamed them, they'd been through a lot, and they kept looking at everything with tense apprehension. The jungle hadn't been gentle—not that it ever was.

At last, I found a tree covered in a network of thick vines that made something like a living lattice all the way to the lowest branch. It would be easy for novice climbers to handle. One by one, I sent the men upward and told them to wait for me.

Aubren's leg was getting weaker and he was losing blood because of the poor bandaging, so I waited to send him up last and climbed along beside him. I could see his hands shaking as he reached for every handhold. His jaw was rigid and the veins in his neck stood out against his darkly tanned skin. His forehead beaded with sweat, making his shaggy hair stick to his face.

At the very top, his wounded leg suddenly gave out. He slipped, losing his grip and began to fall backwards.

Without thinking, I lunged out, grabbed his arm, and roughly dragged him back against the side of the tree. For a few seconds, we just hung there together, panting as bits of bark fell the long distance to the jungle floor below. That was too close for comfort.

"H-heights don't agree with me," Aubren stammered weakly.

"Just a little further. We're almost there."

He looked at me, his brow drawn up in frantic distress. "If I don't make it, please take the rest of my men on to see the Queen. They must reach her. W-we need her help."

"That's not going to—"

"No! You have to promise me, Reigh. I have a duty to my people. I cannot fail them."

We stared at one another in silence. I got this weird feeling, like maybe I'd seen him before. Only, that was impossible.

Slowly, I nodded in agreement.

With his jaw set in determination, Aubren started climbing again. I watched him go, shakily scaling the distance to the first limb where the rest of his men were waiting. They helped haul him over the edge and made a path for me when I made my way to join them.

It took a lot of patience, coaxing, and time to get the soldiers used to using the tree paths. They didn't like the idea of hopping from one branch to another, even if there was more than enough room. I guess humans in Maldobar didn't do a lot of that kind of thing. They weren't very good at staying quiet, either. Progress was slow, very slow, and it was nearly dawn by the time we finally arrived at the spot I had in mind for us to stop.

A steep cliff jutted upwards, right against a group of trees whose limbs butted up and curved around the mossy rock face. The cliff was riddled with big ferns and flowering plants, but there were also lots of flat open spaces to perch and watch the jungle floor as it sloped downwards into a deep gorge.

But I was looking for the cave.

Kiran had brought me here once, a long time ago. He showed me where the cave was and how to secure it. He told me that if I ever got lost, I needed to try my very best to follow the river and find my way to this spot. This was a safe place, a hideout, where I could wait to be found and I wouldn't have to worry about anything bad finding me.

I'd avoided the cave before for that exact reason. I figured it was probably the first place Kiran would come looking for me. Now it was our best shot at surviving long enough to see Mau Kakuri.

The cave had a narrow entrance that was hidden from plain view. You had to know exactly where to look. Brushing back two big fern fronds, I saw it. My body went slack, and I let out a deep sigh. So far, so good.

There was a big, mossy stone rolled in front of the entryway to keep other animals from taking up residence in it. Normally, I could have handled that on my own. My injured shoulder was slowing me down, though, so I had to get a few soldiers to help me roll it out of the way.

"Okay," I told them. "You can light a torch inside. It will be safe."

Aubren eyed me skeptically. Maybe he didn't like the idea of squeezing through that narrow passage into a dark, unknown place. "You're certain?"

I nodded. "I'm going to collect plants."

"Plants?"

"Yes, you know ... " I struggled to think of the right words. "For medicines. Herbs?"

Aubren seemed to understand as he smiled and patted my good shoulder. "Smart boy," he said again.

I was starting to like that kind of praise. Kiran never praised me for anything. Enyo said it was tough love because he didn't want me to get too cocky. Maybe it was, although it still would have been nice to get a little approval every now and then.

When I returned to the cave, my arms were full of firewood and a bundle of fresh herbs I knew I could use to make poultices and quick medicines to fight infection. The soldiers were pleased to see me, and gathered around as I began to make a fire in the middle of the cave.

The chamber was large—a lot bigger than the entryway suggested. There was plenty of room to stand and move around, and there were a few old bedrolls and animal hide blankets stored at the back that had been left behind by other travelers.

Once the fire was lit and the stone was rolled back over the doorway, the soldiers seemed to relax. They began peeling off their layers of armor and unfurling the bedrolls for the more severely injured members of their party. I watched silently as I sat, stoking the small fire. It was still surreal to see them, so many humans, just going about their business. They were completely different from elves—more so than Kiran had told me. They were much bigger in build, brawnier, and many of them had short beards. It made me rub my own chin, which had a few days' worth of short, rough stubble on it now.

Elves couldn't grow facial hair, and I'd felt like a huge freak when I'd first started growing some. Enyo had even teased me about it once, saying I might start growing hair all over until I looked like a big walking hairball. After that, I'd asked Kiran to teach me how to shave it off.

"So tell me, how does a human boy with hair as red as a ripe tomato wind up living in Luntharda, dressed like a Gray elf? Do your parents live with the Gray elves, as well?" Aubren asked as he sat down next to me. He wasn't looking so good. His face was a little ashen and he was still breathing hard.

"No, not exactly," I replied as I pulled out my medical kit and got to work preparing medicines. "You're going to have to roll up your pant leg so I can see the wound."

Aubren made painful grunting sounds as he obeyed. The wound itself looked gruesome. There was a deep, jagged bite mark right in the muscle of his calf. He was lucky, though, even if he didn't feel that way. The bite hadn't severed any major arteries and it was clotting well on its own. All I had to do was clean it, apply a good herbal poultice, and wrap it securely. Kiran would be able to do more when we got back to Mau Kakuri, but at least he wouldn't die of infection before then.

"I might have spared myself this if I hadn't given up my greaves," he muttered. "We had to shed a lot of our gear early on so we could move more quickly."

A wise decision on their part. According to Kiran, human armor wasn't practical for anything in Luntharda except making you harder for a Greevwood tree to digest.

"So where are your parents, then?" Aubren asked again. I guess talking helped take his focus off me poking around the gaping holes in his leg while I assessed the full extent of the damage.

"I don't know. Somewhere in Maldobar, I guess. I was abandoned as a baby. The Gray elves took me in."

"I see." He winced as I began pouring water from my water skin over it and cleaning out the dirt and grime. "Then why were you out here on your own? I didn't think Gray elves traveled alone."

I avoided his eyes and pretended not to hear him. Taking some of the herbs I had gathered, I used the sharp end of one of my blades to cut and mash them into a slimy green paste. I smeared it over his wound, even when he flinched and hissed in pain.

"It might sting at first, but it will help with the pain and will keep it from getting infected," I told him. I took a glob of it on my finger and held it out to him. "Here, you should eat some, too. It will give you back your strength."

Aubren eyed the green goo doubtfully. Okay, so it looked gross—like a big slimy green plant-booger. Not to mention it tasted really, *really*, bad. But it would help, I was sure about that.

He shuddered and gagged as he let me swipe the goo onto his tongue. I let him have a few sips of water to wash it down. After that, he lay back on the stone floor, seeming to relax as the remedy took effect.

I finished my work by cutting up one of the animal hide blankets into a long, thin strip that I used to tightly bandage his calf. Kiran might insist on some stitches on the larger gashes later. I wasn't sure how much more pain Aubren could withstand right now, though. Humans weren't as strong as elves, even if they were bigger, and I didn't want to push him too far. I'd give it some time, see how the wound reacted to my remedy, and then decide if he needed more intensive treatment.

I went around to the other wounded soldiers, doling out the green herbal goo to any who needed it. I cut more bandaging strips out of the blankets, wrapped wounds, and even had to apply a few stitches to more serious gashes. It was hard work and all the while, the blood loss from my own injury was beginning to make my head fuzzy. I had no adrenaline left to keep me going, and I barely made it back to Aubren's side before I collapsed onto my rear. The shaking in my body had gotten worse and my face was dripping with sweat.

"Here," Aubren said as he sat up and moved closer. "Let me see. I'm no medic, but maybe you can talk me through it."

I hesitantly slipped off my black leather jerkin and tunic. I could feel the fabric sticking to my skin, soaked with my own blood. I didn't know how bad it was. I didn't want to look. Unfortunately, being the only person in the vicinity with any medical training meant I didn't have a choice.

My leather jerkin had protected me from the worst of it. There were a few deep punctures where the snagwolf's teeth had broken through to my skin, but for the most part, it had been the crushing force of his jaws that had left my shoulder badly bruised. As far as injuries went, mine were minor.

I shuddered and handed Aubren my water skin. "Just rinse it off and smear some of the herbal paste on it."

"You're sure?"

"Yeah. It'll be fine."

Aubren obliged. After he'd cleaned out my wound and dabbed some of the poultice on it, I talked him through how to properly apply a bandage to my shoulder. It was still looser than I would have liked. I guess he was worried about hurting me. I still gave him credit for trying.

"So, what made you want to run away from home?" he asked suddenly.

I froze and flashed him a panicked glance out of the corner of my eye. How had he known that?

"Relax. I was a teenager, once. I know it can be hard at times. You want to prove yourself as a man, even if your parents feel you aren't ready. And in your case, being raised by an entirely different race, I can only imagine you've had to deal with more than your fair share of challenges. It can't be easy."

"No," I agreed quietly. "It isn't."

"But I'm sure your family, Gray elf or otherwise, is probably worried about you."

I ducked my head in shame. I knew he was right. Kiran was probably freaking out, driving everyone nuts trying to track me down. The only time I'd ever seen him lose his calm and collected demeanor was when something happened to me. There was one time in particular, when I was six or seven, and I'd fallen out of a tree while learning to climb. I'd broken my leg, and Kiran had been more upset about it than I was. It was one of the only times I could recall ever seeing him look scared.

I rubbed the back of my neck sheepishly. "I keep screwing up. I thought it would be easier if I just left."

Aubren smiled warmly. "We all make mistakes, Reigh. Young, old, Gray elf, or human—we all screw up every now and then. It doesn't mean our parents don't love us, though. I'm sure yours would agree with me; family sticks together. We always trust one another, and we never give up on each other. It's what makes family special."

I couldn't meet his gaze because, for the first time, I understood why it bothered me so much that Kiran wouldn't let me call him dad. It was like he didn't want me to be his family. And if he wasn't my family ... then I had no one.

CHAPTER SEVEN

The men settled in to wait, resting and going through what was left of my meager food rations. It wasn't much, although apparently, they hadn't had much to eat since they'd gotten lost. Many of them fell asleep on the cold stone floor, snoring loudly as though this was the first time they'd been able to rest. The cave became quiet then, except for the snoring and the occasional whispered conversation.

I sat by Aubren and kept the fire going, occasionally sprinkling wood splinters and twigs onto it. The light seemed to comfort them and the smell of the wood was fragrant. I'd chosen it on purpose. It wouldn't smoke much, and Kiran had told me that the smell of it was soothing. So far, that was proving to be true.

"What was that thing you were speaking to? That black ... smoke creature," Aubren whispered suddenly. He was stretched out on the ground next to me, his eyes closed, expression calm, and breathing steady.

My mouth twitched.

"I've heard stories since I was a boy about a young man, a dragonrider about your age, who could do things—strange, miraculous things."

"Lapiloque," I guessed.

Aubren didn't open his eyes as a smile slowly crept across his features. "We called him Jaevid."

"I'm not a dragonrider," I reminded him. Technically, I wasn't even a real scout. I was a kid. Just a dumb, useless, disobedient, ungrateful kid.

"Neither was Jaevid, when it all began. At least, that's how the story goes."

"The Gray elves don't say his name. They believe it's disrespectful," I muttered.

He shrugged slightly. "My people once shouted his name in the streets, now they whisper it. It's not out of disrespect, though. I think they are waiting to see if he will keep his word or not."

That was surprising—to hear that the humans also believed he would return. "And what do you think? Do you think he'll come back?"

Aubren's eyes opened slowly. The corners of his eyes crinkled as he studied the ceiling of the cave. "Before all of this? No. I suppose I didn't believe it. I thought it was just a story, even if my father swore every inch of it was true. But there was never any proof that I could see, and it's our nature to want an explanation for things and to want to believe in a supernatural force that is moving events in our favor. We want to cleave to those ideas to give us hope in hopeless times."

He lifted his head slightly, leveling a puzzled stare in my direction. "But things change. That is, ironically, the only thing constant about our world. And when you came flying out of the trees, and I saw what you could do. I saw that creature appear ... "

I looked away and studied the fire.

"Jaevid promised he would come back. He didn't say how. Are you him? Are you Jaevid reborn?"

I scowled. Okay, so maybe it wasn't *that* crazy of a question to ask. After all, I didn't know anything about the lapiloque's origins beyond stories, either. But I seriously doubted the chosen one of Paligno had done or seen any of the stuff I had.

"No," I muttered. "Definitely not."

"How can you be sure?" he pressed.

I cracked another stick in half and tossed it onto the fire, watching the sparks dance in the darkness of the cave. "Because, in the stories, lapiloque never murdered anyone by devouring their soul. He healed people. He brought hope and life, not fear and death."

Aubren didn't answer, and I was too afraid of what kind of expression I'd find on his face to look at him right then.

"What you saw wasn't some helpful forest spirit. His name is Noh, and I don't know what he is. I do know he isn't good, though. And neither am I. That's why I ran away."

It really sucked to say it out loud—the things I'd been feeling for so long. It made my eyes tear up and my teeth clench. I took a shaking breath and tried to recollect my nerve.

Then I felt a heavy hand on my head.

Aubren was sitting up, turning my head around to look him in the eye. "You saved us not once but twice. You rescued us from those creatures. Then you brought us here and treated our wounds. You could have just left us to die."

I swallowed hard.

"You seem to be a lot of things, Reigh. Whatever you are, however, I don't believe evil is one of them," he said as he patted my head like he was comforting a child.

I was afraid to say anything. My throat was tight and I couldn't get my eyes to quit watering up.

"You want to be taken seriously, like an adult? I think you should go back home and talk to your parents. Explain to them why you left. If it makes you feel any better, I'll go along to make sure they hear you out. Part of being an adult is having the courage to admit when you're wrong."

Aubren ruffled my hair and gave my head a playful shove as he let me go. "Who knows, they might even let you come back to Maldobar with me. I could certainly use a fighter with your skill."

My heart soared at that possibility. "You mean be a dragonrider?"

He chuckled. "I can't make any promises about that. I'm not even a dragonrider, myself. I couldn't get through the basic training. Heights, you know—I get sick every time. But maybe I can put you on a different path than one that leaves you wandering the wilderness alone."

I smiled and looked back at the flames, watching them smolder and hiss as they licked at the new bits of wood. "That sounds good to me."

IT WAS DAWN THE NEXT MORNING WHEN I HEARD VOICES OUTSIDE THE CAVE. I recognized the muffled Gray elven words and instantly got to my feet, nudging Aubren with my toe to wake him. He sputtered and finally seemed to realize what was going on.

The cavalry had arrived.

By the time I got to the entrance of the cave, Gray elf scouts were rolling the stone back and letting the morning light pour in. It was so bright, I tried to shade my eyes with my hand. Through my fingers, I barely made out the shape of a man standing in the entryway, his outline silhouetted against the jungle.

Suddenly, he rushed at me.

I instinctively drew back into a defensive stance. I'd assumed these guys were friendly. Stupid, stupid, *stupid*!

I reached for my blades—which weren't there. Crap. I'd left them lying on the floor near the fire.

When I turned to look back, it was too late.

Kiran threw his arms around me and hugged me so tight I couldn't breathe.

Neither of us spoke, even after he let me go. I didn't know what to say. He'd never hugged me like that before. His brows were knitted and his mouth was mashed together in a hard line that made his chin wrinkle. He studied me wordlessly for what seemed like a long time. Then he muttered under his breath in the elven language. "We will talk later."

Right. We had bigger problems to deal with right now than my latest screw-up. I stepped out of his way and let him see what remained of the human soldiers, who were gathering around to marvel at Kiran and the other scouts curiously.

"The Queen sends her blessings and warm welcome," Kiran spoke to them in the human tongue. He was better at it than I was, and could speak it without an accent. "We were sent by her to take you to Mau Kakuri safely—"

"Kiran!" Aubren shouted, interrupting his speech. He broke through the company of his soldiers with his eyes wide, an excited smile on his lips. He rushed forward and clasped Kiran's hand, pulling him into a gruff hug.

Kiran smiled as he hugged him back. It was weird. I couldn't remember the last time I'd ever seen him smile like that at anyone. He actually looked happy.

I pinched myself to make sure I wasn't hallucinating.

They started talking, laughing, and acting like they'd known each other for years. I guess I shouldn't have been so surprised. After all, Kiran had lived in Maldobar for a long time. He probably knew lots of humans. But something about it was just ... weird.

"And this boy? He's yours?" Aubren asked suddenly, turning the focus back to me.

My face grew hot with embarrassment.

Kiran gave a noncommittal shrug. "I came across him as an infant, not long after I dismissed myself from the court."

Aubren's gaze sharpened as he eyed Kiran a bit more suspiciously. "Is he Holly's?"

The question made Kiran's expression harden, his eyes becoming dark as he looked away. "When I found him, he was no one's."

Holly? Who the heck was Holly? The idea that Kiran might have *known* my parents had never dawned on me before. He'd never suggested he might have known them. But in a matter of seconds, my brain was swirling with a frenzy of questions.

"We should get going," Kiran changed the subject. "We brought shrikes to ensure a speedy return. I hope you can manage that far in flight."

Aubren laughed dryly, like that was a bad inside joke.

I wasn't laughing, though. I was trying to decide if I was upset, shocked, hurt, or just plain furious.

I didn't say anything to either of them as we helped the soldiers onto the backs of the shrikes. The scouts had brought more than enough, anticipating a much larger group of survivors.

The beasts were uneasy. The presence of the human smell made them stir and hiss, their six muscular legs flexing, talons digging into the meat of the tree limbs. Their long tails swished cautiously, while their hides of shimmering scales reflected the jungle like a mirage. They were a Gray elf scout's mount of choice, as fast as lightning, as vicious as a viper.

I'd never ridden on one by myself. And today wasn't going to be the first time, unfortunately. Kiran climbed on to the back of one and beckoned me to mount up in front of him—like a little kid. Great. How embarrassing.

We took off into the jungle, zipping through the trees at a speed that apparently humans didn't have much experience with. They screamed until they either went horse or got used to the abrupt, darting way the shrikes flew through the tree limbs.

We cut a three-day journey down to around sixteen hours. By dusk, we were at the outskirts of Mau Kakuri and seeing landmarks I recognized. Kiran and I were leading the group, and he chose the straightest course without stopping.

I thought we were going to the clinic. After all, more than a few of these soldiers needed medical attention—not to mention myself. But we blitzed over the rooftops, passing our home and heading straight for the royal palace. The closer we got, the further down I sank into the saddle. I was kind of hoping I might just disappear, maybe vaporize into the air like Noh. I mean, sure, I'd run away. But I hadn't done anything *illegal* or punishable by the royal court, had I?

Unless … they had found out about Enyo and I trespassing in their courtyard.

"Kiran," I whispered when we landed in the grand courtyard in front of the palace's sweeping front entrance.

He sent me a silencing glare.

Right. We were going to talk later.

It was after sunset, so the palace was draped in veils of darkness. The alabaster halls were cavernous and cool, and elegant gold braziers stood along the hallways and smoldered with fragrant incenses. The soldiers walked together in a clump like scared goats, staring around at the staggering beauty of the place as though mystified. The Gray elven scouts followed us wordlessly, but as soon as we came to the antechamber that led into the throne room, they stopped, saluted Kiran, and left.

I started to leave, too.

Kiran planted a firm hand on my injured shoulder.

I winced.

I guess he hadn't noticed I was hurt. Aubren's bandaging attempt was covered by my shirt and jerkin. When he saw me flinch, Kiran immediately pulled both to the side long enough to see that I was, in fact, hurt.

His already frigid glare cooled even more. "How bad is it?"

I shook my head. "Not bad."

He snorted and nodded toward the throne room, indicating that I should follow them inside.

"Why?" I dared to ask.

He didn't answer.

As we entered, royal guards dressed in elaborate silks and wearing jewel encrusted scimitars pushed open the two huge wooden doors. Each door was engraved with infinitely complex floral patterns and closed behind us with a thunderous *boom*. My stomach started swimming, and my teeth were rattling. Before us, down a sloped walkway lined with more of those fancy braziers, was a raised stone platform adorned with plush animal skin rugs, low lounge sofas, and intricate silk cushions stitched with gold threads and glittering beads. There, seated amidst the cushions, were King Jace and Queen Araxie.

They stood as we entered, the lengths of their matching navy-blue robes spilling all the way to the floor and pooling at their feet. The Queen wore a headdress of blue and green feathers fitted into a golden crown, and the King had one of a similar style, minus the feathers. They looked at Kiran, the soldiers, Aubren, and me with similar expressions of relief and apprehension.

The Queen was the first to speak. "You are most welcome here, warriors of Maldobar." She spread her arms wide and offered a faint smile. "We understand your journey has been most treacherous. Many were lost. We grieve with you at such a loss."

King Jace nodded in agreement.

Her gaze fixed on Aubren. Her aged smile grew as bright and warm as a sunrise, crinkling her eyes and the corners of her mouth. "How you have grown! I hardly recognize you."

Apparently, I was the only one in Luntharda who didn't already know who this guy was.

Aubren grinned back and offered a deep, respectful bow. "My Lady, you are as beautiful as ever."

"I am an old woman now, my dear," she sighed resignedly.

"And yet I'm certain you could still best me in a duel."

Queen Araxie laughed and glanced back at her husband, who was smirking rather confidently. I guess he agreed.

"I know there is much to discuss, but let's first attend to your injuries. I would see you all fed, bathed, and given any manner of comfort you desire. Then we can speak frankly about the matter at hand." She waved her hand, calling in servants who began helping the more seriously wounded away into the palace.

At last, her gaze fell on me.

I was too scared to move.

"You are the boy who found them?" she asked bluntly.

"Found us?" Aubren chuckled. "We'd all be fodder if it weren't for him. He saved our lives."

The Queen's brows rose. "Is that so? So much bravery from so young a boy ..."

Something strange shimmered in her eyes. I saw her exchange a meaningful glance with the King, who was studying me harder now. He wasn't nearly as friendly looking as she was. His gaze was cold and piercing, and it made me feel about two inches tall.

"Well, I believe honors are in order then," she said and pulled a long feather from her headdress. She walked down the steps to stand before me, her multicolored eyes glittering with interest. She took the feather and lightly brushed it across my forehead before tucking it into my hair. "Let it be known the Queen of Luntharda has named you worthy of praise. You are now a scout, and one most favored in my service."

I could see Kiran's jaw tense out of the corner of my eye. He was gritting his teeth, like he was trying to restrain himself from objecting.

I bowed my head and managed a nervous smile. "T-thank you."

"Where is your bow?" she asked.

"I gave it away. It's a long story, Your Majesty."

The Queen's mouth quirked upward. "Well that will never do. A scout must have a good bow." She looked at Kiran for a moment, studying him silently with her eyes twinkling thoughtfully. She stretched out her hand, beckoning to one of the servants standing against the sides of the room carrying a beautiful bow and quiver. Both looked much finer than anything I'd ever owned and were engraved with the design of the royal seal—the head of a stag leafed in pure silver.

"Then you will have mine. Aubren means well, but I'm afraid he's mistaken. My hands are not as steady as they once were. They've forgotten much of their former strength. This bow served me well even in times of great trouble. I hope it will do the same for you."

I took the bow and quiver carefully, marveling at them before slipping them over my shoulder. I bowed again and thanked her.

"I welcome you both to stay here, as well. Kiran, I'm sure the soldiers would appreciate your expertise to help treat their wounds. My own medics might learn a thing or two from you."

She smiled like she was trying to console him, but Kiran's expression remained grim. Even so, he nodded stiffly. "As you wish."

CHAPTER EIGHT

The palace had a much nicer setup for medical care than our clinic. It was bigger, cleaner, and there were plenty of trained assistants to help with changing bandages, cleaning wounds, and helping administer different medicines and treatments. Even so, the royal medics watched intently as Kiran appraised each and every soldier, examining their injuries, doling out instructions and advice. The medics never questioned him, even the older ones. He had the most experience—especially when it came to battle wounds.

Kiran didn't want me to help him, though. He made me sit down on one of the patient bedrolls and commanded me to take off my jerkin and tunic. He didn't say much while he cleaned out the punctures left by the snagwolf's jaws in my shoulder. He did growl at me to be still when I flinched and cringed as he stitched some of the deeper wounds closed, though.

Okay, it was my fault he was angry, I'd defied him by running away in the middle of the night into the jungle and almost getting killed. Saving a few human soldiers didn't absolve me of any of that. Fair enough.

But I was angry, too. The idea that he might be hiding secrets about my birth parents was infuriating. I deserved to know. I *needed* to know.

Kiran didn't give me much of an opportunity to ask him questions. He bandaged my shoulder tightly, pushed a cup of tea into my hands laced with a bitter-tasting remedy, and went back to treating the soldiers.

It was the beginning of a very long night. Despite all our efforts, one of the soldiers had blood poisoning. I overheard Kiran talking to the medics. They couldn't get his fever to come down. He was in a lot of pain, but the only way to save his life was to … well, cut off the source of the infection.

I won't even try to describe what that sounded like.

Finally, at some point in the early hours of the morning, things got quiet. All the medics had retired, leaving behind their trained, hired servants to keep watch over the sleeping soldiers. The soft sounds of snoring echoed in the cavernous room, and only a few flickering candles gave off warm, gentle light.

Kiran didn't leave with the other medics. He sat down on the bedroll next to mine and started washing the blood from his face, arms, and hands with a wet rag. There was more crimson spatter speckling his silver hair, and his whole body sagged with exhaustion. I wondered if he'd slept at all since he discovered I was gone. Had he even stopped to catch his breath? Or had he been forging on for days on end, relentlessly until he found me?

"You should be asleep," he murmured when he noticed I was watching him.

"Who is Holly? Was she my mother?" The questions burst out of me before I could think about it.

Kiran's eyes darted up to meet mine, his forehead creased with surprise. "No. She wasn't."

My heart sank. "Would you even tell me if she was?"

"Of course, I would." All the stiff, stern lines on his face smoothed, and he bowed his head slightly with a sigh. Kiran scooted over and sat cross-legged next to me, his elbows resting on his knees. "Can you tell me why you left?"

I didn't want to. And as soon as I tried to explain, the words seemed to stick in my throat. I rolled over onto my side so I didn't have to look at him.

"Because I wouldn't let you become a scout?" he asked quietly.

"No."

"Because you wanted to prove yourself to me? Or to Enyo?"

"No."

"Reigh." He put a hand on my arm. His tone was surprisingly gentle. "Talk to me."

I did. I told him why I left—that I didn't think I could stop Noh from growing stronger, and that I knew my presence here in Mau Kakuri was putting everyone at risk. I was better off alone. And a very small, very childish and naïve part of me, had hoped I might find my parents somewhere in Maldobar.

When it came to telling him about seeing Noh again while fighting the snagwolves and the mysterious woman's voice I'd heard in the dark—I hesitated. In the past, I'd always been perfectly honest with him about everything that happened, especially when it came to stuff like that. After all, I assumed he could help me or protect me somehow. Now ... I knew that wasn't the case. Whatever was happening to me, Kiran couldn't stop it any more than I could.

When I finished, he looked at me squarely, the dim candlelight catching over his multihued eyes. "Reigh, where you came from doesn't matter. Those events are set, and no one can change them. It's where you are right now, and what you plan to do next, that matters. The past belongs to time, the future is still yours."

"But it matters to me! I want to know why I am the way I am. I want to know what Noh is, and why he's bound to me. Maybe my parents know somethi—"

"No," he interrupted with a growl. "Leave it alone. I mean it."

I was stunned. I rolled over to find his expression closed and dark again. We sat in silence, me gaping at him while he glowered down at the floor.

At last, he looked up with a grim scowl. "You must not look for your parents, Reigh. Not yet."

"Why not?"

He shook his head. "The time will come for that soon enough. For now, try to enjoy things as they are."

As they were ...? I didn't know what that meant. How could I enjoy not knowing who or what I really was? It sounded stupid, like he was telling me I was too young or naïve to understand. I frowned and rolled over onto my side again.

"Aubren thinks I'm some sort of reborn lapiloque," I muttered angrily.

He snorted. "Is that so?"

I didn't answer. The fact that he dismissed it so lightly made me even more frustrated. Something was wrong with me. Something big—something dangerous. And whatever it was, Kiran knew and had no intention of telling me.

I OVERSLEPT. THAT—OR KIRAN HAD SLIPPED A LITTLE SOMETHING EXTRA INTO my medication to make sure I didn't go sneaking off in the night again. If that was the case, it worked. I slept like a corpse, and by the time I finally cracked an eye, it was nearly noon. My stomach was rolling with hunger, and the pain in my shoulder was nothing more than a dull ache.

I sat up, rubbing the grogginess from my eyes. Around me, the clinic bustled with activity. The medics and their helpers were going around administering meals, clean bandages, and more medications. The man with blood poisoning had improved greatly, despite having his arm amputated. He even seemed to be in good spirits. Not dying tends to make the whole world seem brighter, I suppose.

I peeled off the bandaging from my shoulder to get a look at my own injuries. Kiran's stitching job was as efficient as ever, and the wound was no longer angry or inflamed. Thanks to his care, and whatever mixture of herbs he'd used, it seemed to be healing already.

Kiran, however, was nowhere to be seen. The more I looked around, the more I realized another face was missing, too—Aubren.

I bent down to grab my jerkin and tunic so I could get dressed. Instead of finding my old scout's clothes, tattered and caked with dried blood, I found a brand-new tunic and black leather jerkin neatly folded beside my bedroll. Both were nicer than my old ones. The tunic was midnight blue, almost black, and made of fresh silk with intricate, silver, star designs stitched onto the sleeves and collar. The jerkin was black, to match my other gear, but it was made of many layers of tanned faundra hide. The outermost layer had details crafted from shrike scales in the shape of the royal stag's head, with elegant antlers sweeping up each side.

Somehow, I doubted these had come from Kiran. The scales shimmered like mirrors in the light when I put it on. It brought a wicked grin to my face; I'd never worn anything this awesome before.

With my kafki on my belt and my new bow and quiver strung over my back, I strutted out of the infirmary hall and started looking for Kiran. The palace was huge, and I got lost more than twice in the airy marble halls. The whole place smelled faintly of incense, and there were numerous hallways that were open to the cool, moist air that flowed in from the falls. Elegantly crafted covered bridges arched over some of the rocks, revealing curtains of water and swirling mist.

I rounded a corner, trying to find my way back to the throne room. I had a feeling that was where I'd find Kiran and Aubren, probably talking business with the King and Queen. Not that I had any expectations of being included in that discussion, but I wanted to hear about what was going on in Maldobar. What were Aubren and his men doing risking their lives in the jungle? Whatever was happening in the human kingdom, it must have been bad.

The sight of her, standing in a small courtyard beneath a willow tree, stopped me dead in my tracks. I wouldn't have seen her if not for the dress she was wearing—a beautiful billowing gown with long bell sleeves. The dress was pastel colors in every hue of the rainbow, and looked so light that the breeze from the falls made it ripple and swirl around her. Her hair was a polar shade of silver and hung down her back in smooth lengths like bolts of satin.

I couldn't see her face—not at first. She stood with her back against the trunk of a willow tree, looking up into its limbs as though deep in thought.

Then she looked right at me.

I froze. My face started to get warm. Busted.

Her eyes were creepy. One was a bright, crystalline shade of blue. The other was green. It made it hard to decide which one I should look at. The rest of her, however, was really pretty. She had a small, round face and ears that were only slightly pointed. Whoever she was, she was a halfbreed—half human, half Gray elf.

"I can hear you there," she said suddenly. "I don't know your sound. Who are you?"

"My what?"

"Your sound. Everyone has one. A way they breathe, a rhythm to their movements. It's like music, and everyone's is different. But I don't recognize yours." She smiled slightly and her strange eyes panned away, staring at the ground right in front of me.

"You mean you can't see me?" I asked, like a complete moron.

Her tiny smile grew wider. "Of course not. I suppose that means you aren't an assassin or another one of those pompous suitors, then. They always know I'm blind and tend to be ridiculous in making sure I know they are okay with it."

"Oh."

"So, who are you?"

I blushed harder and scratched at the back of my neck. "My name is Reigh. I'm Kiran's so—er I'm his ... "

She tilted her head to the side with a confused wrinkle in her brow. "His what?"

I sighed. "I'm not even sure anymore. Pet, maybe?"

That made her giggle, which in turn made my head spin and my face flush even more. She looked young, maybe even close to my age. "You're funny, Reigh."

I dared to take a few steps closer, brushing back some of the willow fronds as I joined her under the tree. "Funny-looking, maybe. Not that you'd know."

She laughed again and her strange, mismatched eyes twinkled with enthusiasm. "My name is Hecate."

I stuck out a hand to shake, mimicking the human greeting. Then I remembered she couldn't see it and awkwardly drew it back. Thank the gods she couldn't see that. "So, other than young and funny, what else do I sound like?"

She pursed her lips. "Hmm. You have a certain warmth and kindness in your voice. It makes me think you would make friends easily, but you are a little cocky. So maybe you've got a short temper. Your heartbeat gets faster whenever you come closer, so you must think I'm pretty or maybe scary."

"Definitely scary. Terrifying, really."

She giggled and pointed her gaze directly at my chest, which was about eye level for her. Now that I was close to her, she probably wasn't an inch over five feet.

Suddenly, her expression twisted. Her eyes widened and she drew back slightly. "T-there's something else. A whisper. A voice like ... "

She didn't get a chance to finish. Someone shouted behind me, startling both of us. To my surprise, Hecate lunged forward and awkwardly grabbed my sleeve as though she were afraid and using *me* as protection.

My chest swelled a little with pride.

Someone was coming down the hallway, calling her name over and over. Any second they were going to come around that corner and find us.

"It's my bodyguards. They'll make me go back to my room," she said weakly. "Please. I don't want to go back there. Not yet. I never get to go outside anymore."

Like I said, no one has ever made the mistake of calling me a genius. I didn't even ask for an explanation. Grabbing Hecate's hand firmly, I dragged her away from the tree and down another hallway. We took off at a sprint, me leading the way.

She was much smaller, and so frail I was a little concerned she might faint. Her cheeks were rosy and she was out of breath when we came to a huge atrium where four halls intersected. The domed ceiling overhead was a giant stained-glass design of a flower, and off to the left I spotted the familiar set of giant double doors leading to the throne room.

I took us slowly down the hallway, looking for a side entrance, maybe something the servants used, so we could see inside. Down a narrow passageway, I found a small door that led up onto a platform. A big tapestry covered it, but we could hear conversations. I recognized Kiran and Aubren's voices right away.

When the Queen spoke, Hecate squeezed my hand tight. Sadness crept over her face as she whispered, "My grandmother is in there."

"Grandmother?" I choked. "You mean you're a princess?"

The sadness in her eyes intensified and she didn't answer.

Suddenly, the tapestry was snatched back, exposing us. Hecate gave a yelp of alarm before she hid behind me. My body went stiff, paralyzed with shock. I still had a firm grip on her hand as I looked up ...

... directly into the scowling face of her grandfather, King Jace.

CHAPTER NINE

Behind the King, I caught a glimpse of Kiran. His pasty expression was one of pure mortification. I watched him bury his face in his palm and slowly shake his head. He was probably hoping this was just a nightmare and he'd wake up.

I was kind of hoping that, too.

No such luck, though.

"Eavesdropping, are we?" the King's sharp gaze seemed to pierce right through me. "And with my granddaughter, no less."

"We weren't, I promise." Hecate's voice was quiet as she stepped out from behind me. "We just got lost. I went out for a walk and got turned around. I asked this boy to help me find my way back to my room."

"The ignorant leading the blind," the King snorted. "I can't think of anything more disastrous. This boy is a guest here, Hecate. He doesn't know where he's going, either. Where are your bodyguards?"

Her expression drooped and she shifted uncomfortably. As far as liars went, Hecate wasn't one of the best I'd ever seen. I guess we had that in common.

"It's all right, Jace. They can join us," the Queen called suddenly. She was sitting amidst the silk cushions, across from Aubren and Kiran.

"They're only children," he protested.

The Queen's smile was strangely cryptic. "So were we, once."

King Jace didn't push the issue. With a dissatisfied sigh, he pulled the tapestry back further and nodded for us to go ahead. I slunk past him and made a wide berth with Hecate trailing behind me. When he noticed she was holding tightly onto my hand, the King's eyes narrowed dangerously. Yikes.

Hecate released her hold on me when Queen Araxie insisted that she sit beside her, and I went across from them to settle down between Kiran and Aubren. Kiran was still gaping at me in disbelief, like he couldn't decide if he should smack me over the head or throttle me.

But hey, how was I supposed to know she was a princess?

One look at Aubren, and I realized his eyes were fixed on Hecate, wide and mystified. His lips parted and he cleared his throat, looking down as though he were embarrassed. His face was even a little flushed across the nose.

At first, they kept the conversation light. Servants brought in silver platters of freshly cut fruit, roasted nuts, and grilled fish rolled in delicious vegetable leaves. They were probably meant to be finger foods we could all snack on, but I went ahead and started stuffing my face. I couldn't remember ever eating anything that fancy or delicious.

Then the adults got down to the business at hand.

"You know why I'm here," Aubren said bleakly. "My father might be too proud to call for aid, but I can no longer turn a deaf ear to the cries of my people."

"What has Felix said?" King Jace's attention—finally—wasn't focused on me. He didn't look any happier though as he listened to Aubren explain.

"Our relationship was strained even before, but after the first wave of enemy forces struck our shores not six months ago, my father has closed himself off inside the castle at Halfax and is determined not to let the royal city fall. He's recalled most of the dragonriders there to hold it. Meanwhile, the rest of the kingdom is left to be ravaged as the enemy marches uncontested."

"Who are they?" Queen Araxie sounded worried.

"That's just it, we know very little about them. What we have learned has come at a great price. They call themselves Tibrans, and it seems most of their forces are comprised of slave soldiers captured from other kingdoms they've already overtaken. Their leader is a man who calls himself Argonox. He sent an emissary to my father's court mere days before the invasion, to announce that we would be given one opportunity to peacefully surrender and be added to their Empire."

King Jace sank back in his seat and rubbed his forehead. "I can imagine how Felix responded to that."

Aubren didn't answer right away, although his eyes blazed with quiet anger as his hand clenched around his half-empty goblet of wine. "My sister urged him to fortify the Four Watches by calling out any able-bodied dragonrider, even those in retirement. My father refused and when she rebelled, he banished her from Halfax. She now fights as a rogue, leading a company of other riders who are loyal to her. They've all been branded outlaws, but they are the only reason we held Southwatch for as long as we did. I've been able to communicate with her in secret. She's made a makeshift base for her operations in the mountains near Blybrig Academy."

"Wait a minute," I interrupted and pointed a finger at Aubren. "You mean *your* father is the King of Maldobar? You're a prince?"

Everyone stared at me—even Hecate—like that should have been obvious.

Kiran swatted me over the back of the head.

Aubren, on the other hand, chuckled. "I suppose I should have mentioned that sooner. I am Aubren Farrow, oldest son to King Felix Farrow of Maldobar."

"Oh." I swallowed hard. That meant Kiran and I were the only non-royals in this gathering. Talk about a lot of pressure.

Aubren took a deep breath, and the mood darkened, as he slowly lifted his gaze to the King and Queen with a glint of desperation in his eyes. "The Tibrans have burned everything from Southwatch to Mithangol. We had concentrated our forces there, hoping to drive them back to their ships, but they struck our soil again from the east. Northwatch has been overtaken, along with Dayrise, Eastwatch, and the Farchase Plains. The Tibrans come in numbers we cannot count. Their war machines are beyond anything even our best dragonriders can contest. In months, they have reduced our forces to nearly nothing. Without your help, I fear Halfax will fall and with it all of Maldobar."

The silence was heavy. I looked to Kiran, trying to gauge by his expression how bad this was. The answer I got wasn't what I was hoping for. His forehead was creased with deep, hard lines and his mouth was drawn tight into a frown. Though he hadn't said a word, his chest heaved slowly with deep, wrathful breaths that made his nostrils flare.

It was bad—*extremely* bad.

"Can the Tibrans be reasoned with? Can we call for a council with this Argonox?" King Jace asked.

Aubren looked back down at his cup. "I tried sending a messenger to him, asking for that very thing soon after my sister was banished. The messenger was immediately sent back to me ... one piece at a time."

The King and Queen exchanged another look, this one more worried. Between them, it seemed like Hecate was growing smaller and smaller. She'd stopped eating and was sitting with her head bowed low, her expression twisted with a look of fear.

"Please." Aubren put down his goblet and got on his knees. He leaned forward, bowing his head nearly to the floor to show the deepest of respect and humility. "Please help us. I know you owe us nothing, and we've no right to ask such a thing of you, but I came to beg for your aid."

The silence was uncomfortable. I was human, sure, but I knew what the Gray elves thought about foreign wars. They did not like getting mixed up in other people's battles and problems. It just wasn't done—at least, not unless some personal offense had been committed.

You know, like stealing one of their sacred, divine artifacts and almost ending the world.

I knew what the answer was going to be even before Queen Araxie spoke. "Aubren, my dear, please understand me. I feel great sorrow for your people, but I can't go against the laws of my own. We abstain from war unless we have been provoked directly. That has been our way for centuries. I will send out a decree, inviting any of my warriors who are willing to go with you to fight, however I doubt the numbers will be significant enough to help you."

Aubren's shoulders drooped and his face blanched with despair. "Then I beg that you take me to the place where Jaevid rests. He promised my father he would return when we were in need. Now is that time. Let me ask him for help."

"Aubren," the Queen started to object.

"I know you don't think it will work," he interrupted, his voice cracking with emotion. "But I told my men I would not return until I had tried everything. And unless I do this, I haven't kept my word."

"It's not far from here. We could manage the journey in a day if we went by shrike," King Jace pointed out.

The Queen flashed him an exasperated glare. "We have tried many times to wake the lapiloque without any response. I seem to recall you reminding me of that fact."

"But we aren't Felix's heir," King Jace countered. "That promise wasn't made to us."

Aubren's jaw tensed.

They were at a stalemate. No one spoke as the Queen and King sat, staring each other down until, at last, a small voice interrupted.

"Let him try," Hecate murmured.

Aubren raised his head to stare at her, eyes wide.

"Is that what the gods have told you?" The Queen shifted uneasily.

Hecate shook her head, making her silver hair swish. "No. It's not that. But he came so far and has sacrificed so much to be here. Many have died for this chance. It would be cruel to turn him away now, and you are not cruel, grandmother."

Aubren's cheeks and nose had gone red again.

The Queen pursed her lips, considering Hecate for a moment before finally nodding in consent. "Very well. We will give it one day."

"Thank you, My Lady," Aubren lowered his head again.

"Thank your fiancée, Aubren." The Queen arched a brow, a coy smirk playing on her aged features.

Aubren sat back stiffly, still blushing as he stole quick glances in Hecate's direction. "Y-yes. I am ... most grateful."

Wait—*fiancée*? I stared between them, Hecate and Aubren. Was this some kind of joke? Were they teasing him?

I didn't get a chance to figure it out.

"I should go with him," King Jace murmured. "If it does work and he awakens, there should be at least one person there he recognizes."

"I agree. And we will tell no one of this attempt to awaken lapiloque," the Queen said firmly. "Only you and my most favored scout will accompany Aubren there."

The King arched an eyebrow suspiciously. "Your most favored scout?"

Queen Araxie smiled, panning her shimmering gaze directly to me.

My stomach hit the soles of my feet. I was really wishing, at that moment, that I didn't have a mouth full of food.

"Of course," she said with a satisfied smile. "Reigh will be your security escort."

I WAS HOPING I WOULD FEEL EPIC, SADDLING UP MY OWN SHRIKE TO RIDE OUT under the cover of darkness on a secret mission for the Queen to save Maldobar. But as I sat atop the squirming, snarling beast—I couldn't get my teeth to stop chattering. My throat was tight and my hands were so sweaty I could barely grip the saddle. Something in my gut told me this was a bad idea. I wasn't ready yet. It was one thing to go off by myself. Now I had other people—important *royal* people—counting on me to protect them.

Next to me, Kiran was talking me through how to maneuver and communicate with the shrike, which was the fastest route to take, and what to do if we came under attack. I'd already been through scout training. I knew all of that already. And yet, now that I was sitting on a shrike, it was like someone had scrambled my brains so I couldn't remember a thing. *What was a shrike? Who was the lapiloque? What the heck was I doing?*

"Reigh?"

Kiran grabbed my arm tightly to get my attention, and I realized I had no idea what he'd even been saying.

"You need to calm down. It's going to be fine."

"A-are you just saying that because it's the Queen's orders so you can't do anything to stop it?"

He gave me a faint, resigned smile. "No. I'm saying it because it's true. You are ready for this. It's not far to the temple grounds, you know the way, and it's only one day. Just remember what I've taught you. Concentrate."

I nodded shakily.

"The Queen's declaration of you as a scout makes you a man now. That means you have to be able to handle yourself in situations like this. So, take a deep breath. You'll be all right." Kiran patted my arm and stood back, making room for our takeoff.

"And if Noh shows up?" I couldn't bear to look at him. "What if he hurts someone?"

"Reigh." His voice was quiet. "I know you. And I know you won't let that happen. You can do this."

I squeezed the saddle harder.

"Now go on. Make me proud."

Those words were buzzing in my head as we took off into the jungle, leaving the palace and Mau Kakuri far behind. Jace and Aubren were riding together, which slowed our pace somewhat since shrikes didn't like to carry more than one passenger. It was safer, though, especially since Aubren wasn't all that great with heights ... or speed, for that matter.

They followed behind me as we zipped through the trees, sticking to the highest paths that kept us far away from the jungle floor. Kiran was right. I knew the way. And even if I got lost, all I had to do was break above the canopy long enough to catch a glimpse of lapiloque's tree. That was our destination.

I leaned down, letting my body lie flush against my shrike's back while his translucently feathered wings flapped rapidly. Their motion was more like the wings of a hummingbird, giving off a low hum that sent us surging forward at incredible speed. They could corner and hover, even fly backwards somewhat, and their mirror-like scales hid them well against the dense backdrop of leaves, vines, flowers, and branches. In Luntharda, there was no other creature that could match the speed of their flight. We were relying on that to get us to the temple without issue.

So far, that was working out fantastically.

As dawn began to break, splintering the canopy with pale shafts of golden light, I knew we were getting close. I hadn't gone up to check—I could just feel it. There was a sort of energy in the air, so thick I could practically taste it, as though all the trees here were holding their breath. It was a silence so deep and complete, breaking it seemed like a crime worse than murder.

About a mile away from the temple grounds, our shrikes started to get skittish. They landed, chirping and shivering with anxiety, and wouldn't go another step. I couldn't decide if that was good or bad. On the one hand, it meant other dangerous predators wouldn't go near this place. But then again, I couldn't shake the sense that we weren't supposed to be here.

"Let's make this quick," King Jace murmured as he climbed out of the saddle and held the shrike steady long enough for Aubren to do the same thing.

"What's the plan?" I looked to him, since of the three of us, he was the only one who'd actually been here before. After all, he'd known the lapiloque. I wanted to ask him about it. Of anyone I'd met, he seemed like he might take a more realistic stance on the whole thing. Although since he'd caught me holding hands and sneaking around with his granddaughter, I doubted he would want to share life stories with me—even if I hadn't meant anything by it.

"We go to the tree and see if there's a way down into the tomb. From there ..." Jace cast Aubren a meaningful look. "I don't think it's up to us."

Aubren nodded, still holding onto the nearest tree trunk to steady himself. His face had gone pasty white and he clamped a hand over his mouth as he retched. I guess flying still made him nauseous.

"And if something goes wrong?" I asked.

"Then we fight." King Jace shrugged like that should have been obvious.

"And if something goes *really* wrong?"

He smirked. "Then we run away bravely."

Right. Well, at least that last part sounded easy.

I checked all my weaponry one last time before tying our shrikes off to a nearby branch so they didn't leave us behind while we were away violating sacred ground. Shrikes weren't terribly loyal by nature—and if things got bad, I seriously doubted they would come sweeping in to our rescue.

We were on our own.

CHAPTER TEN

The temple grounds had been all but swallowed by the plant life around it. Trees had snagged the crumbling stone structures in their roots, slowly crushing them to rubble. Tall ferns had muscled their way up through the paved walkways, and thick vines snaked their way up the statues. The structures were barely recognizable, hidden beneath forty years' worth of moss and other plant life.

But you couldn't miss the tree.

It was monstrous, an absolute behemoth even next to the other giant trees in Luntharda. The base must have been about two hundred feet in diameter, and the trunk thrust straight upwards, breaking the canopy and soaring far above it. Standing before it, gawking up at the staggering size, King Jace, Aubren, and I didn't say a word for several minutes.

Finally, Aubren whispered, "Incredible."

King Jace didn't comment. He started walking toward it, his expression locked into a determined scowl. He marched all the way around the base of the trunk with us tagging along behind him, scouring the area for some crack or crevice that would let us get inside the chamber that was supposed to be buried deep below. After several hours of searching, however, we couldn't find anything. The tree's base sealed off any possible way of getting into that chamber.

All the while, my head throbbed and pounded. I was sweating, and not from exertion or heat. The closer I got to the trunk, the more it seemed like my brain was pulsing against my eardrums. It felt like pressure—as though I'd sunk down to the bottom of the ocean, and it made my skin prickle with wave after wave of shivering chills. I couldn't wait to get out of here.

"Something wrong?" King Jace was eyeing me like he thought I was up to no good.

I swallowed hard, trying to shake off the creepiness of this place. "No. I'm fine. So what now?"

He nodded at Aubren. "He makes his request. Then we see what happens."

Aubren was looking pretty pale, himself. He wobbled up to the tree's massive trunk, struggling to find solid footing amidst all the rocks and roots. King Jace and I stood back and watched as he finally reached out and laid a hand against the trunk.

"It's warm," he said with surprise. "I-it's almost as though it's vibrating. No—pulsing. Like a heartbeat!"

I took a careful step backwards. A tree with a heartbeat, now that was weird even by Luntharda's standards.

"Do you think he can really hear us?" Aubren was gazing up into the tree's outstretched limbs again.

King Jace's expression went tense. His mouth scrunched, and he looked away as though a bad memory had suddenly resurfaced. "Just go on and be done with it."

Aubren squared his shoulders, took a deep breath, and pressed both his hands against the tree. "Jaevid, if you're there ... please, hear me. My name is Aubren, and you knew my father, Felix. You were his most trusted friend. And even if he's not here to ask for it himself, he needs your help. We all do." He bowed his head slightly, his voice holding a tremor of desperation. "Maldobar will fall unless something is done to stop Argonox and the Tibrans. We cannot win against this enemy. I've seen with my own eyes what they are capable of. I know the depth of their treachery and malice. Please, Jaevid. Please keep the promise you made to my father. Help us in this fight."

I wasn't sure what was supposed to happen. We all stood in uncomfortable silence, watching and listening for anything to happen. Nothing did.

The tree didn't move. The temple around us remained quiet and completely indifferent to our presence.

At last, Aubren pulled his hands away from the tree. "Will you do nothing?"

A few more minutes passed, and he turned away. As he walked back toward us, I could see his mouth twitching and his brow furrowing, as though he were steeling himself to keep his emotions in check.

There was nothing more any of us could say. The answer seemed clear. If Jaevid was somehow in that tree, he had no intention of coming out.

"We should go back," King Jace decided aloud.

"Isn't there anything else we can try?" Aubren pleaded. "I came all this way. So many of my men died to get us here."

The King grasped his shoulder. There was a sympathetic sorrow in his gaze. "I knew Jaevid, just as I knew your father during the Gray War. Believe me when

I say, it was not in his heart to stand idly by while people suffered. Helping others, healing them, was as important to him as his own life. If there was a way for Jaevid to come back, if he had any control over it at all, I believe he would have already done it by now."

Aubren let out a shaking sigh. His face screwed up as he clenched his teeth. "It's not right. Why would he make that promise?"

"I don't know," King Jace admitted.

We left the temple grounds tired and even more frustrated than before. I had to admit, the further away from the tree I got, the better I felt. My head stopped pounding and all my muscles relaxed.

When we arrived back to where our shrikes were waiting, napping in a patch of sunlight, we settled down to let them rest while we ate and drank from the rations of food we'd brought along. Sitting in a circle, none of us seemed to feel much like talking. It was weird, though, to just sit there and not say anything. So, as long as King Jace wasn't leering at me, I decided I'd ask a few of those questions that had been nagging at my brain.

"So, you really did know the lapiloque? Like, he was an actual person and not just a story?"

The King glanced over at me briefly. "Yes. And you can call him Jaevid, if you wish. I'm sure he'd prefer that, regardless of what Gray elf custom demands. I was his instructor, one of the ones who trained him to be a dragonrider."

"You were a dragonrider, too?"

He gave a half-smirk. "A long time ago, yes."

This was getting interesting. "So? What was he like?"

"When I first laid eyes on him, I thought he was one of my former comrade's attempt at a very bad joke. He was a halfbreed, and probably less than half your size. He'd never lived here, in Luntharda. In fact, you probably know more about Gray elf life and customs than he did."

I couldn't stop grinning. "No way."

"Absolutely. I felt a little less sorry for him after Gray elf puberty finally put more meat on his bones. But it didn't do anything to make him meaner, which probably would have served him better at the academy. Blybrig Academy is no place for the small and timid, neither is the battlefront." King Jace rubbed his wrinkled mouth thoughtfully. "He was about your age, maybe a year or two older, when we first came here to the jungle. I'd see him do strange things even before that, though."

I leaned in closer. "What kinds of things?"

"He could heal people with his bare hands. He saved my life that way more than once. But he could do much more than that. By the time it was all said and done, I think everyone here and in Maldobar had much more respect for what being the lapiloque really meant—and for the ancient gods we all assumed had faded from this world eons ago."

"Did he know he was the lapiloque? I mean, like when he first started having those powers. Did he know what he was supposed to be?" I shifted uncomfortably.

King Jace cast me another brief, appraising look. "No, I don't believe he did. And sometimes it seemed to scare him. It was a definite shock for the rest of us. We don't see much in the way of miracles in Maldobar, usually—not that we don't need them. Now more than ever, it seems."

"Oh."

"Jaevid tried keeping his abilities from everyone, even from the people who loved him—the people he should have been able to trust. I think that caused him a great deal more suffering. It seemed to haunt him." His eyes flickered away, back in the direction of the tree. "He didn't have a choice about what he went through, but he did have a choice about whether to go through it alone. He *chose* to be alone for most of it. And I doubt he would recommend that path to anyone else."

Somehow, I had a feeling King Jace and I weren't talking about Jaevid anymore. I looked down at the piece of stale bread in my hand and thought about that. Kiran knew about me—the things I could do that no one else did. He'd warned me ever since I was little *never* to tell anyone or show them what I could do. Now, things had begun to happen that I didn't even want to share with him because I was afraid. I was bottling it up, hiding it, just like Jaevid had. Maybe ... that wasn't the right thing to do, after all.

What if someone needed me the way Maldobar needed Jaevid?

AUBREN STAYED SILENT AS WE JOURNEYED BACK TO MAU KAKURI. NOT THAT I blamed him, really. I could only imagine what he was feeling. His features sagged in a somber, listless frown. His dark blue eyes panned aimlessly around us, as though he were still searching for a miracle.

It seemed the jungle was fresh out of miracles for now.

For some reason, the whole situation put a fire in my blood that refused to calm. It shouldn't have mattered. It didn't involve me, right? Why should I care what happened in Maldobar? Life in Luntharda was going on as usual.

And yet ...

Fury blazed through my body and my jaw ached from grinding my teeth. To think that this Jaevid guy had made a promise like that—one he couldn't even keep. Seriously, why would he do that? He was the lapiloque, the spokesperson for the god of all wild things. People trusted what he said, probably more than anyone else. Why get their hopes up? Especially now, when things were so dire for Maldobar. It wasn't right.

Under the cover of night, we swooped low over the rooftops of the royal city on the backs of our shrikes. I'd never seen it from the air like this. The misty breeze was cool against my face. All the streams and little rivers that ran from the base of the falls all through the city shimmered in the moonlight. Colorful glass lanterns hung like globes of warm light in the dark, marking sloped bridges and city squares.

It was breathtaking, and yet my head still swam with anger as we landed on one of the palace's raised courtyards. There was a small party waiting to welcome us back. Among them, I saw the Queen dressed in billowing green robes. Her hopeful expression shattered into sympathy and sadness when she realized Jaevid wasn't with us.

Kiran was there, too. He was the only one smiling faintly as we touched down. I guess he was glad to see I hadn't been maimed, eaten, or chopped into a million pieces.

I climbed down off my shrike and started unfastening my gear from the saddle. I wasn't used to riding for so long, and my back was aching. Two long rides in a day was a lot even for a seasoned scout.

"I take it things didn't go well?" Kiran asked quietly as he stepped in to help me with my bag.

I shook my head. Out of the corner of my eye, I saw the King and Queen embrace and begin speaking quietly to one another. I suspected they were probably having a similar conversation.

"Well, I am glad to have you back home." Kiran patted my shoulder reassuringly. "I bet you're hungry."

"Gods, yes." I sighed.

Our group moved inside, and Aubren left with the King and Queen while Kiran and I were left to our own devices. We'd been given a big suite to use for the night that was prepared especially for us. There were two bedrooms, a bathroom, and sitting room all adorned with the finest things you could imagine—animal pelt rugs, polished white marble, silk sheets, feather pillows, and even a new change of clothes for both of us spread out on a table. I took my time soaking in a tub of warm water to wash the sweat and jungle grime off my skin. I'd been hoping it would help ease my temper, and yet that anger still simmered in my soul.

Afterwards, I changed into clean clothes and let Kiran twist my hair into a soggy red braid down my back. I couldn't braid it very well myself. My hair wasn't like a Gray elf's—it was thicker, heavier, and coarse. Having it braided just made things easier and kept it from getting in my way.

"What did you think of the temple grounds?" he asked as he knotted off the end of my braid.

I shrugged and moved to put on my boots. "It felt like I didn't belong there."

"It feels that way to most everyone. That's why we have left it untouched. I suspect the lapiloque prefers that it isn't interfered with."

I clenched my hands. "Jaevid doesn't prefer anything. He's dead. And he's not coming back."

I caught a glimpse of his disapproving scowl.

"It's time to be realistic. Maldobar is in actual danger right now. We can't rely on someone's dying promise from forty years ago to do anything about it." I growled as I snatched up my kafki and belted them to my hips.

"Reigh, I would take the lapiloque's word over an army of a million men."

"Then you're an even bigger idiot than Aubren," I snapped. "The way I see it, either he's a liar or a jerk— 'cause either he can't come back or he can but he's choosing not to. Either way, I'm not going to get sucked into believing something that obviously isn't true."

Kiran opened his mouth to argue, but I didn't give him the chance. I stormed out of the room and slammed the door behind me. My stomping footsteps echoed over the cavernous palace halls as I started looking for the dining hall. I was seeing red, not paying attention to where I was going.

"*We could help them,*" a familiar voice hissed from the dark.

I felt the familiar chill of Noh's presence creep up my spine.

"*Death is our business. We are very good at death.*" He snickered.

I glanced sideways to where I could see his red, bog fire eyes flickering in the shadows. He prowled out of the gloom, materializing in his usual shape of a big black wolf with a grinning, toothy mouth.

"What are you saying? That I should go to Maldobar and let you kill Tibrans?" I narrowed my eyes at him.

Noh stalked around me in a circle. Every time his misty body brushed against me, I got another terrible chill. "*War is a game, my master. Victory goes to the best killer. And in that game, we are king.*"

I tried to think of a good reason to say no. I knew he wasn't saying this because he wanted to help Aubren or Maldobar. Noh wanted to kill. It's all he ever wanted. But it wasn't a bad idea.

"I have to know you'll obey me," I said. "Without question. Without hesitation."

Noh's smile widened. His smoky black form rippled with delight. "*Always, my master.*"

CHAPTER ELEVEN

Sitting in the royal dining hall, I looked down at the fancy arrangement of food on my plate and wished I felt like eating. It smelled wonderful, and I was starving. But I was so nervous I couldn't even think about it.

All around the long dining table, guests of the King and Queen sat on the floor with intricately stitched silk cushions as padding. Aubren and the rest of his men were wearing new Gray elven clothes of colorful silk. They eyed the spread of food curiously, as though they weren't sure what most of it was or how they were supposed to eat it. They liked the sweet berry wine, though, and had no problem diving right into it.

Any other time, I would have been driving them nuts with questions about Maldobar. There was so much I wanted to know about it, the dragonriders, and what sorts of things they ate and drank there. But at the moment, I just wasn't in the mood.

Across the table, the mismatched gaze of Hecate was fixed on me like she was studying me—only, I knew she wasn't. She couldn't see me at all, so she must have been listening. I wondered if she could hear the way my heartbeat was racing or how my thoughts were running around in circles in my brain like a vortex.

Sitting beside her, Aubren was still staring vacantly down at the table. His brow was burrowed deeply and his entire demeanor was still somber. I guess he was probably trying to figure out what to do now that he'd run out of options to help his kingdom. He hadn't said a word yet, and was the only one of the humans at the table who wasn't on their third glass of wine.

Next to me, Kiran was still angry. I could tell because of the pulsing vein that was standing out in the side of his neck. I could practically taste his anger in the air. He wasn't finished with our argument, and I had a feeling he was already plotting out what he was going to say as soon as we were alone again.

The Queen's calm voice filled the tense silence. "As promised, I sent out a decree calling for any able scouts or warriors who were willing to go with you to Maldobar's defense to come right away."

Aubren looked hopeful for a second. "And?"

The Queen sighed. "As I feared, my people are reluctant to leave the jungle. It has been a long time since the end of the Gray War, and with your father's help we have rebuilt much, but our numbers are still miniscule. I can't go against the customs of my people. Our warriors, as you know, are all volunteers. It's their choice if they want to fight or not."

Aubren leaned forward, resting his elbows on the table and covering his face with his hands. "So not even one person volunteered?"

Queen Araxie placed a comforting hand on his arm. "Please don't despair. We will open our borders and have scouts waiting to help any refugees who wish to come here. And we will give you any weapons you might desire to take with you. Shrikes, too, if you wish."

Shrikes and weapons weren't going to help. Even I knew that. But Aubren forced an anguish-ridden smile and thanked her politely.

I took a deep breath. It was now or never. "I'd like to volunteer."

Everyone stopped eating and stared at me.

"W-with your blessing, of course, Your Majesty," I added quickly.

The King and Queen exchanged a glance. Beside me, Kiran's eyes looked like they might pop right out of their sockets. And Aubren, well, he just sat there with his mouth hanging open.

"We need to discuss this," Kiran began to object.

"There's nothing to discuss. I want to go. I want to help them fight the Tibrans."

"You're too young," he started to shout. "You've only been a scout for one day! And you've never fought in actual combat!"

"He's right," King Jace agreed. "Your bravery is admirable, Reigh, but you're just a boy."

I clenched my teeth against all the things I wanted to scream at them. Boy? I was a scout, wasn't I? Didn't that make me a man now? I had just as much right as anyone in Luntharda to volunteer.

"And it was just a boy who saved us from Hovrid and the wrath of Paligno's Curse," Queen Araxie spoke softly. Her color-changing eyes gleamed with memory as she studied me. "A boy ended the Gray War and saved the lives of millions around the world. Perhaps a boy can save Maldobar, too."

I sat back and blushed.

"I grant you my blessing," she said. "If it pleases Aubren, of course."

Aubren didn't answer right away. He was still gaping and glancing around at all the mixed expressions of approval and rage he was getting. Kiran gripped his dinner fork like a weapon, and King Jace glared at his wife like he'd just been betrayed.

"Very well, then." Aubren turned a grateful smile to me at last. "We'll leave in a few days, once my men can manage the journey. If you change your mind before then, it's all right. I would understand if you decided to stay here with your family."

That was just it, though, I wasn't leaving my family—I was setting out to find them.

ALONE IN OUR ROOM, KIRAN WAS EERILY CALM. IT WAS REALLY FREAKING ME out. He took his time removing his boots, unfastening his formal leather jerkin and vambraces, and settling into a chair by the fireplace.

He took out his long bone pipe and began packing it with fragrant dried leaves. Having that long, slender pipe sticking out of the corner of his mouth made him seem even more the stoic old warrior. His stern, chiseled features were sharpened by the glow from the fire and the dancing of the flames reflected in his multihued eyes.

I didn't hang around until he was ready to give me the sever tongue-lashing I suspected was brewing. Retreating immediately to my own room, I hesitated in the doorway. Movement caught my attention.

There was a face looking in through my balcony window.

I clamped a hand over my mouth to keep from screaming like a scared little kid.

It was Enyo—curse her.

She put a finger over her mouth, gesturing for me to be quiet. Once I managed to collect my nerve, I shut my bedroom door and slipped quietly out onto the balcony to join her.

"You scared me to death. How did you find me? Geez, how did you even get up here?" I kept my voice down as I leaned over the edge of the balcony, sizing up the extreme climb she must have made. We were nine stories off the ground, at least.

With the soft, moist breezes from the falls billowing in her dark hair, Enyo suddenly threw her arms around me. "I'm so sorry, Reigh. I know you didn't want to see me anymore. But Kiran came to our house looking for you. He said you ran away. He was so upset; he thought I might know where you went. And then I heard about the human soldiers coming here, that you saved them somehow ... "

I relaxed in her embrace. "It's okay, Enyo. I'm fine, really."

She squeezed me harder. "You're so stupid. I can't believe you ran away."

"I didn't think it was safe for me to stay here anymore. I don't want anyone else to get hurt. Especially you and Kiran."

She glared up at me. "You're my best friend. It doesn't matter what you can do—"

I covered her mouth with my hand. "Don't say that. You don't know what I can do."

Her eyes bored into mine. Slowly, I took my hand away from her mouth and found her frowning hard.

"You don't trust me?" she asked.

"It's not that."

"Then what? I thought we could tell each other anything."

"You don't understand; it's not that simple."

Enyo crossed her arms and cocked her chin up challengingly. "Just because I haven't gone through the change yet doesn't mean I'm dumb, you know. You don't have to treat me like some insignificant little child."

"I know."

"So, what is it then? What are you so afraid of?"

I shut my eyes tightly and turned away. "I'm not like you. I'm not like anyone else, okay? I can ... feel death."

"What?"

"I don't know how to describe it. If someone is about to die, or if someone has died, I just know. I can sense it. Sometimes, I can even see it, like their life is a bright spot that's wavering and going dark. It's been that way ever since I was little. That's why Kiran wants me to work with him at the clinic all the time—you know, not just because he wants to keep an eye on me. It's also because I can tell which of the patients are going to make it and which ones won't. And sometimes, if I lose my temper, bad things happen."

"What kind of bad things?" Her voice was softer, as though she were afraid someone might hear us.

I didn't want to tell her. I didn't want anyone to know because, honestly, there were a few things that not even Kiran knew about. But before I could stop it, the truth came pouring out of me like a spewing geyser.

I sat down on the edge of the balcony with her, our legs threaded through the railing and watched the falls pouring endlessly over the rocks below as I told her as much as I dared about my dark friend who liked to lurk in the shadows.

"So that creature, the one that looked like you, he's some kind of bad spirit?" she guessed.

"I guess. It's hard to say. Noh calls me master and follows me everywhere. I've been seeing him since I was a toddler. Kiran suspects he's been with me since I was born, haunting me all the time. Until recently, no one else could see him. And he's never looked like me before. Usually, he just appears like a black wolf."

"Do you think he's the reason you can feel death?"

I shrugged. "I don't know."

"So that time in the jungle, when the stag was going to kill us, you set Noh loose?" Enyo's gaze caught mine. "He was the one who saved us?"

I nodded.

"And you can control him?"

"Most of the time, yes. But lately, I dunno, it's like he's getting stronger. He appears more often. He thinks we should go to Maldobar and fight the Tibrans."

Her brows snapped together instantly. "What?"

"I already volunteered. I'm going back to Maldobar with Prince Aubren."

"You can't. You'll be killed!"

"Enyo—"

"No! Reigh, do you even hear yourself? Is it even you that wants to go, or is it just Noh? How do you know he's not manipulating you?"

"Because if I don't, Maldobar is going to be destroyed. Prince Aubren said it himself. That's the whole reason he came here. They don't stand a chance against the Tibrans. They came here to beg for help because otherwise, their whole kingdom will fall. We even went to the old temple to ask Jaevid."

Her eyes grew wide. "You *what?*"

"Yeah. Aubren went to ask him to keep his promise to help Maldobar. And you know what happened? Nothing!"

Enyo shrank back, her face clouding over with anger. "T-that's not how it's supposed to work. He said when we needed him, he would return."

"Just give it up already. He lied! He isn't coming back. So, someone has to help Maldobar before it's too late." I growled as I started to get up. "And I guess it's going to be me."

Enyo grabbed onto my sleeve. "And if it goes wrong? If you can't control Noh anymore? What then?"

I lost my steam and stopped, scrunching up my mouth while I tried to think of a good comeback.

"I'm not saying you won't be able to help. Maybe you're right. Maybe you can destroy all the Tibrans," she whispered. "But what if you can't stop there? What if Noh destroys what's left of Maldobar in the process?"

I swallowed hard. When I looked back at her, Enyo's bright eyes were gazing up at me earnestly. I got a weird feeling, seeing her that way. The weird kind of feeling you shouldn't have about a girl who's only supposed to be your best friend.

"I'm sorry, Enyo. All those things I said before—that I couldn't stand you—they weren't true. I hate this. I hate being a monster."

Sadness clouded her face and she let my sleeve slip out of her grasp. "You're not a monster, Reigh."

I tried to smile. "Guess we'll find out, won't we?"

She looked at me bleakly, her chin trembling. I could tell she was trying to keep it in. Silly girl, she always tried putting up a courageous front. I took her chin and turned her a little so I could kiss her cheek.

When I leaned away, her face had turned bright pink.

"Better not try following me. I mean it," I warned.

She opened her mouth, but no sound came out.

I went back inside, locking the balcony door and closing the drapes. I knew she could find her way back down. She was crafty, and a much better climber than I was—obviously. There's no way I would have even tried scaling the side of the palace like that.

Dang. I was going to miss her.

CHAPTER TWELVE

There are a lot of scary things in Luntharda—but nothing ever frightened me as much as Kiran did when he was angry.

He hadn't spoken to me for two whole days. Not a word. Not a cough. Not a sneeze. Not even a whistle. It was like I might as well have been invisible. And while before I would have been okay with having some space, the fact that I was about to leave my whole world behind to go to Maldobar and fight in a war made his silence beyond terrifying.

We left the palace long enough to go home so I could pack my things and say my goodbyes. The Queen had given me a new full set of scouts' robes all made from the finest materials in varying shades of black, royal blue, and emerald green.

The morning we were supposed to leave for Maldobar, I put them on piece by piece, taking the time to admire myself in the mirror before I strutted out into our living room. I was hoping Kiran would say something—I would have even been glad for an insult at that point. Just something so I'd know he was aware I was still alive.

But he didn't even look up as I walked past.

I pretended to rummage around in our pantry for something to eat, and then peeked back around the corner to watch him. He was just sitting there, on his favorite cushion, puffing away at his pipe and flipping through one of the thick medical journals he'd brought with him from Maldobar years ago. The pages were as yellow as dying leaves and crinkled whenever he turned them.

I cleared my throat, then quickly ducked away to see if he would look.

He didn't.

I tried it again.

No response.

My frustration mounting, I narrowed my eyes and briefly entertained the idea of hurling a loaf of bread at him. Then I noticed what he was wearing.

Kiran was dressed in his scout's clothes.

"Father?" I used the forbidden word as I emerged from the pantry.

At last, his gaze raised and met mine.

"Can we talk?" I tried my best not to sound like a scared little kid.

The resigned way Kiran took his pipe out of his mouth and let out a heavy sigh told me I'd failed in that. He gestured to the seat next to him. "Come on, then."

I crept across the room and quickly sat down.

"Reigh," he began, "I need to apologize to you."

Okay, now I was *really* scared.

"I shouldn't have been so quick to argue against your desire to go to Maldobar. I suppose it's natural you would want to help your kinsmen or to find your parents. And while I do fear for your safety, I'm not within my right to forbid you from going. As I said before, being a scout now makes you a man, and that means you are free to make your own choices."

I tried to swallow without choking.

"But you need to understand, that also means you will have to endure the consequences of those choices—which may very well be something I won't be able to save you from."

"I understand," I rasped. This wasn't at all the verbal smack down I'd been expecting.

"I've volunteered to go with you as far as the border, to help guide you and the rest of the soldiers there as safely as possible. But once we reach that boundary, we will have to say our goodbyes." Kiran looked at me squarely.

I chewed on the inside of my cheek, wondering why he was saying all this now and why he'd been so silent the past few days.

"What is it you wanted to talk to me about?"

I couldn't remember for a moment. Once again, I was wondering if Kiran knew who my parents were. If he did, then why wouldn't he tell me? What was he hiding?

My gaze wandered down to my boots. I sat, fiddling with the buckles, and tried to explain. "I'm sorry, too, for running away. And for volunteering for this without talking to you about it first. I keep disappointing you. I shouldn't have said those things about Jaevid. I know you knew him, and that he was your friend. I just got so frustrated."

"I've had my share of doubts over the years. Don't think for a moment I haven't. You're right; I did know Jaevid. Just because we think we need him so desperately now doesn't mean we genuinely do. Maybe he can see things we can't, opportunities for hope we don't yet know about. That's what I choose to believe, anyway." Kiran sighed again, more deeply this time. "As for running away, I'm only disappointed that you decided your only option was to leave rather than trying to talk to me about it. I had no idea you felt things were so bad."

I hung my head. "I just didn't know what else to do."

"Reigh, I don't expect you to be perfect. I'm certainly not. And even if you feel you can't talk to anyone, I hope you will always know you can talk to me about anything. I may not be your father, but I could not love you more if you were my son."

I had to change the subject. Kiran was being unusually open and it was beginning to terrify me worse than the silence.

"I feel bad for Aubren," I murmured. "He came here looking for a hero."

Kiran's mouth curled into a smirk. "I suppose he'll have to settle for you."

I smirked back. "Right. Never send a hero to do a monster's job."

THE SUN WASN'T EVEN UP, BUT WE WERE READY GO.

The Queen had given Aubren and his men new Gray elf styled weapons and armor, and even lent us some of her fastest shrikes—which none of the soldiers, including Aubren, were very thrilled about—to get us to the border faster. We also had enough food and water to get us through the journey. Kiran was in the lead, riding alone so that he could guide us on the safest path. I was next in line, Aubren clinging to my back like a scared kitten. He had a death grip on my shoulders even before we took off. According to Kiran, I was in charge of making sure he didn't die before we got him back to Maldobar. That included falling off the saddle, getting eaten by something, or wandering off and getting lost.

Human princes were turning out to be a lot of trouble.

The rest of our party rode behind us, doubling up with other scouts or attempting to ride on their own. We kept a close eye on them to make sure they could handle it. Riding a shrike isn't easy, even if you're lucky to get one of the more docile ones.

As the dawn began to break, Kiran gave me a nod and gestured skyward. It was time to take off. I sank down into the leather-crafted saddle and patted my shrike's scaly, shimmering neck. The creature snapped his jaws, hissing and fluttering his translucent wings with eagerness. All six of his muscular legs flexed, his long tail swished, and in a flurry, we took off into the jungle.

Aubren only screamed for a few minutes, which for him was progress. I tried to get him to focus on what was ahead instead of the deadly, thirty-story drop from the trees.

Kiran pushed us hard. We didn't stop until late in the afternoon to let the shrikes rest while we got a bite to eat and something to drink. The soldiers wobbled around like newborn fawns after riding for so long. Their legs weren't used to it. Mine weren't either, but I tried not to waddle even though my legs and calves were cramping like crazy. Rule number one of being a scout was you had to look cool. Okay, so maybe that wasn't an *official* rule. But it was certainly a given.

It hurt worse when we got underway again. I was sure I was going to have bruises where Aubren was gripping my shoulders the whole time. I guess he didn't remember that I had been gnawed on by a snagwolf a few days ago. Even with the herbal remedies helping my wound heal faster, my shoulder was still tender—especially with a grown man wrenching on it.

Needless to say, late that night when Kiran finally gave us the signal to stop, I was beyond ready for a break. I waited until Aubren had dismounted and was off helping his own men get settled onto the broad, lofty branch where we were going to make camp before I staggered down off my shrike's back. The animal grumbled and shook himself, flicking me an irritated flare with vivid, glowing green eyes.

"Tell me about it," I muttered back as I rubbed my sore shoulder. "And we have to do it again tomorrow."

Dinner was meager. While we'd brought along enough rations for everyone, dried meat, roasted nuts, stale bread, and some sundried fruit wasn't the appetizing spread I wanted. Still, it filled the gnawing emptiness in my gut.

The limb we were camping on was about twenty feet wide and had a nice flat area for everyone to sit and get comfortable. It was plenty of room, even for a group our size, and far above the dangerous jungle floor. Kiran spread out his bedroll next to mine, and then drew straws for who would stay up for first watch. It was safest to do it in pairs, just to make sure no one accidentally nodded off on the job.

Aubren and I drew the short straws.

Everyone settled in for the night. Men curled up on their bedrolls, or propped themselves up on their bags, and passed around a wineskin filled with strong berry liqueur. Soon, the soft sawing of snores filled the cool night air. Even Kiran was wheezing quietly, stretched out on his side with his arms folded and his favorite curved dagger within reach.

Aubren and I sat down on the edge of the limb. It was so dark we couldn't see the jungle floor. I guess that's why the height didn't seem to bother him so much —that, or he was just too tired to care.

All around us, Luntharda was making a harmony of night sounds. Frogs and nocturnal birds made eerie calls through the network of vines and plants that clung to the sides of the trees. Fireflies lit up the gloom with spots of colored light in pink, green, and blue. In the distance, I heard snagwolves yipping to each other. They were on the hunt for an easy meal.

"This place is terrifying," Aubren said suddenly, keeping his voice down so as not to wake the others. "But it is undeniably beautiful."

"I guess Maldobar is different?"

"Very much so." He nodded in agreement, and then glanced at me with a curious arch in his brow. "You've really never seen it?"

I fiddled with the sheath of one of my kafki blades. "No. At least, not that I remember. Kiran said there aren't any trees like ours, that most of the land is open and flat, or with small rolling hills covered in grass. He said there are mountains like heaps of rock so tall they scrape the sky."

"Well, he's not wrong. It is beautiful, too, but in a much different way," he replied. There was a subtle, sad smile on his face. "I didn't thank you before, but I am grateful."

"For what?"

"For volunteering to come back to Maldobar with us. You have courage beyond your years," he said quietly.

"Don't thank me yet. I'm not sure if I can really help you or not."

His smile widened, although there was a hazed darkness in his eyes. "If you fight as well as you did against those wolf-creatures, I suspect you'll do just fine."

"Maybe. Kiran was right, though. I've never fought in a real battle before. I've never even fought against another person. Not for real, anyway. I've sparred plenty of times but it doesn't count when the other person isn't trying to kill you."

"No, I suppose it doesn't."

"Anyway, I don't know how useful I'll actually be. I'll try, though." I sat back, leaning my weight against my hands and watching the eerie stillness of the canopy overhead. No wind got through, so not a single leaf rustled. I cleared my throat. "So ... you're engaged to Princess Hecate?"

He swallowed. "Yes. Well, actually, I was engaged to her three elder cousins, first. Not all at the same time, of course. My father negotiated a marriage for me with a princess from Luntharda. I suspect this was to further strengthen our alliance. But one by one they all met a premature death."

"I remember that—when the last one died, that is. No one ever said what happened, but there were rumors about an illness. The whole city was in mourning after. That must have been five years ago."

Through the gloom of the night, I could just make out the sorrow on his face. "I'd never met Hecate before this," he spoke quietly. "Maybe it's selfish, but I tried not to talk to her at all. I've never written to her or asked to visit."

"Why not? She's nice." I rubbed the back of my neck. "And just for the record, the whole hand-holding thing wasn't a big deal. We're not ... you know."

"No, it's not that. I suppose I'm a coward. I met the last three princesses, her cousins that I was supposed to marry before. They were all kind, lovely women, too." He let out a slow, despairing breath. "Hearing that they had died was terrible. Knowing them before hand, even liking them a little, made it all the worse. I suppose I just don't want to go through that again. I don't want to get my hopes up."

I wasn't sure what to say to that.

"Besides, what must she think of me? I'm a hand-me-down fiancée, more than fifteen years older than her. We were never supposed to be together." He leaned forward and rubbed his brow. "Our father made it no mystery that while I am the older sibling, it will be Jenna who eventually wears the crown. She is his chosen heir, not me. Even my own father has found me lacking. And then I had to humiliate myself in front of Hecate's grandparents, begging for help to save my kingdom. Not exactly the best of first impressions."

"Don't worry too much about it." I patted him on the shoulder. "Besides, you don't look *that* old."

Aubren chuckled. "I was surprised to learn Kiran had adopted you."

"Really? Why?"

"He served my father as an ambassador and advisor for a long time when I was younger. But once I was old enough to stand and hold a blade, my father urged him to teach me to fight. Kiran tried, but insisted to my father I didn't have a fighting spirit." He rubbed the dark stubble on his chin thoughtfully. "I realize in the Gray elf culture, that's not such a bad thing. Men can be other things besides warriors and scouts. It's not quite the same in Maldobar—not for princes, anyhow. I may not be destined to wear the crown, but I am expected to be able to fight to defend it."

"You're not that bad with a blade," I said. "You held your own against the snagwolves. That's not easy."

Aubren shrugged. "I can fight, and I did learn. But I think what Kiran meant and what my father didn't understand, was that while I could wield a blade with competence, I have no taste for violence and no love for the glory of battle. I much prefer diplomatic solutions, which aren't always popular when your kingdom is known for being a source of great military brute strength. Most likely another reason I wasn't my father's first choice as heir."

"Yeah. I guess I can see that."

"Now my sister, on the other hand, she's a lot more like my father. You remind me a bit of her, too. She's fierce, driven, fearless, and as stubborn as an old mule. She soaked up Kiran's teachings like a sponge, and it wasn't surprising to any of us—except my father—that she wanted to be a dragonrider like he had been. He was appalled. To this day, I'm not sure he approves. But trying to stand against her is like trying to tame a hurricane."

"But you said she was one, right? A dragonrider?" I studied him. The idea of dragonriders had always intrigued me. I just assumed all human soldiers could ride them. After all, plenty of Gray elf women were warriors, scouts, and could ride on shrikes if they wanted.

"After years of begging and tumultuous arguments, he finally agreed to let her go to Blybrig Academy to learn to be a dragonrider. She was the first female student to attend. And on her first day, she had broken three boys' noses and sent one to the infirmary with a broken jaw."

"Bravo." I laughed quietly.

Aubren was smiling. I could see his eyes glinting with satisfaction. "Indeed. My father had warned her that the other students wouldn't like that she was there. I think maybe he was hoping she would be discouraged and would come home. But that stubbornness of hers knows no bounds."

"So, what about you? Where will you go now?"

He let out another unsteady breath. That spark of joy in his eyes snuffed out by worry. "I suppose I will try to find my sister. I don't know how many riders she still has fighting for her. Perhaps together we can work out some sort of a plan to collect what remains of our forces and make a final stand against Argonox before he can overrun another one of our cities. Apart from that ... "

His voice faded before he finished. He didn't have to, though. I could read the defeat in every corner of his expression. Getting help from the Queen of Luntharda had been his Plan A. Plan B was trying to resurrect Jaevid. So now he was on Plan C with not much hope and a limited amount of alphabet left to work with.

"We'll figure something out." I tried to sound encouraging.

He forced another smile for my benefit. "Yes, one way or another."

"So why did it surprise you that Kiran took me in?" I asked.

"Oh, because when I was young he never seemed very comfortable around children, especially young ones. I remember when my sister was an infant, he held her like she might be explosive. She threw up right down the front of his shirt. It was funny to watch. I suppose those nurturing instincts didn't come naturally to him then. He must have changed a lot to go from being intimidated by merely holding an infant to charging headlong into single parenthood."

The idea of Kiran being covered in baby vomit made me smirk. I wondered if I'd ever done anything like that when I was a baby. "Yeah. I guess I broke him in pretty good."

"It's a shame he never married. I suppose losing Holly was more than he could bear."

"Holly? She's the one you thought was my mom, right?" I probed. "Kiran said she wasn't."

Aubren's mouth tensed, quirking downward as though maybe he wasn't so sure about that. "Well, her hair was red, like yours. She ran a medical clinic in the royal city, and was very talented with healing and tending wounds. Somehow their paths crossed during the war. He never said it around me, but I think he loved her quite a lot."

I could tell by his tone that this story wasn't going to have a happy ending. "What happened to her? Why didn't they just get married?"

"I don't know," he replied quietly. "She died young, or so I heard. I don't think she ever married, either."

I glanced over my shoulder to where Kiran was lying. Somehow, he was able to scowl even in his sleep. "I used to wonder why he never had a wife. I just assumed it was because of me."

"Love is a complicated and powerful force," Aubren said. "It can either sustain or destroy you. Sometimes both ... even at the same time."

CHAPTER THIRTEEN

"*Wake up.*"

The sound of whispering woke me up suddenly. I squinted angrily through the dark at the bedroll next to mine where Kiran snored faintly.

Chills swept over my body, rattling me and instantly made my pulse race. It wasn't Kiran.

"*Something is coming.*"

I snapped to my feet, snatching up my kafki and startling a few of the soldiers awake. The two who were keeping watch turned around to stare at me with bewilderment.

"What's going on?" Kiran slurred drowsily as he sat up.

"Shh!" I commanded, freezing in place as I slowly surveyed the area around us. The jungle was dark, calm, and silent—nothing out of the ordinary.

"*It's close.*"

My body got another jolting chill. This was new. Noh was always there, hiding in the shadows and in the back of my mind, but he'd never given me a warning like this.

Just in case, I drew both of my kafki and sank into a fighting stance, my eyes still keen on the jungle around us.

When Kiran saw me get ready, he jumped to his feet, drew his bow, and nocked an arrow. "What is it, Reigh?"

"I'm not sure yet." Around me, the noise of soldiers getting up and rummaging around was making it hard to focus.

"*Close, very close.*"

I shut my eyes tightly.

Then I felt it—like a white-hot splinter in my mind. A source of hostility. A threat.

I opened my eyes and whirled around, just in time to see a monster burst out of the foliage and onto the branch. Our shrikes let out feral screeches of alarm and took off in a flurry.

The huge beast lumbered forward on four long, two-toed legs with wicked black talons the length of my forearm. Its green and black scaly body rippled with muscle, and its long whip-like tail lashed in the air with a deafening popping sound.

"It's a surtek!" Kiran shouted to the rest of the scouts. "Aim for the mouth!"

Arrows started to fly. Men shouted.

The monster reared up and let out a furious battle screech. Its eyes were tiny, and its mouth wasn't all that big either. Inside it were rows of tiny jagged teeth.

But it was the pincers you had to worry about.

On either side of its flat, scaly green jaws were huge pincers like horns. They had rows of points inside them like the teeth of a saw, and they snapped together angrily as arrows zipped past its head and bounced off its thick hide.

"Fall back! Form ranks!" Aubren shouted at his men.

Kiran grabbed the back of my tunic and started dragging me backwards away from the creature. He was screaming in elven, barking commands to the scouts who were still firing arrows as quickly as they could.

I looked back, just as the surtek snapped its tail again.

It wrapped around the leg of one of the men and dragged him in closer. Those deadly pincers got him, squeezing him in a death grip. Then came the shock—a burst of electricity stronger than a bolt of lightning. You could feel it in the air, a deadly surge of current meant to kill.

I didn't want to see. But I knew even if I shut my eyes and covered my ears, it wouldn't help. I felt the soldier's soul leave his body like a tearing sensation straight through my chest. It sent another cold wave of shivers through me.

We couldn't win. We couldn't outrun it. More people were going to die. Someone had to do something.

I had to do something.

I ripped away from Kiran's hold on my shirt.

"Reigh! No!" He reached for me again, missing by inches.

I charged straight for the surtek, my blades raised to strike.

The surtek screeched and lashed its tail in my direction. I could hear the crack of the whiplash and felt it close around my legs. Instantly, I skidded to a halt and took a swing—slicing off its end.

The monster roared in pain and fury. I kicked away the dead end of its tail and dodged as it snapped those pincers mere inches from my face. I could practically taste the electrical current popping across my tongue.

It moved like a blur, lunging, snapping, while trying to flog me with the now bloody stump that was its tail.

I tried to keep up. I dodged and rolled, springing out of the way of every strike.

Suddenly one lucky swing from that tail-stump struck me right across the chest. I went flying end-over-end like a ragdoll over the edge of the branch. I lost my grip on my blades as the wind rushed past me. I was falling—plummeting. Leaves and vines scraped my face. I could have sworn I heard Kiran shouting my name.

Then, the wind was knocked out of me as I hit another branch. I coughed as spots swirled in my vision.

I was lying flat on my back, staring up at the branch overhead where I'd been just a few seconds before.

The surtek was coming straight for me. Using those long talons, the beast scaled down the tree and sprang, pincers open wide.

I clambered to my feet, glaring up at the monster with my teeth bared. No more games. I'd tried it Kiran's way. Time to try things *my* way.

"One blast," I whispered. "That's it. No one else dies. Got it?"

Noh's sinister laugh rang out, and I couldn't tell if it was real or just in my head.

The surtek gripped me in its pincers, ripping me right off my feet and into the air again. Its gaping maw was directly below me, ready to swallow me whole once I'd been shocked to death.

I squeezed my eyes shut. My hands curled into fists. I felt cold—horrible, hopeless cold overtake me. It surged through my veins, and made every muscle in my body go rigid.

I threw my head back and yelled. The surtek's pincers began to turn black. The animal screamed in panic as the blackness spread quickly, engulfing its body, and sticking like tar. There was no escaping it.

I snarled at the beast and grabbed the pincers, pouring every ounce of my will into a blast of my power.

With one last pitiful shriek, the surtek's body suddenly went stiff. It froze in place, still holding me aloft in its pincers. Then it began to shrivel up. Its body warped and shrank like a sun-dried grape, leaving nothing but bones and a big mummified corpse.

The fragile, skeletal body of the surtek couldn't support my weight. I hit the ground again and landed on my rear end. Looking up, I watched as the rest of the corpse began to crumble into a heap of black ash.

"You lose," I whispered.

It was the first time using my power hadn't rendered me unconscious. Every time before that, letting him off the chain was costly and something I didn't dare do except as a last resort. It left me drained and useless, usually unconscious for a few hours. But as I staggered away from the surtek's remains, I could tell something was different. My head swam, my vision spotted a little, but I didn't pass out.

This dark power within me—Noh's power—was getting stronger.

As I climbed back over the edge of the limb where Kiran, Aubren, and the rest of our companions were waiting, I could read the telltale signs of fear on every single one of their faces. Even Kiran was looking me over with a deep furrow in his brow. He was the first to speak up as I stumbled toward them, tripping over someone's abandoned bedroll.

"Are you all right?"

I stooped to pick up my weapons and slipped them one at a time back into their sheaths at my hips. "Fine."

Kiran grabbed my shoulder firmly, forcing me to stop and look at him. "I'm serious. Are you okay?"

That's when I realized he wasn't asking about my physical health; he wanted to know if Noh was still around.

I looked away, briefly catching a few apprehensive stares from the rest of our group. "I'm fine. So long as no one starts gathering pitchforks and lighting torches."

His jawline relaxed and he let go of my shoulder. "Try not to take it personally."

I stole a quick look at Aubren to see if he was as pasty looking and terrified as the rest of his men. Of them all, he was the only one studying me as though he were trying to figure me out. Good luck with that, buddy.

Under Kiran's stern instructions, everyone got busy packing up our belongings so we could be on the move before the sun came up. I helped four of the scouts round up our shrikes, which had fled to other trees to watch us get eaten alive. Like I said, they aren't inherently loyal creatures. Sometimes I wondered if they had much of a brain at all.

By the time we got back, everyone had calmed down and was ready to go. Aubren didn't say much as I helped him climb onto our shrike's back, and part of me wondered if he was having second thoughts about letting me tag along with him to Maldobar. Then again, he might have just been upset about losing another one of his men. Either way, he must have been distracted because he didn't scream when we took off this time, although he was still gripping me hard enough I'd have more bruises to show for it.

We rode hard all day and the next, stopping overnight again to let the shrikes rest. This time, we put four people on night watch shifts instead of just two. Kiran was insistent we keep the noise down and not use any more torches than was necessary to get everyone settled in. The less noise and light we made the better.

I noticed that everyone except Kiran was making a wide berth around me now. The soldiers watched me from a distance, their eyes wide and haunted. The other scouts had never been very buddy-buddy with me before, and now they were even less willing to sit and talk to me. Even Aubren didn't have much to say, although I wasn't sure if it was because of what I'd done or because we were getting closer to his kingdom.

It was late on the fourth day when I noticed the light was changing. It was brighter somehow, and the air felt cooler and much less heavy with humidity. We were getting close to the border.

We passed markers carved into the trees, symbols that reminded us of the boundary line ahead. Some of the marks looked very old and warned about the dangers of dragonrider patrols. Those marks, Kiran told me, had been put there during the Gray War.

I don't know what I was expecting to see when we got to the boundary line. After all, I'd heard others talk about it before. Some of them made it sound horrifying. Others made it sound beautiful. To me it just seemed abrupt.

One minute we were in the thick of the jungle, surrounded by the familiarity of the giant trees and overwhelming tapestry of plant life. The next, I was standing on a limb, staring at a landscape that was unlike anything I had ever laid eyes on before. Vast rolling plains covered in snow rippled like a clean white blanket in every direction until they were interrupted to my right by mountains of gray stone with peaks crowned with white. Before me and to my left were more of the rolling plains as far as my eyes could see.

The wind moved fast over the flat land, and it was frigid—which was a totally alien feeling. I'd never seen snow, never smelled frost.

"Look there," one of the soldiers called to the rest of us. He was pointing to a small black smudge on the horizon off to our left. "Northwatch still burns."

Aubren's eyes flickered darkly. "We must assume the Tibran forces are still there, which puts us well within their striking distance. We will have to tread carefully."

"It would be safer to wait for the cover of darkness to move in the open," Kiran agreed. "You plan to make for Barrowton?"

"Yes." He nodded grimly. "But we can't linger there for long. We will press on into the mountains and try to make our way to Westwatch."

"That's a very long journey, Aubren, even with shrikes. They won't do well in the cold, either."

"Couldn't we get dragonriders to take us?" I suggested.

"Perhaps. But it might take a few days for them to reach us. There aren't any dragonriders housed in Barrowton. Usually, they're all kept at the Four Watches. Although my father has now recalled all of them to Halfax—except for those who defected and followed my sister. I'll have to dispatch a messenger to summon them." Aubren rubbed his chin, which was now sporting the beginnings of a beard. That and the dark, sagging circles under his eyes made him seem much older. "But dragonriders will undoubtedly draw the Tibrans' attention. Not to mention any time we spend in Barrowton will already be borrowed. I'm sure the city is attempting to prepare for a Tibran attack."

"You're short on alternative options," Kiran muttered. "And shorter on time if these Tibrans move as fast as you say."

Aubren's gaze locked onto him and there was confidence glowing in his eyes. "Then it's good we have a secret weapon on our side."

At dusk, everyone gathered to say our goodbyes. Some of the soldiers had made friends with our scouts, particularly the females. The men stared at them with mystification, like they'd never seen anything female before. And while the female scouts seemed to like the attention, I never saw any of them reciprocate the interest.

Kiran kept his farewells to Aubren brief. They both wore similarly somber expressions and exchanged quiet conversation, pointing to this and that and occasionally me.

At last, Kiran came over. "Are you ready?"

"Yeah," I lied, pretending to check the saddle on my shrike.

"Aubren will be counting on your instincts and skills. It's important, Reigh. Remember what I've taught you."

I nodded as I avoided his gaze. I didn't like goodbyes, and this one really sucked. There was a lot I wanted to say, but every time I thought I'd found the right words my throat seized up and I couldn't do anything but clench my teeth and look away.

Kiran's eyes steeled and his jaw went tense. Suddenly, he wrapped a hand around the back of my head and yanked me into a stiff hug. "You know that you are always welcome to come back home to me, boy."

"I know," I said.

"Keep them safe."

"I'll try."

Kiran reluctantly let me go and gave my shoulder an awkward, gruff pat. Then he looked at Aubren. Neither of them spoke, but I could sense an understanding pass between them as they stood apart, their expressions a mirrored image of grim resolution.

"You'll take these shrikes and make for Barrowton. Release them there and they will return to Luntharda," Kiran spoke at last. "May the favor of the gods go with you, Aubren. If I were a younger man, I most certainly would."

Aubren's smile was bleak. "I know. And if I didn't already owe you so much, I might ask you to go in spite."

Kiran closed his eyes.

The atmosphere was tense as the soldiers, Aubren, and I climbed aboard our shrikes and prepared to leave. The sun had disappeared behind the mountains, turning the snowdrifts orange and then red as blood. I tried to concentrate, to keep my focus on what we were about to do.

But I couldn't stop staring up at the sky as night closed in.

Stars, thousands and thousands of them, sparkled overhead. I'd never seen so many. And as the moon rose, it seemed so close I might be able to reach out and pluck it from the air.

Then Aubren, who was sitting behind me sharing my shrike once again, gave a whistle. It was time. My heart dropped into my stomach. I looked around for Kiran, having second thoughts. I was making a mistake—I was leaving behind the only home I'd ever known.

When I spotted him, standing at the back of the company of scouts who were waving farewell to us, I felt like I was going to be sick. He didn't look happy, or proud, or satisfied. He was looking back at me with his mouth set in a hard line and his forehead crinkled with worry.

That was the last glance at him I got. With a fierce burst of wind off the wings of our shrikes, we took to the open air.

The safety and cover of Luntharda was gone. There were no trees to shield us, no dangerous jungle to deter our enemies. Nothing but the cold, empty air lay between us and a small point of light on the horizon—the city they called Barrowton.

CHAPTER FOURTEEN

It was a sprint. The shrikes didn't like the cold air any more than they liked being out of the cover of the jungle. They hissed and chirped, complaining to one another and flocking close together as we zipped through the air. I wasn't exactly thrilled, either.

My first impression of Maldobar? I seriously needed some warmer clothes as soon as possible. My hands were going numb, and the blistering wind made my eyes water and my nose and cheeks feel raw.

Below, the landscape shimmered under the moonlight. The snow-covered hills rippled; rising and falling like wrinkles in a white blanket. It was beautiful, and strangely haunting. So much blank white emptiness was bizarre.

All of a sudden, a hard, violent chill bolted up my spine. This wasn't from the cold. I sat up, heartbeat pounding in my eardrums as I looked around for Noh. I didn't see him.

But I heard him.

"*They're coming.*"

I twisted in the saddle, scanning all around. But there was nothing—no sign of anyone or anything for miles in every direction. "Who is? I don't see anything," I shouted over the wind.

Aubren was staring at me with eyes as wide as moons, like I was out of my mind. I guess he couldn't hear Noh.

"*Below. Underneath,*" he growled in my mind.

I shut my eyes tight and tried to feel if there were any other living spirits around us. Panic blurred my concentration and jumbled my thoughts.

Then behind us, someone shouted.

Aubren and I both turned, looking back as two of our comrades disappeared—snatched right out of the air by massive flying nets.

Far below, big trapdoors were popping up out of the hillsides everywhere. One second it was flat snowy ground and the next a dozen hidden panels flew open, throwing snow in the air, and revealing a strange wooden contraption that fired nets made of thick metal wire. The nets howled through the air at blistering speed and snagged two, three shrikes at a time, twisting around their wings and dragging them back to the earth.

"Spread out!" Aubren yelled right in my ear. "Fall back to the jungle!"

But it was too late.

All around us, our comrades were netted, one right after the other. The shrikes were in a frenzy of terror. I could hear the men screaming as they fell. Below, soldiers in weird bronze-colored armor were pouring out of the trapdoors like angry ants from an anthill.

Suddenly, we were the only ones left in the air. In wild desperation, our shrike did a quick twist and tried to make a break back to the boundary of the jungle. We were picking up speed, the wind moving with us.

Then the hillside directly in front of us exploded. Five trapdoors hidden under the snow opened with those net-throwers aimed right for us. I caught a glimpse of Aubren wrenching a golden signet ring off one of his fingers and throwing it away as hard as he could about two seconds before I saw a net hurling straight toward us.

I WOKE UP LYING ON MY BACK, THE METAL NET MASHING MY FACE. I COULDN'T move. All I could do was look around at the unfamiliar faces that marched by. They were dressed in bronze suits of armor with a snarling lion's head engraved across the chest, and wore dark crimson cloaks and helmets crowned with a short mohawk of white hair.

Tibrans.

They were carefully removing the nets, working together to capture everyone who had survived hitting the frozen ground—including our shrikes. They tied the shrikes' wings down, strapped their jaws shut, and dragged them away one by one. The Maldobarian soldiers didn't get any special treatment. I watched them struggle and try to escape. But eventually everyone was caught and chained up as well.

A sneering face eclipsed my view.

It was a woman—at least, I *thought* it looked sort of like a woman. It was hard to tell past the black tribal tattoos that swirled around the left side of her face, her wide jawline, and the way her hair had been cut so that it was nearly down to her scalp. Her nose was crooked like maybe someone had broken it once or twice. She glowered down at me, her dark eyes studying me through the net.

"This one's alive," she rasped the human language in a gravelly, deep voice. "What about the other one?"

"Unconscious," someone answered. "But alive."

She leaned away, her eyes narrowing into black, calculative slits. "Very clever of them to abandon their human armor for these fancy savage scraps. It will make it more difficult to identify which one is the prince. But we have other means of discerning that. Strip them of their weapons and bring them to the interrogation chamber. Then I want these hatches recovered immediately." Her mouth curled into a menacing grin of excitement, as though the idea of getting to torture someone was a thrill.

"Mistress Hilleddi!" Someone shouted for her and she went striding away, her hand resting on the massive, double axe that was hanging from a leather belt strung across her hips. She was wearing similar bronze armor as the rest of the Tibran soldiers around her, except hers had been modified. Instead of a breastplate, she wore something like a bronze bra. The shoulder pauldrons had long spikes sticking out of them, and there were similar spines running down the armor along her back and the sides of her legs.

As the woman moved away, shouting and cursing at her minions, I got a better look at the burly beast of a woman she was. She stood a solid foot taller than most of the men who scurried around her like scared puppies. Her neck was almost as thick as her waist, and her bare arms, torso, and thighs bulged with veiny muscle.

When I'd tried to imagine what human girls looked like—Mistress Hilleddi wasn't exactly what I'd had in mind.

The Tibran soldiers pulled the net off me. Right away, my instinct was to flee. I staggered to my feet and spun around, looking for a break in their ranks that I could sprint through, until I got tackled from behind.

I hit the ground so hard I lost my breath. My head spun and I was paralyzed with fear. A crushing weight bore down on my back, pinning me to the snow while my arms were wrenched around and cold metal shackles were clamped around my wrists. They took my kafki blades, my bow, quiver, and all my gear.

Someone grabbed my long braid and used it to drag me to my feet.

Next to me, I saw Aubren. He was lying on his back on the snow, still unconscious, and already bound with chains. There was a deep cut across his brow that had stained some of the snow around him pink with blood, but except for that, he seemed okay.

Our shrike, on the other hand, wasn't getting up. We'd landed on top of him, as best I could tell, which is why Aubren and I had survived the impact. The shrike wasn't as lucky.

One by one, those of us who had survived were forced into the open hatches that had once been hidden under the snow, while those who were too wounded to walk, or still unconscious, were dragged by their ankles. Tibran soldiers flanked us on every side, armed with short swords, crossbows, or bronze-tipped spears.

As soon as we were all inside, the big wooden machines used to launch the nets were rolled back and the hatches were cranked closed again. A few hours of wind kicking up the snow would hide them again and no one would be the wiser. It would be liked we'd been wiped off the face of the earth.

The Tibrans had been very busy digging tunnels—lots and lots of tunnels. They weren't very wide, but they were tall enough to wheel those machines through with ease. Torches lit the way every few yards and I quickly lost all sense of direction as we were forced to walk through their dark, damp, earthy maze. Sometimes it felt like we were going down, sometimes it seemed uphill. After a few minutes, I gave up trying to remember.

"They'll kill us for sure," I heard one of the Maldobarian soldiers whisper.

"We're doomed," someone else agreed.

"Silence!" A Tibran soldier whacked me over the back of the head with what I suspected was the blunt end of his sword.

I staggered and almost fell, my vision going dark for a moment.

They took us into a big open chamber where stalactites dripped from the ceiling like long, jagged stone teeth. The walls were stone, too, as though their tunneling had accidentally intersected with a pre-existing cave system. Iron rings had been driven into the walls and connected by heavy chains, perfect for chaining up a string of prisoners—which is exactly what happened to us.

They propped Aubren and two of the more seriously wounded members of our group against the wall, but chained them nonetheless. As I looked around, I realized that only five of us, not counting Aubren and myself, had survived. The shrikes weren't anywhere in sight, and I didn't see any evidence that any other prisoners had been here.

Across the room, a line of Tibran soldiers stood against the opposite wall. They were all armed with crossbows primed and aimed right for us. It seemed like a lot of trouble to just bring us down here to shoot us, so I dared to guess they were insurance to prevent anyone from making a daring escape.

Minutes passed. Then hours. I was sore from the crash landing, but I didn't dare sit down or drop my guard. On either side of me, the Maldobarian soldiers didn't move, either. Their expressions were hard and focused, as though they expected that whenever this finally ended, it would end very badly for us.

A noise down the corridor made everyone stir suddenly. It was a creaking, grinding sound like squeaky wheels. The light of torches lit up the passage and suddenly Mistress Hilleddi stepped into view. Behind her, being dragged on a low, flat cart by several of her soldiers, was another strange machine.

"Good evening, gentlemen," she purred as she walked slowly down her line of captives. She took her time examining each one of us. When she got to me, she stopped. The torches made her dark eyes glitter wickedly. "Perhaps you're wondering why you're still alive. Allow me to explain. You're here because of a rumor—a rumor Lord Argonox heard that the Prince of Maldobar was seen fleeing from battle into the wild wood."

She leaned down, putting her face uncomfortably close to mine. There was a stench of old meat on her breath. Or maybe that was just the way she smelled in general—I couldn't be sure.

"It was said he went to beg the help of the gods. Or perhaps to even seek help from your pointy eared neighbors to the north. Personally, I don't believe in gods, just as I despise rumors and those who run from battle like cowardly little children. But my brother is more superstitious. He believes in gods and magic. He commanded me to keep watch in case the spineless prince dared to show his face here again."

She grabbed my chin. Her fingers were too strong for me to pull away. "Normally, I would relish ripping the truth out of each of you one by one. But time is of the essence, so let me make this very easy. Since I'm sure your infantile prince is too cowardly to step forward himself, the first person to tell me which one of you he is will be set free. The rest of you will make excellent target practice for my new recruits."

No one said a word.

She was so close I could see my own reflection in her eyes. They were like bottomless pools of black tar—there was no color to her irises at all.

She squeezed my chin harder. "If you refuse because of some idiotic sense of loyalty to the gutless worm you call a prince, then I will greatly enjoy the alternative. Now, what'll it be, boys?"

CHAPTER FIFTEEN

No one was talking.

Minutes passed while Mistress Hilleddi paced in front of us like a hungry lioness, snarling and threatening us with what was going to happen if no one spoke up. Down our line, I could see Aubren out of the corner of my eye. He was still out cold. He must've taken a nasty blow to the head during our landing. Blood was caked all over his face from the gash on his forehead, but I could see him breathing every now and then.

"Time is up! No takers for my bargain, I see? This is why I love these noble kingdoms. They make for much better sport!" Hilleddi laughed in her throat and snapped her fingers to the soldiers behind her. They started moving that weird-looking machine into place in the middle of the room.

"Hmm. Who shall we take first? What about you?" She lunged forward suddenly, grabbing one of the men down the line by the front of his tunic and yanking him up onto his toes so she could sneer into his eyes. "You positively reek of fear. Are you the prince?"

The Maldobarian soldier spit in her face.

The room was silent, as though everyone were holding their breath.

With her free hand, Hilleddi wiped the spit from her cheek and grinned. She dropped the man onto his knees, giving him one swift kick to the gut on his way down. Something that sounded a lot like a bone cracked.

I cringed. Behind me, I twisted my hands against the shackles.

I could kill her—I knew I could. Just one word to Noh and this would all be over. Except there were the other Tibrans with their crossbows to think about, not to mention I had no idea where we were or how to get out of the chains. Those things, however, weren't my biggest concern.

If I let Noh out again, if I let him kill Mistress Hilleddi and the rest of her bronze armored entourage, I wasn't sure I could get him to stop there. I'd never let him kill that many at once before. I could just as easily kill the rest of my companions. I was second-guessing myself. I didn't know how much control I really had over him. It was a weakness I couldn't escape, and one Noh might exploit.

I couldn't take that risk. Not yet. I had to hope there was some other way. Maybe if I could get closer somehow ...

"Very well, then. Let's show the rest of them how the game is played." Hilleddi twirled a finger in the air and pointed to one of her soldiers. "You there, come here. Remove your helmet."

The soldier obeyed. When he took off his helmet, I was stunned to see he looked about my age. His head was shaved to the scalp, and there was a marking freshly branded into the side of his neck. The skin still looked angry and swollen around it; I couldn't make out what it was supposed to be.

"Drop your weapons," Hilleddi commanded.

The soldier put down his round bronze shield and crossbow, then unbuckled his sword belt and placed them all on the ground.

"Good. Now get in."

Hesitation flashed in the young soldier's eyes. He looked at her, then at the machine, then back to her.

Hilleddi took a threatening step toward him. "I said, *get in*."

We watched him obey silently, standing up on the top of the rolling wooden platform. In the center was a wooden chair, which was where the other Tibran soldiers fastened him. It was tilted back uncomfortably far, like the sort of reclining chair Kiran used when he was going to extract a tooth. The other soldiers locked his arms and legs down with metal clamps. There was another that went around his forehead, holding his head firmly in place. I could see him shaking. His eyes were wild and his nostrils flared with fear as he watched Hilleddi approach.

Another soldier brought her what looked like a collar. It was bright gold and set in the center was a strange looking round plate, almost like a mirror. All around it were intricate designs made of that same gold, depicting twisted, tormented faces on one side and joyful happy ones on the other. When she fastened it around the soldier's throat, the mirror turned black. It seemed to churn with smoky dark movement and I got a chill I knew wasn't coming from Noh. This was something far more ancient.

"We've found many curiosities on our conquests, so many trinkets and artifacts from across the world. But this one, by far, is my favorite." Hilleddi stroked the collar affectionately. "The Mirror of Truth; that is what we call it. The only trick in demonstrating how it works is, well, you must tell a lie. And you are such a good, loyal servant, aren't you?"

The soldier nodded frantically, although he was beginning to fight the restraints.

"Yes, of course you are. Fortunately, there's one question all men lie about." Her voice became a whisper as she leaned in closer to him. "Do you love me?"

"Yes, Mistress," the soldier cried out desperately.

He must've known what was coming.

I couldn't bear to watch. It was bad enough to feel it the way only I could. Watching it was just too much. I turned away and squeezed my eyes shut until the soldier's screams finally went quiet.

While the Tibran soldiers unfastened their dead comrade's limp body and dragged him down from the chair, Hilleddi began prowling down our line again. There was a fresh smirk on her lips as she sized each one of us up from head to foot, like she was selecting fruit from the market.

"The Mirror cannot be fooled. It is indifferent to crowns and kingdoms. Tell the truth, and it will release you. Tell a lie, and even if you don't know it's a lie, it won't matter. All the Mirror cares about is whether the words that leave your lips are true or not. But perhaps you think you'll give me no answer at all and that will save you." She hummed as she pulled a long, curved dagger from her belt and began flipping it in the air, tossing and catching it by the hilt every time. "Getting men to talk is my specialty. It's my favorite game. So the only *real* question is who looks the most princely, even in those tacky savage clothes?"

Down the line, I saw Aubren's head loll forward. His eyelids flickered and he started to groan. He was finally waking up.

And Hilleddi was walking straight toward him.

I didn't know how much Aubren understood about our situation. Obviously, it wasn't good. But as he drowsily sat up and looked at all of us, the Tibran death machine, and the already deceased soldier, I saw realization dawn on his face.

"Come on, little prince. We don't have all day. My brother grows impatient quickly. I tell you what, if the real prince is the first to step forward and reveal himself, then I will honor his show of courage and let the rest of you live."

She didn't have to be strapped to that stupid mirror for me to know she was lying. I seriously doubted any of us was going to be walking out of here alive if she had anything to do with it.

But I saw Aubren start to open his mouth. What choice did he have? If there was any chance he could save the rest of us, that idiot was going to take it.

"It's me!" I shouted suddenly. "I'm Aubren, Prince of Maldobar!"

Everyone stopped to stare at me.

Hilleddi's smile bloomed with wicked delight, as though she somehow knew I was lying and was just thrilled at the idea of using her favorite killing toy again. She made her way back to me slowly. Looming over me, she reached around to grab my long red braid and brought the end of it up to her nose. She took a few long sniffs and her eyes crinkled in the corners as her grin widened.

"Say it again, boy."

I clenched my hands into fists against the shackles. "Why? Did I stutter the first time?"

"Strange, I was expecting someone older. But I thought I sensed something different about you," she purred, and kept flicking the end of my braid back and forth under her nose. Creepy.

Behind her, I could barely make out Aubren's face as he gaped at me in horror. I tried not to focus on him. "So, you got what you wanted. Are you going to let them go?"

"Of course," she said and dropped my hair. "Right after I make sure you're telling the truth."

I did my best to look unfazed. I just had to get her alone, further away from everyone. Just for a second—if I could just get my hands on her for a second.

One snap of her fingers and the Tibran soldiers were on me like attack dogs. Aubren started to shout and fight against his chains, demanding they let me go and that he was the real prince. The other Maldobarian men did the same, shouting and declaring they were the prince, not me.

I guess they were trying to save me. I wished they'd knock it off.

"Noh," I muttered, "where are you?"

I got no reply. Uh oh.

"Noh! Answer me!"

Crap. My mind was empty. I listened for his voice or any clue that he was there, but got nothing except my own blinding panic. Maybe he couldn't get through to me. Maybe I was so overwhelmed I couldn't hear him—not that that had ever happened before. There's a first time for everything, right?

I fought as the Tibrans forced me down into the chair. They took off my shackles only to begin strapping down my arms and legs and closing that metal brace over my forehead. I couldn't move and couldn't see anything but the ceiling overhead. Aubren and the rest of my companions were still shouting, trying to distract Hilleddi.

Suddenly, her face appeared over me.

My body went stiff with fear. This wasn't part of the plan. Desperately I tried to wiggle one of my hands, just an inch or two and maybe I could reach her.

Just one touch, that's all I needed.

I felt the cold metal of that golden collar as she fastened it tightly around my throat. The places where it pressed against my skin tingled. I clenched my jaw and glared at her.

"Feisty, aren't you? You certainly have a royal's pretty face, even with that scar." She put her big ugly face in front of me again. "Say it again. Do it loudly, so they can all hear you."

Aubren was screaming at the top of his lungs. "No! He's not the prince! It's me! I'm the one you want!"

I felt the distinct prick and pressure of a blade against my forearm.

"Say it, or I start cutting off fingers," Hilleddi hissed. She dug the dagger in a little more, just to get the point across.

"I-I ... " My voice broke.

"Come on, little prince. Don't be shy." Her dark eyes gleamed with pleasure, as though she knew what was about to happen.

I was about to die.

"It's me," I repeated. "I'm the Prince of Maldobar."

CHAPTER SIXTEEN

There was a loud metal clunk.

I could hear it because everyone else in the room had gone completely silent. Even Mistress Hilleddi was scowling down at me with her mouth scrunched up into a snarl of disappointment.

As soon as I spoke those words, the golden collar went slack around my throat, fell off, and clattered noisily to the ground.

I was alive. I didn't understand how or why, but I was alive.

Before anyone would argue or demand a redo, I heard a loud commotion enter the room.

"Mistress! There's been an attack on the entrance tunnels!" a man panted, like he'd been sprinting to get here. "It's the dragonriders! They've found us!"

Hilleddi growled a furious curse. She vanished out of my line of sight and I was left staring up at the dangerous, dripping points of stalactites dangling overhead.

"Take them all to the containment block. Except that one—I want the prince brought to my chambers immediately!" Over the rattling of weaponry and armor, I could hear her barking orders at her men. Were they leaving? What was going on? I started wriggling in the chair again, but it didn't do any good.

A pair of Tibran soldiers appeared above me right on cue and began removing the restraints. They grabbed my arms, one on each side of me, and dragged me to my feet. I saw another soldier coming for me with those iron shackles in his hand.

Big mistake.

"*Noh!*" I shouted at the top of my lungs.

This time, his presence and power descended on me like a rush of cold wind. Darkness rose off my skin, boiling in the air like a column of churning black mist. From the depths of the darkness, Noh's menacing red eyes flickered. The hissing sound of his laughter filled the cavernous room, rattling the stalactites on the ceiling.

The Tibrans' ranks became chaos. Some of them began running from the chamber, while others drew their weapons or fired their crossbows at the cloud—which of course, did nothing. Hilleddi was apparently the only one who recognized that *I* was the actual problem.

I caught her gaze through the chaos, her dark eyes narrowing on me with intent.

I smirked back at her and winked. Better luck next time.

Before anyone else could remember me, I lashed out with every shred of Kiran's training I could remember. I snatched my arms free of the two soldiers who held me, kicking into a roll and sweeping the legs out from under the third soldier who had the shackles. As he fell, I ripped the sword out of the sheath on his belt and kicked him the rest of the way to the ground.

Hilleddi was coming for me. The ground practically shook under each of her steps. She made a bellowing noise like an angry bison, her double-axe drawn and ready to chop me in half on the first swing.

I dropped down into a spring directly toward my Maldobarian comrades. I was aiming for Aubren.

She was right on my heels, the wind screaming off the axe as she swung it.

The axe came down so close it brushed my back—but I didn't stop at the wall. I ran *up* it, kicking off hard and launching myself into an aerial backflip.

I landed behind her just in time to see her mighty axe smash through the chain that held all my friends against the wall.

"Head's up!" I shouted to Aubren, who was already on his feet. I threw the sword to him.

He jumped, sweeping his shackled arms under his legs and catching the sword in mid-air. He didn't have long, but with that sword, at least he could crack the chains off our comrades.

"You!" Hilleddi yowled and spun around, her wild gaze meeting mine.

"Me, indeed. Shall we play?" I smirked and spread my arms wide, taunting her.

She screamed a curse and reared back her axe to take another swing at me. "You filthy little whelp!"

The axe came down, aimed for my head. I bared my teeth. I was going to destroy her, just like I had the surtek. All I needed was one touch—one touch and she was mine.

My rage boiled over. In an instant, I lost control. Something inside me snapped and Noh's power broke through my body, washing over me like an icy flood. It was different this time and so cold that I could barely breathe, my frantic breaths turning to puffs of white fog. Everything seemed to slow down.

Suddenly, Hilleddi stopped. Her gaze turned from me to something else—something behind me.

Something *bigger*.

Her expression blanched with terror under all those tattoos.

Noh rose up behind me, his form swelling into a monstrous black beast. It was as though we were one; I could feel his presence and power as clearly as I could feel my own body. When he moved, I moved. Our minds were melded, fused by the darkness. He let out a snickering laugh—or was it my laugh? I couldn't tell anymore.

I smiled. His smiling maw grew wider, as well. It was filled with jagged teeth. His smoky black body changed as it grew, beginning to resemble a hybrid of the surtek we had killed not long ago and a fox. His long tail lashed. One swipe took a line of Tibran soldiers and flung them across the chamber like toys.

Hilleddi's gaze met mine once more. From a few yards away, I could sense her thinking—considering me carefully. She may have looked like a barbarian muscle head, but she wasn't stupid.

She rushed at me again.

I shouted. At the same time, Noh let out a booming, screeching roar that rattled the chamber. Tibrans fled in every direction, clambering to get out. Overhead, the stalactites started to fall like lethal stone missiles, crashing down all around us. Stones and boulders flew through the air. Dust choked out the light of the torches.

Something hit me hard over the back of the head and I was instantly dazed. I crumpled to my hands and knees, managed a few wheezing breaths, and collapsed.

I WAS STILL IN A DAZE, MY VISION FUZZY. I COULDN'T SEE WHO WAS CARRYING me, but I could hear frightened voices shouting and the muffled sound of something roaring.

Noh? It couldn't be. I didn't feel his presence anymore.

As my mind cleared, I realized it was Aubren who was carrying me on his back like a limp sack of flour. We were running. All around us, the ceilings shook and rubble poured down on our heads like there was a battle raging on the surface.

Before us was a maze of dimly lit tunnels. Behind us were the shouts of Tibran soldiers. They were chasing us and firing their crossbows. Arrows zipped past us, bouncing off the stone walls or lodging in the dirt floor at our heels. We were screwed.

I squirmed on Aubren's back. "Put me down! I can run!"

He immediately dropped me and I fell into a sprint next to him.

We turned a corner, then another. The Tibrans were gaining on us. When we came to a four-way-intersection, everyone wasted a good four seconds arguing over which way to go. We took a right and kept going.

Right into a line of Tibran soldiers. They stood in a phalanx formation, using their bronze shields as a barrier.

We tried to turn around, to run back the way we'd come, but it was too late. The Tibran soldiers chasing us had caught up. More arrows launched from crossbow strings whizzed past my face. One of our companions fell immediately, and Aubren grabbed me by the scruff of my tunic and forced me to stand behind him to shield me from the fire.

So much for my great plan.

Then the whole tunnel began to shake. Overhead, rubble poured down over us like an avalanche as something huge broke through from the surface. The Tibrans fired at it blindly. Aubren threw himself over me.

Suddenly, two massive, scaly, clawed feet burst down through the ceiling of the tunnel. They snagged one of our friends and lifted him away. Another set of clawed feet appeared, and another, and another. One by one, they plucked us out of the ground and carried us up—up into the pale moonlight above.

"Hang on!" Aubren shouted. He grabbed me like a puppy and tossed me in the air so one of those big scaly feet could grab me. All I could do was cling to the toes and scream as I was swiftly yanked skyward.

I couldn't see what happened to Aubren. The moonlight dazed me, and I stared around at the blurred images of sky, snow, and scales.

Dragons.

There were dozens of them everywhere, soaring on powerful bat-like wings and spitting plumes of flame at the Tibran soldiers below. Their muscular bodies spun effortlessly through the air, their scales shimmering in the silver starlight as they dove and roared, attacking the soldiers who were firing at them with those net-throwing machines.

It took one net, sometimes two, to bring down a dragon. They were bigger than a shrike—much bigger.

I looked up at the dragon that was carrying me in its claws, ready to give a stupid grin and wave up to the rider.

Only there wasn't one.

The dragon wasn't even wearing a saddle.

The beast craned its head down, looking at me briefly with bright blue eyes. They were eerily intelligent, almost curious.

"H-hey there," I stammered. "You're not gonna eat me, right?"

The dragon tilted its head and made a funny clicking, chirping sound. Its big eyes blinked and nostrils puffed like it was smelling me. Then it went back to flying with strong wings pumping furiously against the wind. It soared for the horizon and all around us I saw more dragons join in. They were all different colors and patterns. Some were red, while others were yellow, silver, or blue. Some had stripes. Others had markings like the big jungle snakes in Luntharda. Some were even spotted like a leopard.

The ones directly around us all had one thing in common, though. They were all carrying my companions.

"Reigh! Are you all right?" I heard Aubren shout suddenly. A huge blue dragon had him. It was bigger than any of the others with long black horns and spikes that ran all the way down its back to the tip of its long tail. The horns around its face were tipped with orange, and it had big yellow eyes that seemed to glow when it looked my way.

"I'm okay! For now," I called back. "What's going on? Where are the riders?"

Aubren was gazing around in awe. "There aren't any," he answered at last. "These dragons are wild."

CHAPTER SEVENTEEN

The dragons carried us away from the battle. They flew fast and so high up none of the nets the Tibrans launched could ever reach us. In the distance, I saw a spot of light on the horizon. Barrowton. We were nearly there.

We were carried almost to the city before the dragons finally began to descend. They soared in circles like vultures, taking turns swooping down and dropping us into the snow one at a time until Aubren was the only one left.

I stood back with the others, watching as the biggest dragon—a blue one with bright yellow eyes—landed with a *boom*. Aubren stumbled back away from it as the dragon let him go, slipping and landing on his rump in front of the rest of us.

It was unbelievable. I'd always imagined what dragons might look like. Kiran had tried to describe them many times. But they were incredible. None of the descriptions did them justice.

Their bodies were muscular and compact, built sort of like a mixture of feline and bat, with two front wing arms that boasted two toes crowned with curled talons. Their hind haunches had paw-like feet with long toes, big dew claws, and more of those lethal talons. Instead of looking like a serpent, their short snouts, pointed ears, and long tails made them seem even more feline—even if they were covered in scales and spikes.

The blue dragon lowered its horned head, looking at us with those dazzling yellow eyes. Everyone scurried back away from it, even Aubren, who was crawling backwards across the ground like a crab.

Now that we were closer, I could see there was a thick black blaze running down the length of the dragon's body. The rest of it, however, was a deep royal blue color. It also had two long fangs that dripped below its jaws, like a tiger.

The blue dragon didn't seem afraid of us at all, even if he was supposed to be wild. And it didn't seem threatened by us, either. It snorted and snarled at any of the other dragons that swooped down too close to us, like he was protecting us.

"Y-Your Majesty," one of our comrades stammered as he grabbed onto Aubren's sleeve. "Is that ... ?"

Aubren didn't answer right away. His whole face was flushed and his eyes were wide with an emotion I couldn't identify. "Yes," he replied in a hushed, awestruck voice. "I think it is."

"Who?" I looked for anyone to clue me in.

"Mavrik," Aubren clarified. "The one ridden by Jaevid Broadfeather."

At the sound of that name, the blue dragon let out a thundering roar. He reared his head back and shot a plume of fire that lit up the night sky. I took a *big* step backward, just in case he decided to roast us on the spot.

The dragon apparently had other plans, though. He regarded us one last time with a snort, and then reared onto his hind legs, spreading his black wings wide, and sprang back into the sky to join the rest of his kind.

They circled a few more times and then soared away, Mavrik leading the flock. The sound of their wing beats faded into the distance. We stood there in the snow, only a mile or so outside of Barrowton, watching in silence until we couldn't see them anymore.

"But that was forty years ago," someone protested. "That would make him—"

"A king drake," Aubren finished for him.

"But why would they come save us?"

"Do you think it's possible? Did Jaevid send them?"

"Don't be ridiculous!"

"Well, how else do you explain a whole flock of wild dragons just showing up like that?"

"He did something like that before, didn't he? In the last battle of the Gray War?"

Questions started to fly. Things got heated. No one could agree on why the wild dragons had come to save us. For some, it was a miracle. For others, it was pure luck. To me, it seemed a little too bizarre to be luck. But I wasn't sure I believed Jaevid had sent them, either.

At last, Aubren raised his hand for silence. "There'll be time to debate later. We have to get to the city immediately. The healthy will help the injured. Let's move out."

Everyone began to obey.

It was an uphill walk through the snow to reach Barrowton. No one said much. I guess everyone was still processing what we'd just been through. I certainly was.

Somehow, I'd managed to beat Hilleddi's Mirror of Truth. Privately, I decided Noh must have had something to do with it. That's the only explanation that made sense to me. He'd helped me beat it and bought me enough time for ... for the dragons to arrive? Argh, that didn't make sense, either. I couldn't summon dragons.

After a few minutes of trudging through the snow, I got the unsettling feeling I was being watched. Next to me, Aubren was staring in my direction.

"Scared of me now?" I muttered. I wasn't sure if I wanted him to hear me or not.

"Somewhat," he conceded.

"Sorry," I mumbled.

Aubren cocked an eyebrow like he was confused. "What for?"

"I would've done something sooner, but I was afraid of that."

"That I'd be frightened of you?"

"No, that I'd lose control and accidentally hurt you guys, too." I kept my head down. "That's why Kiran never wanted me to show anyone what I could do."

Aubren drew closer and fell in step right next to me. "I can understand that. But I can also knock you out again. That seemed to neutralize things fairly well."

I rubbed the sore knot on the back of my head. "Yeah, I'll say."

"Reigh." He lowered his voice as though he didn't want anyone to overhear. "We aren't the only ones who know what you can do now. Hilleddi has seen it, which means Argonox will be looking for you, too."

"Why?"

"The Tibrans are fond of taking prisoners. Most of their army is made up of captured slaves from other kingdoms. They force them to fight under threat of death. They've done that very thing to some of our own men and even a few dragonriders."

"So, you think Argonox is going to try to make me fight for him?" I scoffed at the idea. "Yeah, right. There's no way I'd ever agree to that."

Aubren looked away. I could tell by his expression he wasn't so sure.

I had a hard time not taking that offensively since it was basically like calling me a liar and a potential traitor. Sure, I was new to this whole war between kingdoms thing, but I wasn't about to switch sides.

"At any rate, I'm grateful. Thank you for saving us," he said quietly. "I know Kiran would be proud of you, too."

I shrugged and shot him a quick, sulky scowl.

He caught me in the act. I expected him to frown back, but instead he just cracked a smile and ruffled my hair. "C'mon, don't look like that."

I swatted his hand away and tried in vain to smooth my hair back down. "Stop it! Geez, why do people always do that?"

"Do what?"

"Pet me like I'm a little kid, or a dog, or something."

"I don't know." He chuckled. "Maybe because you pout like one."

I WAS EXHAUSTED WHEN WE FINALLY ARRIVED AT THE GATES OF BARROWTON. The city looked more intimidating up close—like a stone fortress perched on a snowy hilltop. Looking up at the tall gray walls made me feel insignificant. Gray elves didn't build walls that big. I'd never seen anything like it.

Far up on the ramparts, I spotted a few groups of soldiers. More were stationed on the turrets on either side of the gates. When they spotted us down below, they started shouting to one another. I heard the banging toll of a bell somewhere high in the towers. Slowly, the big gates groaned open and more Maldobarian soldiers stepped out to greet us.

Aubren greeted them first. As soon as he introduced himself, the soldiers bowed and saluted him with great respect. They looked happy to see us as they escorted us into the city. I turned to watch as they began to close the massive gates again, dragging them into place by two huge cranks that were being turned by teams of what I could only guess were horses.

I'd never actually seen a horse before—not live ones, anyway. I'd seen plenty of them in pictures. Kiran had told me humans liked to ride them, and some could run quite fast, although not as fast as our faundra. Others, like these, were bigger and stronger so they could be used to pull heavy things. Their legs where thicker and their bodies more muscular, and they had long manes of hair on their necks.

Inside the outer walls were another set of even thicker walls, like a double ring of protection. These had holes cut in them near the top with something that looked like a big rainspout sticking out. I wasn't sure what that was meant for, though probably not rain.

Through the second set of gates, the city of Barrowton was bustling with activity. There was a nervous energy in the air, so I stuck close to Aubren's heels and stared around at all the people who were walking the streets. Some of them were herding flocks of cattle while others drove big wagons pulled by more horses. Women walked with children in their arms and groups of soldiers marched back and forth. Their clothes were strange. The food displayed in the shop windows looked weird, too, although it smelled okay.

I expected to see humans everywhere. After all, Maldobar was a human kingdom. And while there were a lot of them, sweeping out the front steps of their shops or hanging laundry out the second and third story windows, I saw plenty of Gray elves and even some halfbreeds, too. All of them stared at us as we went past—probably because of our clothes.

"Why are there so many Gray elves here?" I asked Aubren quietly.

"During the Gray War, this city was burned to the ground and utterly destroyed. It was the site of a great battle that cost both our kingdoms immense casualties. My father wanted it to be the first site of our efforts for a peaceful future, so he ordered that the city be rebuilt. It would serve as a safe haven in times of trouble, and people worked year-round to build it. My father decreed that anyone who signed on to work and help with the construction, be they elf or otherwise, would be given their choice of a paid salary or a new home within the city. Many of the Gray elves that had fled to Maldobar during the war came to live here for that reason," he explained with a smile. "It's become something of a melting pot since then."

"A melting pot?"

"Yes, it means a place where many cultures have mixed. After this place was such a success, my father decided to do the same thing with another city further to the east, called Dayrise."

I paused, turning in a slow circle to look all around as we walked through a city square. There was a large fountain in the center with a familiar figure sculpted into it. I knew his face now—and not just because it had the same scar over one of his eyes. I'd seen him plenty of times in Mau Kakuri in paintings, engravings, and tapestries. It was the lapiloque, Jaevid Broadfeather. In this sculpture, he was standing tall wearing a suit of armor, holding a scimitar regally against his chest and looking up toward the sky.

Aubren glanced at the fountain as we walked past, and I saw his brow crease and his expression darken. "The whole city is made like a fortress and is highly defensible. The idea was that, if war ever came to Maldobar again, many people could come here for refuge," he went on. "The governing Duke is one of my oldest friends."

The deeper we walked into the city, the tenser the atmosphere became. Shopkeepers were boarding up their windows. People were stacking bags of sand in alleyways like makeshift barricades. Soldiers were going door to door, dressed in full armor and carrying battle-ready weapons.

Ahead of us, behind one last fortified wall, was the keep. It was a tall rectangular building, with turrets on every corner and narrow windows. Royal blue banners fluttered on either side of the iron front door, each of them stitched with the image of a golden eagle grasping swords in its claws. The door was opened for us as we got close and the soldiers who had been escorting us stopped, saluted, and turned to go back to the city.

"Aubren!" a voice called out suddenly.

We all turned to look.

A man who looked like he might be in his late twenties was running toward us, waving his arms. He wasn't all that tall—average sized, really, and a few inches shorter than Aubren—but he had a powerful build underneath his noble clothing and black leather jerkin. He had shaggy, wavy black hair that hung around his squared, firm jawline. When he glanced my way, I caught the glimmer of his fierce green eyes.

He grasped Aubren by the shoulders, laughing and giving him a shake. The two men embrace roughly, patting one another on the back. "Gods and Fates, it's good to see you." The man chuckled. "After Northwatch fell, I feared the worst. What on earth are you wearing?"

Aubren laughed with him. "It's a long story."

"Save it, then. I prefer to pair long stories with good ale." He looked around at all of us and when he got to me, he paused. The corners of his mouth quirked up. "And who is this?"

"Reigh," Aubren answered for me. "He's come from Luntharda to fight with us."

"Well that explains the hair," the man said. "A human boy taught to fight by the Gray elves? Sounds lethal, indeed. A pleasure, Young Master Reigh. Welcome to Barrowton. I am Duke Phillip Derrick, but you can call me Phillip if you like."

He offered to shake my hand and reluctantly I obliged. I didn't think dukes were the kinds of people who shook hands. They were nobles, weren't they? Only, this guy didn't act very noble. He went around to each member of our group to offer a handshake and confident smile.

"Welcome, all of you. I wish we were meeting under better circumstances," Phillip said at last, and gestured for us to follow him into the keep. "But time is against us and there are far too many Tibrans on my doorstep for my liking."

CHAPTER EIGHTEEN

The rest of Aubren's men were excused to join the ranks preparing to defend the city. Phillip assured them they would be fed, given new armor and weapons, and a chance to rest before they got to work. Those who were wounded would go directly to the infirmary to be treated. The men seemed happy about this, and I sort of expected I'd be joining them, since I wasn't a noble. But Aubren insisted I stay with him.

I was given a room all to myself in the keep, and it was almost bigger than the whole house Kiran and I had shared in Mau Kakuri. The bed was huge and there was a set of brand new human-styled clothes spread out on it. I even had my own bathroom.

Phillip had invited us to join him for dinner, so I had to get cleaned up. A couple of lady servants in clean white dresses came in to help me get ready. I had to ask one of them to show me how the bathtub worked. There were all these knobs and I couldn't get the water to get hot.

"Sorry, it's different in Luntharda," I said as I stripped down out of all my filthy scout's clothes and undergarments, leaving them in a pile next to the door. It would all need a wash and some repairs now, anyway.

When I turned around, the servant girl who had been drawing the bath dropped the bar of soap she'd been unwrapping. Her whole face blushed bright pink and she covered her eyes. "Ah! Y-yes, of course. Please excuse me!"

Before I could get a word out, she darted out of the room and shut the door. Well, that was weird. What was her problem? I scratched my bare rear end and tried to figure it out.

Pfft, oh well. I had about made up my mind that all human girls were odd.

Scooping up the bar of soap she'd dropped, I climbed into the tub and started scrubbing the grit off my skin. Another servant came in, this one much older than the first one and her pudgy, wrinkled face sagged around her mouth and eyes. Her skin was like tree bark, textured with age, and her hands were knobby and callused. She sat down on the edge of the tub, pulled a wooden brush from her apron, and started trying to get the knots out of my hair.

"What's wrong with the other girl? Did she get sick or something?" I asked as I sank down and let the hot water sooth my sore joints.

The old woman gave a raspy laugh. "I assume she's not accustomed to being flashed the private bits of a young man."

I winced as the brush snagged on a tangle. "Oh ... wait, so humans don't have public baths?"

"No, child. We prefer to bathe alone. We also cover ourselves in the presence of young ladies, even if they are only servants, and we don't prance around naked. You might try to remember that next time."

Now I was the one blushing. "Oh. Oops. Uh, sorry about that, then."

The old woman sighed. "My goodness, all this hair. What a mess."

I blushed harder and sank down lower in the tub. "Gray elves don't cut their hair."

"I see." She didn't sound convinced that was a good excuse.

Once I was clean, the old woman turned her back long enough for me to climb out of the tub and wrap up in a towel. She followed me back out into my bedroom and waited while I got dressed. Then she sat me down at a dresser and started massaging some kind of oil into my scalp and brushed it through my hair. It smelled funny, but not in a bad way.

"It's cedar wood, tea tree, and olive oil," she rasped in her throaty voice.

I wasn't paying much attention. I was looking at my reflection in the fancy gold-framed mirror hanging behind the dresser. Kiran didn't have any fancy furniture at home. He had one mirror, which I used to shave sometimes, and I hadn't done that in several days now.

My chin and jaw were flecked with lots of dark stubble, and I still had a pretty noticeable scar across the bridge of my nose from where the stag had slashed me with his antlers. I ran my finger across it, tracing the rough, raised skin while the old servant woman began weaving my hair into one long braid. The scar made my face look wild, even now that it was clean. Once she was done braiding it, my dark red hair hung all the way down to the base of my back. There were dusky circles under my eyes.

I looked almost as tired as I did savage—just as Hilleddi had said.

"Why such a sour face?" The old woman was eyeing me in the mirror.

I frowned and sank back in the chair. "I came here because I thought I'd fit in better than I did in Luntharda. I wasn't very good at being a Gray elf. And now it turns out I'm not good at being a human, either."

"Why do you say that?"

"I keep embarrassing myself," I mumbled. "I just wanted to fit in, you know? Just once, I wanted to feel like I wasn't the odd man out. I thought maybe if I were useful ... "

"Well, I'm no expert in Gray elf culture, but I do know a thing or two about us round-eared folk. I don't think flashing your naked rear end to one servant girl is a ruinous mistake, considering you didn't know any better." The old woman chuckled and poked me in the back of the head. "You young men are all the same. You focus too much on what you're not—you forget to see what you are."

I glared up at my reflection again. I already knew what I was and it wasn't anything good. An orphan. A monster. Cursed. Haunted by an evil spirit I could barely control. The list went on and on.

"Up with you. It's nearly dinner time." The old woman poked me again, and when I stood, she muscled around me. She was surprisingly nimble for someone so ancient. She straightened the collar of my borrowed, human-styled tunic and picked a few bits of lint off my shoulders.

"Will you tell that other girl I really am sorry about before?" I rubbed the back of my neck and looked down.

She smiled, making her drooping mouth seem a little less saggy for a moment. "Yes, if you like. Now go on. It's bad manners to be late to dinner."

BIG SURPRISE—I GOT LOST ON THE WAY TO DINNER. I DIDN'T RUN INTO ANY princesses this time, though. And it wasn't completely my fault. As it turns out, human castles are much different than Gray elf palaces, and the Keep of Barrowton was no exception. It was taller, narrower, and there were very few windows. A grand stone staircase spiraled to every floor, lit by chandeliers with hundreds of candles—and no one had bothered to tell me which floor the dining hall was on. Since you couldn't see out, the walls were adorned with big tapestries stitched with images of mountains, valleys, beautiful meadows, and scenes from great battles. The ceilings had paintings of clouds, dragons, and figures that I could only guess were gods and goddesses.

Following my nose and the fragrant aromas of a freshly cooked feast turned out to be the most effective tactic for finding my way around. The smells of freshly baked bread, roasted meats, herbal seasonings, and things I didn't even have a name for practically dragged me down the correct path toward the dining hall. Aubren and Duke Phillip were bound to be waiting for me. I was already late. I rounded another corner quickly, walking fast and not paying attention—

and smashed right into a servant girl carrying a platter of fruit. Grapes went flying, apples rolled across the floor, and I got smacked in the face by the prickly end of a pineapple.

"I'm so sorry! I didn't see you there," she apologized and began frantically trying to recapture the grapes that were making a break for it down the hallway.

"No, it's totally fine. I wasn't paying attention," I said, attempting to help her pile all the runaway fruit back onto the tray. One of the apples had rolled away, making its escape to the far end of the corridor. I jogged in pursuit just as it came to a stop outside the dining hall's door. On my way to grab it, I heard Aubren and Phillip's voices faintly coming from the other side.

"So, she did come here." Aubren sounded relieved.

"Yes, only a few days ago. I was afraid we might suffer her rage when she found out you had gone to Luntharda without her," Phillip replied. "Not that I'm complaining. I find her most beautiful when she's angry."

Aubren chuckled darkly. "You're crazy. Crossing my sister is as good as a death wish."

"I know, I know. It doesn't matter, though. She still looks straight through me as though I'm not even there. All my compliments fall on deaf ears and she makes no effort to hide that she's using me for whatever value I might be to her and her riders. That cruel streak must run rampant in your family," Phillip complained. "I suppose that's why I was very surprised to find you letting that redheaded kid tag along with you. Taking up babysitting, are we?"

I froze with my hand around the apple, squatting down behind the door.

"Hardly," Aubren replied dryly. "Kiran found him as an orphaned whelp, or so he claims. Kiran might fool everyone in Luntharda with that shoddy story, but I've known him too long to be duped so easily."

"I didn't think Kiran had any children of his own. Granted, there was that one girl. Didn't she have red hair as well?"

"She did," Aubren agreed. "But I don't believe this boy is his child at all. He has none of the marks of a halfbreed."

"True. So what do you suspect?" Phillip's voice got quieter.

For a moment, no one said a word. I was afraid maybe they'd somehow realized I was listening to them. But after nearly a minute, Aubren took a deep breath. "Did I ever tell you how my mother died?"

"Only that she passed in childbirth. It wasn't so surprising, considering her age. I remember my own mother mourning for her. She said it was often too much for older mothers to go through a birth."

"Indeed. The pregnancy as a whole took a toll on her. I was too young to fully realize it then. It was only after that I realized how weak she had become, and how frail. She could barely walk across a room at the end. She hid it well. She kept smiling—I suspect because she didn't want to scare us. She pretended to be preoccupied with other things. She must have knitted a dozen blankets sitting in her bed."

"She was a strong lady, I do remember that."

"She was. But the night she went into labor, my father forbade my sister and I to enter their room. I think he must have known the delivery would be difficult. He didn't want us to see her that way." Aubren's tone was gravely serious. "I never knew exactly what happened; only that it had been too much for her. Jenna and I sat outside the door, trying to listen while Kiran watched over us. It sounded like chaos inside. I could hear my mother straining. And then there was silence—a strange silence. Kiran ran inside to offer his help, and it was as though utter chaos broke loose. My father began screaming like a wild animal, like he'd gone completely mad. I couldn't even understand what he said. Jenna and I were so afraid we ran back to my room and hid in my closet. We must've stayed there most of the night, scared out of our minds."

My face started to get hot. I was squeezing the apple harder and harder, not daring to move an inch.

"The midwife told us later that our mother had succumbed to the labor, that it was just too much for a woman her age to bear, and that the baby had been stillborn. It never even took a breath." Aubren was whispering now, his voice so faint I could scarcely hear him. I leaned closer and pressed my ear to the door. "I never had any reason to question it. My father, the midwife, and even Kiran told the exact same story—but without giving away any more detail. They wouldn't even tell me if the baby had been a boy or a girl. They buried my mother with the baby in her arms, wrapped up so no one could see it. But I couldn't resist. I wanted to see it. I wanted to know if it was a brother or a sister I had lost—to take just one glimpse of its face. So, I pulled back the blanket just to take a peek."

Aubren hesitated again. His voice caught like he was having a hard time getting the words out. "I remember when I saw it, I couldn't believe it was real. I'd never been so terrified in my life. It had only been a few days and yet the baby looked all wrong. It was tiny, shriveled, and shrunken. It was ... *mummified*."

The apple fell out of my hand and hit the floor. It rolled away, but I didn't go after it. I was staring at the door, barely breathing.

"What are you saying?" Phillip asked dubiously.

"He's the proper age. Kiran was very vague about where he'd come from. It was less than a week after that Kiran departed from Maldobar. True, he'd been talking about retiring for quite some time, but the timing is a little *too* convenient. You know as well as I do that after that night, my father was never the same. He's been all but mad with grief. If there was another—"

"Another what? Another child? Gods and Fates, Aubren. Think about it. How could that be possible?"

"I don't know. But that boy can *do* things, Phillip. Things you've never even dreamed of in your wildest nightmares."

"Like Jaevid?" His voice brightened with hope.

"No," Aubren replied. "Nothing like Jaevid. When I first met him, I thought that maybe he was. I thought maybe he could help us. But what I saw him do in Luntharda was only a small taste of his power." I heard a chair creak across the floor. "Now I am honestly afraid of what I have brought here. I am afraid of what might happen if I put him in battle and he unleashes the full extent of it. Even he admits that he can barely control the power within him. And worse, I am afraid that he might be my—"

"He doesn't look much like you or Jenna." Phillip was quick to interrupt. He still didn't sound convinced. "Although, your mother's hair did have a reddish hue, if I recall correctly. But let's be reasonable here, Aubren. You're suggesting that Kiran somehow stole a newborn baby with your father and the midwife standing right there and swapped it with a mummified one?"

"I don't know how or why he did it. But he was there—he was in the room."

Phillip's laugh twanged with anxiety. "So? That doesn't mean this boy has any relation to you. Why jump to that conclusion?"

"Because he said it himself," Aubren snapped in a soft but sharp voice, proceeding to tell Phillip about how we had been captured by the Tibrans, how they had interrogated us, and finally about the Mirror of Truth. He admitted that while he had taken a blow to the head, he had been able to figure out what was going on when I told Hilleddi I was the prince.

I should have died right then and there.

"Maybe it was just a fluke," Phillip suggested. "Magical weapons and artifacts like that are faulty and inconsistent. You can't expect them to be accurate all the time."

"No!" I heard a banging sound as someone, probably Aubren, had slammed their fist down on the table. "I can't explain it. I've no real proof; I know that. I just *feel* it. He is my brother."

My heart was beating so hard I was afraid it might punch right out of my chest. I backed away from the door. I wanted to run. To get away before I had to hear anymore.

"And if he is?" Phillip asked quietly. "What then?"

"Then I have failed him in the most absolute and profound way one brother could fail another. I should have come looking for him. I should have been the one to raise him and take care of him, not Kiran. He's spent all his life pining for his lost family, thinking we had abandoned him, and I never knew he existed."

Suddenly, someone placed a hand on my arm. I flinched and spun around, almost knocking the servant girl over a second time. The platter clanged loudly again, and the conversation inside stopped.

"I-I'm so sorry, sir," she stammered. "You can go in, if you like. They're waiting for you."

I glanced at the door then shook my head. "Actually, I'm not feeling very good. Can you tell them I'm just going to stay in my room tonight?"

She gave me a hesitant, worried smile and nodded. "Of course. Should I have your dinner brought up?"

I backed away from her slowly and took one more, hard look at the door. "No. Thanks. I don't have much of an appetite anymore."

19

CHAPTER NINETEEN

I didn't go back to my room. Not right away, at least. I walked the halls of the keep, wandering from floor to floor while servants and soldiers passed me. Some of them stared, and I couldn't help but be a little paranoid. Maybe they knew who I was, what I could do, or that I was probably Aubren's—

No. I couldn't accept that just yet. If Aubren was right, if he was my brother, then I really was a *prince*. It was weird to even think about it. I didn't like the idea of being made into a social spectacle like that. The shadows were safer for someone with a problem like mine.

Unfortunately, there was only one person who could tell me if any of that stuff was true, and he was back in Luntharda. My blood boiled at the idea that Kiran had been lying to me all these years. Had he stolen me? Was it some kind of plot? Just what the heck was going on?

A familiar face caught my eye and made me stop. I was standing before another big tapestry. It was a scene from the Gray War.

I'd heard the Gray elves tell this story many times, as though it were a legend. The lapiloque, Jaevid Broadfeather, was standing on what was supposed to be the temple grounds deep in the jungle of Luntharda. He and another man, who must have been Jace before he became the king, were bound up and about to be executed as traitors. At the last second, something amazing had happened. The tapestry showed Jaevid walking with his arms outstretched, directly toward the shining image of the ancient god, Paligno.

Paligno looked like a mixture of many animals. He had the body of a horse, the legs and wings of a bird, the tail of a lion, scales like a lizard, and long white horns sweeping back from his head like a stag. He'd been stitched in shining threads so the god seemed to be glowing and glittering with power. All around him were Gray elves cringing away and shielding their eyes. Some were even bowing with their heads to the ground.

That was the moment when Paligno had chosen Jaevid as the lapiloque—officially, anyway. It was said a lapiloque's power wasn't complete until he was chosen.

I wondered if that went for evil gods, too.

"If anyone wants to choose or claim me, or however it works, now would be a great time," I muttered.

Of course, I didn't get an answer—not even from Noh.

I must have walked for hours. My stomach growled angrily because I hadn't eaten any dinner and I was so tired I found myself wanting to sit down in every chair or sofa I passed. Eventually, I wandered back to my room and found the door standing open. Aubren and the old servant woman from before were standing there, having a heated conversation.

"What do you mean he didn't come back here?" Aubren's voice was raised in panic.

"I'm deeply sorry, Your Highness. I didn't see him after he left for dinner." The servant woman bowed her head in apology.

"Miss Harriet, please, you must have some idea where he went. Did he say anything strange?" Aubren pressed her.

I scowled and cleared my throat. "I'm right here."

The two of them stared me down. Aubren looked surprised and relieved. Miss Harriet—well, honestly it was hard to tell. Her face was so wrinkled her subtle expressions were nearly impossible to interpret.

"You missed dinner." Aubren frowned. "What's going on?"

"Nothing. I'm fine." I muscled my way in between them to get into my room.

Aubren followed me inside. I saw Miss Harriet flash me a sympathetic look from the hallway right before he shut the door. Now we were alone and Aubren didn't look happy with me at all.

Okay, so I had ditched on dinner. And snubbing a dinner invitation from a duke and a prince probably wasn't a good thing. But if we were going to start comparing wrongs here, he wasn't exactly blameless.

"You don't look fine," Aubren said as he followed me into the sitting room. "You were listening to us, weren't you?"

I stopped. My hands clenched. Slowly, I turned back to face him. "And if I was?"

His expression fell. The hard lines in the corners of his mouth softened and he let out a sigh. "If I had any concrete proof, I would have said something to you first, Reigh. All I have is a suspicion. I didn't want to give you false hope."

"It's just as well. I don't want to be a prince." I stared down at the toes of my boots.

"Why not? I realize I'm no prize candidate for a brother but—"

"That's not the reason," I muttered. "You said it yourself; you really have no idea what you've brought here. I don't even know. But whatever I am, it's definitely not anything good. I'm a disaster waiting to happen, don't think I don't know that."

"Good can be a relative thing sometimes. What's good for the hunter isn't good for the deer," he said as he made himself comfortable in one of the parlor chairs. He leaned his elbow on the armrest and rubbed at his chin, his eyes gleaming thoughtfully.

"Noh said something like that to me once," I mumbled. "A spider is only a monster to a fly."

"He's not wrong."

"I know. I'd just rather not be a monster or a hunter." I sank into the chair next to his and slumped down till my chin was resting on my chest. "And I hate spiders."

"Well, let's not get ahead of ourselves." He cast me a tired smile. "The thing to do is ask my father. If you were stolen from us somehow, he's never said a word to anyone about it."

"What about Kiran?"

His gaze hardened. "He's spent a long time lying about this and trying to cover it up. I don't expect him to tell me the truth, even if I backed him into a corner."

My chest felt heavy. I couldn't decide if I was angry, upset, sad, or excited. There was a chance I had a family—one that truly wanted me. Maybe I hadn't been abandoned. Maybe I'd only been lost, or stolen. Aubren was right about one thing, if the King of Maldobar was my father, why hadn't he tried to find me? Did he know I was missing? Did he even care? I gnawed on the inside of my cheek while those questions rolled through my mind.

"What's he like?" I asked. "The King, I mean."

Aubren made a face like that was a loaded question. "He used to be a very good man, who loved to joke and tease us. He had a laugh you could hear from every corner of the castle. He was also very dedicated and straightforward. When I was a boy, much younger than you are now, he would take me on hunts and horseback rides. He taught me to wrestle, told me stories, and taught me everything he knew about navigation and tracking in the wild. Some nights he would sneak down to the kitchen with me late at night so we could have a midnight snack. A few times he let me ride a dragon with him—although I think that was to test if I'd make a good rider or not. Still, he was a very good father. I never had a doubt that he loved us."

That didn't sound so bad. "What's different about him now?"

"After my mother died, it was as though part of him died with her. He stopped talking to us. He didn't laugh or smile anymore. We didn't play games, or go on hunts, or even have dinner together. He didn't leave their room unless it was for business. Sometimes I didn't see him for weeks on end. He became like a phantom in the castle." Aubren took in a deep breath. "Then a lot of things seemed to go wrong. Jenna and I became a constant source of disappointment to him. Whenever we did speak, it always ended in an argument. I hated those days. I did everything I could to avoid fighting with him," he recalled. "Jenna wasn't as mindful of his temper as I was. She didn't back down when he would raise his voice. He couldn't break her. I doubt if anyone can."

I swallowed hard and looked at the fireplace. A few thick logs were smoldering and crackling in a nest of white ash. The heat from it warmed my face even from across the room. "Hilleddi is going to come looking for me, isn't she? She's going to come here and attack Barrowton."

Aubren didn't answer. He was staring at the fire, too, the flames flickering in the centers of his dark blue eyes.

"We need to have a plan," I said. "Something better than just blockading ourselves in here and hoping the dragonriders show up before they burn the whole city down."

He flicked me a quick sideways glance. "What did you have in mind?"

"Something crazy," I muttered under my breath. "Something absolutely insane."

THE BROAD SIDE OF A SWORD'S HILT CAME SMASHING RIGHT AGAINST MY FACE, knocking me into a daze. I stumbled, tripped, and fell flat onto my back. Before I could come to my senses, the point of the sword was pricking against the end of my nose.

"You've got to stay off your heels when you take a blow. You do that and a follow-up strike will knock you flat on your back, like so. That's as good as a death sentence." Aubren leapt back a few paces to reset the match, his wooden sparring sword raised at me. "Again."

I groaned and sat up. My whole body screamed in protest. There weren't many parts of me that didn't hurt. We'd been stuck here two days. Two days waiting for word to come from Aubren's sister and the rest of her dragonriders. To pass the time, Aubren had decided to test my skills in battle.

"Tibrans don't fight like elves, Reigh," he warned. "They fight more like humans—like us. But their armor is thick. Their shields are heavy. They will hit you hard and from all sides. They outman us on the battlefield five to one, on a good day."

I grabbed my own practice sword, which had been knocked out of my hand at least a dozen times this morning, and dragged myself to my feet. "Can't we take a water break?"

He smirked. "I thought you were the Queen of Luntharda's most honored scout?"

"Yeah, maybe in Luntharda. Here I'm just ... existing." I touched my nose gingerly, testing to see if it was broken. "Am I bleeding?"

"No, not yet. You gave it your best try, though. Come on," he urged and poked me in the arm with the tip of his wooden sword. "One more round. Then we'll take a break. I'd like to see you win one match."

I narrowed my eyes. "Fine."

I dove in, swinging wide to feint an assault. He saw it coming, and stepped in to make a strike of his own while my guard was down. I pitched backward suddenly, bounding off the floor and hurling myself into a backflip. I pulled my knees in close to my body and kicked him square in the chest as I went over.

I landed in a low crouch, my sword still clenched tight in my hand, and immediately rushed him again. Rearing back my blade, I aimed for the winning blow.

Aubren blocked. The impact made my teeth rattle. And too quick for me to react, he swept my legs out from under me. I dropped my blade when I hit the floor again, but that didn't mean I was out of the game yet.

"That's cheating." I snarled. "I'm not used to a human sword."

He smirked. "There's no such thing in a real battle, kid. Those fancy elf blades of yours are as good as gone now that the Tibrans have them. So you'll have to improvise."

"Okay, then."

I curled my body into a ball for a kick up. When I landed, I slowly stood and rolled my shoulders, one by one. I flexed my empty hands, spreading my fingers wide, and summoning just a *tiny* bit of my power. Darkness gathered around my open hands like swirling clouds of black. They took form, boiling inwards and morphing into the shape of two long, black scimitars. It only took a few seconds and there they were, just as I visualized in my mind—two blades as dark as night and as sharp as razors resting comfortably in my grip.

Aubren's eyes went wide.

I rushed him once again, and this time I wasn't faking. I struck hard, tearing through different combinations and strikes in a flurry that kept Aubren on the defensive.

His jaw clenched as he strained to match me. Something had changed. Uncertainty and panic wafted off him so strongly I could practically smell it.

A grin wriggled its way up my lips. I just couldn't help it. This was *fun*.

I came down hard, knocking Aubren off balance. While he stumbled, I swung an arm out wide. The scimitar in my hand exploded into a puff of black mist, swirling and instantly snapping back into a new shape—a long black whip. I snapped it in the air, letting it wrap around one of his arms. One solid yank and I brought him face-first into my knee.

The blow rattled him. Aubren crumpled slowly to the practice mat and dropped his blade. He stayed on his hands and knees, breathing heavily, trying to collect himself. Then I saw him raise one of his hands in a gesture of surrender.

"Talk about cheating," he panted.

"You said to improvise." I let my shadow-hewn weapons dissolve into the air and crossed my arms smugly.

"That's not really what I had in mind." Slowly, he started to get up. He had a round, raised, knee-shaped lump beginning to swell on his forehead. "How long can you sustain those weapons? Doesn't it drain you to use that power?"

I shrugged. "I'm not sure. I've never tested it. Kiran didn't want me to. It does drain me a little, but not as much as when Noh ... well, you know."

Out of nowhere, the doors of the small sparring gymnasium we'd been using flew open. Duke Phillip burst in, red faced and out of breath. His eyes looked at both of us with frantic desperation.

"What is it? What's happened?" Aubren was already halfway across the room, running toward him. "Is it the Tibrans?"

"N-no," he stammered. "I mean yes! I mean—your sister is here!"

"What?" Aubren and I both asked in unison.

"They've come to warn us! The Tibrans have attacked the western border. They're marching this way!"

CHAPTER TWENTY

We left our sparring equipment behind and followed Duke Phillip out into the front courtyard of the keep. There, other soldiers and people from the city were gathering, crowding around to watch as five dragonriders landed. It was difficult to see. Everyone was pushing and shoving around me, and I was too short to catch a glimpse of what was going on. The thunderous beats of dragon wings and roaring filled the air. The crowd started shouting.

Aubren's strong hand grabbed the back of my neck. He was looming over me, his expression tight and fierce as he started muscling his way through the crowd. He kept his hand on me, trying to make sure I didn't get lost.

When we broke through the front of the crowd, I immediately got a blast of angry dragon breath in my face. Not the fiery kind, thank the gods. Just a big snort of stinky, hot breath that made me gag. The dragon snarled, showing rows of jagged teeth that might have had a few bits of his enemies still stuck between them.

"Keep back," Aubren warned as he steered me out of the way.

Five dragons stood together, fully dressed out in their battle gear. They wore big, beautifully crafted saddles between their wing arms and the base of their necks. Each saddle was made to fit flush against their bodies, over their spines and rippling scales. I didn't see any kind of bridle or reins, but the saddles did have a peculiar looking pair of handles on the front, and deep leather pockets on the side where the riders stuck their legs from the knee down.

The dragons hissed and bared their teeth at the crowd while their riders dismounted. One after another, dragonriders dressed in gleaming armor stepped off the beasts. They each wore helmets and long, royal blue cloaks with collars made out of white fox fur. Swords hung on their belts and their breastplates were engraved with Maldobar's royal seal depicting the eagle with its wings spread wide.

I assumed they were all men—which was dumb considering I should have known better—until the rider in the center of the gathering took off her helmet. Hair like bolts of golden silk fell, flowing down her back. Her eyes were a dangerous shade of stormy blue, and her heart-shaped face turned to pan the crowd with a bold, indifferent expression. She was tall, staggeringly beautiful, and looked about as friendly as the dragon that had snarled at me just a few minutes earlier.

The crowd booed, yelled curses, and called her names, and some even hurled rotten fruit in her direction. One of the other riders quickly moved to stand in the way, holding his cloak out to protect her from the garbage. Some of the soldiers from the keep were trying to keep the angry mob back, using their shields like a barrier.

None of it seemed to bother her. Or if it did, she never let it show. She strode proudly through the crowd with her head held high, shoulders back, and gaze focused squarely ahead. She walked straight toward us and stopped, slipping a hand free of her riding glove so she could shake hands with Duke Phillip and exchanged a stiff nod with Aubren.

Then her gaze fell on me.

Her brow furrowed slightly. She tilted her head to the side slightly, studying me up and down without ever saying a word.

Suddenly, some of the crowd broke free of the soldiers who were battling to keep them back. They were flinging potatoes and screaming, calling the dragonrider princess vile names Kiran never taught me.

The princess's dragon, which also happened to be the one that had growled at me, let out a bellow of rage and a blast of flame into the air. It made a few members of the angry mob stop, some even ran away in fear, but others pressed on, undeterred.

"Hurry, we must get inside." Aubren squeezed the back of my neck harder.

Together, Aubren, Phillip, the princess, and I walked quickly into the keep, while the rest of the dragonriders followed behind, but stayed by the doors to stand guard until the mob was dispersed. Duke Phillip barked out orders to his own men inside the castle, commanding them to do whatever was necessary to make them go—even if that meant locking them out of the city altogether. He had an angry flush to his face as he led us to a private parlor on the second floor. Servants had put out a long table of snacks for us and were still pouring four goblets of wine when we arrived. Phillip dismissed them and commanded that the doors be shut. We weren't to be disturbed.

The parlor was quiet. The atmosphere was tense. Aubren had taken a seat in one of the wingback chairs, and was scowling as he gripped the armrests in quiet rage. Phillip was pacing back and forth like a panther in a cage.

Only the princess seemed calm. She didn't look bothered that the crowd outside had just tried to mob rush her. She sat her helmet down on the coffee table and began removing the heavier pieces of her battle armor. She tossed them all onto a sofa and unbuckled the cloak from around her neck, folding it and placing it on top of the pile. Under all that metal, she wasn't very big. She was tall, yes, and she did have broad shoulders. But her body was lean and long-limbed. She had a slender neck and elegant arch to her back. When she walked, it was like she floated with her long golden hair spilling down all the way to the base of her back.

She looked up at me all of a sudden, catching me red handed gawking at her. A small, impish smile put dimples in the corners of her mouth. "You're a bit young to be a soldier."

I blushed. "I-I ... "

"He's not a soldier." Aubren's voice was quiet and sharp.

I couldn't decide if that should offend me or not.

The princess blinked. "Oh?"

"My name is Reigh." I decided to speak up. "I came from Luntharda. A-as a volunteer, I mean. To help."

Her smile widened. "That explains the hair, then."

My face got hotter. "It's traditional for Gray elves."

The princess nodded as she walked over to me, planting her hands on her hips. I could sense her sizing me up and almost had a heart attack when she thrust a hand out for me to shake. "I am Princess Jenna Farrow," she said. "But Jenna will do. An ally of Maldobar is a friend of mine."

My hand must have felt like a limp noodle as I shook hers. Her grip was like a snagwolf's jaws.

"Why do you look so embarrassed?" she teased. "Don't tell me that's the first time you've seen a princess get pelted with garbage?"

I swallowed. It totally was.

"I was the first woman to ever join the dragonrider ranks officially. I went through the same training as any other rider. There are many people in Maldobar who don't agree with that. I know in your kingdom, women may fight and become warriors if they choose, but that isn't the case here. My people despise it, and hate me for it, as well." Her gaze flicked to Aubren while she explained. "Even more so because of my social standing. They think a princess should wear beautiful gowns, sit still, behave, and always look pretty."

"O-oh."

Jenna giggled and winked one of her dark blue eyes at me. "But between us, sitting still is overrated and I'd rather wear pants any day."

Things calmed down after a few minutes and everyone got something to eat. I could still feel tension in the air, though, and it took me a little bit to realize that *I* was the problem. They wanted to talk business and war strategy—just not in front of me.

"Maybe you could go and make sure they are taking good care of Phevos for me." Princess Jenna was at least trying to be discreet about telling me to scram. "He's very temperamental and doesn't like being cooped up. Make sure they feed him well; he hasn't had much to eat in a few days."

"Right." I knew it was a bogus errand. Sure, I was probably close to ten years younger than everyone else in that room, but I wasn't five years old anymore.

As I left the parlor and closed the door behind me, I felt like I'd just been kicked out of a secret clubhouse or something. I wondered if Aubren would tell her about me, or rather, how much he would tell her. Knowing they'd probably be discussing me only made me more anxious and frustrated as I dragged my feet through the halls of the keep.

One thing was certain: I wasn't going to see about her dragon. No way. That thing would probably do worse than snort at me if I got close to him again. I wasn't going anywhere near any more dragons.

I decided to go up to the roof. I wanted a breath of fresh air, to clear my head, and maybe I'd be able to see Luntharda in the distance. I climbed the stairs up, going all the way to the top level of the keep. Past a pair of reinforced iron doors, I found the roof. It was wide and open. A few soldiers were stationed along the corners to keep watch. Each one of them carried a big bronze horn, and they ignored me completely as I walked past.

The wind was strong and cold. It snatched at the flags hoisted to the top of tall poles on each of the four corners of the building. Overhead, the sky was bright and as blue as a bird's egg. Clouds like puffy clumps of cotton floated over the valley to the east, casting shadows on the snow below. To the west were the mountains, still crowned with white. To the south, I could see more mountains in the distance, and to the north the distant solid green wall of jungle that I knew was Luntharda.

Seeing it put a pang of sorrow through my heart. I wondered what Kiran, Hecate, and Enyo were doing right now.

Out of nowhere, the whole building shuddered under my boots. I spun around, expecting to see some form of a Tibran attack hailing down upon us. What would it be this time? A catapult? A monster? I didn't have a weapon—no sword, bow, or scimitar.

I ran right into the end of a short, scaly snout. Two familiar, big, blue eyes the same hue as the sky stared at me.

I gave an undignified, I'm about to die, please someone save me scream. Thank the gods Aubren and Jenna weren't there.

Scrambling backwards, I flailed my arms and tried to get away. The heel of my boot caught on an uneven stone tile and I went down, landing flat on my back.

Those big eyes appeared over me again. Cat-like pupils widened and that short snout sniffed me so hard it sucked up some of the front of my shirt.

"Gods and Fates," I squeaked. "Please don't eat me."

The dragon made a humming, purring noise. It pulled back some and perked its small, scaly ears. Wait ... Why was that look so familiar? Then I realized—this was the same wild dragon that had pulled me out of the Tibran's tunnel and saved my life. It was back, and alone this time.

"What do you want? Look, I'm really grateful for before. You saved my life, and I appreciate that. But I don't have any food." I tried to bargain with it as I cautiously sat up.

The dragon flopped onto its belly in front of me, making the roof shudder. I swallowed, my heart still pounding in my ears as we stared at one another. What was this? A greeting? Not that I was any sort of dragon expert, but there was something impatient about the way it was staring me down.

This dragon was smaller than some of the others I'd seen. It had a more slender body, and its scales were shiny like they had a pearlescent coating on them. Their lime green color faded gradually into electric yellow along the dragon's belly. Its back, snout, tail, and legs all had dark green stripes like a tiger, and there was a line of long yellow spines down its whole body. Two big horns on the dragon's head curved back and sloped inward, like a stretched-out S-shape.

The beast was looking up at me and twitching the very tip of its tail, like it was waiting on me to do something.

"I ... uh ... " I tried taking a step backward, away from it. "I'm just gonna go back inside now, so you should probably go back home."

The dragon scooted closer and lay flat again, making a chirping sound.

"I'm not sure what you want."

It snorted. Its hind haunches wiggled, like a puppy trying to get someone to play.

Crap.

It scooted again, this time intentionally bumping its big nose against my knees. I tripped and fell forward, landing square on the dragon's head. The monster yipped in delight and immediately stood up, tossing me backward so I landed right on its neck. Thankfully, I didn't get impaled on any of those spines. I landed right between two of them, and barely had time to hang on for dear life as the dragon rose, spread its wings, and took off.

The last thing I saw were the four watchmen at the top of the tower rushing in to try to help me. They yelled and waved their arms, blowing their horns—but they were too late.

CHAPTER TWENTY-ONE

I screamed until I was hoarse.
Clinging to the dragon's neck, I squeezed my eyes shut and tried to pray to whichever of the gods might be listening that I wouldn't fall or be carried back to a dragon nest and devoured.

"Reigh!" someone shouted suddenly.

I cracked an eye open. At first, I thought maybe I was dead, or terror was making me hallucinate. But I recognized Jenna sitting astride her big dark purple dragon, soaring right next to us.

"Help me!" I shrieked. I wasn't sure she'd hear me over the rush of wind. I could barely hear her even when she swooped in closer.

"Calm down! She's not going to hurt you!"

She? I looked down at the dragon underneath me. It was peering back with big, curious blue eyes.

"Just get me down!" I yelled again.

"She's chosen you, Reigh! She wants you to be her rider! You have to talk to her if you want to get down." Jenna was grinning like a madwoman as she steered her own dragon away, soaring back toward the keep.

Talk to her? Great. Fantastic.

"Hey, c-can we land somewhere and talk this over? I'm not really, you know, cut out for this kind of thing. It's nothing personal, but I don't want to be a dragonrider." I felt stupid. This was ridiculous. As if the dragon was actually going to be able to understand me.

She let out a ferocious little grunt, snapped her wings in suddenly, and we went rocketing toward the ground like a lime green comet.

I screamed again, and it was even less dignified than before. Wrapping my arms and legs around her scaly neck as far as they would go, I hunkered down and tried not to sob. "Stop! Please!"

She did the opposite of stopping. The green dragon started spinning like a top, swirling through the air, and slinging me around like a ragdoll. I could barely keep my grip. My legs started to slide off.

"O-okay! You win! You hear me? You win! I'll be a dragonrider! Whatever it takes! Just put me down!"

Suddenly, she slowed down. The ride became smoother. When I finally dared to open my eyes again, we were soaring in a slow circle around the keep. Jenna and her dragon had landed on the roof to watch us. She was waving at me and still smiling from ear to ear.

"Easy, girl." My voice shook and my teeth chattered. "Be gentle with me."

The dragon finally spread her wings and cupped them, making a few graceful flaps as she stretched out her hind legs and landed on the roof.

As I scrambled down from her back, one of my boots snagged on her spines. I fell the last few feet and landed in a heap.

As I lay there, on my back again, staring up at the sky and trying to figure out why I wasn't dead, I felt something warm and slimy swipe the side of my face. Dragon spit. She'd *licked* me.

"Yuck!" I bolted to my feet and started wiping the thick, sticky goo off the side of my head.

Jenna was gripping her sides, howling with laughter. "Aw! You've got a girlfriend."

I glared up at the green dragon, who was making content purring sounds. "You have got to be kidding me."

"You should see your face!" Jenna was still cackling.

"How do you even know it's a girl anyway?"

"Look at the dewclaws on the hind legs," she explained through giggling breaths. "Smaller ones mean it's a female."

I tried wiping the dragon spit onto my shirt, but it only made my hand stick to my tunic like wet paste so I had to peel it off. "Ugh. Gross. Out of all the soldiers here, why did she pick me?"

"You'll spend the rest of your life asking yourself that question." Jenna's expression had gone misty and distant as she beamed at us. "Welcome to the ranks, Master Reigh. What'll you name her?"

"Nothing. I'm not naming her and I'm definitely not riding her again," I growled. My face was burning with embarrassment and I couldn't wait to get out of there—just as soon as I got the rest of the dragon spit out of my ear.

I turned around to leave, looking for the exit doors, when the floor in front of me erupted into flames. I stumbled to a halt and glared back over my shoulder.

The dragoness was glaring back at me, her nostrils flared and her ears slicked back.

"I don't think she's going to let you just walk away, Reigh," Jenna warned.

"She held me hostage!"

"She chose you. It's an honor, one of the highest to be had in Maldobar," Jenna said firmly. "By right of our laws, it means you are a dragonrider."

I crossed my arms and faced the green dragon again. "Fine. You want me to be your rider? Then you better promise not to do that to me again. I don't negotiate with kidnappers."

She gave another snort, licking her toothy chops. I took that as an agreement.

"So, what does this mean? I have to go to the academy or something?" I glanced at Jenna, who was giving me another one of those appraising stares. It was different than before, though. I wondered how much about me she knew now.

"Maybe, in time." She sighed and came over, grabbing one of my arms to drag me closer to the dragon. "Normally, Blybrig Academy, where all dragonriders are trained, would welcome you and train you. But this war is far worse than our kingdom has ever seen before. The academy has been closed for a state of emergency. So, for now, ride her … forge a bond with her. The closer your bond, the better you will fight together."

Jenna forced my hand against the dragon's nose. She held it there and gave me a hard look. "You are *very* lucky, Reigh. Most riders don't even sit in a dragon saddle until their first day of training. Anything you can learn now will be of great use to you. Being chosen by a dragon is a high honor. She will be loyal to you until the day she dies. It's a bond stronger than love. I can only compare it to the connection between a mother and child. It's soul-deep. Do you understand?"

I didn't, but I nodded anyway. When I looked at the dragon again, meeting her sky-blue eyes, I got a strange tingly feeling in my stomach.

"Being a dragonrider does not mean you simply have the option of zipping around on a dragon, doing as you please. It's much more than that. To be one of us means you stand with us. We are a brotherhood—a family bound by honor. We defend our own and we hold tightly our oaths to do whatever it takes to protect Maldobar. That is our legacy."

I could feel the gravity of her words settling over me like a heavy weight—the weight of hundreds of years of tradition. I couldn't comprehend being a part of that. Who was I? Why would I be chosen? How could I possibly live up to that kind of standard?

"What will you call her?" Jenna asked softly.

I thought for a moment and then decided out loud, "Vexi."

"Is that a Gray elf word?"

"Yeah." I smirked. "It means 'troublemaker.'"

BARROWTON'S KEEP HOUSED THE DRAGONS IN A STABLE THAT HAD BEEN BUILT into a highly secure vault hidden underground. As we walked across the open courtyard that was secluded behind the keep and blocked off by tall iron bars, Jenna explained to me that while it would have been better to have the dragons up high, inside the keep, where they could take off more easily, it also made them an easier and obvious target. According to her, the Tibrans had war machines unlike anything else they had seen before. Their range was extensive. And they knew the strength of the dragonriders was the greatest threat to them.

"As soon as we appear in battle, all focus of the enemy's assault is on us. They know that if we can be disabled, the rest of the army will quickly fall into chaos," she said as she guided us to a place in the rear of the keep where a wide, open tunnel seemed to slope gradually downward. It looked almost like the mouth of a cave, only there were steel tracks laid into the floor. They reminded me somewhat of the mining carts the Gray elves used to haul gems out of the ground; only these were much larger.

"The launching system here in Barrowton is unique and untested, for the most part. It works out well enough on paper, and in the few trial runs that were done when it was constructed. But we've yet to use it in battle. This whole place was designed to be an impenetrable and highly defensible fortress, you see."

Yeah, I was beginning to grasp that now. It was obvious from the outside that it was meant to be defensible. It had two outer walls, an inner set of walls, with turrets and ramparts teeming with soldiers and a whole network of underground tunnels.

Jenna led us down into the dark through the wide opening. Vexi didn't seem to like it, even if there was plenty of room for a dragon twice her size to get through. She stuck right on my heels like a stray puppy, lumbering along with her head so close that I could feel her damp breath rustling the back of my hair. Occasionally she made uncomfortable chittering noises and nudged me roughly with her snout.

Jenna's dragon, Phevos, didn't seem to care. He followed us from a distance at an indifferent pace, and his presence only seemed to make Vexi more nervous. She kept herself between me and the other dragon.

At the end of the sloping passage was a big, cavernous room. Soldiers were bustling back and forth, rolling carts and driving wagons full of supplies. The distant bellow of another dragon echoed from somewhere in the distance.

"This is the launch dome. Here the riders are prepared to go into battle," Jenna explained. She pointed out two huge cranks on either side of the passage. They reminded me of the ones pulled by horses to open the gates of the city. "The launcher is spring-loaded with tension. It can deploy only one dragon at a time, but the speed should be more than enough to get them airborne. Then the launcher is quickly reloaded. We estimate it can launch one dragon every two minutes."

"Whoa." I turned in a slow circle, taking it all in.

"This way." She waved me on. "I'll show you where you can keep Vexi."

I had a lot of questions. I just didn't know where to start with any of them. How was I even going to be a dragonrider? I didn't have a saddle or any money to buy one. According to Kiran, dragonrider gear didn't come cheap. I didn't have any armor—I didn't even have my own weapons anymore.

Jenna brought us to the dragon stables. The stalls were spacious and the air was warm. It smelled like new hay and animal musk. Vexi crouched down low behind me, curling her tail around her legs and slicking her ears back. Her big eyes peered around at all the other dragons, some of whom had poked their head out of their stalls to get a look at her.

I patted her head. "Guess you're the new kid, huh?"

She made an uneasy grumbling sound.

"It'll be okay. I'll stay down here with you, if you want."

Her gaze met mine and she pressed her head harder into my palm. It made me smile. Okay, she was still a troublemaker, and I didn't quite trust her not to take me hostage again, but it was hard not to like her.

Jenna showed me how to guide Vexi into an empty stall and get her settled. Vexi chirped at the nest of hay and immediately began nosing around in it. She turned around four times and curled up, lying her head down and letting out a big dragon-sigh.

"Good, eh?" I chuckled.

She chirped.

"Workers come by to feed them fresh meat daily. Dragons are quite efficient eaters. They prefer their food whole, and are partial to fish, but they are scavengers and in desperate times will eat just about anything to stay alive. They can go months without eating, if necessary. But of course, we'd never make them wait more than a day. They get pretty cranky when they're hungry."

"I don't know much about them," I admitted as I sat down next to Vexi's head. "I grew up in Luntharda. We don't have any dragons there."

Jenna was leaning in the doorway with her arms folded over her chest. She was watching us, a distant, thoughtful expression on her face. "Aubren told me. He told me quite a lot about you."

I looked down.

"He said you've saved his life more times than he could count. He also insists that you're quite brave for so young a person and perhaps a better sword fighter than he is. He seems to have a great deal of faith in you."

"I wish he didn't," I mumbled. I started tracing my fingers over Vexi's bright green scales, outlining the stripes on her head. She purred with delight.

The hay crunched and when I looked up again, Jenna was sitting across from me. "It's okay to be scared, you know."

I met her gaze.

"I'm scared," she said. "Right now, right this second. When I left Westwatch, the rest of the dragonriders there were deploying to try to stop the Tibrans from burning the port cities along the western coast. Many of them are my friends. I've known them for years. I think of them as brothers. And I don't know how many of them will survive. I'm scared for them. I wanted to go with them, to fight alongside them, but I have a duty to the kingdom. I had to come here to warn Aubren, Phillip and the others."

"You could go back. Maybe it's not too late," I suggested.

Her delicate brow furrowed, her jaw stiffed, and her lips puckered slightly. "I want that more than anything. But Aubren tells me that the Tibrans are practically on Barrowton's doorstep. I must stay here in case the city is attacked. With the dragonriders at Westwatch already engaged, we can't expect any reinforcements from them if things should go badly. There are a lot of people living here depending on us to protect them."

"The same people who hurled rotten food at you and cursed you?"

The corner of her mouth turned in a half-smile. "Yes. I fight for them, too, even if they are too foolish to see it. It's true; there are lots of people in Maldobar who still don't think women should be allowed to be soldiers or dragonriders. But I was chosen, just as you were. Phevos chose me, and not even my father could refute that. I was meant to be a dragonrider—so I will be the very best one I possibly can, even if no one ever blesses me for it."

"Aubren doesn't seem to mind it," I said. "In fact, he seems really proud of you."

She laughed quietly and looked away. "Yes, well, over the years we've learned to encourage, support, and protect one another through anything—whether we agree with it or not. Our parents either can't or won't, so it's what we have to do." She fidgeted with a lock of her hair, winding it around her thumb. "Since they came here, the Tibrans have been hell-bent on kidnapping someone from the royal family to hold as hostage. I can only assume that's so my father will be forced to negotiate the surrender of the royal city and, in essence, the whole kingdom."

I rubbed the prickly stubble on my chin. That must have been why Hilleddi was so determined to figure out which one of us was the prince. She wanted a hostage to deliver back to Argonox.

"My father wanted Aubren and I to stay with him in Halfax, to hunker down and hide like rabbits in a hole." Jenna's jaw tensed as she bit down hard on every word. "But I refuse to hide. I won't abandon my people to suffer and perish. I will fight for them until my very last breath."

We sat quietly for a few minutes, watching Vexi drift off into dragon dreamland. I was thinking about what an epically huge mistake that poor dragon had made by choosing me. Couldn't she sense that there was something wrong with me? What would she do the first time she saw Noh?

Jenna must have been thinking about her comrades in battle. There was a grim heaviness in her demeanor and a dark sense of worry in her eyes. It put a crease right between her eyebrows.

She looked a lot like Aubren. They had the same eyes, similar color hair. But where Aubren's features were more squared and broad, Jenna's was distinctly feminine and almost angelic. Her face was deceptively gentle looking for someone who could have crushed my fingers to dust with one handshake.

"My brother tells me you have a touch of destiny in you." Her voice was barely a whisper. "I wasn't sure what he meant until I saw her choose you."

"Destiny," I replied. "Or darkness."

"Maybe in your case, the two go hand in hand." Jenna was staring me down once more, determination like dragon fire flickering in her eyes. "But that doesn't mean you don't have a choice about the path you take—as long as you're prepared to live with the consequences."

"I guess." I sighed and looked back down at Vexi. "She is pretty awesome. Too bad I can't ride her. I don't have a saddle."

Jenna grabbed one of my cheeks, stretching and pinching it. She had another one of those wry, teasing grins on her face. "We'll just see about that."

CHAPTER TWENTY-TWO

"Jenna, wait! You can't do this!" a familiar voice shouted in the hall.

Groggily, I raised my head off my pillow and squinted into the dark. Two seconds later, someone kicked down my bedroom door.

One of my feet snagged in my sheets as I scrambled out of bed. I fell flat on my face just as Jenna appeared in front of me. Smooth, real smooth.

"Get up, Reigh. Get dressed. We're leaving." She started barking orders, still wearing her nightgown.

"Jenna, please! Stop and think for a moment. We have to talk about this." Aubren pleaded with her as he followed her into the room—also wearing his pajamas. Geez, why was everyone having a pajama party in my room?

"They are my brothers! More so than you ever were!" She spun on him, her eyes blazing with rage. "I will not abandon them!"

She turned on me next, picking my boots up off the floor and flinging them at me one by one. "I said get dressed, idiot!"

"Uh, what's going on?" I ducked for cover as a boot whizzed past my head, missing me by mere inches. Something told me she'd missed on purpose.

Aubren's expression had gone cold, as though Jenna's words had struck a kink in his armor. "Westwatch is burning. We just received word," he replied quietly.

Jenna was picking up my clothes and throwing them at me. "If we hurry—"

"*It won't matter!*" Aubren roared with a fury I'd never heard before. "You heard the report. The tower has fallen."

Jenna stopped dead in her tracks.

He clenched his fists, his thick shoulders bowing up as he faced her. "It took at least a day for that messenger to make it here. You know that as well as I do.

He said the tower was already under siege. It wouldn't matter if we left right now. They are already gone!"

"My men can hold longer than a day," she fired back.

"They didn't at Eastwatch." He took an aggressive step toward her. "And not at Northwatch, either! Leaving this fortress would be idiotic and you know it. Here, we have a chance. And any one of your men who survived at Westwatch will know it, they'll come, and we need to be here to receive them."

The two were practically nose-to-nose, although Jenna was about half a foot shorter than her older brother. I cringed and waited for the fists to start flying as they snarled at one another.

"*He* could have done something." Jenna threw her arm out to point at me. "You know it. He could have stopped them, or at least given them a fighting chance. You should have taken him—"

"How was I supposed to know they would attack us from the western coast? They've only come from the east until now! I'm not a fortune teller, Jenna!"

"G-guys?" I tried to break things up.

It didn't work. Or maybe they just didn't hear me.

"He came here to help. So, let him help! Let's take him out there right now and let him slaughter them like the barbarian cattle they are!" She lunged at me faster than I could evade and seized my arm. "You've got that demon magic inside you, right? Can you do it? Can you kill them all?"

"I-I-I—"

I squirmed and tried to get away, but she just squeezed my arm harder. She was much stronger than I was, and it scared me. Her eyes flickered with wild emotion as she stared me down, waiting for me to do something.

"Let him go," Aubren warned.

She ignored him and twisted my arm harder. "Show me. Prove that you can do it."

A cold chill tingled up my spine. I bit back a curse and tried to will Noh away. It shouldn't have surprised me—with so much anger and negative emotion swirling around. He always did like a good fight.

"No," I growled, both to her and Noh. "I'm not some mutt you can order around. You have no idea what you're messing with, or what you're asking me to do. I can barely control this thing inside me as it is. If I go out there and try something like that, there's a good chance it won't stop with Tibrans. I'd probably end up killing more civilians than enemy solider before it was over."

Jenna let go of my arm, her eyes wide. I couldn't tell if she was surprised or on the verge of a nervous breakdown.

"Aubren's right, we need to stay here and prepare. It sucks. I know you feel like you're turning your back on them. But now we have Tibrans coming at us from two sides. Did you ever stop to think that maybe this was their plan? They're probably hoping to draw you away from here, and me too. It would make this place even easier to conquer, and you'd be running out of places to hide. Think about it—you're the one who said what Hilleddi and Argonox really want is to take one or both of you hostage."

Across the room, I saw Aubren's demeanor soften. His shoulders relaxed and he bowed his head slightly. "If you're right, we should anticipate an attack very soon."

I sincerely hoped I wasn't. It wasn't like I was some great war-planning mastermind. It just made the most sense to me, one monster to another, to try to lure all the best fighters away from the one place where they stood a chance to make a meaningful stand.

Fresh tears rolled down Jenna's face. Her jaw trembled, and she hid her face in her hands.

Aubren put his arms around her and hugged her tight. She curled against him and started to sob. He patted the back of her head, comforting her like he would a small child.

I let out a breath of relief.

Aubren narrowed his gaze on me. He didn't say anything—but he didn't have to. I got the message. Time was running out. I needed to get it together and figure out how to use my power without losing control.

I might be the only chance they had of surviving this.

I COULDN'T SLEEP.

Aubren managed to convince Jenna to go back to her room and try to rest. He was going to talk to Phillip and make sure that first thing in the morning the city began lockdown procedures. The gates of Barrowton would be shut permanently. The civilians would be advised to stay inside and take cover until further notice.

I was supposed to be resting, too. But after a few hours of tossing and turning, watching the moon silently sail past my bedroom window, and asking myself if I could do this or not—I finally gave up. I got dressed in a basic dark blue tunic, black pants, and my boots. I didn't even bother putting on my belt. After all, it's not like I was going outside. Not technically, anyway.

I crept out into the hall and snuck from shadow to shadow, dodging guards, soldiers, and servants until I got down to the sublevels of the keep. Things were quiet upstairs. Down here, however, the Maldobarian soldiers were on high alert. It wasn't easy sneaking my way past them all—lucky for me, being sneaky was a vital part of being a Gray elf scout.

Vexi lifted her head drowsily when I cracked open the door of her stall and slipped inside. She chirped happily and flicked the end of her tail.

"Shh!" I pressed a finger to my lips. "Don't let them know I'm here."

She tilted her head to the side, cocking her ears like she didn't understand why I had to worry.

I trudged across her nest of hay and flopped down beside her, propping myself up against her neck. "It's a long story. Basically, I just don't want anyone to come down here and preach to me about what I have to do anymore."

I felt the heavy puffs of her breath in my hair as she sniffed me.

"You know, I seriously don't get why you picked me," I said as I scratched her under the chin. "But it's kinda nice to have a friend. You know, one that doesn't want me to kill people for them, anyway."

She purred happily and wrapped her tail around me as she plopped her big head back down into the hay.

I tried not to think about it. There was so much going on. I was far away from the only home I'd ever known and all the people who'd cared about me there. It was moments like this, when I was feeling especially crummy, that Enyo always seemed to pop by to cheer me up. I missed her a lot. It made the center of my chest ache like there was a big hole in it.

And Kiran ... Where did I even start when it came to him? I missed him, yeah. He was the closest thing to a father I'd ever known. At least, that's what I'd always thought. Now I was forced to question why he wanted me in the first place. Had he stolen me from the castle? From my real parents? Why would he do something like that? It obviously wasn't because he was dying to be a parent because he refused to let me call him my father. So why?

And now I had Aubren trying to treat me like a kid brother, or just a kid—honestly, I couldn't tell which. I had no idea how much he'd told Jenna about me, and I was too afraid to ask. She apparently knew about my power, so he'd told her that much. She wanted me to use it to avenge the dragonriders and kill the Tibrans, which wasn't all that different from what Aubren wanted, as well.

I growled angry Gray elf curses under my breath and scratched the back of my head. The hay was itchy. I was anxious. I couldn't get comfortable here, either.

So, I did something stupid.

"Noh," I muttered. "Are you there?"

At first, there was no answer. Then I felt that shiver of cold. I could see my breath in the air. Around me, Vexi stirred. Her nose twitched and her ears perked. Suddenly, her head shot up and her eyes focused on a corner of the room where the shadows were especially thick.

"*Yes, master?*" Noh's voice echoed like a whisper in the air.

Vexi started to growl softly.

"When we were captured by the Tibrans, you know, and I was bound to the Mirror of Truth ... " I hesitated and scratched the back of my head again. "Did you do something to make the mirror go screwy? What I mean is, did you save me then?"

Noh stepped from the darkness like he was just passing through a doorway. This time, he didn't look like a wolf. He looked like a darkened reflection of me. It caught me off guard. He was even wearing the same clothes as I was, although they were all black. His skin was a dark gray and his hair, while it was still a long, braided mess like mine, was as black as a moonless night. His bottomless red eyes flickered as they stared me down from across Vexi's stall.

"No."

I pushed Vexi's tail out of the way and stood up. Gathering my courage, I walked toward him. "So, the mirror didn't kill me because I was telling the truth?"

Standing eye-to-eye with him was beyond creepy. He even had the same scar across the bridge of his nose. Geez, no wonder everyone treated me like a kid, I really did look like one.

"*So it would seem,*" was his reply.

"We have to come to an agreement here, okay? I need to be able to use this power without it getting out of hand."

He smirked, showing off his pointed canine teeth. "*You still don't understand, do you? Silly master.*"

"Understand what?"

"*It is not me you cannot control, it is yourself.*"

I frowned. "What is that supposed to mean?"

"*You think you desire control, but what you need is understanding. You cannot have one without the other. I am you, what hides within you, what you hope no one else sees. The darkness of your heart. The thing all men fear.*" He stretched out a hand and touched a finger to the center of my chest. A pang of violent cold ripped through my body, leaving me breathless. "*We are one, you and I. Two souls, one body. That is our inheritance.*"

I tried to push his hand away from me, but every time I touched him, my hands passed right through him like mist.

"*Don't fret. Soon, she will claim you—and hers is the only family that will matter. The ritual must be done, you see. Without it, our power will never be complete and you will never have the control you seem to crave.*" He laughed and tapped a finger against his temple. "*We cannot sync until it is done.*"

The memory of that woman's voice that had whispered to me in the dark—right after saving Aubren and his men from the snagwolves—resurfaced. I hadn't heard her again since then. Was that it? Was that the key?

She'd said something about a ritual, too. And blood ... pure blood.

"Until what is done? What is the ritual? Who is she?" I started to yell. "What the heck are you talking about!"

It was no good. I dove at him, but Noh had vanished and I wound up tackling nothing but empty air. I stood in the stall, breathing hard and looking around in case he reappeared somewhere else.

At last, I met Vexi's worried gaze. Her blue eyes blinked, regarding me cautiously.

"Sorry, girl." I sighed as I sank down to sit in the hay far away from her. "I should've warned you there was something seriously wrong with me. It's not too late, right? You could leave and find someone better."

A heavy, scaly, green dragon snout landed in my lap. Vexi stared at me with eyes the size of dinner plates, making worried chittering sound as she pushed her snout against my chest.

My eyes got misty. I ran a hand across her head and gave her a scratch behind the ears. "Guess you're pretty stubborn, huh?"

She closed her eyes again and scooted the rest of her big dragon body close to wrap around me again. I leaned back against her side and listened to the deep, muffled *thump, thump, thump* of her heartbeat right in my ear. It was soothing, like a soft dragon lullaby, and eventually it lulled me into a deep sleep.

CHAPTER TWENTY-THREE

I awoke to the sensation of the whole world shuddering around me like an earthquake. The stacked stones of the walls and floors groaned. Little bits of debris and rubble showered down upon my face and dust swirled in my eyes. Geez, how long had I been asleep?

Behind me, Vexi unfurled from her nest and let out an uneasy growl.

People were shouting outside her stall. Commotion and the faint tolling of bells accompanied the low blast of warning horns.

Oh no. That could only mean one thing.

I ran to the door of Vexi's stall and rolled it open, sticking my head out into the corridor just in time to see Jenna and her company of dragonriders rounding the corner. They were fully outfitted from boot to helmet in their battle armor, long blue cloaks fluttering behind them. They each carried their helmet under their arm and walked single file, parting the flurry of panicked soldiers who were running up and down the corridor.

Jenna and I locked eyes as she strode past, but she didn't stop.

"H-hey! What's going on?" I called after her as I jogged to catch up.

"Isn't it obvious?" she snapped back. "The Tibrans have finally come to lay siege to the city. They're attacking from both sides and they've brought more war machines than ever before."

"You can't go out there! There's only five of you." I grabbed her arm and dragged her to a stop. "You'll be killed!"

Her steely gaze met mine and for a second, I thought she might backhand me across the face. Since she was wearing her riding gauntlets, it would have left a mark and maybe even knocked a few teeth loose.

She put a heavy hand on my shoulder instead. Her gaze softened and her mouth curved into a faint, bittersweet smile. "This is what we do, Reigh. This is what it means to be a dragonrider. Every person in Barrowton is counting on us. Live or die, we have to fight for those who can't."

Jenna pulled away, leaving me standing in the corridor while she and the rest of her men went to mount up. I was numb. All around me, the keep shuddered again, as though being hit by something enormous. Men shouted. Rubble sprinkled over my head.

I looked back to the stall were Vexi was peeking at me, leaning her big head out so she could watch me with one big eye.

For a moment, everything seemed to stand still. Something clicked in my brain—like a switch had been flipped. Now was the time. I didn't have any weapons. I didn't have any fancy armor. Heck, I didn't even have a saddle. But I did have a dragon and a few wicked tricks up my sleeve.

I made my choice.

I hid in Vexi's stall, peering through a crack in the door while the other dragonriders rode past on their way to the launch dome. I waited until they had all gone around the corner and out of sight before I rolled Vexi's stall door all the way open. Racing down the hall again, I grabbed the first piece of rope I came across and darted back to begin tying it around Vexi's neck.

"This is nuts. Yep. This is crazy. I am insane," I muttered as I crawled onto her back, trying to find a good place between her spines to sit. My hands were sweating and shaking as I tied the other end of the rope around my waist. It wasn't a saddle. Not even close. But maybe it would keep me from dying if I fell off? Here's hoping, anyway.

"Okay, girl. Are you ready to do something stupid?" I leaned down to pat her neck.

Vexi gave an answering snarl. I felt her strong body flex under me as she stood and immediately bounded out of her stall.

The last dragonrider was being deployed from the launching system when we arrived on the scene. They had him standing on a big wooden sled while the cranks held tight, pulled by draft horses. The dragon hunkered down, wings folded in tight, and the rider was sitting low in his saddle with his body flush against his mount.

Then, together, the soldiers released the ropes binding the horses to the crank wheels. The huge wheels spun and the wooden sled went rocketing up the passage toward the blaze of daylight. It fired the dragonrider and his beast out of the tunnel like an arrow. The dragon spread its wings, catching the wind, and soared out of sight.

"Okay, that's terrifying." My teeth were chattering.

Vexi crawled forward while the cranks were hooked back to the horses and pulled tight again. The soldiers quickly began winding the wooden sled back down the ramp and into place.

I got a few hesitant looks from the soldiers manning the launcher as I went past. Probably because I wasn't dressed for battle. I didn't even have a jerkin on, for crying out loud. But I did have a dragon, so for them I guess that was good enough.

My hands were slippery from sweating; I couldn't get a good grip on Vexi's already slick scales. My heart was pounding so fast I could barely breathe. I tried to get as flat against my dragon's neck as possible, wrapping my arms around her in a bear hug.

Vexi flattened herself down on the wooden sled just like the dragon before her had. She folded her wings in close to her body and lowered her head, her ears slicked back and her eyes narrowed.

Somewhere in the back of my mind, my common sense reminded me that this was an *extremely* stupid thing to do and I was probably going to die in the next two minutes.

Good thing I've never been all that smart.

"Okay, we can do this," I whispered. "We can totally do this. No big deal."

It was a *very* big deal.

The cranks released and suddenly we were being hurled out of the end of that tunnel like a projectile into the midday sky. Vexi twisted her body into a spiral and then spread her wings wide, catching the wind and soaring upward.

Below me, the scene of battle was nothing short of horrific. Under a gloomy sky, the Tibran army had surrounded the outer wall of Barrowton. There were so many soldiers it was like looking at an angry ant colony. They were using massive catapults to throw black orbs over the walls, which exploded into a spray of liquid inferno.

"Dragon venom." I guessed. Kiran had told me all about dragon fire. It wasn't really fire—it was a sticky, highly acidic venom that combusted explosively whenever air got to it, making it almost impossible to put out. You had to wait for it to burn itself out once all the fuel was used up.

The soldiers inside Barrowton were firing volleys of arrows, but the effort seemed futile. The Tibran soldiers had come in overwhelming numbers. Another explosion of fire and burning venom rocked against the keep. In the distance, I saw Jenna and her dragonriders making calculated passes. They were trying to take out the catapults.

I leaned down to call up to Vexi. "I've got a plan. Ready for this?"

It was hard to tell how much she really understood. I didn't know how dragonriders usually communicated with their mounts. Kiran had never explained that to me—although he'd told me that Jaevid could speak telepathically with his. Part of being the lapiloque, I guessed.

I wasn't that lucky. So, I had to improvise.

I smirked and set my eyes on the closest of the catapults, squeezing the rope tighter. "Time to fight fire with fire."

I GUESS JENNA WAS SURPRISED WHEN VEXI AND I WENT ZIPPING PAST HER into battle. I couldn't see her face because of her helmet, but I got the impression from the way she started frantically waving her arms that she wasn't exactly thrilled about me being here.

We didn't pull over to debate it, though. Vexi darted through the sky, spinning and rolling, dodging arrows and nets that were being fired from below. We did a wide pass, circling one of the catapults closest to the city wall. It was firing shot after shot at the keep, trying to break it down.

I squeezed my legs around Vexi's body to get her attention and pointed at the black orbs being hurled through the air. "Let's go for it!"

She snorted in agreement, pumped her mighty wings, and went in for the strike.

The timing had to be perfect. As the catapult's long arm was cocked back, I watched the Tibran soldiers roll another huge black orb onto the spoon-shaped bucket at the end of the arm. I clenched my teeth. We just had to wait for the right moment.

"Now!" I yelled at the top of my lungs.

Vexi whirled through the air, picking up speed and falling into a steep dive. I felt her sides swell as she took a breath. The catapult's arm released, beginning to fling the black venom-filled orb into the air.

The air around me exploded. There was an acrid smell and a flash of heat as Vexi detonated the orb like a bomb with her breath before it could even leave the bucket, sending burning dragon fire spraying through the air and all over the Tibran soldiers.

And all over my back.

I cried out in pain as Vexi wheeled upward again, a hailstorm of arrows zipping past us and glancing off her scaly hide.

I couldn't see how bad the damage was, but it felt like my whole back was ablaze. I tried to twist to see, but the movement was almost more than I could stand. That's the problem when you decide to play with dragon fire—you gotta be ready to get burned.

Below us, the catapult was in cinders. Unfortunately, there were dozens more being slowly positioned all around Barrowton. Sure, my plan had worked, but we'd only taken out one. Trying it again might actually kill me.

In the distance, I heard another huge explosion. Fire belched into the air and I saw Jenna and her dragon soaring upward as another catapult was destroyed.

She had seen what we did—and now she and the rest of her riders were copying us!

Catapults started going up like torches one after another. The Tibrans scrambled to regroup and tried desperately to shoot down the dragonriders.

"Let's go again," I called down to Vexi.

She turned her head to look back at me disapprovingly.

I didn't have to be the lapiloque to figure out what she was thinking. I was already hurt. It was beyond dumb to take that chance again, right?

Why does everyone keep expecting me to do the smart thing?

"Not with fire this time," I bargained. "I wanna try something new. Just trust me!"

She did. Or at least, enough to give it another try. She began beating her wings faster, picking up speed as we set our sights on the next catapult.

As we got close, I let go of the ropes and let my weight fall back against the tension of the knot tied around my waist. I spread my arms wide, closing my eyes and drawing my focus inward. Just moving my arms made my back feel like it was being scalded.

I bit down hard and forced myself to concentrate through the pain as I called upon the darkness within me, drawing out my power like I had in my fight with Aubren. It was hard with so much chaos and the rocking motion of Vexi's wing beats bouncing me all over the place. Yet I could feel it, like a spot of cold pressure between my open hands.

I reared back, visualizing the swirling mass of darkness taking the shape of a spear. As soon as I felt it go solid in my hand, I opened my eyes and hurled it straight at the black orb about to be launched from the catapult bucket.

The shadow spear hissed through the air, leaving a trail of black mist behind it. Vexi immediately did a mid-air about face and started to retreat, but I wasn't about to miss it. I turned back just as my shadow spear struck the orb.

The explosion sent out a blast wave of darkness that spread through the air like ripples on a pond. It blew the catapult apart in a shower of burning venom. Then it tore through the surrounding Tibran ranks, reducing the soldiers closest to it to nothing but heaps of black ash.

Vexi was fast—but she wasn't *that* fast. She couldn't outrun the blast wave. When it struck us, it sent her flipping end-over-end through the air. I felt the rope tethering us together snap.

I tried to grab onto her, reaching for any part of her I could, but my sweaty hands slipped right off her neck. I caught a glimpse of her green scales hurtling away from me as I twisted in the air, plummeting straight toward the ground.

CHAPTER TWENTY-FOUR

I shut my eyes tightly and told myself it was okay to die. It wouldn't be so bad. Sure, I was young. There was a lot of stuff I hadn't done yet—including kissing a girl. But hey, at least I'd have a few good stories to tell when I got to the other side, right?

Then a strong arm snagged me around the waist and snatched me out of midair. I wheezed as the sudden impact knocked the breath out of me, looking up into the frenzied glare of the last person in the world I expected to see.

"Hang on," Kiran shouted as he hauled me over onto the back of his shrike with him. He pulled my arms around his waist tightly.

All around us, other Gray elf warriors riding shrikes were streaking through the air like tongues of lightning. I couldn't believe it. They were joining in the fight!

"You came?" I called up to him in disbelief.

He didn't answer. Now wasn't really the time to chat, though, so I tried not to take it personally.

"Watch out for the machines throwing nets!" I warned, pointing below. "We have to stop them from tearing down the wall!"

Kiran nodded and heeled his shrike into more speed. He drew back his bow and started firing arrows in rapid succession, taking out the Tibran soldiers who were trying to reload one of the net-throwers.

Right on cue, Vexi dove in for a strike. One burst of her burning breath demolished the machine. She flashed me a toothy dragon smile as she soared away, following us from a distance as we began making more passes.

We made quick work of six more net throwers, although in the sea of

Tibran forces that were crashing against Barrowton's outer walls like the sea against the shore, it didn't seem to make much difference. We couldn't keep this up forever.

We didn't even get the chance to try.

The sudden, panicked screech of a dragon made my insides go sour.

I whirled around just in time to see a net snag around Vexi's head. She clawed and tried to hover, but another net wrapped around one of her wings. She started to go down, kicking and clawing to get free until she landed with a thunderous boom in the middle of that boiling sea of Tibran soldiers.

"No!" My whole body pitched violently and I kicked away from Kiran, leaping out into the open air before I could even think about it.

"Reigh!" Kiran shouted and reached for me, missing by inches.

I was falling again—but I wasn't scared this time. I wasn't going to die.

I didn't have to concentrate. My power came to me instantly, snapping in the air around me and taking the shape of two huge black bird wings. I could move them, like extensions of myself, and I used them to fly straight for her.

The Tibrans were prodding at her with spears, trying to find the right place to stab to kill her quickly, before she could shower them with flame.

Right as one of them went in for the killing blow, I kicked down and snapped the staff of his spear in half. With one punch from my shadow-coated fist, the soldier went flying backwards and crashed through a stunned line of his comrades.

I landed next to Vexi, spreading my black-feathered wings and snarling at them. Raw dark power sizzled off my body. I wasn't myself. I could see and hear, but my body was out of control.

I flexed, spreading my arms outward and sending out a pulse of darkness much like when my shadow spear had detonated the black orb of venom. More Tibrans went flying, and the ones closest to me were reduced to heaps of ash.

That got their attention. Some of them immediately dropped their weapons and ran. Others tried to form ranks, linking their bronze shields together and pressing in.

"Go ahead," I growled. "Just try to touch her."

They fired bows. One flex of my hand sent a focused blast that made all the arrows disintegrate in the air long before they could ever touch Vexi or me.

"Care to try again?"

They threw spears—and I did the same thing.

"I don't have time for this."

I couldn't stop. It was like Noh had taken over my body completely. He was the one talking, the one suddenly cutting through the Tibran ranks like chaff. The sensation of so many deaths made me reel and left me totally delirious. I couldn't concentrate at all. I was out of my mind.

And I had no idea how to make it stop.

Terror gripped me like a chokehold. What if I couldn't stop? What if it stayed like this forever? What would happen to me? What if—

I felt someone grab me from behind. Powerful arms wrapped around me, pinning my arms to my sides.

"Reigh, you have to stop this now!"

I knew his voice. But I couldn't stop it. Another wave of power surged out of me, tearing past all my willpower.

His arms went slack.

I whirled around, looking straight into Kiran's eyes. He seemed surprised at first, like he wasn't sure what had happened. Then I saw realization come over his features. He gave me a warm smile as one of his hands brushed over my cheek.

"I am so sorry, my son."

His whole body faded, instantly dissolving into a fine black mist right in front of me.

Kiran was gone.

Whatever happened next, I couldn't remember. The roar of battle, the heat of flames, and the dull gray sky all turned to a muddy blur. I blacked out.

The next thing I knew, I was waking up, lying on my side in my bedroom at the keep. I bolted upright, my body pouring a cold sweat as I called out for Kiran. The fight with Jenna, the battle—maybe it had all just been a nightmare.

"Reigh, please, you have to lie down," a soft voice cooed to me. "Careful. Don't lie on your back."

I was still dazed when I looked over to find a beautiful Gray elf lady sitting on the edge of my bed. Something about her was eerily familiar. Only, I was sure I'd never seen her before. That is—until she smiled.

"Enyo?"

She nodded slightly.

"W-what happened to you?"

I looked her over slowly, carefully. She wasn't anything like the small, dark-headed little girl I'd left behind in Luntharda. She had *changed*. Her black hair was now the color of freshly fallen snow, and her once childish frame had transformed into that of a slender, elegant woman dressed in the cream-colored robes of a healer. Her smooth, oval face reminded me of the sculptures of goddesses I'd seen in the Gray elf temples. And yet, I could see ghostly traces of my childhood friend in her features as she arched one of her brows at me. It was her, the girl I...

"Don't be ridiculous, you know how Gray elves mature." She rolled her eyes. They caught the candlelight like diamonds.

"I'm sorry, I just had a terrible dream," I said as I started to lie back on the bed. Moving again sent a pang of sharp pain through my body, pain from the where the dragon venom had burned me.

I knew, even before I saw her expression fade from that exasperated smile to a look of sorrow. It wasn't a dream.

"N-no," I stammered and choked. "I-I didn't. I wouldn't."

Enyo closed her eyes and bowed her head. Resting in her lap, I saw Kiran's bow.

Suddenly, I couldn't breathe. Tears blurred my vision. I wanted to scream but nothing, not a single sound would come out.

"Your dragon is safe," Enyo said softly. "We came when we learned that Westwatch had fallen. King Jace wouldn't stand to see the dragonriders fail. He made a proclamation that he would be joining the fight and many others followed him. He is here now, speaking with the other nobles."

I still couldn't speak. Inside, it felt like I had swallowed a mouthful of dragon venom. My whole body burned. I squeezed my eyes shut as I tried to keep it in. I didn't want to lose it. Not now—not in front of her.

"The battle is over. Barrowton's walls still stand and its people are safe, for now. The Tibrans who survived fled in fear. But it is expected they will return very soon in far greater numbers. For now, you need to rest. You were badly injured."

"Get out," I rasped.

"Reigh?"

"Just go."

The bed shifted as Enyo stood up. I felt her take one of my hands and place Kiran's bow into it, gently rolling my fingers closed around it. "I'll be right outside if you need me."

Her footsteps retreated. When I dared to look again, I saw her hesitating in the doorway—like she wanted to say something else.

Whatever it was, she never said it. Her eyes fluttered closed and she turned away, closing the door behind her.

CHAPTER TWENTY-FIVE

The damage was much worse than I'd anticipated. By the time I managed to hobble across my bedroom floor to the dressing table and turn around to see my back in the mirror, I was in so much pain I nearly fainted. I peeled back the corners of the bandage to assess how bad it was.

My skin was scorched, blistered, and raw. There were a flew places where it had been melted away, revealing spots of naked flesh and muscle. So yeah, it was severe.

I couldn't do anything, couldn't go anywhere. I collapsed on my way back to the bed, crumpling to my knees, and buried my face in my hands to stifle my own screams. My body shook out of control. Every fiber of my body cried out in agony, but I bit down hard. I didn't want Enyo to hear. I didn't want her to come in here again and see me like this.

I didn't deserve anyone's comfort.

She and Aubren found me there the following morning. I was still sitting on the floor staring out my bedroom window, feeling nothing as I watched a red sun rise over the mountains. Part of me had hoped I wouldn't live to see that dawn. It only seemed fair after what I'd done.

Aubren helped me get back in bed so Enyo could change my dressings. She talked, making idle conversation that I guess was supposed to distract me from the fact that it felt like she was peeling my skin off every time she removed a bandage. Apparently, Kiran had hired her to take my place as his assistant and was beginning to teach her all his healing methods.

"The job seems to suit you," Aubren said with a friendly smile.

"I've wanted to learn to become a medic for a long time. My mother was a very talented scout, and she hoped I would follow in her footsteps. I tried to for years, but it never felt right. The moment I woke up after my change, I knew I had to be honest with her. Being a scout wasn't what I wanted. And as soon as I started to learn about the healing arts, making medicines, and caring for patients —it was like coming home. This is what I was meant to do," she replied. "Of course, my mother was a little surprised. I'm not sure she's convinced I made the right choice, yet."

I had nothing to say about it. It was taking every bit of concentration I had to keep from yelling curses as she began applying what smelled like a healing herbal salve to my back. It would speed the healing process, cutting the time in less than half. That's what I kept telling myself. And the sooner I was able to walk around, the sooner I could ...

"Kiran began learning the healing arts here, when he served in my father's court as an ambassador and advisor. There was a very talented medic in the city named Holly. She trained him for years." Aubren rubbed his chin thoughtfully.

"That explains why so many of his medical texts are in the human language. I wish I could read them. Kiran was a very good teacher, but I still have so much to learn." Enyo was applying new bandages, carefully covering each of the open places where the dragon venom had melted away my flesh.

"I'm sure you'll do fine," he reassured her. "You speak the human language very well."

"O-oh, thank you!" Enyo's voice had an excited, girlish tremor in it. I'd heard that before whenever she talked to one of the older male scouts.

"Will you both just shut up," I growled.

Aubren stared at me with his eyes wide.

Behind me, I felt Enyo pause in her work. "Reigh, I'm sorry, I didn't think ab—"

"I said *shut up!*" I snarled louder.

Aubren's expression had gone cold. His eyes narrowed at me dangerously, like he was silently daring me to make a scene. "Calm down. I know you're in pain, but don't take it out on her."

"Get out. Both of you just get out!"

They did. It took a few minutes because Enyo had to gather up her medical supplies. But eventually, she hurried out of the room with tears in her eyes and Aubren's hand on her shoulder. I couldn't decide which upset me more.

By evening, I could tell the pain was starting to subside. I could sit up without wanting to vomit, anyway. The next day, I could finally stand up and walk across the room. Enyo came back in every morning to change my dressings, just like before, but she didn't try talking to me again. She was sulking. Or she was afraid of me. Either way, it was probably for the best. I didn't have anything to say to anyone.

Kiran's bow sat on my bedside table, right next to the one the Queen had given me, until the morning of the third day when I felt well enough to get up, change my clothes, put on my boots and belt, and begin packing what few belongings I had. It wasn't much, just a few changes of clothes. I slung the bag over my shoulder and reached for the bow—*his* bow.

My hand hesitated, hovering over it. I couldn't stop my face from screwing up. Tears blurred my vision and I bit down hard on my tongue to keep from making a sound.

No. I couldn't use it. I didn't deserve to even touch it.

"What are you doing?" I heard Enyo's voice from the doorway. "You should be resting. You aren't well."

"I'm fine." Gritting my teeth, I picked up Kiran's bow and quickly disassembled it, packing it away with the rest of my gear. Then I picked up the one the Queen had given me, slung it across my shoulders, and started for the door.

"Reigh, wait." She grabbed my arm.

Enyo was standing so close that I found myself staring directly down into her eyes. Her brow was drawn up into a look of desperation, tears welling in her eyes. I tried not to notice she was gorgeous, or that the feeling of her hand on my skin made my heart race.

"Don't you trust me at all?" she pleaded. "You are my best friend. Please, just talk to me."

"It's me I don't trust," I muttered as I pulled away.

I made it all the way out of my room and into the hallway before she caught up with me and planted herself in my path. "But where are you going?"

"Home, where I should have been all along."

"You mean you're—?"

"Going back to Luntharda." I sidestepped around her and kept going down the hall.

"But what about the Tibrans? What about Aubren and the others? They still need you."

I stopped. "No. They don't."

"Reigh, that's not—"

"No!" I whirled around suddenly, fixing her with a scorching glare. "I never should have come here. It was a mistake. It's been a disaster from the very beginning. I'm done. I'm not fighting in anyone else's wars. I can't stay here any longer, not for one more minute."

Enyo's eyes narrowed and her forehead crinkled slightly as she glared back at me. "So, you'll go back and do what?"

"Run the clinic, what else? I'm the only one who's qualified."

Her lips parted and she blinked slowly in surprise.

I started walking away, but I only got a few more feet down the hall before I heard her running to catch up.

"I'm going with you, then," she declared.

"Pfft."

"I am!" She crossed her arms and pursed her lips stubbornly. "You can't do it on your own. You'll need help."

I rolled my eyes. "Fine. Just stay out of my way."

I DIDN'T TELL ANYONE ELSE I WAS LEAVING. I DIDN'T WANT TO HAVE TO explain myself and it wasn't hard to guess how Aubren and Jenna were going to feel about this. I was a convenient pet for them to have around. A useful tool of war. They'd have to find another blunt object to wail the Tibrans with.

I wanted to get out of this place without someone pinning me down to interrogate me or tell me what I *should* be doing. And as I led the way down through the keep's maze of corridors, I got the impression that Enyo was hoping I would change my mind. She followed close behind, flicking me worried glances whenever she thought I wasn't paying attention.

I pretended to ignore her.

Nothing was going to change my mind.

When we arrived at the big door of Vexi's stall, Enyo started to fidget. She stood back as I began to heave the heavy door open, groaning as the wounds on my back burned in protest. My vision spotted. I felt lightheaded. The door was halfway open when I felt my legs go numb and I started to fall.

Something warm and scaly caught me. I looked up, realizing that Vexi's big head was under me, keeping me from falling the rest of the way to the floor. She made a worried murring sound.

I let her help me back up, using her head to steady myself on my feet again. "I'm fine, really."

Vexi snorted like she didn't believe me.

"She's so beautiful." Enyo whispered, her face the picture of awe. "Can she really understand you?"

My dragon and I exchanged a glance. "I guess so."

Kiran had always told me that dragons weren't like horses or faundra. They weren't even like shrikes. They were smarter than other animals. They had thoughts, opinions, and personalities like people.

I walked around to Vexi's back and eyed that place between her spines where I knew I could sit. I hesitated again. The last thing I remembered from the battle was ... well, let's just say Vexi had still been trapped under the net and we were surrounded by Tibran soldiers.

But what about after that?

"You said the Tibrans were afraid of me," I said as I turned enough to watch Enyo's expression. "Why? They weren't running from me before everything went dark. What happened? What do I not remember?"

She swallowed hard. Her eyes flickered with fear. She was afraid of me, or at least of whatever I'd done. "Reigh, does it really matter?"

It did. However, if she didn't want to tell me, fine. So be it.

I grabbed Vexi's spines and pulled myself onto her back, then stretched out a hand to help Enyo up.

She still hadn't put a toe across the threshold of Vexi's stall. She stared at me, at my dragon, and at my outstretched hand. Her cheeks flushed and she shook her head. "I ... "

"If you want to go with me, then hurry up."

Enyo paused, thinking it over. Finally, she muttered a Gray elf curse under her breath and quickly trotted over to grab my hand and climb up behind me. Her arms snaked around my middle, clinging to me and squeezing handfuls of my shirt. Great, now I was the one blushing.

She squeaked with alarm when Vexi stood up, hugging herself against me tighter as my dragon began prowling out of the stall. I was having second thoughts the whole way to the launch dome. It was rude to bail out without even telling Aubren or Jenna where I was going. I hadn't exactly been a shining example of honor here lately, though. Cowardice and humiliation weren't so far fetched for someone who had just murdered their own father.

The soldiers working the launcher didn't ask any questions. I guess if you are riding a dragon, everyone does their jobs and doesn't bother you with questions. I could get used to that.

"Hold on tight," I told Enyo as Vexi positioned herself on the wooden sled.

She hugged me harder.

I hadn't bothered with a rope this time. After all, I didn't have any intention of doing any fancy aerobatic flying. This was strictly a transport mission. But as I heard the cranks draw tight and one of the soldiers give the order to release the launcher, my stomach churned with nerves. Crap. I should have grabbed a stupid rope.

The launcher released and hurled us through the tunnel toward the daylight. I squeezed my whole body against Vexi's neck as hard as I could, trying to lie down flat against her as the wind whipped past us. Behind me, Enyo was gripping me so hard it was killing my back.

Suddenly, we were in the open sky. Vexi spread her wings, caught the wind, and began wheeling in a gentle circle. I let my body relax.

Enyo was still clinging to me, her face pressed against the back of my neck, her frantic breaths puffing on my skin. It made my insides feel like jelly. She'd held onto me before, but things were different now. She was different.

I didn't enjoy it for long, though. The higher we climbed, the more of Barrowton I could see. The Tibrans were gone—or at least, the living ones were. What was left behind, all around the city, was a sea of black like the earth had been scorched. Even some sections of the city walls were stained black. I thought it might be left over from the catapults or the dragonriders, but as we swooped low, I saw the black dust swirl. It wasn't scorch marks. It was *ash*. Scattered throughout it were empty helmets, breastplates, shoes, and shields—and not just from Tibran soldiers.

My heart went cold.

Gods and Fates ... what had I done?

CHAPTER TWENTY-SIX

I got Vexi to land at the boundary where Maldobar and Luntharda met. We touched down gently, and I helped Enyo climb down before I swung my leg over and slid down to the ground. Traveling by dragon was a lot more convenient than a shrike. Her flight was much smoother and she could go higher —so high no Tibran net thrower could possibly catch us.

Standing before the looming tree line, I caught a waft of all the familiar smells of the jungle. The damp smells of rotting wood, rich soil, humid air, and exotic flowers. It smelled like home.

I started for the trees.

Vexi let out a shriek of unhappiness, leaping over me and landing right in my path. She stamped and puffed, growling like she didn't want me to go.

"I'm sorry, girl. I'm leaving. And I'm not coming back." I started walking around her.

She zipped back into my path again, blowing a furious dragon snort right in my face.

I glared up at her. "I said no! Look, I appreciate the gesture. But you picked the wrong guy. I'm not a dragonrider. I'm not even a good person. So, move!"

Her scaly ears slicked back and she showed me her teeth, belting out a roar of defiance.

Fine. So, we were doing this the hard way.

"I don't want you," I yelled. "Get out of my sight—*now*."

She stopped growling and blinked her owlish blue eyes at me in confusion. Her ears swiveled and her snout twitched.

I stormed around her, marching straight for the tree line. I could hear Enyo's footsteps crunching along right after me. As soon as we crossed into the jungle, I heard Vexi let out another frustrated roar.

I didn't look back.

We hadn't exactly come prepared for a journey. Fortunately, Enyo had said that King Jace was at Barrowton. That meant he had brought a company of warriors with him—and that meant there would be more of them camped out near the boundary waiting for marching orders and to relay news back to the Queen.

Finding them was easy, mostly because they found us first. Scouts running perimeter patrols escorted us to their base camp. They knew who we were, although they were surprised to see us, and granted my request to borrow a shrike and enough provisions to get us back to Mau Kakuri. I didn't mention Kiran, even when they asked me how he was. When my back was turned, I overheard Enyo delivering the news that he had fallen in battle.

She didn't tell them *I* was the reason.

We left as quickly as possible. It was a long journey back and I didn't want to waste any time. Even being back in the jungle, shielded under the canopy of trees, I didn't feel any more at ease. My soul was restless inside me. I couldn't sleep. I couldn't sit still. Every second we wasted might be one I decided to look back, reconsider, or really think about what I was doing.

We flew hard during the day, breaking only twice to eat and let the shrike rest. At night, Enyo and I slept on separate bedrolls. I faced away from her, not wanting to run the risk of idle conversation.

She changed my bandages in the morning and slathered my back down with healing salve, all without saying a word. Privately, I wondered how bad the lasting damage would be. I'd have scars, of course. I might even lose some of the sensation back there.

I kept thinking about how if that spray had killed me, Kiran would still be …

We arrived at Mau Kakuri three days later. The city was the same as I remembered—still tucked away in a tranquil part of the jungle under the misty ambience of the falls. I guided the shrike to the front of the clinic where Kiran and I had lived ever since I was a baby. It hadn't changed—not that I'd been away all that long.

So why did it feel like I'd been gone for ages?

I climbed down but stopped Enyo before she could do the same. "Just go home. I'm sure your parents will be glad to see you're back."

She frowned. "Won't you need help settling in? We have to prepare to receive patients again."

"There'll be time for that tomorrow." I swatted the shrike on the rump, sending it off in a flurry of mirrored scales and fluttering wings.

I just wanted one night alone without someone's sad, sympathetic stare pinned at my back.

I unlocked the front door of the clinic and stepped inside, quietly closing the door behind me. I locked it—just to make sure Enyo didn't try to come sneaking in when I wasn't paying attention.

The house was a tomb of memory. The air smelled strongly of herbs that were hung up to dry so they could be made into medicines. Kiran's shoes were lined up neatly in the foyer along with a few of mine, as though he'd expected I would come back someday. He'd cut lots of firewood and left it piled in its usual place on the far wall. His books and texts were stacked by the side of the fire pit where he always sat to read and smoke his favorite pipe.

Sitting on top of the stack was a crumpled piece of paper—an old drawing of two wobbly looking stick figures holding hands. The taller one had silver hair, while the shorter one had red. It was something I'd made for him when I was a child.

I choked out loud and covered my mouth to stifle the sound. Tears welled in my eyes and I turned around to slam my fist against the door. I did it over and over, until my knuckles were bashed and bleeding and there was a deep dent in the wood.

"Reigh!" Enyo's voice cried out from the other side of the door. She'd come back. "What's going on? Let me in!" She knocked furiously.

I let my head fall forward until my forehead came to rest against the door. "Go away." My voice broke.

There was a long pause and I started to suspect she'd gone.

"I know you're ashamed," she said quietly. "I know you don't want anyone to see you this way. I know you're hurting. You miss him."

I closed my eyes.

"So do I," she whispered. "I miss him, too."

My hand fumbled at the door lock. As soon as it was open, Enyo pulled the door back and pounced at me. She threw her arms around my neck and drew me in against her. I buried my face against the side of her neck.

We held each other for a long time. I wasn't sure how to let go. I was afraid if I did, she might disappear, as well.

At last, Enyo pulled back enough to brush my bangs out of my eyes and wiped the tears from my face. "Don't think for a single second that you're alone now, you hear me? You're not. I'm right here. I'm not going anywhere."

I cringed at those words.

She kissed my cheek gently. "Come on, let's get your hand cleaned up. I know you haven't been sleeping. You need to rest."

Enyo insisted on staying at the clinic with me. It looked bad, most likely, but I swear we slept in separate rooms. Or rather, she stayed up sitting by the fireplace, reading one of Kiran's medical technique journals he'd translated into the Gray elf language.

I went to my room, and stretched out on my old bed. It felt too small now. The whole room did, in fact. The window was open and outside I could hear the constant rumble of the falls. Usually, it was the perfect white noise to lull me quickly to sleep.

I was exhausted. I wanted to rest. But sleep came restlessly. I tossed and turned, staring at my closed bedroom door for what felt like hours until at last I drifted off.

And a nightmare swallowed me instantly.

I OPENED MY EYES TO THE INSIDE OF A DIM CAVE. OVERHEAD, STALACTITES dangled like stone fangs. Before me was nothing but darkness, as though the cave went on forever in every direction.

My pulse raced. For a moment, I thought I might be back in that awful Tibran interrogation chamber. I took a step back, and my boots sloshed and splashed noisily. There was standing water on the floor.

When I looked down, I saw my reflection rippling on the surface.

I looked like Noh—or rather, some twisted version of him. My hair was black and my eyes were glowing like red fires, just like his. I had two immense black-feathered wings on my back, and black spiky horns poking out of my hair. They started just above my ears and went all the way down my back. My hands were stained black all the way up to my elbows and my fingernails had become hard and long like claws.

I staggered back in panic, turning in a circle as I attempted to wipe the black stuff off my hands. It wouldn't budge. It was as though my skin had been stained with ink.

"Hello? Is anyone there?" My voice echoed off the cavern walls. "Where am I?"

Out of the corner of my eye, I saw a point of white light. Without thinking, I ran for it. Maybe it was a way out.

It wasn't.

A square, milky-colored slab of stone stood only a few yards away. I couldn't be sure, but it looked like it might be a Gray elf sarcophagus. There was a bust of a person engraved on the top of it, and the whole thing seemed to emanate a soft white light.

Sitting on top of it with his back to me, was a guy in a dark blue tunic. At least, I assumed it was a guy. I couldn't see his face. But his muscular build and the broadness of his shoulders made me think it was a man. He had shaggy ash-gray hair that came to his shoulders, and he was leaning over like he was resting his elbows on his knees.

"Hey, are you stuck here, too? Do you know the way out?"

He didn't answer. He didn't even move. It was as though he couldn't hear me. I got a weird feeling, like pins and needles under my skin.

I started walking up to him. "Hello? Can you hear me?"

"*I've been waiting for you.*" A woman's voice suddenly filled the cave, sending out ripples across the water.

I staggered back. I knew that voice. It was the same one from before.

"M-me?"

"*You've been lazy, boy. You've been reckless and stupid.*"

"Hey!" I shouted, looking around to try to find where the voice was coming from. "Who are you?"

"*But no more. You are my chosen one. My champion. My harbinger. Soon you will carry the staff of my judgment and all will bow before it.*" The woman's voice oozed with delight and she gave a wicked laugh. "*But first you must complete the ritual. You must find the crystal, harbinger, and give an offering of pure blood.*"

"What are you talking about? Who are you?"

"*I am your Matron. Your mother. Your master. You will call me Clysiros,*" the voice replied. "*Now go and do as I command. Awaken he who sleeps and complete the ritual.*"

I turned back, looking over my shoulder and past one of my black wings to see the guy still sitting on top of the sarcophagus. His head fell forward slightly, as though he were hanging it in anguish. I still couldn't see his face, and I didn't get the impression that I knew him.

"I don't understand," I shouted at the empty air. "Tell me what's going on! Who is that? Who are you? What do you want from me?"

I didn't get an answer.

Suddenly, the ground fell out from beneath me. I was swallowed up by a vortex of swirling black water—falling farther and farther away from the light until there was nothing.

Just the darkness and me.

"Reigh, wake up!"

Enyo was shaking my shoulders. I felt it an instant before she smacked me hard across the face.

I bolted awake, dazed by the candlelight. I looked around frantically, my gaze finally settling on her. I was in my room, still in my bed. My sheets were soaked with sweat and my heart was trying to pound out of my chest. A dream? I checked my hands just to make sure.

They were back to normal. The black marks, claws, wings, and horns were all gone. Slumping forward, I buried my face in my hands with relief.

"Reigh, what happened? You were yelling. I couldn't get you to wake up." Enyo's voice trembled with concern.

I tried to remember. It was all a haze now. I just remembered that voice, a woman's menacing voice calling to me in the dark. And something about a crystal.

"I'm sorry," I rasped. "I'm fine. It was a dream."

Her mouth drooped into a frown. "About Kiran?"

I caught myself before I could answer. Should I tell her? Studying her face, I could see the evidence of worry, apprehension, and fear.

"Yeah," I lied. "It's fine now. I'm okay. Sorry for freaking you out."

"You're sure?"

I rubbed my cheek. "Well, my face stings now."

"Don't worry. I went easy on you; it won't leave a bruise." She brushed one of her cool palms over it, making me go stiff.

"*Har har har*, so funny."

"Seriously, are you sure you're okay?"

I forced a smile, purely for her benefit. "Yeah. I'm gonna try going back to sleep."

She seemed to buy it. Her face brightened and she gave me a cautious smile as she left, taking the candle with her. I almost asked her to leave it. The light was a comfort. But I didn't want her to suspect that I wasn't okay. I waited until after she closed the door behind her to lie back down and rub my forehead with the heel of my hand. I was hoping I could rub that voice out of my mind.

No such luck.

Clysiros—the name was stuck in my brain like a thorn. I'd never heard it before. I didn't know if she was someone important, but I had a feeling I knew exactly where I could find out.

CHAPTER TWENTY-SEVEN

Early the next morning, I got up and got dressed. The clinic was quiet. There weren't any patients here, yet. Now was as good a time as any.

I crept downstairs, tiptoeing through the main room where Enyo was curled up on a sleeping pallet next to the fire. There was a book still open, resting in her hands, and she was breathing softly. I paused as I passed her, studying her placid expression. Her lashes fluttered as she dreamed.

I couldn't leave her like that.

Squatting down, I slid my arms under her back and knees and carefully lifted her off the floor. I carried her up the stairs, into Kiran's room, and laid her down on his bed. I tucked the blankets in around her snuggly.

As I brushed my fingers lightly over her cheek, she sighed and mumbled something I couldn't understand. A strange pressure settled in my chest, like a hand was squeezing around my heart. It hurt—in a good way—which made absolutely no sense to me.

I closed the door and went back downstairs. I sat on the front step and tied up my boots. Around me, the jungle made its waking up sounds. Birds, bugs, and frogs sang. The city was just beginning to rouse. As I walked the streets, I saw shopkeepers beginning to open. Bakers were already putting out their fresh pastries. Street merchants were rolling out their carpets on the sidewalk and arranging their wares on them.

I'd seen it all before, hundreds of times. Some of the shopkeepers even waved at me as I went by. I tried to smile back, but I couldn't find the strength.

I made my way to the front gates of the palace. There, two royal guards stopped me and demanded to know what I wanted.

I frowned at them. "I need to see Queen Araxie."

"Hah!" One of the guards laughed in my face. "You think you can just waltz up here and demand to see her?"

"I'm her favored scout. Or maybe you don't remember? Kiran is my father. I've come all the way from the battlefront in Maldobar to see her." I bit at the words angrily, narrowing my eyes at them. "Stand aside."

"What proof do you have? You aren't even dressed like a scout. You're just a kid!"

I flexed my arms, flinging them out wide. One small blast of my power sent both royal guards flying through the air like scarecrows. They landed on their rear ends on either side of me, mouths agape in horror.

I straightened my shirt collar, dusted off my sleeves, and stepped through the gates. Neither of them said another word.

Nobody else gave me any trouble as I walked into the palace. The other guards who saw me stood perfectly still, gripping their spears and bows hard, watching me carefully for a false move. Lucky for them, I hadn't come here looking for trouble.

I remembered the way to the throne room, and I was nearly there when I heard someone calling my name.

"Reigh! It is you!" Hecate walked toward me, her mismatched eyes fixed right on me. "I felt it the moment you came through the gates. You came back?"

I looked down, my face burning with embarrassment. She couldn't see me—I knew that. Still, I had been hoping she might not be anywhere nearby to hear what I'd come to say to her grandmother.

"It's a long story." I tried to be vague.

She stopped a few feet away from me with the lengths of her long, white and pink gown pooling around her. Her expression became tense as her brow furrowed ever so slightly. "What you did outside, I felt that, too."

"I'm sorry." Only, I wasn't.

"What's going on? That voice ... the whispering voice ... it's so much louder now. I can hear it." She tilted her head to the side slightly, as though she was listening. "What does it mean? Who is the harbinger?"

My jaw dropped. "I-is it a woman's voice?"

Her head bobbed slowly.

I gulped. "Maybe you're the one I should be talking to."

"About what?"

"I need to know if there's anything in the royal library about a woman," I replied. "A woman named Clysiros."

Hecate led the way through the halls of the palace, guiding me to the royal library where all the ancient texts and scrolls were kept. She explained that it was one of the few rooms she knew how to get to without her attendants. "It's been much easier to come and go as I please with my grandfather away. He's so stiff about the rules. He doesn't want me going anywhere without an escort, not even the library."

"Not to be mean, but why do you like the library. You can't read the books, right?"

She gave a small, haughty smile. "Not to be mean, but I think I use them better than seeing people do. I don't *read* the books. I *listen* to them."

"How exactly does that work?

"It's difficult to explain. I told you, I hear things—things no one else can." Her brow creased as we stopped where two halls intersected. She thought for a moment, and took an abrupt left and kept going. "It helps for me to make physical contact. It makes things much clearer. When it comes to books, if I hold them, I can hear the voice of the writer. Sometimes I can even ask them questions."

Okay. That was weird even by my standards.

"Here," Hecate said. She stopped right in front of a tall door with a rounded top. There was a silver half-moon shaped panel with the head of a stag engraved on it hanging over the door.

I opened the door and took her arm to guide her inside. "So how long have you been able to do that?"

"As long as I can remember. My cousins had the same ability. We were all born this way. But eventually it became too much for them. It drove them mad."

"What did?" I studied her troubled expression.

"It's like listening to a chorus that never ends. Some days are better than others. If I try, I can focus on one voice, like yours. It's easier if it is especially strong. But most days I am overwhelmed. Day or night, sleeping or awake, I always hear them. It's exhausting. And no one seems to know any way to make them quiet." Her brow creased with distress as she turned her face away. "I've tried everything. My grandfather seems convinced that sitting alone in my room undisturbed will make it better."

"Does it?"

Hecate shook her head. "He cannot hear them, so he doesn't understand. What sounds like silence to everyone else is a raging orchestra of chaos to me."

I felt bad for her. That didn't sound like fun at all. Somehow, though, it was comforting to know I wasn't the only weirdo walking around these days. "So, does anyone know why?"

"Why what?"

"Why do you hear these things?" I clarified.

She drew her bottom lip into her mouth, nibbling at it for a moment. "I don't know. Some have theories. My grandmother suspects it's something to do with the gods, maybe even a punishment for the things our family did during the Gray War. But no one knows exactly."

"Oh."

"Reigh, did he ..." She started to ask, but her voice fell silent before she could finish the question.

"Did who what?"

Hecate swallowed, her mouth pressing into an uncomfortable frown. "Did Prince Aubren say anything about me?"

"Uh, um, well." This was *not* something I wanted to get caught up in. Since when was I qualified the middleman in their relationship?

"Did he find me disappointing?" She asked again.

"What? N-no! Of course not," I rasped. "He didn't give me that impression at all."

"He never spoke directly to me while he was here, except for that one moment at dinner. And only then because my grandmother insisted upon it. I don't even know if he looked at me." Her tone had gone soft, as though she were ashamed or afraid someone else might overhear. "I was afraid he might find me ... less suitable as a bride than my cousins. I'm younger. I don't know if I'm as pretty. I was hoping he would at least introduce himself, or let me touch his hand so I could hear him. From afar, his sound was so conflicted and wrought with worry, I couldn't get a clear impression of him."

I rubbed the back of my neck. Was I supposed to tell her everything Aubren had said? Was that even fair? Love games were not my thing. I had my own problems in that department. "Look, I'm no expert here, but I think Aubren's a nice person. Honestly, he's kind of worried you'll be disappointed with him, too. Maybe there's a lot you two have in common."

"Maybe so." Hecate's expression brightened slightly. "Come, let's see if we can find that name."

The library was a literal labyrinth of shelves and cubbies crowded on every wall. There were rows upon rows of them, all crammed with papers, scrolls, rolled up maps, and dusty tomes. I stared at it in awe. There was no way we'd ever have time to search every shelf. It would take a lifetime just to get down one aisle.

"Clysiros." Hecate repeated the name. Her whispering voice sent chills over me, like there was some sort of spell to it. Her sightless eyes panned the room and she took a small step, then another. She started walking slowly down the center aisle of shelves. Her lips moved, making shapes like she was repeating the name over and over.

I hung on to her arm, eyeing the long shadows that were cast by the huge stained-glass window overhead. Something about them felt off, as though they were quietly mocking me.

Hecate stopped suddenly. She turned, going down an aisle to the right and taking very slow, careful steps down it. When she stopped again, she faced the shelf and reached into one of the cubbies. I heard papers crinkling inside.

She shrieked and drew her hand back like she'd been bitten by something.

I stepped between her and the shelf, ready to smash whatever might come popping out. All I saw was the corner of an old, yellow, ragged-looking piece of paper. I carefully pinched it between my fingers; dragging it the rest of the way out like it might bite me, too.

It was just a piece of paper, though.

Once I was sure about that, I held it up to the light.

"That voice," Hecate whimpered. "It's the same."

The paper had no words on it—at least, none that I could read. They had been written ages ago, so the ink had almost completely disappeared over time. What I could see, especially when I held it up to the light, was a drawing. It was a picture of a woman in a long black gown adorned with tiny pinpricks of white, almost like stars. Her eyes had been colored in so they were completely dark. Black spiked horns protruded from her head, peeking out of her flowing dark hair, and she had three sets of feathered wings—two of black, and one of silver.

Resting in her hands was a jewel. The picture was so old; I had a hard time discerning what it really looked like. It was just jagged, black, and oddly shaped like a cluster of ... crystals.

My stomach went sour.

"She keeps saying the same thing." Hecate groped forward until she found my hand. She clutched it and I could feel her shaking with fear. "*Awaken he who sleeps and complete the ritual.*"

I squeezed my eyes shut.

"What does it mean?"

When I opened them again, I set my gaze on the face of that woman in the picture and growled, "It means I have to leave now."

CHAPTER TWENTY-EIGHT

Hopefully the Queen wouldn't add theft to my growing list of crimes. I'd blown her guards over, entered the palace without invitation, met in secret with Princess Hecate, and now I had that piece of paper with the drawing on it folded up in my pocket—and it wasn't even noon yet. At this rate, I'd be burning the jungle down by dinnertime.

But first, I had a bone to pick with "he who sleeps."

There was only one person in the world I knew she might be talking about. And frankly, I was sick of him. It was time to put an end to this once and for all.

I already knew the way to the stable where the royal family kept their prized shrikes. I'd been there before with Aubren and King Jace. It wouldn't hurt to borrow one for a little while, right? I mean if I was going to be arrested for any of that other stuff anyway, this would just be a good story to tell the guy in the cell next to mine.

I slipped into the stable without any of the guards seeing me. Then I nabbed a saddle, crept into one of the stalls, and got the shrike ready to go. It was kind of bittersweet. I wished I could be riding Vexi instead. Hopefully she was okay and had gone back to wherever her home was with the other wild dragons.

The shrike gave an excited trill as we took off, which alerted all the guards and stable hands nearby. We were already long gone by the time they came dashing over to try and stop us. I gave them all a smirk and a wink as I zipped away into the jungle.

The trees whipped past us as the shrike's translucent wings hummed in the air. It sprang from limb to limb, kicking off the branches and tree trunks as it flew. The sun hadn't been up for long. I could make it before dusk if we pushed hard and didn't pause to rest.

There was no stopping me now.

My blood was on fire. I gripped the saddle so hard my palms ached. I kept my eyes sharp as the shrike took a brief dive above the canopy, bursting through the foliage into the sunlight. There, looming in the distance, was the prize—the lapiloque's tree.

"Faster," I urged the shrike. I wanted to get there before I changed my mind or my better sense caught up with me.

The sun had just begun to set when the shrike finally landed on a branch on the edge of the temple grounds. The beast was tired. As soon as I was out of the saddle, it flopped down to pant and growl in complaint.

"Sorry," I muttered. "Don't worry, the trip back won't be anything like that."

If I even went back.

Honestly, I had no idea what I was doing here. From where I stood on the edge of a branch, I could see the overgrown temple grounds below. The tree was still there, enormous, and not budging.

My whole body flushed with anger. Beyond this forest, his kingdom and everything he'd claimed to love was being destroyed. And yet here he was, the lapiloque, the great Jaevid Broadfeather—chosen one of the god Paligno—doing absolutely nothing about it.

I climbed down to the jungle floor, which was a terrible idea considering I didn't have any weapons on me. Luntharda's vast assortment of hungry predators wasn't my concern right now. My boots hit the ground and I started running, smacking fern fronds out of my way and jumping over boulders. I scurried across the temple grounds until I came to the base of the tree and skidded to a halt.

The monstrous tree was just as we'd left it. I could feel the faint aura of power wafting off it, pulsing like a heartbeat.

My lip curled. My insides writhed and anger crackled over my tongue. Stupid tree. Stupid legends and myths, giving people false hope. Enough was enough.

"I'm sick of you!" I yelled at it. "You hear me, Jaevid? *I hate you*! None of this would have happened if you had kept your promise. You're a liar."

I curled my hands into fists, drawing upon my power for what I sincerely hoped would be the last time. I hated it—being this monster. I didn't want it. After this, I never wanted to use it again.

"This is it. No more," I growled under my breath. "You hear me, Clysiros? You stay away from me. I'm not your harbinger. I won't be anyone's weapon. I'm finished."

I thrust both of my hands against the tree trunk and poured into it every ounce of power in my body. I gave it all, every last drop. It felt like my insides were being scrambled. My head swam—but I didn't stop. Not until I felt that pulse within the tree suddenly stop.

I jerked my hands away and stumbled back.

There was an unnatural silence, nothing in the jungle made a sound. No birds. No insects. No wind.

Only my heartbeat thrashing in my ears.

Then, right where I had touched the tree, its bark began to turn black. The blackness spread, growing bigger and bigger until it surged over the entire trunk. Far overhead, the leaves turned brown and began to shrivel. One by one, they began dissolving into black ash.

The trunk came next. From top to bottom it began to fade away, dissolving into ash that slowly faded away in the air. I couldn't stop it. In a matter of minutes, the tree was completely gone.

The only thing left was a deep, dark, open pit.

WITH MY KNEES SHAKING, I WOBBLED TO THE EDGE OF THE PIT AND PEERED down. It was so deep I couldn't see the bottom. But there was an old, cracked stone staircase that spiraled around the chasm, leading down into the gloom.

I had the weird sensation I had seen this before somewhere. I just couldn't remember where. For some reason, I just *had* to go in there. I needed to see what was at the bottom.

Before I knew it, I was walking down that staircase. The deeper I went, the more the sunlight and jungle became a distant memory overhead. The air was cool and damp. It smelled of old soil, roots, and rotting leaves.

I raked my sweaty hair out of my face as I stepped off the last of the stairs. I was standing before the gaping mouth of a tunnel and, far at the other end, I could see a faint glow of light. It made my entire body shiver and every hair on my body prickle.

Slowly and cautiously, I crept down the tunnel. It was so quiet. The air was musty, like no one had been down here for a long time, which probably had something to do with the giant tree that had been covering it until a few minutes ago.

Part of me expected to find that dark woman, Clysiros, waiting for me on the other end of the tunnel. But when I got to the other side, I stared around at a massive cavern chamber. It looked a lot like the one from my dream.

And just like in that dream, dead in the center of the chamber was a white stone sarcophagus.

Only, there wasn't anyone sitting on top of it this time. There wasn't any water on the floor, either, which was a huge relief. I kept an eye out just in case as I hedged toward the gravesite. The white stone shimmered in the dark like pearl. It filled the whole room with a soft, ethereal glow.

"This is it?" I asked myself out loud as I stood over it.

The stone vault didn't look like anything special. It just looked like a normal burial vault that the Gray elves used to bury their loved ones before the Gray War. There were plenty of them in the older cities.

On the top was an engraving, an extremely detailed bust of Jaevid lying on his back, his expression serene and eyes closed, with his arms at his sides. He looked younger in this sculpture than he had in any of the others I'd seen. He had that same scar over one of his eyes, which was a fairly easy way to be sure of who it was.

I didn't know why, but seeing him look so calm and content pissed me off even more. I curled my lip in disgust and reached out to thump his statue in the cheek—just for spite.

The stone cracked under my fingertip like an eggshell.

I bounced back in terror. I-I'd barely touched it!

The place on his cheek began turning black, just like the tree's trunk had. The darkness spread, consuming the whole sculpture of Jaevid and beginning to dissolve it. Black ash boiled into the air, swirling and curling like a plume of smoke that stung my eyes. I covered my face and looked away.

Then I heard someone cough.

My eyes flew open wide and I gaped at the place where Jaevid's bust had been. Lying there in its place was a person—a live person. His mouth opened wide and he sucked in a deep, desperate breath. Then he coughed hard, like he'd been holding his breath for a long time.

About forty years, to be exact.

I was paralyzed with shock, my mouth still hanging open. It wasn't possible. Seriously, I'd barely touched it. I hadn't done anything. I hadn't even used my power on it.

I watched Jaevid try to roll over and sit up. He was weaving drowsily, squinting around, and still coughing and gasping for breath. Suddenly, he started to topple forward.

I immediately rushed forward to catch him.

"Whoa, there. Take it easy." I helped him sit down at the base of the marble slab. "Deep breaths."

He blinked up at me, his brow drawn up in a confused daze. He kept looking around as though he were expecting to see someone else in the room.

"W-where are they?" he asked in the human language. His voice was weak and hoarse.

"Who?"

His pale gaze seemed to focus for an instant. He—Jaevid Broadfeather—looked me square in the eye. "I don't remember. I just thought there would be someone else."

"Sorry, it's just me." I wasn't sure if I was supposed to apologize or what. I'd just murdered his sacred tree and, well, raised him from the dead—accidentally.

"You're him, right? You're Jaevid?" I wasn't sure. After all, it could have been a trick.

It certainly looked like him, though. At least, mostly. He seemed way younger than he did in all the paintings, sculptures, and tapestries I'd seen over the years. In fact, he looked like he might be close to my age. He also didn't look very chivalrous, knightly, or regal like he had in all those sculptures.

His black cloak was ratty and dirty like it had seen better days, and his silvery-gray hair was a wavy, shaggy mess. He had that distinct halfbreed look to him, with pointed ears that were a little shorter than a normal Gray elf's peeking out of his hair. His skin was a dark bronze color like theirs, too, and his features were sharp and defined. But his jaw was wider and more human looking. And his eyes, well, they were such a light shade of blue they almost looked like ice.

"That was my name, I think." He seemed to be sizing me up, as well. "Who are you?"

"Reigh." I wasn't sure if I should try to shake his hand or not. Did you shake hands with legendary war heroes? Not to mention I'd come here to, you know, destroy his final resting place.

He glanced around the room again, his eyes panning everywhere like he was still hoping to see someone else. "Where am I?"

"Luntharda," I answered. "At the old temple ruins. You mean you don't remember anything?"

He reached up to touch his face, exploring it like he had no idea what he even looked like. He did the same thing with his clothes, looking them all over and dusting the black ash off where it was still stuck to him. When his hand struck the hilt of his scimitar, I saw him hesitate. He gripped it firmly, then drew it slowly from the sheath and brought it close so he could examine it. He brushed his thumb over the stag's head engraved on the pommel.

"I'm not sure," he answered quietly and slipped the scimitar back into its sheath. "It's like trying to remember a dream. Some things are clear. But others ... " He closed his eyes, his brows drawing together and his mouth set into a hard line.

"Hey, just take it easy. You've been down here a while. It might just take some time to—"

"How long?" he interrupted.

"Uh ... " I wasn't so sure I should tell him that.

Jaevid staggered to his feet, leaning against the marble slab behind him for balance. He was still weak; he could barely stay upright. And yet he looked at me with a fierce desperation blazing in his eyes. "How long?" he demanded.

"Forty years, give or take."

His chest shuddered with a frantic breath. He started to wobble forward, but didn't make it two steps before his legs buckled. I dove out and caught him again to keep him from falling. I looped one of his arms around my shoulders and helped him sit back down.

"N-no," he pleaded. "No, I can't stay here anymore. Please, you have to help me. I have to find them."

"Who?"

His eyes got cloudy. He looked lost and confused, staring around us at the dark until he finally admitted, "I can't remember."

"We're the only ones here. But you're right; we can't stay much longer. It'll be dark soon. I don't know how much you remember about Luntharda, but being on the jungle floor in the dark is the last place anyone wants to be."

CHAPTER TWENTY-NINE

It was well past nightfall by the time I helped him hobble up out of the pit, going up all those steps one at a time, and making our way across the temple grounds. The best scenario we could possibly hope for was making it to the tree without being found by anything looking for an easy midnight snack. Jaevid had a weapon, but I seriously doubted he could use it. He could barely put one foot in front of the other.

Jostling him a little bit to steady my balance and adjust his weight on my shoulder, I focused on the tree. "Just hang in there, okay? We're almost there."

"I ... I feel something," he said hoarsely as his head bobbed and lulled against me. "It's coming this way."

"What?"

I stopped dead in my tracks, looking around as the haunting sounds of snagwolves yipping to one another echoed through the darkened jungle. I caught glimpses of their glowing eyes winking at us in the dark.

They had us surrounded.

"No," I growled under my breath. "No, no, no. Not now."

The snagwolves started to close in. One popped out of the foliage directly in front of us, its mossy hide bristled. Then another came from behind. More and more emerged from the thickets, circling us and baring their jagged teeth.

One of the snagwolves lunged, jaws open wide for the kill.

I squeezed my eyes shut and braced for it. There wasn't time to do anything else. We were goners.

Suddenly, I heard a deep, concussive sound like the low toll of a bell. Green light exploded in the air, blinding me even through my eyelids. The snagwolves howled in fear. The sounds of them yipping and screeching in terror faded into the distance.

The flash of light left me seeing spots. I rubbed my eyes and when I could see clearly again, I realized Jaevid wasn't leaning against me anymore.

He was standing tall with his shoulders square and one of his hands outstretched. His palm was still glowing with a faint greenish light and his gaze sharpened into a lethal glare. Slowly, he lowered his arm and turned to look at me—about two seconds before he fainted. His eyes rolled back and he toppled backwards like a puppet with its strings cut.

"Hey! Don't you dare die on me!" I rushed over to check his pulse.

He wasn't dead, thank the gods. But he was completely out of it, so I had to pick him up and fling him over my back. It set the sensitive areas where my wounds were ablaze with a painful reminder that I wasn't fully recovered yet.

I struggled to scale the tree, foot by foot, inch by inch. My body burned with exhaustion. My hands trembled and slipped and my legs cramped. I stopped to catch my breath, to curse Jaevid for weighing so much, and then I started climbing again.

It probably took an hour or more. When I reached the limb where my shrike was still waiting, I collapsed face-first onto it. Jaevid's unconscious body was on top of me and I roughly pushed him off, lifting my head to spit out dirt and leaves.

This day was *not* going as planned.

After lying there for a minute or two to catch my breath, I forced myself to get up again. Grabbing him by the ankles, I dragged Jaevid further onto the branch. I took off his cloak and rolled it into a bundle that I used to prop up his head. That was the best I could do for him at the moment. I didn't have any water, food, or even a blanket to make either of us comfortable.

Sitting down next to Jaevid, I crossed my legs and stared up at the big empty hole in the jungle canopy where his tree had been. Moonlight poured through it, illuminating the ground where the pit was. It made the dew-covered plants sparkle like they'd been sprinkled with diamonds. I could even see a few stars, which was kind of nice. It gave me something else to think about in between doing life-checks on Jaevid every few minutes.

I'd come here intending to put an end to all the myths about Jaevid ever coming back to life. Now he was lying about two feet away from me. I couldn't decide if this was a stroke of good luck or a huge mistake. I did decide one thing, though, and that was that I absolutely—without a doubt—could not tell him why I'd really come here. He was the chosen one of the forest god, lord of all living things. That wasn't the kind of guy you wanted on your bad side.

"*Not to mention he wouldn't approve of our differences, don't you agree?*" Noh's voice whispered in the back of my mind. "*The lord of life and the harbinger of death. What a recipe for disaster!*"

Next to me, Jaevid's face twitched. He stirred, almost as though he could hear Noh, too.

I clenched my teeth and tried to will him to be silent.

It was already going to be a long night without Noh making it worse.

JAEVID WOKE UP BEFORE DAWN. HE ROLLED OVER ONTO HIS SIDE AND groaned loudly, clutching his head. It made me jump and have a tiny heart attack since I had been nodding in and out of sleep for the past few hours.

"Where am I?" he croaked.

"Still at the temple grounds. Sorry, but you weigh a ton and carrying you up this tree was about all I could do."

He pushed himself up slowly and went on rubbing his forehead. "My head is killing me."

"Yeah, I don't doubt it," I mumbled. "Nice trick with the snagwolves, though."

My borrowed shrike began to stir, making heavy puffing sounds. It was eager to get going. I hadn't brought anything to feed it.

Jaevid's eyes went wide as he stared at the creature. "That's a shrike," he said.

"Yep. So, you do remember some things, after all."

He turned to stare at me next. "Who are you?"

"I already told you, my name is Reigh."

"No, that's not what I meant." He shook his head. "Why did you awaken me? How did you do it?"

Those were two excellent questions and I didn't want to answer either of them. "It's kind of a long story. Maybe we should start with what you do remember and go from there."

He frowned suspiciously, his eyes crinkling at the corners. "I remember ... faces. There was a war. Someone was trying to ..." His voice faded to silence and I saw his shoulders curl forward, withdrawing as though he were afraid. "It's still too hazy. None of it makes any sense, like scattered puzzle pieces in my mind."

"Look, it really doesn't matter right now. Don't worry about it. What's most important is getting you to Mau Kakuri as soon as possible. Queen Araxie will know what to do." I showed him a confident grin.

He smiled back, but it looked painfully forced. "Araxie—that name does sound a bit familiar."

"Good. See? It'll be fine. She'll know much more about how to help you than I do."

"I suppose I owe you a debt of gratitude, Reigh, for awakening me." He slowly turned his head down and away, staring vacantly at the end of his scuffed-up boots. "Thank you."

I tugged at my shirt collar. It felt too tight for some reason. "That's really not necessary. It was kind of an accident."

"Forty years," he muttered. I could hear the weight of those words even as he said them.

Until that moment, I'd never really thought about how waking up was going to be for him. He was a hero. A legend. He was supposed to be someone we could all count on to come riding in on his famous blue dragon and save us from whatever happened to be destroying the world that day. Tibrans, in this case.

But forty years was a long time. Odds were, anyone he'd known before was either dead or so old they'd be dead sooner rather than later. I studied his profile, watching as his eyes rolled closed and he bowed his head slightly. He was alone in a way I knew I couldn't understand.

"We should probably get going," I suggested.

"Yes," he agreed and began to stand. He wobbled a little, but the more he moved around the more stable he seemed to get. At least I wasn't going to have to carry him anymore.

"Ever ridden a shrike before?" I asked as I climbed up into the saddle.

He approached the creature with uncertainty. For a few awkward seconds, Jaevid and the shrike stared at one another. Then he smiled, petted it on the head, and climbed into the saddle behind me.

"Not that I remember," he replied.

Weird.

"Okay, well you better hang on tight, then. We're going fast. It'll take all day to get back to Mau Kakuri."

"Whatever you say, Reigh," he agreed and grabbed on to the back of my belt.

I nudged the shrike with the heels of my boots. The animal gave an excited screech as it crouched down low, its strong legs coiling for takeoff. I stole one last glance back over my shoulder to where Jaevid Broadfeather was sitting behind me. He flashed me another forced smile. Then we took off into the jungle like a comet, leaving the old temple grounds far behind.

CHAPTER THIRTY

Under any other circumstance, returning to Mau Kakuri after I'd basically broken into the palace, assaulted a few guards, consorted with the princess in secret, and stolen one of the queen's shrikes, was probably an extremely bad idea. I would have been better off staying as far away from there as possible. Not to mention, the rest of the Gray elf citizens in Luntharda were probably going to notice that a certain enormous tree-shaped landmark was now missing on their horizon. Whoops.

However, with Jaevid sitting in the saddle behind me, I had more than enough reason to think that past transgressions might be overlooked. Or, at the very least, they wouldn't kill me for it.

Hopefully, anyway.

Three scouts intercepted me before I could cross the boundary back into the city. They were probably one of many who had been put on patrol to watch for me in case I did come back. They surrounded us from every side, their mounts snarling and snapping bony jaws dangerously. Their bows were drawn, arrows pointed right at Jaevid and me.

"Wait a second," I protested. "I can explain!"

"Silence," one of the scouts shouted back. "Dismount immediately and drop all your weaponry!"

"All right, all right. Just don't shoot." I got down first and Jaevid followed. We both stood between the scouts with our hands in the air in a gesture of surrender. I hadn't brought much in the way of weaponry with me. Jaevid, on the other hand, was relieved of his scimitar and a long hunting knife before the scouts were satisfied.

Then one of them actually looked at the blade Jaevid had been carrying. I watched him studying it, surveying the peculiar design, and noticing the royal seal on the pommel. That wasn't just anyone's scimitar.

Suddenly, the scout's gaze shot up to look right at Jaevid. He paled. The other two men with him quickly noticed his reaction and came over to see what the problem was. All told, it took them about five minutes to work it out.

"Lapiloque," they gasped in unison.

Two fell flat on the ground, prostrating themselves before Jaevid—who honestly looked bewildered. The third inched forward, his knees shaking as he offered the scimitar back. "Y-you are truly him? You are lapiloque?"

Jaevid seemed unsure, but he gave them another one of those thin, uncomfortable smiles as he took his blade back. "I am."

The third scout dropped to his knee in reverence. "May the gods be praised!"

"That's really not necessary." Jaevid was blushing slightly and patted the man on the shoulder. "Stand, please, all of you. We need to go to Mau Kakuri. I need to see Queen Araxie as soon as possible. Can you take us there?"

"You, yes." The scout nearest to him confirmed with an eager smile. That smile immediately vanished when he looked at me. "He is a criminal, my lord. He broke into the palace and stole from the royal stable. He must be taken to stand trial."

Great. What a way to make a first impression. Granted, it wasn't exactly offbeat from my usual antics, but Jaevid hadn't known that. Fantastic.

He shot me an exasperated look. "You might have mentioned that before, Reigh."

I forced a chuckle. "Yeah, well, it didn't seem relevant at the time."

He rolled his eyes. "We can address his crimes later. For now, I require his presence. Please, take us to the palace."

The scouts exchanged quiet murmurs and unsettled glances, but they didn't question him. They did, however, decide to make me ride with one of them—my hands bound behind me—just for good measure. I guess they weren't willing to take it on divine faith that I wouldn't try to run if I got the chance.

It was impossible to tell from Jae's expression what he might be thinking as we crossed the final distance and broke through the last line of foliage into the city itself. Mau Kakuri was breathtaking, even for a jungle paradise. He didn't smile, though. In fact, he appeared to be even more confused as the scouts landed in the city street right before the palace gates. Two of them ran on ahead to alert the rest of the palace. The last stayed behind to guard me. He grabbed the cord that had been tightly tied around my wrists and shot me a punishing glare.

I thought about elbowing him in the gut, just for good measure. He had a lot of nerve, treating me like that. If he was a scout, then he knew who my father had been.

I shuddered at the very thought of Kiran. Thankfully, it didn't linger for very long because Jaevid was slowly approaching the palace gates just as a chorus of horns blew throughout the complex. It started a chain reaction and within minutes, bells, chimes, and horns were ringing out all over the city. People came running out of their shops and houses, crowding into the streets and clambering in our direction. They gathered in throngs, hundreds of men, women, elderly, and children—all pushing and shoving to see him.

And Jaevid, well, he looked lost.

Standing in front of the city gates in his tattered, dirty clothes with nothing but a cloak and a scimitar, he stared back at everyone with wide eyes. His forehead crinkled and his brows drew up in a look of distress. I could see him breathing faster, backing up step-by-step until the gates opened suddenly behind him. Startled, he spun around to face the front steps of the palace itself.

The royal family came out one by one. First Queen Araxie, then King Jace. Behind them was Princess Hecate with a few of her personal bodyguards. I knew she couldn't see what was going on, but the look on her face me told me that she probably knew more about it than the rest of us who could. Her misty eyes were welling with tears and she had a fierce grip on the arm of her nearest bodyguard.

Everyone was composed for about six seconds.

Then, the Queen suddenly broke into a run. She sprinted down the paved walkway from the front of the palace to the gate, moving faster than I thought an old woman in those kinds of clothes possibly could. I guess she hadn't lost all her spirit, yet.

She stopped barely a foot away from Jaevid, the wrinkles in her face lifting as her eyes widened and her mouth opened. She didn't speak. No one dared to breathe a word. Around me, the crowd and city bells had all gone eerily silent—as though everyone was holding their breath and hanging on the one and only question that mattered:

Was this really him?

The Queen raised a trembling hand to touch him, cupping his cheek tenderly as her whole face twitched with emotion.

Slowly, Jaevid's tense brow relaxed. He stared back at her, his mouth opening slightly and then closing again. Placing his hand over hers, he held her palm against his face and closed his eyes. "It's been a long time, cousin."

She let out a loud, frantic sob and threw her arms around Jaevid tightly.

A deafening cheer went up through the crowd all around us. It was like the whole city of Mau Kakuri exploded into celebration. People threw ribbons and flowers in the air like confetti. Women sobbed against one another, shedding tears of relief and joy. Men beat their chests and shouted war cries. Children danced to the sounds of the music as the tower bells began ringing again.

Jaevid Broadfeather had returned.

HARBINGER

The Dragonrider Legacy Book Two

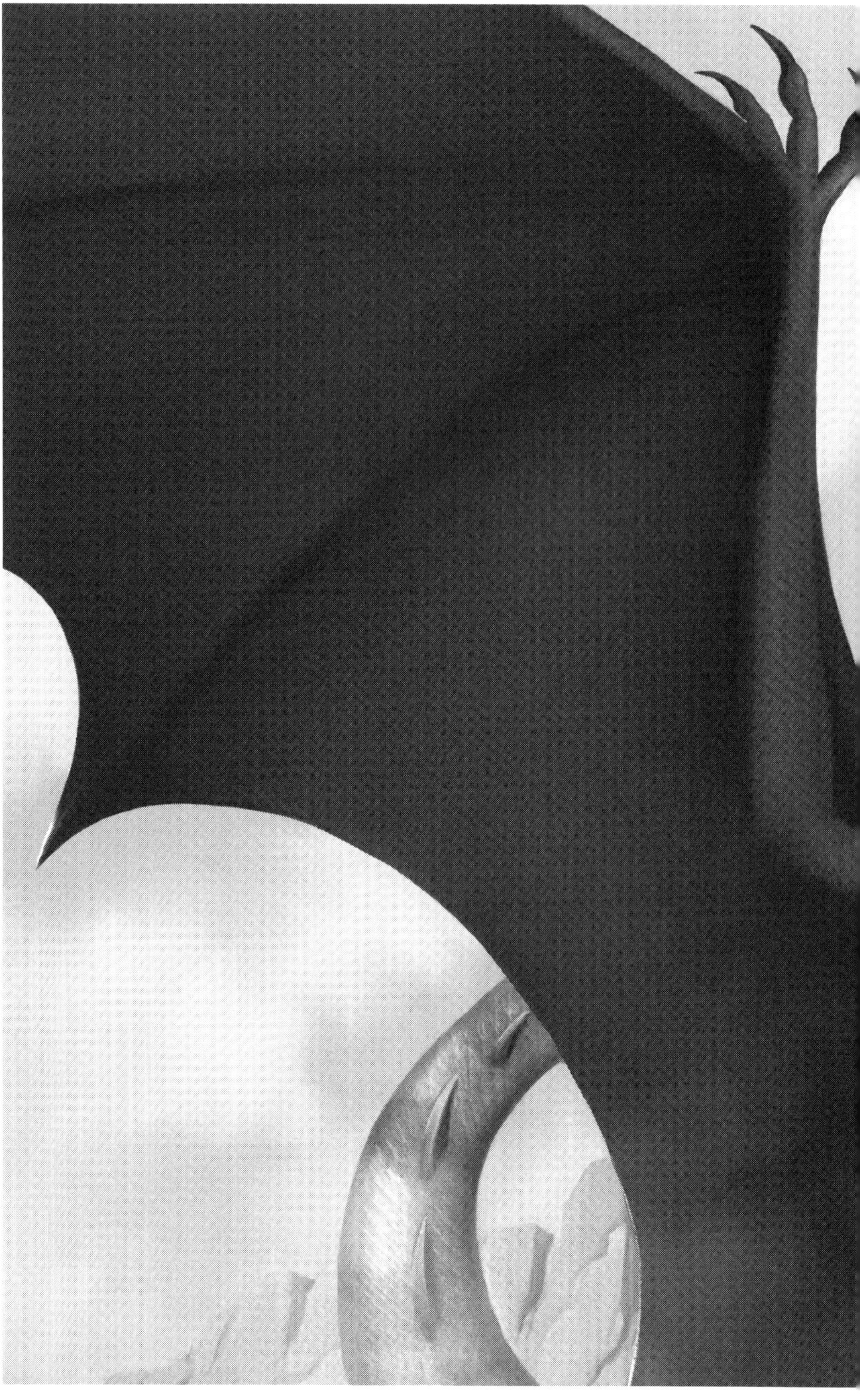

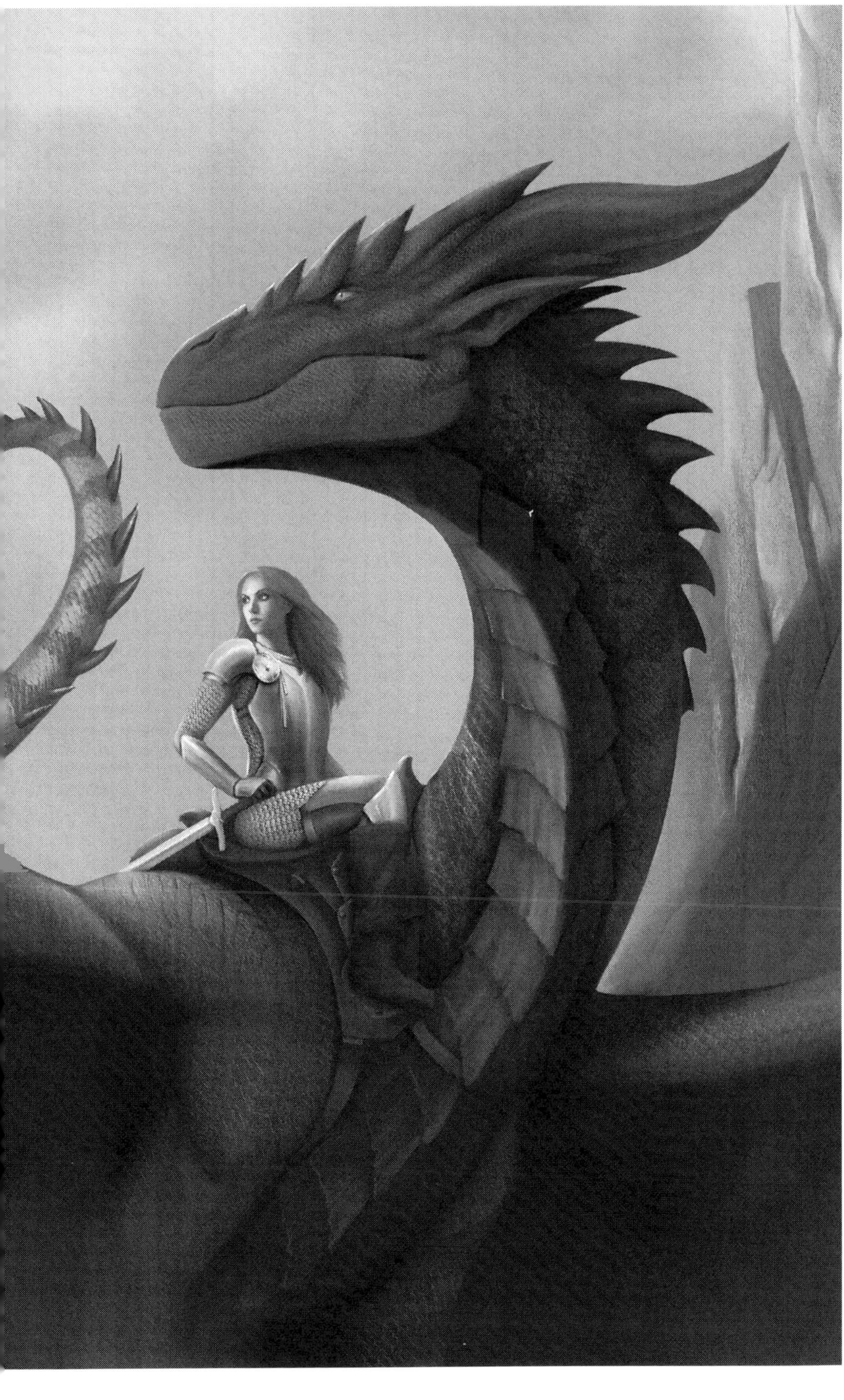

PART ONE: JENNA

CHAPTER ONE

I heard him before I saw him—which was nearly always the case with Phillip.

"Good morning, my love!"

I stole a quick glance over the top of the book I was studying, one centered on aerial battle techniques, as Duke Phillip Derrick swaggered into the parlor and leaned against the arm of the sofa beside me. He peered over my shoulder, invading my space to see what I was reading. Or maybe he just wanted to see what I would do if he let his cheek brush mine.

"I've asked you not to call me that," I muttered, fully aware of the futility of having this discussion *again*.

"I'll stop when it stops being true," he replied.

He probably thought he was being clever, using lines like that.

Calling him *ridiculous* would have been the understatement of the century. It was just a cruel, inconvenient coincidence that he also happened to be one of the better-looking men I knew. That hadn't always been the case, however. When we'd been children, which hadn't been all that long ago, he had been tall, gangly, and awkward. He'd had buck teeth, a face covered in freckles, and a regular riot of loose, black curls on his head that had stuck out all over the place.

Now, in his late twenties, he'd changed quite a bit. He didn't have the buck teeth anymore. In fact, his were obnoxiously perfect and straight now. I got a good look at them every time he flashed me one of those roguish, coy smiles he most likely thought were charming.

There were still a few freckles dusted across his cheeks and nose, almost invisible now because of his tanned skin. His hair, however, was no less a mess than it had been when we'd been little. It was still as black as pitch, wavy, and tended to poke up if it was even the least bit humid. He wore it a bit longer now, almost to his shoulders, so that those loose curls framed his squared jawline in a pleasing way. Something about how they shone in the light made you want to run your hands through them, just to see if they were as soft as they looked.

Not that I'd ever tried it myself. I had a firm no-touching policy with Phillip. The cheek brushing was a test, I knew. If he tried that again, I'd be forced to smack him to reinforce my rules.

"More battle plans?" he asked.

"We know the Tibrans will strike again soon," I replied. "Without Reigh here to help even the odds, we'll have to try some new techniques. I only have four riders at my disposal, counting myself. That doesn't leave us with much hope when the next attack comes. If the Tibrans have proven anything, it's that they bounce back quickly and fiercely. We can wager with confidence that their next assault on this city will be far more brutal."

"Ah." Phillip shifted and looked down at his boots. "Well, for what it's worth, I have the utmost faith in you."

So much for keeping the conversation light.

Truth be told, I was no good with that sort of thing. Social grace and appropriateness might as well have been foreign tongues. Being a princess didn't grant me an innate sense of grace; and when it came to interacting with other nobles, I had a long track record of embarrassing myself.

It was easy to play it off like I didn't care what they thought about me, most of the time. I think many people, even my own brother, believed that ruse—that it really didn't bother me not to be very refined when comporting myself in court. But there were moments when I wished I could come up with the right things to say; moments when I wished I had just a single ounce of social confidence. Half the time, whenever I opened my mouth, it was the soldier in me who spoke rather than the princess.

I managed to smile back at him slightly, which was a huge mistake.

Phillip grinned and leaned in closer like he was trying to dazzle me with his sharp, vibrant green eyes. "You're so lovely when you smile, Jenna."

I immediately scowled. "Stop that."

"Stop what?"

"Whatever it is you're trying to do." I raised my book up again and all but buried my nose in the crease of the pages. "Go away, please. I'm very busy."

He sighed. I felt his presence withdraw from looming over my shoulder. For an instant, I dared to hope he really had gone away.

I should be so lucky.

The couch where I sat minding my own business and hoping for a few minutes of quiet to read and plan suddenly lurched. Phillip flopped down onto the opposite end of it, reclining back and staring at me while he scrunched up his mouth and rubbed his chin.

"You'll fall for me one day, you know." He sounded so sure. "Maybe not tomorrow, or next month, or next year—but eventually. My love for you knows no limits. I'll wait forever, if that's what it takes."

I resisted the urge to hurl my book at him. One well-aimed shot and I was pretty sure I could break his nose with it. If I'd thought for even a second that might humble him a little, I might have tried it. "You're impossible."

"Impossibly handsome, maybe." I could hear the smirk in his voice without looking.

I rolled my eyes. Like I said—ridiculous.

His antics weren't a recent development, though. Phillip had been antagonizing me this way for years, baiting me for any response he could possibly get. I thought he honestly just liked getting me riled up and he'd discovered that flirting with me shamelessly was an easy way to do it.

This game of his had started when I'd turned thirteen. I'd grown from my own awkward childhood body into adolescence and finally become a figure of interest for young men in the court. Hooray for puberty, I suppose. Most girls would have been delighted to suddenly be regarded as beautiful. I was cautiously intimidated by those kinds of compliments, however, especially from the boys my age.

I wasn't sure how many of them actually saw *me*—or were just looking for an easy leverage point to get to the crown. Fortunately, my father, King Felix Farrow of Maldobar, was protective. He wouldn't allow most of the suitors who wanted to spend time with me to come anywhere near our family. I was grateful for that. It felt like I might be safe to make some of my own life choices, after all.

And then Phillip began professing his undying love for me.

He was older, the son of a longtime family friend, and I'd known him literally since birth. He and Aubren, my older brother, had been partners in crime for as long as I could remember. We'd all played together as children. He was already inside my father's barrier of family trust, so when he started to show interest in me, everyone just seemed amused by it. Perhaps they assumed we would be married eventually, anyway.

I found it completely annoying and humiliating—like he was making a joke out of me.

Now, more than ten years later, nothing had changed in that department. Phillip was one of the only men in my father's court that still didn't seem thrown by my determination to follow what I knew to be my destiny and become a dragonrider. It wasn't a womanly thing to do—hefting swords, smiting enemies, riding in a dragon's saddle. At least it wasn't in Maldobar. I was undeniably good at it, though, and that only seemed to make my father even more irate. He'd been staunchly against it from the very beginning. But when my dragon, Phevos, had chosen me—that had left no room for anyone's objection, not even the king's.

I was born to be a dragonrider—in body, in heart, and now in destiny.

"Would you go for a walk with me?" Phillip asked suddenly.

I lowered my book so I could glare at him. "Why?"

He put on one of his rare, businesslike frowns. If he'd known I found that look slightly less annoying than any of his other expressions, he might have used it more often.

Of course, I would die before I ever told him that.

"I'm having the catacombs and undercrofts below city opened for anyone who wants to begin moving there in the event of another attack. I've encouraged those with young children, or any who might have difficulty moving quickly, to depart now. I've also opened two of the escape tunnels for anyone who may want to escape to the mountain passes. We know those paths are clear of Tibran forces—so far. They should be safe," he explained. "Like you said, we have to accept the reality that the Tibrans are going to come back. I'd like to go see how everything's progressing."

I arched a brow. "That's so ... *responsible* of you."

His brow puckered with a wounded expression. "I can do my job, you know. My love for you hasn't blinded me from all the things your father expects of me as duke. I mean to take care of the people here as best I can."

"And that's the only reason? Worry for their welfare?"

Phillip made a snorting sound, as one side of his mouth curled up into a half smirk. "That and the remote chance you'll hold on to my arm or hand while we walk."

I closed the book and narrowed my eyes. "Don't count on it."

※

I TOLD MYSELF THIS HAD ABSOLUTELY NOTHING TO DO WITH PHILLIP—I needed to get out of that stone fortress for a little while, breathe the free air, and think about the battle plan that was taking shape in my brain. So as soon as we stepped outside the front doors of the keep, I took a deep breath. The smell of smoke was still thick on the wind. The courtyard before us was crowded with soldiers working to refortify the walls, bolster the gates, and arm the catapults that had been lashed onto the ramparts.

We weren't going to win this fight. I knew that. One look at the somber, focused frown on Phillip's face and I suspected he was aware of that fact as well. Our forces had been all but devastated by the first Tibran attack. Barrowton had endured, but that was only because of Reigh.

Aubren had been right about him—he was a dangerous boy. Useful, maybe but dangerous nonetheless. He'd killed almost as many of our own troops as he had Tibrans with his demon magic. Having him in our midst was a risk.

I had no illusions of glorious victory here. I only had three riders, besides myself, to work with. They were good men and seasoned riders. But we were still going to lose, so the only question was how.

Phillip was right to invite his people to begin evacuating and taking safety measures now. The smart ones would accept and be long gone by the time the hammer fell. For the rest of us, who had no choice but to stay and fight it out to the bitter end, things looked grim.

I chewed on my bottom lip as I walked beside him, down the steps and through the gates, into the city beyond. Here, the cobblestone streets sloped steeply downward. Barrowton had been designed to be the stronghold of the north, a place of safety and refuge, and a great amount of care had gone into the design. The city itself sat on a manmade, cone-shaped hill with the keep at the very top. It was difficult for an invading enemy to move uphill, and it gave us a slight advantage on all sides. Archers could rain down arrows from any of the three sets of high stone walls that encompassed the city like rings around a bull's eye.

"The outer wall was severely damaged during the last attack," Phillip said as he stopped in the center of an intersection. Around us, four streets came to a large square where a fountain stood in the very center. "My men are doing their best to repair the damage, but I think it's safe to say that we will have to fall back behind the second wall next time. I've asked them to focus their efforts on making sure the second and third walls hold for as long as possible."

I nodded. Walking slowly around the huge fountain, my eyes were involuntarily drawn up to the all-too-familiar image of Jaevid Broadfeather engraved into the granite, high upon a pedestal. His statue stood tall and proud, dressed in dragonrider armor and holding a scimitar against his breastplate as he gazed toward the north—toward Luntharda. The lengths of his cloak had been cut to look as though they were blowing in the wind, and the detail on his face was so lifelike it was nearly haunting.

"Still hoping for him to return?" Phillip asked suddenly. He'd snuck up behind me again.

I quickly looked away. "No."

"He insists he's given up, but I think Aubren still believes Jaevid will come back."

"He's always believed it, even when we were little. That's just who he is—a believer." A bittersweet smile crept over my lips. I looked up at Jaevid's stony face again and tried desperately not to hope. "My father told us stories about him every night. He made it all seem so real."

Phillip sighed. He was standing right next to me, his arms crossed and those raven-black curls blowing around his face. His annoyingly perfect brows were furrowed ever so slightly.

"What about you? Do you believe?" I asked quietly.

He flicked me a look with those electric green eyes. It might have made any other girl swoon when he grinned like that. "I believe the universe always balances itself out. Every right, every wrong, in the end it will all even out. We may not live to see it happen. But it will."

"So Reigh appearing instead of Jaevid is the universe balancing itself out?" I snorted and turned to continue walking down the sidewalk.

He shrugged as he fell in step beside me. "Maybe so."

I wasn't so sure I agreed. I still didn't know what to make of Reigh. My brother had dredged him up from the depths of the jungle when he'd gone on that desperate and futile errand to try to get help from the Gray elves. I knew they wouldn't help us—not that I blamed them. Ours was becoming more of a lost cause every day.

Still, finding Reigh had seemed like it might be a brush of fate. He was a human teenager who had apparently been raised with the Gray elves since infancy. Odd? Yes. I'd never heard of such a thing. Not that Gray elves were incapable of that kind of compassion, but the one who had raised him was a man I knew well from my own childhood. Kiran had been an ambassador in my father's court for years. He'd taught me to fight, to meditate, and to appreciate the value of nature's balance. But Kiran taking in an orphaned infant was ... shocking. He'd never been married, as far as I knew. I couldn't even picture him changing diapers and handling a baby—especially on his own.

Perhaps that was why Reigh was strange, too. That boy couldn't even speak the human tongue without an elven accent. That and his wild red hair, cute childlike face, and somewhat cocky demeanor all hid a powerful darkness I'd now witnessed lurking inside of him. Aubren had brought him here hoping he would fight for us, but you only had to gaze out beyond Barrowton's outermost wall to see exactly what kind of devastation that boy was capable of.

I didn't dare say it, many might not agree, but to me his mysterious disappearance seemed like a blessing in disguise. That is, so long as he didn't show up fighting for the Tibrans. If that happened—Gods and Fates—I shuddered to think of what that would mean for us.

When at last we reached the outermost wall, Phillip led the way up into one of the turrets, so we could stroll along the high ramparts, examining the work being done to repair it. Outside, beyond the wall, was a scene of utter desolation beyond words. That was Reigh's handiwork. The smell of the smoke was intense, tinged with the sharp flavor of smoldering dragon venom and singed flesh. It made my eyes water.

Phillip covered his nose and mouth with his hand. He didn't look out across the battlefield for long, and he gagged as his face went a bit pale. He wasn't used to these things. He'd never seen death like this.

Until recently, I hadn't either. Now I was beginning to learn that this sight—endless burning fields of death and despair—was what the Tibrans always left in their wake. And if they had their way, all Maldobar would be this way.

I couldn't allow that to happen.

CHAPTER TWO

"You're suggesting that we just leave you behind?" Aubren had gone stiff. Sitting across from me at the dinner table, I could see an angry little vein standing out against his forehead.

"I'm suggesting that the only chance the citizens who still remained in the city have of safely making it to the mountain passes is if the dragonriders hold the Tibrans back and then destroy the tunnels on this end, so they cannot pursue you," I replied. "That includes me."

My brother's mouth scrunched up and his nose wrinkled. "I won't do that. I won't just run away while you and your men stay here and—"

"This is what we are meant for, Aubren," I snapped. "And we will do our job with pride. It is an honor to die protecting the people of Maldobar."

Phillip interrupted. "Guys, please, let's take this down a notch. I've known you both long enough to know that your arguing will never solve anything. You're like two angry cats in a bag." He cleared his throat and took a moment to rub his hand across his forehead. "Based on what we saw today, I think Jenna and I can agree that a good number of Barrowton's citizens have taken my advice and are already either evacuating or taking refuge in the catacombs under the city. I'll issue a decree in the morning warning those who remain to be ready to fall back behind the third wall at the sound of the warning horns. We'll save as many as we can. But should the third wall fall, this keep will be the only safe place left. We'll have to evacuate as well."

I poked nervously at the prongs on my fork. "The dragonriders and I will hold the Tibrans off for as long as we can," I promised.

"You're sure that's the only way?" Phillip studied me carefully.

"Yes. I've been over the plans a hundred times. It's the only way to be sure the Tibrans can't follow you. You'll be able to make it to the mountains."

Aubren slammed a fist down on the table, rattling the china. "I will *not* go without you, Jenna. What will I tell our father?"

"Tell him that if he'd spared even a dozen of the riders guarding Halfax, maybe we would have stood a chance." The words tasted bitter on my lips, and I couldn't keep my voice from sounding punishing.

It was too much. I didn't like having them both staring me down that way. Without ever touching the food on my plate, I stood up and left the dining hall.

I waited until I was behind the closed doors of my private chambers to let out a ragged breath. It was almost impossible to keep the emotions from surfacing. All the uncertainty, the fear, the dread, and the burning resentment of my father—all of it ate away at my insides. I didn't understand how he could just stand by and allow the Tibrans to burn city after city without sending any of his forces to help us. He had almost every dragonrider in Maldobar guarding Halfax, the royal city. Meanwhile, his people burned. Soon, his children would burn, too.

My face flushed, and my hands were sweaty. I was terrified. I leaned against the door for a moment until I could catch my breath. Breathe—I just had to breathe.

Wandering farther into the room Phillip had lent me, I rang for a servant to draw a bath. I waited until the servant had finished adding in scented salts and oils and departed before I undressed, though. I wasn't fond of this part. To me, it seemed most women were proud of their bodies. It was their social weapon, something they could use to manipulate and coerce.

My body wasn't like that. At least, not anymore. Perhaps it could have been, but I'd chosen a different path—a path riddled with scars.

I tried not to look at my reflection in the mirror on the wall as I closed the bathroom door and began to undress. I unlaced the sides of my leather jerkin and pulled it over my head, slipped out of my tunic, and stepped out of my boots and pants. Out of the corner of my eye, I saw the edge of the jagged, gnarled, freshly-made scar that zigzagged down the curve of my back. It went from the back of my shoulder all the way down to my hips. *Gruesome* hardly did it justice. Just the sight of it made my heart wrench. No man—not even Phillip—would be able to look at that without cringing. It wasn't beautiful.

Pair it with the rest of me, which was flecked with nicks, cuts, and scrapes, and you weren't left with someone whose body would be alluring to most men. Not the noble, wife-seeking sort, anyway. My face and neck were protected well by my armor, so they were still mostly unmarked. But my hands weren't soft or slender. They'd been hardened by the hilt of a blade, and I knew I could trust their strength, even if I couldn't trust anything else.

Sinking into the fragrant, steaming waters of the bath, I sat back to let the warmth relax my muscles. It took a long time to wash and detangle my hair.

Despite having chosen what was deemed in my kingdom as a "man's profession," I still preferred to keep it long. Just because I'd elected to wear a dragonrider's gauntlets instead of lace gloves didn't mean I didn't enjoy some more feminine habits—fixing my hair being one of them.

Suddenly, someone was knocking on the bathroom door.

I jerked upright and grabbed the closest towel to cover myself. "Who's there?"

"Jenna?" Phillip's voice was muffled by the door.

I deflated. "Go away!"

"Are you all right?"

"I was until you interrupted," I yelled back.

"Maybe I should just come in and make sure ... "

"Gods and Fates, Phillip, if you open that door, I swear I will break your neck."

He was quiet for a moment, and I braced myself in case he really was *that* stupid.

"Seriously, though." His voice had become quieter. "Are you all right?"

I swallowed hard against the thick knot of emotion in my throat. "I'm fine." My voice cracked a bit.

"Really? 'Cause that would be truly astounding if it were true. No one else here is fine right now, Jenna. We're all staring death in the face."

Slowly, I put the towel down and sank back into the tub. I let the hot water rise all the way to my chin. "You don't understand because you're not a soldier. I'm a dragonrider. I can't be afraid of death."

He chuckled. "You're also human. Anyone with a pulse would be afraid—soldier or not."

I watched some of my golden hair swirl in the water around me. For a brief, fleeting moment of pure insanity, I entertained the idea of letting him come in.

What? Was I losing my mind?

"I just don't want you to think you have to do this alone," Phillip said. "I may not be a soldier, but I hope you know I'm your friend. I'm here if you want to, you know, talk."

I laughed out loud. I couldn't help it. "Are you asking me to have a real, adult conversation about feelings with you? I'm not sure you're qualified for that."

"You know I do mean it, right?" His tone was suddenly serious. I didn't like it.

"What?"

"I really do love you, Jenna."

Suddenly, the atmosphere was intensely awkward. It made me wince, and I was thankful he couldn't see it. Why did he always say things like that? What was *I* supposed to say? I ... he ... *argh!*

"Go away, Phillip." My tone lacked the authority and determination I'd been hoping for.

A few more uncomfortable seconds passed. Then, at last, I heard him mutter softly as his footsteps retreated from the door. "As you wish."

The silence that came after wasn't as comforting as it had been before.

A SOUND WOKE ME IN THE DARK. IT WAS THE EERIE, HIGH-PITCHED WAILING warning sirens.

Panic shot through my body.

I bolted upright in bed and ran to the window, throwing back the heavy drapes to stare into the horror of the night. From where the keep stood high upon the crest of that cone-shaped hill, I could see down across the city, beyond the walls. They were here.

The Tibrans had returned.

I could see them approaching like an encroaching ocean of blazing torches. They were coming at us from every side, stepping over the ashes of our dead. I could hear the pulse of their war drums. My heartbeat raced in that same frantic rhythm.

I took a deep breath.

It took me three minutes to dress for battle. I'd done it so many times now I could manage it without having to concentrate. As I tied my hair up into a ponytail, I took a few fleeting seconds to stare at my reflection. There were dusky circles under my eyes. I'd lost weight because of the stress, so my cheeks looked sharper. Somehow, it made me look vulnerable despite the dragonrider armor I had buckled against my body.

I scowled, grabbed an untouched pot of lip rouge from the vanity, and drew war lines under my eyes, on my chin, and across my forehead.

Snatching my royal blue cloak off the bedpost, I slung it around my shoulders so that the fur collar was pulled around my neck. I buckled my favorite weapons —a pair of short leaf-shaped blades that Kiran had taught me to use when I was a child—around my hips and grabbed my helmet.

My three remaining dragonrider companions waited for me, already outfitted and ready to go, right outside my bedroom door. Well, most of them. Lieutenant Eirik Lachlan was still buckling his sword belt and yawning. Eirik had been my friend ever since we'd begun our training as fledgling dragonriders together. We were the same age, and he had taken a liking to me after I'd dislocated his shoulder during our first sparring match.

He was brawny, sturdy, and came from a long line of proud dragonriders. I enjoyed his crude, brutal honesty almost as much as he enjoyed ale. He had softer, almost boyish, features, which the tavern girls and barmaids seemed to appreciate rather enthusiastically. His brown hair was cut somewhat short on the sides, but a bit longer on top so that he could style it just so. And while he insisted it was meant to make his helmet fit more comfortably—we all knew otherwise. He took a little *too* much time at the mirror, combing it and arranging it just so for that style to be strictly utilitarian.

Eirik was the wing end to a man everyone called Haldor, although I'd heard rumors that wasn't his real name. It didn't matter much to us what he called himself—he was a brilliant archer and could speak three or four languages. He'd graduated from the dragonrider academy a class ahead of ours, and while I'd never dared say a word about it, I found him handsome.

His skin was a much darker shade of olive brown than I was used to seeing because his mother had come from one of the eastern desert kingdoms. The Gray elves had the same sort of warm golden hue to their complexion, although not quite so dark as his. Haldor's hair was as fine as silk, jet black, and his eyes were a peculiar light amber brown that almost seemed gold in the right light.

His deep voice rang with a faint touch of the same accent I'd heard from his mother once. She'd dazzled the court at one of the officer's balls, dressed in a brightly-colored gown that fit to the curves of her body like a silk glove. It reminded me a bit of how the Gray elves dressed, with such vivid colors and exposed skin, but Haldor's mother had also adorned her eyes, cheeks, and hands in detailed designs drawn with black kohl. There were tiny gemstones glued along the arches of her brows, across her forehead, and on each finger. It kept the men of court thoroughly distracted throughout the night—which seemed to embarrass Haldor. He got ribbed about it in the barracks for months.

The last of our group was Calem. He had been my wing end for some time now, and while he was the youngest and rarely said a word, he was perhaps the most brutal fighter among us. I'd never seen anyone best him in sparring. He had a deceptively pretty, almost angelic face—which I'd heard had caused him to be the victim of relentless teasing when he'd been a student at the academy. He was lean in build and his straight hair was the color of corn silk. I'd honestly have never seen him smile once, but he seemed set on staying at my side as long as I allowed him to—which I didn't mind, considering how well he fought and flew. He tended to lurk at my back like a tall, silent specter and rarely said a word unless someone asked him a direct question.

We were an odd bunch of misfits. I suppose when they had decided to join me in exile, rather than staying behind in Halfax with the rest of the dragonriders to defend the city, my father probably hadn't considered it much of a loss. But I trusted every one of these men with my life, and I knew they held me in the same regard. They didn't care that I was a woman, or a princess, or anything other than a capable dragonrider.

As I stepped out of my chambers and closed the door, I glanced at their faces. We'd already lost one of our company in the last battle. No one had spoken about him yet. We would, eventually, drink to his honor. Not yet, though. There was still work to be done.

"So? Everyone ready to die?" Eirik chuckled hoarsely. He was finally finished getting dressed.

Haldor rolled his eyes.

Calem just stood there, staring into the distance like he was lost in his own private world of thought. It was terrifying how he could go from doing that to cutting someone's head off in about two seconds.

I smirked back at them. My whole body relaxed, and all my apprehensions dissolved. Just knowing they were there, watching my back and fighting by my side, gave me all the confidence I needed.

I stuck my helmet under my arm and turned to lead the way, striding down the halls of the keep. "Absolutely. Let's go kill some Tibrans."

CHAPTER THREE

We split off once we reached the lowest level of the keep, where our dragons were housed right next to the launching contraption that would fire us, one by one, into the air like a giant slingshot. I'd balked at the idea when I'd first seen the launcher. I didn't like the idea of my dragon and me being hurled into the air like a stone from a slingshot. Once I saw the machine in action, though, I had to admit that it was effective. It had the added benefit of catching our enemy off guard.

Well, last time, anyway. Now they'd likely be expecting it.

Phevos raised his head as I came into his stall and he greeted me with anxious chirping. I watched my dragon unfurl himself from the far corner where he'd been crouched, most likely waiting for me to appear. Even down in the bunker beneath the keep, you could hear the warning sirens wailing outside and the distant sound of catapults firing. Battle sounds weren't unfamiliar for either of us. He knew I would be coming.

I rubbed the plated scales on his head as I walked around to check his saddle. I went over every buckle and strap quickly, making sure nothing had been damaged or knocked out of place. Normally, I didn't leave him in it any longer than necessary. At eighteen years old, he was a young dragon, and the weight of it still made him anxious. But I hadn't bothered removing it after the last battle because I'd known full well we would be riding back into combat very soon.

"Hello, handsome," I crooned as he pushed his big purple snout against my side. His strong, scaly body was a gorgeous, deep eggplant purple color dappled with vivid, teal-green stripes. The large black horns on his head were curved like those on a ram, and he had smaller jagged black spines running down his spine all the way to the tip of his tail. The leathery membranes of his wings were nearly black as well, and there was more of that vibrant teal color flecking his legs, as though he'd accidentally stepped in paint. He had big, intelligent, golden eyes that tracked me constantly as I moved around him, buckling my bag crammed full of emergency supplies into place on the back of his saddle.

Phevos snorted in agreement, blasting my face with moist, smelly dragon breath as he tried licking my cheek. I smiled and grabbed a hold of one of his ears, giving it a playful tug. "Such a big, beautiful boy. What did I ever do to deserve you, hmm?

"Phillip would be jealous."

I glared over my shoulder to see my older brother, Aubren, standing in the doorway of my stall. Quickly, I turned my back, so he wouldn't see me blushing with embarrassment. "Phillip is a moron."

"I won't disagree with you there," he replied. His tone carried a heavy tension, as though there was something else he'd come here to say—something much more serious.

"Come to beg me to stay behind?" I muttered as I fidgeted with my saddle straps.

Suddenly, a warm hand fell over mine and held it tightly against the side of my dragon. Aubren was standing right beside me, his presence far more invasive than ever before. It wasn't like him to be so aggressive. Something really was wrong.

"Jenna, please be careful," he said quietly, his tone strange.

I froze, waiting for him to continue.

"I won't ask you not to go. I know you believe you must. But please, Jenna, please don't let this be the last time I see you. Sometimes it feels like you're all the family I have left in the world."

My stomach twisted into knots. I stared at his hand, much larger and broader than mine. I bit down hard because, honestly, I felt the same way. Our mother had passed away while laboring to birth a stillborn child. After, our father had grown distant. Even Kiran had left us by then. So Aubren and I had been forced to cling to one another. We didn't have anyone else.

His hand slipped away from mine. I felt his presence retreat.

When I dared to turn around, I found him hesitating in the doorway of the stall, his broad back to me and his head bowed slightly like he might be looking down at the tops of his boots. "I'm not evacuating," he said quietly.

I swallowed hard.

"I'm the only one fit to lead the infantrymen who will be defending this city. So, I intend to stay with them for as long as possible. As long as I'm alive, I will see to it that every last man, woman, and child has an opportunity to evacuate into the mountain passes."

My body felt strangely cold, even under all my armor.

Aubren looked back at me, flashing a brief, thin smile that had died long before it ever touched his eyes. "I am proud of you, my sister. Perhaps I've never done a very good job of showing it. But of the two of us, you have always been far braver. I am confident you will make a fine queen."

"That's not—"

He cut me off with a wave of his hand before I could finish. "There was something else I came here to tell you in case I don't have the opportunity to tell you later. I think you need to know."

I watched his expression cloud over with a darkness I didn't understand. "What? What is it?"

"The boy I brought back from Luntharda. Reigh—I believe he might be our brother. I'm not sure how, but I think Kiran was up to something. I didn't want to tell you this until I had some real evidence, but now we're out of time."

I struggled with what to do with that information. That boy was my little brother? How could that be possible? Had my father had a love affair? When? With who?

I guess Aubren could read my puzzled, frustrated expressions more easily than I'd anticipated. He smiled, chuckled, and waved his hand again like it didn't matter. I guess now, with the city of Barrowton about to be overrun, it really didn't.

"Take care of yourself, Jenna," he said softly. "If not in this lifetime, I'll see you again on the other side."

THAT WASN'T HOW I'D WANTED TO LEAVE THINGS WITH AUBREN. I SHOULD have said something—anything—to let him know I loved him. Gods and Fates, I loved that idiot more than anything.

But the moment was gone and so was he.

The wind howled past my helmet as Phevos and I were hurled into the sky by the launcher. With his powerful hind legs curled, my dragon waited until the launcher reached the very end of the tunnel to spring forward with the momentum of the wooden sleigh that had flung us out into the air. He spread his mighty wings wide, catching the wind and climbing steeply into the sky.

I moved with him, gripping the handles of my saddle and flexing my legs to lean into his speed. I could feel every one of his powerful muscles working around me, his strong wing arms pumping, his sides swelling with deep breaths, and his tail whipping to counterbalance the added weight of me and the saddle.

Overhead, I saw Haldor and Eirik already aligning to begin their first pass. Our plan was simple—we were going to give the Tibrans hell as they approached the city and then keep them pinned between the second and third wall for as long as possible. With so few of us in number, there wasn't much more we could do. Our last act, of course, would be to destroy the entrance to the evacuation tunnels so that the Tibrans couldn't pursue any of the fleeing citizens into the mountains. Until that time came, we had to stall our enemy. Every minute gave someone else a chance to get to safety.

I steered Phevos into a steep turn, looking back as the launcher spat out the last of our company. Calem sat astride his white and silver dragon, a lithe female he called Perish. It was a fitting name. She was known for being extremely high-spirited and temperamental, and she'd killed the last two riders who had tried to own her. Calem's family had gotten her at a discounted price, both because of that nasty reputation and the fact that her near-albino coloring was less than desirable for most dragonriders. It made her very easy to spot.

Perish swooped into formation behind me like a sterling comet, her scarlet eyes glittering, watching us for cues.

I gave Calem a series of hand signals, communicating to him what we were about to do. He gave me a thumbs-up in reply. Time to go.

Below us, the battle was already underway. Maldobarian soldiers on the ramparts fired catapults into the oncoming hoard of Tibran warriors. They'd brought a force larger than I could have imagined in my wildest nightmare. They came like a flood, thousands upon thousands of soldiers carrying bronze shields and pikes. Within minutes they would be at the outermost wall.

I set my jaw and twisted the saddle handles, adding a bit of pressure against Phevos's hide to tell him how to turn and move. He dropped into a steep, blitzing dive. We made a low pass, moving in perfect unison with Calem and Perish, and I gave both handles an inward twist. Immediately, I felt Phevos's sides swell as he took in a deep breath. As soon as we were within range, he opened his mouth and poured out a shower of burning venom upon the first two ranks of Tibran soldiers.

Behind us, I heard Perish doing the same. The sound of the roaring flames from their burning venom mingled with the roar of battle. The wailing sirens. The snap and boom of catapult fire. The cries of men as they burned. The clatter of sword and shield. The pulse of war drums.

This was a dark symphony I knew all too well.

Calem and I made pass after pass, scorching the Tibran ranks until their numbers overwhelmed ours. We couldn't douse them fast enough to stop their progression. They reached the first wall and broke upon it like waves upon a rocky shore. But as Phillip had warned, that outermost wall had taken a real beating in the last battle. The gates were compromised, and they fell quickly to the brunt force of the Tibran army.

Right on cue, Haldor and Eirik fell into formation beside Calem and me. They gave me the signals, gesturing that they were ready. It was time to hold the boundary.

I gave them all a dragonrider salute—clasping my hand into a fist and holding my arm across my chest.

Every one of them saluted back.

Then, as one, we spiraled downward to begin our attack.

Out of the corner of my eye, I saw Haldor reach back and pull his bow from his saddle sleeve and notch an arrow. Not many dragonriders could wield a bow in flight and hit anything with it. He was a crack-shot, though. He rose, standing in the boot-sheaths that held his legs to the saddle, and began firing one shot after another. He picked off a dozen Tibran cavalrymen as they rode in through the gate on ironclad horses.

It was hard not to be impressed.

We dropped in low, flying swift figure-eight patterns around the gate where the bulk of the Tibran soldiers were forced into a bottleneck. We set them ablaze, and they fired volley after volley of projectiles in an attempt stop us. They flung clay orbs filled with dragon venom from slingshot-like contraptions. They also had a rolling, horse-drawn machine that could fire spears like arrows. All of this we had seen before. We knew how to dodge, how to pitch our flight patterns so that we were more difficult to hit.

But when *she* appeared—it was something none of us had ever seen before.

CHAPTER FOUR

Through the licking flames that engulfed the gateway of the outermost wall, the silhouette of a monstrous beast appeared. I couldn't tell what it was until it lumbered through the opening, bearing a rider on its back. It looked like a reptile, maybe some distant cousin to our dragons, but it had no wings. Rather, it crawled along on thick, muscular legs and had a long tail that was tipped with a bony, club-shaped growth. The creature was dragging iron chains that were bolted through the flesh of its forelegs. The chains were handled like reins by the rider, who stood on a raised platform fixed to the creature's back. It was made from a mixture of twisted metal and something white that I couldn't identify. When we made another pass, however, I saw it much more clearly.

They were bones. That saddle, platform, or whatever they called it had been crafted from bleached skulls and bones bolted together.

I saw the rider look up at us with a delighted sneer from the back of her monster. I had seen her in combat before—one of the leaders of the Tibran Empire.

They called her Hilleddi.

The creature she rode was much larger than our dragons, more than double in size. It lumbered clumsily, making its way toward the second gateway. The form of the monster's head, with no eyes and a dome-shaped protrusion of bone that looked like it was made for bashing, gave me an idea of what was in store for us. That creature was a living battering ram.

I couldn't resist a snarl.

Phevos and I dove in, ready to blast her with dragon flame. Calem and Perish were on our tail, and I could see Eirik and Haldor already taking up a defensive position around the second gateway. We surged toward her, our dragons flying side by side. They breathed in at the same moment, unleashing an inferno upon Hilleddi and her pet.

Suddenly, an explosion rocked the air in front of us. It sent us flipping end over end through the air. Phevos struggled to regain control, trying to twist himself in midair to take the brunt of the blow as we slammed against the ground.

A chaos of rubble and scales blurred my vision. My ears rang. My body ached and tingled. I was dazed—unsure if I was alive, dead, or somewhere in between.

Then Phevos stirred, starting to get up. He was all right—just stunned. That made two of us.

I looked up hazily through the eye slit in my helmet to see Hilleddi and her monster prowling straight for us. They were less than two hundred yards away. We didn't have much time.

"Get up," I coaxed Phevos as he shook himself and snapped his jaws angrily. "We have to get off the ground!"

I still didn't understand what had happened. What was that explosion? Where had it come from?

Then I saw Eirik and Haldor swoop in to our defense. They made a swift pass between Hilleddi and me, and their dragons spat two plumes of burning venom at the monster she rode. An instant before the flames could touch them, her monster opened its massive maw and returned fire with something—a ball of wild energy that sizzled and snapped like electricity. It hovered, suspended in the air for a fleeting second until the flames touched it.

Then it exploded with bone-rattling force.

I braced against the shockwave is it rolled over us, hunkering down against Phevos's back. When the dust began to settle, I squinted to find my dragonrider brothers.

To my right, Calem and Perish were getting up, already flaring for takeoff. They both looked okay. On my left, Haldor and his mount were shaking off the impact and beginning to stand as well. But Eirik—I didn't see him anywhere.

I looked back.

As the dust cleared, I spotted him. Eirik's dragon had been thrown farther than the rest of us. He must have taken the full force of that creature's attack. I could tell just by how it was lying that it was already dead. Its wings were splayed out and its head twisted around at an awkward angle. Then I noticed that it was lying on its back—saddle down.

And I couldn't see Eirik anywhere. That meant ... he hadn't gotten out of the saddle before impact. He was pinned underneath with over a thousand pounds of dragon crushing down on him.

A scream of rage and panic tore out of my chest.

Haldor must have heard me, even over the roar of combat. He kicked out of his saddle and began sprinting the distance to where Eirik's dragon lay. Any other time, that would have been a stupid thing to do, but I knew what he was planning, and I wasn't about to let him try to do it alone.

I unbuckled myself quickly and sprang out of my saddle. Phevos nipped at my shoulder, growling disapprovingly. I wasn't supposed to leave him in the heat of battle like this. Spinning around, I grabbed his scaly snout and pressed my lips against his nose. "Hold them off as long as you can!"

It was hard to say just how much of what I said he understood. But our bond was strong, and he was no mere dumb animal. When I turned to run, I heard Phevos take off. He let out a thundering cry that made Haldor's dragon rise to join him. I watched over my shoulder for a moment as our dragons zoomed toward Hilleddi and that awful creature. This time, however, they didn't spit flame. They attacked it outright, going in with their claws and fangs bared.

I dove into a sprint toward where Haldor was already trying to roll the dead dragon over. He shouted as he strained, stepping back and throwing off his helmet in frustration. I skidded to a halt beside him and began to help.

Together, we fought and struggled. My fingers slipped, even with the resin-coated palms of the riding gauntlets helping me get a firmer grip. My back creaked. I let out a string of curses until—at last—I could feel the weight of the dragon's body beginning to shift.

"L—nnngh—mmph!!" A muffled cry came from under the dead beast.

It was Eirik. He was still alive.

Hearing his call for help gave me a new rush of adrenaline. I pulled up even harder, and Haldor joined in the effort. Little by little, we managed to roll the dragon's limp body over. Suddenly, a hand shot out from under it. Without a second of hesitation, I grabbed it and began to pull while Haldor strained to keep the dragon's weight off him. He wasn't going to be able to keep it up for more than a few seconds on his own, so I was ruthless as I dragged Eirik out of the way.

I had just gotten his legs free when Haldor's strength finally gave out. He dropped the beast with a yelp and a thud—but it was all right. Eirik was free.

The three of us lay in the dirt for a moment, panting and shaking off the astonishment of what had just happened.

Then I heard Haldor rasp, "We've got to keep moving."

He was right. Behind us, our dragons were still brawling with Hilleddi's monster like two cats fighting a much bigger dog. They were doing a good job of keeping her occupied—for now.

"Can you stand?" I asked Eirik.

"C-Can't f-feel my l-leg," he stammered from under his helmet. I bent down to slip it off his head. Underneath, his face looked all right. There were no obvious head injuries. Even so, his pupils were dilated, and his skin looked ashen. His breathing was rapid and shallow. He was in shock.

Looking down, I could see that his armor was probably the only reason he was still alive. His breastplate, pauldrons, and thick belt had prevented him from being mashed flat by his dragon's dead weight. But one of his legs had been crushed even inside his riding greaves and boots. It was badly broken. He wouldn't be able to walk, much less ride.

"I-Is it bad?" he wheezed.

I bit down hard. "No worse than usual."

"Y-You're a t-terrible liar." He chuckled weakly. His expression became strangely distant, and he looked over to Haldor. "Y-You gotta l-leave me here. G-Get out while y-you can."

Haldor's expression sharpened. He opened his mouth like he was going to protest. Before he could get a word out, the ground shuddered beneath us. Perish landed only a few yards away, her white wings spread and her mouth open as she hissed.

Load him up. I'll get him out. Calem gestured to us using our code of hand signals.

We didn't stop to ask questions. Haldor and I got Eirik onto his one good foot and helped him limp over to Perish's side. He swooned and sagged between us, barely conscious as we hauled him up into the saddle in front of Calem.

I patted his cheek and smiled. "Don't you dare die on us now, you hear? Remember, war heroes who are wounded in battle are rewarded with a kiss from the queen when they return. Since there is no queen, I guess you'll have to make do with me."

I saw a bit of lively color rush back into his cheeks. "C-Careful. I'll hold y-you to that."

Haldor and I backed away as Perish flared for takeoff. She shot skyward, streaking away and disappearing over the second wall. I glanced sideways to my last remaining dragonrider brother.

He was already fitting an arrow into his bowstring. "Shall we, then?"

I drew my two blades from the sheaths at my waist and nodded. "We shall."

WE HELD THE LINE AS LONG AS WE COULD—LONG ENOUGH TO GIVE OUR friends time to evacuate. But two dragonriders against Hilleddi's monster and all the forces of the Tibran Empire wasn't a fair match.

Fighting back to back, Haldor and I cut through ranks of Tibrans. Their bronze shields were broad and thick, their short swords were sharp and fast, but we had spent years in training for a moment just like this. They came at us from every side, and nearby I could always hear the bellowing roars and snarls of our dragons locked in combat with Hilleddi's mount.

Haldor brandished his bow until his quiver was empty. Then he drew his sword and took up one of the shields from a fallen Tibran soldier. His reflexes were lightning fast, and his face was drawn into a feral, blood-spattered snarl.

The bellow of another dragon drew my attention upward where Calem and Perish were wheeling overhead. They were ready to rejoin the fight. It was time to change tactics again.

I reached into my belt and took out a thin, silver whistle. It wasn't unlike a dog whistle, and the sound was so high-pitched, no one else would be able to hear it. As soon I blew into it with repeated short blasts, Phevos answered me. He let out a high-pitched returning call.

"Get ready!" I shouted to Haldor.

The dragons zoomed low over the battlefield, headed straight for us. At the last possible second, I sheathed both my blades. Haldor ran up next to me and we both jumped skyward, hands outstretched. I may or may not have used a few dead Tibran soldiers as a springboard, too. They didn't seem to mind.

Phevos and Haldor's dragon snapped their wings in tightly and rolled over, spinning in the air like two scaly arrows. They turned so that their saddles faced down. We jumped.

For one breathless moment, I was hanging in the air, reaching with all my might toward the saddle as it passed above me. My palms caught the saddle handles. I clenched my teeth and hung on.

Phevos snatched me off my feet at an incredible speed. But the instant he felt my weight, he rolled back over and spread his wings. Arrows and spears zipped past us. I crammed my feet down into the boot sheaths to anchor myself and gave quick hand signals to Haldor.

Calem and Perish dropped in beside us, wanting an injury report. I signaled back that we were fine. No injuries—so far.

Eirik? I asked with my gestures.

Evacuating with the civilians. He'll be okay, Calem replied.

That was a relief. I could think straight again when I cut my gaze back down to the battle below. Hilleddi was making steam straight for the second gateway on the back of that ugly beast. Behind her, the Tibran forces were rallying again. Soldiers were pouring through the gateway by the hundreds. They had brought along more of their war machines, catapults that flung even larger versions of those clay orbs filled with dragon venom.

This was going to be ugly.

So far, they hadn't met with much reprisal except from us. That was part of the plan. I'd advised Aubren to use what remained of his infantrymen wisely. We needed to hold the second and third wall. They were the priority. What we were doing now was just buying them as much time as possible to prepare.

I quickly relayed a new strategy to my two remaining dragonrider brothers. They signaled they understood and immediately wheeled away in unison to fall back to where the soldiers were still bottlenecked coming through the outermost gate. They continued pouring their venom over the heads of the Tibran soldiers, slowing the progress and giving our comrades as much time as possible.

Phevos and I, on the other hand, streaked straight for the second gateway. We made a graceful landing at one of the two large turrets overlooking the gate far below.

One of the infantrymen rushed out to greet us, giving me a hasty salute. "Your Highness!"

"They're going to try to beat down the gate," I warned him. "Pull all the men back and send out the cauldrons. We have to bring down that creature at all costs."

"Yes, ma'am!" He gave another swift salute and ran away to carry out my instructions.

I patted Phevos's scaly neck. I could feel him panting. His mouth was gaping open and his fangs dripped with globs of his burning venom. He turned his head so one of his bright golden eyes glanced back at me.

"Ready for this?"

He blasted a furious snort through his nostrils, slicked his ears back, and licked his jaws. I took that as a "yes."

CHAPTER FIVE

The Tibrans were inside the city now. They filled the streets with the roar of combat and the throbbing beat of war drums. I could only pray that all the citizens of Barrowton who had been living between the second and third wall had chosen to evacuate when they'd had the chance. There was nothing we could do for them now.

Hilleddi's huge, lizard-like beast was lumbering down the main street leading to the second gate, knocking over buildings and crushing the sidewalks under its monstrous weight. Behind her was a torrent of her soldiers, many hauling their war machines, and even more on horseback. They were carrying the red banners of the Tibran Empire into yet another one of our cities.

Just the sight of it made me sick with hate.

Phevos let out a shriek of delight as Haldor and Calem landed their dragons on either side of us, taking up position on the second wall.

Out of venom, they both signaled to me. *You?*

Two blasts left, maybe three, I replied.

Our dragons didn't have an endless supply of their burning venom. They could carry quite a bit at once, but not even close to enough to take on a force like this without reinforcements. It took time, days, for their bodies to generate more.

In an ideal world, there would have been a hundred other riders behind us ready to take up the fight. But there were only three of us now, and Phevos was the only one who still had any venom left to burn. We were going to have to make it count.

From where I was sitting, I could see that Haldor's dragon, a large blue male he called Turq, had taken a few arrows to his scaly hide. He wasn't hurt too badly —but it was still going to slow him down. Perish looked all right, though. She was still hissing and snarling at the soldiers approaching below us like she wanted to have another go at them.

On any other occasion, I might have let her have her wish. But I had one task left for them—the only thing that really mattered.

Fall back to the evacuation tunnel, both of you, I ordered. *Aubren and I can hold them here long enough to make sure that any remaining evacuees have a chance to escape. When the third wall is breached, collapse the tunnel and get out.*

Haldor's eyes narrowed disapprovingly. *What about you?*

After a few uncomfortable moments, I signed a reply. *I won't leave my brother behind. If we make it out alive, we will meet you at Cernheist.*

Now Haldor and Calem had both turned to stare at me. I couldn't see Calem's face because he was still wearing his helmet, and yet I could sense he didn't like this plan any more than Haldor did.

I scowled at them dangerously. Neither of them had ever treated me as though I were fragile before. Now was not the time to start.

Go now, I ordered.

Calem obeyed first, giving his dragoness the signal. She spread her white wings and took off toward the keep.

Haldor was still casting me a hard, unhappy look. His mouth twisted like he was trying to decide if he was going to obey or not. I suppose, of them all, he must have felt most responsible for what might happen to me. He was the only one of us who had been a seasoned rider before this madness had begun. He was the oldest, probably the smartest, and sometimes the most stubborn.

Not today, though.

At last, he clasped his hand over his breastplate in a dragonrider salute and took off to follow Calem.

I watched him soar away. Only when I was sure he was gone did I allow myself to let out a slow, trembling breath of uncertainty. I tried to swallow it, to push down the fear and panic that swelled up inside me. It put a coppery taste in my mouth.

Then I leaned down against Phevos's body, and we surged out into the open sky. Three good blasts of flame, that's all we had left. And I knew exactly what I wanted to do with them.

As we zoomed over the ramparts, I saw the Maldobarian soldiers wheeling four huge cauldrons into place directly over the gateway. The bottoms of the iron pots were still red hot, and the bubbling contents filled the air with a putrid smell.

Far below, Hilleddi's monster had stopped right before the second gateway. It was so massive; I didn't see how the creature was going to be able to fit through it even if they managed to break the iron-plated gate down. Hilleddi snapped the chains hard with her burly arms, yanking hard on one that was connected to its lower jaw. That forced the creature to open its maw and unleash another sizzling, popping ball of energy. It burst in the air and sent out a shockwave that rattled the very foundation of the city.

But the gate held fast.

Hilleddi sneered angrily. She yanked on all three chains this time, and her monster reared back to bash its dome-shaped skull against the gate. The impact made the whole wall shudder. Our infantrymen began to shout orders down their battle lines. Archers took aim and sent down a hailstorm of arrows over the Tibran forces.

One of them struck Hilleddi. She stumbled, losing her footing for an instant as an arrow lodged deep into one of her bare thighs. But rather than crumpling in pain, that hulking beast of a woman just snarled down at it, grabbed the shaft of the arrow, and ripped it out of her leg as though it were nothing.

She snapped the chains again, sending her mount into another frenzy. The lizard bashed its head against the gate again. And again. And again.

On the fourth try, the gate began to give. I could see it faltering, cracking more and more with every strike.

Suddenly, a horn sounded along the wall.

The cauldrons were in place. Our soldiers began cranking the mechanized bases, tilting them over. Four waterfalls of boiling black oil washed over the enemy—the beast, Hilleddi, and the first several lines of Tibran soldiers.

I could hear their screams of pain and terror even from my saddle, high above the battlefield.

"Okay, boy. Light 'em up!" I twisted the saddle handles and sent Phevos into a rolling dive.

We zipped through the air like a spear, flaring only fifty feet above our panicked enemy's lines. Phevos breathed in deeply and let loose a burst of flame. The oil caught. Our enemy burned.

As we retreated skyward, I looked back to see if Hilleddi had survived that attack.

She was looking right back at me, her armor and bare skin spattered with black oil. Our eyes met through the chaos, and I saw her mouth curl in a menacing smile. She pointed right at me. I knew what that meant.

Hilleddi was coming for me.

IT TOOK A MOMENT FOR THE TIBRANS TO REGROUP AFTER BEING DOUSED WITH burning oil. Our archers were still doing a good job of making the most of that moment, keeping them scattered while our troops rallied for open war behind the second wall.

I found Aubren sitting atop a white horse carrying our father's banner in one hand and his sword in the other. The golden eagle of Maldobar shone against a field of royal blue. But the sight of it wasn't inspiring to me. It made resentment twist sourly at my insides. My father should have been sitting there—on that horse—preparing to defend his people.

All around Aubren, other knights on horseback were forming a line three-deep in the main street right in front of the third and final gate. They were the cavalry and our last real hope. This was where we made our final stand and did everything we could to keep the Tibrans from breaching the third wall.

Phevos flared to land right before them, startling the first line of horses who reared and whinnied in panic. I noticed that the rider mounted directly beside my brother seemed to be having an especially hard time keeping his horse under control. He also wasn't holding his shield up properly, and his helmet looked a bit big for him. He must have been a civilian, one of a few who had volunteered to take up arms and hold the city as long as possible.

"How long?" Aubren shouted to me.

"Soon," I called back. "Get ready. Hold fast until you see that big monster fall. I'm going to give them the bitter bite!"

Aubren's face paled. "Jenna—no! That's too dangerous!"

I wasn't interested in any of his brotherly speeches about my safety. As if we had time for that nonsense. With a quick salute, Phevos and I took off again, flying low through the city streets. We streaked past the city square where the statue of Jaevid stood atop that stone fountain, and I made a deliberate effort not to look at it.

As the second gate came into view, I reached down to touch a hand to Phevos's strong neck. I didn't know how this would end. But I wanted him to survive.

"When I'm gone, you don't stick around here for even one more second, do you understand? Get out of here. Fly far, far away from this place. Find somewhere safe."

Phevos flicked a look back at me, chirping and chattering. I couldn't tell if he understood or not.

Suddenly, I heard it—the rumbling, booming sound as though the earth itself had been split open. Immediately, warning began to wail all along the ramparts. Hilleddi's monster had broken through the second gate. The Tibrans were advancing.

Beneath me, Phevos snarled and let out a vicious roar.

We soared over the heads of our comrades, still flying low over all the Maldobarian infantrymen who were braced for combat. They cheered at the sight of us, and Phevos let out another trumpeting cry.

Then I saw her.

Hilleddi was still standing atop her bone platform as her war beast came lumbering through the shattered gate, splattered with oil. It took out the sides of the stone walls as it pitched and bellowed, worming its way through an opening that was too small.

Our infantry hurled round after round from catapults at the creature when at last it squirmed through. It took one of the large stone projectiles squarely to the head. The hit looked good. The creature staggered as though it were dazed, and I dared to hope it might fall.

But that dome-shaped skull must have been thicker than any of us had realized. The monster shook off the blow and continued, crawling forward as its relentless rider snapped the chains again.

Piercing that skull from the outside wasn't an option. Fortunately, I had an insane idea—one we called "bitter bite."

I stood up and quickly unbuckled from the saddle. Squatting down on Phevos's back, I waited until I felt him cup his wings a bit, flaring for a rapid deceleration. Suddenly, he took a sharp left turn. I let myself pitch forward and ran headlong down the length of his long tail. Five or six steps down, I couldn't find good footing, so I jumped and curled my body into a ball. I hit the ground at a roll and stood, whirling around to draw both my blades.

I looked up, directly into the gaping mouth of that monster. It loomed over me, enormous and still dripping with burning oil. I'd never seen an animal so huge, so alien, or so terrifying.

"Devour her!" Hilleddi screeched. She snapped the chains again.

Her monster rumbled and roared in reply. It blasted the air around me with hot, rancid breath.

I saw the creature's giant mouth open wide, a literal abyss of toothy darkness ready to swallow me whole.

CHAPTER SIX

I let the creature eat me.

Wet, sticky, smelly darkness closed in from every side. I could feel its massive, soft tongue wriggling under my boots. Thank the gods it didn't have any chewing teeth that I could see. That would have been a problem. But I didn't intend on hanging around to find out for sure.

As soon as I was able to get my footing on its wide, disgusting tongue, I flipped my blades over my hands and drove them both straight up—through the roof of its mouth. I rammed both blades in all the way to the hilt.

Immediately, the monster started trying to spit me out. My ears rang as it bellowed in pain.

"Bit off more than you can chew?" I laughed like a maniac as I ripped my swords free and went back for a second blow.

I must have hit something crucial because suddenly, the slippery, slimy world around me began moving wildly. I rattled around inside the beast's mouth like a mouse in a toothy cage. I smacked the roof of its mouth, bounced off its tongue, over and over.

With a final thunderous *BOOM,* it stopped.

Lying on my back, I couldn't see anything except for the inside of the monster's mouth directly above me. The little bit of daylight seeping through its teeth only faintly illuminated it. I couldn't hear the beast breathing anymore.

Everything was still.

Slowly, I staggered to my feet and began looking for my weapons. I only found one of my swords, though. The other one had either been slung out of the creature's mouth in the chaos or swallowed. Either way, it was gone.

I started pushing and pulling at the monster's teeth, using my whole body to begin prying its jaws apart. Once I could get an arm through, I began wrenching myself through the crack and back out into the daylight.

I was met with a crowd of Maldobarian soldiers as I stumbled out of its mouth. They stared at me with wide, astonished eyes, their mouths hanging open.

I took a quick look around for Hilleddi. Surely, she'd be storming in to avenge her war beast any moment, right? But the platform where she'd been standing was empty. Hilleddi was nowhere in sight.

Now was my chance to regroup.

"Has anyone seen my dragon?" I asked as I wiped some of the monster's nasty, bloody slobber off my face.

One of the soldiers standing at the front silently pointed a shaking hand off to the left.

"Thanks." I sheathed my one remaining sword, raked some of my slobber-soaked hair out of my face, and went marching off to find him.

Hilleddi's troublesome war beast was dead, but the battle raged on through Barrowton. Shops and homes burned. The cobblestone streets ran with blood. War horses ran in panicked herds, their saddles empty and their banners aflame.

Aubren's men were playing it smart. They held the cavalry in reserve, guarding the final gateway, while the rest of their infantry brothers fought guerilla style through the city—hiding in buildings and making deathtraps of the city squares as the Tibrans tried to advance. I had to give Aubren some credit. He didn't have the mind of a killer. He was much more like our mother, who didn't enjoy warfare at all. Despite that, both he and his men were holding out a lot longer than I had anticipated.

Maybe, just maybe, we would be able to get out of this alive. We wouldn't win, of course, but we might live to tell about it.

I darted down an alleyway, zigzagging through the narrower streets with my eyes on the sky as I made my way back in the direction of the third gate. That was where we'd planned to make our last stand, and I knew Aubren would still be waiting there. I just hoped Phevos would be waiting for me, too.

The echoing sounds of combat rang out from the larger streets. Soldiers were marching in formation, the thunder of their footsteps mingled with the clash and clatter of sword and steel. The *snap*—*whoosh*—*BOOM* of catapult fire rattled every street corner.

Sprinting as fast as I could, I cut through a backstreet that emptied into the large city square where Jaevid's fountain stood in the center. I skidded to a halt and checked the skies for Phevos again. But he was nowhere to be found.

All around me, Maldobarian soldiers locked blades with our Tibran enemies. The air was heavy with the coppery tinge of blood. I was less than half a mile from the third gate, and any moment now, I expected to see Aubren's cavalry come thundering through the street on horseback.

Suddenly, the warning sirens behind the third wall began to wail in the air. They were a slightly higher pitch than the rest and created an eerie harmony with the others. Immediately, I looked up toward the keep, and my heart stopped for an instant.

I could see fire in the windows.

The Tibrans had breached the third wall already? But how? Hilleddi's beast was down. It was dead—I'd made sure of that.

Panic and anger welled in me like a torrent of flame.

A Tibran soldier tried to rush me, using his round bronze shield like a battering ram. I must have looked like an easy target, even if I was dressed in a dragonrider's armor and cloak—a little woman with long, golden hair standing all alone.

I spun on him with a crazed snarl, dropping into a crouch and sweeping his legs. As he fell, I grabbed his shield and snatched it violently into a twisting motion that broke his arm. He screamed with pain, trying to get away from me. He'd picked the wrong little woman to mess with today.

One plunge of my sword ended his suffering.

The thundering clatter of hooves over the cobblestones drew my gaze up. Some of Aubren's men rode right past me through the city square, pursued by Tibrans on their ironclad war steeds. Their line had broken. They were attempting a retreat—but had nowhere to go.

Something had gone wrong; I just didn't know what. We had lost our last chance to defend the third wall. Everywhere I looked there were Tibrans rushing in. I was alone and outnumbered.

Squeezing the hilt of my sword, I backed up against the side of Jaevid's fountain and watched as Tibran soldiers began to encircle me. They had me cornered, pinned in the center of that city square. But I could see apprehension on their faces. They probably recognized my cloak—they knew I was a dragonrider. I was never truly alone.

All I had to do was get my whistle from my belt.

Before I could even reach for it, however, I heard a feral screeching sound coming from beside me. Instinct made my senses snap into focus. I dropped to a knee and ducked as a mace hummed right over my head. I could feel the wind from it and caught a glimpse of the spiked ball as it passed mere inches from my head. It cracked against Jaevid's statue, lodging deep into the stone of one of his legs.

I kicked into an evasive roll, coming up into a squat with my sword ready for a counterstrike. Before me, she emerged through the ranks of Tibran soldiers like a lumbering giant. She pushed them aside like pesky children, snatching a shield from one and flinging him to the ground as though he were a ragdoll.

Hilleddi towered head and shoulders over the rest of the men gathered around, looming like a giant as she stomped toward me. Her neck was nearly as thick around as her head, her biceps bulged under the weight of the shield and battle-axe, and her movements were jerking and beastly. She'd shaved away all the hair on one side of her head, leaving the other only an inch or so long. The left side of her face was covered in tribal markings, and her armor—if it could even be called that—seemed more like a ceremonial afterthought that left her torso and legs exposed.

She leered at me and crinkled her crooked nose. Her dark, wicked eyes flickered with excited malice. "Well, if it isn't Maldobar's pretty little princess. I hear you like to play at being a warrior."

Slowly, I rose to stand and lowered the tip of my sword. I narrowed my gaze at her challengingly. "Yes. Didn't you notice? I had a very good time *playing* with your war mount."

Her mouth curled in a delighted snarl. She swung her axe wide, gesturing to all the soldiers gathered around us. "Not one of you lot better move a muscle! This whelp is mine."

Hilleddi dove at me like an angry bear, swinging her double-headed battle-axe wildly. I waited, steeling my nerves until the last second before ducking and evading her wild assault. Her axe sailed right over my head as I dipped under her arm.

Her weapon was heavy. She was committed to the swing. That was the weakness I had to exploit. Standing up behind her, I flipped my sword and caught it by the blade, taking a half-swording hold so I could use the hilt like a club. Then I wailed her over the back of the head with the pommel as hard as I could.

She was stronger—bigger—and could probably cut me in half with one blow even through my armor. But if she wanted to kill me, she was going to have to work for it. I hadn't lived through the hell of the academy to die at the hands of a barbarian mongrel like her.

Hilleddi staggered, catching herself against the fountain and dropping her shield. When she faced me again, I saw blood trickling from the corners of her smirking mouth. "Clever little tramp, aren't you?"

I tilted my chin up and spun my blade back over to grip it by the hilt. "I doubt it takes much to be smarter than you."

She snarled again, turning and kicking her shield away. She grabbed the handle of the mace—which was still lodged in the leg of Jaevid's statue—and ripped it free with one tug. She spun on me then, brandishing both weapons and prowling forward with her brawny shoulders hunched. At the last second, she surged toward me to make another frenzied attack.

I had to be careful. Every hit had to count. I couldn't overpower her, so I had to outlast her until she made a critical mistake.

While Hilleddi swung wildly, flinging her weapons through the air in my direction again and again, I dodged and kept light on my feet. She chased me around the square, like we were doing laps around the fountain. Whenever I could, I ducked in to plant a calculated blow—one at her throat and another at the wound on her thigh where she'd unceremoniously ripped an arrow out during battle.

Her strikes began to slow. She was breathing hard, favoring that wound on her leg. But when our eyes locked, I saw no surrender in her.

Suddenly, Hilleddi reared back and hurled her axe directly at me. It spun end over end, rocketing toward my face. I pitched to the side to avoid it, but when I came up, she was already waiting for me. I took the full force of her mace against my side. It crunched through my armor like it was cheap tin. Pain shot through my body. I felt something pop—bones breaking.

I landed on the ground at her feet, dazed and tasting the coppery flavor of blood on my tongue. Squinting through the haze and winking spots in my vision, I could barely make out the shape of her boots stomping toward me. Oh no. I clenched my teeth, trying to will my body to stand. Get up—*now*!

But I couldn't.

Hilleddi lifted one of her monstrous feet and stomped it right into my face.

I managed to angle my face away in time to spare my nose. But once again, my brains felt scrambled. I couldn't clear the darkness that was swallowing my vision. This was it. I was down—and she was one swing of that mace away from spattering the feet of Jaevid's fountain with the insides of my head.

"My brother ordered me to spare you if I could. I suspect he wants you for a trophy." Hilleddi scoffed as she used to the toe of her sandal to nudge my chin. "Just this once, I don't think I'll grant his wish."

Vaguely, I could see her rearing that mace back for the final swing. Past the end of her spiked iron weapon, I could barely make out the shape of Jaevid's face on that statue. I wondered if I would see him in the afterlife. Perhaps I could plead with him to keep his promise.

The mace came down with bone-splintering force, aimed right at my head. I closed my eyes.

Suddenly, someone was shouting. A man? Through my fog of pain, I could have sworn I knew that voice.

When I opened my eyes again, there was a person crouching over me like he'd materialized out of thin air. He had a shield strapped to his arm, and he threw it up clumsily to deflect Hilleddi's killing blow. The impact made him cry out, and I saw a huge dent form in the back of the shield where the mace had hit on the other side.

"You!" She screeched like a feral cat.

"Get up, Jenna," the man rasped breathlessly from under his helmet. He looked down at me through the eyeholes cut in his visor.

I caught a glimpse of familiar, vivid green.

Oh, gods—it was Phillip!

"Look out," I cried out to warn him when I saw Hilleddi lunge again—but it was no good.

She grabbed him by the shield and sent him flying into Jaevid's statue. He cracked off the stone hard and landed in a heap in the shallow water at the base of the fountain. She was on him again in an instant. I saw her flailing that mace again and again. He managed to block the first few blows, but then the fourth split his shield.

The fifth blow hit him across the shoulder, crumpling his shoulder pauldron and drawing blood. He cried out, still shouting at me, "Run, Jenna! Run now!"

Terror shot through me like a cold tongue of lightning.

She was about to beat Phillip—*my* Phillip—to death.

"*No!*" A roaring shout tore out of my throat and I was on my feet. All sense of pain and injury was gone from my mind. All I knew was the white-hot taste of revenge crackling over my tongue.

Hilleddi drew back, preparing for another swing—a killing blow—when I drove my sword straight through her burly bicep. She let out a howl of rage and surprise, and I quickly wrenched my blade sideways with ruthless force.

Her arm, mace and all, clattered to the ground.

"Never turn your back on me, you ugly wench," I growled as she spun to face me.

Hilleddi rushed me like an enraged bull, eyes bloodshot and nostrils flared. The bloody stump where her arm used to be didn't seem to bother her at all. I kicked off to meet her, taking three long strides before I sprang into the air with my blade swung wide. I saw her eyes go wide and her nostrils flare with sudden realization about a second before the point of my sword met her neck.

CHAPTER SEVEN

I stood over Phillip and defended him until my last bit of strength was spent. Without Hilleddi to command them, the Tibrans were much more cautious when dealing with me. They'd fought enough dragonriders before to know that one of us was worth a hundred of them in battle. But the Tibran soldiers attacked in calculated waves, and soon I was overwhelmed. For each one I cut down, there were five more to take his place.

Until at last, it was over.

One stiff blow across my cheek from a sword's hilt put me on the ground right next to Phillip. His shoulder had been crushed by Hilleddi's mace. He couldn't even sit up.

The Tibrans could have killed me. All my strength was gone. I couldn't move from where I'd fallen. But rather than ending it with a blade in my heart, they pinned me down and tied my arms behind my back. I was going to wind up a trophy of war after all.

They did the same to Phillip, and I heard him screaming and wailing in pain when they moved his injured arm. All I could do was clench my teeth and wait for it to be over. Once our arms and legs were bound, we were thrown onto the backs of horses, covered with black blankets to hide our identities from anyone who might try to rescue us, and carried away through the burning remains of the city.

I couldn't see anything but the flurry of horse hooves and blood-spattered cobblestones blurring by as I lay on my belly. I could still hear, however. The warning sirens had gone silent. Now there was nothing but the crackling of flames and the shouts of the dying.

It was impossible to resist hoping that Aubren, Haldor, or Calem would suddenly sweep in to rescue us. But the city had fallen faster than we had ever expected. If they had followed my orders, Haldor and Calem were already flying for the safety of the mountains while my brother made that same journey with hundreds of civilians in the tunnels.

That left me with only one burning question—but I didn't get a chance to ask it until Phillip and I had been delivered behind enemy lines and loaded into the back of an armored wagon. It had no windows and only one door that bolted closed from the outside, so when they locked us inside, it was pitch black.

"Phillip?" I called out to him in the darkness, trying to scoot my way closer to him.

"You know, this isn't exactly how I envisioned our first time alone in the dark together," he rasped.

When I found him, I let my leg bump his, so he would know I was there. "What happened? How did the Tibrans get past the third wall so quickly?"

He wheezed as though he were having a hard time getting a breath. I wondered if that wound had affected one of his lungs. "It all happened so fast. There was an explosion."

"From outside the gate?"

"No, it was from the inside. They kept shouting—something about the tunnels." His voice grew quieter. "I-I'm cold."

"You're going into shock." I tried to make my voice soft and comforting as I scooted in close enough that my side pressed against his. It hurt. From the fresh agony coming from the wound on my side and my own difficulties breathing, I could guess that a few of my ribs were broken. "Just try to take deep, slow breaths. It's going to be okay."

"L-Liar." He chuckled weakly.

I felt his head loll against me, resting on top of mine as we sat alone in that hateful dark place. I didn't understand why he was here—he should have evacuated with everyone else. He wasn't supposed to be wearing armor or slinging shields around or ... trying to save my life.

"I thought I was too late," Phillip muttered in a broken voice. "I saw you lying there. I thought she'd already killed—"

"Hush, now. You just need to try to focus on calming down and slowing your breathing."

"Will they torture us?" He sounded genuinely terrified. It was a somber reminder that unlike me, he'd never been trained to handle that sort of thing.

"You? No. I don't see why they would." After all, he didn't know much that would have been useful to them. He was a duke, sure, but he was no war strategist.

"But me ... " I stopped and swallowed hard. My mouth felt dry just thinking about it. I *was* valuable to them. Aubren had told me some of what had happened when the Tibrans had captured him and his men before. He'd explained how they'd seemed almost desperate to figure out if there had been a member of Maldobar's royal family among them. They'd also seemed quite fond of torture, especially when it came to those royals. Hilleddi's venomous words about being a war prize for her brother burned in my mind.

"You don't need to worry about that," I finished at last, gritting my teeth. "I can take care myself."

"I do worry, though. I always worry. You are the most important person in my life."

I bit down harder. "Why, Phillip? Why do you *always* say things like that? Even now, when we're about to—"

"You know why."

I couldn't see him in the dark, so I just glared in the direction his voice was coming from. "You're not being serious. You're never serious. You treat me like a joke, just like when we were children."

"Is that really what you think? That I'm just making fun of you or something?" He sounded surprised.

"Well, aren't you?"

"No. I mean, not all the time. I do joke sometimes—maybe more often than I should. But I always thought you could tell the difference."

I frowned and looked away, letting the silence serve as my answer.

"So, all this time, you thought I was mocking you? Geez, no wonder you hate my guts." He sighed.

"I don't hate you."

He chuckled hoarsely, tensing up some as though it hurt. "I guess if you did, you would have stood back and let that beastly woman smash my head in like a spring melon, eh? What an ogre she was. I don't think I've seen a more alarmingly repulsive person in my life."

No argument there.

"Where do you think they're taking us?" he asked. I could hear him still struggling for every breath. I couldn't see him, so I didn't know how badly he was wounded. I didn't know if he'd even survive to get wherever it was we were going.

That fact clamped down on me like a cold hand at my throat.

"Maybe to some sort of prison camp or to wherever Argonox has been hiding out," I guessed carefully.

Honestly, I had no idea. But since I was the only experienced soldier of the two of us, I knew I had to keep morale up. If these were our last hours alive, I didn't want him to spend them petrified of what horror awaited us when they dragged us out of this rolling prison cell.

"You want to know the first time I realized I loved you?" Phillip broke the heavy silence. I could hear that mischievous smile in his voice.

"Phillip," I warned. He was right—I couldn't tell when he was joking and when he wasn't.

"It was at your brother's debut ball," he said between rough breaths. "We were all there to honor Aubren. He was supposed to be the center of attention since it was his debut to the royal court as a man. But the moment I saw you step into that ballroom, it was like the whole world had shifted under my feet and I couldn't think of anything else except how to make you mine."

I closed my eyes tightly and hoped he couldn't hear how my heart had begun to pound sloppily. I remembered that night, too—for an entirely different reason. I had still been begging my father to let me go to the dragonrider academy. After yet another monstrous argument right before the ceremony had begun, I had still been hot with rage and determined to sulk when I'd come into the ballroom.

"I'll never believe there's anyone else I could be happy with," he murmured. Fatigue, pain, and maybe blood loss had begun to slur his words. "There is only you, Jenna. I am yours; I've always been yours."

My cheeks burned, and I was thankful he couldn't see it. I'd never dreamt any man would say something like that to me. I was still a princess, yes. But in the eyes of most of the men in the noble court, becoming a dragonrider was essentially the same thing as deciding to become a man. You couldn't be both—not in their eyes.

Phillip, though ... It was as though he still saw me as something fragile and beautiful beneath all my armor.

"Tell me again." The words slipped past my lips before I could consider them.

I felt his body tense slightly where he sat so close to me. "W-What?"

"You know what." My heart thrashed wildly in my ears. "But not here. Not now. Afterward, when we're both safe and I can look you in the eyes and know you really mean it. I want you to tell me how you really feel about me."

"I ... I ..." Phillip fumbled for words. I had never heard him do that before.

"I'm serious, Phillip. You have to stay alive. Do you understand?"

"J-Jenna ..." he slurred my name one last time.

"Phillip?"

No response.

I nudged him with my shoulder, but he didn't make a sound. Instead, his full weight slumped over against me. Pain from my injuries, mainly my shattered ribs, shot through my body. I could barely keep us both upright.

"Phillip! No! Wake up. You need to stay awake," I cried out as I tried jostling him again. "Wake up, right now! Don't you dare give up on me! I need you to stay alive. I need you ..."

I had no idea how much time had passed, or where we'd gone after the wagon had carried us away from the smoldering remains of Barrowton. But when the doors of the wagon opened, and bright light from torches glared down upon me, I knew we were underground. The air smelled thick, humid, and earthy. It was tinged with the flavor of smoke, almost like scorched metal. Voices echoed from all around, bouncing off the stone walls and mingling with other sounds. Horses, footsteps, the clanking of metal armor—all were sounds I knew well.

"How many?" a gruff man's voice asked.

"Two," another replied. "Captain says they're priority targets."

"Dead or alive?" A hand suddenly grabbed one of my ankles and started dragging me out of the wagon.

I screamed and kicked. More men gathered, swarming around to fling me out of the wagon and onto the ground. Squinting up into the light of their torches, I finally got a clear glimpse of them—Tibran soldiers.

"Alive." One of them chuckled.

An older man wearing an ornate bronze helmet crested in dark red horsehair leaned down to peer at me. "This is her? The Maldobarian princess?"

"So they say." His comrades didn't seem so sure.

"She'll have to go to Argo, then." The older man rubbed his chin and frowned. "What about the other one?"

They were dragging Phillip out of the back of the wagon, too. He hung from their grasp, limp as a wet rag, and didn't put up any resistance as they tossed him onto the ground next to me. He landed with a *thud* and was motionless, not making a single sound except for labored, rasping breaths.

It took everything I had not to look at him, not to show any kind of concern. I didn't know what they would do if they found out who he was, or that I had a relationship with him. Would they torture him, too? Would they kill him outright?

"Is it the prince?" The older man asked.

"No. He's already here. They sent him on to Argo ahead of us. Bet he never guessed he'd wind up back here again, eh?" The Tibran soldiers joined in a chuckle, as though that were a joke.

Wait—Aubren was *here*? Oh, gods. He'd been captured, too.

My heart sank to the soles of my feet.

The older man in his crested helmet nudged Phillip with the toe of his boot. "This one's just a common foot soldier. Look at his armor. It's not even the proper size for him. Probably another volunteer from the city folk." He scowled and gestured to a few of the soldiers around him. "He won't be any use as a recruit. He's already half-dead as it is. Take him to a holding cell and we'll see what Argo wants to do with him. If he dies, cut him up and feed him to the switchbeasts."

"What about her?"

"You know the orders. If either of Maldobar's royal brats ends up in custody, they go straight to the tower." He sighed. "Strip down her armor, make sure she doesn't have any concealed weapons, and maybe clean her up a little. He may want to keep her."

A few of the soldiers were murmuring, chuckling darkly as they gazed down at me. It was like being circled by a pack of ravenous wolves. With my hands still bound at my back by the wrists, and my side splitting with pain every time I took a breath, there was no way I would be able to fend them all off if they attacked me.

"*Hey*—not a finger on her otherwise. You know Argo will have your neck if you mess with his prize," the man snapped. "Now get moving."

CHAPTER EIGHT

The Tibran soldiers took every piece of my armor—my greaves, gauntlets, even my boots. I stood, shivering in my socks and undergarments, as they checked my body over for any concealed weapons. I bit back a curse when they snatched the silver whistle from around my neck. That was my way of calling Phevos. It had taken us years to work out our own language of signals with that whistle. Now I could only hope he'd found safety somewhere far away from the reach of the Tibrans.

... If there was such a place.

My face was tender, especially around the place where Hilleddi had attempted to kick my skull in. When one of the soldiers started wiping at it with a rag, tears immediately welled in my eyes. I cringed away from the pain of his touch, biting down hard against the urge to whimper.

"It's all right. I know it hurts. I'll try to be quick," he murmured quietly so none of the other soldiers would hear. He was surprisingly gentle as he took my chin in his fingers and kept gingerly wiping at the blood and grit smeared on my face.

I dared to look at him and my heartbeat skipped. He was a Gray elf, a teenage boy probably about the same age as Reigh. All his silver hair was gone—shaved down to the scalp to expose his pointed ears and the freshly branded mark seared into the dark golden skin on side of his neck. It was still swollen and red. I'd seen that brand before. That was how the Tibrans marked their slave soldiers. When our gazes met, I caught a glimpse of absolute terror reflected in the depths of his multicolored eyes.

We were both captives here, but I knew better than to expect him or any of the other slave-soldiers to do anything to help me get out of here.

I was on my own.

Flanked by more Tibran soldiers on all sides, I walked the cold stone passageways through their compound. They were fond of this tunneling method of moving men and supplies and had all but perfected it as a means of invasion. The tactical soldier side of my brain could appreciate that strategy. It made their movements difficult to track and their numbers impossible to estimate. No one really knew how they were able to do it with such speed. A beast or creature, perhaps? Or maybe another divine artifact they'd come across? Until Barrowton, I'd never seen their tunnels used to make a direct siege on a city before. The Tibrans were full of horrific surprises.

A cold blast of air hit my face like an icy slap when we emerged from the tunnel. I squinted into the daylight, trying to get my bearings. One look upward at the fifty-story tower that loomed overhead like an ominous black spike was all I needed. I knew the stronghold of Northwatch the instant I saw it. The Tibrans had besieged this city weeks ago, and yet the fires of war still smoldered in the city streets, throwing up plumes of foul black smoke that turned the sky dreary gray.

Aubren had lost more than half of his infantry and cavalrymen here trying to defend this city. If our father hadn't recalled all the dragonriders back to Halfax, they might have been more successful in holding it. After all, this fortress had withstood more than twenty years of war before, and at the time we'd only had Tibran forces coming in from one of the coasts. But Aubren had warned me not to bring my riders here. He didn't want to risk leaving our western coast unguarded. And without dragonriders to support his ranks, Northwatch had fallen.

Looking around at the remains of the city, now overrun with Tibran soldiers, encampments, and war machines, I felt sick. Just the sight of their red banner fluttering from the tower's battlements made my stomach turn and my pulse surge with rage. That banner was like a poison spreading through my homeland. I despised it with every fiber of my soul.

The company of heavily-armed soldiers walked me to the front gates of the tower, a sword aimed at my back in case I got any bright ideas about escaping. The gateway had been built to be heavily fortified, and yet the Tibrans had made their own modifications to it as well. The entrance was small, the size of a doorway barely large enough to march two men through. That had been intentional, funneling any potential invading enemy into two-abroad. Besides, the *real* entrance was fifty stories in the air: a platform and wide passage into the tower where dragonriders could land their mounts without any interference from the ground.

Vicious snarling and barking pierced my eardrums from either side the second my bare feet crossed the threshold of the entryway. Two hounds as big as horses lunged at the length of iron chains with their mouths foaming and their red eyes fixed upon me. Their tails and ears were cut down to nothing, and their snouts were snubbed and disfigured. Another inch of chain and they could have mauled me to death. I had to walk in perfect line with my escort to avoid their snapping jaws. Where in the world had the Tibrans found such creatures?

The interior of the tower was as I remembered it from my own service as a dragonrider. A central shaft ran from top to bottom of the enormous structure, featuring a crank-operated elevator system that was used to move supplies up and down the various floors. It wasn't designed for moving people, but no one had warned the Tibran soldiers about that—or maybe they just didn't mind the risk of losing a limb if you happened to get it caught in the wrong place.

I cut my eyes around to the company of armored men around me as they put me in the center of the elevator's broad platform and flanked me on all sides. One of them still had a sword at my back. Occasionally I felt the prick of it against my bare skin.

I'd deal with that first.

The crank's metal gears began to grind and groan, putting tension on the ropes and hauling the platform aloft with us on board. I waited until we were moving fast, blurring up the floors. This had to be quick. No mistakes.

Sucking in a breath, I dropped into a crouch and threw myself into a backward roll. I hit the soldier with his sword drawn as hard as I could, throwing him off-balance. He stumbled, his sword clattered to the ground and arms flailing as he stumbled back. *Crunch*—the fluttering end of his cape snagged in the ropes, chains, and gears and he was yanked off the platform.

I swept my shackled hands under my legs and dove for the sword. The rest of the soldiers were panicking now, drawing their weapons on me. Three against one; I liked those odds.

"It's rude to keep a lady waiting, you know." I snarled as I grasped the hilt in both hands, licking the front of my teeth. "Who's next?"

AUBREN—I *HAD TO FIND MY BROTHER.*

That was my one and only objective as I sprinted down the twisting hallways of Northwatch tower. I was barefoot, my wrists shackled, and still wearing nothing apart from my undergarments, so it was far from the ideal situation. But I did have a sword, and so far, the Tibran soldiers hadn't caught up to me. The few who had survived my escape from the elevator were still hot on my trail and gathering reinforcements as we played a frantic game of cat and mouse through the tower. I knew this place far better than they did, which turns to take, where the hidden passages were. But that wouldn't help me find Aubren ... or escape the tower altogether.

There were only three ways out of this place. One was the platform where riders landed their dragons. There was also a small hatch that opened to the roof, although unless you had a dragon waiting on you or an amazing talent for climbing the exterior of the tower, that wasn't going to help. The last exit was the one I'd come in through, the one guarded by the two hounds.

I set my jaw and rounded another corner. First things first—I needed to find where they were holding Aubren. Maybe with his help we could ...

I came to a halt right in front of a passageway that should have led from the dragonrider level down to the infantry portion of the tower. Only that passage no longer existed. It had been completely blocked off by crudely-installed iron bars. I spun in a circle, looking around for somewhere, anywhere else I could go. Down the hallway behind me, the rattle of armor and shouts of Tibran soldiers approached. They were searching every corridor. It was only a matter of time.

Gods and Fates. I was trapped.

"Princess?"

I whipped around, sword raised.

It was him—the same young elf who'd wiped the blood from my face. He stood only a few yards away, hesitating at the other end of the corridor with his hands raised in surrender.

"I don't want to kill you," I growled through panting breaths.

"Well, that's good news," he said with a nervous smile. "I'd rather neither of us died."

"Then let me pass."

He slowly started to drop his arms back to his sides. "And what then? Your Highness, there is no escape from this place. Take it from someone who has already tried." His strange eyes glinted like opals in the gloom as he studied me. "I would let you go if I knew of some way out of here. I'd do everything I could to help you escape. But it isn't possible. Even if you made it out of the tower, they have thousands of men encamped around the city. War mounts the likes of which you've never seen. I don't want to watch them kill you. Please don't make me witness that."

I swallowed. My grip on my sword faltered. I was tired. The pain from my ribs was nearly more than I could bear, and the rush of adrenaline left my body trembling.

"T-They'll kill me anyway," I rasped. "Better to die on my feet, fighting to my last breath."

The elf boy took a few cautious steps toward me, little by little closing the gap between us. "If they intended to kill you, you'd already be dead."

"Then they'll torture me first."

He stopped in front of me with his brow crinkling and his mouth pressing together into a worried line. "Please, Your Highness."

My vision blurred and dimmed. I couldn't breathe. Every attempt was agony. "M-My brother, Prince Aubren, where is h-he? Where are t-they holding him? I have to ... "

Before he could answer, my knees buckled. The sword slipped from my hands and I slumped forward. The floor rushed up, but before my knees met stone, the bronze-clad arms of the elf soldier caught me.

"You're hurt." He sounded surprisingly concerned.

"Phillip." My soul cried out his name even as it passed over my lips. He was somewhere here, too. Lost, maybe dying. He needed me just as much as Aubren did.

And I couldn't do anything to help either of them.

My head lolled against the elf's shoulder as he picked me up. Every muscle in my body was slack with exhaustion. I clung to consciousness as he carried me through the hallways of the tower, back toward the chaos of the Tibran army.

Back into hell.

CHAPTER NINE

I awoke to the soft, flickering glow of warm candlelight. Before me was a room I only vaguely recognized. I'd stood in it maybe three times, and only briefly. It was the finest room in the tower, the chambers of Northwatch's former colonel. Only it had been drastically redecorated to suit someone else's tastes.

And he was standing right in front of me, leaning against the broad window. The moonlight and hard shadows from the candles that burned about the office made it impossible to see his features. I could only make out a vague outline of his face: —a hard, squared jawline, short hair, wide shoulders, and a muscular frame. The soft light flickered off the surface of his breastplate and shoulder pauldrons, making the bronze shimmer like molten gold.

I snapped upright, surprised to find that I wasn't chained or tied to the chair where I sat. I was, however, still naked except for my meager undergarments. Well, that and a crimson cloak that had been unceremoniously draped around me. The collar was lined with a mane of long, golden fur and the hem trimmed in embellishments and depictions of lions.

"Most impressive." He spoke in a deep, smooth voice. "I heard you took down eight of my men in your effort to escape. They're still cutting the remains of one of them out of the elevator mechanics. You also killed my sister and her favorite war mount singlehandedly." His laugh was rich but decidedly cold. "You are deceptively beautiful for so dangerous a woman. It's enchanting."

I narrowed my eyes. "Argonox, I presume? Give me a blade and I'll show you exactly how *enchanting* I can be."

The outline of his cheek moved as though he were smiling. "My name sounds so mundane when you say it. Most people whisper it, as though it were a curse."

"I don't believe in curses. Fairy tales are for children." Without bonds or chains to stop me, I tried to stand. Agony immediately shot through my body from my broken ribs. I wheezed, faltering as my legs threatened to buckle again.

"Ah, yes. Your injury must be quite painful; however, I'm told it's not life-threatening. In any case, I suggest you sit and take rest while you can."

I squeezed the armrests and tried to breathe through the discomfort. "W-What is this? Planning on torturing me yourself? Save your efforts. Nothing would please me more than to take every shred of valuable information I know to my grave."

He laughed again and pushed away from the window. As Argonox stepped into the candlelight, more and more of his features came into view. He was … so much younger than I expected. He looked nothing at all like Hilleddi. He was about the same height as my brother, just at six feet, but there was something deceptively soft and handsome about his face. His light brown hair was trimmed short, the front combed back away from his forehead and his strong jaw flecked with short stubble. He studied me with deep-set eyes of cobalt blue a slight smirk tugging at the corners of his mouth.

"You seem surprised," he observed, his smile widening.

I was. Argonox didn't resemble the monster I had painted in my mind at all. I searched every corner of his face for the subtle traces of cruelty that had to be hidden somewhere in his features. To do the things he had done, and was still doing, to my kingdom—it *had* to be there somewhere.

"And what do you think?" He arched an eyebrow.

"What?"

"You're sizing me up, aren't you? Evaluating? I'd like to know what you think," he said. I leaned back, turning my face away when he crouched down in front of my chair so that we were eye level. "Well?"

"You don't look like a tyrant. But then, you're the first one I've met, so maybe it's only that I have an unpracticed eye."

"Perhaps." His tone was light with amusement. "You, on the other hand, are one of many princesses I have met. Would you like to know what I think?"

I curled my lip. "I don't care what you think."

He moved with startling speed, gripping one of my wrists and bringing my palm to his face. I squirmed, trying to wrench it free, but his hold was like a vise. "I think you have incredible potential—far more than your senile father would ever acknowledge. They tell me that women in your kingdom are not permitted to choose a soldier's path. And yet here you are, making fools of my men and whetting my appetite to see what you might truly be capable of." He studied my fingertips for a moment, then slowly panned his eyes up to meet mine. "Rumor has it a dragon chose you, that you are a true dragonrider who shares an unbreakable bond with one of those scaly beasts."

"What difference does that make? There are dozens of others who've been chosen."

"Ah, but you are different. You are a treasure far surpassing any gold or gems my armies might unearth in this soggy little patch of land you call Maldobar. Your spirit burns like star fire. I can see it." He forced my hand to graze the side of his face and dragged my fingers across his lips. "I can taste it."

"Take your filthy hands off me," I hissed.

"What if I told you this war could end tonight?" he murmured. "Right now. Right this very second."

"W-What?"

"You could end it, princess. You could save thousands of lives, bring this senseless war to an end, and take your rightful place in this world." My pulse boomed in my ears and my blood boiled in my veins as he forced my thumb back and forth over his bottom lip so that I could feel every word he spoke vibrating off my fingertip. "Become my queen. Stand at my side and Maldobar will know prosperity forever, guarded by the power of my empire. You would become legendary. A queen for the ages. A goddess."

I sucked in a sharp, shallow breath. He was asking me to marry him? Why? He couldn't possibly be interested in having me for a wife. There was something else, something more he wanted. There had to be. It couldn't be *that* easy.

I held still, studying and searching through his face. I let the dark pools of his sapphire eyes swallow me whole. I needed to see it—the monster behind the man.

Argonox leaned in closer, his grip on my wrist loosening. "You hold me in suspense, princess."

I bent in toward him as well and slowly slipped my hand away to place it on his cheek. His gaze sharpened into a cold, satisfied smile. "My lord Argonox," I whispered softly, "I would marry the south end of a sow before I ever gave you my hand in marriage."

Then I punched him across the jaw as hard as I could.

The effort was almost too much. The pain in my side went white-hot and for a few seconds I couldn't even breathe. I wheezed and slumped back against the chair, trying to blink away the stars in my vision.

Not that it wasn't worth it.

Argonox stumbled back, catching himself on the edge of a large mahogany desk as he rubbed his face. Seeing that I'd split his lip was satisfying, but only for a moment.

"Excellent." He laughed wildly as he wiped the blood from his chin. "I knew you would be good for sport. It's so much more fun this way, isn't it? Let's make it even more interesting."

He paced calmly across the room to the door that led back out into the hall and knocked on it three times. It immediately swung inward, and three armed guards clambered in, leading my brother by a chain around his neck as though he were a dog. Aubren's face was so battered, one of his eyes had nearly swollen shut. There were heavy iron shackles around his wrists and ankles, and his clothes were torn to blood-spattered shreds.

"Aubren!" I tried to stand, to go to him, but the fresh agony in my side only got worse the more I moved.

His face went pale when he saw me. "Gods and Fates. Jenna, what are you doing here?"

"Your sister and I were just discussing her future," Argonox interrupted, striding casually between us. "I must say, having now met you both, I have to agree with your father. She is clearly the better choice for the throne. Especially now that you've proven yourself to be utterly useless in bringing me what I asked for."

I froze, trying to sort out what Argonox was talking about. What he'd asked for ... ?

"Oh, I see. You didn't tell her, did you?" Argonox strolled over to my chair, combing his fingers through my hair as he passed. "Well, now's your chance. Go on. Tell her what you promised to give me in exchange for giving you the throne of Maldobar."

"T-That wasn't why!" Aubren lurched against his bonds, cursing and struggling for a moment. A quick gesture from Argonox and one of the guards smacked him over the head with the blunt end of a sword. Aubren stopped fighting then. He sagged against his bonds, blood dripping from a new cut across his brow.

"We're all waiting," Argonox purred. "Either you tell her, or I will. I doubt my version will be as forgiving as yours."

Slowly, Aubren raised his head. His eyes were wide with desperation and his chest heaved with frantic breaths. "Jenna, please, just listen. I only wanted to stop this war before it destroyed everything we love. I thought I could save our people and put an end to the carnage ... if I had something to offer that was more valuable than adding Maldobar to their empire."

"Aubren," I rasped. "What are you saying?"

His whole body shook as he sobbed. "I-I promised I would bring him Jaevid. I thought I could resurrect him—that he would keep his promise to us and come back to life. Then I could bring him back here and it would all be over. The Tibrans would take him and leave. We would be spared."

My mind went eerily quiet. I couldn't think or even process that. The foul sting of bile singed the back of my throat. I bit down hard, suppressing the urge to gag. "You were going to betray Jaevid Broadfeather?"

"Indeed." Argonox was laughing again. "But it seems that legacy ended long ago. Whatever remains of your beloved hero now is useless to us both. As you so eloquently put it, 'fairy tales are for children.'"

Tears welled in my eyes, blurring my view of my treacherous older brother. I couldn't even stand to look at him. Even if Jaevid was now nothing more than a memory, the very idea that Aubren would have done something like that was unfathomable.

"You really think Jaevid would have ever agreed to fight for you?" I turned my glare to Argonox.

He smirked down at me, blood still oozing from the split in his lip. "I didn't intend on giving him a choice. You see, princess, in my many conquests I've traveled this world over time and again. I've unearthed ancient relics, divine artifacts, and powerful talismans the likes of which your people have never seen. They are of particular interest to me. After all that, I suppose you could say I've learned to pick out the scent of truth in every legend. Divine power has its own distinct stench." Argonox moved around to plant his hands on the arms of my chair and put his face mere inches from mine. "Your people believe Jaevid Broadfeather was special. But based on everything I've seen and heard, he was nothing more than a shoddy sorcerer given a bit of magic by that artifact you call the god stone. When it was destroyed, so was his source of power, and he died like any other mortal man. Thus ends another fairy tale."

"T-That's not ... " The words hung in my throat. I'd never been a believer like Aubren. I didn't put as much faith in those old bedtime stories our father had spun. Overly embellished versions of the truth—that was what they were to me. Sure, Jaevid had been real. He had fought bravely and ended the Gray War. But did I honestly believe he was some sort of demigod?

And if he was, then what did that make Reigh? A demon?

"None of this really matters now, though, does it? Whatever Jaevid was, he's obviously not going to fulfill that prophecy of a glorious return, toting the banners of justice and victory. Believe me. No one is more disappointed in that than I am. I was looking forward to a proper challenge." Argonox chuckled, grabbing my chin and forcing me to meet his gaze. Behind him, I heard Aubren struggling against his bonds again. "Which brings me to my next question: the scent of a fairy tale. Where is the boy who destroyed two legions of my soldiers at Barrowton? All accounts claim he was human, so clearly it wasn't Jaevid. But they all agree it was a dragonrider—one of yours, I can only assume. Another sorcerer as well. A timely alternative, and one that absolutely reeks of divine power."

"Jenna, no! You can't tell him anything!" Aubren shouted. The guards holding his chains silenced him with another crushing blow upside his head.

"My men are calling him an angel of death," Argonox whispered. "Whatever artifact or power he has will be mine, one way or another. This would be so much easier if you were to become my bride. Then we would all be on the same side, wouldn't we? But you've put me in a very *difficult* position."

I took a sharp breath, holding it as he moved in closer until I could feel the heat of his breath against my mouth. I squeezed my eyes shut, gritting my teeth.

"So, would you like to reconsider your answer?" he asked softly. "Or are you going to force me to rip the information I want out of your darling brother while you watch?"

Delirium and pain were my only salvation as I lay in the gloom, trying to remember how I'd gotten here in the first place. All I could recall was sitting in that chair, listening to my brother's garbled screams, and then nothing. It was all a blur. Had I told Argonox who Reigh was? Or where to find him? Gods, I hoped not. But for the life of me, I couldn't be sure.

Staring ahead, all I could see was the flickering light of torches in the hall outside my cell—a cell that had once served as a cramped room to house dragonriders in the tower. Now instead of a door, there was an iron grate barring the entrance. The stone floor was cold beneath me, and the glass of the narrow window on the far wall had been smashed out to let the bitter wind howl in. The Tibrans hadn't given me anything more to wear, so all I could do to try to stay warm was curl into a ball against the floor. With my knees drawn to my chest and my arms curled in tight to cover my bare midriff, I shivered and watched the hallway. By dawn, I might be dead from hypothermia, although that sounded much better than having to face Argonox again.

The sound of footsteps from outside my cell made my pulse race. My entire body shuddered with terror. I was paralyzed, too afraid to move, as the steps came closer. The dark shape of a man dressed in armor appeared outside my cell.

"Princess?" a gentle voice called out to me.

I recognized the shape of his nearly-bald head and long, pointed ears. It was the same soldier from before. A frantic sob made me shudder again. "P-Please ... help me."

"I can't open the door. Only Argonox himself has the key to your cell. He doesn't trust anyone else with it, not even his own soldiers," he whispered as he knelt down and reached through the bars toward me. "Come closer. Hurry, I can't stay for long. Someone will notice."

It took every shred of my strength and will to get on my hands and knees. I crawled across the cold stone and seized his hand, clinging to its warmth desperately as I collapsed against the bars. Through the faint light from the torches burning along the corridor, I could see the lines of distress and worry on his face.

"Princess, you're freezing," he murmured as he gripped my hand harder and brought his other palm to my cheek. "Here, take this."

I was reluctant to release him, but the elf slipped out of my grasp and began unbuckling the long red cloak from the shoulders of his armor. He passed it through the bars and tried wrapping it around me. I balled myself up in the thick wool fabric as best I could.

"Your Highness, I wanted you to know that I—"

I interrupted. "Jenna."

"What?"

"Please, just call me 'Jenna.'"

He swallowed hard and started over. "Jenna, I didn't want to turn you back over to them. I swear, if I knew some way to get you to freedom, I'd gladly die making sure you made it there."

Studying him—his wide, frightened eyes, straight, symmetrical face, and olive-toned skin—I wondered how on earth he had wound up here as a branded slave-soldier. The Tibran armor didn't suit him at all. It was bulky and rounded, a stark contrast to his sharp elven features. But then, he didn't have the look of a warrior or a killer, either. I wondered if he'd even been in real combat before.

"What's your name?"

He bowed his head slightly and looked down. "Aedan."

I managed a small smile. "You speak the human language very well. You don't even have an accent."

"I'm not from Luntharda. I mean, not really. My grandparents stayed in Maldobar after the end of the war and my family has been here ever since. I was born here. We live—er, well, lived—on the Farchase Plains." His mouth pressed into an uncomfortable line and his jawline tensed. "That's where I grew up. I'd never been anywhere else until the Tibrans came."

"And your family? Where are they now?"

His tone grew stiff and I could see the flames of memory sparking in his eyes. "Gone. All of them. The Tibrans burned our farm just like all the others. There's nothing left of it now."

The air seemed to grow colder as we sat there on opposite sides of my cell door. He didn't say a word for nearly a minute. Then his strange, multicolored eyes met mine. "Argonox is mounting a force here unlike anything the world has ever seen. I don't know why, for sure. Some do know, or suspect, but they won't dare speak of it. More and more ships are landing on the eastern coast. Thousands of soldiers are coming through the tunnels."

"He's looking for someone," I replied. "A boy named Reigh. He may have killed my brother trying to find out where he is."

Aedan shook his head. "Prince Aubren is still alive. He's not in good shape, but Argonox won't let him die. Not yet."

I clenched my fists. "Of course. He still needs leverage to force my father into surrender."

"I'm so sorry, Miss Jenna." He bowed his head again. "I came as soon as I heard. Orders were just passed down. Argonox has ordered for you to be sent to the experimentation division."

"The what?"

"I've heard about it before. He's curious about the bond between riders and dragons—particularly the ones who were chosen by their mounts." His voice became so quiet, I could barely hear him. "He dissects them. He wants to find out what makes them different, why they are more desirable partners for the dragons. It's despicable."

I swallowed against the raw, burning sensation in the back of my throat.

"I'll do what I can to delay it," he insisted. "With any luck I can buy some time for the other dragonriders to rescue you."

No one was coming for me. I knew that. With Eirik grounded, that only left Haldor and Calem able to get to Northwatch in time—and I'd ordered them both to stay in Cernheist. I was alone now unless my father suddenly had a change of heart.

"Aedan, what happened to the other human man? The one who was brought in with me? His name is Phillip and h-he's my ... "

"He's still alive. They took him to the weaponry division." He shifted, beginning to pull away as though he didn't want to tell me more.

I lunged at the bars, seizing the front of his breastplate and dragging him in again. "What are they doing to him?"

Aedan's mouth opened and closed, his eyes as round as two pale moons. "He, uh, he's being fed switchbeast venom."

"What does that mean?" I snarled. "Explain it! Now!"

"I-I don't know for sure! I'm not allowed in there. I only know what I've heard the other soldiers talk about," he stammered. "A switchbeast is a kind of monster, something the Tibrans brought here with them. Its venom does something to you. Makes you change. Honestly, I don't know anything more than that, I swear."

Slowly, I let my grip on his breastplate relax. My head drooped forward to rest against one of the cold iron bars. "This venom ... is it painful?"

"I, uh, I'm not—"

"Tell me."

He let out a shaky breath. "Yes."

I closed my eyes. "They're torturing him."

Aedan didn't speak as he stood. I could sense his hesitation. I debated asking him to kill me and maybe Phillip and Aubren, too, if he could manage it. End our suffering. Take away all the leverage Argonox might use against Maldobar. That would be better, wouldn't it?

"Do you believe the stories about Jaevid?" I tried to speak through the sobs that strangled my voice. "Your people called him 'lapiloque.'"

"Yes," he answered quietly.

"Do you think he could hear us if we cried out to him? Even from so far away? Even from a place like this?"

His warm hand touched the top of my head. "I don't know, Miss Jenna. But if you want, I'll stay a bit longer, and we can give it a try."

PART TWO: REIGH

CHAPTER TEN

For the record, nothing about my current situation was going as planned. Shocking, I know. Usually my plans went off like clockwork.

I'd gone to lapiloque's sacred tree with a very short agenda—destroy the stupid tree, maybe yell a few curses while I stomped on the ashes, and then leave. Waking up the legendary, demigod war hero was *not* something I'd set out to do. And yet here we were, standing on the front steps of Mau Kakuri's royal palace, while the king and queen of Luntharda continued to stare at us in dumbstruck awe.

The look on Jaevid Broadfeather's face wasn't much different. His movements were jerking and abrupt, almost defensive, and he stared around at the celebrating crowds of villagers with his eyes wide and expression blank.

"Jaevid, I can't begin to express how relieved and happy we are to see you again." Queen Araxie shifted her weight, her eyes welling with emotion as she looked him over from head to toe.

Jaevid gave a stiff nod and a quick, thin smile, and then flicked his gaze to her husband, King Jace.

If Jace scowled any harder, it might've singed my eyebrows right off my face. His weathered features were drawn into a deep, relentless frown, his jaw tense and his eyes narrowed slightly. By the look of his attire, which was a more kingly, intricate version of a scout's leather riding armor, he'd only just gotten back from his visit to Maldobar. He must have departed Barrowton right after Enyo and I had to have made it back here already. I wondered if the disappearance of a certain large tree had something to do with that.

"Let's go inside. We can speak in private." The queen stretched out her hand, gesturing for us to follow. A tired smile deepened the wrinkles around her mouth.

Young guardsmen dressed in gold and white silk robes pulled the palace doors open so we could enter. Everyone began to move inside—all except for me. Yeah, I was still a prisoner—for now. It was getting harder and harder to resist the urge to do something violent and immature. My wrists were still bound at my back, courtesy of the scout warrior who had discovered us in the jungle.

Jaevid hesitated, staring at me with an eyebrow arched. "What about him?"

Everyone else paused as well.

Queen Araxie's expression sharpened with a look of parental disappointment. I was well acquainted with that look. "Reigh? You were the one who stole from my stables?"

"*Borrowed*," I corrected. "I brought it back—and him, too, if anyone cares." I nodded toward Jaevid.

When all eyes tracked back to Jaevid, he shrugged. "It's true."

"*You* revived him?" Jace's expression went steely. "How?"

"Uh, well, yes. I did. But it was sort of an accident. I didn't know I could do it. I just, um ... " I tried frantically to think of a way to make it sound like I hadn't gone there just to destroy the sacred tree out of spite in a childish fit of rage and self-loathing. Not one of my finer moments.

"I helped him," Hecate volunteered in a quiet voice. She stood between a pair of royal guards, apart from our group, with her head bowed and hands clasped in front of her. A beautiful gown of shimmering sky-blue satin swept over her petite form, and her long silver hair was pinned into a series of intricate braids. Copper beads and flowers had been wound into it, and there were decorative designs painted on her cheeks and forehead in gold.

The instant she spoke, Jaevid's expression changed. His mouth opened slightly as his eyes darted over her form, as though he recognized her somehow. Only ... he'd been dead, or asleep depending on who you asked, for forty years. There was no way he could have met her before now.

"Reigh came to me wanting to know how it might be done," she spoke quietly. "I told him what to do. He was desperate, and we were both unsure it would work. But I thought he should try. After all, we need Jaevid's help. We need a miracle, and there wasn't time to get anyone's approval."

And here I'd assumed Hecate couldn't bluff. She came off so meek and tentative all the time—I'd just assume skills at deception wouldn't come naturally to someone like that. It must have been those wide, sightless doe eyes that made her seem so innocent. I'd never been so relieved to be wrong. She was a *much* better liar than I was. I officially owed her one.

"Is that true?" Jace shot me a dangerous look with his lip slightly curled.

I cringed.

"If that is the case, then we are all in your debt now, Reigh. Release him at once," Queen Araxie ordered.

I heard the scout growling angry words under his breath as he obeyed. With my hands suddenly free, I rubbed the sore spots on my wrists where the bonds chaffed my skin. "From the queen's honored scout to a thief wanted for crimes against the crown in twenty-four hours and now the awakener of demigod war heroes. That has to be a new record."

Jaevid arched an eyebrow. "I'm a demigod?"

I choked. "Uh, well, some people said you were."

Come to think of it, I wasn't sure what to call him. Lapiloque? Lieutenant Broadfeather? Sir Jaevid, Savior of the World?

"Just 'Jae' will do," he said before I could decide. "They called me that before, I think."

"Only your friends did," King Jace corrected, his demeanor softer. "Though I'm sorry to say most of them are as old as I am now. Haven't aged as well, either. Gods, your brother, Roland, looks like the back of an old boot."

The queen covered her mouth, stifling a laugh.

"O-Oh." Jaevid blinked in surprise, like he wasn't sure if that was a joke he should have gotten or not. The king chuckled and gave him a few gruff pats on the shoulder. It even made Hecate smile a little.

"Right. Well, then, Reigh, I suppose this makes us friends," Jaevid said at last as he turned back to me, one hand outstretched as an offer for me to shake.

I froze as our gazes locked and I searched his pale eyes, looking for any sense that this might be bad idea. Did I *want* to be friends with this guy? If he really was Jaevid, the chosen one of the god Paligno that presided over all living things, what was he going to do when he found out about my dark passenger? He was the hero. I was the monster. We weren't meant to be allies ... right?

The longer I waited, the more awkward it became. Jaevid's brow creased slightly, his head tilting to the side. "Is everything all right?"

I couldn't afford to let on. Not now—not in front of everyone. The king and queen had never seen what I could do. They didn't know the half of what I was capable of. Not even Hecate knew, although she probably had more of an idea about it than most. She was blind, yes, but she could hear things others couldn't, whispers from somewhere beyond our world or understanding.

One glance at her and I could see the tension rising in her face. Her lips pressed together tightly, mismatched eyes of blue and green staring earnestly toward the ground at my feet. I saw her give the tiniest of nods, like she was urging me to get on with it.

Fine. I'd just have to trust her on this.

"No, uh, just wondering if this means we have to wear matching shirts or something." I forced a laugh and took Jaevid's hand to shake it quickly before letting go. "I'm not sure I'm ready for that kind of commitment."

King Jace smirked and folded his arms over his chest. "The way things usually go with Jaevid, you might consider adding a big bull's-eye to the design."

The queen snorted and gave her husband an elbow to the ribs. "Come on, then. Forty years without a bite to eat? I can only imagine our guest would like some dinner."

THE KING AND QUEEN LED THE WAY THROUGH THE WELL-GUARDED DOORS OF the palace and into the cool, marble foyer beyond. There, everything became quieter as the celebration in the city outside died away to a muffled rumble. Jaevid walked close beside me, occasionally stealing glances in my direction as we ventured down the airy halls, passing pillars of alabaster and jade.

Servants were already spreading out a lavish feast onto the low tables at the far end of the grand throne room when we entered. It was the same place I'd sat and dined with them before, when Aubren and his men from Maldobar had come to ask for help. Just as before, cushions of velvet, silk, and exotic animal hide had been placed around on the floor, so we could sit comfortably.

My mouth watered at the sight of the food and the delicious fragrance of roasted lamb in a spicy red sauce, fresh vegetables, crisp flat bread baked with sesame oils and rich herbs, sharp spices, and buttery rice. There were bowls of brightly-colored curry dishes and trays of pastes made from candied fruit for spreading over the flaky breads and pastries. My stomach growled and squirmed, and I spotted Jaevid chewing at the inside of his cheek while his gaze slowly panned over the spread.

As we sat down, the servants poured everyone goblets of sweet berry wine and cold water. But no one was supposed to eat until the king and queen started eating.

Somehow, I wound up sitting right next to Jaevid. I was beginning to suspect he was following me on purpose. I guess he'd taken that friendly handshake more seriously than I'd anticipated. He made himself comfortable, taking off his tattered cloak—which had a few big rust-colored stains on it I was almost certain were dried blood. The tunic he wore underneath it had stains, rips, and grime on it, too. Not to mention it was outrageously old-fashioned.

"Please." The queen gestured to the feast, her gaze still fixed on him. "Eat as much as you like."

I assumed the invitation went for me as well, so I snatched a piece of the flat bread from the nearest platter and started loading it down with helpings of rice, curry, and lamb.

Jaevid, on the other hand, blinked owlishly as he stared back at the queen. His mouth opened like he was going to speak, but his brow furrowed, and he swallowed hard, looking across the table toward King Jace.

"I-I'm sorry," he stammered quietly, his expression going tense as his shoulders hunched and he seemed to withdraw. "Your faces and voices are familiar. I ... don't remember how I know either of you."

"What?" King Jace froze where he had been unbuckling the leather breastplate from around his torso. His brow snapped into a scowl. "You don't remember anything from before?"

Jaevid shrank back farther, ducking his head lower. "Well, some things are clear, but others are jumbled. I know she was my cousin." He nodded slightly in Queen Araxie's direction. "But everything is so ... blurred. I can't sort out what was real and what wasn't. I remember there was a war. Fighting. So much suffering—" He stopped suddenly as he reached to press a hand against his shoulder. Honest shock drained the color from his face as he probed his fingers at something hidden there under his clothes. Jerking the neck of his tunic to the side revealed a scar, like something leftover from a stab wound.

"There was a war," Queen Araxie verified, her voice soft and gentle. "Between Maldobar and Luntharda. We call it the Gray War now. You ended it, Jae. You destroyed the god stone, took its place, and sacrificed yourself to save us. Do you remember that?"

He stared back at her, brows raised and expression utterly blank.

The atmosphere around the dinner table was thick with worry. Jace was rubbing his bearded chin and frowning deeply. Hecate sat perfectly still with her head bowed. Even Araxie was studying me and nibbling on her bottom lip.

"Tell him, then," I suggested. "Tell him what happened. Maybe it'll help piece together whatever fragments of memory he does have left."

So, they did.

It took a while. After all, it wasn't every day a guy went from essentially being a doormat for their abusive, deranged father to becoming a dragonrider and saving the world. Queen Araxie told as much of it as she had witnessed firsthand, but King Jace had to fill in the gaps, especially for the parts that had happened in Maldobar when Jaevid had been a dragonrider. Araxie hadn't known him then. In fact, the Gray elves hadn't even known Jaevid had existed at all until he'd been shot down in combat at Barrowton.

I'd heard all these tales before. Kiran had told them to me like bedtimes stories—about how Jaevid had come from an unkind human household. He'd been chosen by a wild dragon and had survived being brutally tortured by the Gray elves who'd believed he'd been an assassin sent to kill off what remained of the royal bloodline. Back then, humans and elves hadn't mixed. Being a halfbreed like Jaevid would have basically made you a social outcast. Halfbreed children were regarded as disgusting mutants—something that never should have existed. Now, obviously, things were different. Still, halfbreeds weren't common in Luntharda, although I'd seen more than a handful in Barrowton during my visit.

Once, the tales of Jaevid's adventures had filled my kid-sized brain with wonder, courage, and the desire to be a hero like that myself. Whenever Enyo and I had acted out those epic battles, I'd always wanted to be him. I'd wanted to be the underdog who rose against the odds and claimed glorious victory.

But sitting next to Jaevid now, watching his features become creased, tense, and stiff as the story of his life was laid out before him—I started to realize what it must have been like to be there in those moments. I'd been in a real battle now. I'd felt the harrowing pain of loss. He'd walked through that same kind of hellfire to end the Gray War numerous times. And now he was reliving it.

Little by little, his head bowed lower and lower until he was sitting, his shoulders hunched forward, and his chin nearly on his chest. His shaggy, ash-colored hair fell over his brow to hide most of his face, but I could still see that his mouth was mashed into a tight line as though he were clenching his teeth.

Then Queen Araxie started bringing him up to speed on our current situation, which wasn't good. She told him about Prince Aubren, who had come here looking for help to save Maldobar from invasion by the Tibran Empire. Things were bad—worse than they knew, really. I'd seen it firsthand, how the Tibrans fought and what they were capable of. I'd looked into the eyes of our enemy. Maldobar was doomed to fall unless something was done. This was worse than anything Jaevid might have faced in the Gray War.

But we were all counting on Jaevid to be able to save us—just like he had before.

When all the storytelling was over, Jaevid sat in complete silence. He didn't move, although I could see him taking in quick, sparse breaths every so often. His hands curled into fists on the table.

Too late, I began to wonder if this was too much for him to take in all at once. They were stacking a lot on his head right away. I mean, Gods and Fates, he'd only been awake for a day now. First, rehashing his whole life in excruciating detail, and then explaining to him that he was supposed to be the world's great savior and battle an enemy he'd never even seen before. If it were me sitting where he was, hearing all of that, I probably would have been ready to throw up and run from the room screaming.

"Where is Felix?" he asked suddenly, raising his head. "I know that name. I remember him, I think. Something about a promise?"

No one seemed eager to answer that question. If they'd really been best friends, like the stories said, then it was only natural he'd want to know what had happened to him. And the promise—well, that was bound to come up sooner or later.

"It was the last thing you ever said to him," King Jace replied in a quiet voice. "You promised him you would return when he needed you."

Jaevid's gaze flickered in my direction. "And yet you were the one who was able to wake me up? Why?"

My neck suddenly got hot and itchy. I scratched at it, acutely aware that I was beginning to sweat. "Uh ... well ... that's, um ... "

King Jace leaned across the table, his eyes locking on to me with a look that reminded me a little of being stared down by an angry dragon. "Talk, boy. Now is not the time to be testing my patience."

I swallowed hard. "I-I don't even know if it's true. Aubren said I would have to ask King Felix directly. He's the only one who might know."

"Know what?" Now the queen was giving me a disapproving glare as well.

"There's a chance, a small one, that I might be related to him," I muttered. "King Felix, that is. I, uh, I might be his son."

Queen Araxie froze in her seat, her eyes wide like two opal moons. Next to her, Hecate's mouth opened slightly. Jaevid frowned, as though he were confused.

"You don't say!" King Jace's booming laugh caught me off guard. He slapped his knee and nudged his wife with his elbow. "Well that explains a *lot*, don't you think?"

I blinked. "It does?"

"Indeed. I thought I recognized that cockiness and pride." He went on chuckling. "Not to mention the innate ability to lodge yourself right in the middle of every world-ending disaster within a hundred-mile radius."

My face was burning as I looked back down at the half-eaten platter of food in front of me. "Yeah, well, I don't know if it's really true or not."

The queen interrupted with a pensive frown. "I don't understand," she said. "Julianna passed away in childbirth. They said her child was lost as well. They buried it with her. We were there, Jace. We saw her in the coffin and the baby, too."

"We saw a baby, or a bundle of cloth shaped like one." Jace shrugged. "So, it was swapped somehow, and Kiran brought him here. That's not so farfetched, is it?"

The queen didn't look convinced. She frowned at me, her eyes still glittering with suspicion. "I suppose we will have to ask Kiran when he returns from Barrowton."

Those words hit me like a knee to the gut. A hard knot lodged in my throat, blocking my air and making my eyes tear. I felt hot and cold at the same time, and every muscle in my body jolted with a chill.

They didn't know Kiran was dead. They didn't know I had killed him. How— how could King Jace not know? Hadn't anyone told him at Barrowton? Why would they keep it a secret? Or ... had they not known it yet, either? Kiran was never one to inject himself into royal matters unless someone commanded him to, so it made sense for him to avoid that kind of attention. But surely, by now, they knew he was dead.

"Felix is still alive?" Jaevid changed the subject.

"Yes, as far as we know, and still the King of Maldobar. But if things keep progressing this way, he may not hold that title for much longer," Araxie answered softly. "But the Tibrans are relentless, and we've had no news in days now. Kiran left with a small group of our warriors when we heard that Barrowton was expecting an attack. Jace followed with as many reinforcements as we could muster. Based on everything we had heard, it was doubtful the city could withstand an assault. Very few dragonriders had been spotted there—not nearly enough to hold the city."

"Our first wave of reinforcements was able to reach the city before the battle was over," King Jace added. "But not before the Tibrans unleashed some manner of ... creature onto the field. It killed as many of their own soldiers as it did Maldobarians. A miscalculation on its destructive force, I can only assume. After that, they began a full retreat."

I swallowed hard, fighting to gulp down the burning lump that rose in my throat. He was talking about *me*. I was the one who had killed all those men—although, not for the Tibrans, of course. I was trying to help, trying to save Vexi, when everything spun out of control. Had Aubren told them a Tibran weapon had done all that to cover for me?

"Not that any of us believed for a moment that kind of backfire would deter them," the king continued. "Tibrans are not so easily discouraged. They'll try to take Barrowton again—if they haven't already. Prince Aubren and Duke Derrick were determined to evacuate the city and save as many as they could before that hammer fell, however."

Jaevid's eyes darkened. He clenched his teeth so hard a vein stood out in the side of his neck. Neither of us was enjoying this conversation anymore.

I cleared my throat, although my voice still cracked when I spoke. "Uh, maybe we should take a break here."

Queen Araxie drew back in confusion, almost like she found the suggestion utterly ridiculous. Then her gaze paused on Jaevid. I guess she could see his distress as plainly as I could. Her expression saddened, and she nodded. "A room has been prepared for you both. You are welcome here as long as you wish."

Jaevid's smile looked painfully forced. His hands were still clenched.

"I think he should stay with me," I said. "At the clinic, that is."

Now the king and queen were both glowering at me. Right, okay, I know that probably really sounded stupid to them. He was a famous demigod war hero. At first glance, it made way more sense that he should be housed in the palace with as many royal comforts as he could stand, not at my cramped little medical clinic. Except in every story I'd ever heard Kiran tell about him, he'd always emphasized that Jaevid was modest. He was a simple kind of person who didn't like being in the spotlight or being given any extra attention because of who he was. Formalities, riches, and grandeur made him uncomfortable—according to Kiran, anyway. I was acting on a hunch that being here might have been part of the problem. After all, I hadn't seen him relax since we'd walked through the door.

At my suggestion, Jaevid's mouth quirked slightly in a *real* smile. He closed his eyes and nodded slowly. "I would prefer that, if it's all right. I mean no insult, and I'm grateful for your hospitality. Truly, I am. I just ... need some time to think."

"Don't worry about it." King Jace let out a deep sigh. He'd known Jaevid back then, during the Gray War, so maybe he got it, too. "As far as we are concerned, this city is as much your home as it is ours. You can do as you like." Then he looked at me. "Just try not to make a spectacle out of it. For the time being, let's keep his presence at your home just between us."

"Of course," I agreed. The last thing I wanted was the whole city of Mau Kakuri knocking down my front door to catch a glimpse of everyone's favorite war hero.

CHAPTER ELEVEN

Dinner seemed to drag on forever. Sleeping rough in the jungle the night before had my back aching and a belly full of warm food had made my mind sluggish. King Jace talked on and on about some of his memories from when he and Jaevid had been captured in Luntharda. He made being tortured sound like it wasn't that big of a deal. Starvation? No problem. A few broken bones? A minor inconvenience. Almost being beheaded on the temple steps? Ah, well, it had just been a misunderstanding.

Jace was a strange old guy, even for a human.

Jaevid didn't eat much and stayed quiet while everyone else talked. His gaze was distant, as though he were a thousand miles away. Every now and then, he would steal a quick glance at Hecate. Then his body would stiffen, his brow twitching and creasing, until he finally looked away again. It was like they were having a conversation the rest of us couldn't hear.

When the meal was over, Queen Araxie hugged Jaevid tightly again and kissed his forehead. King Jace offered him a firm handshake and a few rough pats on the back. Hecate bowed slightly, murmuring a quiet farewell.

During all that, Jaevid never said a word. He had a thin, anxious frown on his lips as he picked up his bloodstained cloak, tied it around his shoulders again, and came to stand next to me. For whatever reason, he seemed more comfortable around me than he was with them. It was like having a much taller shadow following me around.

At King Jace's suggestion, we slipped out of the palace through a cramped secret tunnel that led us underground. It twisted and turned, seeming to go on forever. Jaevid had to crouch over and shuffle along with a hand on my back so we didn't lose one another in the dark. I walked with my hands out in front, groping through the gloom until it ended at a small door. The smell of cool, crisp moisture and moss filled my nose before I even opened it. The sound of rushing water gave me an idea of where we might be.

Pushing the door open, I squinted into the silvery moonlight that hit the mist around the falls and made the air sparkle. We were standing on a ledge right beside the falls, nothing between us and the glistening spires of the palace except for empty air and the pouring falls. Before us, the city of Mau Kakuri was bathed in glittering veils of mist and starlight.

"Beautiful," Jaevid whispered.

I smirked. "After you save the world again maybe you can retire here."

"You think I can do it?" He arched an eyebrow.

"What? Beat the Tibrans? Save Maldobar?"

He nodded.

"Well, if you can't, then we're basically toast, right?" I regretted those words instantly. Jaevid's expression went from curious and marginally content to utter despair in a matter of seconds. "I, uh, I'm sure it'll work out. Besides, you're not alone. You've got the support of Luntharda and Maldobar this time."

Looking back out over the city again, Jaevid didn't answer. A sad, distant smile made his sharp features soften as he sighed. "Sure. What's the worst that can happen? I die again?"

I choked, trying not to laugh. "Was that a joke? Did the great Jaevid Broadfeather just make a death joke?"

He started laughing, too. "I guess so."

Things felt more relaxed as we made our way into the city. Most of the celebrations had been moved indoors after the sunset. We both had the cowls of our cloaks pulled up to hide our faces from the few people still out celebrating in the street. Windows into houses and taverns revealed crowds still toasting, eating, and joining in excited conversations—probably retelling all of Jaevid's wild adventure stories. No one paid us much attention, though.

When we got to the front door of the medical clinic, I opened it and gestured for him to go inside first. He had to duck to get through the doorway. He really was tall, especially for a halfbreed. Gray elves were typically on the short side, and halfbreeds almost always shared that trait as well. Not Jaevid, though. He was easily three or four inches over six feet.

It was cozy inside the clinic. Enyo had left embers to smolder down in the fire pit, and the smells from her dinner were still lingering in the warm air. Only a few oil lamps were lit, making the shadows heavy and the atmosphere seem dim and close. More of Kiran's medical journals were spread out across the floor like she'd been studying again. I didn't see her anywhere, though. Maybe she'd gone to stay with her family for the night rather than be here alone.

Together, Jaevid and I took off our boots and cloaks and left them by the doorway. I watched my guest step carefully into the house, looking all around with a strange expression, as though he were wondering if he should have recognized any of this or not.

I decided to clear that up for him. "You've never been here before, by the way."

Jaevid winced. "O-Oh. Okay. Good. I was just thinking that it doesn't look familiar. The palace didn't, either."

"This city was just a small village before the war, so most of the buildings here probably didn't even exist then," I explained.

"I suppose a lot has changed in ... forty years." His voice hitched, catching at the number.

"That's what I've been told." I sighed, picking up a few more logs from the timber box near the door so I could stoke the fire back to life. It filled the room with more light and made things seem a little less depressing. "Make yourself at home." I nodded to the seat across the fire pit.

Jaevid Broadfeather sat down at my home hearth, his arms folded guardedly across his middle. I spotted him once again probing at that scar on his shoulder, his brow furrowed, and his mouth skewed, as though he were still struggling to remember where it had come from.

"Look, it's okay," I said. "I get that this is a lot for you to take in. So, if you have questions, or you're not sure about something, you can ask me. I'm not gonna judge you."

"Thank you. I appreciate that." His expression dimmed. "Everyone's expecting so much from me, and I'm not sure if I'll be able to live up to that. The list of things I know is disturbingly short."

I smirked. "Well, I didn't know you before, so I don't have any expectations. Except maybe for you to take a bath. No offense but going forty years without one doesn't smell so great."

His face flushed. "O-Oh. Yes. I suppose I should."

"You can borrow some of my clothes, too, if you want. I'm shorter, so they probably won't fit right, but it'll get you by until we can find you something else."

"Thank you, Reigh." I got the impression by the tone and the earnest way he was staring at me that he wasn't just thanking me for the clothes.

I shrugged. "It's the least I can do after, you know, what I did. It's my fault you're in this mess now, right?"

"How did you do it? How did you awaken me?"

I had *really* been hoping he wouldn't ask me that. I didn't have Hecate's bluffing skills. I turned my face away, pretending to be filling one of our bronze teapots with water so he wouldn't see me grimace. "It was sort of an accident. I don't know how to explain it."

"How old are you?" He had a strange edge to his voice.

"Sixteen. I'll be seventeen in a few months."

"I know you said we've never met, and I guess it's impossible that we would have. You wouldn't have been born when I was, er, alive before." He was rubbing that scar again. "I just get this weird feeling that I know you. You seem very familiar somehow."

I hesitated, my body cringing up involuntarily. "Well, if Prince Aubren is right and I'm, you know, related to King Felix of Maldobar ... that could be why." It was only explanation that made sense, but not one I had fully come to terms with yet. If everything Aubren suspected was true, then I was also a prince of Maldobar—and a direct descendant of Jaevid's best friend. Maybe I looked like him, or at least favored him enough to call back some of those memories from the depths of his mind. Regardless, I wasn't exactly up for an open debate about my parentage.

"I suppose." He sighed. "I'm not sure of anything anymore. My head feels like a grape being squeezed in someone's fist. I can't concentrate. The more I try, the more my thoughts scramble."

"Some senility is expected for a man of your age." I tried teasing him a little, just to lighten the mood. "But if it's any consolation, you look okay for someone everyone thought was a corpse a few days ago."

Jaevid smirked back. "I suppose I do smell like a corpse, though."

"Yep, no argument there. The public bathhouse is probably closed for the night. But you can use the basin upstairs. It's the first door on the left." I nodded toward the staircase. "Help yourself."

OKAY, SO IN RETROSPECT, I PROBABLY SHOULD HAVE GONE UP WITH HIM AND made extra sure Enyo wasn't there. My bad. I was still a little thrown off because of the whole "having the one and only Jaevid Broadfeather in my house" thing.

The sound of her scream from upstairs made me jump. Commotion, thumping noises, thuds, and Enyo screeching like an angry hawk came from the stairwell. *Oh no ...*

Dropping the tea steeper, I'd been stuffing full of fragrant dried tealeaves, I bolted upstairs as fast as I could.

Jaevid was on the floor opposite from the washroom with Enyo looming over him in a defensive stance, her hands balled into fists. Her long, silver hair was dripping wet and her face was flushed with anger.

Oh, and she was naked. Well, mostly naked. She had a thin silk shawl wrapped around her, but it only barely covered everything.

"Reigh!" She gasped as she saw me clambering up the stairwell. "This mongrel broke in. Probably trying to steal medicines or money. He tried to corner me in the washroom!"

Jaevid was groaning and holding his face.

Enyo curled her lip in disgust and gave him a kick to the ribs, just for good measure. "Hurry up and get your sword! I'll hold him here until the city guards get—"

"Enyo, stop!" I rushed in between them and helped drag Jaevid back to his feet. He was dazed, but the instant he looked at Enyo, his whole face turned beet red and he turned away, covering his eyes.

I didn't get it at first. Sure, she was pretty, but she was also kind of terrifying when she was snarling like an angry shrike. Then I remembered what an old servant woman in Barrowton had told me about nudity. Humans weren't comfortable with it, and Jaevid had grown up in Maldobar, raised mostly by humans. I guessed it was only natural that he'd be a little shocked and embarrassed to see her like that.

"Oh, gods," he rasped. "I-I'm so sorry. I didn't know there was anyone else here."

"It's okay." I shot Enyo an exasperated glare over my shoulder.

She glared back. "What's going on? Who is this?"

"He's my guest, not an intruder." I stepped out of the way, so she could see him. "Jaevid, this is Enyo. Enyo, meet Jaevid. If you can manage it, try not to punch or kick him again. He's had a rough day."

Her face paled. Her eyes widened and her mouth dropped open.

Jaevid still wouldn't look at her. With his eyes pinched shut, he just nodded once and went on rubbing his jaw. There was blood on his chin. She'd split his lip wide open with one punch. "Nice to meet you," he rasped.

"Oh," Enyo breathed the word shakily. For a moment, she looked like she might faint. Then her wide, shimmering eyes flicked to me. "How? When? I-I heard the commotion in the streets, but I had no idea it was ... I mean, I just assumed it was something to do with the war in Maldobar, not ..."

"It's a long story," I mumbled. "Before we dive into that, why don't you put some clothes on and do something about the damage you did to his face, eh? I've got to find him something to wear."

"Oh! Oh, Fates." She gasped again, horrified. She clamped a hand over her mouth as though she'd just remembered. "I-I punched him. I punched Jaevid Broadfeather in the face!"

CHAPTER TWELVE

Everything had calmed down again as we settled downstairs, gathering around the fire pit and waiting for the water to boil for tea. Jaevid was avoiding eye contact as he joined us around the fire pit. His cheeks and nose were bright red, and his bottom lip swollen and bloody. Likewise, Enyo couldn't seem to sit still. She shifted her weight, nibbling on the inside of her cheek and stealing glances at him now and again.

"I am so sorry, Lord Jaevid. Honestly, I had no idea you were here." Enyo spoke softly, scooting closer to sit by him with a tray of medical tools. She kept her head bowed in respect, and her hands shook as she picked up a cloth off the tray. "May I tend to your lip?"

He blushed and hardly seemed able to look at her. "I—yes, thank you. But please, you can both just call me 'Jae' if you want. 'Lord' sounds a little formal. Besides, I'm not really lord of anything."

Now Enyo was blushing, too. For some reason, that *really* got on my nerves. I watched as she laid out a few things to treat Jaevid's split lip. It was swollen and probably needed at least one stitch. She patted it gently with that clean cloth to wipe away the blood.

My heart pounded as Enyo gingerly leaned closer to him to examine the damage. I didn't like it one bit—the way she was looking at him. Like he was special. Like she was enjoying being close to him. Why the heck had I suggested she do this? I was the medical expert here. I'd spent years apprenticing under Kiran. Stupid, stupid, *stupid*!

How could I compete with that? Jaevid was older than me by a year or two and probably better-looking by female standards. He had those sharp, perfectly-defined elf features and a piercing gaze that reminded me somewhat of Jace's. That must have been a dragonrider thing. His hair was chopped off short, right above his shoulders, and was ash gray color—a bit darker than the normal white-silver of the elves. Not to mention he was taller with wider shoulders and a more leanly muscled frame.

And I was just ... me. Luntharda's resident human screw-up. The guy who'd gotten her in trouble practically every day since we'd met.

I rubbed my jaw and tried to think of something, anything else. Why did this even bother me so much? Why did it matter how she treated him? It wasn't like I ...

As Enyo went on cleaning the split on his lip, I saw her avoiding his gaze in a coy, bashful manner. She'd never acted like that around me. Great. It didn't matter what I felt. I didn't stand a chance now.

I cleared my throat and glared down at the fire. "You can have my room for the night. Maybe if you can rest, some of those memories might come back."

Jaevid couldn't answer while she was preparing to put one stitch on his bottom lip.

"Memories?" Enyo glanced between us, her brow crinkled.

"He doesn't remember much from before he, well, I'm not sure 'died' is the right word for it."

He nodded slightly in agreement.

"Oh, I see." Her expression became sympathetic. "Because of the foundling spirits?"

I arched a brow. "The what?"

"You know, the ones from the final battle? When he destroyed the god stone?" She looked at Jaevid like she was hoping he might back her up.

He just stared back at her, frosty blue eyes wide. He still couldn't speak until she'd finished doctoring his lip.

"You really don't remember, do you?" She smeared a bit of healing salve over the place where it had split and then gingerly reached out to take his arm. "May I?"

Jaevid blinked as he allowed her to take hold of his arm, unlace the vambrace there, and roll back his sleeve. On the inside of his forearm, covered by a grimy old bandage, was a mark. It looked almost like a brand, or tattoo, of swirling black designs that went from his wrist almost to his elbow. The instant I saw it, I got a strange feeling like pins and needles under my skin. There was something odd about that mark, almost as though it had an aura all its own.

"I only heard this tale once, from one of the old storytellers who used to sit in the market square. My mother said it might not be true. Foundling spirits can be unpredictable and treacherous. They're almost as old as the gods and have incredible power." She brushed her fingers over his arm. Maybe she didn't mean anything by that, or perhaps she was just mystified by the sight of that design—

either way, it was clear that touching him that way made Jaevid even more embarrassed.

I gnawed furiously on the inside of my cheek.

"The story said that you made a bargain with the foundling spirits. They agreed to help you bring the god stone through the dangers of the jungle and protect your loved ones, but at a high price," she said.

"What price?" I pressed.

"My memories," Jaevid finished suddenly, clarity dawning on his face. "I remember that. They wanted some of my memories, the ones from my ancestors."

"Do you think that's why you can't remember anything now?" I asked.

He shook his head. "I'm not sure. Everything is muddied, like I can't focus. I'm ... " His voice died away before he could finish.

"Tired?" Enyo guessed with a gentle smile.

He ducked his head as though he were ashamed. "After forty years of doing nothing, is that bad?"

She laughed. "I suppose we can grant a night of sleep. We'll let it slide, just this once." She regarded him so warmly, so affectionately, that it made my blood boil.

They went on talking, and I got the feeling I might as well have been invisible. Why did that bug me so much? Why did I even care how she looked at him? Before I could sort it out, Jaevid dismissed himself to go upstairs, wash off, and rest. I'd loaned him my bedroom for as long as he planned to stay here. No way was I putting him in the room with Enyo.

Now that we were alone by the glow of the fire, Enyo let out a deep sigh and slumped back to rest her weight on her palms. "I can't believe I punched Jaevid."

I snorted. "What's the big deal? You've hit me plenty of times."

She shot me a look. "Only when you deserved it."

"You never bandaged me up after, though. Or looked at me like that."

Enyo blinked in surprise. "Like how?"

I didn't want to explain it—it just made me more frustrated. "Forget it. It doesn't matter."

She was still staring me down, though. "Reigh, what happened? You disappeared for two days, do you realize that? I didn't know where to even begin looking for you. And then you come back, out of the blue, with Jaevid Broadfeather?"

I kept my mouth shut.

"Tell me what happened, please. You did this, didn't you? You awakened Jaevid."

When I didn't reply, she touched my arm.

I couldn't help but look at her then. "It was kind of an accident, okay?"

She looked puzzled. "An accident?"

"I didn't go there with the intention of waking him up. I know that's what everyone is going to think now, but that's not what happened."

"Where did you go?"

"To the tree, the one at the old temple grounds. I—" my voice caught, and I checked over my shoulder to make sure Jaevid wasn't anywhere in sight. "I went there to kill that stupid tree, not to bring him back to life. I used my power on it, to make it rot and die. But when it disappeared, I found Jaevid's tomb. I went down there, you know, just to see if he was there. I didn't do anything to him, I swear. He looked like a statue, like he was made of stone. So, I just thumped his face a little and the next thing I knew, he woke up."

"You went there to kill that tree? Why? Why would you do something like that? Especially if you didn't know you could wake him." Enyo frowned, her eyes searching mine. "I know you're upset about Kiran, but that's no excuse to—"

"It's not that," I barked at her. There was so much she didn't know about me, where I'd come from, and what I was really capable of. If she didn't prefer Jaevid now, she would after she found out.

"Then what is it?"

I turned away and started to get up. "Nothing."

She wrenched my arm and yanked me back. "Don't you dare lie to me, Reigh."

I took a deep breath. She wanted to know? Fine. "I wanted to destroy that tree because if he had been there, if he'd woken sooner, none of this would have happened. He could have fought at Barrowton. He could have stopped the Tibrans and Kiran would still be—"

I stopped. My expression skewed with pain and I bit down hard to keep it in. "I just wanted to stop everyone from expecting me to fill his shoes somehow. I can't do that. I'm not like him. I'm not a hero. I'm not even a good person."

Enyo touched my face. I felt her cool, smooth palms slide over my cheeks as she leaned in to touch her forehead to mine. "You're stupid sometimes. You're reckless. You're ridiculous, too. But I don't believe that you're a bad person, Reigh. I'll never believe that."

"I murdered him, Enyo. I murdered Kiran," I rasped. "The king and queen don't know. They think it was a monster fighting for the Tibrans. And, gods, I might as well have been, right? I killed just as many Maldobarian soldiers as I did Tibrans. I killed my own father!"

She paused as though she were thinking it over, choosing her words carefully. "You lost control. This power you have, while I don't understand it, I can see that it is strong. It could overtake you again, just like it did that day. You have to be stronger. You can't let it own you like that ever again. Maybe that's why Jaevid has come back now—to show you how."

"That woman. She called me her Harbinger."

Enyo's brow creased with concern. "What woman?"

"The one I keep seeing in my dreams," I replied. "She said her name was Clysiros."

Recognition flickered over Enyo's face the instant I spoke that name. Her body tensed, and she held my gaze with wide, fearful eyes.

"You know that name?" I dared to ask. "Do you know who she is?"

Her lips pressed together, and she took a deep breath. "That old storyteller, the one I mentioned before, I used to visit him all the time when I was little. I liked his stories because sometimes he told ones I'd never heard before. He knew things no one else did. The last time I saw him, he told a tale about the ancient gods. It was about how the world began, how the gods of the earth and sky were lonely, so they came together and had two children.

The first they called Paligno, who was the god of life. He filled the dormant world with plants and animals, beautiful things that pleased his parents." Enyo hesitated, her multihued eyes catching in the light from the fire pit and sparkling like two fiery diamonds. "But the other child was much different. She was the exact opposite of her brother. They called her Clysiros, and her touch brought death to all the things Paligno had created. The god of the earth was so disgusted by her, he banished her from ever setting foot upon the ground he ruled. But her mother, the goddess of the sky, loved her. She recognized that while death was terrifying to most, it was also necessary. The sky goddess hid Clysiros away in the stars, protecting her there."

"And?" I asked, breathless.

She shook her head, her mouth scrunching thoughtfully. "I never heard the ending of the story. My mother came in to get me, and when she heard which story he was telling, she immediately took me away. She told me never to utter that name again and never tell anyone what I'd heard. I'd forgotten about that until now, when you said it."

"But why? Why doesn't anyone talk about her? Clysiros, I mean."

"I don't know. After that, I never saw the storyteller again. I suppose he could have passed away. He was quite old, after all." She flashed a worried glance up at me.

I was just trying to let that sink in for a second. I'd never heard that before. I wondered if the king or queen had. And Kiran—had he known?

"Reigh," Enyo whispered. "If it's true and you are seeing Clysiros, then maybe you are like Jaevid."

"No," I snapped. "He's like Paligno. He heals people, brings life and hope to them."

She stared up at me silently, a mixture of apprehension and the smallest trace of fear in her eyes. It was as though she didn't know if she should run or hold perfectly still. Would I hurt her? Would I lose control again?

"I'm the opposite," I whispered. "I ... am the Harbinger of death."

Even after the house became quiet and still, with Enyo snoozing away in Kiran's old bed and Jaevid borrowing mine, I couldn't find any peace for myself. I'd made a pallet on the floor beside the fire pit, but I didn't expect to be sleeping tonight, anyway. Too much was happening for my mind to relax. Everywhere I looked, I saw memories. Kiran hadn't been my real father, but he'd been the only parent I'd ever known. He had raised me from an infant. With him gone, this place felt so empty. Part of me kept hoping that somehow, some way, he'd come striding through the door with that signature scowl on his face and start lecturing me for being so reckless.

Only I knew that wasn't possible. He was gone. And regardless of what Enyo said, I knew that was my fault.

Once I was sure everyone else was down for the night, I got up and pulled my boots on. I sat out on the front steps. I soaked in the gentle night sounds of the city. Frogs and insects sang in the tall reeds. Fireflies winked like warm yellow spots against the jungle. The rumbling whoosh of the magnificent waterfalls pouring down the steep cliffs behind the palace was constant. Everything was so familiar. It made all that chaos, blood, and agony in Maldobar seem like a faraway nightmare that I could easily ignore. I didn't have to go back. It wasn't my fight. I never should have gotten involved in the first place.

Except I knew better than to think the Tibrans wouldn't come here, too. I'd seen their brutality with my own eyes now. I knew what they were capable of. Maldobar would fall and then that ruthless Tibran woman who called herself Hilleddi would come looking for me here. She had seen what I could do, she knew I had power, and I wasn't stupid enough to think she wouldn't tell their leader, Argonox, about me. I was a threat they couldn't afford to ignore, and Luntharda wasn't the military powerhouse Maldobar was. The wild jungle and all its natural horrors was our biggest defense. We could run, hide, and use our environment to drag out the inevitable, but eventually ... they'd find us. They'd find me.

And what then?

"*Then we crush them, eat them, burn them!*" Noh's voice rippled over my brain, making me shudder.

His wispy dark form came slinking out of the gloom like a huge wolf made of licking, flickering black shadows. His glowing red eyes watched me, and his wide canine mouth was smiling with rows of jagged white fangs.

"You know the truth, don't you?" I growled at him under my breath. "Am I really Clysiros's 'chosen one' like Jaevid is for Paligno?"

The mention of her name made his form ripple like a reflection on a pond. When he didn't answer I let out a sarcastic snort.

"And what does that make you? My nasty little sidekick? A perk of being some sort of death-dealing monster?"

He still didn't answer as his shadowy form came striding closer, sitting back on his wolfish haunches and studying me with ominous, flickering red eyes.

"If that's the case, then you might as well move on to someone else. I meant what I said to Clysiros at that tree. I'm done. I won't use my power again. I'm staying here and running the medical clinic. I'm not fighting any more battles or wars. I don't want anything to do with it." I scowled down at the tops of my boots. "Besides, with Jaevid here now, they won't need me anyway. I'm sure he can handle it."

"*And if he fails?*"

His reply made me look up again. "What's that supposed to mean? Jaevid's fought in battles before. He's trained for it. He was a soldier, a legitimate dragonrider, for crying out loud. I'm nothing like that."

Before me, Noh's form rippled and changed. It moved with fluidity like smoke on the wind, blurring and reforming into another shape—one I'd seen him take before. He looked exactly like me. Well, a darker, shadowy, red-eyed version of me. His skin was a dark, charcoal gray color and his hair as black as night. When he smiled, I could see that his incisors were pointed.

"*And yet, in us, he has met his match.*" Noh sounded deliciously confident.

I narrowed my eyes. "Who are you—really?"

He stretched out one of his shadowy hands toward me, fingers spread wide. "*I am you,*" he replied. "*You are me. We are one. Two souls, two minds, one body. That is the mark of the Harbinger.*"

I didn't understand. Mark? What mark? No one had ever mentioned anything like that to me.

Even as the doubts sparked in my brain, I couldn't ignore a strange pull toward him—like a hook lodged deep in my gut. It tugged at something, a sensation I couldn't explain. I had the uncontrollable urge to put my hand against his, just to see if it really was the exact same size as mine.

But before I could move, a commotion from the jungle broke my concentration. Overhead, the glimmer off translucent wings caught in the moonlight. A single shrike came streaking out of the jungle, passing right above our street. It was alone and flying high, bearing a rider headed straight for the palace at an urgent speed.

"*News from the battlefront, no doubt.*" Noh's form flickered with delight. He licked his chops hungrily.

"Something else has happened."

"*They'll be coming for him,*" Noh hissed in agreement. "*Seeking practiced hands to strum the instrument of war.*"

"I'm sure." Frowning, I turned to look back at the front door of the medical clinic—my home, my refuge. "And something tells me they'll want to make it a duet this time."

CHAPTER THIRTEEN

Hours—that's what we had left. The king and queen would soon come knocking, either personally or by sending one of their messengers. It only made sense to let Jaevid enjoy those hours resting. I passed the night sitting at the fire pit, watching the flames dance in the dark, and skimming Kiran's old medical journals. He'd almost finished translating another one from the human to Gray elf languages. It was tedious work, going back and forth between the two languages, and his unique knowledge of the medical practices and terms in both kingdoms was unique.

I got to the end of the final page he'd translated and stopped, running my fingers over the heavy parchment pages. There was still a lot left to go in this journal—a lot of work left unfinished. He'd stopped mid-sentence. And while I could probably read the rest of it in the human tongue and translate it, it just felt wrong to tack my sloppy handwriting on to the rest of his neat, perfectly-uniform script. I'd spent most of my life right here at his side training to be a medic. Until Enyo, I had been the only apprentice he'd ever taken on. At least, for any length of time. If he'd been teaching Enyo, then she'd barely had enough time to learn how to properly apply a bandage. I was the only one qualified to run this place now. But considering I was to blame for his absence ... would he have even wanted that?

That question stuck in my brain like a thorn, keeping me awake until the sun began to rise. My back was aching along the area where I'd been burned by dragon venom during the battle at Barrowton. Two nights without much sleep was wearing on me. My clothes and hair stank from sweat. I needed a bath.

All I needed was a clean shirt from the spare closet in Kiran's room. That was it. I'd only intended to go in long enough to grab one, so I could change after I took a quick turn in the washroom. Enyo was still sound asleep in the bed when I crept in. I didn't want to wake her. But one glance at her made me pause, my body freezing up with a hand on the closet door.

She was curled up on her side with her long, silvery hair spilling over the pillows like bolts of white silk. It made a beautiful contrast to the warm, golden color of her skin. Soft rays of morning light fell over her face, and her eyelids fluttered as though she were dreaming.

Gods, had she always been that beautiful?

The longer I stared, the more an intense squeezing sensation pulled the breath from my lungs and made my heart start to pound. My face grew hot just thinking about how she had smiled and acted so bashful and friendly with Jaevid. It wasn't fair. I ... I didn't want her to look at *him* like that.

I took a step closer to the bedside and let my fingertips lightly graze the curve of her cheek.

She'd always been the voice of caution and reason, which I'd deliberately ignored. Nearly every time we'd gotten into trouble, it was because I'd dragged her off somewhere we weren't supposed to be in the first place to do something we weren't supposed to be doing. And then I'd left her behind here in Luntharda to chase the idiotic idea of finding my human family somewhere in Maldobar.

Talk about stupid.

I let out a sigh and started back for the closet.

A hand grabbed my wrist, pulling me to a stop.

"Reigh? Is everything okay?" Enyo mumbled as she blinked up at me groggily, still holding on to my arm.

"I—I, uh."

"Haven't you slept at all?"

"No," I confessed.

"I told you sleeping on the floor was a bad idea. Your back is still sore, isn't it?" She propped herself up on one arm, tugging on my arm a little. "Lie down here."

Gods, Fates, and all things holy. Was this really happening? I opened my mouth to make a witty and confident retort—but nothing would come out. My face felt like it was on fire.

"Don't be stubborn." She sighed. "You need to rest. I know you've hardly slept at all since we left Barrowton."

"O-Okay." I tripped around trying to kick my boots off and then stood awkwardly at the side of the bed while she scooted over to make room.

It wasn't a very big bed. Bigger than mine, but still ... Kiran never had, you know, *those* kinds of guests. I knew there was absolutely no way I was going to be able to sleep, not with her curled up right next to me. As I sank down into the mattress, I could easily pick out the warm spot where she'd been lying mere seconds before. The pillows smelled like her, too. I didn't get any time to contemplate that, though. As soon as I got settled, lying on my side with my back to her, Enyo started snuggling me. She slipped an arm around my chest, hugging herself up against my back. Her breath tickled in my hair right next to my ear.

My heart pounded out of control. I should say something—something good. Something intelligent and maybe a little romantic. Suave, but casual.

"I, uh, I'm thinking of making eggs for breakfast."

Crap.

"Reigh?" Her voice came in a soft, barely audible whisper.

I took a deep breath, trying to steady my frazzled nerves. "Yeah?"

"I love you."

My heart hit the back of my throat so hard, I couldn't speak. Had I heard that right? There was only one way to be sure. My hands were sweaty and shaking when I rolled over to face her. Her captivating, multihued eyes met mine in the pale light of the morning. She was blushing, too.

"Say something, please." She squeezed her eyes shut. "It's so embarrassing if you just stare like that."

I couldn't. I wanted to, but everything I wanted to say kept getting tangled up in my brain. Words—what were words? Smoke was probably coming out of my ears.

I kissed her instead.

Enyo took in a breath of surprise as I moved in closer, sitting up just enough that I could lean over and press my mouth against hers. There was a slim chance I'd taken her words the wrong way. She might have meant love in a brotherly way, in which case she might break my nose or knee me in the groin—both if she was especially angry. I was willing to take that risk, though.

Her lips moved against mine and she reached up, grabbing handfuls of my hair and dragging me in closer. My pulse was starting and stalling wildly when I slipped my arms around her. But the second I started to get confident, Enyo pulled back. Her brow crinkled as her eyes searched mine.

"Don't ever suggest that I like Jaevid more than you again," she commanded. "I mean it. I know you think this power you have is evil, and that you're not a good person because of it, but I don't believe that. I never will."

"Why?" The question tore out of me. "You realize that doesn't make any sense, right? You saw what happened at Barrowton. And I've done nothing to make you—"

"Because you are *my* somebody, Reigh. Don't you understand that? You're the one person in the world that makes me feel whole. You're the quiet voice in my head, the fire in my soul that makes me want to be brave, and the funny thought that makes me smile." The morning light glittered in her eyes, making them shine like aquamarines as she ran her palms over the sides of my face. She brushed her thumb over the scar on the bridge of my nose.

"Funny as in funny-looking or ... ?"

She giggled and pinched one of my cheeks. "See? Reigh, you really are stupid sometimes. It's like you think you're all alone in the world. But all you need to do is look down. I'm here. I'll always be right beside you."

I was debating making a quick joke about how far down I'd have to look—since she was still short compared to me. Her lips against mine wiped those thoughts away instantly. One kiss and I was hers. Nothing else mattered ... because she was my somebody, too.

We curled up together in the middle of the bed, nestled in the pillows and blankets. She put her head on my chest and entangled her legs with mine. Her breathing slowed, coming in gentle puffs as she drifted off asleep again.

Drinking in the serenity and silence, I kept my arms around her and my nose burrowed into her soft silver hair. I honestly didn't know if I could make her happy. She was everything I'd ever wanted, and everything I knew I'd never deserve. But in that moment, I knew I'd happily kill myself trying to be the guy she claimed I was.

I'd do whatever it took to become the hero she believed I could be.

ENYO AND I HAD JUST SAT DOWN TO EAT A LATE BREAKFAST. OKAY, SO I WAS showing off a little. Expertly-fried eggs, freshly-baked bread from the bakery down the street, hot spiced tea, sweet butter, and an assortment of jellied fruit preserves were spread out around for us to share. I was stirring a spoonful of honey into my tea when someone knocked on the front door.

In an instant, reality burst the bubble of happiness I'd been reveling in all morning. I sighed. "I'll get it."

"Who is it? Are you expecting a patient?" Enyo looked worried.

I didn't want to answer that. "Just keep eating. I'll handle it."

Of course, it wasn't a patient. I was anticipating a troop of Gray elf warriors waiting outside my house. But when I opened the door, I found the king and queen standing on my doorstep alone. They hadn't even brought an escort.

Okay, that was weird.

"Where is he? Where is Jaevid?" Queen Araxie asked with a tremor of worry in her voice.

"Inside," I replied. "Still asleep, last I checked."

"Then we'll be joining you until he wakes up." King Jace muscled his way past me. "Breakfast smells delicious."

The queen followed with an apologetic smile.

Enyo's face paled like she might pass out as the two royals entered my cramped sitting room and sat down next to her at the fire pit. Her hands trembled as she began pouring some of the tea we had been sharing and offering it to Queen Araxie. "G-Good morning, Your Majesties."

"If only it were." Queen Araxie sighed as she took a teacup from Enyo. There were tired creases around her eyes, like she hadn't slept last night, either.

I plopped back down next to Enyo and went back to eating my breakfast. "Something to do with the scout I saw returning from the jungle last night, right?"

Everyone, Enyo included, stared at me with similar expressions of wide-eyed surprise.

"I saw him heading for the palace." I shrugged and stuffed a piece of bread into my mouth.

King Jace nodded, his mouth locking into a somber frown. "There was another battle. The Tibrans came in overwhelming numbers. Barrowton has fallen."

A cold, tingly sensation climbed my spine and made my teeth chatter. I bit down hard, willing it away. "When?"

"Only two days ago. Our scouts report that the whole city was overrun." Queen Araxie's voice was quiet. I could feel her gaze on me without having to look up. "We don't know much yet about who might have survived. But the scout was quite certain that Kiran was killed in battle. I am so sorry, Reigh."

My stomach lurched. My body went cold. I couldn't breathe, or think, or even move. Immediately, my eyes darted to Enyo, who was staring back at me with a pasty, haunted expression.

"He went to Barrowton with a small number of our warriors to help defend the city. He must have arrived just after you left. I didn't seek him out during my visit. There were so many wounded from the previous battle—I just assumed he'd gone out to give medical attention to as many as he could," King Jace explained, as though he actually knew what had happened. He put a hand on my shoulder. "We know what he meant to you; that's why we thought we should come give you the news personally."

I clenched my teeth so hard, my jaw ached. The weight of his hand on my shoulder felt like a thousand pounds. Guilt split through my brain like hot iron spike. Guilt—and shame.

When I finally dared to look up again, I could see Enyo studying me carefully out of the corner of my eye. I could almost hear her voice in my head screaming at me not to lose it. I had to stay calm. The king and queen had no idea about Noh. If he showed up now, I doubted that would go over well.

"There will be a time to grieve for his death," Queen Araxie assured me. "But right now, we must find some way to help Maldobar. Jaevid must go there as soon as possible. Without his help, it will fall, and we don't have the warriors or resources to stop it."

"We will send as many warriors as we can to fight at his side," King Jace agreed. "I have no doubt many will volunteer now that he's come back. We can prepare a sizeable force."

"No," Jaevid's voice replied firmly.

I choked on my tea.

Everyone whipped around to find Jaevid standing at the bottom of the stairwell. His features were hardened into a stony frown and his pale blue eyes somehow reflected the heat there without ever looking warm.

"N-No?" The queen's voice broke. All the color drained from her face.

"Jaevid, whether you remember it or not, those are your kinsmen dying out there," King Jace snarled suddenly. "Your dragonrider brothers—the citizens of Maldobar—people you swore to protect!"

Jaevid raised a hand to silence him. "I'm sorry, that came out harsher than I meant it to. Of course, I will go to Maldobar, but I won't take any of your fighters with me. They should stay in Luntharda, in case things don't go as planned."

I had to agree with him there. Putting more soldiers in the Tibrans' path was essentially like tossing them into a meat grinder. They were taking down dragonriders, so it's not like a few shrikes would do any better. It wouldn't end well, and there was no sense in giving Argonox any more slave soldiers to use against us.

"You're going alone?" I snorted and shook my head.

Jaevid's piercing gaze settled on me. "No. *You* are coming with me."

"What?" I balked. "Like hell I am! If you want me back in Maldobar, it'll have to be you dragging my dead corpse because there is no way I'm—"

"Paligno spoke to me in a dream last night," he replied, his tone still eerily calm. "He revealed to me what's happened in Maldobar. We don't have much time. Your brother and sister need you. Argonox has them both at Northwatch. They were taken prisoner during the battle."

Thankfully, I wasn't the only one sitting there with my mouth hanging wide open. Queen Araxie and Enyo wore similar expressions. I felt a little less stupid when I couldn't do anything more than make unhappy noises as a response. The Tibrans had captured Aubren and Jenna? What could I do? How was I supposed to find them, let alone do anything to—

"*Brother and sister?*" Enyo shot me a threatening look.

Oops. I hadn't told her about the possibility that I might be some sort of lost son of the King of Maldobar. I mean, of course I was going to tell her ... eventually. But I didn't know quite how to or where to begin. When it came down to it, I didn't have any real proof yet.

I didn't have to scramble for an excuse right then, however.

"It's true, then. You really have replaced the god stone." King Jace interrupted as he leaned back and folded his arms over his chest. "Seems as though you've gotten your memories back."

"Not entirely," Jaevid murmured, his expression dimming. "My interaction with Paligno brought some things back to the surface. A few flashes of memory and a handful of names. I remember Felix—he was my friend. I loved him like a brother. And I remember you and Araxie, though you've obviously changed since then. I recall being here in Luntharda, going to the temple, and ... " He paused, and his brow furrowed. "I remember saying goodbye. Then there was nothing. Just a darkness like endless night. I could sense that time was passing, but I didn't know how long it had been when I awoke."

Heavy silence hung over us for nearly a minute before Queen Araxie dared to break it. "Forgive me for being indelicate, but what does you being the god stone mean for us, exactly? I don't understand."

"It means that I carry Paligno's essence within my body. Our minds can be melded so that we think as one. If I concentrate, I can see what he sees and feel what he feels. He can share his thoughts with me, and I with him. It's not a constant thing, and I can't read his thoughts unless he allows it." Taking a step closer, Jaevid tipped his head in my direction. "It's similar to the connection you will have with your goddess through Noh."

I made a few more shocked, unhappy choking sounds.

The king raised his hand, his expression snapping into a scowl aimed right at me. "Wait a minute—who is Noh?"

Great.

Jaevid's gaze softened, becoming almost sympathetic as he spoke. "It's time, Reigh."

Time? Who was he to tell me it was time for anything? Just because he was a great war hero from some bygone era and Paligno's chosen one did *not* mean he got to give me marching orders. "No." My lip twitched in a snarl. "I am not going back to Maldobar, and last time I checked, you didn't have the authority to command me to."

"This isn't a choice either of us gets to make. Surely, you understand that after what happened in Barrowton."

My skin prickled with a cold sweat.

"Clysiros has chosen you, and both of us have been called upon to stop the bloodshed. We need to go. We must fight this together if Maldobar is to survive."

"C-Clysiros?" Queen Araxie sucked in a sharp breath, regarding me with sudden horror.

Now he'd gone too far.

I threw my plate of food down, letting it smash against the stone floor before I slowly rose to my feet. My hands shook as they curled into fists. Every muscle in my body was tense as I glared at him and bared my teeth. "Get out of my house."

Jaevid didn't even blink. "Paligno told me you would be scared, just as I was. But I'm giving you a gift, whether you are willing to see it or not. I'm giving you a reason—a purpose for being what you are. This is what you were born to do."

White-hot rage crackled over my tongue and my mouth filled with a coppery flavor, like sucking on an old coin. My body, though, had gone as cold as ice. I couldn't hold it back. The shadows were growing thicker, soaking up the light in the room and swallowing it whole. My breath turned to white fog. Out of the corner of my eye, the vague, flickering shape of a wolf went slinking along the farthest wall.

"You have no right," I growled. My body flexed beyond my control, arms drawing up in a curling gesture that made the shadows dance and take form. Noh's cold laughter cracked in the air. The queen and Enyo leaned in closer together, their eyes wide with fright. King Jace moved in front of them as though he might try to shield them.

Suddenly, the wooden beams of the ceiling and walls groaned. They creaked and shuddered, sprouting branches and leaves that filled the inside of my house with living greenery. Vines the size of jungle pythons burst through the windowpanes, climbed the walls, and snaked around my feet. Jaevid stood before me with his hands also raised before him. His eyes flashed like green lightning against the gloom of my shadows. "I have the only right." His voice thundered through my living room.

I tried to resist. With my teeth clenched, I poured every ounce of my will against the anger that rose like a bitter wind and ripped through my lungs. There was no stopping it.

"You think you can oppose me?" Noh's form burst from the ground before me, swelling like a churning black tide. I could feel his delight—his desire for blood—as if it were my own. He wanted to feast. His red eyes flickered, and his jagged fangs glittered as he surged forward, jaws open for the kill.

A blast of white light blinded me. The impact rippled through the air, blowing me back onto my rear end. My head cracked off the floor. I sat up in a daze, trying to shield my face and squint through the light that radiated in the air like someone had dropped the sun into my living room.

I could just make out the shape of Jaevid rippling in the center of that light. He had Noh by the throat and was holding him in the air as he kicked and squirmed, toothy jaws still snapping.

"I am not your enemy," Jaevid said, his voice eerily calm. "And I am not your rival." My body shuddered as his gaze slowly panned over to stare right at me. "This is not the time to let fear rule you, Reigh. You must make a choice about who you are—right now. Either you will embrace Clysiros as your patroness and learn to use your power, so we can rescue your family and end this war, or you will let the Tibrans destroy them. I can't do this without you. What's it going to be?"

CHAPTER FOURTEEN

My head was pounding when I woke up, lying on my back in my childhood bedroom. The familiar, spicy aroma of Kiran's special chaser root tea wafted past my nose. He'd always made it when we had a patient with a head injury or concussion. It was the best cure for a headache. Trouble was, take too much of it and it could make you extremely drowsy. Take *way* too much of it, and you were basically a drooling lump until it wore off. Kiran had never let anyone mess around with it. Apparently, there had been a few instances in the past of elves slipping it to someone because it made them easy to take advantage of. Not good.

For a minute or two, I thought it might have all been a dream. The Tibrans, Aubren, Jenna, Hilleddi, the battle at Barrowton, and Jaevid returning from the dead—all of it was just a figment of my overexerted brain. That meant Kiran was still ...

"How are you feeling?" Enyo's voice whispered over me. She was sitting at my bedside, holding a cup of steaming hot tea and doing an excellent job of looking worried.

All my hopes came crashing down around my ears.

"You passed out. Jaevid checked you over but said you probably just used too much power too quickly. He said you might have a headache when you woke up."

I muttered a few of my favorite Gray elf curses under my breath. "Where is he now?"

"He went up to the roof a few hours ago."

I arched an eyebrow. "What's he doing up there?" If he was messing up my perfectly-organized herb garden with his forest powers, there would be blood.

"Chatting with a deity, I imagine." She flashed a nervous smile. "He asked to see Princess Hecate. It was so strange. The king and queen left right away." Enyo sighed shakily, looking down into the cup of tea. "Reigh, you—"

I cut her off. "I was going to tell you. About my family. Everything just got so messed up. I don't even know if it's true or not."

She hesitated, nibbling on her bottom lip. "It's all right. I understand. I can't imagine what all this is like for you."

"A scorching abyss comes to mind," I rasped as I tried massaging my throbbing temples. It didn't help. "I guess the fact that I'm still here means the king and queen don't intend on putting me to death for the whole 'being chosen by an evil goddess' thing."

Enyo shifted in her seat, clearing her throat and still nibbling on her lip. Then she stood and carefully placed the warm clay cup into my hands. When I moved to take it, she put her hands over mine and squeezed lightly. Her palms felt clammy and sticky, and I could see her brow crinkling with uncertainty.

"I think you need to go to Maldobar with Jaevid," she said at last.

Those words sent a jolt through me.

She squeezed my hands harder. "Jaevid is the only one who can help you with Noh and Clysiros. He can follow you to places no one else can. He can stop you from going too far."

"I have duties here as well. I can't just abandon the clinic. This place was Kiran's legacy. This was his life's work. It's the only thing left of him now."

"I will look after it for you," she argued. "I know I'm not fully trained yet, but surely the royal palace would be willing to spare a senior medic to help me until you get back."

I didn't like it one bit—the idea of turning my back on this place again. This clinic was all I had left in the world. These walls were the only place I truly felt safe. Not to mention the fact that I'd be leaving Enyo again, too. I couldn't. Not now that we'd finally, you know, cleared the air.

"Please, Reigh. Don't be stubborn. Not about this."

"And if I die in combat? You'll be all right with that?"

She scowled. "Of course not. But I'm not okay with you living like this, either. Always looking over your shoulder. Being afraid of your own shadow. This is no way to live. I want more for you. I want you to be happy." Her eyes watered, and she looked away. "I want *us* to be happy."

Us—she'd said that word with such emphasis. It made my stupid heart start to pound again and I stretched out a hand to touch her chin, gently guiding her gaze back to meet mine. "What are you saying? That you'd want to hang around with me forever?"

"Hmm. Well, when you put it like that, I suppose I don't have any other plans. I might as well stick around to look after you. I'm the only one qualified, anyway."

"I don't deserve you," I murmured.

The corners of her mouth quirked into a breathtaking smile that made my thoughts tangle up like cobwebs. She blew my mind like other people blew dandelion puffs. "No one does, according to my mother. But if you defeat the Tibrans and save Maldobar, she'll be forced to reconsider it."

"I'll see what I can do." I laughed, letting my eyes fall closed as she leaned in to touch her lips softly against mine. Warm, soft, inviting—kissing her was a taste of pure sunlight.

BRAVE THE JUNGLE ROADS BACK TO MALDOBAR, SOMEHOW MAKE IT TO Northwatch, break into it and battle past a few thousand angry Tibran soldiers, rescue Aubren and Jenna, and make it back to ... well, somewhere safe. That was it. That's as much of a plan as I could come up with as I crammed every sword, weapon, and dangerous pointy object I could find into my travel bag. How, by all the gods, we were going to pull this off, I couldn't even begin to imagine. But based on all the stories I'd heard over the years about Jaevid—if you were going to do something insanely dangerous and potentially epic, he was the one you wanted on your side.

Enyo took over packing the medicinal supplies and food rations while I went up to fetch our resident war-ender. If Aubren and Jenna really did need my help, it was best not to waste any more time, right?

I found Jaevid sitting on the edge of the roof. His head was thrown back, his eyes closed and a blissful smile on his face while his legs dangled over the drop. He wasn't alone. Around him perched a whole flock of exotic, brightly-colored birds. Finches and sparrows were fluttering all around him, and a large parrot was perched on his shoulder, nibbling playfully at his pointed ear. There was even a thalcrowe, one of Luntharda's most notorious birds of prey, sitting nonchalantly at his side with talons like razors. The sight of that feathery, thirty-pound monster stopped me dead in my tracks.

"It's all right," Jaevid said, his eyes opening to stare back at me with a strange grin.

"So you say," I muttered as I hedged a little closer. "I've seen thalcrowes snatch baby faundra right off the jungle floor. Just—bam—gone."

Jaevid chuckled. "Not much of an animal lover, are you?"

"Not when it comes to the ones that could claw my face off, no." I sat down on the other side of him so that Jaevid was between the thalcrowe and me.

"Dragons would fall into that category, I guess." There was a suggestive edge to his tone. "Vexi might do just that when you see her again. She's not happy with you. I'm not sure I'll be able to talk her down."

I flushed until even my neck felt hot. "H-How do you know about her?"

Jaevid laughed again. "Well, it's kind of a long story. After I talked with Paligno last night, a few other things happened. I can hear Mavrik again. He's been reminding me of some of our adventures."

"Mavrik? As in ... your mount? The dragon you rode in the Gray War?" I swallowed hard. I remembered vividly my last encounter with him after he and a pack of wild dragons had rescued us from the Tibrans. Mavrik was an impressive beast, to put it lightly. He was a king drake now, far bigger and stronger than any other wild dragon.

"More like a friend, really." Jaevid shrugged. "I can communicate with him much like I can with Paligno, although it doesn't tire me out nearly as much."

I snorted. "Yeah, chatting with a deity always wears me out, too."

Jaevid just grinned. "It will. You'll see."

"What does he have to do with Vexi? Did she go back to the wild dragons or something?" Part of me hoped she had. That was her home. And since I had no plans of becoming a dragonrider, it was the best place for her.

"More or less," he answered. "She's one of his favorite hatchlings, so he looks after her. Spoils her a little, I think. I was able to talk to her some, although her presence is harder for me to channel."

"Wait—are you saying Vexi is Mavrik's daughter?"

His grin widened. "Lucky you. I suppose that practically makes us family."

I sighed. "No offense, but I'm not exactly cut out for the whole dragonrider thing."

"Neither was I in the beginning."

"Yeah, but you didn't accidentally kill people when you lost your temper."

Jaevid's eyes darkened some and his jaw tensed a little. "I did once. And I came close to it several other times." He met my gaze with a half-hearted shrug. "Or so Mavrik tells me, anyway."

I had to scrape my jaw up off the floor. Jaevid had killed somebody by lashing out and losing control over his powers? No one, not even Kiran, had ever told me that story before.

For the first time, I felt a little less monstrous.

"Hey, uh, I wanted to say sorry for losing it before." My voice cracked a little under the crushing embarrassment. "The last time I went to Maldobar, everything went wrong. I screwed up. I did something ... terrible."

"I know," he answered quietly. "Vexi showed me."

"And you still think it's a good idea for me to go back?"

"It doesn't matter what I think. You're supposed to be there. That's what destiny has chosen for us. We are supposed to fight this together, and I'm willing to trust that and you." His pale blue eyes studied me as though trying to read my mind. "But for what it's worth, I think this is your chance at redemption. I'd like to see you take it. So, do you think you can trust me?"

I had to think about that. The Jaevid I was getting to know now was nothing like the one in all the legends and stories I'd been told. Maldobar really needed that regal, victorious hero depicted in all their sculptures and tapestries if they were going to survive—but the guy sitting next to me was a far cry from those images. I just hadn't decided yet if that was a good or bad thing.

"Well, the way I see it, you've got the royals and citizens from two different kingdoms trusting in you to save their butts. That's pretty compelling." I rubbed the short, scratchy stubble on my chin. "And Enyo trusts you. She's a much better judge of character than I am, so that's two strikes in your favor."

"Sounds like I'm scoring well." The thin scar that sliced over his left brow, eye, and down to his cheek crinkled when he smirked.

"Just promise me one thing. If this goes badly, if I lose it and you can't make me stop—you have to end it before I do something like that ever again. I won't be the villain in this story. I don't want that to be my legacy. Not because of me, you know, but for Kiran and Enyo's sake. I don't want to smear either of their names by association."

Jaevid's smirk faded. We stared at one another, me studying his strange mixed features. It was easy for me to pick out which parts of him were Gray elf and which were human. Other parts, however, were caught somewhere in the middle. His ears, for example, were pointed, but much shorter than a full-blooded elf. His shaggy hair was a shade somewhere between black and the traditional Gray elf silver. Its color reminded me of ash or soot.

"You have my word," he replied at last.

I nodded. At least that was settled.

We sat in silence for a few minutes, the birds still pecking and fluttering around Jaevid. It was getting late in the day. We only had a few hours left before sunset.

I cleared my throat. "What's the plan, then?"

"Jace and Araxie agreed to let me speak to Hecate. Then we leave."

"Right. And, uh, what's talking to her going to do?"

Jaevid's gaze panned over the city spread out before us, his pale blue eyes catching in the filtered light from the canopy. "We're going to need her before it's over. She's the mediator. She can channel the voices of the divine. It's the only way to talk to your goddess."

I nodded like I had some clue as to what that meant. "Okay. Well she did mention she hears voices."

"I have to teach her how to focus it. Paligno gave me instructions. It won't be easy—and I doubt Jace will approve. But we don't have a choice. By the time we finish your ritual, my hope is that she will have practiced enough to be able help us with a meeting."

"A meeting?"

"Something has to change. First Hovrid and now Argonox. There was another who came before, centuries ago, who called himself the God Bane. They all wanted the same thing—to seize the power of the gods. They all spread slaughter and mayhem, leaving a path of destruction behind them." Jaevid rubbed at his lip, which was still a little battered from Enyo's punch. "If there's ever going to be lasting peace, then all divine power has to be put out of reach of mortal hands."

"Sounds easy enough."

"Not exactly," he murmured. "The gods require some sort of manifestation upon the earth for them to effectively maintain power here. Like it or not, we need that power. Paligno brings life. His very essence kindles the fires of creation, healing, and the birth of new things. Clysiros brings death and decay, and while that might frighten most people, they are necessary. You need both to maintain a cycle of balance."

I blinked. "I, uh, didn't expect you to take the 'death isn't evil' stance."

Jaevid shrugged. "Nothing is meant to live forever."

"Does Clysiros have a stone? You know, like Paligno did? Like the one you destroyed?"

He nodded slightly. "It's not a stone, per se, but it's essentially the same thing. We'll need it to complete your ritual. The rules that govern Clysiros are different from those that Paligno had to follow for me to manifest his power. It's going to be complicated."

Somehow, the way he said that made me think he was up to something. Maybe it was his tone, or the way he refused to meet my eyes as he spoke. Regardless, something was off. Jaevid wasn't telling me everything.

"We'll have to come up with a different solution for the gods' presences here," he went on. "But until then, there are other things to work out."

"Yeah," I agreed. "Like the fact that Northwatch is currently crawling with Tibran soldiers."

"Mavrik has been briefing me on the situation. He's watched their progression since they first landed, anticipating my return." Jaevid rubbed the back of his neck. "Aubren and Jenna are being held in the tower, which unfortunately was built entirely around the idea of keeping unwanted people out. Even with dragons to help us, we would be hard pressed to get inside. They've already sealed all but one of the landing platforms dragonriders used to use to get in and out of the tower. If we did manage to get in, we might be cornered there if they close off all the remaining exits."

"Well, that ... sucks."

"No kidding. And then, of course, there are the war machines and the possibility that Tibran scouts might tip Argonox off to our approach. According to Mavrik, the entire northern region is crawling with their spies. They'll be watching for us."

"Okay, that really sucks."

Jaevid laughed again. "On the plus side, we have a double dose of divine power at our disposal."

"There is that." I chuckled and arched an eyebrow at him. "So? Any bright ideas?"

His icy-hued eyes glittered with wild energy, looking eerily similar to those of the thalcrowe perched at his side. "Just one."

CHAPTER FIFTEEN

By nightfall we were ready to go. All our bags were packed. Our swords and knives were sharpened, and our quivers stocked with arrows. We had everything we needed—except maybe any hope of success. Seriously, how were the two of us supposed to break into Northwatch like that? It was insanity.

But, hey, doing insane and potentially lethal things was becoming a trend in my life. Why stop now?

Sitting around the fire pit again, Jaevid, Enyo, and I ate our last meal together without saying a word. Enyo sat closer to me than usual, her brow creased with worry. My hands were unsteady, and I didn't want her to see it. I had to at least appear confident—for her sake and my sanity.

Jaevid, on the other hand, was the picture of thoughtful calm. The warm light from the crackling embers made hues of gold and red dance across his pale blue eyes while he ate. His brow was locked into a pensive frown, as though mentally he was a thousand miles away. I wondered which god or dragon he was talking to this time.

A knock on the door interrupted the silence. No one moved. Then Jaevid lifted his gaze to meet mine from across the hearth. He nodded slowly.

I took a deep breath and got to my feet.

King Jace and Queen Araxie were on my doorstep again. Neither one smiled when they saw me. No surprise there. After all, the last time we'd been together, they had seen me lose control of Noh and found out I was the chosen one of the goddess of death. I had no new assurance to offer them that it wouldn't happen again, even with Jaevid there. I was a disaster waiting to happen, and now they knew it, too.

Hecate stood between her grandparents, her lovely face pale and her visionless eyes darting rapidly in the direction of every sound. Her chest rose and fell with frantic, shallow breaths. I wondered what she was hearing that made her so scared. Paligno? Clysiros? Noh? Or something worse?

"We need to hurry." Jaevid's voice nearly made me jump out of my skin. He was standing right behind me in the doorway, looking at them over my shoulder. For a guy well over six feet, he could move as quiet as a cat.

Queen Araxie's mouth hardened, but she didn't speak. She led the way inside with her husband right on her heels. They kept Hecate close between them, as though trying to shield her from something. Probably me. I tried not to take that personally.

Enyo snapped to her feet, visibly flustered at the appearance of the royal family returning to my living room. I had to remind myself this was still a new experience for her. I was getting used to nobles, royals, and all manner of famous faces hanging around at my house. Maybe Argonox would come knocking next and save us the trouble of hunting him down. A guy can dream, right?

"I apologize for the rush, but there isn't time to explain everything." Jaevid said, offering our guests a thin smile before he faced Hecate. She stiffened as he took slow steps toward her, as though she could somehow sense his presence drawing closer. "But we cannot do this without you, Hecate. Your gift is the key. Will you help us?"

"Gift?" Queen Araxie's voice broke, her expression riddled with pain. "How can you call it that? Do you have any idea what it has cost our family? My granddaughters snuffed out like candles in the wind, one by one, and no healer could do anything to help them. Now Hecate hears the voices, too. She grows weaker every day. This is not a gift—it is a curse!"

Jaevid stopped her with one look, his eyes flashing like the cold steel of a blade. The queen snapped her mouth shut, her chin still trembling with grief.

"I think you should wait outside," he suggested, although his tone didn't exactly invite anyone to disagree. "Enyo, please go and make sure no one else enters."

The queen sucked in a sharp gasp. Rage flickered in her multihued eyes. She looked like a dragoness about to spit flame until her husband put a hand gently on her arm. King Jace guided her outside, whispering to her in a comforting tone until their voices faded beyond my front door.

Enyo followed behind them, her face the picture of petrified worry when she hesitated in the doorway and looked back at me. I could read the doubt in her face—the reluctance to leave my side. I didn't quite understand what I'd ever done to earn that kind of devotion from her, but by all the gods I never wanted to mess it up.

I forced the best "I'll be fine" smile I could muster.

Her shoulders drooped, but she turned to leave anyway. I suppose I should have known she wouldn't buy that. She knew me too well.

Then it was just the three of us alone with nothing but the sound of the embers crackling in the hearth.

I cleared my throat. "Not to be an insensitive jerk, but you did say we were short on time. So let's get on with this."

"Did you really mean that?" Hecate flicked a quick glance in Jaevid's direction. "That my condition is a gift and not something bad? It's never brought my family anything but grief and suffering."

"Those of us who have these divine powers learn that it's more complicated than just being good or bad. Our power is a gift—a tool—and how we use it decides if it's a curse or not." Jaevid stood right in front of her, taking her small hands in his. "I'm going try to teach you how to use yours. It may frighten you, but I promise I won't let any harm come to you."

"I-I can't," she whimpered. "Every time I focus on it, the voices get so loud and—"

"Please," he coaxed gently. "I won't let them overwhelm you. I'll be right here beside you. And once this is over, you will be able to silence them yourself. Will you be brave for me?"

She was shaking like a frightened child in her dainty royal gown. But she took a deep, shuddering breath and slowly bobbed her head. "I'll try."

"Very good." He smiled warmly. "Now tell me, what do you hear?"

"T-There are so many." Hecate took a frightened step closer to him, shivering and cringing with her eyes shut tight. "Who are they? What do they want?"

"Spirits," Jaevid replied. "Some of those who have passed, some of those who have yet to be, and some who have been since the dawn of time. The Gods, the Fates, those who reside in the Vale, and beyond the Sivanth."

A cold puff of wind, like the breath of a ghost, prickled at the back of my neck. Not an unfamiliar sensation to me, but somehow this was different.

"I need you to listen to them. Let the voices come. Hear their words, but don't focus on them. Let them move past you like current in a stream. They can't touch you, can't affect you." Jaevid slowly began moving away, letting his hands slide away from hers.

Hecate's entire body froze. I couldn't even tell that she was breathing anymore. Her gaze was fixed straight ahead, staring blankly at the middle of Jaevid's chest as her irises began to glow. They shone like two rings of molten gold. Her lips parted, and the sultry female voice that left them wasn't her own. *"Come to me, my Harbinger."*

My stomach dropped. I knew that voice. The familiar sensation of cold chills surged up my spine like a bolt of lightning. Every muscle in my body tightened with a jolt. My heartbeat flourished. I bit down hard, resisting the pull of the shadows.

That is, until Jaevid turned his glare on me, his eyes glowing like two green lanterns. "You have to hold him back, Reigh."

"You think I'm not trying?" I growled through clenched teeth.

"Try *harder*."

Right. Easy for him to say.

I wheezed and strained against the weight—as though someone was standing on my chest. But the urge was too strong. I couldn't resist it. Noh shot out of my subconscious and materialized before me like a rumbling black storm front. His laughter crackled in my mind as he swallowed up all the light in the room. My mind scrambled. All my thoughts became a flurry of chaos. I was being sucked down into a whirlpool of cold darkness. Air—I needed air. I was drowning. I thrashed in wild panic, trying to claw my way to a surface that didn't exist.

A STRONG HAND SUDDENLY SEIZED MY WRIST AND PULLED. I COULDN'T SEE who it was, and I didn't care. I latched on to that hand with all my strength. When my head broke the surface, I took a frantic gulp of air.

"You're all right. That's it. Breathe." Someone dragged me, coughing and sputtering, out onto solid ground. I was too busy blinking water from my eyes to see who it was.

I collapsed onto the grassy bank and wheezed.

"You always did have a flair for the dramatic." He chuckled over me. Raising my head, I looked straight into the eyes of a face I knew all too well.

Noh crouched before me, his elbows resting on his knees. When he smirked, every hair on my body stood on end. Once again, he looked human. Only this time, he looked ... normal. He looked exactly like me. Well, except that he was dressed differently. Rather than my scout's attire, Noh wore baggy robes made of silk as black as pitch. The big bell sleeves were stitched with flecks of silver like stars, and there was a wide black belt around his torso. He wasn't wearing any weaponry in plain view—he didn't even have shoes on. And yet, somehow, he managed to look menacing.

I raked my soggy bangs away from my face. "W-What's going on? Where am I?"

"It has many names in the mortal realm. The in-between. The world between worlds. The silver shores. The valley of spirits." Noh grinned impishly. "But we call it 'the Vale.'"

Shambling to my feet, I tried to make some sense of that as I looked around. Gray stone buildings, salt and pepper colored grass, and a bleak colorless sky didn't offer me much hope. It was as though all the color had been drained away from this place and left it every bit as dreary as it was disturbing. In fact, the only thing that had any color at all was Noh and myself. The pool of water I'd just been dragged out of looked like a well of ink—so dark you couldn't tell the depth. Despite the whirling current that had nearly drowned me, the surface looked strangely calm.

"How do I get back?" I swallowed hard. Part of me already knew the answer, but I was hoping for an alternative to going for another swim.

"You only just got here." I could hear that wry, slightly sinister smirk in the tone of his voice without ever having to look at him. "Not curious about your kingdom at all?"

"My ... kingdom?"

"Of course." Noh gave an exaggerated, flourishing bow. "Everything from the Well of Souls to the Sivanth is our territory.

"I, uh, I don't know what any of that means."

His eyes twinkled with delight. "Then it's long past time you learned."

Gesturing for me to follow, Noh began strolling away down the white cobblestone path that led between the drab stone structures. Everything about this place was so bland and featureless; it put me on edge. There was no source of light. No sun or moon. Just a blank gray sky without clouds or stars. There were no plants, no trees, no birds—nothing.

"Not much to look at, is it?" Noh chuckled, as though he could read my mind.

I stopped to turn in a slow circle as we passed through a small courtyard. There was a fountain in the center, but it had no water running through it. "I guess redecorating is out of the question."

"The spirits wouldn't notice if you did," he replied.

I opened my mouth to ask who that was exactly. And then I saw them—a group of three people standing in the courtyard directly in front of us. They looked human and normal enough. Well, except that their bodies were completely translucent and just as colorless as the rest of this place. They stopped talking and stared at us as we went past. One of the men bowed his head.

"Ghosts?" I guessed.

Noh shrugged. "They come and go. It was never intended for any of them to stay here for very long. Once they pass through one of the Wells, they can either decide to cross the Sivanth and face the Fates or remain here until their essence fades."

"The Sivanth? What does that mean?"

"It is the gateway—the place of judgment where the two Fates decide the eternal reward of every soul. If a soul is found to be pure and unmarked by misdeeds, it is allowed to enter Pareilos, the Kingdom of the Gods. But if the soul is tainted by many sins, then it is banished to Desmiol to burn for eternity as one of the stars." He shot me a dubious glance. "No one has ever told you this before?"

I rubbed the back of my neck, trying to process all that. It was a lot to absorb. "No. I guess the Gray elves are a little superstitious when it comes to the gods."

He pursed his lips. "A healthy fear can be good, but in excess it breeds ignorance."

Noh's pace quickened as he led the way deeper into the eerie city, and he kept looking back, as though to make sure I wasn't falling behind. I tried not to stare as we passed more and more spirits. There were hundreds of them—humans, elves, and races I'd never seen before. Some talked quietly together, others simply stood in silence, but every one of them looked at us as we went by.

"Why are these people here, then? Shouldn't they be going to the Sivanth to be judged?"

"Some are waiting for loved ones to join them. Some are afraid to face the Fates." Noh glanced back at me again. "They have their reasons. But staying here forever is not an option. If they linger for too long, they will disappear and become nothing."

"Well, that's depressing."

He chuckled. "Death usually is."

"So ... what are *you* doing here?" I may not have been the brightest guy, but I could put together that he wasn't just another deceased soul loitering around here.

"I'm here because of you."

I stopped.

It took Noh a few seconds to realize I wasn't following him anymore. When he did, he turned back around and stopped before me. Facing him was like standing in front of a mirror. I couldn't decide how to feel about it. It was creepy, yes, but it was also sort of ... incredible.

"You're not a demon, are you?" I asked.

"No."

"Or a dark spirit?"

One corner of his mouth twitched. "That's a matter of opinion, really."

I squeezed my hands into fists. "Who are you? Tell me the truth."

He tilted his head to the side slightly, studying me. "I'm you, and you are me. We are one and the same. Two souls, one body."

"That's not an answer."

"It's the only answer." He took a step closer, reaching out a hand toward me like he wanted me to touch my palm to his. "Allow me to show you."

I drew back. This was already a lot to take in, and frankly none of it made sense to me. Everything I'd seen from Noh so far pointed to one conclusion: I couldn't trust him. Why start now? I didn't know what he was, what he wanted from me, or if he had some plan to kill me and possess my body. Letting him do anything to me was an invitation to disaster.

"Our minds are not yet synced. They won't be until the ritual is complete. But

I can show you things this way. It's a way of sharing memories," he explained, his eyes narrowing and mouth curling into a cold smile. "And I have quite a lot to share with you, brother."

CHAPTER SIXTEEN

My eyes flew open just as I managed to suck in a desperate breath of air. My body shuddered, shaking and thrashing out of control until I realized I wasn't submerged anymore. Okay, the whole drowning in the Well of Souls thing was beginning to get *extremely* old. There had to be an easier way to move between those realms. That was a problem for another time, though.

"Thank the gods!" Enyo screamed and threw her arms around me, knocking me back onto the floor again.

I wheezed and panted, trying to loosen her grip so I could get another breath. "Y-You're ... choking ... m-me!"

She stammered back with tears streaming down her face. "We thought you were dead. You weren't moving. And Jaevid couldn't bring you back!"

Behind her, the rest of my captive audience was gaping down at me with pasty expressions. Even Jaevid looked rattled, although he was the next to come and crouch down beside me. "What happened?"

My frazzled brain struggled to make sense of it. It was hard to remember at first. Then the floodgates opened. Memories and flashes blurred through my brain, assaulting my senses and making my stomach roll. I doubled over and buried my face in my hands.

"Reigh? What's wrong?" Enyo was still hysterical.

"I-It's nothing. I'm fine." I forced myself to lie. "I just overdid it again."

That answer seemed to appease everyone—except Jaevid. He stared down at me, his expression sharp. When our eyes met, I knew he was onto me. Maybe he could feel that something was different now. I was different.

I knew what I was, and what I had to do.

"Will you be able to travel?" he asked.

I took a few more deep, steadying breaths and nodded. "Yeah. I think so."

The look Enyo gave me was nothing short of fractured. She squeezed my hand, desperation still flickering in her beautiful multicolored eyes. "How can you go now? Please, at least rest a few minutes."

I brushed a hand over her soft, warm cheek. It wasn't fair. One look like that from her was like smashing my heart into jelly. I hated this—disappointing her. Worrying her. Making her upset. I didn't deserve her affection. "I'll be fine," I murmured, leaning in closer to touch my forehead to hers. "Wait for me, okay? And look after this place. I'm counting on you."

She sniffled and bobbed her head.

"All right." I cleared my throat as I got to my feet, trying to shake off the way my head was still spinning. "Ready when you are."

"Good." Jaevid stood, too, and turned to the royal family. "Hecate, you'll keep practicing on your own, won't you? We're going to need you to be ready when I send word."

"I'll do my best—I swear it." She smiled weakly.

"Then it's time for us to go."

We gathered our belongings, our travel bags and weapons, and set out into the city alone. The night was calm. Mau Kakuri was sleeping peacefully. And yet every step I took made my heart pound faster and faster. Images from the Vale swept through my brain. Noh's words, the things he'd revealed to me, made my blood run like icy slush in my veins. Glancing sideways at Jaevid's somber, focused expression, I had to wonder if he truly knew what I was. Sure, Paligno had probably told him some things about me—maybe even about Clysiros as well —but did he *really* know? Would he even want my help if he did?

"Something on your mind?" His glacier-hued eyes flicked in my direction.

I cringed. "No."

He frowned but didn't push the issue.

It wasn't like we didn't have enough other stuff to worry about anyway. Imagining what lay ahead was the only thing worse than knowing what I was leaving behind. Enyo, the clinic, my home—everything I'd ever known. I was turning my back on it again. That realization turned my stomach sour.

When I'd left to join Aubren in the war against the Tibrans, I had expected Maldobar to change how I felt about Luntharda. And it had—just not in the way I'd expected. Instead of replacing Luntharda as my home, going to Maldobar had just confirmed that I belonged here. Maldobar was a different world, and not one I was sure I'd ever feel at home in.

A small company of scouts greeted us when we reached the main gate. King Jace had arranged for us to take shrikes from the city perimeter. It would be a long flight to the border, and every second we wasted was one second longer

Aubren and Jenna spent in Tibran custody. That realization settled over me like a cold rain. We'd lost valuable time because of my inability to keep my power in check, and now there was still a solid three-day ride between the border and us.

"This won't be necessary," Jaevid said as he ran a hand over one of the shrike's glistening scaly sides.

"But, Lapiloque, it is a very long journey through the jungle to reach the boundary," one of the scouts protested. "Shrikes are the fastest way to travel there."

His mouth quirked into a half-smile. "Is that so?"

If that was a joke, I didn't get it. I stood back with the other scouts, watching as Jaevid took a few confident strides toward the gate. He stopped, facing the dark expanse of the jungle beyond with his sharp eyes panning like an eagle searching for prey.

A prickle of unease made the little hairs on the back of my neck stand on end.

Jaevid drew back the sleeve of his tunic, quickly unfastening his vambrace to expose the mark on his skin hidden beneath it. That mark, according to Enyo, had been put there by the foundling spirits when Jaevid had made some sort of deal with them. Raising his arm so that the mark faced toward the jungle, Jaevid curled his hand into a fist.

Instantly, the ambient noise of jungle went completely silent. The frogs and insects stopped singing. The night birds hushed. The cold chill on my neck spread, making me shudder. I took a *big* step back, and the rest of the scouts did the same. Nearby, the shrikes began to screech in panic, bucking at their tethers and clawing to get away.

Then I heard a voice, Jaevid's voice, muttering quietly. He was biting words through clenched teeth. I couldn't understand what he was saying, but as he spoke, the mark on his arm sparked to life. It burned with a brilliant green light, flashing like lightning in the night. It crackled and sizzled along his arm, spreading over his entire body before it burst into the air, sending out a shockwave of power that knocked me onto my heels. It doused the braziers burning by the gate and sent the shrikes into another panic.

"W-What was that?" One of the scouts stammered as he ducked behind me to hide.

Before I could make a guess, the jungle rumbled before us like a hungry beast. My body shook. My heartbeat thrilled at the presence of wild, primal power. I could feel them coming, drawing closer by the second. Their eyes winked into view amidst the shadows of the giant tree trunks—bright spots of white and green that shone like stars. Strange noises echoed in the air, the calls of creatures I couldn't identify.

Two of them approached, seeming to materialize from the gloom without a single sound. Their sleek, canine bodies were roughly the same size as the shrikes and resembled fox's or jackal's. They had tall pointed ears, long bushy tails, and slender legs with small paws. Their jet-black fur caught the ambient moonlight filtering down through the canopy and revealed the tapered feathered wings that were folded against their backs.

The one nearest to me was covered in swirling markings of bright red and turquoise and many of the feathers on its wings were that same combination of colors. It eyed me, bright eyes twinkling and tapered snout twitching with tall ears perked.

The one that approached Jaevid, however, was more brightly colored. Its black pelt was mottled with yellow, green, and blue. The shape and color of its wings reminded me of a parrot, and even its tail had some of those long feathers mixed in with the rest of its fur.

Jaevid smiled at the creature, stretching out his hand so that it could sniff him. "Hello again, Pasci."

The spirit yipped in response, slicking its ears back and pushing its snout against his hand.

"Friends of yours?" I couldn't keep the flavor of sarcasm out of my voice.

"More or less." He chuckled.

"You do realize the foundling spirits are tricksters, right? They can't be trusted. I can literally tell you twelve stories of them luring children to their deaths."

"Good thing we aren't children, then." Jaevid smirked as he rubbed his hand along one of the spirit's bright-feathered wings. "Sometimes stories are just stories, Reigh. And anyway, they fly much faster than a shrike."

Okay, so he'd been right about the fast part.

I had a difficult time fathoming that anything could fly faster than a shrike. But the foundling spirits didn't tire like normal animals. They flew hard, fast, and without making a single sound. We made incredible time through the jungle, twisting through the limbs of the trees, bounding and gliding from bough to bough like shadows in the night. We flew all night and into the following day. By evening, we had already reached the midway point. At this rate, we'd reach Maldobar sometime tomorrow afternoon. The only downside was the lack of a saddle or anything to hold on to except fistfuls of their silky fur. Riding like that for so long had my back aching, my hands throbbing, and every muscle in my body howling for a break. Not to mention my stomach was practically turning itself inside out with hunger.

When we finally stopped for a break, I fought the urge to drop to my knees and kiss the ground.

We set up camp in a small clearing, even though all my training as a scout told me camping on the ground was a terrible, awful, suicidal idea. Having two ancient, divine earth spirits and one full-fledged demigod made me feel a little better about it, though. Hard to argue with that kind of muscle, and it was good to have my feet on solid ground for a few hours.

I shuffled stiffly through unpacking my bedroll near the small campfire Jaevid had made from dry twigs, moss, and bits of limbs. Spreading it out on a nice flat spot, I turned around long enough to grab the water skin out of my bag. My sore back was begging me to lie down. It was all I could think about. When I went to sit down and get comfortable, however, I discovered a big, feathery fox creature had taken up residence on my bed.

"Come on, seriously?" I groaned. "Where am I supposed to sleep?"

The spirit tilted its head to the side, big ears pricked and listening. "You're a foundling spirit. Do you even sleep at all?"

It yipped at me in what I could only assume was defiance, fluffing its feathers and making itself more comfortable—on *my* bed.

Great.

I noticed Jaevid wasn't having the same issues with his own foundling spirit. He was sitting by the fire, the creature relaxing casually behind him so that he could lean back against its side. I noticed he was biting back a grin as I stomped over to sit down on the other side of the fire. "Having trouble?"

"It's personal, isn't it? Because I'm the Harbinger?"

He laughed.

"I knew it," I grumbled.

Jaevid went back to poking the fire with a stick, making sparks dance up into the night. "Still not much of an animal lover, eh?"

"Considering most of the ones I've met have tried to kill, eat, or otherwise maim me ... No, not exactly." I shot the foundling spirit curled up on my bedroll one last spiteful glare. "Now they're stealing my bed and getting fleas on my pillow."

"Perhaps it's for the best. We can't stop for long." His mouth stiffened into a tense, firm line. "And ... we should talk about what happened at the clinic."

I swallowed and immediately locked my gaze on to the toes of my boots. Anything to avoid having to meet that intense, peer-into-your-soul look on his face. I didn't like the idea that he might be able to read my expressions better than I could read his.

"What did you see in the Vale?"

My body cringed involuntarily at the word. How did he even know about that? *Creepy.* "What does it matter?"

"A lot, considering our next order of business after rescuing Aubren and Jenna will be finding a way to complete your ritual," he said. "We won't be any help to Maldobar unless we are both working at our fullest capacity. Right now, your power is too unstable. I doubt anyone needs to remind you that in this state, you'd do more harm than good."

I shot him a glare. "And yet you just did it anyway."

"Talk to me, Reigh." His demeanor softened into something like sympathy. "You don't have to walk through this alone. I could feel your soul leave your body when he took you. It was like you had died. And yet your heart never stopped beating. I couldn't bring you back."

The memories swept back over me, making my pulse race and my skin feel flushed. "That was the first time I'd ever been there. To the Vale, I mean." I leaned forward, letting my elbows rest on my knees. "I saw Noh. I mean—really *saw* him. He showed me the Vale, the Well of Souls where people cross over from the mortal world. There were hundreds of them there, the spirits of people who had passed away."

"And?"

I shook my head slowly, too ashamed to meet his gaze again. "And then he showed me what I am. Where we came from. He took me back to the moment when it happened." My jaw clenched. "He's not a demon. He's not a dark spirit, either. All my life that's what I believed he was. Kiran never told me any different. But Noh ... he was a person. He was my brother."

Jaevid didn't push me to continue. It was hard enough to think about this, and someone hounding my heels for every tiny detail wasn't something I was prepared to tolerate. Even so—the words boiled in my throat like a poison. I had to get them out.

"King Felix is my father. I am a prince of Maldobar. Aubren and Jenna are my brother and sister, just like I thought. But that mummified baby Aubren saw when they buried our mother wasn't just a decoy or substitution. That's all that was left of him, of Noh, after I ... " My voice caught. I hated seeing those images in my head. It was like a nightmare that repeated over and over, driving me to the edge of my sanity. It made rage and disgust blaze through every part of my body. "Noh said that was the price we had to pay—the cost of being the Harbinger of Clysiros. We were twins, and my first act in this life was taking his so that his soul joined with mine. Two souls, two minds, in one body—one to stand in this world and the other to guard the Vale. That's the birthright of the Harbinger."

Jaevid's expression had become grim. "Did Kiran know this when he took you in?"

I shuddered at the thought. "I don't see how he couldn't have. Kiran was there. He saw everything. Noh showed me how it happened—our birth. King Felix wouldn't even touch me. Kiran took me out of Maldobar after that. It wasn't clear if he did it because King Felix ordered him to, or if he just felt sorry for me being tossed out into the street like a piece of trash." Anger made my eyes sting and blurred my vision. "And it doesn't matter. I don't blame Felix for throwing me away. Look at what I've done. I killed my mother and my twin brother before I ever took my first breath in this world. I murdered Kiran. I butchered hundreds of Maldobarian soldiers who were looking to me for salvation."

Jaevid didn't speak. He sat perfectly still, watching me with the reflection of the flames dancing in his piercing eyes.

Maybe it was stupid to tell him this. But hey, if he was about to go marching off to save Maldobar with me, he deserved to know exactly what he was getting himself into, if he didn't already. I let my head sag toward my chest as I clenched my fists. Not even Enyo knew this stuff about me, and I hoped she would never find out. "I hate it—this thing I am. How could anyone ever look past it? What I am is ... disgusting."

"You're not disgusting."

I clenched my teeth as I looked up to meet Jaevid's gaze. "How can you say that?"

"We are what we were made to be, Reigh. And I don't believe anyone was made to be disgusting." He offered a faint, almost sad smile as he began fiddling with that stick again, poking it into the fire. It sent more showers of glowing embers floating skyward like fireflies. "I still don't have many memories of my life before. But there are a few moments that have resurfaced. One that is most clear was something your father, Felix, said to me. We don't get to know where our purpose will take us or how our story will end. He said that 'we just have to go on faith. Faith in the cause. Faith in the people we love. Faith that however this ends, we'll have done everything we possibly could to make things right.'"

I snorted. "Jaevid, how can I possibly make any of that right?"

"One step at a time. Although if you're open to suggestions, I'd recommend starting with not letting your other siblings die at the hands of Argonox." He gave a small shrug, as though that should have been obvious. "By the way, you can call me 'Jae,' you know."

"Like we're friends or something?"

He smirked but didn't reply. I took that as a yes.

I stole a glance back over my shoulder to where a certain fox-mutant was snoozing away. "So, friend, how about using some of that demigod influence to get the foundling spirit off my bed?"

"Nice try. Being friends doesn't mean I'll solve all your problems."

"Right, just the ones involving deities, foreign armies ravaging the countryside, and the end of the world."

Jae laughed. "Exactly."

CHAPTER SEVENTEEN

We took a couple of hours to rest, eat from our rations, and discuss our plan once we reached the border where the tangled jungle of Luntharda met the sweeping mountain valleys of Maldobar. With any luck, the Gray elven outpost just inside the jungle boundary would have a few rations to spare for us. They might even have some valuable information on the situation in Northwatch, or an idea of how we could get inside. We could regroup there long enough to get our final preparations together ... then it was time.

My stomach was already in knots when we mounted up and took off again. The idea that we might be too late, that Jenna and Aubren would already be dead, was enough to make me want to vomit. My mind raced as we blitzed through the trees as quick as ghosts in the damp, flowering foliage.

It was nearly sunset when I caught the scent of the frosty, Maldobarian air leaking in through the canopy. We were close. Just that scent took me back to my first encounter with the Tibrans—being shot down on our way to Barrowton and nearly butchered by Argonox's beastly right hand, Hilleddi. I clenched my teeth. If she came for me this time, I wouldn't hold back. I'd happily deliver her to the Fates myself.

The expressions on the faces of the scouts manning the small outpost were priceless when they saw us. I wasn't sure what freaked them out more—that I was riding on a foundling spirit, or that the Lapiloque was riding on the one next to me. Several of them fell onto their faces, prostrating themselves before Jaevid as we dismounted. It took a few minutes to talk them back to their feet.

I had to give him some credit; Jae didn't use his prestigious past or title to take advantage of anyone. Money, jewels, all the prettiest women in Luntharda rubbing his feet—he probably could have gotten anything he asked for. But as he spoke to the scouts gathering around us in awe, all he requested from anyone was to speak to whomever was in charge of running the outpost.

Our foundling spirit friends didn't stick around once we started into the outpost. They didn't give us much of a farewell, either. One second, they were there, sniffing at the Gray elves who gawked at them from a safe distance—and then they were gone. Fast, silent, and without a trace.

The Gray elves brought us into the compound without delay. Night was closing in, so they were anxious to get back to their patrols. Walking along the lofty rope bridges that were strung between the trees, we made our way to where the lead scout had set up his command center. Unfortunately, I recognized him right away.

Lurin was one of the apprentices Kiran had trained to become an official scout. He was older, although no taller than I was, and had always been one of the first to mouth off about how I—a human—had no sense in trying to be a scout. I got the impression he didn't think I should be living in Luntharda at all.

Lurin's color-changing eyes narrowed and his lip curled when we entered. He didn't seem to register that Jae was there at all. "What are you doing here, human?"

I crossed my arms and nodded in Jae's direction. "I'm with him."

It was satisfying to watch Lurin's face go pale when he realized who was standing beside me. His face went nearly as white as his hair and he immediately gave a formal bow and salute. "Lapiloque, I-I was not aware you would be coming here."

Jae raised a hand, dismissing the formality. "We won't be staying, I'm afraid. Our mission is urgent. I understand that the Prince and Princess of Maldobar are being held captive in Northwatch. We're going to need every bit of information you have about the Tibrans' occupation there."

Lurin's brow creased with concern. "Surely, you don't intend to try to rescue them."

"No," Jae replied. "I intend to succeed."

Lurin flushed all the way to the tips of his pointed ears. "My lord, that city is overrun. The Tibrans have been mounting a force there in numbers we cannot even count. To go there would be madness."

"I don't intend to lay siege to it," he clarified. "All I need is a quick way in and out. The more discreet, the better."

Rubbing his pointed chin, Lurin paced back and forth. "Most of the Tibran forces are in and around the city. They ran out of room to house them within the city walls, so they had to resort to building temporary camps outside. These camps are well-guarded, though. I haven't been able to get my scouts within two miles of them." He stopped, turning to face us. "Their tunnels are the best way into the fortress. The Tibrans use them to move soldiers and war machines in secret, but the network also delves under the walls. I have good intelligence that one such tunnel leads nearly to the front gate of the tower."

"The tunnels are suicide," I said firmly. "I've been in them before. They're crawling with more Tibrans than an angry anthill. Not to mention it's impossible to navigate them unless you have a map or know their layout."

The planets must have aligned at that exact moment because Lurin gave me a nod of agreement. "I've already lost several scouts in an effort to map them. It's impossible."

"Maybe not," Jae countered. "Do you have anyone on the inside now who can help us get into the tower itself once we make it there?"

Lurin scratched at his brow. "There was someone sneaking us messages, but we've since lost contact. It's been weeks since we heard anything."

"How were you getting word from them?" he pressed.

"One of the resident nobles in the city kept messenger birds. He had a lover in Aular and would send her notes that way. We intercepted one of them by accident before the city was under siege," Lurin explained. "Afterward, we got more messages from someone calling themselves 'Your Lamb.' They were strange—phrased to sound like nothing but love letters. But we were able to identify a hidden code. They used elven words for some things, and the first letters of each one would spell out information. That's how we learned about the timing of the Tibran patrols around the city, where they have their war machines positioned, and even when they were mobilizing to mount another attack."

I arched an eyebrow. "And you have no idea who this Lamb person might be?"

"No." Lurin shook his head. "It might have been the noble, one of his servants, or even a sympathetic Tibran soldier. They use mostly slaves captured from other kingdoms to do their fighting for them. It's not too farfetched to think one of them might know our language."

"Do you still have any of the messenger birds you used to send these messages?" Jae's expression had become dark and pensive.

"Well, yes, but how does that—?"

"Bring it to me," he commanded.

Lurin tripped all over himself to pass the order on. It was refreshing to see him humble for once, and a little satisfying that I'd gotten a front row seat to watch it.

As soon as he was gone, I leaned over to Jae to whisper. "A bird? How is a bird going to help us? Tell me this is not that one grand idea you had."

"Of course not." Jaevid shot me a look. "I can talk to it. Demigod, remember?"

"Riiiight." I tried not to laugh, but it still came out as a choking snort.

"What?"

"Nothing." I snickered. "I just can't wait to see the look on Lurin's face when you do."

"You're enjoying this, aren't you?"

"What?" I feigned an insulted gasp. "Me enjoy you interrogating one of the blockheads who constantly mocked and bullied me as a child? Never! And frankly, I'm wounded you'd even suggest it."

Jaevid rolled his eyes.

"I don't suppose you could tell him the bird is a sacred, ancient forest spirit he now has to pay homage to for the rest of his life?"

"Not a chance."

I SAT OUTSIDE, MY LEGS THREADED THROUGH THE WOVEN RAILING OF THE deck that overlooked the jungle below. Jae was inside, still meeting with Lurin and some of the other scouts ... and the bird. It wasn't something he needed me there for. And, being the only one standing around without some variant of gray hair and pointed ears, called back uncomfortable memories from my youth. Maybe because Lurin was there, and he'd been one of the guys from my past I'd hoped I would never run into again.

From where I sat, I could barely make out cracks of open daylight between the trunks of some of the trees. We were only a mile or so from Maldobar. Here, the air was cool and moving, tasting faintly of the chilled winds beyond the jungle. It was early spring in Maldobar. When I'd left, there was still snow on the ground. My last memory of the place, apart from the scorched desolation I'd left at Barrowton, was telling Vexi to leave.

I pursed my lips at the thought. Vexi was a wild dragon. She'd picked me to be her rider—which was arguably the worst choice she could have made. I still didn't understand why. I wasn't a soldier. I barely passed as a scout. I couldn't understand what that was supposed to mean for me. What kind of dragonrider would I make?

The sound of footsteps and voices approaching interrupted my thoughts. Jae and Lurin were saying their farewells. My old elven rival still looked flustered and embarrassed as they shook hands. I took some small amount of satisfaction in that as I got up to meet Jae.

The bird, a pigeon, was perched on Jae's shoulder with a little scroll of paper tied to one of its scaly orange feet. I barely got a look at it before it took off into the jungle, making steam toward Maldobar.

"Well?"

"I'm sending word ahead of us to find this Lamb person. With any luck, they will be able to help us get into the tower," Jaevid replied with a sigh.

I tried not to dwell on the idea that my survival hung on whether a pigeon with a brain the size of a pea would deliver a message. Gods and Fates. "All right. So, what's next?"

"We figure out how to get to the tunnels." He led the way down one of the staircases wrapped around the tree trunk. It spiraled down to the jungle floor, depositing us right in the middle of the encampment.

"Okay. Suicide. Got it."

Jaevid's fingers brushed the hilt of his scimitar. "Nothing so dramatic. But we are going to need your companion's help to get inside."

"You want Noh to help us?" My stomach clenched. "Not that I wouldn't enjoy cutting up more Tibrans, but unless you mean to carve our entire path to Northwatch in blood—"

"Noh can do a lot more than just kill," he corrected. "But since you haven't completed your ritual, it'll be risky." He flicked me a glance, as though silently asking if I was willing to push my luck that far.

"If you're suggesting it, then it must be our best option. What do you want me to do?"

Jae stopped walking and faced me, his mouth set in an uncomfortable line. "You've already seen that he can bring you into the Vale. But just as he can materialize anywhere in this world at will by crossing over from the Vale, he can also move you to a different location."

I frowned. "Is this something Paligno told you about?"

"Yes," he admitted. "It's called valestepping. Noh can create a portal within himself that we can step through, bringing us from one location to another instantly using the Vale."

"What's the catch?"

Jae shifted, his brows drawing together as he looked down. "It's one of your most costly talents, even with the ritual complete. It could kill you, Reigh. I'll do my best to feed your soul enough of my power to do it, but I can't guarantee it'll work."

It took a few seconds for that to sink in.

"And that's not the only risk," he added.

"Of course not."

"Noh could almost certainly get us within the tunnel, but we will have to get close. The shorter the distance, the less likely it is to harm you."

I had been joking about the whole suicide thing, but this was beginning to sound like exactly that. "How close are we talking about here?"

Jae grimaced. "Two hundred yards would be pushing it."

My shoulders sagged. "*This* is your idea? Get us within firing range of any half decent archer in the Tibran army, have Noh magically poof us into tunnels packed with angry soldiers, and hope there's some mysterious, sympathetic party named Lamb there to help guide us to the tower at Northwatch?"

"Yes." He ran a hand through his ash-colored hair as he looked up. "I'm open to suggestions."

I dropped my arms to my sides and gaped at him. "You're insane. You do realize that, right?"

"I doubt you're the first person to tell me that."

I was ready to bet money on it.

"Good, as long as you're aware." I let out a deep sigh and gestured ahead, toward the boundary line between Luntharda and Maldobar. "Well, we're wasting time. Let's go try not to die."

PART THREE: JENNA

CHAPTER EIGHTEEN

Thunder shook the tower around me.
 No, not thunder. This was something else. Something I knew from the deepest corners of my soul. My eyes flew open.
It was a bellowing war cry—a dragon's mighty roar.

My heart seized in my chest, sending a bolt of pain through my body. Staggering to my feet, I limped to the only narrow window in my cell. The Tibrans had taken their time trying to break me. Argonox was most likely hoping that throwing me to his wolves would soften my resolve and make me more willing to negotiate. He was wrong.

No sooner had I wrapped my hands around the cold iron bars than the huge, blue scaly body of a monstrous dragon surged past, swooping through the air on powerful leathery black wings. Plumes of orange and red flame exploded against the darkness of the night, revealing the smoke rising from the city. Dragons, dozens of them, were descending upon the outer city limits of Northwatch.

The tower shuddered again. I lost my balance and fell, landing against the cold stone floor of my cell. The eerie wail of the war horn began to scream in the night—a sound that was meant to call our men to arms now screeched to warn our enemies. The shouts of men, clatter of armor, and stomping of boots echoed down the corridors. Whatever was happening, it was focused on the city. Surely, my father wasn't thinking of trying to retake Northwatch with all the riders we had left.

Back on my feet, I pressed my cheeks as far as they would go between the bars of the window, straining to see anything I could. The thatched roofs in the city below were burning. Tibran legions were forming ranks, scrambling to position their spear- and net-hurling war machines to fire at the dragons that made diving passes and showered the streets with scorching venom.

A feral scream tore past my lips, ripping past all the agony that crippled my body. Tears made cool trails over the flushed heat of my cheeks as I tried to shake the iron bars. If those were my dragonrider brothers—I would have given the very last breath from my body without hesitation to be out there fighting with them. Just let me out! Give me a blade! I would carve every bit of my dignity back out of Tibran flesh.

"Miss Jenna!"

I turned at the sound of Aedan's voice. He appeared at my cell door, gripping a tall, spear-tipped halberd in one hand. His face, armor, and hands were coated in a fresh spray of blood that dripped from his chin and shoulder pauldrons.

"What, by all the Gods and Fates, is happening out th—?" My voice died in my throat as two other young men stepped in to flank him on either side.

With long, scruffy red hair tied in a ragged braid down his back and his squared, boyish face sporting that mischievous grin—I knew Reigh right away. He wore a similar spray of crimson across his body and there were dark, heavy circles under his light amber eyes.

But the man on Aedan's other side, standing a head taller than the other two, just the sight of him made my heart stop. His eyes caught the torchlight like aquamarines and his dark silver hair framed his strong jawline as it fell to his shoulders. I could just make out the faint line of a scar running from his left brow, over his eye, to the top of his cheek. There was something undeniably forthright about the way he stared back at me, and it put a warm shiver down my spine.

I knew that face, that scar, that look.

My legs buckled, and I crumpled to my knees. I couldn't hold back the sobs. Jaevid Broadfeather had answered my prayer.

"I couldn't get the key to the door. Argonox guarded it too closely." Aedan looked to the others, his face blanched with frantic terror. "Can you open it with your magic?"

"Move," Reigh growled as he shoved the other two out of his way. He stepped forward to grip the bars of my cell, his face twitching and his jaw clenching.

"Reigh." Jaevid's voice rang with concern. "You've pushed yourself too much already. If you do much more, you'll—"

"Back off! I didn't come all the way here just to leave her in this hellhole because of a stupid locked door." Reigh squeezed his eyes shut. "I can do this." His body shook hard, convulsing with his spine curled and his head thrown back. He let out a cry like the howl of a beast, and the places where his hands touched the bars began to swirl with black smoke. The iron shriveled, decaying and rusting in a matter of seconds. The rot spread until it consumed the entire cell door, leaving nothing but a heap of ruddy ash on the floor between us.

Reigh jerked back suddenly, bearing pointed canine teeth like an animal as the colored rings of his eyes glowed like red coals in the gloom. He doubled over, wheezing and gasping for shallow breaths as though he were in pain. But when Jaevid rushed over to help, he cringed away and snarled. "Don't touch me! I'm fine."

Jaevid's fractured expression suggested otherwise.

"Miss Jenna, we have to hurry. They're closing down the tunnels and barring the exits as we speak." Aedan crouched down beside me, his brow drawn into a look of worry. "Can you walk?"

"She has two broken ribs, a fractured jaw and ankle, several infected cuts, and a concussion," Jaevid said firmly as he moved toward me, purpose in every step. "Not to mention she's severely dehydrated. She's lucky she can stand at all. I'll carry her."

"C-Can't let me have one moment to look awesome, can you? Just had to show off your divine power, too?" Reigh wheezed.

Jaevid didn't retort. Before I could object, he swept under my back and knees, lifting me easily into his arms. He carried me out of that putrid Tibran cell as though I were something delicate.

I choked on my words, unable to keep the tears at bay. I threw my arms around his neck and hugged myself against him. I was terrified it wasn't real—that I'd wake up and find myself back in that cell again. But every frantic breath filled my nose with his earthy smell. With my head against the crook of his neck, I could hear his heart beating. Jaevid Broadfeather was holding me. Everything about him was strong, warm, and alive.

He was ... *real*.

Reigh was standing upright again, although his face was as pasty as a corpse and the circles under his eyes seemed darker than ever. "Okay, Lamb, where's Aubren?"

Aedan opened his mouth to reply.

"Phillip." My voice was so weak, I wasn't sure anyone would hear me, so I gripped the front of Jaevid's tunic to get his attention. "P-Please. Find him."

"What? You've got to be kidding. Phillip is here, too?" Reigh's eyes went wide before shooting Aedan a scorching glare.

He swallowed. "I ... well, technically, yes, but—"

"And when, exactly, were you planning on sharing that with the rest of us?" Reigh shouted in his face.

Aedan shrank back, his strange elven eyes flicking anxiously back and forth between the rest of us. "I-I didn't think it mattered. The message only mentioned the prince and princess. And that man is ... he's not ... I mean ... "

"Out with it!" Reigh bellowed again.

"He's not himself anymore." Aedan's voice trembled with fear. "They took him into the containment block for the final phase of the switchbeast transition.

He's been inside a whole day. There might not be anything human left of him by now."

My stomach wrenched, but I had nothing to throw up. "Please, gods, we can't leave him here," I begged. "I won't abandon him!"

"We don't have time to get them both," Aedan urged. "Prince Aubren is being held in solitary detainment on the first floor. The fastest way there is the freight elevator, but the longer we wait, the more soldiers will be down there to reinforce the primary entrance into the tower. We must go now!"

The constant wail of the battle horn crushed down over us like a stone fist, filling the silence. My heart stopped and started, threatening to let the panic kill me.

"Go," Reigh murmured suddenly. "Get Phillip. He's closer by, isn't he?"

Aedan's jaw went slack. "Yes, but—"

"You two find Phillip and take him and Jenna out of here through the roof exit."

"And what about you?" Jaevid's jaw hardened, his eyes burning with quiet rage.

"I'll stick to the original plan and get Aubren. I'm *not* leaving my brother here."

From across the dim corridor, the two young men locked gazes. The air was practically sizzling with raw tension as they stared one another down like a pair of angry wolves.

"You could die," Jaevid warned.

Reigh smirked. "There are worse things than dying, especially for the Harbinger." He glanced my way, his smile fading for an instant. His eyes flickered, searching mine, as though he wanted to say something. Then he winked and flashed a halfcocked grin that made my insides go numb. "Just make sure she makes it. Don't worry about me. I'll catch up."

AEDAN LED THE WAY DOWN THE HALLS OF NORTHWATCH TOWER. WE MOVED fast, but with extreme caution. Whenever a company of Tibran soldiers came close, Aedan signaled and Jaevid immediately ducked into the nearest alcove or doorway, clutching me against his chest. I clung to him, my body shaking out of control. If they found us, I wouldn't be able to fight. I didn't even know if I would be able to run. I was helpless and depending on him to get me out of here alive—a helplessness I hated. Breathless seconds ticked by and we waited for Aedan to whistle, signaling us to move again.

Meanwhile, a thousand questions buzzed through my head like a swarm of wasps. How was any of this possible? What had brought Jaevid back now? Would

Reigh make it? Would we? Was my brother still alive? And Phillip ... what had Argonox done to him? Would we make it to him in time?

All my racing thoughts stopped instantly as we rounded a corner into what had once been the roosting area of the tower, used to house dragons for the riders stationed here. Like everything else, the Tibrans had wasted no time repurposing it for their schemes. Now the stalls were sealed like cages, and through the bolted doors came the muffled snarls, growls, and calls of animals I couldn't identify. There was a strange, acrid smell mingling with the ambient stench of blood in the air.

Jaevid shuddered and came to a halt, his arms tightening around me as his expression skewed.

"What is it? What's wrong?" I had to know.

"These creatures." He grimaced. "Something's not right. They're strange. Their presence feels almost human, but it isn't. I can't explain it."

"Are you all right?"

His mouth twitched briefly into a halfhearted smile. "I'll manage."

"Here!" Aedan called to us. He was standing in front of one of the stall doors, tugging futilely at the heavy chain and padlock that had been put there to keep anyone from going in ... or out.

Jaevid stooped long enough to put me gingerly back on my feet before he eyed the door. "You're sure this is the one?"

"Without a doubt." Aedan nodded. "Can you break the lock? Or maybe the chain?"

"I'm afraid corroding metal isn't one of my talents," he admitted as he eyed the large rolling door that sealed the stall from roof to floor. "Luckily, the rest of it seems to be made of wood. That, I can work with."

"We should stand back," Aedan warned as he grasped my arm. He tried to gently urge me to move away.

I shrugged him off. "No! I want to see! I have to know if Phillip is—"

"Miss Jenna, please." His wild, bizarre elven eyes searched mine earnestly. "If the venom has overtaken him, your friend will most likely attack us. He won't remember anything about who he was before. He will be one of them—a switch-beast—and they are incredibly fierce, especially when cornered."

I struggled to steel myself. "I don't care. I need to see him."

A loud crack made us both turn. Jaevid stood before the massive wooden door, his hands stretched toward it. His jaw tensed. His eyes narrowed. He clenched his teeth and the palms of his hands began to glow with ethereal green light. The wooden boards of the door responded immediately. They groaned and swelled, beginning to bend and sprout leafy branches that twisted toward the ceiling. Jaevid parted the door right down the middle like a living curtain.

As he dropped his arms to his sides, I limped forward toward the opening in the door as fast as I could on my injured ankle. Each step was agony, but I would see him—no matter the pain or risk.

"Phillip!" I screamed his name into the total darkness of the cage. The air reeked of blood, and my bare feet stepped in something wet and warm. Gods, where was he? "Phillip, you answer me right this second!"

A strong hand fell on my shoulder. I jumped and almost fell, but Jaevid held me steady. "Straight ahead," he said softly.

Aedan came to the doorway carrying a torch that filled the cell with revealing light, but he refused to take a single step further. His face had gone pale and his knuckles were white as he gripped the shaft of his halberd.

The light was enough, though.

Directly in front of me, I could make out the shape of a table. It looked like one of the long, heavy wooden ones they used in the dining hall. But this one had been modified, made into some sort of experimentation table. Holes had been cut for restraints to keep a subject contained.

Stretched out on it, lying on his back, was a figure I didn't recognize. He was shackled down by his wrists, neck, arms, knees, and ankles, the metal of the chains clamped down so that they bit into his flesh. There was blood everywhere, splattering the table and dripping from the corners onto the floor. It was too dark to see the man's features clearly, but this person couldn't have been Phillip. He was too tall. He must have been seven feet because he spanned the entire length of the dining table.

Then Aedan lifted the torch higher. More light came in.

I screamed.

The man on the table was not human. His bare skin was an unnatural shade of slate gray that slowly transitioned to black at his hands and feet. A hundred tiny white spots peppered along his corded arms, legs, and strangely-shaped chest reflected the light and glinted like diamonds, making odd patterns. His frame was strange, with shoulders that seemed too wide and a torso that was longer and narrower than a normal man's.

His chest rose and fell with frantic, shallow breaths—but otherwise, he lay perfectly still. I dared to move closer. I searched his face for what felt like an eternity. It was all wrong. His cheeks were never so sharp. His jawline had never been that rigid.

My hand trembled as I touched some of his jet-black hair to brush it away from his face. His hard, fierce brow was locked into a scowl so that his eyes were pinched shut. The longer I looked, the more of those shining spots that flecked his forehead and cheeks I noticed. My fingertips grazed the elongated point of his ear. It wasn't like an elf's. It was longer, sharper, angled more like the edges of a knife.

Tears blurred my vision.

Somewhere, under all that deformity—it *was* Phillip.

"What have they done to you?" My voice shook. I covered my mouth to stifle a sob.

One of his hands twitched.

My breath caught. Hope made my heartbeat stutter. Was he ... ?

A flash of silver was my only warning.

Phillip's eyes flew open, his feline pupils narrowing to hair-thin slits. He lunged against the bonds holding him to the table, snapping the thick chains as though they were nothing. A hand shot forward. He grabbed my throat with crushing force, the sharp black claws where his fingernails used to be digging into my skin.

I couldn't scream. My air was cut off. I pulled desperately at his wrist and fingers, trying to get a breath. I fought and flailed. But he didn't let go. My vision tunneled. I could just barely see his eyes glowing like two sterling moons in the dark.

Aedan cried out.

Jaevid lunged.

A burst of green light blinded me, and I felt Phillip's grip suddenly release. Dropping to the floor, I wheezed and gasped. My neck burned like it was on fire. It hurt so badly, I couldn't bear to touch it.

"Jenna!" Jaevid came to his knees in front of me, invading my space to examine my neck. "It's all right. Let me look. Can you breathe? Where does it hurt?"

I couldn't answer. My chest constricted, and my throat closed. I wanted to cry, but even swallowing was agony.

"You need to listen to me," Jaevid whispered. "Look at me, Jenna. You need to calm down. Try to take a breath."

I forced my lungs to work. Cold air filled my body. My mind started to clear.

"Very good. Now do it again."

Aedan was standing over us, brandishing his halberd and torch. His eyes never left the table where Phillip was lying motionless again. "Is he dead?"

"No. Just unconscious." Jaevid's expression darkened. "He'll have to stay that way until I can examine him. But this isn't the place. Our time is almost up."

"You want to take him with us?" Aedan balked. "Are you mad? What if he wakes up again?"

"He won't. Not until I allow it." He put an arm around my middle and hoisted me to my feet. "You'll have to carry Jenna. I'll get Phillip. Hurry up. Let's move."

CHAPTER NINETEEN

We were too late. As Aedan and Jaevid stepped back out into the corridor beyond Phillip's cage, the air rang with the sound of bowstrings going taut, swords being drawn, and shields clanging as they formed a phalanx before us. Clinging to Aedan's back, I counted twenty-five strong. The archers were a problem, but if I could just get my hands on a sword ...

Then it no longer mattered.

Argonox stepped from the midst of his soldiers, the lengths of his crimson cloak billowing at his boot heels. The torchlight gleamed off the snarling lion's head engraved upon his bronze breastplate. His cold eyes examined us, and I could only imagine what he must have thought of our scruffy company.

When our eyes met, his mouth twisted into a smirk. "What interesting friends you have, princess. And here I thought your father would send the best of his cavalry to your rescue. But this is just shameful." He drew the short sword from his belt and gestured to Aedan with the point. "Hand her over now, slave, and I'll consider welcoming you back into my ranks rather than letting my dogs feast on your flesh."

With my arms around his shoulders, I could feel Aedan's breathing hitch. His eyes darted wildly at the soldiers before us. He took a step back, bowing his nearly-shaved head slightly.

"Miss Jenna ... can you run?" he asked in a whisper so soft, I barely heard it.

I squeezed my arms around him tighter. I was a dragonrider. We did *not* run.

"You've got to try. We won't be able to hold them for long."

"No," Jaevid said suddenly as he put Phillip's limp body down. When he stood, he squared his broad shoulders and faced Argonox with a steely-eyed glare.

"Hah!" Argonox sneered. "You think you can save her? Some miserable wretch plucked from the Maldobarian gutter? I've had more impressive warriors licking the bottom of my boots while they begged for mercy. What chance do you think you stand?"

Jaevid dipped his head slightly, but his eyes never left Argonox. The cold fire in them made my blood run like icy slush as he drew his scimitar. "You want to know who I am?"

Argo's expression twitched. His eyes scrunched thoughtfully. And I saw it, dawning on his face as plain as day. Suspicion. Hesitation and concern followed swiftly.

"I am no Gray elf, nor am I human. I am both and neither. I am a hand-chosen Dragonrider of Maldobar. I am a brother adopted by kings," Jaevid declared as he prowled forward. "I am descended from those who speak for the gods. I am the one who delivered my people from the hands of deception and horror. I am he who has walked with the ancients. I hear the voices of the earth and weave the strands of life. I have shaken hands with death and kindled the fires of destiny. I am Jaevid Broadfeather, and you *will* fear my name."

Argonox's lips peeled back into a snarl of wild delight. He gave a command, and chaos erupted into the corridor. Arrows flew. Men shouted. The Tibran phalanx line advanced. Over it all I could hear him shouting, "Take him! Now! I want him alive!"

The volley of arrows zipped toward us. Aedan shrank back, angling himself between the incoming threat and me. I hugged him tighter, fighting the urge to shut my eyes in the face of death. I didn't want to die, but I didn't want Aedan to sacrifice himself for me, either.

Jaevid moved like a phantom of divine fury. One wave of his hand made all the wooden shafts of the arrows freeze in midair. With a flourish of his wrist they spun, suddenly unleashed back upon the Tibrans who had fired them. Jaevid dropped into a crouch, the blade of his scimitar glowing with the same raw power that thrummed from his body. He drove it down into the solid stone floor like a knife through warm butter.

The tower quaked. All the wooden cages up and down the corridor burst into splinters.

"G-Gods," Aedan breathed in awe.

"No," I rasped. "Just one."

With his gaze blazing like green starlight in the gloom, Jaevid yanked his blade free and advanced. More than a dozen creatures came prowling from the cages he'd opened, their silver eyes glinting with primal hunger. They looked feline, almost like panthers with sleek, muscular bodies as black as pitch. Their dark hides were flecked in the same sparkling dots that dappled Phillip's skin.

Each one was easily six hundred pounds, bearing jagged fangs and bristling the long black spines that ran from their snouts all the way down their backs to the tips of their whip-like tails.

The Tibran line broke at the sight of them. The men screamed in terror as the switchbeasts surged past Jaevid to attack with blitzing speed. They easily bounded over the barrier of interlocking shields, pouncing and dragging their shrieking victims down like panicked goats.

It was complete slaughter.

And amongst it, Argonox fought like a bronze-plated fiend. He was no less skilled in combat than any dragonrider I'd ever seen. He cut through his own ranks and monsters to carve an escape path in their blood—but not before looking back to lock gazes with Jaevid. Wrath like fire made his face go red. His nose wrinkled, his nostrils flared, and his mouth bent into a bitter scowl.

This wasn't over.

It had only just begun.

AEDAN, LIKE MOST GRAY ELVES, WAS ON THE SHORTER SIDE OF AVERAGE WHEN it came to stature. Not that he was puny. In fact, he didn't seem to have any trouble at all carrying me. And as soon as Jaevid gave us the signal to go, he ran as fast as a startled doe—even with my added weight on his back.

Gripping the shoulder straps of his Tibran-styled breastplate, I hung on with my legs wrapped around his waist. Every step jostled me, sending a shock of pain from my broken ribs. But there was no other choice. I'd never be able to keep up on my own, not in this condition.

Behind us, Jaevid wasn't fairing much better. He carried Phillip again and struggled to keep pace. Every time I dared to look back, he was fighting to manage Phillip's big, bulky form.

We darted through the tower, winding a path I knew all too well from my time here as a newly-graduated dragonrider—headed upward to the top level of Northwatch. There was an exit there hidden on the roof and closed off by iron bars. It was only a small hatch used for a single-post lookout, like the crow's nest on a ship. You could scarcely fit a grown man in armor through it, let alone a dragon or any sort of war machine. But it was a way out, and that was all we needed.

Clambering through the winding stairwells, we climbed up farther and farther toward the sky. There was no time to stop and catch our breath, but Aedan grew slower with each step. He was breathing hard, sweat beading on his brow and running down the sharp angle of his cheeks. My stomach swam with guilt that he had to carry me like this. I was a dragonrider; I should have been an asset, not a burden.

"Almost there!" Jaevid called up to us. I looked back as we rounded the last staircase, just in time to see him come to an abrupt halt. His body stiffened as he stood straighter, his eyes suddenly going wide as he stared all around at the near-dark of the stairwell. I tried following his gaze—to see whatever had startled him—but there was nothing.

"What's wrong?" Aedan asked in a panting whisper. "Tibrans?"

"N-No." Jaevid's face flushed across the nose. He blinked owlishly, panning his awestruck gaze slowly back to us. "I know this place."

"You were stationed here during the Gray War," I verified. "You don't remember that?"

"No." His expression dimmed, features falling into despair. "My memories from before are scrambled. It's like trying to piece together a nearly-forgotten dream. Sometimes they come so clearly, and other times ... " His voice faded to shattered silence.

Aedan and I exchanged a glance. Jaevid Broadfeather didn't remember who he was? *That* was a problem.

"But this place," he continued. "I've been here, right in this spot, before. There was someone else. A girl, I think."

"Beckah Derrick," I reminded him.

His gaze darted back up to mine, realization dawning in his face. "I love her."

My throat ached from Phillip's chokehold as I swallowed hard. "Yes. You did."

Jaevid opened his mouth again, as though he was about to ask something, but out of nowhere the tower rumbled and quaked violently. It shook Aedan from his footing. He staggered back, barely catching himself against the wall before we both went tumbling backward. I gripped his shoulders harder and hung on for dear life. "Jaevid, please tell me that was you."

His mouth hardened, face locking into a somber scowl. "No," he growled deeply. "We have to go. Now."

It took them both to pry the hatch open. A bitter cold wind howled in through the narrow exit. Freezing rain stung my eyes and made my cheeks and nose go numb. Overhead, I could see nothing but a dark, churning sky.

Until *he* landed.

Amidst the wail of the battle horn, cracks of thunder, and the distant roar of combat, the concussive thump of wing beats drew closer. A dragon's trumpeting cry blasted through the air. The king drake dropped from the clouds like a mighty demon. Lightning snapped in the air behind him, illuminating deep blue scales, curved black horns, and eyes of piercing yellow.

The dragon landed and immediately poked its huge snout down through the opening, nostrils puffing in deep breaths of our scent.

Aedan gasped back, once again putting himself between any possible danger and me.

Jaevid, however, surged forward and let out a yell—a shout of wild relief. "Mavrik!"

He lugged Phillip up the last few steps, his eyes never leaving the beast. At the last second, he let Phillip's unconscious body slide off his back, so he could throw his arms around the monster's head. The drake purred and chattered, his yellow eyes closing as he nuzzled Jaevid's chest.

"I have missed you, too, my friend." Jaevid's voice came in a rasping murmur as he rested his forehead against the dragon's. "I am ... so sorry to have left you for so long."

The dragon puffed a snorting blast of air at his face.

"All right, fair enough. We'll work it out later." He smirked as he leaned back and scratched the beast's scaly chin. "Thank you for coming to our aid. Are the others here?"

Mavrik chirped and his big yellow eyes flicked to where Aedan and I watched. Behind him, a glimmer of green scales caught my eye as a slender dragon zoomed past. Vexi had come with them. But I didn't see my dragon, Phevos, anywhere. Was he all right? Had he fallen at Barrowton?

Jaevid's broad shoulders sagged. "No, Reigh isn't with us. He went to find Aubren. I can still sense his presence, but we can't wait. Argonox already knows we're here. Phillip is in dire shape and Jenna is wounded. It's now or never."

The king drake gave another snort and made a long series of clicking, chattering sounds before he pulled his head out of the passageway. It made Jaevid sigh. "If Vexi wants to stay behind, then I understand. That's her choice." He motioned to us. "They're ready."

"They?" I assumed he meant more wild dragons. Perhaps they were going to carry us to safety like they had my brother. But as Aedan helped me hobble up the last few steps, out into the fierce bitter wind atop Northwatch tower, my heart stopped.

The shape of a white dragon soaring like a pale ghost against the stormy sky made my breath catch. Behind her, another dragon of light blue flew in perfect synchronization. Perish and Turq spiraled in an emergency descent straight for us.

My brothers had come back for me.

Agony tore through my body as I ran out to meet them. I hurled myself through the air, jumping the last few feet to catch Calem's hand. He seized my palm and hauled me up and into the saddle in front of him in one smooth motion. With one of Calem's strong arms wrapped around my waist to keep me firmly grounded in the saddle, Perish spread her white wings and leapt into the turbulent sky. We were up in seconds, flying higher to avoid the onslaught of Tibran ground fire.

The others couldn't be so quick. With Phillip still unconscious, Aedan had to help drape him over Haldor's saddle and strap him down before they could take off. Behind them, I saw movement beyond the hatch. Tibran soldiers stormed through one at a time, forced into a funnel by the narrow passage.

Jaevid spun, scimitar drawn to hold them back while Aedan scurried onto Mavrik's bare back. It was a mad race. Every second was torture to watch. More and more soldiers poured out onto the platform atop the tower, encircling him with blades and shields. The wind howled at his back, spitting frigid rain and whipping his shaggy hair around his face.

From his saddle, Haldor began to pick off a few of the soldiers with his bow. The wild winds and sheeting rain of the storm made shooting difficult, though. He lost more shots than I'd ever seen him miss before. Meanwhile, the Tibran soldiers advanced, attempting to pin Jaevid in their middle and cut off any possible threat.

Suddenly, Jaevid sheathed his weapon and dropped to his belly on the ground —right as a blast of burning dragon venom hit the bulk of the soldiers around him. Mavrik was up with Aedan still clinging to his back. The king drake shot another plume of fire, lashing his tail and sweeping several soldiers from the tower's edge. Fifty stories is a long way to fall.

With his black wings spread wide, Mavrik held fast long enough for Jaevid to leap back to his feet and run over, sidestepping and jumping around burning Tibrans all the way. As soon as he was secure, the massive blue drake shot skyward. He dove headlong toward the storm, past clouds snapping with lightning and battering winds. And we followed without hesitation. I looked around in vain for Phevos, still hoping to see that familiar glint of purple scales. He wasn't anywhere in sight. My heart wrenched in my chest, torn in agony at the idea he might be gone.

Without padding or armor, I couldn't stop shivering. The frigid air chilled me right down to the bone. Huddling close to Calem was my only shelter. Once we broke through the clouds into the smoother air above the storm, he sat back in the saddle long enough to unbuckle his heavy navy-blue cloak and wrap it around me tightly.

Calem had been my wing end and partner in combat for years. He was someone I knew I could count on, even if he was less experienced than the rest of us. Through the glass slit in his helmet, I saw his gray-blue eyes looking me over as though searching for any apparent damage.

I tried to force a smile, but my chin trembled. It probably looked more like a child trying not to sob.

"*You're okay now. I've got you,*" he said using the dragonrider code of hand signals.

I hurried to signal back. "*Where is Phevos? Did he make it to Cernheist?*"

"*He's fine. Stayed behind to guard the city. He wasn't happy about it, but the king drake wouldn't let him follow. Promised him we'd bring you back safe.*"

I shut my eyes tightly and buried my face into his cloak. My body shook from adrenaline, relief, and a lingering chill as I leaned against him. Phevos was safe. He was alive and waiting for me.

Safe had become such a loaded word. While Argonox lived, and as long as there were Tibrans in Maldobar, none of us were safe.

We were just out of reach ... for now.

CHAPTER TWENTY

We flew above the large storm system that spanned most of the northern border of Maldobar. It stretched out below us like a carpet of boiling gray smoke. Portions of it flashed with bolts of lightning that occasionally jumped from cloud to cloud like rigid fingers of light. It was a wild and beautiful thing.

Spring storms weren't an uncommon sight for Maldobar. They blew in from the west and lingered for weeks. Sometimes they even brought late snows. This one gave us the perfect cover for retreat. The distant shape of Luntharda and the stars overhead were all we could navigate by, but that was more than enough for a trained dragonrider. Orienteering was one of the first things we learned at the academy. I'd spent countless hours poring over maps and star charts, learning to find my way from a dragon's saddle.

Mavrik led us west, past the smoldering remains of Barrowton. I was glad we couldn't see it through the cloud cover. Just the thought of our failure there made my mouth taste of cinders. How many people had we lost? How many had made it to the mountains for safety?

I looked across to Haldor and Turq. Phillip's body was still motionless where it was tied down in front of him. Jaevid had promised he wouldn't wake up. My hand came to my neck, feeling the bruised, tender skin left by his chokehold. I'd never known Phillip to try to hurt anyone before. But if Jaevid hadn't been there, he would have ...

I clenched my teeth against the urge to cry. I wouldn't grieve—not yet. Not until I knew *my* Phillip was gone. There might be some of him still trapped somewhere inside that creature he'd become. And if there was even one tiny fragment of that Phillip left, I wouldn't give up.

Cernheist came into view late the next morning, although it was difficult to tell because of the bleak weather. Below the storm, the white jagged peaks of the Stonegap Mountains were shrouded by the toiling gray skies. You couldn't see the sun at all.

Here, the rain had become a heavy snow. Summer was as short-lived as it was mild this far into the mountains. The people here led a different sort of life, cut off from the rest of Maldobar unless they dared to brave the icy mountain passes riddled with bears, wolves, and mountain cats. Cernheist was one of the larger settlements due to the thriving mining industry. Most of the precious metals and stones came from the northwestern most mountains, and Cernheist sat closest to the largest gold mine in the kingdom. If you could stand the horrible weather and didn't mind tunneling around in the dark like a goblin, a person could make a good living there as a worker in the mine.

Perched on the steep incline of a jutting mountainside, the city looked small compared to Barrowton or Halfax. Most of the buildings were huddled at the crest, overlooking a vertical drop to a large frozen lake below. I could make out the shape of the keep, where the governing noble lived.

Although I didn't know her personally, Baroness Adeline Marden had an infamous reputation as a recluse at court. Her husband had died young, leaving her to manage things alone. She rarely left her city—not that I blamed her, considering what a trek it would be to get anywhere. My father had told me that she was a bright, yet incredibly shy woman. I could only hope she would welcome us.

After all, we were bringing trouble right to her doorstep.

The lights from the city burned warm and welcoming against the stormy sky as we began our final approach. Mavrik started a spiral pattern above the keep, circling for a landing, and the rest of us followed suit. Our dragons held pattern like a flock of huge vultures, taking turns to land in the small front courtyard one at a time.

Anyone could tell this place wasn't made to house dragons. Everything about it was subdued, unassuming, and without the usual grandeur of a noble home. There were no lavish gardens or ornate walkways. The exterior walls were made of the same slate blue stone as the mountains around them, making the keep itself look like a part of the wilderness. Blue Maldobarian banners depicting the king's golden eagle fluttered from the foreword ramparts. Apart from those, there was nothing fortified about the keep—not that it was necessary considering the back portion of the structure hugged the edge of that staggering drop to the frozen lake below. No one would be making a tactical approach from that side.

Servants dressed in heavy wool clothes hesitated when our dragons landed.

Their eyes were wide with awe, and even the men were reluctant to get too close. They probably didn't see dragons very often.

Calem climbed out of the saddle first, then he reached up to help me down. I tried to manage it. But as soon as I put weight on my injured ankle, it caved. I crumpled and Calem barely caught me before I hit the ground.

"It's all right. I've got her." A manservant had mustered the courage to come over and help. He looped my arm around his shoulder as I hobbled along, trying not to put any more pressure on my foot than necessary.

The others were dismounting, too. Haldor and Jaevid had to work together to untie Phillip and carry him toward the entrance from the courtyard. Aedan and Calem followed, lugging bags of gear.

Before me, the open doors of the keep made my heart feel crushed and renewed all at the same time. We were here. We were safe. But we were on borrowed time. How long could we really stay before the Tibrans came for us?

The servants took us to the great hall, a spacious room with cavernous ceilings that boasted bare wooden beams adorned in carvings of bears, wolves, and the occasional dragon. Two wrought-iron chandeliers holding a hundred lit candles hung on either end of the space. Their warm light shimmered over the granite floor, inlaid with design work of green turquoise and red jasper. The place had a natural, earthy feel to it—something I preferred to the gaudy grandeur of most noble houses.

"Your Highness, I welcome you."

Everyone turned at the sound of a woman's soft greeting. Baroness Adeline walked toward us, her dark eyes studying me. She wasn't as old as my father, maybe in her forties, but the lengths of her black hair were flecked with traces of gray.

I managed a smile. "Thank you for taking us."

"Of course." The baroness nodded slightly, her features softening into a motherly smile. "I must admit, when your companions told me of their aspirations of stealing you back, I was not convinced they would be successful. Northwatch was a mighty fortress, even before the Tibrans took it. I'm very pleased to be proven wrong." Her keen gaze shifted to where Phillip sagged between Haldor and Jaevid, taking more time to consider him before she spoke. "I'm afraid I can only offer you the most basic of comforts. I've never had many visitors. But you are all welcome here. The North Wing is at your disposal for as long as you want. My servants will see to your needs."

"What about the dragons?" Jaevid asked.

Baroness Adeline studied him for a moment as well. I could have sworn I saw her blush. "They'll be taken to the stables in the caverns beneath the keep. I've already had my stable master move the horses. It'll be cramped, but they'll be warm and safe from harm."

"I can't tell you how much we appreciate this," I rasped, emotion shaking my tone.

She waved her hand dismissively, making the fur-trimmed sleeves of her green dress swish. "Please, Your Highness, you don't need to thank me. It's my honor to aid the kingdom. I only wish I could do more. We'll speak again when you've all had some food and rest."

"Jenna!" Eirik burst out into the main room of the North Wing as soon as we entered. He was balanced with a crutch under one arm, hobbling along with one entire leg sealed in a plaster cast from thigh to toes. "You look as pitiful as I do!"

I cried out, shouting his name as soon as I saw him. We limped to one another and I threw my arms around his neck to hug him tightly. "You idiot, I thought we'd lost you."

He chuckled. "Bah, you know me. I'm like a weed—hard to kill and always popping up where I'm not wanted."

"Gods, look at your leg." I wiped my face and leaned back to get a better look. "You're practically a statue. How are you feeling?"

"Hot meals, warm bed, and pretty servant girls giving me sponge baths every night—I can't complain too much." Eirik shrugged and gave me a wink.

"As you can see, his horrible sense of humor is still firmly intact," Haldor mumbled as he trudged past to collapse onto the nearest sofa, armor and all.

"Someone has to keep things light," Eirik countered. "You lot are about as cheerful as a two-week-old corpse."

"There isn't much to be cheerful about right now, I'm afraid." I sighed.

"We're alive," Aedan pointed out in a quiet voice. "That's something."

Eirik nodded in agreement.

I couldn't bring myself to argue with it. My body ached. I was starving, thirsty, and in so much pain, I could hardly think straight. Aedan was quick to take up where the servant had left off, helping me wobble to the nearest of the bedrooms that had been opened for us.

It took the rest of the day for everyone to get settled. Space was limited. We would have to share one central washroom, but luckily many of the bedrooms had multiple beds.

Haldor and Eirik were already sharing a room. Calem and Aedan took another, although it took some convincing. My usually-silent wing end didn't like the sight of a Tibran slave soldier. Not that I blamed him, but under the armor and slave brand, Aedan was a Maldobarian—not a Tibran. He'd proven that several times over now. It helped that he was all too eager to wrench that bronze armor off and toss it piece by piece into the flames of the huge hearth in the main room. Stripped down to the tattered, bloodstained rags he wore beneath, Aedan looked much less threatening.

I was the only one to receive a private room because Jaevid had insisted on sharing with Phillip. No matter how I argued, he wouldn't back down and see reason.

Okay, so maybe it was safer for him to be the one to stay with Phillip. Jaevid could stop him if he lashed out again. But it was my fault Phillip was in this state to begin with. He was my responsibility. I should've protected him. I should've found a way to get him out before the Tibrans had gotten their filthy hands on him. If he hurt anyone, it should be me …

Things got quiet as night closed in. Servants came to turn back the beds and bring us more than enough food to eat, although most of us chose to eat in our rooms. The atmosphere was heavy. Silent tension hung thick over us like smog. We were all bracing for what we knew would come sooner or later. It was only a matter of time.

Lying on my back in the soft bed, I tried not to think about what would happen next. I tried to force myself to relax. My strength was gone. I had nothing left. And yet sleep was out of the question because of how my body throbbed in agony. My ribs caused me pain with every breath. I couldn't bear anything to touch my fractured ankle. Every time I closed my eyes, it felt like the whole room was spinning.

A soft knock on the door made me flinch and my hand snap to my hip, reaching instinctively for a blade that wasn't there. After a few breaths, the panic passed. I should've sat up. It wasn't appropriate for a princess to be seen sprawled out unceremoniously on the bed like that. But just the thought of moving that much made my breath catch because of how it would hurt. Burn appropriateness and let it rot.

The door cracked open slightly.

"Jenna?" Jaevid sounded unsure.

"I'm here. Come in."

He entered quietly followed by a younger girl I didn't recognize carrying a bathing pitcher and basin. She was petite, probably half my size, and her long, wool dress hung off her shoulders a little, as though it were too large. She couldn't have been more than sixteen, about Reigh's age, but then again, her stature might have made her seem younger than she was.

When she caught me staring, her heart-shaped face shone with a friendly smile. "Hello, Your Highness. My name is Miri. I'm Adeline's niece. She asked me to come and make myself useful. We're a bit shorthanded on staff. It's so exciting! We've never had so many visitors at once."

"Oh." I forced another obligatory smile. Seeing lovely girls like that always filled me with a mixture of anxiety and envy. I'd never been that dainty or pretty. At least, not in my opinion. I wondered what it was like to be so effortlessly fragile. That was the sort of woman most men wanted, right? Her presence made me want to cover my unpolished, callused hands and all my various nicks and scars.

"Please, call me 'Jenna,'" I mumbled. "If one more person calls me Highness today, I will lose my mind and throw myself out that window."

Jaevid turned his face away, as though trying to hide his smirk. I saw it, anyway.

"What?"

"Nothing." He cleared his throat, still fighting that grin as he pulled a chair to my bedside.

"Must be a very amusing nothing, then."

He finally let it slip. "It's just that, well, you remind me of someone."

I didn't get a chance to ask who. Miri came over to begin adjusting the pillows and help me sit up straighter. It hurt like the fires of hell were burning along my ribcage. My whole body trembled as I bit hard against the curses writhing on my tongue.

"Forgive me, Your—er, I mean, Jenna." Miri's smile was tinged with sympathy as she brushed some of her fluffy, light brown hair away from her eyes. Most of it was tied back into a long braid down to her waist. But her bangs had escaped and framed her face with wavy curls.

"It's all right." I blinked wearily up at Jaevid. "I guess you've come to put me back together?"

He arched an eyebrow. "Does word spread that fast here?"

I looked away. "No. But my father used to tell your stories all the time. He said you could heal people with just a touch."

Jaevid didn't reply. When I glanced back in his direction, I saw something complex and troubled cross his brow. It dimmed the light in his pale eyes.

Miri was apparently oblivious to the tension as she stood by the nightstand, ringing a washcloth in the basin. "I've been getting to know your friends. I always thought dragonriders would be stoic and fierce. You know, the silent, brooding sort. But they're so friendly! Eirik is very funny."

"Please don't tell him that. We'll never hear the end of it."

"I won't," she promised with a giggle as she folded the wet cloth and hung it over the rim of the basin. "Will that be all, Master Jaevid?"

He bowed his head slightly. "Yes, thank you. Please tell Eirik I'll be tending to him next."

Miri beamed and all but danced out of the room. I was beginning to wonder if anyone could be that cheery and nice or if there was something wrong with her. Perhaps it was just that I didn't spend much time around other girls these days. Not that I minded. For whatever reason, I had never felt all that comfortable around the other noble girls, especially the ones close to my age. It always felt like I was being silently judged purely on my appearance, and in my eyes ... I would never be able to measure up to standard in that regard.

Jaevid let out a heavy breath as he turned to face me in his chair. "Jenna, before I do this, we need to talk. I would say it could wait until after but repairing this much damage to your body might leave you delirious for a bit. It's best for you to rest afterward. We have to discuss it now."

I swallowed hard. I had a feeling I already knew what this was about.

"Phillip is stable, for now. But on my first attempt to peer into his soul and see what consciousness it holds, be it man or beast, I couldn't find anything. It was just chaos." His brow furrowed, and I could see lines of fatigue and worry in the corners of his eyes. "Chaos and fear. It's as though he is still at war with that venom."

I closed my eyes. My chin trembled, so I clenched my teeth and fought to keep my composure. "He's ... never going to be the same, is he? We were too late."

"I was able to stop the progression of the venom, but I can't undo what's already been done to him," he admitted. "The physical changes won't get any worse—"

I stopped him cold. "No. You know that's not what I meant. I don't care how he looks. I just want to know if the man I ... " I choked on my words and struggled to get control again. As soon as I opened my mouth, a sob escaped. The words poured out and I was helpless to stop it. "I-I always took him for granted. He was so theatrical about everything. He'd look at me with that dumb, crooked grin on his face, and I just assumed he was teasing or trying to embarrass me when he told me how he felt." Tears ran down my face. Every hitching, sobbing breath was like a white-hot knife in my lungs. But I couldn't stop. I couldn't keep it in anymore. "I just want to know if he's still in there somewhere. Does the Phillip I knew even still exist?"

Jaevid put a hand on mine. "I haven't given up, Jenna. I don't want to give you false hope, but if there is anything I can do to keep his mind intact, I'll do it."

All I could do was bob my head.

"Aedan talked me through what the Tibrans were doing with the switchbeasts. Their bite contains venom that changes you into one of them. Usually it's a very fast process and the victims lose themselves quickly, essentially becoming an animal with no memory of being anything else. But by giving it to subjects slowly, the Tibrans hoped to make warriors infused with switchbeast speed and strength." He squeezed my hand firmly. "The fact that there is even a chance that anything of him might be left is a miracle, Jenna. Phillip fought hard. He resisted the venom for days. He may still be fighting, even now. Let's be strong for him now, all right?"

Looking over at him, I still couldn't speak. I squeezed his hand back instead.

"I'm going to try working with him again after I've seen to the others." Jaevid leaned in, using his thumb to wipe away the tears on my cheeks. "Let's get you fixed up."

Talking about lost memories brought a question back into my mind—something he'd only mentioned in passing while we'd been escaping from Northwatch. "Do you really not remember anything about your life before this?"

He tensed. His jaw stiffened, and his shoulders drew up ever so slightly. It only took a few seconds for his expression to close up completely. Turning his face away, he muttered, "I don't know anymore."

I decided not to push him. It had been a tough day for all of us. I didn't envy where he was sitting in the slightest. Everyone would be looking to him for answers now. He was the one who was supposed to save us all, right? He was supposed to have all the answers.

"Will this hurt?" I asked instead.

Jaevid's expression softened again as he turned back toward me. "No. Just lie back. Take a deep breath and let your body and mind become calm. I'm going to fix it all."

CHAPTER TWENTY-ONE

I gasped awake to the distant sound of combat. Swords clashing. Men shouting. My pulse raced. Had the Tibrans come already? How had they found us so quickly?

My body was shaky and strange, tingling along the areas Jaevid had healed, as I dragged myself out of bed and fumbled for the first thing I could find to use as a weapon—the bathing pitcher. I wobbled out of the bedroom like a newborn fawn, staggering into the main room ready to join the fight.

"Gods, Jenna," Eirik chortled loudly.

I blinked around in bleary confusion. Where was the fight? All I could see was Haldor and Aedan wrapped up in a complex wrestling hold on the floor as though they'd been sparring. All the furniture had been pushed back out of the way, and Eirik, Miri, and Calem were standing by watching. Jaevid, however, was nowhere to be seen.

"I-I heard ... fighting," I rasped.

Eirik laughed so hard, he started choking. Miri giggled and patted him hard on the back.

Calem's expression never changed—as usual. He came striding smoothly over, snatching a loosely-knitted wool blanket off the back of a sofa on his way. "You might consider putting something on," he murmured as he plucked the bathing pitcher from my hand and draped the blanket around me.

I blushed right down to the tops of my knees. I'd completely forgotten to get dressed. The Tibrans had taken all my clothing and armor except for my undergarments, so I'd stayed wrapped up in Calem's cloak until last night when I'd gone to bed. I was still nearly naked, brandishing the bathing pitcher in my linen underwear and top.

"Thank you," I whispered as I hugged the blanket around myself tighter. "Where's Jaevid?"

"He's with Phillip," Calem's deep voice replied.

My heart lurched. Glancing up, I studied the piercing glint of the firelight in his gray-blue eyes. It was silly, I supposed, to think I might have found some clue as to how things were going hidden in his face. Calem wasn't the most expressive person.

"Where? In their room? I'm going in." I whirled around.

Calem caught me by the arm, the strength of his grip startling me to a halt. He met my gaze, a slight furrow sharpening his already-serious brow. "He asked that no one go in until he's finished."

"Finished what?"

He shook his head slightly. "He didn't say."

Cold chills shivered over my body. What was happening in there? Was Phillip awake? What if he needed me?

"We should get you cleaned up!" Miri's voice rang like a cheerful chime of bells as she skipped over and took my arm. "Don't worry. Aunt Adeline sent down something for you to wear. Right this way—I'll show you."

As she led me toward the washroom, I heard the sparring match between Haldor and Aedan resume. Haldor was barking instructions at him as though he were trying to give him a crash course in hand-to-hand combat. Glancing back, I saw Aedan kick backward into a roll, landing on his feet and snatching up a long wooden shaft that looked suspiciously like a mop handle. He brandished it with incredible speed and even scored a few whacks across Haldor's jaw. Impressive.

"He said he was a shepherd—that his family raised sheep in the Farchase Plains," Miri explained in a quiet voice. She had paused to watch them as well. Then I saw her eyes track to Eirik again.

"Seems like Aedan's full of surprises," I agreed. "And I owe him my life. I owe them all, actually."

Her fair cheeks turned rosy. "We don't get visitors here often. It's nice to hear laughter again."

It only lasted a second or two, but I saw it—that look in her eyes as she watched Eirik laugh and taunt Haldor. Even if I wasn't any kind of expert when it came to social grace, that look was one I knew all too well. I forgot my own misery for a moment.

"Eirik is handsome, isn't he?" I turned my face away, fighting a sheepish smile as we closed ourselves inside the privacy of the spacious washroom.

Miri made panicked, sputtering noises. "I-I, um, well—I hadn't thought, I mean I *did* think that, but—!"

I smirked. "If you like him, you should tell him. Days like these don't guarantee a second chance, you know."

She hung her head a little. "I know. I'm just no good at talking to men like that. Or anyone, for that matter. We don't leave Cernheist very often. Aunt Adeline mediates between the merchants and miners, so she works nonstop. They're constantly giving her trouble. We don't throw many parties or balls and it's been ages since we went to one elsewhere in the kingdom." She sighed and went to arrange several towels and bottles of scented oils on the edge of the large stone tub. "I understand it's a long journey, but sometimes I feel like I'm smothering to death in this place. I'd love to go out, maybe see some other parts of the kingdom."

Shrugging off the blanket, I dared to look at my reflection behind the sink. Horrifying didn't even begin to describe it. My hair was scrunched up and tangled into filthy, ragged clumps. It would take an eternity to get all the knots out. While my injuries were gone, I still had heavy, haunted circles under my eyes. My skin looked ashen because of the sheen of sweat and grime caked onto it.

"Gods," I grumbled as I leaned in to study the tired redness in my eyes. "I look awful."

"It's not that bad," Miri consoled as she tested the bathwater. "I'll help with your hair! I'm good at braiding." She swished her own intricate braid proudly.

I decided not to admit that I couldn't braid my own hair. Not like that, anyway. I could manage exactly three hairstyles on my own, and I was currently sporting one of them. Disheveled, down, and a messy ponytail were the extent of my skill set. My mother would have been sorely disappointed.

I felt a bit less like a goblin after a bath. When it was clean, my hair was a burnished golden color. Miri wove the top portion of it into a fishtail braid and combed the bottom half out smooth so that it hung down to my lower back.

Of course, Baroness Adeline had given me a dress to wear. Not my first choice of clothing, especially if I had to take up arms and fight later. But beggars couldn't be choosers and the baroness had already been so generous with us.

I slipped into a white linen chemise and leggings before working the soft wool dress over my head. It was a pale, dove gray with a velvet lavender bodice that laced up the front. The sleeves came to my wrists and were laced up the back to be form-fitting. Thick socks and short boots lined with fleece kept my toes warm, but I still shivered with anxiety. I hadn't worn something this feminine since my mother had been alive. Scrutinizing my reflection, I tried not to blush and cringe. I could just imagine what the others would say.

"You look lovely," Miri crooned with a dreamy sigh. Standing beside me, her head barely came to my shoulder.

"I never wear things like this," I admitted as I turned toward the door. "But thank you. Your aunt has been very gracious to us."

She beamed and fell in step beside me as I left the washroom, hands clasped behind her back. As soon as we reappeared in the main room, all eyes turned to me. Haldor blinked a few times, like he thought he might be hallucinating. Even Calem furrowed his brow slightly—which was more expression than he normally showed about, well, anything.

I resisted the urge to run out of the room screaming.

"I'm dead, right?" Eirik swaggered over to us, his arms crossed as he surveyed my change of wardrobe. "That's the only reason I can imagine I'm seeing *this*." He waggled a finger, gesturing to my outfit.

My cheeks blazed, and I raised a fist in front of his face. "Do I need to remind you who you're dealing with? I can re-break that leg."

Eirik raised his hands and ducked his head in surrender. "Not at all, dragonrider! I'm well aware of who would win that match."

"I'd still enjoy watching it," Haldor said with a half-smirk. "Someone beating Eirik's face in has yet to bore me."

"Says my wing leader! The rider I was supposed to partner in battle until death!" Eirik feigned a wounded expression. "How's that for comradery?"

Haldor rolled his eyes. We were all well acquainted with Eirik's melodramatic sarcasm. Miri seemed to be catching on to it as well. She covered her mouth, bashfully hiding her smile. That only seemed to fuel him on. He followed Haldor and the two men bickered like angry chickens, exchanging playful arm-punches until Eirik swung a bit too hard on one of his blows. Then it devolved into another sparring match on the floor.

Miri and I stood back with the others to watch. The commotion attracted a few servants, who stuck their heads in to watch, too. Maybe this was a little more rough-and-tumble action than this place was used to, but that was the price you paid for harboring dragonriders.

I couldn't enjoy it for long, though.

My heart sank, and my gaze was instinctively drawn away to the hallway that led to our rooms. My insides wrenched and squirmed, making my hands feel jittery. Not knowing what would happen to Phillip had my mind in knots.

"It's been over a day," Calem muttered, reappearing at my side again. "Aubren has not returned."

I closed my eyes.

"How long do we wait?" he asked. "And at what point do we discuss a second rescue attempt?"

I didn't have answers to either of those questions. But that wasn't what scared me. Far more terrifying than the idea of Argonox still having possession of my brother was the notion that he might have Reigh, too. Reigh was dangerous. He was an unlit fuse—a catastrophe waiting to happen. And the last thing in the world Maldobar needed right now was to have that sort of power fighting against us instead of with us.

"We'll wait for Jaevid," I replied at last.

Calem's face had resumed its usual calm, cool indifference. "And if he doesn't know what to do?"

I shuddered at the thought. "Then gods help us all."

My anxiety was a monster I'd yet to tame. It was like a wild wind, whipping around me, ripping through me—leaving me tangled, frantic, and utterly exhausted. And it never stopped. No matter how I tried, those racing, ripping, whipping thoughts never calmed. I was stuck in my own private storm.

That storm drove me from the laughter and lively conversation of the others. Normally, I'd have gone to Phevos. He brought me comfort and stability in moments like this. But I couldn't bear to be too far from Phillip. If anything changed, if Jaevid came out, I wanted to be close by. I wanted to be the first one through that door.

Sitting alone in the study, I curled up in one of the reading chairs near a tall, skinny window and drew my legs in close to my body. I tried not to think about Phillip—and failed miserably. I scoured my brain trying to remember the last thing I'd said to him in the back of that Tibran wagon. Had it been nice? Gods, I hoped so.

The glass windowpane before me was caked with frost and ice around the edges. It offered a view of the bleak frozen lake and the dark shapes of the surrounding mountain peaks. Everything beyond this castle seemed so lifeless, entombed in a never-ending winter. The storm outside kept the skies dark and the air far below freezing, but for now the snow had subsided. I wondered how Miri hadn't lost her mind after staying here day after day. No wonder she was lonely.

A warm hand touched my shoulder. "Jenna?"

I startled, cringing away with a gasp.

Eirik shifted uneasily. His mouth was pressed into a tight, uncomfortable frown. I knew that look. There was something he didn't want to tell me, but he had to.

My stomach dropped. "What is it? What happened?"

"He's asking for you. It's time." He wouldn't meet my gaze as he rubbed a hand through his dark brown hair. I noticed he was wearing his weapon of choice sheathed across his back—a two-handed longsword over fifty inches long.

My throat constricted, seizing up on anything I tried to say.

Eirik must have been able to read the panic on my face because he offered a hand and a half-hearted smile. "Come on. You know I've got you. We all do. You're not in this alone."

I wished that were true.

Taking Eirik's hand long enough to get to my feet, I walked slowly behind him out of the study. We crossed through the main room and down the hall toward the room that Jaevid and Phillip were sharing. No one had come in or out of there all day.

The closer we got, the louder my heartbeat thrashed in my ears. I couldn't bring myself to meet the gaze of Aedan or Miri as we passed. Their apprehension and fear were palpable enough already. Seeing it would only make it worse.

Haldor and Calem stood on either side of the door like two gargoyles. Haldor gripped his bow with an arrow already fitted to the string. Calem stood disturbingly still, hands resting on the pommels of his dual scimitars that hung at his hips. I didn't have to ask why they were there. If this went badly ... it had to be stopped as quickly as possible.

The memory of what had happened last time rose up in my mind. I could almost feel his hand around my throat, threatening to crush the life out of me. Would that happen again? Would anyone be able to stop him if it did?

I held my breath as Eirik opened the door to let me go in first. He followed, closing it behind us. There was sobering finality in the click of the bolt as he locked it.

The room was nearly dark. Jaevid had pulled all the drapes over the windows to blot out the sunlight, and only one oil lamp burned on the bedside table. He sat in a chair at the foot of the bed, hunched over with his elbows on his knees and his head bowed.

Laid out before him, covered mostly by a downy padded quilt, was all that was left of Phillip. Physically, I couldn't tell that he had changed from the state we'd found him in at Northwatch. But seeing him again transformed into this distorted mixture of man and beast hit me hard. His immense stature, tightly-muscled frame, slate-colored skin, and strangely feline features were the same as when we had found him in Northwatch.

My breath caught. I clenched my teeth, trying to will myself closer, but my feet wouldn't budge.

"It's all right." Jaevid sounded exhausted. "I haven't woken him up yet. I thought you should be here for that. You know him better than any of us. You'll be the best judge of how stable he really is."

"I thought you were a healer," I whispered. "You ... couldn't undo any of what this did to him?"

Jaevid raised his head to meet my stare. His eyes were bloodshot and ringed with dark circles. Guilt soured my stomach. That question had sounded ungrateful—which wasn't at all what I'd intended. We'd all been resting, eating, and roughhousing while he'd been in here working.

"It's the venom," he replied. "I can heal injuries, but what this has done to him isn't a wound. It's changed his physical being. I can't reverse that."

I took a steadying breath. "Thank you."

He blinked. "For what?"

"For trying. For not giving up." I nibbled my bottom lip. "Just tell me what to do."

Standing next to me, Jaevid put his hand on my back and steered me to the bedside. I couldn't stop myself from shaking as he guided one of my hands to touch Phillip's. That contact, the warmth of his skin against mine, made my heart swell with hope.

I laced my fingers through his and squeezed. I tried not to look at how each finger was tipped with a pointed black nail that looked more like a claw.

"I'm ready," I whispered.

Jaevid didn't reply. He placed his palms over Phillip's forehead. Warm green light glowed between his fingers, only lasting for a second or two. Then Phillip's eyelids fluttered. His mouth twitched, and his brow furrowed. The sound of his breathing got louder and more agitated.

Jaevid moved back, giving us some space. He gestured for me to stay put—but I had no intention of going anywhere. Not now. I had to know.

The scrape of a blade leaving its sheath broke the silence, coming from behind me where Eirik stood by the door.

Phillip's eyes flew open, vertical pupils narrowing to slits. A beastly snarl rumbled from his throat as he sprang into a crouch, snatching away from my touch. He scrambled to get away from us, backing up until he fell off the far side of the bed and crawled into the corner. His movements were fast and fluid, more like an animal's than a man's.

"Phillip! It's okay," I cried out. "You're safe now."

He bared pointed canine teeth, hissing as he tried mashing himself farther into the corner of the room like a frightened feral beast. His long tail flicked and curled around his legs as he sank down into a squat, strange eyes darting between the three of us. I could see fear in the human features of his face. It was primal, feral, but it was still something I recognized.

"He's afraid," Jaevid said quietly, confirming my suspicions. "Talk to him again. Let him hear your voice."

"Phillip, do you remember me?" I steeled my fractured nerves and cautiously moved a few steps closer. "Do you remember what happened at Barrowton? You saved me. Hilleddi was going to kill me. But you came just in time."

I rounded the corner of the bed and stopped. Phillip had turned his face away, practically mashing his dark, sinewy body into the corner as far as he could. One wide, petrified silver eye still stared back at me. He was panting hard and his whole body shivered, making those gleaming flecks along his arms, legs, and chest shimmer in the lamplight.

"They got both of us," I continued, keeping my tone soft. "They took us from Barrowton. We were trapped inside the back of that wagon and ... you told me about that night at Aubren's debut ball. Do you remember?"

His head turned ever so slightly to look back at me.

"I'm so sorry, Phillip. I'm sorry I couldn't save you."

His long, pointed ears perked up as he tipped his head to the side a little.

"Please," I begged. "Don't leave me. I need you. I've always needed you. You have to remember."

He blinked owlishly, head tilting the other way. Meanwhile, his sterling eyes squinted, and his brows knitted.

I chanced a few more steps closer before coming to my knees in front of him. My hand shook as I stretched it out into the open air between us.

Turning his face away again, Phillip's lip twitched into a half-snarl. Then his expression scrunched. He shut his eyes tightly and shook his head, burying his face in his hands. I could hear his teeth clicking as he gnashed them.

My heart pounded wildly. "Phillip?"

He let out a low, thunderous growl—then a gasping, choking pant.

Gradually, inch-by-inch, his hands lowered. His gaze tracked around the room until it met mine again, pupils wider and mouth slightly open.

I held my breath.

"J-Jenna?" His voice was huskier, laced with an inhuman growl. But it was *his* voice.

Tears welled in my eyes. "I'm here."

He dropped back onto his rear end, sitting with long legs sprawled and his back against the corner. "W-Where? Where am I?" Suddenly, his gaze roamed down to his hands, his legs, and his ... tail.

Phillip let out a feline shriek of horror.

"It's okay!" I lost myself and darted in closer, taking his face into my hands. "Just calm down. It's okay now. You're all right."

"Are you insane? How exactly is this all right?" He wheezed, staring back at me with terror. "G-Gods ... what did they ... what did they do to me?" He started to sob.

My composure broke. I threw my arms around his neck and hugged him tightly, burying my face against the side of his neck. His shuddering, broken breaths and racing pulse engulfed me as he hugged me back. For a few minutes, it was all we could manage—just sitting there, holding one another. It was all I'd thought about, all I'd wanted, since the moment we'd been separated.

"I'm a monster," Phillip rasped.

"No, don't say that. It's not that bad."

"Not that bad?" He seized my shoulders and held me at arm's length. "I have a *tail*, Jenna! And my hands, my skin ... Gods, look at my feet!"

He wiggled his bizarre toes. They did resemble cat's paws somewhat. Each toe was tipped in a curled black claw much longer than the ones on his hands—which might have passed for normal at first glance apart from their color. The whole of his foot was longer, and I'd noticed when he moved that he tended to carry his weight on the balls of his feet.

Okay, so they were a bit strange—maybe even stranger than the tail. But not by much.

My shoulders sagged as I laughed.

He took it the wrong way. "This is funny to you? What the hell, Jenna?"

I couldn't help it. And I couldn't stop. I laughed so hard I choked. "I-I'm sorry," I wheezed. "It's not funny. Not really. I'm just so happy."

He frowned, arching one of his eyebrows in a dubious look he'd given me a thousand times—usually right before I did something reckless. Seeing it again was more than I had dared to dream of.

"I was so afraid you were gone. I thought I'd lost you forever." I leaned forward to rest my forehead against his shoulder. "But you're here. And you're worried about having a tail."

Phillip's body twitched with a sarcastic snort. "You say it like it's a perfectly normal problem to have."

My body relaxed against him. My eyes felt so heavy, as though the fear and dread building up to this moment had been the only forces sustaining me. With them gone, I was drained.

"Oh, hush," I murmured as I embraced the calm, simple weariness. "We've never been very good at normal, have we?"

"No," he replied softly. "I suppose not."

CHAPTER TWENTY-TWO

Explaining Phillip to the servants, staff, and of course—Baroness Adeline—was going to be a challenge. No one in Maldobar had ever seen anything like him, and to be perfectly honest, he looked scary. The slate gray and black skin speckled in tiny shining flecks, intensely fierce features, and fang-like incisors were a lot to take in. Not to mention he was essentially a giant compared to the rest of us.

The servants tending our chambers were terrified of him, even after Jaevid explained that he wasn't going to hurt anyone. I believed that with every fiber of my being. I knew when I looked into Phillip's eyes I was seeing the man I'd grown up with. But the others didn't know him like I did, and even my dragonrider brothers regarded him with tense uncertainty when he came out into the main room.

It was strange to see all seven feet of him cowering behind me, looking at the others with his slender ears drooping and his peculiar, steel gray eyes as wide as moons. The clothes Miri had brought for him only barely fit. The tunic was stretched to the seams over his hard, muscular shoulders and the sleeves were much too short. The pants had the same problem, only coming to about his calf, and we'd had to cut a hole for his ... um ... tail.

Miri and I had given up entirely on packing his misshapen feet into boots, although being barefoot didn't seem to bother him. He had soft, feline-like pads on the balls and heels of his feet, as well as one on each toe. His toes were shaped more like paws, and since he moved with his weight supported on the balls of his feet, wearing boots or shoes would have prevented that and probably made things more awkward for him.

"I can feel vibrations in the ground," he muttered as he flicked a glance down at me. "And the smells—the sounds!"

"The venom's had an effect on many things." Jaevid approached us with a smile, offering a heavy iron poker from the fireplace. "Try this."

"I've never been very good with weapons," Phillip mumbled as he took it reluctantly.

Jaevid's smile widened. "I don't want you to fight with it. I want you to break it."

"Break it?"

"Yes. Just humor me. Try cracking it in half."

Phillip swallowed, glancing around at the rest of us. My dragonrider brothers, Aedan, and Miri had all gathered around to watch. I must admit, I was curious, too.

Phillip swished the end of his tail. The black fur on it was as sleek as it was shiny, catching the light like silk as he flicked it back and forth. I wondered if he was even conscious that he was doing that. Would he be upset if I tried petting it?

Taking the fire poker in both hands, Phillip furrowed his brow and started to concentrate. The iron poker snapped in half instantly—as though it were as brittle as a toothpick. He dropped the pieces in surprise, his ears drooping a little more. "I-I'm sorry. I didn't mean to, uh," he stammered.

My jaw dropped.

Eirik let out a nervous bark of a laugh.

Aedan looked like he might bolt from the room at any second. Of all of us, he was the only one who had any experience with switchbeasts. Maybe that was why he was standing a lot farther back than the rest of us.

"You'll have to be mindful of your strength," Jaevid warned as he stooped to pick up the pieces of the poker. "We're much more fragile than you are now. It'll take some getting used to."

"So long as he doesn't snap anyone's hand off when he shakes it." Eirik snickered.

Phillip's expression dimmed. I caught him stealing another peek in my direction, and it was as though I could read the worry written all over his sharply-featured face.

"You won't hurt me." I smiled as I took his hand. "I trust you."

Phillip turned his face away and didn't reply.

Baroness Adeline had requested that everyone join her for dinner tonight in the keep's dining room. I had no doubt as to what she wanted to talk about. It was the same thing weighing on all our minds now: What should we do next? If Reigh and Aubren hadn't escaped, should we mount another rescue attempt? Or should we leave them to their fate? Should we try going back to Halfax to reason with my father or spend our efforts attempting to rally a force large enough to take back Northwatch?

The latter wasn't even an option, really. After what it had taken just to get Phillip and myself out of that hellhole, trying to take on the brunt of the Tibran army was nothing short of insanity. We only had four battle-ready dragonriders at our disposal, counting Jaevid. Eirik was no longer injured, but he didn't have a dragon anymore. Even with a demigod on our side, it seemed hopeless.

"I ... think I prefer to stay here," Phillip murmured. He settled down on the rug right in front of the crackling hearth with his legs crossed.

I frowned. "Aren't you hungry? It'll be fine, I promise. They'll get used to it, you'll see."

He shook his head a little. "No. It's not that. I just need a moment to think," he murmured. "Besides, I don't have much to contribute to a war meeting. The only city I knew anything about defending is gone."

My heart sank. I hated seeing him so hopeless.

"Come on—don't make that face." He forced an awkward smile.

"I'm not much use at a war meeting, either. What if I stay and keep him company?" Miri offered.

That did make me feel a little better about it. I didn't want him to sit up here all by himself. "All right." I sighed.

Out of the corner of my eye, I saw Eirik's mouth scrunch unhappily and his eyes narrow. He didn't say anything, and I had a suspicion he wasn't only worried about her safety.

"Let's not keep our hostess waiting, then," Jaevid suggested. He led the way out of the North Wing with the rest of us following like chicks behind a mother hen. Eirik stuck close to my side and was unusually quiet. He still hadn't shaken off that scrunched look of discontent.

I decided to dig at him a little. I still owed him for that comment about my dress. "So, Miri thinks you're very funny."

His whole face flushed beet red. "She said that?"

I shrugged, suppressing a smile. "She may have. Or maybe she was talking about Haldor. I can't remember."

Eirik's expression soured into a pout. "You're cruel."

"And you're a terrible flirt," I quipped.

"It's not like that. I'm not just messing with her."

"Oh?"

"I ... like her. She's ... you know." He shrugged and looked away.

"Eirik Lachlan, the poet." I covered my mouth to stifle a laugh. Somehow, attracting the attention of the rest of our group seemed a little *too* mean, even for him.

"Oh, shut up." He sulked. "I keep thinking of things I could say to her. Nice things. But whenever there's a chance my mind goes blank and I end up staring at her and not saying anything."

"You're an idiot."

"I know."

I nudged his shoulder with mine, offering some playful reassurance. "When did this happen? Before or after I got here?"

"Before," he confessed. "She took care of me when I was injured. I must have looked like a lost cause, pathetic with my leg all crunched up, but she looked after me anyway. She sat by my bedside. Fed me. Talked to me. She even brought in some cards so I could teach her to play."

"And have you thanked her?"

He started gnawing on the inside of his cheek. "No. Maybe I should."

"That might be a nice gesture." I nudged him again. "Open with that. And then tell her she's pretty, or compliment her smile, or tell her how much her kindness meant to you. Something simple."

Eirik arched an eyebrow suspiciously. "Just like that, eh?"

"Sometimes simple is best," I replied. "And in your case, simple is probably the only thing you can manage. So, skip the poetry and romantic ballads for now. Clearly you're not ready for that."

"Did I mention you're cruel?"

I grinned. "You have no idea."

BARONESS ADELINE HAD A GRAND SPREAD LAID OUT FOR US IN THE DINING room. The rich, savory smells of roasted lamb and goose, succulent puddings, spiced boiled potatoes, and freshly-baked bread made my stomach howl. We'd eaten well on hearty soups and stews in our chambers, but this was a real feast. I couldn't wait to dive in. I hadn't eaten food this good since I'd been in Halfax.

From her seat at the head of the table, the baroness gazed around at all of us with a thoughtful purse to her lips. She was a quiet woman, petite like Miri, but with a much more cautious demeanor. Apart from those few streaks of gray in her hair, she was still lovely for someone closer to my father's age. Maybe the lack of sunlight and cold air in this part of the kingdom had helped preserve her youthfulness. I wondered why she hadn't bothered trying to remarry. Surely she could, even if she was too old to bear children. She already had an heir in Miri, right? And it shouldn't have been too difficult for a woman with her connections to attract a whole flock of worthy suitors.

Her dark eyes fixed on Jaevid when he took the seat next to hers. I sat on her other side, and the rest of our company filled in the remaining chairs—except for the two on the other end. Phillip's and Miri's. The baroness flicked her gaze to those empty seats, seeming to notice her niece's absence.

"I'm pleased to see you all mended and healthy again." The baroness smiled, once again staring at Jaevid. "Miri has kept me informed on your progress. I hope she's been useful to you."

"Yes, she's wonderful!" Eirik answered—a little *too* quickly.

I kicked his leg under the table and shot him a look. Down, boy.

"And Duke Phillip Derrick? How is he getting on?" she continued without missing a beat.

Haldor shifted in his seat. Eirik cleared his throat and fidgeted with the tableware. Calem, as usual, didn't even blink. I quietly envied his ability to reveal absolutely no expression whatsoever while my face grew hot and I shrank down in my seat some.

"He's ... still coming to terms with what happened," Jaevid replied. I marveled at his ability to be both vague and honest at the same time.

"The staff tells me his physical appearance has not changed." Baroness Adeline didn't mince words.

Jaevid stiffened. "Unfortunately, no. I'm afraid that in that regard, there is nothing that can be done. He won't deteriorate any further, but what's been done to him will remain."

"That is truly a shame." The baroness let out a small sigh, gesturing for the servants to begin serving us our first course. "He would have made an appropriate suitor for Miri."

My stomach clenched. Under the table, my hands curled into fists. Out of the corner of my eye, I saw Eirik's jaw stiffen.

Jaevid spoke up. "Actually, I think he already had someone in mind to court. Not that I'm much of a judge—I hardly know him. But during my efforts to stop the venom from taking his mind, I spent a lot of time immersed in his thoughts." He met my gaze from across the table. "There was a certain lady who appeared many times."

My cheeks burned. I stared down into a plate of food as a servant slid it under my nose.

"Is that so?" The baroness's eyebrows lifted as though she were surprised. "She will be greatly distressed to hear of his condition, then. I doubt he will be able to stay on as duke in his current state."

"He can't even walk down a sidewalk in his current state," Haldor mumbled under his breath. "Not without people scattering in terror."

I wanted to give him a good kick as well. He was too far out of reach of my leg, though. And ... well, he was right. Even if by some miracle we won this war, retook Barrowton, and could rebuild it—Phillip might not be up to the task of taking his place as duke again. Not that I wouldn't encourage him to try.

As ridiculous as he'd been with me, Phillip had always done his part to be a good leader. He'd carried the torch of my father's mission to peacefully unify humans and elves proudly. People liked him. The Barrowton citizens had trusted him. I wondered if that would really change just because he looked different. It didn't seem fair. What had happened wasn't his fault.

"At any rate, that's not why I asked you here tonight." The baroness waved her hand, dismissing the subject as she took up her fork. "There is much unrest amongst my people here about what will happen if the Tibrans attempt to take this city as well. We are not prepared to wage a war. Cernheist has never seen battle before and our location doesn't generally attract outside parties. The only soldiers here are the ones who came as refugees from Barrowton, Westwatch, and Austlen, and many of them are too wounded to fight."

Jaevid took up his goblet of wine with a nod. "Don't worry about that. I will do what I can to help them. It would help if we could send out a decree for any wounded infantrymen or dragonriders to be brought to the city squares. It'll be faster than if I go door-to-door."

"You can heal so many?" Baroness Adeline blinked at him in surprise. "Does it not tire you?"

He shrugged. "It does. But being a little tired is a price I'm willing to pay if it puts more blades between the Tibrans and this city."

Her eyes narrowed with a small, approving smile. "Then consider it done. You can start in the morning. Hopefully, the weather will not make things more difficult for you."

"We'll do the same with the other wounded—the city folk and villagers—but only after I've seen to the soldiers," he added. "We don't know how much time we'll have."

"Speaking of time," Haldor said, interrupting. He was the only one who hadn't started eating yet. "How long are we going to wait before we count Reigh among the lost? It's been nearly two days."

"It is a long journey on foot to come here from Northwatch," the baroness said. "The mountain passes alone are quite treacherous for the inexperienced. That's why the merchants drive me mad with their endless hazard pay negotiations."

Jaevid shook his head. "They wouldn't be coming on foot. Reigh's dragon stayed behind. I've tried seeking out her thoughts, but either she's intentionally blocking me or ... something else has gone wrong."

I swallowed against a cold, hard knot of uncertainty in my throat. "Can you tell if they're alive? Reigh and my brother?"

"Yes. It's faint, but not beyond my sight," he said. "Both your brothers are alive."

I dropped my fork. "Both?"

Closing his eyes, Jaevid took in a deep breath. "I doubt Reigh would want me to tell all of you this. But considering what we could be facing, it's only fair that everyone is aware of what we might be up against."

"I-I don't understand." My brain frazzled at the idea. Aubren had mentioned something in passing about that boy possibly being our brother. At the time, I hadn't been able to process that new information. There were other, more important things to focus on—like surviving. But I never could have dreamed that he might have actually been right. How? Why had our father never told us about this?

Jaevid gestured to Aedan. "Thanks to some valuable insight into how the Tibran Empire operates, I can guess what might happen if Argonox were to take control of a powerful being like myself or Reigh. The experimentation he did on Phillip using the switchbeast venom is just a taste of what goes on within their ranks."

Heavy silence settled over the table. No one was eating now. Every eye fixed upon Aedan, who sat rigidly in his chair with his face scrunched in anguish. His brow creased, eyes shut tight as he started to speak. "Argonox is a monster in more ways than you know. He has an appetite for power beyond just what he can win with numbers and brute force. Some of the other slave soldiers came from places thousands of miles away. They say he's searched every kingdom he's conquered, stealing all the divine relics and magical devices he can find. He warps their purposes, uses them to test on different subjects. He wants to find a way to weaponize these divine powers. He wants to make himself a god!"

"Wait a second." Eirik raised his hand with a frown. "Why does that sound so familiar?"

"Because it happened once before," Calem growled. His gray-blue eyes narrowed as he stared Jaevid down. "We fought an enemy who called himself God Bane with that same agenda. He tried to take Maldobar and it was the dragonriders who put a stop to it. We all hear this story during our training at Blybrig Academy."

"But that was over three hundred years ago," Eirik protested. "No way God Bane and Argonox could be the same person. No one lives that long. Besides, the god stone was in Luntharda at that point, right? If he was looking for divine relics, he was attacking the wrong kingdom."

Memories swelled in my brain like a roaring ocean wave, sweeping me back to Northwatch tower. I'd stood face-to-face with our enemy. Argonox had said many things, and men like that always liked to talk themselves up. To gloat in front of the poor helpless woman. But ... something he had said pierced my mind like a wasp's sting.

"Become my queen. Stand at my side and Maldobar will know prosperity forever, guarded by the power of my empire. You would become legendary. A queen for the ages. A goddess."

I ground my jaw against the urge to gag.

"There's another possibility." Jaevid's voice was soft, but it carried a finality that chilled me to the marrow. "He came to Maldobar in search of a different relic—the same one that Reigh needs in order to complete his ritual and be able to fully channel and control his power."

No one at the table said a word.

"Just as the god stone once held the essence of Paligno, the essence of Clysiros is contained within a crystal. To the untrained eye, it might look like onyx or volcanic glass."

My lungs constricted. I couldn't breathe. My pulse roared. I knew *exactly* which crystal he was talking about. I had seen it almost every day of my life.

Jaevid stared back at me from across the table again, as though he could read the blurred, panicked thoughts racing through my brain. "It sits in Halfax, placed in the royal throne."

Once again, no one spoke.

After a few uncomfortable minutes, Jaevid turned his gaze back to the baroness. "Knowing that, and seeing what Argonox has accomplished so far, you can imagine what he might do with someone like Reigh—especially if he were to take control of the crystal as well."

"What can we do?" My voice would hardly come out as more than a shaking whisper. "Can we destroy the crystal? Remove it from play?"

Jaevid's mouth tensed. "The same rule applies to it that applied to the god stone. The essence of the gods must be present on earth in some form. If we destroy it, the only other natural place for it to manifest would be within Reigh."

"And if Argonox has him, then we've handed him a weapon of immeasurable destruction." Haldor slumped back in his seat. "Gods and Fates bless us."

"King Felix knows about this crystal, then?" Calem was as direct as ever.

Eirik shrugged. "He must, right? Why else would he focus all his forces on keeping Halfax secured."

Of course. Gods, why had I not seen it before? Father had to know—both about Reigh *and* the stone. That must have been why he'd sent Reigh away after he'd been born. Living in obscurity, lost to that immense jungle, seemed like a much safer alternative for someone with power like his.

"I had hoped to take Reigh to Halfax immediately following our rescue attempt at Northwatch," Jaevid went on. "I thought having us both fighting against Argonox would be enough to finish this quickly and cleanly—before any more damage could be done. Knowing that there is any chance at all we might have to fight against Reigh ... "

His voice faded.

He didn't need to finish. Most of us had already seen what that boy was capable of at Barrowton. The thought of him fighting for Argonox made my blood run like ice water.

"What do we do?" Eirik's voice had an irritated edge. "Sure, it's bad, but we can't just sit here. Waiting and doing nothing while fate creeps up on us is not the dragonrider way."

"No, it isn't." Jaevid agreed. "And we don't know for sure that Reigh and Aubren haven't already escaped. But we now must think of the safety of the people here as well. If we leave, they are defenseless."

"We have nowhere else to go." The baroness's expression had become desperate.

Jaevid put a reassuring hand on her arm. "You do. You can go to Luntharda. Surely there must be a road that will take you there from here."

She frowned. "Well, yes, there is. It was a trade route long before the Gray War that ran between here and Luntharda."

"It wasn't reopened after the war ended?"

"No—but it had nothing to do with the elves. That path is extremely dangerous, especially this time of year. The slopes are unstable because of the spring melts. Avalanches are common and the stonehide bears are ravenous after hibernation. We would be traveling with elderly and children."

"The animals will not touch you." Jaevid's voice carried that firm, commanding sense of certainty one might expect. If anyone could dissuade hungry bears or predators from the hunt—we all knew he could. "I will send word to Mau Kakuri. They will let you take shelter in the jungle."

"Some might argue that's trading one death for another," Haldor muttered. "That jungle is no sanctuary."

Aedan crossed his arms. "I'd take it over going back to the Tibrans any day."

"It's not as though we have any other choice," the baroness agreed. "We are cut off from every other side. The Tibrans have taken everything on the western coast from Bowfin to the Canrack Islands. Some say Blybrig still stands, but who can know for sure? No messenger we send ever returns. With Barrowton lost, there's nothing else we can do."

I didn't envy her position. I supposed, being the crowned princess, I could have offered some advice or even insisted she do as Jaevid told her. But Baroness Adeline knew better how to handle the citizens here. These people weren't your typical city folk who worried about who held the throne—they had built their lives for generations in this unforgiving part of the kingdom, cut off from everything else. No doubt my father was merely a distant figure to them; someone they heard about but who didn't really have an effect on their lives. They'd been kind and generous with us. Forcing the hand of their baroness might send the wrong message. This was her choice to make. I wouldn't take it from her.

Leaning forward, she put her face in her hands for a moment and rubbed her brow. "Very well. I will send out a request for every man, woman, and child within this city to go to Luntharda, as you suggest. We'll leave as soon as the storm lifts. With any luck I can negotiate with the merchants to let us use some of their wagons for the young and feeble."

Jaevid narrowed his eyes. "If they give you a hard time, send them to me. I'll handle it." Then he looked back to the rest of us. "I should still have time to see to the injured. But we need to prepare as well. We'll need weaponry, armor, and other outfitting."

"Where are we going?" Haldor cocked an eyebrow, looking more curious by the second.

"With any luck, to Halfax."

CHAPTER TWENTY-THREE

The rest of dinner passed like a blur.

Everyone talked more about what we would do to help the citizens of Cernheist prepare for their perilous journey through the mountains and what we would take with us on our mission to Halfax. Reaching the royal city would be a miracle in and of itself. We would have to somehow make our way across the entire kingdom. Dragonriders flew that distance all the time. It took about ten hours with typical weather conditions, or eight if the winds favored. Taking potential storms into account, it might take us two days if we were forced to land to wait out bad weather.

The kicker was knowing next to nothing about how many and what kind of Tibran legions might stand in our path. Ground legions, for the most part, wouldn't be a problem. Weather permitting, we could fly high enough to stay out of range for archers. But if they had war machines, namely the ones they used to shoot dragons out of the sky, then we had an issue.

The fact that there were so few of us was perhaps the only advantage we had. Our company was so small, maybe we could pass without ever being noticed.

"The last official report we received from Halfax said the city's western front was still clear," Haldor recalled. "I suppose Tibran war machines didn't roll well through the swamps. It slowed their ranks to a crawl. They were forced to go farther south, around the marshlands."

"If we did happen across some of them stuck in the mud, I'm not sure I could resist the idea of bathing them in dragon flame—just for spite," I mumbled.

Eirik chuckled in agreement.

"We'll have to at least try not to draw any attention to ourselves unless we have no other choice," Jaevid cautioned. "The last thing we want is Argonox finding out where we are headed. I can only assume the only reason he hasn't attacked Halfax already is because he was hoping to draw Reigh or me out into the open. That—or he's hoping to cut off all possible points of retreat for Felix so that his first assault is the only one necessary to take the city."

"Could be both." Eirik shook his head slowly. "Either way, he's well on his way to handing our rears back to us on a silver platter."

I hated it—but I had to agree. What chance did we stand? How could we hope to make it all the way to Halfax without meeting resistance? We had barely made it here. The whole eastern coast was alive with Tibran ships like bees around a puddle of sugar water. That had been my last view of my home after Father had banished me.

I could hardly work up enough of an appetite to eat for the rest of the dinner we shared with the baroness. Thinking myself in circles was one of my natural talents, just like worrying about things that were completely out of my control. When the meal ended, I took my time wandering out of the dining hall behind the others. They were so wrapped up in talking about their plans, none of them seemed to notice when I stopped following altogether. Soon the sounds of their voices faded to echoes, and I was alone.

The open stone hallways of the keep had a cold, cavernous feel to them. And for what was probably the thousandth time since I'd left Halfax, I was homesick. I missed my room, my bed, my things, the familiar faces of the servants who had looked after me since I'd been a child, and the oil painting of Mother that hung in the grand foyer. Sometimes, late at night, I would visit her. I'd sat up for hours by the light of a candle, staring up at that ghostly rendering of her face while I talked to her. I told her about Phevos and how I missed the way she would braid my hair. Sometimes, in the silence, it was almost as though I could still hear her voice.

Thinking of her made my heart wrench painfully, remembering vividly the pain of her loss. That pain never faded. I always—*always*—missed her.

When I finally stopped wandering, I was standing in the middle of a long corridor with an arched stone roof. This part of the keep was dim and chilly, and I honestly didn't know where I was anymore. It must have been hours since I'd last seen a servant.

I glanced around, staring back down the way I'd come. It was just as dark and empty as the way I'd been going. Was anyone looking for me? Had the others still not noticed I was gone?

"Jenna?" A voice echoed through the corridor, calling out my name. "Jenna, is that you?"

I turned just in time to see a tall, dark figure running toward me. The faint light from the iron fixtures caught over a pair of eyes the color of pale steel. My breath caught.

Once again, Phillip had found me.

He stopped before me, out of breath and flustered. His wavy, black hair was falling out of the stumpy little ponytail. Usually, he only tied it back like that if he was reading or horseback riding. Now, it made his long ears and strange, sharp features seem more obvious.

"What happened? Why are you wandering around down here?" He panted. "Did you get lost? Gods and Fates, do you have any idea how worried I wa—"

I put my arms around his waist and hugged him, resting my forehead against his chest.

"J-Jenna?"

"I love you, Phillip."

He sucked in a sharp breath. With my head still against his chest, I could hear his heartbeat start racing even through his shirt. "W-What ... ? I, uh, I'm not sure what you ... um."

Leaning back, I stared up into his bewildered expression. His vertical pupils went so wide, they were nearly round. Even with his skin that strange, soft gray color, I could still see his cheeks and nose turning bright red.

"Tell me again," I whispered.

"But, Jenna, I—"

I let him go and took a step back. "If you're about to say something about how you look, don't. Just, please, don't insult me like that. I know it isn't the same, but there are parts of me that I hate, too. There are parts of myself that I am utterly ashamed of—things that no man would ever consider beautiful. I have scars, Phillip. I am damaged, beaten, broken-down, and nothing at all what a princess should be like. But my feelings for you aren't conditional to whatever either of us look like." I crossed my arms. "Are yours?"

His mouth snapped shut. The end of his tail flicked a few times. At last, Phillip let out a heavy breath, his ears drooping slightly. "No, they aren't."

"Then tell me again."

The way he stepped in toward me, leaning close enough that I could feel the touch of his warm breath on my face, made my stomach swirl. He slid a hand along the curve of my jaw, cupping my cheek, and my heart hit the soles of my boots. My eyes fluttered closed.

"Jenna?" He used that hand to tilt my head back farther. I could have sworn I felt his lips brush mine ever so lightly.

"Yes?"

"I love you," he murmured softly.

My insides turned to jelly.

"Every scar you think is unsightly. Every mark you consider horrible. Every flaw you believe you have—I love *every single part* of you."

Phillip's mouth pressed against mine, still soft and smooth. The instant we touched, it sent a jolt through my body and my legs went numb. I leaned against him, gripping the back of his tunic. His strong, solid arms came around me suddenly, lifting me off my feet and backing me up against the wall. With his newfound strength, pinning me there didn't seem to take any effort at all.

Not that I resisted.

I wrapped my legs around his waist and kissed him back, combing my fingers through his hair along his scalp. It made his body shudder with a deep growl of delight.

I didn't want it to end. But it had to. We couldn't stay in the hallway all night. So finally, Phillip put me gently on my feet and stood back, breathless again. His hair had come free of that ponytail and hung around his jawline, covering all but the last inch of his long, pointed ears.

For a moment, all we could do was stare at one another.

"We should go back." He didn't sound thrilled with that idea.

I wasn't, either. "I guess so."

Together, we began the long walk back to the North Wing.

"Why did you come down this far by yourself?" Phillip asked as he strode along beside me. I could tell by his tone he was treading lightly, not wanting to upset me.

I smiled down at the floor. "I started thinking about Mother."

"Are you all right?" He sounded worried.

I wasn't sure how to answer that at first. Was anyone here all right? "Mother was always the one person I knew I could talk to whenever Father and I disagreed, or I was feeling overwhelmed," I replied at last. "Being here, not knowing what will happen next, I guess I just let it get the better of me."

"Oh. I see."

After a bit longer of walking in silence, I noticed his hand brushed mine a few times, like he was testing the waters. Finally, he seized it and wound our fingers together.

"I ... I know what you mean." He said like it was a confession.

"What?"

"When he came back from dinner, Jaevid caught me trying to leave." Phillip rubbed the back of his neck with his free hand. "Miri had fallen asleep while she was reading and ... it just seemed like the right thing to do. I'd taken a dagger, some of the food they'd brought us for dinner, a blanket—whatever I could find that I could use—and threw it all in a pillowcase. I thought I could be long gone before you came back."

Wait ... what? This ridiculous man, who had driven me nearly insane for years, chasing after me like a bloodhound while professing his undying love and devotion, was trying to *leave* me? Now?

"Why?" I demanded. "Why would you leave like that? Without even talking to me about it?"

He shook his head a little, his face screwing up slightly as though he were in pain. "Jaevid said the same thing. That I shouldn't go yet—not without talking to you first."

I tried gulping back my anger. But unfortunately, a nasty temper was something my father and I shared.

I stopped, keeping my grip on his hand so he was forced to either stop or drag me down the hall like a ragdoll. He was not going to get out of this—not that easily. I deserved an answer. "Phillip?"

He stopped as well but kept his back to me. The thick muscles of his back had gone tense under the tight fabric of his too-small shirt. "Because I'm ashamed." His voice was so quiet, I could barely hear it. "I know you say it doesn't matter how I look now, but Jenna ... it *will* matter to other people. I see how the others look at me. It's as though they're all just waiting for me to make a wrong move."

"It's just going to take some time for them to adjust, Phillip."

"No. They don't trust me—and I don't blame them. I'm not sure I trust myself, either. Jaevid says the venom won't affect me anymore, that my mind will stay intact, but how can he really be sure? What if he's wrong? What if I forget again and—?" His body jerked, shoulders cringing up as he bowed his head. "If I hurt you, I'd never forgive myself."

Letting go of his hand, I stormed toward Phillip, stood up on my toes, and grabbed the end of one of those pointy ears.

"H-Hey! Oww! Those are sensitive!" He growled as I dragged his face down far enough that I could look at him eye-to-eye.

"First of all, forget everyone else." I glared at him. "Second, I trust Jaevid. If he says you're going to be fine, then I believe it. I don't see how you could get a more professional opinion about it than his."

Phillip swallowed hard, staring back at me with big, slightly-frightened eyes. Once again, his pupils were wide enough to nearly blot out the silver color of his irises.

"And finally, I am a bloody dragonrider, so don't act like I'm some fragile little damsel who can't take care of herself. You got your one free shot at Northwatch while I was wounded. That won't happen again. So just try to hurt me—I dare you."

He started to protest. "Jenna, I-I—"

I let go of his ear and stood back, trying frantically to blink away the tears that welled in my eyes. "I can't believe you'd just leave like that without even telling me. You're ... Gods, you're such an idiot!"

Phillip tilted his head to the side, watching me. "I'm sorry. I wasn't thinking straight."

I looked down at the floor between us. Maybe the dim lighting would hide the way my face screwed up. It wasn't fair. Why did getting this angry make me cry sometimes?

"You forgive me, don't you?" His voice was closer, and his breath tickled my cheek again.

"No," I growled, gritting my teeth. "Not unless you swear you won't do it again."

Phillip seized my chin and turned my face up to plant a quick, rough, passionate kiss against my lips. When he pulled back, my mouth was still puckered, and my face was flushed and hot all the way down to my neck.

"I swear."

He was smirking when I finally raised my gaze to stare back at him. "I mean it. Don't you dare try to leave me ever again, Phillip Derrick. Because if you do, when I find you—and make no mistake, I *will* find you—it won't be pretty."

"I know." One of his rough, claw-tipped thumbs brushed gently under my eye, wiping away one of those stupid, embarrassing tears. "Does this mean I finally get to call you mine?"

"Fine. But for the record, you are completely ridiculous. And annoying. And sometimes infuriating." I smiled and flicked the end of one of his ears again. "And those are all my favorite things about you."

Waiting was agony.

Even with more than enough to keep us busy, a thick fog of suspense hung in our midst. We hoped to see Reigh and Aubren arrive or, at the very least, receive word that they had escaped and were waiting for us somewhere. But after two more days, there was still nothing. Not a single sign of them. Jaevid insisted he could still sense their life forces—so neither of them was dead—but they were far away, faint, and out of contact. Even Vexi, Reigh's dragoness, was unable to answer his calls.

The waiting continued.

I slipped away as often as I could to see Phevos, who was initially unhappy that I'd waited so long to visit him. My purple monster sulked and gave me his shoulder, ears slicked back as he refused to look me in the eye. He puffed little agitated snorts when I called his name and smacked his jaws ... until I'd bribed him several times with fresh cuts of raw fish. Salmon had always been his favorite. He couldn't resist the aroma of the fatty orange and white striped filets I waved in front of his nose. It only took four to make him purr and lay down, so I could rub his scaly head again.

Seeing him gave me a tiny bit of peace amidst the tension. Sitting with him down in the undercrofts, I traced my fingers along the teal stripes that adorned his dark eggplant-colored hide. His massive head rested in my lap, so heavy it made my legs tingly from cutting off the circulation, but I wouldn't ask him to move. As a hatchling, I'd lugged all twenty pounds of him around in my arms and snuck him through the castle and into my bed more times than my father knew about. He could crush my legs off if he wanted; he was still my baby.

Days passed without any news, and Jaevid seemed to sense everyone's growing anxiety. He began delegating work out to the rest of us in what I suspected was an attempt to keep us occupied. He put Calem and Eirik to work acquiring our gear and supplies for the journey to Halfax. They had to come up with some sort of saddle he could use on Mavrik as well. Aedan, Phillip, and Miri were charged with researching the route that led from Cernheist to Luntharda—which wasn't easy. It had been decades since anyone had gone that way, so finding a map or text would mean combing the keep's archives. Fortunately, none of them seemed to mind spending a day amidst books. I tried not to be too jealous.

Jaevid asked Haldor and me to accompany him into the city to help him make the rounds to every city square in Cernheist, healing people. It took nearly a whole day just to deal with the soldiers. He could only heal one person at a time, and while the effort didn't seem to drain him all that much, the weather took a toll on us all. The storm was growing worse by the hour. The skies were darker, and the temperatures plummeted until my face was numb and my fingers tingled painfully even under thick gloves. By evening, the snow was falling in sheets again, and we were forced to return to the keep.

I sat in the main room, hugged up as close to the hearth as I dared without risking a singed eyebrow. Phillip came to sit down with me, wrapping a wool blanket around us both and rubbing my hands between his. Part of me was totally embarrassed to have him doting on me like that. His special attention had not gone unnoticed by my dragonrider brothers. I caught Eirik grinning at me wolfishly more than once, his eyes practically glowing with mischief. But Phillip was so warm—I couldn't refuse. Every inch of him seemed to resonate an unnatural, almost feverish heat. Not to mention his size now made it all too easy for him to wrap around me like a living barrier of star-freckled muscle. Sitting with my back against his chest and his arms draped lazily around me, I found myself nodding off to the soothing crackle of the flames in the hearth.

"We won't be able to go back out tomorrow if the weather doesn't improve," Haldor said to Jaevid over mugs of warm cider. "We can't ask them to bring their sick and injured out into the city squares under these conditions."

"I agree," Jaevid murmured. "We have no choice but to wait it out. The good news is while the storm has us locked in place, it's also likely preventing the Tibrans from making any progress as well. We are all forced to a standstill."

Haldor sighed. "That's something, I suppose."

"I counted fifty-three infantry soldiers, but only thirty-eight that would be battle-ready." Jaevid was rubbing his jaw and brow, his speech a bit slurred from exhaustion.

"Why so few?" Phillip asked.

"Some had complications before we could get to them," Haldor explained.

"Amputations due to blood poisoning, gangrene, frostbite, or simply wounds to limbs that they believed were unsalvageable. Turns out no one was counting on a divine healer paying them a visit here." He flashed Jaevid a grin.

"I bet." Eirik chuckled. "Did anyone faint? Fall on their face and start praying to you? Offer you their firstborn?"

Jaevid blushed. "No, nothing like that. They were just a little surprised, that's all."

"Liar." Haldor snorted.

Jaevid smirked over the rim of his mug. "Excuse you, but unless the dragonrider code has changed over the past forty years, then I believe any story I tell only has to be ten percent true."

"Hah! He's got you there!" Eirik crowed with delight.

Haldor just waved a hand and made a *pffft* noise.

"I may be old, but I'm not senile." Jaevid looked smug as he took another sip of his cider.

I wasn't about to question that. He'd taken to the task of deciding our next moves without missing a beat. And if he was recalling the dragonrider code, then maybe he was also remembering more of his past as well. I wondered exactly how much he did remember now, but it didn't seem like the right time to ask. Except for Aedan, I was the only one here who knew about his scrambled memories. I didn't feel right about revealing that to the others. Some truths weren't mine to tell.

"If the snow lets up tonight, we'll see about going out again tomorrow as planned," Jaevid went on. "Otherwise, we'll just have to wait."

"I hate this feeling, like I'm sitting on my hands until something happens," Eirik grumbled as he stood up and stretched. "I'm going to bed."

"Make sure it's your own." Haldor heckled him as he wandered out of the room.

Eirik shot him a poisonous look that might have made a point—if he hadn't been blushing as red as a tomato. From her chair by the fire, I saw Miri duck her head like she was trying to bury her nose in the crease of her book.

Haldor and Jaevid chuckled and went on talking quietly while they finished their mugs. When they decided to turn in for the night, Calem followed. Eventually, Miri got brave enough to emerge from the crack of her book and wished us all a goodnight before retiring to her own chambers.

After that, I could barely keep my eyes open. Phillip finally insisted it was time for us to go to bed as well. I'd nearly forgotten Aedan was still there, curled up on the sofa with a heavy quilt pulled all the way up to his chin. He stirred some when we stood but never woke up.

I draped the blanket we'd been using over him as well and left him alone. Aedan had been through a lot. We all had, of course. But looking at his nearly-shaved head and that brand-shaped scar on the side of his neck reminded me that the fact that he was lying there, sleeping peacefully, was nothing short of a miracle. If I'd seen him on the battlefield, I might have burned him along with the rest of the Tibran soldiers standing nearby. I would have never known who he was or why he wore the Tibran armor.

I wondered how many of our own I had already burned.

That thought haunted me as I wished Phillip a goodnight and lay down in my own bed. The room seemed empty and cold. It was unbearably quiet except for the faint howl of the stormy wind outside the window. My mind, more restless than ever, raced as I tossed and turned. I thought about Aubren and Reigh. Were they safe? Were they sleeping somewhere warm tonight? I didn't want to imagine that the sight of Aubren in Tibran chains would be the last time I ever saw him.

Knowing that he would have betrayed us all, betrayed Jaevid and handed him over to Argonox like that, filled me with conflict. I wanted to be angry. I wanted to hate him. How could he have been so stupid? Did he honestly think Argonox would ever honor that agreement? Aubren had never given me the impression he even wanted to be King of Maldobar. So why? Where had this come from? Did I even truly know my own brother?

It felt as though my brain was being torn in half as I lay awake, struggling to make sense of it all. Whatever the case, I was certain about one thing: I wanted them back—*both* of them. And if they couldn't escape Argonox on their own, then I was going to find some way to get to them—even if that meant I had to burn a path through every rank of Tibrans between here and Northwatch.

24

CHAPTER TWENTY-FOUR

Years of training to become a dragonrider at Blybrig Academy had done more than chisel me into the perfect killing machine. It had also made me an incredibly light sleeper, which was unfortunate when you slept in barracks surrounded mostly by men—some of whom snored a *lot*. I'd almost gotten used to Calem's familiar wheezing. Since he was my wing end, we usually roomed together. Being a princess and a woman didn't entitle me to my own room at any of the places I'd been posted for duty. Not that I would have had it any other way. Fair was fair, and special treatment was not something I wanted or expected. I'd signed on for this, fully aware that I would be the subject of scrutiny and abuse simply because I was a woman attempting to survive what had always been deemed a "man's profession."

That said, earplugs would have been nice.

A faint scuffling sound woke me instantly. My eyes popped open and I tensed. My hand instinctively reached for the place next to my bed where I usually kept my sword. Naturally, it wasn't there. I wasn't in dragonrider barracks.

Sitting up in bed, I raked my hair away from my face and squinted around the bedroom. Everything was dark. The storm outside the window didn't allow any moonlight to filter in, so I could only barely make out the faint dark shapes of the furniture. Maybe it was just the wind? My groggy mind was willing to accept that explanation as I snuggled back down into the blankets.

Then I heard it again. Soft, faint scraping. It was coming from under my bed.

I lunged for the nightstand and quickly lit a candle. Hanging over the edge of my bed, I sat the candle on the floor and peered around for the culprit. I was expecting a mouse, or even a rat. Both weren't so uncommon in big castles like this. They found all kinds of nooks and crannies to hide in.

Then I saw it—a big, long, hairy leg.

Then another.

And another.

So many hairy, spindly legs.

Clamping a hand over my mouth, I sprang back onto my bed and drew my legs in to my chest. It was a spider. A *huge* spider. What kind of demonic spider could live in a place like this? Wasn't it too cold for them here?

My mind raced. I didn't have anything within reach to smash it with, should it decide to explore my bed. Going back to sleep was not an option when the idea of prickly spider legs tangling in my hair was a very possible threat.

Help—I needed help. Or a very large boot. Unfortunately, my boots were sitting right beside my socks out in the main room. They'd been soaked from trudging around in the snow all day, so I'd left them by the hearth to dry.

I could make it to the door in four long strides if I tried. I gathered my nightgown in my hands, counted to three, and ran. I ran like a banshee out of the room, slamming the door behind me. Out in the hall, I darted for the first door I could think of.

Then I stopped.

Gods and Fates, was I really about to ask Phillip for help? I stepped back and wrenched the end of my nightgown in my fists. Staring up at his door, I tried to rationalize. Maybe I could find a boot or a book or something and go back in and—

The knob creaked. I shrank back as the door cracked open and Phillip stuck his head out into the hall. "Jenna, is that you?" He squinted down at me. "I thought I heard a door slam."

"H-Hello. Um, I mean, good evening."

He rubbed his eyes and yawned. "It's the middle of the night. What's the matter?"

"Ah, yes. It is. I know ... it's just that ... " I couldn't bring myself to look at him anymore. So instead, I stared down at my bare toes and gnawed on the inside of my cheek.

"What is it?" He sounded genuinely concerned.

"I think there's a spider under my bed." I blurted it out before I could talk myself out of it. When he didn't reply, I winced and slowly raised my gaze up to meet his again.

Phillip was staring down at me, his mouth hanging open. "A spider?"

"Yes. I'm not sure, but it looked like one. I heard a noise under the bed. There was something crawling around." I tried my best to make it seem legitimate, but the more I explained, the more absurd it sounded. "There were legs, Phillip. Lots of legs."

He raised an eyebrow. "You're aware that you are, in fact, a dragonrider, right? You've reminded me of this on numerous occasions—tonight, even."

My eyes narrowed into a glare.

"You've killed people. Dozens of them. Not to mention monsters that looked like they'd crawled straight from the deepest pits of the abyss."

"Of course, I know that. But it's a spider."

"So?"

"A very *big* spider." I crossed my arms and looked down again. "If you aren't going to help me, then at least let me borrow one of Jaevid's boots."

Phillip blinked a few more times, as though he were trying to process this. Then he sighed loudly and pushed the door the rest of the way open. "All right. A moment to put on my pants, please."

I blushed. I tried not to stare as he wandered back into his room—wearing only a pair of cotton underpants. Gods, had I ever seen him that way before? Even before the tail? It was ... distracting, and too much. I couldn't look away, so I turned my back and waited.

When Phillip emerged again, he was wearing pants and carrying a short sword still dangling from its sheath and belt.

"You're bringing a blade?" I asked. "What about a candle? It's dark in there."

He shrugged and flashed a wry grin. "Well, you said it was a big one. Might as well be prepared. And believe it or not, my eyes seem to work better in the dark now. At least, well enough to spot a spider."

"It is! Stop laughing, I mean it! You'll see."

"So, the mighty warrior princess is afraid of spiders." Phillip chuckled. "I've literally known you since birth, Jenna Farrow. How did I not know this about you?"

"It's not like I advertise it. Can you imagine what the others would say?" I frowned. "And it's your fault, you know. Yours and Aubren's. You used to put spiders in my shoes to scare me when I was little. It was awful."

His brow puckered, looking perplexed and surprised. "And that really bothered you this much?"

"Of course, it did! I was five years old!"

Phillip pursed his lips thoughtfully as we stopped in front of my door. "Well, then I suppose I owe you a spider-killing or two, don't I?"

I rolled my eyes. "Just kill it, please."

"Okay. Stay here."

He disappeared into my bedroom, shutting the door behind him. The sounds of scuffling and commotion made me startle. I couldn't decide if that was necessary or if he was just making fun of me. I backed away from the door, just in case. Minutes passed. When the door opened again, I felt my cheeks go cool as the color drained from my face.

"Well, that was a big one, I'll grant you that," Phillip muttered as he emerged.

"I knew it! Where is it? What did you do with the body?"

He chuckled and raised his hands in surrender. "Relax. I tossed it out the window. It's dead, I assure you."

Rubbing my arms, I leaned around him to peer back into my bedroom. "I don't know if I can sleep in there now."

"Because of one spider?"

"I hate spiders, Phillip! *Hate* them! Which is your fault, by the way. You don't understand ... "

He made a face. "Clearly."

Just the thought of it made me shudder. My skin still crawled like I could feel hairy legs tickling up my spine. "And where there's one there's always more. Skittering around. Making webs. Laying eggs. It's absolute evil."

Phillip rubbed his chin. "Mmm, you're right. They could be anywhere. Under the dresser. In the armoire. There might be a whole nest of them in your mattress."

I glared up at him in total mortification. "Why would you even say that?"

"I suppose you could stay in my room." He waggled his eyebrows.

"What?"

"Well, I can't guarantee a completely spider-free environment, but I promise to kill any that dare to come out of hiding."

I narrowed my eyes. "You're teasing me."

He showed me a gentle, disarming smile. "Only a little." Then he offered me one of his large hands. The glittering specks shone against the gray-to-black gradient on his forearm.

"I-I don't know if this is ... I mean, I'm not ready for ... " My words got all tangled.

"Oh relax, love. If it makes you feel any better, I'll sleep on the floor." He wiggled his fingers. "Come on."

I slid my hand into his. The instant our palms touched, my stomach fluttered, and I couldn't bear to look up at him again. Why did touching him make me feel like that? Dizzy and self-conscious, like I couldn't put an intelligent sentence together.

Jaevid was oblivious, sound asleep in his own bed, as I crawled under Phillip's blankets. They were still warm and smelled like him. I waited until his back was turned to steal a sniff or two of his pillow. Tail and claws aside, he still smelled good.

True to his word, Phillip took a spare blanket and pillow out of the armoire and made himself a pallet on the floor next to the bed. It was hard not to feel guilty. The stone floor must have been cold and uncomfortable.

I peered over the edge of the bed at him. "Are you sure you're all right down there?"

His mouth twitched into a smirk. "Is that an invitation?"

My heart skipped a beat. "N-No! I meant, well, maybe you could sleep in my bed."

"Tossing me in there with all the spiders, eh?"

"Never mind," I grumbled.

We lay in silence for a long time. I started to wonder if he'd fallen asleep. Then Phillip's voice called softly up to me again. "Jenna?"

"Yes?"

"I'm sorry about the spiders in your shoes. You know, when you were little. I probably did a lot of stupid things like that, thinking it was all in fun." He cleared his throat as though he were anxious. "I had no idea it made that much of a difference to you."

Rolling over onto my side, I peeked over at him again. "It's okay."

"You're sure?" His bizarre silver eyes were watching me carefully. "It's just that, you've always made such a point that I should never mistake you for anything but a dragonrider. I assumed a fear of, well, anything was out of the question."

"Being a dragonrider doesn't mean I'm not human. You should see how Eirik is with cats."

"And here I thought it would be girls that had him running in terror," he mused. "But I see your point. So ... we're all right, then? About the spiders?"

I smiled. "Yes. But don't be surprised if I try to get my revenge."

One of his cheeks turned up into a handsome half-grin as he closed his eyes and let out a deep, satisfied sigh. "I'll look forward to it."

"DON'T LOCK YOUR KNEES. KEEP MOVING. THAT'S IT," HALDOR SHOUTED, stepping wide around the area where Aedan and Calem were sparring.

Once again, they had moved all the furniture in the main room to accommodate some combat practice. So far, they'd only knocked over one porcelain vase and a small statuette with their efforts. But that was the trouble with dragonriders. They tended to break things when they got bored. And we were now on our second day of being confined to the keep because of the storm. It had everyone restless.

Not that we didn't have enough to keep us busy in the meantime. With this much extra time at our disposal, the craftsmen in Cernheist had been able to come up with something decent in the way of armor for Aedan, Jaevid, and me. They'd even come up with a sort of reinforced leather breastplate for Phillip, although I could tell by the look on his face that the idea of wearing armor made him uncomfortable.

There weren't any official tackmasters living in Cernheist since there wasn't much of a market there for dragonriders needing saddles. But we were able to track down one old leatherworker who agreed to try putting together a temporary saddle that Mavrik could wear. It wouldn't be as fine as the ones the rest of us had, but Jaevid could get by without having to ride bareback.

After receiving several reports of refugees suffering grievous wounds, Jaevid ventured out into the city again to try to heal some of the worst cases. Haldor and I had gone along, but it was exhausting and bone-numbing work, marching around in the frigid wind tracking down one patient after another. In the end, we were only able to find and treat four of them before we were forced to return to the keep again.

Jaevid seemed deeply frustrated by that failure. He'd taken to sitting in a corner of the room, his brow locked into a pensive scowl as he stared down at the floor. The way his pale eyes flickered back and forth, it made me wonder what he was thinking. Or maybe he was seeking out the council of some spirit or god? With him, it was impossible to tell.

The rest of us were still watching the sparring match, however.

Haldor had all but taken Aedan under his wing and was teaching him more sophisticated techniques with a halberd—or for practice purposes, an old mop handle. "Don't get timid," he shouted again. "Use your reach—your reach!"

Aedan flashed him a heated look and set his jaw. His expression sharpened, and so did his movements. He moved faster, feigning in and darting back while whirring the length of that mop handle at astounding speed. I'd never seen anyone use a halberd like that before.

It worked. Calem wasn't sure what to make of those techniques, especially when Aedan took to the air, springing through the air as agile as a deer. Calem was brutally fast with his dual scimitars and quickly threw up a parry. Aedan didn't stop for a second. He instantly whirled into a follow-up strike and managed to knock Calem onto his heels. A leg-sweep put him flat on his back with Aedan crouched over him, staff poised for a killing strike.

The fight was over.

Until Calem flung his blades away and blurred through a floor-wrestling maneuver. He brought Aedan to the ground, wrenched the staff from his grip, and wound him into a crushing pin. He held Aedan there, letting him feel the power of his grip for a moment, before finally letting him go.

"Nice try." Eirik chuckled. "Calem's been taking it easy on you. No one can beat him in the sparring circle."

Calem didn't respond to the praise, not even to gloat over his victory. Getting to his feet, he brushed the dirt off his shirt and ran a hand through his platinum-colored hair. By the look on his face, you'd think he had just finished a stroll in the garden rather than a fierce sparring session.

"Shut up, Eirik. He's getting better." Haldor offered a hand to haul Aedan up. "Not bad for a shepherd boy."

Aedan was rubbing the side of his neck where Calem had pinned him. "I used a staff in the fields some. Dah taught me to fight with it, you know, in case there were wolves. I never fought a man until the Tibrans—" He stopped short, his face flushing as he winced.

"Don't worry about it." Eirik patted him gruffly on the back as he went past. "Dah—is that the elven word for 'father'?"

Aedan blushed harder and nodded. "Sorry, I forget sometimes. My parents didn't speak the human language well, but they sent me to a tutor in the city. She taught me human customs and to read and write. But at home, I still used the Gray elf language."

Phillip, who had been sitting quietly next to me on the sofa with his long legs tucked beneath him, suddenly perked up. His ears pricked forward, and he smiled, beginning to rattle off words in elven with startling speed.

Even Aedan looked surprised at first. Then he smiled back—probably the biggest, happiest smile I'd seen from him so far—and laughed as he replied in the elven language.

They went back and forth like that until Aedan seemed to notice how the rest of us were staring at them.

"I didn't know you spoke the Gray elf tongue." I gave Phillip a nudge.

Phillip tipped his chin up with a proud grin. "Well, of course. I was brought up to be duke, after all. Many of my subjects were elves. It wouldn't make much sense not to be able to talk to them, now would it? And besides, it was great fun to be able to curse at my father without him understanding it."

I playfully elbowed him again. "You didn't!"

"Oh, I most certainly did."

"I'm sure the esteemed Commander Derrick was thoroughly impressed by his son's creativity." There was a sarcastic edge to Haldor's voice as he strode by with a grin.

"Oh yes," Phillip replied, mimicking his tone. "He demonstrated it all over my backside a few times."

"Wait—are you talking about Lieutenant Derrick? *Sile* Derrick?" Jaevid interrupted suddenly. He was sitting up straight in his chair, staring at Phillip with wide eyes. "Sile Derrick is your father?"

"*Was* my father," Phillip corrected. "He passed away not three years ago."

Jaevid's expression dimmed, his jaw going slack as his eyes became distant. "Oh ... I'm sorry. I didn't know."

"What's to be sorry for? He lived a good life, thanks in part to you. After the war ended, King Felix made him the Academy Commander at Blybrig. He got to spend his days yelling at fledgling students, which I'm sure I don't have to tell you he enjoyed thoroughly. He lived to be a cranky old man with a terrible pipe-smoking habit, father of four children, three of which he saw to adulthood, and two who made him a grandfather several times over." Phillip's tone softened. I caught him smiling in my direction. "We should all be so lucky."

"I guess you were born much later, after I ... " Jaevid's brow creased, as though he weren't sure how to finish that.

Phillip just laughed. "Indeed. You were only around to see Beckah and Nora. Thea and I were born later. If I'm not mistaken, Nora is especially indebted to you. Without your aid, she and Mother both would have perished during the birth—or so the story goes. My father only told it about a hundred times."

Somehow, the look on Jaevid's face didn't make me think he was listening anymore. His demeanor had gone dark as he sat eerily still, staring down at the floor. His mouth was twisted into an uncomfortable frown, as though he'd tasted something bitter.

"Is everything all right?" Phillip tipped his head to the side slightly. "Was it something I said?"

Jaevid didn't even look up. "No. It's nothing. I'm just tired." He got up hastily and started for the door, as though he meant to leave the North Wing altogether. "Please excuse me."

CHAPTER TWENTY-FIVE

"I thought I might find you here."

Jaevid looked up in surprise as I entered the chamber where his magnificent blue dragon was curled up on a bed of clean hay. All our dragons were being housed here, kept sheltered from the wind and cold in a series of caverns beneath the keep that had likely once been entrances into the mines. More recently, they had been used for stabling horses, and the air still smelled of a rich mixture of animal musk, hay, and grain.

Normally, housing our dragons together in one space would have been asking for trouble. They didn't usually get along well in cramped quarters. But since one of them, Jaevid's dragon, was the king drake—he kept the peace and they all seemed content to let him be in charge.

At the sound of my voice, Phevos raised his head and chirped musically. He got up and stretched both his legs, then his wing arms one at a time, then came lumbering over to press his scaly snout against my chest. I scratched at his chin and behind his ears, making him purr as he sucked up the front of my long tunic with his curious sniffing—looking for any traces of more salmon I might have brought along.

"I'm sorry, I didn't mean to worry you." Jaevid spoke quietly as he watched us. "Your dragon—he's very fond of you."

"Is he? Well, that's good to hear. It's mutual," I crooned as I rubbed Phevos's horned snout. "Have they been feeding you enough? You're my handsome, wonderful, strong boy, aren't you? Perfect in every way."

Phevos clicked and chattered with approval, his golden eyes rolling closed with a happy grumble when I scratched his favorite spot right between his ears.

He sat back on his haunches and started scooting in closer to wrap himself around me.

"He was worried about you when the Tibrans took you," Jaevid added. "They've been well taken care of here."

I sat down across from him, letting my back rest against Phevos's side. One flop of his giant, purple tail across my lap knocked the wind out of me. It made Jaevid chuckle and even Mavrik, the king drake, snorted like he thought it was funny.

"I was worried about him, too." I patted his tail.

Phevos blasted my face with another hot, stinky breath before he laid his head down next to me.

"I've been so overwhelmed since we got here." I flicked a quick glance up at Jaevid. "I can't imagine what you must be feeling."

His expression skewed again. He pressed his lips together, jaw tensing as he looked away.

"Jaevid?"

Gradually, he raised his pale blue eyes to meet my gaze. I could see it all: pain, worry, and something like sorrow all crushing down over his features. His sharply-handsome face made it difficult to discern what exactly he might be thinking, so I wasn't sure what to say.

Thank the gods Phillip was a bit more transparent.

"Whatever is bothering you, I hope you know you can talk to me about it," I coaxed. "I won't tell a soul. I haven't told any of the others about your memories."

Jaevid didn't reply, but his dragon made a concerned chirping noise and nudged at his back. The two exchanged a heated glare, and finally Jaevid sighed. "I guess sometimes I catch myself forgetting how much time has passed. I know it's been a long time, but to me it still seems like ... only yesterday. And then there are moments when it suddenly snaps back into focus and I'm reminded that everyone I knew, everything I felt comfortable with, is gone."

I idly traced the outlines of the deep purple scales on Phevos's tail. "Not everyone."

"Most of them, though." He rubbed his brow. "And I can't decide what's worse—remembering them, what they meant to me, and realizing they're long gone, or not remembering them at all." A short, humorless laugh escaped his lips as he buried his face in his hands. "I don't even understand what's going on in my own head anymore. Maldobar is burning down around me and everyone is looking to me to save them from an enemy I know next to nothing about, but I can't stop thinking about how terrified I am."

"Terrified of what? Of Argonox?"

He looked up at me, his expression so broken and anguished I barely recognized him. "No. That would make more sense, I guess," he muttered. "What scares me more than anything is knowing I have to face your father. I have to account for not being there, for not ... doing more to help."

I nibbled on my bottom lip, watching the flurry of conflicted emotions that passed over his face.

"If he turns me away, if he doesn't forgive me, then—" Jaevid's voice caught and he looked down again, gritting his teeth. It took him a minute or two to collect himself enough to speak again. "Ever since we left Northwatch, things have been coming back to me more and more quickly. I remember your father so clearly. He wasn't much younger than you are now. When I look at you, it's hard not to see him. You have a lot in common."

I frowned. "I've heard."

"For what it's worth, he didn't get along well with his parents, either."

"The boys have been running their mouths, I see. Telling you all about my dramatic falling out with my father?" I rolled my eyes and went back to fiddling with Phevos's tail spines. "Bunch of gossiping hens."

"Regardless of what Felix may have told you about me, I'm not an idiot. I can tell there's something up between you two. No one talks about it, but it's there. It's the same between you and Aubren. You make a face, the one you're making now, whenever someone mentions them," he explained. "I won't ask what happened, but believe me, I know how Felix can be. He's as stubborn as an old mule sometimes. Or he was when we—er—*he* was younger."

I leaned forward, letting my chin rest on my palm. "He never said that, you know."

"Said what?"

"That you were an idiot. A little insane, maybe. But never stupid." I cast him a satisfied grin. "I used to compare myself to you all the time when I was a fledgling student."

His brow rumpled with confusion. "To me? Why?"

I shrugged. "You know, because you were the first halfbreed to attend the academy. I was the first girl. I used to tell myself, 'If Jaevid could do this, so can I' whenever things got hard or the others tried to push me around. I would think about all the stories my father told us about you." I let my gaze settle on Phevos's scaly, sleeping face. "And then something changed. I changed. I glimpsed the ugly face of war, I saw what men like Argonox did to innocent people, and ... your stories started to seem more like fairy tales than history. I didn't want to believe you ever existed. I wanted to forget all about you."

"To be fair, I'm sure your father exaggerated things a *lot* in those stories."

"Maybe so." I had to grant him that. "But then the Tibrans took us from Barrowton. And when I had no strength left and no one else to turn to for any hope at freedom, you were the only person I could think of to cry out to. And you were the one who saved me."

When I looked up again, Jaevid was blushing. Even the tips of his ears were pink. "I-I did have some help, if you recall."

"True, but that's not my point." I met his gaze and offered him my most confident smile. "It's been forty years. The world has changed. Maldobar has changed. My father has probably changed, too. But all of that happened because of you and the sacrifice that you made. Even if we never see eye to eye, I know my father has not forgotten what you did for us. I don't believe for a second that he would turn you away."

Jaevid's broad shoulders steadily relaxed as he closed his eyes. His mouth curved into a calm, gentle smile. "I hope you're right."

As sun set that evening, the storm finally began to break. It stopped snowing, and even the relentless, howling winds had died down to a faint whine. Everything outside was encased in a thick layer of ice and snow, but now you could see the surrounding mountain peaks, jagged valleys, and pine forests all dusted in white as the sun set behind them.

It was decided—we would leave at dawn.

After so many days spent in waiting, sitting on my hands just hoping the weather would change, the sudden realization that we would be leaving put me on edge. I was glad to finally have a legitimate excuse to refuse to wear the dresses Baroness Adeline kept sending for me to wear. It was back to thick, weather-treated leggings, pants, layers of socks, boots, and long tunics over a thermal undershirt. Thank the Fates for that. As usual, all were made to fit the shape of a man's body, so they were strange on the different angles of my frame. It wasn't anything I hadn't gotten used to at the academy, however.

I sat on the edge of my bed, testing the fit of a pair of new boots that laced up the back from my ankles to my knees. They weren't regulation dragonrider boots, but they'd get me by. Besides, technically, I wasn't a dragonrider for the king now. Father had banished me, so I was a rogue. I could wear what I wanted.

A soft knock on the door made me look up. "Yes?"

Miri entered as quickly as a shadow and began spreading a long, black cloak out for me at the end of the bed. It was far nicer than anything a dragonrider should have been wearing into battle. Made of fine, soft velvet and lined with silver fox fur—I almost felt bad it would most likely wind up stained with blood.

"I hope this will be warm enough," she said as she stood back, keeping her head low. "My aunt says she is sending heralds through the streets all day, advising everyone to join us and take refuge in Luntharda."

It was no good. I could hear the emotion in her voice without having to see her face. Something was wrong.

"Miri?" I stood up to approach her.

She immediately waved a hand, as though trying to brush me off. "I-It's nothing. I'm all right."

"No, you're not. What happened?"

She puffed a few deep, steadying breaths and then managed an awkward, forced smile. Her eyes were red and swollen from crying. "I just wish you didn't have to go. It's so dangerous. I wish it didn't have to be this way. He said it's better if we never saw each other again, but it's not ... is it?"

"Who said?" My temper caught like dragon flame. "Was it Eirik?"

Miri's smile collapsed like a dying star. Her chin trembled as she hid her face against the crook of her elbow.

Eirik Lachlan—that *idiot*! What had he done to this poor girl? *Argh!* Give some men even an inch of a uniform and suddenly they think they can walk over anyone they want.

"You wait right here," I snarled, jabbing a finger at my bed. "I'll sort this out."

"B-But, wait!" She began to protest, but I didn't stand by to hear her out.

I stormed from the room, tasting cinders as I started my search. It didn't take me long to find him sulking in the study, leaning against the window with an unusually pensive frown creasing his forehead.

"You!" I slammed the library door behind me to get his attention.

"What? What happened?" He jumped, eyes as wide as saucers.

"You did, apparently." I fixed my glare on him, fists clenched. "What did you say to Miri? Did you dump her right before we're about to leave? You rotten little ... If I find out you took her to bed while planning to leave her all along, I swear by the Fates, I will—"

Eirik threw his hands up in surrender, leaning away when I got in his face. "No! Gods, Jenna. It was nothing like that, I swear!"

"Then start talking."

Slowly, he lowered his hands until they sagged limply at his sides. With his head hung, he didn't have the smug look about him I'd been expecting. "I never touched her. Not that I didn't want to, but I couldn't even talk to her without acting like a fool. I've never met anyone who makes me feel that way. And then after what her aunt said at dinner the other night, it just made things even worse. I couldn't stand the thought of her being with anyone else." His eyes closed while his brows drew together in a look of absolute misery. "Then I realized her aunt is right. Miri is the kindest, most beautiful person I've ever met. She deserves the best ... and I can't give her that."

"What?" I sputtered.

"My family has been in the ranks of dragonriders for generations, but we aren't wealthy. We aren't nobles—you know that. Our only legacy comes from whatever glory our ancestors won in battle, and we all know that sort of fame usually only lasts as long as the people who remember it firsthand," he replied. "Baroness Adeline is never going to let her only heir be with a man like me—

someone with no title or anything but a few acres of soggy farmland in Two Rivers to his name. With Feena lost at Barrowton, I don't even have a dragon to rightly call myself a dragonrider anymore. I have nothing to offer her."

My temper fizzled, doused by the sincere anguish on his face as his head bowed lower and lower until I couldn't even see his face anymore. I'd known him for years and had never once seen him so upset. He'd been less worried about losing his own leg.

I put a hand on his shoulder. "Have you even talked to Miri about this? What if she doesn't care? What if she wanted to be with you anyway?"

"You think the baroness would ever allow it? I'd basically be asking her to elope, to betray her whole family. A man of honor would never do that. I may not be the finest the king's riders have to offer, but I do have some sense of honor."

Looping my arm around his neck, I dragged him in to a rough hug, being sure to mess up his neatly-styled hair as much as possible in the process. "For crying out loud, you were only supposed to tell her she was pretty. Couldn't even manage that, could you? You really are hopeless, you know that?"

"Yes. I know," he moaned.

"And if you wanted a noble title, all you had to do was ask."

Eirik choked. "No! I wasn't asking for that!"

"Am I really supposed to hear a story like that, told with such conviction from one of my very best friends, and not do anything?" I smirked.

"I'm not noble material, Jenna. You of all people should know I'd never fit in with those kinds of people."

"I don't either." A soft, teary voice interrupted us from the doorway. Miri was standing, wrenching the hem of the loosely-knitted blouse she wore over her dress. Her wide, doe eyes shimmered with tears as she stared at him. "I've never fit in with anyone. Not until you came here."

I could have knocked Eirik over with a stiff sneeze. He was frozen under my arm, scarcely breathing, and his face had turned a disturbing shade of red.

I tried nudging him back to consciousness before he started bleeding from the ears. "Well? Aren't you going to say anything?"

He made a few sounds that might have been words in some ancient, forgotten language. Or it might have just been the panicked garbling of a man about to pass out. I couldn't be sure.

And suddenly, there wasn't time to sort it out.

The tall window behind us exploded, sending shards of glass flying past my head like daggers. I felt the heat of flame against my back as I was thrown across the room with Eirik. The keep shuddered on its stone foundation. Books, papers, and scrolls were snatched from their shelves. The furniture toppled. I could hear shouting and more things shattering in the main room.

Somewhere else in the chaos, Miri screamed.

My ears were ringing with a high-pitched tone. There was blood in my mouth and dribbling off my chin. I'd nearly bitten my lip clean through on impact.

Eirik, who had cushioned my landing, was coughing and wheezing for breath. "M-Miri?"

I looked up immediately and spied her lying on the floor right up against the door. With my vision spotting and ears still screeching, I dragged myself off Eirik and tried to stand.

He kicked off the ground and instantly bolted to where Miri lay. His hands shook as he brushed her hair from her face, calling to her. "What do I do? Do I move her? Is she dead?"

I joined him in trying to prop her upright. She had a nasty-looking bump on the side of her forehead, but no other injuries that I could see. "Not dead. Just unconscious. She's still breathing." I stared around the room as the sounds of screaming and deep roaring echoed from somewhere outside the keep. "Take her to her the baroness. They need to take cover."

"From what?" Eirik shouted again. "What the hell is happening?"

I didn't know. All around us, puddles of liquid flame licked and crackled. I choked on the intense, acrid smell in the air. It was a stench I recognized right away.

The smell of dragon venom.

CHAPTER TWENTY-SIX

We weren't ready for this.

There was barely time to buckle on the pair of short swords I'd been given by the baroness and sprint for the hall. Servants ran past, crying out and sobbing in terror as they scrambled for whatever shelter they could find. Some were still trying to put out the flames while others struggled to carry out the wounded. It was total mayhem.

The keep shook again, and the muffled sound of a dragon's roar set my blood ablaze. We were being attacked by one of our own? Why?

There wasn't time to figure out the details. I—we—had to get airborne. I left the North Wing, tearing down the stairwells and hallways to the entrance to the caverns. On the way, Jaevid and Haldor fell in step beside me. It wasn't until I reached Phevos that I realized Calem was right on our heels.

"What are we up against?" I called to Jaevid as I climbed into my saddle. I had no armor, no helmet and no clue what kind of a fight we were in for.

"I don't know," he shouted back as he threw his temporary saddle over the base of Mavrik's neck. "I can barely sense the dragon at all."

"Another Tibran divine artifact?" Haldor guessed with a snarl as he joined in helping Jaevid tie his saddle down.

I hated that idea, but it seemed the most likely.

Jaevid started giving us rapid instructions. "The city has no defenses for this kind of warfare. Go on, see if you can draw them away, and we'll catch up!"

Calem and I gave a dragonrider salute. In a flurry of growls and dragon wing beats, we left the cavern like two enormous bats and took to the evening sky. The bitter wind stung my eyes as we picked up speed, climbing rapidly. Phevos's strong body rippled beneath me, forearms flexing and rolling with each stroke of his wings. I could feel his heart pounding against the sides of my legs even through the saddle. His golden eyes flashed, catching in the crimson glow of the setting sun. That same light reflected over Perish's pearly white scales, staining them scarlet.

Below, the flames from the keep choked the sky with a plume of black smoke. The destruction wasn't as bad as it seemed from the inside, though. Only the North Wing had been struck so viciously. The rest of the burning spray was cast at random, as though it were meant to cause more panic than damage.

And then our enemy appeared.

I saw only a flash of her, a blur of green scales, and my heart dropped like a stone to the pit of my stomach. Vexi wheeled in a broad circle over the city, angling herself to make another dive run at the panicking, defenseless townsfolk below.

I ground my jaw, squeezing my saddle handles fiercely. From that distance, I could barely make out the shape of a rider on her back, sitting in a strangely crafted saddle. I couldn't tell who it was—I had to get closer.

"*Split run,*" I signaled to Calem. "*Take her to the lake.*"

He confirmed, and together we rolled in to pursuit.

We picked up speed and altitude, breaking out wide and dropping into a rapid descent. The air pierced through me like spears of ice. I couldn't bear to keep my eyes open at that speed, so I ducked my head and tried lying flat against Phevos's back to get out of the wind. He knew what to do. We'd practiced this maneuver hundreds of times. I trusted him.

Together, we blitzed past Vexi and crossed right in front of her, narrowly missing her with two short bursts of flame. She was forced to throw on the breaks to avoid our spray. Flapping wildly, she shrieked and shook her head.

I could tell right away something wasn't right. Her cries didn't sound like a dragon's usual battle roar. She sounded frightened—as though she were in pain. Through the wind and flame, I dared to look back as she took up pursuit.

It was no saddle she wore. Whatever the Tibrans had put on her, it wasn't only meant to make her rideable. It was meant to make her obedient. There was a bridle made of black metal fixed over her head. It fit like a muzzle with a spiked crossbar right across the back of her mouth. One jerk of the reins by the rider on her back made her squeal in pain, toss her head violently, and eventually submit.

I'd never seen such barbarism in all my life. Whoever that rider was, outfitted from head to toe in bronze Tibran armor, he had just scheduled himself to become the next pile of ashes.

Perish and Phevos darted ahead, leading Vexi away from the city, up the steep incline, and past the keep. Drawing their wings in tight, they swirled downward over the edge of the cliff where the keep was perched and plummeted toward the frozen lake below.

They flared at the last second, powerful hind legs swinging out to catch the surface of the ice in a hasty landing. Even with their claws, it was hard to get a grip on such a slick surface. They flopped clumsily, finally coming together to face off with Vexi.

She all but crashed into the lake's surface, still fighting that muzzle and yelping every time the rider jerked the reins to make the bit pinch at her lips and tongue. She beat her head against the ice and clawed at it. Blood from her mouth stained the snow pink.

"Stop it!" I screamed.

The rider on her back ignored me. He pulled the reins tighter, forcing her to hunker down and shudder in pain while he stepped off her back onto the surface of the lake. Rather than flee, Vexi remained crouched, her scaly hide shivering. I'd never seen a dragon act like that. She was absolutely terrified of him.

With his face still obscured by a bronze helm, the rider strode toward us across the ice. My lip twitched as my hands writhed on the saddle handles. But something made me stop. Morbid curiosity, I guessed. I wanted to see who was under that helm. Another lackey? Or had Argonox himself come out to challenge us?

The rider drew his sword and pointed the tip right at me.

A challenge.

Whoever that was, his vendetta was personal.

Phevos growled in disapproval, flaring the spines along his back and bearing his teeth. I squeezed my saddle harder. It was a bad idea. In the back of my mind, I knew something wasn't right. But how could I refuse?

I unbuckled from the saddle and dropped to the ground, landing in a crouch on the ice. The rider was only a few dozen yards away, the burning shape of the keep making a harrowing silhouette behind him against the setting sun.

"Only a coward binds a dragon that way," I hissed as I drew my blades, spinning them over my hands as I stepped out to meet him. "Who are you? Show me your face!"

A deep, amused chuckle echoed from underneath that helm.

I stopped short, braced for a fight. Gods, why did that voice sound so familiar?

Before I could place it, the rider gripped the bottom of his helm and took it off, tossing it onto the ice between us. It skittered and scraped to a halt, the red-feathered mane whipping in the wind.

My heart stopped. My mouth opened, but nothing would come out—not even a breath. Every inch of my body locked up, paralyzed by the sneering face that stared back at me.

"Did you miss me, sister?" Aubren's voice sounded wrong. No, it was *all* wrong. His expression was warped with malice and his movements were smooth and calculated. Nothing about this man apart from his face resembled my brother. All the parts of his eyes were as black as pits of hot tar. They bored into me with a harrowing emptiness that turned my stomach.

"Aubren." I gasped. "What did they do to you?"

His mouth twitched. For a single instant, I saw his demeanor crack. A glimpse of horror, of agony—of the Aubren I knew. He was still in there somewhere.

But as quickly as it appeared, it was gone. Aubren was lost. He raised his hand toward Vexi, flexing all his fingers wide. She wailed, futilely trying to smack her head against the surface of the ice to get free of the bridle. It didn't work. He snapped his hand closed and she let out a shattering cry, drooling a mixture of blood and burning venom as she lurched toward Phevos and Perish in a frenzy.

The dragons clashed, brawling like feral cats, and Calem was caught in the fray.

"Now, sister." Aubren whipped his sword tauntingly. "Let's see who made the better warrior after all."

I DIDN'T WANT TO FIGHT HIM. MY ONLY CONSOLATION AS I LOCKED BLADES with Aubren was that this monster was not my brother anymore. He couldn't be. I'd sparred with him many times throughout our childhood. He'd never fought like this.

Aubren struck hard and fast, his strength enough to rattle my teeth every time he brought his sword down against mine. I parried, stepping quickly to evade his blows and blurring through a mixture of dragonrider and Gray elf techniques. He had me with his reach and brute force. Speed, precision, and patience would be my advantage. I dodged another wild swing, feeling the wind off his sword tip as it passed right before me, narrowly missing my cheek.

"Sloppy," he purred. "Have you gotten lazy?"

I set my jaw. "This isn't you, Aubren. You would never hurt me. Please stop this."

"You know *nothing* about me!" He roared, diving in wildly with another fierce swing. The dark pools of his eyes had begun to leak down his face, streaking his cheeks like seeping inky tears.

Behind us, the dragons brawled. I could hear them spitting flame and snarling, their jaws snapping and claws scuffling over the surface of the ice. I wanted to look, to make sure Phevos was okay, but I couldn't take my eyes off Aubren for a moment. As much as I wanted to believe he wouldn't kill me, every strike spoke otherwise. He was bearing in hard, taking every opportunity to make a lunge for a deadly cut.

I dropped to a crouch and spun, hurling a swift kick upward to hit him square in the gut. He staggered back, and I ran him down with my blades swung wide for a dual assault.

Suddenly, Aubren threw his sword aside. He ripped off his gauntlet and shoved his bare hand at my chest. I saw it an instant before it happened—his hand was covered in a strange mark. It looked like a stain, as though someone had spilled black ink all over it.

The movement startled and confused me. What was he doing? I hesitated, tried to evade. Then a concussive force blew me back through the air. I hit the surface of the lake hard, cracking my head and sliding to a halt.

Lying on my back, my pulse throbbed in my ears and my whole body tingled strangely. I could still feel the force of that impact as though it were echoing through my bones. My lungs spasmed, unable to draw in a full breath.

"Pathetic. And this is to be the next Queen of Maldobar?" Aubren appeared over me, his face contorted into a venomous sneer. He planted his boot on my chest and let the tip of his blade graze my cheek, leaving a fresh cut behind before he rammed it into the ice right next to my head. He leaned down to put his hand right in front of my face. "I think not."

"I-It's okay, Aubren." I struggled to wheeze. "I know this isn't you. I know you'd never hurt me. It's okay."

His face twitched again, more violently than before. His nostrils flared, and his mouth skewed. His hand shook in front of me, inches from my nose. I could see the mark more clearly now. It wasn't as random as I thought. The black splotches were designs, some sort of black pattern like a tattoo that had been stained into his skin. That had to be the reason for all of this. Argonox had done something to him.

It wasn't his fault.

"I forgive you." I let my eyes roll closed.

If he was going to use that power again, whatever it was, to kill me—I didn't want to see it. I didn't want the last thing I saw to be my brother's face.

Not like this.

I TENSED, WAITING FOR THE HAMMER TO FALL—WAITING TO DIE.

When nothing did, I dared to crack an eye open.

Aubren was still standing above me, his expression stricken with terror. Through the darkness pooling in his eyes, I caught a glimpse of him. It was like the warm cognac hue of his irises surfaced again, only for a moment. He shook his head, gritting his teeth and grimacing. His hand still shook, hovering right over my face.

He was still in there. He was fighting this.

I started to reach out for him, but a dark shape blotted out the light over us.

The wind kicked up, blowing snow and bits of ice as Mavrik descended like an avenging force. He snatched Aubren in his claws and tossed him away.

The frozen surface of the lake groaned, splintering with cracks that fanned out like spider webs as the king drake landed, Turq and Haldor not far behind him. Mavrik let out a thundering cry that sent the other dragons scattering to get out of his way like naughty children. They cowered at his presence, lowering their heads with their eyes averted. Even Vexi, though she still clawed at that muzzle, trembled and turned her face away.

From Mavrik's saddle, Jaevid called down to me. "Are you all right?"

I gave a shaking thumbs-up—a gesture that I was, in fact, still alive. My body still felt tingly and strange as I sat up, trying to figure out how I'd survived.

Quick as a shadow, a dark shape leapt down from Mavrik's back and came bounding toward me. Phillip moved with speed and grace like an animal, his silver eyes wild and intense with worry.

"Not me." I pointed weakly toward Aubren, who was already getting back on his feet. "Don't let him get away!"

Aubren heard me. He hunched his shoulders, bringing that hand up again like he was about to deal another destructive blow.

Phillip didn't give him the chance. His lips curled back over pointed incisors as his pupils narrowed to slits. A row of black spikes burst through the fabric of his tunic, rising like quills down the length of his spine.

He crossed the distance in a flash, leaping the last ten feet and landing right on Aubren, feet-first. Pinning him by standing on his shoulders, Phillip growled and lashed his tail. With his ears slicked back, his teeth were bared in a dangerous snarl.

"Watch out for his hand!" I warned as I scrambled to my feet.

Aubren was already trying that trick again, bringing his stained hand up with threatening intent. Phillip seized his wrist before he could send off another blast. He let out a deep, guttural roar as he wrenched Aubren's arm back—the wrong way—breaking it as easily as someone might snap a toothpick.

Aubren screamed. I winced. It wasn't the nicest thing to do, but it effectively took Aubren's strange dark power out of play.

"What's wrong with you? How *dare* you attack your own family?" Phillip roared in his face again. He must have forgotten that even without whatever magic was poisoning him, Aubren might not recognize him like this.

"It's not his fault," I panted as I stumbled to a halt a short distance away. "He's not himself. Argonox has done something to him."

Phillip's snarl faded slightly, but he didn't move an inch to let Aubren up. "Switchbeast venom?"

I hesitated to go any closer, keeping a healthy space between us just in case. "I don't think so. It's not the same. Look at his eyes."

"This wasn't done by switchbeast venom," Jaevid agreed suddenly. He had dismounted and come over to look, the wind snagging in his shaggy gray hair. The instant he saw Aubren, his expression hardened, and his mouth clamped into a grim line. "This is ... No. No, it *can't* be."

Suddenly, Jaevid's face blanched as white as fishbone. His body jerked and his eyes went wide.

A monstrous noise like the bellowing of a demon made us all turn.

There was a creature perched on the top of the burning keep, wreathed in the smoke and considering us with eyes that blazed like red coals. It was a dragon—or maybe it had been, once. It didn't seem possible for it to be living now. It was a grotesque mixture of rotting flesh, bare bleached bone, and scales as black as obsidian. Its massive wings were tattered like ragged black sails and its gaping maw was hardly more than a skull with jagged teeth the size of swords. In size it was comparable to Mavrik, the king drake.

The beast unleashed another thunderous cry and spat a plume of flame several hundred feet in the air. Mavrik recoiled with a defiant hiss, unfurling his wings and prickling all the spines and fins along his body. The rest of our dragons, however, ducked away and began to crawl together as though they were afraid, herding Vexi in their center as though to protect her.

"No," Jaevid breathed again. "No ... please, no."

His eyes were fixed on something. I searched until I saw it, too.

There was a rider on the creature's back—a small, almost feminine looking figure dressed in black armor that gleamed like polished onyx.

"It can't be," I whispered. "It's impossible. Is that ... ?"

Jaevid Broadfeather's demeanor went completely cold. All other emotion died to fury. Rage like the coming of a hurricane smoldered in his gaze as he grasped the hilt of his scimitar and drew it. "Take the others and go to the city. Aedan and Eirik are already there. They will need your help to start evacuating."

"But Jaevid," I began to protest.

"Go now, Jenna." He spoke softly as he stepped forward, his eyes blazing like two green stars. "This is *my* fight."

LEGEND

The Dragonrider Legacy Book Three

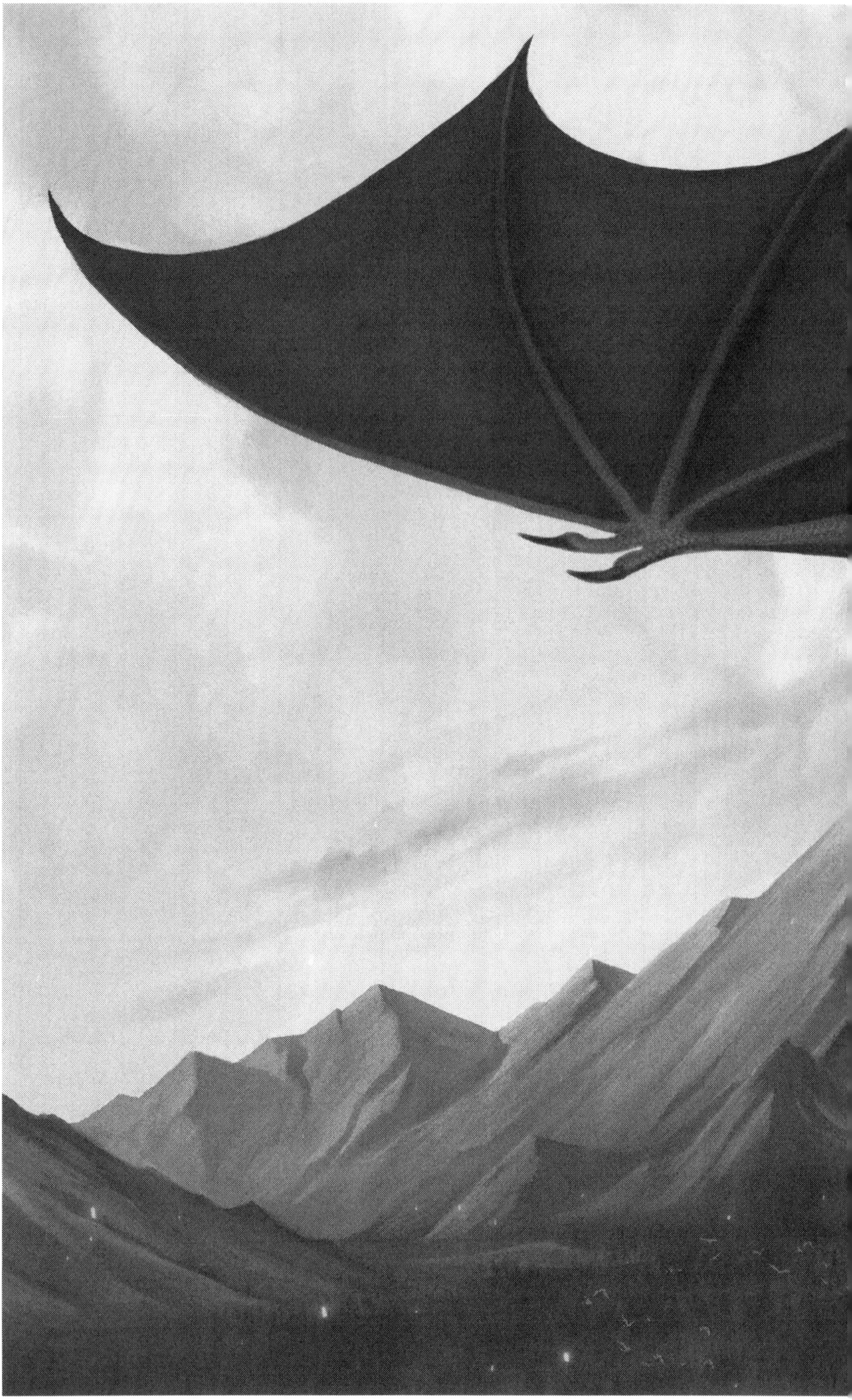

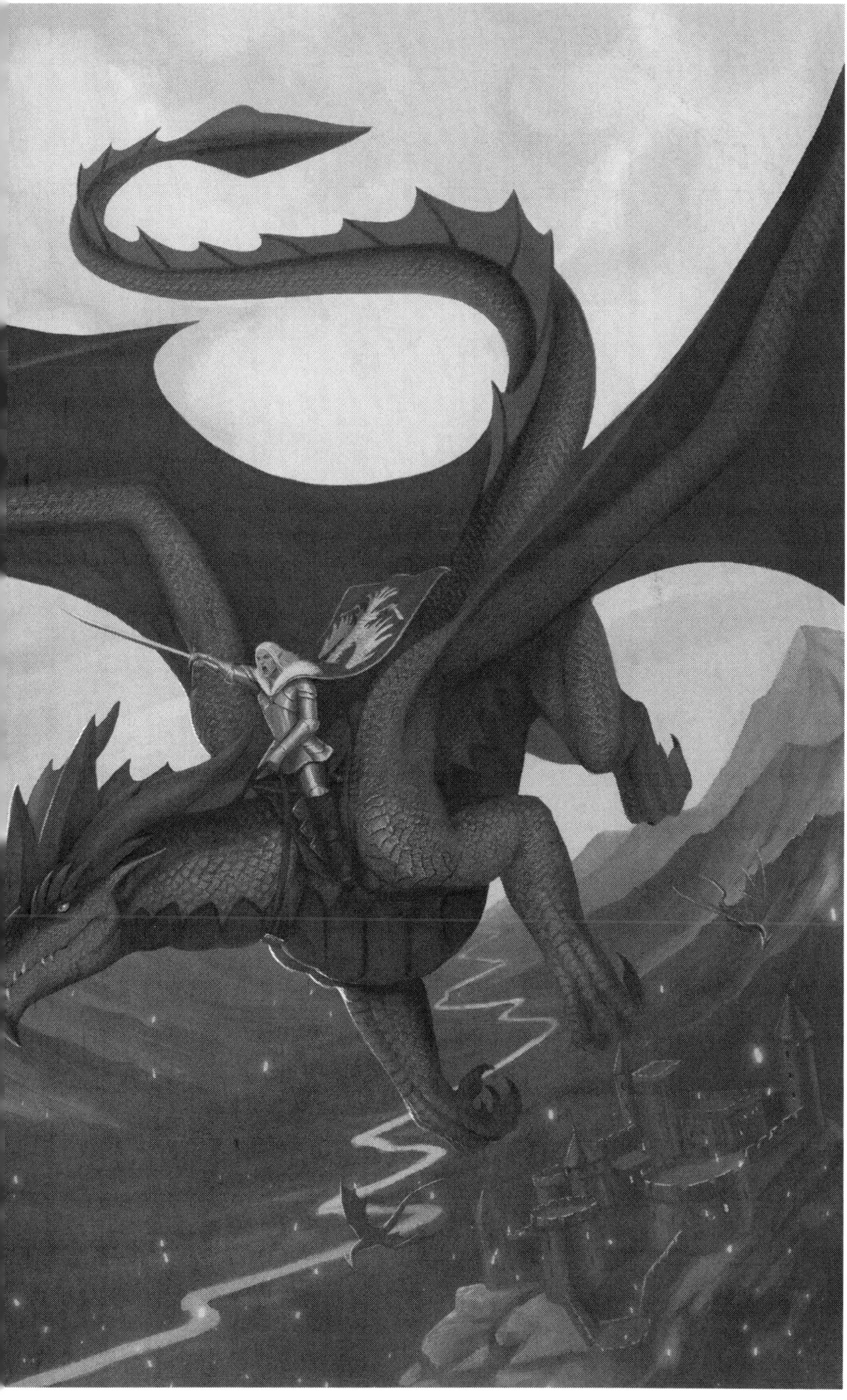

PART ONE: REIGH

CHAPTER ONE

There's a fine line between heroic and insanity—so fine it barely exists. Based on my experience, whether or not you succeeded in your mission was usually what determined which side of that line you wound up on. You succeed, and you're a hero. You fail, and you were a fool for even trying.

I was in dangerously deep "insane" territory.

Granted, this wasn't exactly a new problem for me. I couldn't even blame Jaevid. I'd been winding up in these kinds of life and death situations long before I ever roused him from his divine slumber. The only difference now was—thanks to his explanations about my powers and Noh giving me an impromptu tour through the horrifying secrets of my past—I had more of an understanding of just how screwed I actually was.

It was astronomic, by the way, even by my usual standard of reckless stupidity.

Storming a highly fortified tower crawling with hundreds of furious Tibran soldiers? Idiotic. Splitting up with Jaevid to do this on my own? Insane. Trying to rescue Aubren from this mess and getting us both out alive? Impossible. Thinking I could actually pull this off by myself? Hah! Let's just say, somewhere beyond the Vale, Kiran was probably rolling his eyes. If I did die this time, I was willing to bet good coin he would greet me with a smack to the face and a long lecture—which was something that made a smile tug at my lips.

Gods, I missed him.

Collapsed in the middle of the freight elevator of Northwatch tower, I listened to the ominous symphony of battle all around as the wooden platform made its slow descent. The metal mechanics and gears groaned. Iron chains rattled. The wooden frame creaked. All of it nearly drowned out the distant shouts of the Tibran soldiers, who were now thoroughly aware of our presence in the fortress. The call to arms was blaring in the night. They'd be waiting for me at the bottom of this elevator, ready to cut me down as soon as I showed my face.

But that didn't mean I wasn't going to make them work for it.

Besides, somewhere in this abyss, Aubren was waiting for a rescue. We'd gotten lucky and gained the help of a Gray elf kid named Aedan, who'd been secretly slipping information to the scouts in Luntharda under the alias Lamb. Thanks to him, Jaevid and I had been able to get inside Northwatch tower easily enough. Well, considering what we were up against, anyway. We'd sprung my older sister, Jenna, from her cell, but that's where things started going off track.

Apparently, Duke Phillip Derrick been captured at Barrowton, too, which was not something we'd planned for. He was somewhere in this tower, probably praying for his own miracle, and we couldn't leave him here to die. So, I made the hard choice. I sent Jaevid, Aedan, and Jenna away to find him while I stayed behind to find Aubren.

It had sounded good at the time. Good enough to convince Jaevid, anyway. There was just one small problem ... I'd used a lot of my power just getting us into the tunnels, so we could access the tower. Now I was clinging to consciousness, fighting the swirling spots in my vision while I tried to figure out what to do. Somehow, I had to pull myself together. I wouldn't fail Aubren, even if that meant he was the only one who got to walk away. He was my brother. I would save him.

I stumbled and staggered as I got to my feet, my head swimming and my vision still spotting. Jaevid hadn't been exaggerating when he said that valestepping would drain me. This, I imagined, must be how an insect felt after a little kid shook it up in a jar. I was on the brink of losing it, clinging to consciousness and control.

My mind raced, scraping together a plan. I had to keep it small, make my hits count, and string out my last bit of strength until I could reach Aubren.

Then I'd unleash pandemonium—otherwise known as Noh. I'd go down, and I'd take as many of these Tibran thugs with me as possible to carve a clear path so Aubren could escape. It would work. It had to.

As the elevator clattered and shook toward the bottom of the shaft, I took in a deep breath. My lungs burned. My body screamed in pain, like someone was splitting my head open, as I called more power to my command. I could feel it rising—a deep chill that quivered through every part of me—as though I were being slowly immersed in freezing water.

Darkness gathered around my open hands, swirling and taking the shape of two long scimitars. I closed my fists around the hilts, gritting my teeth and opening my eyes as the elevator came to a shuddering halt.

There wasn't time to count them, but at first glance, I figured there were about thirty angry Tibran soldiers standing between the hall to the left and me. That was where our new ally, Aedan, had advised me Aubren was being held in the solitary confinement cells. Right. Time to get to work.

A Tibran commander shoved his way to the front of the ranks, shouting the order for the archers to open fire. The twang of a dozen bowstrings filled the air with iron-tipped arrows all aimed straight at me.

I dropped into a crouch, gritting my teeth against the sharp pain in my throbbing brain as my blades flickered in my hands, their jagged tips leaving lingering trails of streaking black smoke that hung like dark ribbons in the air. I spun, dancing through maneuvers and feeling the hum of every arrow as though it were a part of myself. Two to the right. One dead center. Six more straight for my head. I cut them out of the air, bringing my blades down in perfect synchronization as my pulse roared in my ears.

My body hummed with dark energy. My nerves blazed. Every movement, every second, brought me closer to the edge.

But there was no stopping now.

"Noh," I whispered. Just the mention of his name sent another wave of chills through my body. "I'm going to need some backup."

"At your command, master." His voice hissed in my mind an instant before I saw him materialize next to me, taking his favorite shape as a black, shadowy canine with tall pointed ears, eyes like red bog fires, and a wide, toothy maw. "Let us teach them what becomes of those who stand in the way of the Harbinger."

His smile was as wicked as it was disturbing, and the sight of him made the front ranks of the Tibran soldiers hesitate. Some of them stopped dead in their tracks, their eyes wide as though considering an immediate retreat.

"Don't get scared now." My mouth twisted into a menacing grin that probably looked a lot like Noh's. "We're just getting started."

It was a mad sprint. I had minutes left, maybe less. I couldn't feel my feet as I ran, hurtling headlong down the narrow corridors and torch-lit halls of the tower's solitary confinement cellblock. Every step sent a surge of fresh agony up my spine. My vision swerved in and out of focus, sometimes dimming until I couldn't see at all.

"Aubren!" I wheezed and gasped, barely able to croak out his name. "Aubren, you better answer me!"

I blitzed past cell after cell, the shouts of prisoners calling to me with haunting, desperate voices through the tiny barred windows on the doors. Sometimes I caught a glimpse of their eyes catching in the dim light, or their fingers reaching out desperately.

I couldn't stop. I couldn't save them all.

"Noh, find him!" I rasped.

His voice whispered in my brain. "*Of course, master. Right this way.*" He materialized like a phantom, trotting along ahead of me, and then vanishing. He appeared again, further down the corridor, taking a sharp right.

The sudden strain of his pull on my power again made both my legs go numb. I fell, barely catching myself before my face cracked off the cold stone floor. My head swam as I lay listening to my own ragged breaths and the sound of Tibran soldiers in hot pursuit. They weren't far behind me.

I set my jaw and willed my legs to work, dragging them into place when they tingled and threatened to buckle again.

"*They are coming.*"

I looked up into Noh's flickering red eyes, burning like hot coals in the dark. "Thanks. I had no idea."

"*We must hurry.*"

"On it," I growled as I heaved myself up again. "How far is he?"

Noh's shaped blurred, the edges of his gaunt, canine body wavering like flame. "*Not very. But his life is waning. He may not be able to flee on his own.*"

"Great." I leaned against the wall of the corridor for a moment and stamped my feet, trying to bring some feeling back to my calves. "Any more good news?"

"*The dragonriders have come. I feel their presence. They are descending upon the roof.*"

"Evacuating?" I guessed. I had no doubt that bringing the dragons here was Jaevid's doing. His divine power allowed him to communicate with any animal with his thoughts, so his plan of calling in an aerial rescue to get all of us clear of the tower was our best option.

Noh's pointed snout dipped in a nod. "*They'll soon be clear of the tower.*"

"Well that's no good. Who's going to stand in captivated horror and awe when we raze it to the ground?" I pushed away from the wall and started limping forward again.

Noh's laughter crackled in my head. "*The thousands of Tibran soldiers encamped outside, perhaps?*"

I smirked. "Good enough for me." At the very least, maybe they'd give it a second thought before they challenged the force of Maldobar again.

The further I ran through the labyrinthine halls of the tower's lowest levels, the less frequent the torches lighting the hallways became. It was nearly total darkness now, and all I could see of Noh were his glowing eyes lighting my path in the gloom. Behind us, the sound of the soldiers grew louder and louder. They were gaining on us.

"H-how much further is—?"

"*Here!*" Noh stopped so suddenly, I nearly limped right past him.

I approached the solid iron door of a cell. It was on the opposite side of the hall than all the others. I could only guess it was an extra special, deluxe solitary suite especially for royal guests. Yeah, right.

"Aubren," I shouted and beat my fist on the door. "It's Reigh. Can you hear me?"

No answer.

"You better not be dead in there! So help me, I will drag your soul back through the Vale if I have to."

Still nothing.

My body burned with a surge of adrenaline and panic. How bad off was he? Would he be able to get out of here, even if I carved a path for him?

Bringing the door down with my power wasn't the problem—it was what came after. I'd be a breath away from losing it, or dying, or collapsing. None of those were good, especially if Aubren couldn't walk out by himself.

This called for a change of plan.

Help. I needed help.

Whirling around, I went to the cell door directly across the hall and banged on it. "Anyone home in there?"

A pair of shimmering, vivid eyes appeared in the tiny window. They stared at me, wild, desperate, and strange. They had rings of golden yellow around the outside of the irises that faded gradually into an electric shade of green. I'd never seen anything like them.

"Who are you?" a feminine voice asked. It was a soft, breathy sort of voice twanged with an accent I didn't recognize. Was she from outside Maldobar and Luntharda?

"Someone who can get you out of here. But only if you do something for me in exchange."

I waited, staring in silence as those strange eyes studied me for a moment. Something about them gave me a swirling, nauseating feeling in the pit of my stomach. Or maybe that was Noh sucking away more of my soul. Who could tell? It was hard to concentrate on anything when I was nodding in and out of consciousness.

"Okay," the voice answered at last. "What do you want me to do?"

"I'm going to open the doors to your cell and the one across from you. The man inside there is extremely important. You have to help him get out of this tower—even if that means leaving me behind. I will make a path for you, so the soldiers don't follow. But he *must* survive. Understand?"

"But where will we go? There must be Tibrans everywhere."

She had a point. "I'll send you as far away from here as I can. Head north, toward the jungle of Luntharda. Once you get there, climb the first tree you can and wait. Gray elf scouts will find you—they're running frequent patrols and will probably be watching you long before you even reach the jungle. They'll take you somewhere safe."

"They won't try to kill me?"

I shook my head. "Any enemy of the Tibrans is a friend of theirs. Just tell them Reigh sent you. You'll be fine."

"Very well, Reigh," she answered faintly. "I will do what I can."

That would have to do.

"Step back from the door," I commanded as I hobbled to the middle of the hall.

"*Master, the Tibran soldiers will be here in minutes,*" Noh warned.

It didn't matter. I only needed one to get this done.

Widening my stance, I set my jaw and spread my arms, a hand aimed at both doors on either side of me. One quick burst. That's all I needed. The mere touch of my power would turn the iron to brittle heaps of rust and ash—the same way I'd freed Jenna from her cell—then Aubren would be free. I could get him out of here. Then I could die knowing I'd at least saved my family.

Jaevid would just have to find a way to save the rest of the kingdom without me.

I squeezed my eyes shut, pressing my will out into both of my hands. The pull was instant, like someone had snatched me under the surface of that freezing water so suddenly I didn't even have time to scream or take a breath. The temperature dropped as the shadows swelled and filled the air with whispering voices. Then again, those might have been just in my head. I couldn't tell. And as my vision tunneled, my lungs constricting like someone with icy cold hands was squeezing the air out of them, it didn't matter.

I was out before I even hit the ground.

CHAPTER TWO

"Reigh!"

The sound of Kiran's voice jolted me awake. I blinked, squinting up into the brilliant rays of sunlight breaking through the vast green canopy overhead. I breathed in deeply, filling my lungs with the sweet, humid air that smelled of moist soil and wild jungle flowers.

Home—I was home.

"Reigh, you're all right." Kiran's face appeared over me, drawn into a look of pasty concern. He seemed ... younger, somehow. It didn't make any sense. "Just lie still," he said in the calm, deep tone he used whenever he was dealing with a frantic patient. His hands shook as he started poking at me, searching my chest and arms for signs of broken bones. "Can you feel this?"

I bobbed my head.

He let out a shaking breath of relief.

I wanted to ask what happened. How could I possibly be back home? Was this some strange manifestation of the Vale? Or was this the paradise that awaited me after death?

"Your leg is going to feel strange. It will hurt. But you have to sit up for me, all right?" Kiran's expression faltered, flickering between panic and relief. With one hand under my back and the other supporting my neck, he helped me sit up.

That's when I realized ... I was *smaller*. Too small. Something wasn't right. It was as though my body had shrunk. Glancing down at my leg, which was lying limply on the ground, I realized why he was so upset. I had a compound fracture. The bone was sticking through the skin of my shin, pearly white against all the blood.

The sight made my body flush and my pulse launch into overdrive. But I didn't feel it. It didn't hurt at all. How was that possible?

"You fell a long way. Your leg is broken. I can fix it, but right now we have to get you back home," he said as he slid his arms under my body and lifted me easily off the jungle floor. "Does anything else hurt? Your neck? Your back?"

"N-no, Kiran." My voice came out small and childish, muffled by sobs.

Suddenly, I remembered. This wasn't paradise or some kind of trick of the Vale. It was a memory. I'd fallen out of a tree when I was little, broken my leg, and once again dodged an early death. After lying helpless on the jungle floor for hours, Kiran had finally found me.

The instant I recalled that distant memory, the world around me seemed to get clearer. I could hear the calls of the birds and feel the coolness of my tears against my flushed cheeks. The familiar scent of medicinal herbs—Kiran's smell—was so close, it brought all my pain, grief, and shame exploding to the surface. I wanted to scream, to put my arms around him, to apologize.

But I couldn't. I couldn't say anything.

"I was so worried, Reigh. You know better than to go off climbing on your own. You're not ready yet." Kiran started in on a lecture even with his face still blanched with worry as he jogged past trees heavily laden with moss and flowering vines. "What if a tigrex had found you first? Or what if you had broken your back? You keep pushing yourself too far and someday you might break what I cannot fix."

"I just wanted to see it again," I whimpered against his shoulder.

"What?"

"The lapiloque's tree. I thought I could get to the top."

Kiran blinked in surprise. "Why didn't you just ask me to take you?"

"You were busy with the scouts. You said you would take me climbing again. You promised. But you never did. You went to train them instead."

"Oh, Reigh," Kiran sighed, the tired lines around his eyes seeming to deepen.

"Do you like them better?" I asked. "Because they're elves, too?"

He halted, staring at me in bewilderment. "Why on earth would you think that?"

"That's what Lurin said. He said you only took me in because you wanted a human pet. He said I'm too stupid and slow to be a scout and that's why you won't let me train with them."

Kiran's multihued eyes seemed to spark and smolder with anger as he started jogging again, faster than ever. "None of that is true. Lurin is an idiot. I will handle him."

"Can I tell him that?"

"What?"

"That you said he's an idiot."

I nearly missed it. Kiran turned his face away, probably so I wouldn't see. But the instant before, one corner of his mouth twitched upward into a smile. "No. I'll tell him myself," he replied. "And if he doesn't listen, then life will eventually teach him that the hard way."

We continued in silence as he carried me through the jungle. All I could do—all I wanted to do—was lie there and stare at him. I wanted to memorize every feature, every detail.

"Kiran?" my tiny, childish voice spoke again.

"Yes?"

"I'm sorry I went climbing alone," I mumbled.

He smiled again, looking down at me with the warmth and parental affection I'd almost forgotten. Gods, it had been years since he smiled at me like that. Not that I'd given him much reason to, but it had almost seemed like the older I got, the colder he became. I wondered if that had something to do with Noh, if he'd somehow known what was in store for me.

"It's all right, Reigh. You're safe now," he replied. "Just promise me you won't do it again. You're always so eager to prove yourself. But a scout must always be careful. He must always remember Luntharda is not forgiving to the naïve and unprepared—nor is the rest of the world, for that matter. There are dangerous things out there, things that will want to kill or hurt you."

"Animals? Like the tigrex?"

"Yes, some are animals," he answered quietly. "But some are men, who are often far worse than any hungry tigrex. They are cruel only for the sake of cruelty."

The memory began to fade, crumbling around me as Kiran lifted his gaze to look back at the road ahead.

"You cannot be like that, Reigh. If you must be cruel, if you must kill, let it be for a good reason. Let it be for something good." His voice was fading fast, growing more distant as his image wavered. "Let it be for something you love more than yourself."

Little by little, it all dissolved away—back into darkness.

Back into hell.

A WARM, ROUGH-PALMED HAND PATTED MY CHEEK, ALMOST COMFORTINGLY. IT felt nice. Right up until it gave me a hard smack.

My cheek stung and immediately my eyes flew open, staring up into the eerie, yellow-green gaze of a young woman stooping over me. "Wake up, boy! You cannot die yet. You promised to get me out of here."

I groaned. My head pounded; the pressure inside making me wonder if I was bleeding from the ears. Groggily, I rolled over and coughed. The numbness had reached my lungs. I could barely get a good breath.

"You must hurry. The soldiers are nearly here," she urged in her weird accent. I raised my head enough to glare at her. "Working on it," I wheezed.

"Perhaps you have overestimated your talents?" She arched an eyebrow, her deep ebony skin gleaming flawlessly in the faint light. With slender pointed ears peeking out through her long, loosely curled locks of black hair, the woman studied me, tilting her head to the side slightly.

She looked like an elf—but not any I'd ever seen before. Her lithe frame was petite but muscular, and there was a bizarre mark on her face. A thin, curved line crossed her forehead and vanished into her hair like a circlet with a small crescent shape right in the center. When she moved, the light shimmered off those markings as though they'd been painted there with liquid silver. Strange—but beautiful.

"What? Melting doors wasn't impressive enough for you?" I rasped as I dragged my tingling, aching body upright. When I stumbled, she quickly darted forward to grab my arm and steady me. Her grip was surprisingly strong for someone who probably didn't stand a single inch over five feet.

"I've seen such tricks. But I take it you've never seen a Lunostri before," she quipped, stepping away again with one of her eyebrows arched.

"How'd you guess?"

"Because you're staring at me like I've got a second head. I suppose it can't be helped. From what little I've seen, the elves in your lands seem quite different. And my people are not explorers. We prefer to keep to our own and let the rest of the world squabble amongst itself. It wasn't until the Tibrans landed that many of us had ever set foot beyond our borders." The young woman crossed her arms and stood farther back to observe me from a cautious distance. I guess she didn't quite trust me yet. Fair enough.

"Is that how you wound up down here?" I asked.

She gave a stiff nod. "Argonox took many of my people into his ranks after he conquered our land. No doubt he plans to do the same here. Don't let him see your power—he's rather fond of adding *special* individuals to his private collection."

I resisted a laugh. Too bad it was a bit late for that.

"Does that include you?" I flashed her another look, studying her ragged clothes and bare feet. It was impossible to tell anything more about who she was or where she'd come from. The Tibrans had likely stripped away anything she owned when they took her prisoner.

Her lips bowed into a secretive little smile. "You could say that. But now is not the time for introductions. I checked on your friend. He is unconscious and severely beaten. It seems Argonox was very thorough with his interrogation. I will have to carry him. But first, you must show me you can get us out of here."

"Go get him, then." I slurred a little as I let my shoulder rest against the closest stone wall. "And hurry."

I closed my eyes as the elf woman disappeared into Aubren's cell. I had to get it together—I had to finish this. A few deep breaths, that's all I needed. Then I could finish killing myself so Aubren would be safe.

Attempting to valestep again was probably beyond idiotic. I'd only done it once to get us into the tunnels, and it had immediately brought me to my knees with a pain like a dragon was doing a tap dance on my head. I wouldn't survive it this time, and yet I knew it was the only way to get them out of here. I'd send them as far north as I could. Hopefully it would be far enough.

Then I would die.

Taking Aubren myself or going along with them wasn't an option. Assuming I even survived the effort of creating the portal, I wouldn't be able to make the journey to safety in Luntharda on my own, let alone carrying Aubren. We'd both die somewhere in the snowbound prairie. So, sending this mysterious elf girl in my place was better. She looked capable. Gods, I prayed she was trustworthy.

Once they were clear of Northwatch, if I was still alive, I would use whatever remained of my power to bring this place down and kill as many Tibrans in the process as possible. If I could make any dent in Argonox's forces, it would be worth it. I'd carve my name into his memory with blood, and he would *never* forget it.

Sounded good, anyway.

Down the hall, the voices and footsteps of the Tibran soldiers grew closer, mingled with the baying of hounds. No wonder they were able to track me so easily.

"*Shall I slow their progress?*" Noh offered with a gleeful laugh. At least one of us was enjoying this.

I shook my head. "Not worth it. Let them come. I need every last drop of power I have left to open the portal."

"Who are you talking to?" The elf woman reappeared from the darkness of the cell with Aubren's limp body over her shoulders. He was easily twice her size, but she didn't shake or waver as she strode out to meet me.

"Death." I chuckled. Maybe that was a bad joke, but it wasn't exactly a lie.

"I hear them! This way!" someone shouted. The soldiers were nearly upon us.

"Well?" The elf woman's bright eyes flashed with urgent panic.

"Get ready." I sucked in a few final breaths and pushed away from the wall.

The hounds were coming. Their claws clicked off the stone, and their snarling and growling echoed off the ceiling. We had seconds.

Widening my stance again, I pushed both of my arms forward with my palms pressed together and squeezed my eyes shut, calling forth every lingering fragment of my power from the furthest corners of my mind and gathering it between my palms. My body twitched, resisting the pull, as my breath caught, my heartbeat thundered in my ears, and everything went numb and cold. Focus. I had to keep calm. This was my last chance, and it had to count.

Slowly, I pulled my hands apart like I was opening a curtain.

I couldn't see it—not with my eyes closed. But I felt it just as clearly as if it were a part of me. The fabric of the living world split, opening to reveal what lay beyond. The Vale. A portal of churning, swirling darkness that led into the realm of the spirits.

"By the goddess," the elf woman gasped. "You ... you are—"

"G-go!" I roared. She could be mystified by my awesome power later. I couldn't hold the portal open forever. With every passing second, my pulse slowed, and my body shook under the strain. My lungs constricted. I couldn't breathe anymore. Something warm drizzled out of my nose and eyes, streaking my face and dripping off my chin.

Blood.

"Go *now*!"

Peeling my eyes open, I stole one last look at her as she darted past, lugging Aubren over her shoulders like a giant, man-shaped sack of flour. Her jaw was set, vivid eyes flashing with a resolute determination I had to admire. She ran straight for the portal without hesitation.

This was it. She was going to make it.

Something whipped past my head, humming through the air. Too late, I realized what it was.

Oh no.

The arrow caught the elf woman right in the back of the calf. She stumbled. Aubren's large frame rolled off her back as she fell forward, arms flailing wildly as though trying to catch herself and hang onto him at the same time.

It didn't work.

The last thing I saw was her long black hair disappearing into the portal as Aubren flopped onto the ground right before it. She'd gone through the portal—or fallen into it, rather—but Aubren hadn't been along for the ride.

No ... *No!*

Something inside me snapped.

My body jerked suddenly, pitching wildly as the coldness under my skin exploded through every part of me. I was finished. I felt my heart stop with one final, desperate thump.

Then nothing—just a strange silence in my ears where my pulse and breathing should have been.

Dark energy hummed through my veins, vibrating through every part of my brain. The world spun around me, smeared with the light of torches blurring in and out of focus. The sound of the approaching soldiers was muffled chaos. My body suddenly went slack as the portal closed, and I hit the floor right next to Aubren.

I barely recognized him, lying only a foot or two away. His entire face was purple and swollen, and there was dried blood crusted around his nose and mouth. One of his eyes had practically swollen shut. Some of the bruises were a deep, angry, fresh shade of purple, while others were turning yellow and green—they were older and already healing. He'd been beaten many times, probably interrogated and tortured. Gods and Fates, was he even alive?

Thoughts swirled through my mind, tossed amidst the churning whirlpool of thrumming power as everything went dark. I'd failed him. I'd failed Jenna, Jaevid, and Enyo, too. We were both going to die here in this putrid hole, far away from the people we loved.

"Sorry," I croaked, not knowing if he'd hear me.

Aubren's brow twitched. Slowly, his eyes opened just enough that I could see him staring back at me. "Reigh?" he groaned. "W-why? How?"

There were a thousand things I wanted to say. He was right about everything. I was his little brother, albeit a lousy one. I shouldn't have left them after that first battle. I was a coward. I'd run away like a sniveling child and hid because ... because I was embarrassed and ashamed. Maldobar deserved better. I should have been there to fight for Barrowton. Maybe if I had, none of this would have happened.

It was too late for all that now, though.

As soon as I opened my mouth to try to speak, someone grabbed a fistful of my hair and yanked my head off the floor. I dangled, delirious and defenseless, staring groggily into the sneer of a Tibran soldier dressed out in elaborate bronze armor. He wore a matching sloped helm with a mane of light red feathers down the middle, the visor raised so he could wrinkle his nose at me.

"We've got you now, Maldobarian rat."

Under any other circumstance, I'd have snapped back with a clever, witty one-liner. I was good at those. Maybe something about how nice he looked in that fancy *pink* helmet. Did they give those to the lousiest fighters in the Tibran armies? Or just the ugly ones?

But I couldn't speak. My lungs squeezed and spasmed for want of just one tiny breath.

"Lord Argonox! I've found him!" The solider dropped me like a rotten apple, sending me face-first back into the floor. Then he used the toe of his boot to poke me in the ribs. "I think he's dead."

As if I would ever be that lucky.

"Turn him over," a deep, smooth voice spoke over me.

Immediately, the soldier roughly rolled me onto my back. It took every ounce of strength to suck in one, short, desperate little breath. Just enough to keep me conscious a few seconds more. I couldn't move. I was helpless, sprawled out in the most undignified way possible, as I stared up at the stone ceiling overhead.

Then an unfamiliar face eclipsed my view.

A man about Aubren's age peered down at me, his slate blue eyes narrowing as he grabbed my chin and turned my face to the side long enough to look at my ears. "My, my. The Fates have smiled upon me today after all." The smile that curled over his lips was nothing short of disturbing. "He's not dead. This is the boy Hilleddi discovered, the one from Luntharda. He turned the tide during our first siege at Barrowton. He's human, although he dresses like one of those elf savages from Luntharda."

"T-the one who serves the dark goddess?" the soldier stammered. "The angel of death!"

Wait—the Tibrans *knew* about Clysiros? And the Fates?

"None other. No wonder your men have had such a difficult time containing him."

"Yes, My Lord. He slaughtered everything on the ground floor. Even the two dread-hounds." The soldier paused as he leaned over me again, trying to peek around his master's head. He swallowed hard. "If he truly is not dead, then perhaps we should take precautions in case—"

"He is no longer a threat, Captain. He obliterated two legions of my finest soldiers at Barrowton—after that, sieging a tower should be elementary for someone playing with that kind of power. He must have drawn out too much of it in an effort to save that shoddy excuse for a prince. A convenient mistake for us. And here I thought today would be a waste." Argonox's smile widened. "Pushed it right to the brink didn't you, boy? A pity no one in this kingdom seems to know anything about divine power."

"What shall we do with him, My Lord?"

"Bind him and take him to the experimental wing. Phoebe will have much work to keep her occupied."

"And the prince?"

Argonox's face disappeared from my view. He sighed as his heavy footsteps began to retreat. "Put him back in the cell." The footsteps stopped abruptly. "No ... wait."

"My Lord?"

"Hilleddi said this boy broke the Mirror of Truth. That he was able to defy it with his dark power." Argonox's voice drew closer again. His eyes narrowed slightly, brow creasing as though he were trying to read my mind. "Coming down here was utter madness. There is no exit from this portion of the tower, and he must have known he was already pushing his abilities to their limits. But rather than escaping with the rest of his cohorts, he came down here. He must have known he would be risking death."

"We have seen such efforts from Maldobarian troops on behalf of their royals before," the captain offered. "They are nothing if not fiercely loyal."

"True, but this goes beyond mere loyalty to the crown." A hand grabbed my chin again roughly. Argonox turned my head, forcing me to make eye contact with him. "And you are no mere soldier. It was not your power that spared you from the mirror, was it? You spoke the truth to it."

Bright spots swam in my vision as I started to lose it. Air—I needed air!

"King Felix has been keeping a dark little secret hidden in that wild jungle." Gleeful realization sparkled in his eyes. "You *are* a Prince of Maldobar."

A greedy, endless darkness dragged me under, snuffing out everything as my mind reeled, whirling with panic at that last glimpse of sheer excitement and delight on Argonox's face. I didn't want to imagine what that meant. Would he torture me? Kill me?

Or something worse?

CHAPTER THREE

"*Reigh? Reigh! Wake up!*"
A loud shout startled me awake, as though someone were bending right over to yell down into my face. But when my eyes flew open, there was nothing. Only empty air. What had happened? Where was I?

I still couldn't move to find out. My whole body was numb and limp, nothing but an itchy, tingly, dead weight. Lying on my back, my vision gradually adjusted to the dimness of the prison cell where I was sprawled on the floor. It was essentially a windowless stone box with one heavy iron door. The smell of cinders, ash, and something else—like scorched metal—wafted past my nose. Each one of my shuddering breaths turned to white fog in the cold air.

"*Reigh? Can you hear me?*" the voice spoke again, so clear it seemed as though whoever was talking should be standing right over me. But there was nothing.

"W-who?" My voice scraped hoarsely through my raw throat.

"*Oh, thank the gods,*" she replied. "*I thought I was too late. It's Hecate.*"

Hecate? But where? I forced my aching eyeballs to roll around, searching as far around the cell as I could without being able to move my head.

"*I'm here, in your head. It's hard to explain. Noh let me in,*" she explained quickly. "*But I can't do this for long. It's still difficult. I'm trying, though. I've been practicing, just like Jaevid said. Soon I can help.*"

"W-with what?"

"*Hush now. Don't waste your strength trying to talk. Just listen. I may not have much time,*" she cooed gently. "*I was able to find out where you are. The foundling spirits are much easier for me to talk to, so they've been helping me search,*" she said. "*The Tibrans have taken you away from Northwatch, further to the south. My grandfather believes you're in Solhelm, at the old estate that used to belong to King Felix when he was still a duke."*

Solhelm? Why would Argonox want to bring me here? Surely Northwatch was more defensible. It was a tower built for war.

"He's been searching for something," Hecate went on, as though she could read my mind. Maybe she could, if she was taking up Noh's usual spot buried somewhere deep in my semi-conscious brain. *"At first, I assumed it was the crystal. But I was wrong. Reigh, he's been combing the estate's cemetery. He's opened almost all of the crypts, even the one where Jaevid was supposedly buried during the Gray War."*

I got a bad feeling about a second before she confirmed my worst fear.

"He's exhuming the bodies of fallen dragonriders. He's even collected the remains of several of their mounts. I think he's planning something terrible. We must find a way to get you out of there before—"

Her voice went silent, as though someone had snuffed her out of my brain like a candle in the night. It didn't matter. She'd said enough. Argonox was digging up old dragonrider graves and raiding them for their bones? That did not bode well for anyone, especially me. I didn't know exactly what he intended to do with them, or me for that matter, but if the past was any clue, I was willing to bet it was going to be something horrible.

Lying alone in the depths of some duke's dungeon, I tried to think of anything I could do to end this before it began. In this state, I couldn't even try to kill myself to prevent Argonox from being able to use my power against my friends and family. I was helpless, cut off from everyone who might have been able to help me. I might as well have been sitting on the dark side of the moon.

No matter what I did, a persistent flicker of hope remained burning brightly in the back of my mind that maybe Jaevid would come for me. He was probably the only one who could at this point. My better sense knew otherwise. Coming here would be suicide.

Tears welled in my eyes until I squeezed them shut, clenching my teeth against the sharp pain constricting my throat. Maybe the end, *my* end, would be quick and painless.

"Enyo." I rasped her name into the dark. With my eyes still shut, I could almost picture her face. "H-Hecate, if you can still hear m-me. Tell Enyo I'm sorry. Tell her I love her. Tell h-her ... it's all going to be okay."

I'D JUST BEGUN TO GET THE FEELING BACK IN MY FINGERS AND TOES WHEN THE cell door banged open. Propping myself onto my elbows, I raised my head shakily to see a company of armored Tibran soldiers file in, surrounding a ... little girl? I blinked a few times just to make sure I wasn't hallucinating.

She couldn't have been more than fourteen, with ginger-orange hair pulled into two wildly curly pigtails right behind her ears. Her face was mottled in freckles, and a long leather apron and soot-stained dress were draped over her scrawny frame. She stared down at me, her wide eyes as blue as birds' eggs, and nibbled on her bottom lip.

She turned to one of the soldiers beside her. "How long has he been like this?"

He shrugged, making his bronze shoulder pauldrons clank.

The girl frowned and rubbed the bridge of her nose. "Bring water right away. If Lord Argonox wants this to work, then it might be in everyone's best interest that he doesn't die of dehydration first."

The soldier obeyed, disappearing back into the hallway. Interesting. Since when did a scrappy-looking teenage girl give marching orders to Tibran soldiers?

"Hello there." She spoke softly as she approached and knelt at my side. "I'm Phoebe. We're going to be ... working together."

I furrowed my brow into the most threatening scowl I could muster. "T-Tibran scum," I growled hoarsely. It sounded more menacing in my head.

Her expression dimmed. "I guess so. I'm sorry we're meeting this way, but Lord Argonox has already given orders." Her lips thinned as she looked away, her delicate brows crinkling with distress. "I'll try to make it as painless as possible."

Painless? What was she going to do to me?

Reaching into one of the pockets of her apron, Phoebe withdrew a strange device—a glass cylinder tipped with a long, thin needle. It was filled with a black substance, and she held it up to the dim light that bled in from the doorway, giving the glass a few taps before turning back to me.

No way! I had to get away from her and that needle.

Floundering backward, I struggled to crawl away over the cold, gritty stone floor. I only managed a few steps before my body gave out, still too numb and weak from hunger and thirst to attempt an escape.

She shook her head. "It'll go much easier if you cooperate, I promise. I just need to—"

"I'll die before I cooperate with a Tibran," I shouted.

Suddenly, a deafening roar shook the cell around us. The stones rattled like chattering teeth, and the soldiers at the door flinched for their weapons.

"Can't you do anything to steady her?" Phoebe barked at the soldiers.

"I'm sorry, Miss Artificer," one of them replied. "She's strong. Even with the bridle in place, she continues to resist."

She? That beastly cry sounded so familiar. Why? Where had I heard it before? Oh, gods, no! They had *my* dragon.

The word left my lips like a scream. "Vexi!"

Another bellow made a shower of dirt spill from the ceiling. I coughed and wiped my eyes, body beginning to quake under the strain of pushing myself upright once more. Everything hurt. My head swam in and out of consciousness. Through the haze, I spotted Phoebe coming closer with the needle poised.

I kicked away wildly, scrambling into the furthest corner of the room, gritting my teeth. If she wanted to stick that in me, she was going to have to fight me first—however pathetic and brief it would be.

"I guess I will need some help restraining him." Phoebe sighed. She motioned to the guards at the door, and two stepped forward.

My pulse thrashed, making my vision tunnel as I staggered to my feet. I barely made it there before the guards grabbed my arms and wrenched me around, crushing my body against the wall.

All I could do was scream. And every time I did, Vexi roared and the room shook, as though she were pitching and fighting to get to me. As the cold pinch of the needle sank into the skin of my neck, I realized what that meant: Vexi had come back. My dragon had tried to rescue me.

And now it was going to cost us both dearly.

PART TWO: JENNA

CHAPTER FOUR

The sight of the black dragon perched atop the keep, its decaying hide rotted away in places to reveal white bone, stopped us in our tracks. Standing on the frozen lake of Cernheist, we gaped up at the undead monster as it let out a shattering cry and spat a burst of burning venom into the frigid air. It was a creature of pure nightmare. It shouldn't have been alive. How? How was this possible?

And the rider ...

The figure seated in the creature's saddle wore armor like polished obsidian. Even from a distance, I could pick out the shapes of golden wings painted onto the shoulder pauldrons and breastplate. How many times had my father described those markings to me during our bedtime stories? More than I could ever count.

But it couldn't be. It was impossible. Beckah Derrick was dead. She'd died a hero's death forty years ago at the end of the Gray War. I'd seen the place where her body was buried on my father's family's land in Solhelm.

"Jenna."

Startled, I turned to glance at Jaevid. Standing tall beside me, his scimitar firmly in his grip, his whole face flushed as his expression closed. His glacier-blue eyes smoldered ominously, and his jaw went rigid. There was no mistaking it. He recognized that beast and rider, too.

"You must take the others away from here," he commanded softly. "I will draw their focus. Make for the mountain pass and do not stop until nightfall."

My body shook with a sudden surge of adrenaline. I couldn't fathom what he must be feeling. Did he remember her? Did he know who and what she'd been to him before?

According to my father, Jaevid and Beckah had been ... much more than close friends. They were not just lovers; their bond went far deeper than just a mere attraction. They were like two halves of the same brilliant spirit. In fact, Beckah had died protecting him. She'd sacrificed herself so that he could complete his mission to destroy the god stone.

So why, by all the Fates, would she come here to challenge him?

As he stepped away, I lunged to grab his arm. "Wait, Jae, you don't have to do this alone. My men and I—we are ready to fight with you. We are dragonriders. We should stand together."

"No." His voice cracked over me like the punishing bite of a whip. "This is not open for debate. You evacuate the city. Defend the people. Protect them at all costs. Their safety is all that matters."

I didn't believe it. Not for a single second. Perhaps he did want to make sure everyone got out safely—but there was more to it. This wasn't duty or heroism. He wanted to fight her alone. This was contrition.

Biting down hard, I seized the front of his breastplate and jerked him down an inch or two, so I could look him squarely in the eye. Demigod or not, he *would* hear me. "You need to remember your place in this mess. If you go out there and get killed over some grand gesture of atonement, then all of Maldobar falls with you. So, fight her, if you think you have to, but don't kill yourself doing it. Please, Jae. We—Maldobar—still needs you."

Jaevid's eyes went round. He blinked a few times, mouth hanging slightly open. Then a thin, sad smile spread over his handsome face. "You sound like him."

I didn't have to ask whom. Once again, he was comparing me to my father, King Felix. "As long as you listen, I don't care who I sound like. Do whatever you think you have to, but come back. Swear that you will."

He nodded once. "I swear."

Throwing my arms around his neck, I squeezed him as tightly as I could. I buried my face against his shoulder, biting against the curses that stung my throat. Then I had to let him go.

Jaevid started for his dragon at a sprint, climbing into the borrowed saddle fixed to the beast's spiny back. Mavrik was an impressive specimen, able to match the undead king drake pound for pound in size. He crouched, powerful legs rippling as his black claws gripped the ice. His wing arms flexed to spread their leathery membranes wide in the freezing wind. With the sunlight dancing off scales of royal blue, he launched skyward with a booming roar. The frozen surface of the lake shuddered, sending out cracks like growing strands on a spider's web.

I watched, captivated by the sight of Jaevid Broadfeather forging headlong into battle as the opposing black drake also took to the air with a screeching cry. My pulse thrashed in my ears, racing so fast I could scarcely breathe. Never in my wildest childhood dreams did I imagine I would see this in person.

But I couldn't waste any more time gawking.

"To work, boys!" I shouted as I whirled back to face my dragonrider brothers. Calem and Haldor were already mounted on the backs of their dragons, waiting for orders. Aubren, after trying to murder me while under the control of foul magic, was now bound and thrown over the back of Haldor's saddle like a prisoner. He kicked and pitched against his bonds when I strode past, as though whatever dark power Argonox had infected him with was driving him to kill me by any means necessary.

I'd deal with him later.

"Easy, girl. I know it hurts." Phillip spoke soothingly to the sleek green dragoness who hunkered before him.

I had not seen Reigh's dragon, Vexi, since Barrowton. The sight of her without that redheaded troublemaker on her back made my stomach turn. Their initial bonding was rocky; Reigh hadn't seemed convinced that the dragonrider path was one he wanted to take. I was willing to chalk that up to him not fully understanding what it meant to be chosen. He'd grown up in Luntharda, after all, so despite being human, the dragonrider culture was foreign to him. He probably didn't understand that Vexi would be loyal only to him for the rest of her life—regardless of how he felt about it.

Still, I couldn't envision Reigh doing anything to hurt her. He wouldn't have muzzled her like that. No, all of this *had* to be Argonox's doing.

What on earth was happening at Northwatch?

Either from terror or fatigue, Vexi didn't resist as Phillip inspected the contraption that had been clamped around her head. Her wide blue eyes panned between us as her emerald hide shivered and her ears drooped. It was a metal bridle, sort of like the kind you might put onto a horse, only with a pinching bit far at the back of the jaw that was angled so it would dig into her sensitive tongue if she rebelled. My blood pressure spiked to think of what sort of person would do this to a dragon.

There had been a time when the Dragonriders of Maldobar had fallen far from our original calling. We'd bred dragons like cattle and treated them as dumb animals. My father had done much in his reign to begin rectifying that. Under his rule, wild dragons could no longer be captured or taken from their natural environment, and it was illegal to steal their eggs or cut wing tendons. But never in our history had we ever stooped this low. This was torture.

Closing his fists around a heavy iron chain at the back of the muzzle that ran behind Vexi's ears and horns, Phillip's thick arms bulged as he gave a swift jerk. The chain snapped like a thread. I blushed and looked away. Phillip's new strength would take some getting used to.

"There we go," he crooned as he slowly started to slide the rest of the device off her head.

Vexi gave a weak, low murring sound and pressed her snout against his chest like a frightened puppy wanting comfort.

Phillip chuckled and ran his hands over her scaly head. "You're welcome, girl. Stay with us, all right? We'll watch out for you."

She chittered sadly in response.

"You can talk to her?" I asked as I stopped next to him, bending over to get a better look at the iron and steel muzzle that had been fastened to her head. It was a crude looking thing—with rough edges and unpolished finishes, as though it had been slapped together quickly and without much forethought.

One glimpse of the marking engraved onto the very top of it, right where the center of her head would have been when she wore it, made my stomach turn. It was a single symbol etched deep into the metal, and it was one I knew all too well. It was the same mark Argonox was fond of branding into the necks of his captured slave-soldiers.

"In a way," Phillip replied, rubbing at the back of his neck. "I suppose it's some kind of mutual animal understanding. I wouldn't say we're ready to start debating politics, though."

"Maybe she can help us figure out what's happened with Reigh," I murmured as I lifted a glare to Aubren. He had gone quiet again and hung limply over the back of Haldor's saddle. I sighed. "But that will have to wait. Jaevid is right. We need to secure the mountain pass and get the city evacuated."

As I stood straight again, the rest of my companions gathered in to listen. "Phillip, you ride with Calem and take point. I'll have the townspeople follow you to the beginning of the pass. Haldor, you guard the rear and make sure we don't leave anyone behind. Keep eyes on Eirik. We'll be counting on him to let us know we've got everyone. Meanwhile, Phevos and I will circle and make sure nothing else interferes. If another one of Argonox's surprises turns up, we will intercept and hold it off as long as possible."

One by one, my riders responded with a dragonrider salute. Phillip nodded in agreement, his arms crossed and long tail flicking anxiously. Behind us, the air shuddered under a sudden burst of green light, flame, and roaring chaos. Everyone turned to look.

Jaevid and Mavrik had reached the keep.

My pulse throbbed in my fingertips as I watched the two king drakes collide midair. With their wings spread and hind legs outstretched to attack with talons, they snarled and snapped as they grappled. They plummeted toward the earth together, only to break apart at the last second and begin another bout of aerial pursuit. It was a deadly dance that reminded me of two eagles battling for territory.

Another burst of green light made me jump back, bouncing off Phillip's chest.

He grasped my shoulders to steady me, and together we watched, frozen in silent awe. Standing in his saddle, Jaevid cast his earthen magic with concussive force, conjuring blasts that sent the wicked undead dragon reeling every time he got too close. It was a game. Jaevid was baiting them—leading them further and further from the city so we could get away without being caught in the crossfire.

Or so I hoped.

"He'll win," Phillip rumbled earnestly.

"He has to," I whispered back.

Every second seemed like an eternity as we worked to get the townspeople and refugees safely out of Cernheist. Eirik and Aedan lead a group of soldiers going door to door as fast as they could to be sure that no one was left behind. Unfortunately, progress was agonizingly slow due to the number of injured, who needed time to get onto wagons, so they could be taken out of the city. There were many women, children, and elderly, too.

Cernheist had become a place of sanctuary for many fleeing the Tibrans. However, it was not a fortress meant for battle. Wheeling far above the frozen lake, Phevos and I watched the surrounding wilderness for approaching Tibran forces, but so far there was no sign of a cavalry or support. Had Argonox really sent just two agents to take the city? I didn't understand that. Then again, a king drake was a considerable force—especially pitted against an unfortified city. There were no city walls or ramparts to guard it or legions of soldiers to defend it. It was vulnerable and Argonox must have known that. He didn't need an army to raze it—just one monstrous king drake and a few good sprays of its burning venom.

We could not afford to give him that chance.

Good thing we had a king drake of our own to match him.

Jaevid and Mavrik pressed in hard, bringing fire and a hailstorm of that glowing green magic whenever the undead mount got in close. So far, they seemed evenly matched. Standing in her saddle, Beckah brandished a strange golden bow. I only assumed the rider was Beckah. The rider's stature seemed petite, but dressed out in full battle armor, it was impossible to tell for sure if it was a man or a woman in that saddle.

Still, that did look like her armor from all the stories and paintings. No one else had ever worn black armor adorned with paintings of golden wings like hers. The helmet was new, however. It hid her face behind a visor painted to resemble a pair of eyes weeping golden tears. None of the stories or paintings referenced anything like it.

Beckah moved on Jaevid with a ruthless precision I tried not to envy. Her aim was deadly, and she fired arrow after arrow with unshaking accuracy. The only thing sparing Jaevid from each strike was his ability to cast some sort of deflective shield with his power. He blocked blow after blow, firing back and snarling out words I couldn't understand over the roar of battle. As far as I could tell, she never answered.

Landing on the top of Cernheist's keep, I let Phevos take a quick breather while I took account of all my men. Perish, Calem, and Phillip made low passes back and forth, guiding the people out of the city toward the mountains. Aedan and Eirik were galloping down the streets on horseback, trying to organize efforts to get everyone moving. Haldor and Turq, with Aubren still in tow, made low circles while they waited to take up the rear position behind the crowd of refugees.

So far, so good.

Suddenly, the keep shuddered beneath us. Phevos flapped wildly, nearly losing his balance and letting out a yowl of panic. I gripped the saddle handles and brought him around, looking toward where Jaevid and Beckah had been dueling in the sky. They were gone. But there was a brand new, dragon-sized hole in the ice of the frozen lake.

Oh gods.

"What happened?" Haldor signaled as he and Turq landed next to us.

I shook my head. I hadn't seen it. My heart thumped with wild panic as I watched the surface of the lake and waited.

The keep shuddered again as the two dragons burst up through the ice, so close I could feel the force of their blows like a shockwave in the air. They were locked in combat, clawing and snapping as they rolled like two feral cats. Mavrik snagged the monstrous black dragon by the back of the head and began trying to get enough leverage to break his neck. Would that even work on a dragon that already looked like it should be dead?

Then their riders emerged from the water, as well.

Jaevid came out first, sputtering and coughing as he heaved himself back onto the solid ice. He lay flat out on his back for a second or two, catching his breath, before staggering back to his feet.

Not twenty yards away, Beckah emerged, too. She leapt out of the water, bow still in hand, and strode directly for him without missing a beat.

Reaching back to draw another arrow from her quiver, she stalked toward him with smooth, even strides.

My stomach dropped.

Jaevid was still reeling, wiping water out of his eyes as he turned to her. His face twisted with a look I wished I hadn't seen. Agony. Sorrow. Rage like the surface of the sun. It was as though he were burning from the inside out as he walked forward to meet her. His whole body tensed, shoulders hunched, and hands clenched as he shouted at her, although I couldn't make out the words over the dragons snarling.

In one smooth, beautiful, lethal motion, Beckah drew back her arrow and fired. Jaevid stopped, his body jerking on impact. Without full armor to protect him, the arrow caught him right in the shoulder above his breastplate.

That was an easy shot. No way she had missed on accident. What then? Was it a warning? Or was it really her under that helmet?

Jaevid grabbed onto the shaft of the arrow and snapped it off, tossing the feathered end aside. He started walking toward her again, still shouting.

"*What is he doing?*" Haldor signaled.

I didn't reply—but I knew. Deep down, I understood not wanting to imagine someone you loved would try to kill you. I'd felt the same way when Aubren had me pinned, ready to land the final blow. Jaevid must have been struggling with that, as well. He wanted to believe that—if it really was Beckah under that helmet—some part of her spirit was in there, fighting to get control over whatever dark power had brought her back into this world. He was gambling on that hope just like I had.

And he was doing it with all our lives—not just his own.

CHAPTER FIVE

Standing less than five yards apart, Jaevid and Beckah stopped. She slid another arrow from her quiver and snapped it into place, drawing the string back to take aim with shoulders braced and firm. At that range, she could pierce his skull easily. She could end it with one shot, and there was nothing any of us could do to stop her.

Jaevid never moved.

Blood dripped from his injured shoulder, leaving a trail of pink splotches and smears across the ice where he'd walked. He faced her, upright and tense, his mouth moving but his words lost to the chaos of their brawling dragons. His eyes closed as he dipped his head slightly. Surrender?

My heart hit the back of my throat. Jaevid, gods, *no!*

Her grip on her bow trembled. She faltered.

My mouth fell open. Was it actually *working?* Was she listening to him? Did she ... remember?

With no warning, Jaevid lunged at her.

Her bow went flying, skittering across the ice and far out of reach. They rolled, wrestling for control. Jaevid wasn't holding back. He worked her into a hold, pinning her down on her back with his knees on her shoulders so she couldn't get up. He grabbed her helmet and tore it off with one quick yank.

Fluffy bangs and a long, messy braid of dark hair framed the face of the beautiful young woman lying beneath him. She stared up with a defiant sneer, though inky tears smeared across her ashen skin and her eyes were stained as black as pitch, just as Aubren's were.

The helmet rolled out of Jaevid's hands. Eyes wide and expression eerily blank, he stared down at her and didn't move a muscle for what felt like an eternity.

Then he threw his head back and yelled skyward. It was a broken, horrible sound that broke over the two dragons still clashing nearby.

My heart shattered as tears blurred my vision.

It was Beckah.

Slowly, Jaevid's shaking hand went to the hilt of his scimitar. He drew it, knuckles blanching as he squeezed the hilt. Gods, was he going to—?

No. I couldn't let him do it. Regardless of what Argonox had made her into, I knew Jaevid loved her. If this had to be done, if there truly was no other way, I would *not* let him be the one to do it.

I owed him that much.

Nudging Phevos, I urged him forward and we leapt from the top of the keep, surging toward them as fast as possible.

Jaevid raised the scimitar, angling it over Beckah's chest. Then he hesitated. I couldn't see his face. Part of me didn't want to. But I had a feeling I knew what I might see.

We were only seconds away. Just a little further. We could make it.

Something exploded to my left and heat scorched the side of my face, singeing my eyelashes. I turned to look, but Phevos whipped over into a desperate roll, angling himself between a burst of burning dragon venom and me. His scales would protect him. Dragon venom doesn't burn through their own hides.

I hugged myself against his neck and hung on as we dropped into an evasive dive just as Beckah's enormous, undead mount hurtled past. Phevos was barely able to flare his wings in time for a rough landing on the surface of the lake. The undead dragon cut in low with Mavrik in hot pursuit, barely skimming the surface of the ice as he sped toward where Jaevid still had his rider pinned.

I screamed—anything to try to warn him—but they were too far and going too fast.

The sound of their approach made Jaevid turn, causing his focus to break. With a twist of her body and a swift kick to his already injured shoulder, Beckah launched herself out of his pinning hold. She left him staggering on the frozen ground and ran to intercept her dragon. The massive beast plucked her up in one fluid motion, and the two sped skyward in full retreat.

Mavrik landed next to Jaevid, taking up a defensive position over his injured rider as he went on snarling at their enemies. Beckah and her black dragon circled once, the beast roaring and breathing a few more plumes of burning venom nearby. Warning shots?

I twisted my saddled handles and Phevos darted forward, taking up a position beside Mavrik with his teeth bared and his tail flicking. If they came back down for seconds, they'd have to contend with two of us this time. She was no longer the only woman worthy of a dragon's loyalty.

And I would end her without hesitation.

After another pass, Beckah turned her mount away to the east—back toward Northwatch. In minutes, they were gone, disappearing into the gathering dusk like phantoms. When the booming wing beats faded, the silence squeezed at my already frayed nerves. It didn't make any sense. Why had she come here? To kill Jaevid? Or just to taunt us? Was this some kind of test to see how easy we would be to kill?

I had no answers, and at the moment, none of it mattered.

Jaevid was hurt. He needed help.

SCRAMBLING DOWN FROM PHEVOS'S SADDLE, I RAN TO JAEVID AS FAST AS I dared on the slick ground.

Mavrik's massive head appeared in my path so suddenly I nearly crashed right into the end of his snout. He bared his jagged teeth, ears slicked back and yellow eyes as bright as moons. I'd seen this before. Dragons were extremely protective of their riders—especially the ones who had chosen them voluntarily. Sometimes they didn't even bother to discern friend from foe. Mavrik was still on edge from the battle, seeing red, and ready to roast anyone who got too close to his injured companion.

Behind me, Phevos gave a protective growl and snapped his jaws. He fumed a long string of popping, chirping sounds that made the king drake hiss.

"It's all right." I raised my hands in surrender. "Jaevid is hurt. I'm sure you can smell his blood. Please, let me help him."

Mavrik studied me with those huge, yellow eyes. They seemed to stare straight through me with intelligence I could hardly fathom. With a heavy snort, he licked his chops and moved out of my path.

I took that as permission to go.

Jaevid sat on his rear, the snow and ice around him splotched with blood. His scimitar lay only a few feet away, so I picked it up as I knelt down beside him. Only an inch or two of the arrow's shaft was still sticking out of his shoulder, through fabric and flesh. I prayed it wasn't poisoned.

Words failed me as I searched his face for some sense of how he was. Catatonic was putting it far too lightly. He stared straight ahead with his broad shoulders slumped and jaw slack. His eyes were empty, expression blank, even when I started probing at the wound on his shoulder to see how deep the arrow's head had lodged into his body.

We would talk about it. We needed to. But not here—not now. There was still work to do.

"Can you stand?" I asked softly.

No response.

Touching my fingers to his chin, I carefully turned his face to look at me. "Jaevid?"

His brows snapped together, mouth skewing. "I-it was ... did you see?"

"Yes," I whispered gently.

He spat a string of curses under his breath, fists quaking as he gnashed his teeth.

"Jae, I can't imagine what you must be feeling right now. But we can't stay here. The others are counting on us. We have to get everyone safely into the mountains."

He drew in a deep, rattling breath and nodded. "Lead on."

"You're all right to ride like this?"

"I've done it with worse."

I stood back as he got to his feet, waiting until I was certain he was able to sit securely in his saddle before I mounted up. Phevos shifted uneasily beneath me, his ears still perked in the direction Beckah and her mount had flown. He chirped and whined, hide shuddering.

I rubbed a hand along the back of his head. "It's all right, love."

Or so I hoped, anyway. We had no way of knowing what Argonox would do now that he had found us. Would Beckah come back with reinforcements? We were putting ourselves in a vulnerable spot. Deep in the mountains, our people would have nowhere to go for cover if we were attacked—especially from the air. It wouldn't take much of a force to overwhelm and destroy every last one of us. Only a small fraction of our company were soldiers. Most were ordinary townsfolk; women and children. Bakers, blacksmiths, carpenters, and cobblers—people who had never once held a blade or had any reason to.

The thought made my throat constrict and my mouth go dry. Fates guard us; we were not in a good position to make any sort of stand. Not with so many innocent lives at stake. But we had no choice.

Together, Jaevid and I took off for the city to rejoin the others.

Cernheist was nearly empty. A long caravan of townsfolk and Maldobarian soldiers filed out toward the steep, rugged slopes of the Stonegap Mountains. The pace was slow. Merchants hadn't traversed this path in years, and this time of year, the ground was still slick and treacherous. The wagons, loaded down with people and supplies, frequently got stuck in the deep slushy drifts and it took an eternity to dig them out.

If Argonox did come for us, we would not be difficult to catch.

CHAPTER SIX

"We can't stay here with them," Haldor insisted as he rubbed his brow. "Every second we do puts these people in danger. Argonox wants us, not some band of refugees. The quicker we leave and draw his focus elsewhere, the better chance they'll have."

"If we leave them, they'll have no means of defense if Argonox sends someone else after them," Calem countered, his deep tone as cool and collected as ever.

Gathered around our tiny campfire, I watched the small pot of boiling water send wisps of steam into the frigid night air. We'd pushed the people as far as we could for one day. Less than twenty miles from Cernheist, we had set up a temporary camp under the cover of a sparse evergreen forest. It wasn't much, but it would do while we waited out the night and came up with some kind of a plan for our next move.

"Nothing has changed," Phillip murmured. "We were attacked, yes, but we were planning on departing anyway. All this has done is put more pressure on us to move quickly."

"Pressure indeed." Haldor snorted and rolled his eyes. "No one said anything about battling undead dragons and ancient war heroes. How do you kill something that's already dead?"

No one answered.

He sighed, head drooping as he let out a heavy breath. "Dead or not, I can't believe she would fight for that tyrant. Gods, how could she turn on her own?"

"You saw how it was with Aubren. You really think he would try to kill me if he were in his right mind?" I flashed Haldor a venomous glare. "That power does something to their minds. She may not have any sense of who she is anymore."

"Regardless, considering the state of Prince Aubren, I think it's safe to assume Argonox has already begun experimentation on how to weaponize Reigh's power," Aedan murmured through chattering teeth. He was burrowed so deeply into his fur-lined coat that only his multicolored eyes peeked out to catch the light of the fire. "We should assume we will meet more such monsters."

As much as I hated to, I had to agree. If Argonox was using Reigh to resurrect soldiers and dragons alike, then our advantage of being the only combatants in the air was gone. We would have to fight more of our own. That was something no dragonrider wanted—to have their own brothers-in-arms, dead or alive, pitted against them. It went against everything we stood for.

"It doesn't do any good to speculate on what we can't know. Let's focus on solving one problem at a time. We still have to make it to Halfax and hope my father will open the city gates to us," I said as I took the small pot off the embers and poured some of the boiling water into a small copper bucket. I'd mashed a collection of medicinal herbs, packed them into tea bags, and lined the bottom of the bucket with them. Then I'd taken my smallest, sharpest dagger and placed it inside, as well. As the bubbling water hissed into the pot, the mixture gave off a sweet, soothing, minty aroma. It would steep the medicinal herbs and sterilize the dagger. "We have to get to that crystal—the one that could quicken Reigh's power—before Argonox does. He cannot get his hands on it."

"Is he still up to it?" Phillip's gaze held mine for a moment, flickering with worry. Jaevid wasn't the only one with ties to Beckah. She had been Phillip's oldest sister, although he'd never known her. She'd died in battle long before he was born.

I shook my head. There were no words I could think of to describe Jaevid's state. I didn't know him well enough to even make a guess. It was impossible to imagine what he might be feeling, and I didn't want to insult him by trying.

"Just don't let any of the townspeople hear you talking about this," I warned as I got up and started back for our tent. "They're already terrified enough as it is. Let's not make it worse."

Phillip gave a forced smile, his pointed ears perked. He was the only one who didn't seem to mind the cold. I could only guess that was because of what the switchbeast venom had done to him.

Most of our group stayed huddled around the campfire, speaking quietly. Phillip, Haldor, Calem, and Aedan could speculate all they wanted. Until Jaevid was himself again, we had no idea what we were truly up against.

Ducking inside our one-room tent, I glanced over to where Miri and her aunt, Baroness Adeline, were huddled together in a corner. The baroness spoke to her in a quiet voice, stroking her hair affectionately as Miri lay propped up on a bedroll, covered with blankets.

Miri was rattled from the attack, but other than a bump on the head, she would be all right. I'd checked her over personally, if only to ease the baroness's concerns that she might have an internal injury. Miri had been lucky. But then again, we all had. It was a miracle none of us had died during that first assault on Cernheist's keep, let alone the events after.

Quarters were cramped in the tent. Not that it was small—it was probably twelve feet across, and it was tall enough that only Phillip had to stoop some to walk around in it. But there wasn't much in the way of privacy. We hadn't intended on staying the night, so there was barely room for all our bedrolls. Fortunately, it seemed not many of us felt like sleeping tonight. Not when there was an undead king drake lurking somewhere in our blind spot.

On the opposite side of the tent, Jaevid lay quietly on his own bed. He was staring straight ahead, eyes glazed and distant. Eirik sat next to him, fingers drumming on the long hilt of his two-handed longsword, which lay across his lap. He was busy gnawing on the inside of his cheek when I knelt beside them.

I didn't have to ask why he was here.

Sure, it might have looked like Eirik was keeping watch over Aubren, who was still bound like a prisoner and gagged in case he decided to start ranting and raving again. But that wasn't the real reason. Aubren had been quiet for a long time, lying perfectly still with his eyes closed as though he were sleeping. No, he wasn't what had my ridiculous best friend on edge.

With every other breath, Eirik's gaze darted to where Miri lay. His brow wrinkled, and he rubbed the back of his neck, muttering under his breath. I could have sworn I heard him giving himself a pep talk. Gods, I hadn't heard him do that since fledgling year. He must have really been worked up.

"She's going to be fine," I whispered as I wrung a clean linen rag in the herbal-infused water. "It's just a bump."

"She keeps shaking." He ran a jerky hand through his hair. "Is she cold? I can find another blanket. Or she can have mine."

I fought back a smile and passed the bucket and rag to him. "Here, give these bags a gentle squeeze. We need to draw out the oils in the leaves."

"What are you—?"

I didn't give him time to object. Getting up, I hurried over to where the baroness was seated right at Miri's side. She looked up with dark circles under her eyes. "Your Highness, is everything all right?"

"Yes. Things are quiet for now. But I've got to, um, dress Jaevid's wound. He'll need a new shirt when I'm finished. His old one was soaked with blood and now I'll have to cut it off him because of his injury. Could I trouble you to ask around some of the other campfires to see if anyone has a spare?"

It was a silly errand, sure, but it worked like a charm. The baroness nodded enthusiastically and left the tent without question. I guess she was eager to feel like she was contributing somehow. I could sympathize. Sometimes sitting still was hardest thing to do. Anyway, it would keep her busy for a few minutes.

As soon as she left the tent, I aimed a grin back at Eirik and gestured for him to come. He practically materialized out of thin air, zipping to Miri's bedside in an instant. I'd never seen him move that fast, not even during our dragonrider training. Silly man.

Returning to Jaevid's side, I tried my best not to eavesdrop or spy as Eirik and Miri began whispering to one another. I failed, of course. How could I not watch? Eirik's tone trembled as he took her hands in his and brought them to his face. Maybe it wasn't right to trick the baroness ... but it was worth it.

"He cares for her a great deal." Jaevid's deep, quiet voice startled me.

I blushed as I went back to wringing the washcloth in the fragrant, herbal water. "Yes. He's an idiot—but a good one."

"You've known him a while?"

"We started dragonrider training together at the academy." I shrugged. "He was my roommate. A poor country boy from a forgotten dragonrider bloodline and the only girl stupid enough to test her luck as a fledgling student," I recalled. "I guess you could say we were destined to be friends. No one else wanted us."

A faint smile ghosted over Jaevid's lips. "Sounds familiar."

"You keep saying stuff like that and I'll be forced to smack you, injured or not." I sighed and gave the cloth one last hard twist. "It's bad enough hearing everyone else say it. But if it's coming from you then it must be true."

"Do you hate your father?"

I hesitated. "No. Of course not. He's my father—I love him. But that doesn't mean I like him right now. He's a hypocritical old fool to even imagine he could stop me from becoming what I was meant to be. He, of all people, should know better. You can't fill a child's head with stories of heroes and glorious battles and then act shocked and angry when she chooses that path. I wanted it even before Phevos chose me. I was not born to stand silently by, blushing and weeping while my kingdom burns. Destiny put a sword in my hand and a dragon's wings beneath my feet. I intend to use both—even if everyone in Maldobar despises me for it."

"A fair point."

"Yes, well, be sure to tell him that when you see him. He won't listen to anything I say anymore." Sliding my arms under Jaevid's good shoulder, I helped him up into a sitting position. He gasped and groaned whenever he moved his injured shoulder. No doubt it was hurting a lot more without the rush of adrenaline and battle to distract him.

I cut away his shirt and tossed the bloody rags aside. Underneath, he wasn't at all what the sculptures and paintings had suggested. He was muscular, yes, but more leanly built. He didn't have any of the heavy brawn I was used to seeing on dragonriders. His deeply tanned skin was flecked with scars, telling tales of battles long past. We had that in common, at least.

Probing around his injured shoulder again, I tried to gauge just how serious this was. About a quarter of the arrow's shaft, plus the barbed point, was still lodged in the soft meat of his shoulder. Now I had to get it out somehow.

"How deep is it?" he asked hoarsely.

"Not far. Lucky for you, I've done this a few times. They made me choose field medicine as my secondary specialty. Little fingers and steady hands are better for stitching wounds, or so they claimed. Just thank that god of yours the Tibrans didn't dip this arrow in poison, otherwise you'd be dead already." Sitting back on my heels, I threw my hair up into a sloppy bun to get it out of my way before I rolled up my sleeves. "I've got to enlarge the wound, so I can pull it out. This is going to hurt."

He sucked in a breath. "Do it."

Taking off my belt, I handed it to him before I fished the sterilized dagger out of the pot of hot water. He put the leather strap between his teeth and gave a firm nod.

Here we go.

Jaevid's body went rigid as I started using the knife to cut a bigger hole in his shoulder. Trying to rip it out otherwise risked losing the arrowhead inside his shoulder. Unfortunately, it wasn't something I could do quickly. I had to be careful. He ground his jaw against the belt, eyes watering and head rolling back as he groaned. But I had to give him credit. He held steady.

When I finished, his whole body was shaking, so I quickly poured him a cup of the herbal tea. "Drink this. It'll help with the pain."

While he drank, I cleaned the wound with the rest of the tea and washcloth. I wiped away the blood as gently as I could before applying a few quick stitches to close it. "It'll be tender for a while," I explained. "I'd say you should take it easy, but I think we both know that's out of the question."

He gave a weary sigh in between sips of tea. The shaking of his hand made it slosh, so I settled in beside him and held the cup. "T-thank you, Jenna."

I stole a quick glance over my shoulder at Eirik and Miri. They were still talking quietly, lost in their own little world. It was as good a time as any. I cleared my throat. There was no subtle or good way to approach this subject. I just had to ask. "Jaevid, are you okay? I know you said the memories were coming back, but this ..."

His jaw went rigid again as his brows drew up. You would have thought I'd rammed my knife back into his shoulder. His pale blue eyes fell closed and he turned his face away.

"I don't expect you to be all right. No one does. We all know who she was and what she meant to you." I reached for his hand, lacing my fingers through his and giving a reassuring squeeze. "You can talk to me. Whatever you say stays between us."

"I-I know I should have ended it. That thing ... it wasn't really her," he rasped through gritted teeth. "I thought I could handle it. I *should* have handled it. Paligno's essence demanded it. I felt his fury as my own. He commanded me to destroy her."

My heart sank at the brokenness in his voice. "Jaevid ... "

His mouth skewed, grimacing between a smile and something anguished. "I couldn't sense her soul anywhere in that body. But her face—Gods. The sight of her underneath that helmet brought the memories back. I wasn't ready for it."

"What do you remember?" I whispered.

Jaevid squeezed his eyes shut again and clenched his hand around mine as though the words were agony on his tongue. "Her smile; that perfect smile lit by the sunrise over a calm sea. The freckles on her cheeks, so many you could never count them all. Her eyes, the same color as the ivy leaves that grow up the sides of my family's old house in Mithangol. Her fingers combing through my hair. The smell of the ocean on her skin. The taste of fresh peaches on her lips." His body relaxed slightly as he let out a trembling breath. "I thought I was meant to be hers forever."

"You don't think that now?"

Jaevid opened his eyes to stare up at the roof of our tent. "I believed she was gone, beyond my reach even as Paligno's vessel. Honestly, I don't know what to think about anything anymore."

He wasn't the only one. "If someone had told me a few years ago I'd be sitting here talking to the famous Jaevid Broadfeather and stitching up his battle wounds, I would never have believed it. We're all living to see things we never thought could be real." I gave his rough, leathery palm one more squeeze before letting go. "Is it destiny that she's been brought back into our world right after you were? Or is it just a cruel coincidence? Who's to say? All I know is, based on what I saw, she had a chance to kill you and she didn't. If that means there is even a tiny piece of her spirit left in that body, then you can't give up hope."

My gaze wandered back across the tent to where Miri was sitting on her bedroll, her petite body curled against Eirik's chest as he put his arms around her. I'd seen him joke, drink, flirt, fight, and cheat death many times in the years we'd spent as friends and comrades. But I'd never seen him like this before. There was a crinkle of subtle desperation in his brow as he held her, as though he were afraid someone might tear her away.

"Love is so much messier than they describe in the stories," I muttered. "Look at us—fighting like fools for it. Bleeding and dying for it."

"Yes," Jaevid conceded softly. "I suppose that's something I can say hasn't changed with time. Love is always messy. And it's always worth it."

Nearby, Aubren stirred and twisted against his bonds. The gag in his mouth muffled his groaning. It took everything I had not to look at him. I wasn't ready to. While I knew he hadn't meant to hurt me, part of me still felt betrayed.

"Do you think you can help Aubren?" I heard myself ask faintly. "Can you undo whatever Argonox did to him?"

Jaevid rubbed his jaw as he studied my older brother. "I'll certainly try. I think most of my memory is more or less intact now, but I don't recall ever encountering anything like Reigh's power before. What little I understand has come directly from Paligno, although it seems not even the god himself knows what to expect. He seemed so certain that this sort of abuse of Clysiros's power would be impossible before Reigh's ritual was complete. But maybe Paligno's divine sister is a mystery to him as well?" He shrugged and glanced my way with a grim frown. "During the Gray War, I saw a glimpse of what abusing sacred power could do. And yet, even at his most powerful, not even Hovrid was able to do things like this. What he began, Argonox seems to have perfected. Turning divine power we barely understand into weaponry that can be used by mortal hands is just ... Gods, it's terrifying to think about."

"And now he's bringing people back from the dead," I murmured. "Does he even need the crystal or the ritual anymore? Is having Reigh enough to doom us?"

Jaevid's expression darkened. "No. Without the crystal, Reigh can only use so much power at a time. It was the same way for me until my ritual was completed. If he pushes it too far, he could kill himself."

"I wonder if Argonox knows that."

"He must. Reigh was already weak when we got to you in Northwatch. Valestepping is incredibly dangerous for him—especially now. But he's still alive to do these things to Beckah and Aubren, so Argonox must be monitoring how much he uses." He lowered his gaze, staring into his nearly empty cup of tea. "I've been thinking about it over and over, asking myself why he would send those two and no other forces. It's as if his goal wasn't to kill us, just to test what they could do."

"You really think *that* was a test?"

Jaevid nodded, gradually panning his eyes over to where Aubren lay. "He could have sent anyone to do this, but he picked two people with strong emotional attachments to us. They had both been poisoned with Reigh's powers in entirely different ways. Aubren was a live victim. Beckah wasn't." His mouth hardened, and his brow furrowed as he spoke in a deep, controlled tone. "I think he was testing to see which of them would make the most effective weapon against us."

CHAPTER SEVEN

When he was ready to deal with Aubren, Jaevid insisted that everyone except for Phillip and myself wait outside the tent. No one questioned him, and even the baroness seemed all too eager to get herself and Miri out of the way. Haldor and Calem spoke in hushed voices, lurking right outside the tent as though they were waiting to respond at the first sound of distress.

My insides squirmed and swirled like live fish were swimming around in my gut as I watched Jaevid take a seat next to Aubren's head. Phillip stood by, crouched with his pointed ears perked and tail slowly swishing back and forth. Every muscle in his powerful shoulders and corded back was drawn taut. I could only guess he was there to be our reinforcement if things went badly.

As if they weren't bad enough already.

Lying on his back, his arms still bound and mouth gagged, Aubren was completely still. Only his chest rose and fell in slow, even breaths. At first, I thought he might be sleeping. His eyelids were even flickering as though he were dreaming. But as I got closer, I could see that inky substance still leaking out like tears running down the sides of his face. His whole body shivered, vibrating ever so slightly.

I bit down hard. Aubren ... how had it come to this? Where was my big brother when I needed him most? Whatever he'd done, however wrong he might have been about trying to bargain with Argonox, he did *not* deserve this. He was and had always been a good person with a much gentler, softer heart than I'd ever had. He probably would have stayed in Halfax, following Father's orders, if I hadn't insisted on—

"Let him hear your voice," Jaevid coaxed, interrupting my thoughts as I scooted in closer. "That seemed to work before."

Work? I guess if you considered "stopped him from killing me with foul magic" as working, then sure—it had worked. I shot Jaevid a glare as I knelt down, careful not to touch Aubren where he lay. I didn't want to make it worse.

Aubren's right arm—the one Phillip had broken—was still in bad shape. The strange black mark on his hand spanned from his palm to his elbow like someone had splashed him with ink. Only, the splotches were not completely random. They seemed that way, at first. But when I looked closer, I could pick out the shapes of swirling, detailed glyphs and designs within the patches.

The sight made my throat grow tight.

"What is it?" The question escaped me in a breathless whisper.

Jaevid's frown deepened, putting stern lines across his forehead. "It's definitely Reigh's power, or some form of it. But there's something different."

Phillip leaned in for a closer look, sniffing the air around Aubren like a curious cat. "Different how?"

"I don't know how much you understand about the afterlife. It wasn't commonly taught when I grew up in Maldobar. Most regarded it as Gray elven paganism or a ridiculous myth," he began to explain. "Our world is separated from that of the gods by a space, an in-between called the Vale. There, spirits await the judgment of the Fates before passing on into the afterlife. Those judged as worthy enter Pareilos, the kingdom of the old gods. Those who fail to meet that standard are condemned elsewhere." His eyes darkened as he studied Aubren's hand. "Desmiol, the prison of lights. We call them the stars."

"You're off it," Phillip balked. "You're saying the stars are some kind of prison of eternal damnation?"

Jaevid shrugged. "Of sorts. Clysiros is also there, banished away from the other gods. Just as Paligno represents life, renewal, and creation, Clysiros governs death, decay, and all that lurks in the darkest places of the world."

Chills prickled along my spine. "What does this have to do with Aubren?"

"Reigh got pulled into the Vale once before by accident. There was nothing I could do to stop it. Because of who he is, he can walk in both places and pass between the two at will." Reaching out, Jaevid brushed some of Aubren's hair away from his face so he could lay a palm against his forehead. "The sense I get from your brother now is similar to when Reigh went into the Vale. It's as though his spirit is trapped there, but every now and then he manages to claw his way back here, if only for a second or two, like someone gasping for breath while drowning."

A soft growl rumbled in the back of Phillip's throat. "If his soul is trapped in that Vale place, then what's keeping his physical body moving?"

Jaevid's head lowered, eyes closed tightly as though he were trying to focus. "I don't know. But it was the same with Beckah. Every time I reach out with Paligno's energy, I get nothing but darkness, anger, and chaos."

I tried to rationalize what this meant. Aubren's soul was gone? Trapped somewhere else? Did that mean he was dead? Could we even save him, or was it more merciful to just end this rather than let him continue to suffer?

The thought made my heart wrench in my chest. I had to look away.

"When this happened to Reigh, nothing I did could bring him back. It seems Paligno's influence ends at the Vale. He is a god of life; normally the realm of the dead is none of his concern. That's Clysiros's territory. So, unless I cross it personally, I don't know if I can help Aubren," Jaevid continued. "I can only think of one way to try. But it will be risky."

Phillip cocked his head to the side. "Riskier than usual?"

He gave a little chuckle. "No, I suppose not. But I'm not sure I'll be a welcomed visitor in the Vale. Still, if that's where Aubren's spirit is trapped, it stands to reason I could go there and set him free."

"And what if you can't?" I blurted. "What if you get stuck there, as well? What then?"

"I'll think of something." Jaevid gave a faint, despondent smile that made me want to jump over and throttle him.

Think of something? Was he joking?

"You can't do this," I protested. "I love my brother. I want him back. But we can't risk losing you over this, Jaevid. We need you if we are going to have any hope of stopping the Tibrans from taking what little remains of Maldobar. Your life, your influence in this war, means more than any of our lives."

"I'll come back, Jenna," he answered firmly. "One way or another, we need to know if this works. We have to find some way to fix it. If we don't, then anyone else infected with Reigh's power will be ... " His voice faded to a somber silence.

He didn't have to finish. I knew what he was thinking. This wasn't just about Aubren or anyone else Argonox might use against us. If Jaevid couldn't save Aubren, then he wouldn't be able to save Beckah, either. He had to experiment somehow.

This was the safest way to do it.

"All right," I sighed in defeat. "Then send me, instead."

Jaevid's eyes went wide. "What?"

"Send me into the Vale," I repeated. "I will find my brother and bring him back."

"*No*," Phillip snarled suddenly, lunging forward to seize my forearm. "Jenna, I will not let you do this."

I snatched my arm away. "I didn't ask for your permission."

"It's too dangerous," Jaevid agreed, his tone severe.

"Too dangerous? And yet you were ready to jump right in? If this is about the fact that I'm a woman and I shouldn't be put in danger—"

"It's about the fact that I am the vessel of Paligno's essence," he interrupted. "I carry the spirit of a deity within my—"

"A deity you just finished saying would have no power or authority there," I fired back, cutting him off. "How does that make me any less qualified? He's *my* brother. He's never even met you. My voice brought him back once, and you said it might do it again. If he were able to see me, then maybe—"

"Guys?" Phillip whimpered.

Jaevid ignored him. "And just how are *you* planning on bringing him back? You have no idea what you might be facing in the Vale."

"And you do? How were you going to do it?" I snapped. "And another thing—"

"GUYS!" Phillip roared.

My mouth snapped shut. Jaevid cringed. Together, we fell silent and looked at Phillip. He was glaring at us; arms crossed and pointed ears slicked back. "If you're quite finished, he's awake."

Aubren lay calmly between us with his breathing slow and steady. His eyes were open, and he stared straight ahead listlessly. His skin was turning ashen, and dark circles had gathered under his pitch-black eyes. The sight made my chest go tight. Was he dying? Were we losing him to the Vale? What if we couldn't get to him in time?

"Aubren?" Jaevid leaned in closer, studying my brother's face. "Can you hear us?"

No reply.

Carefully, Jaevid touched Aubren's forehead. The contact made my brother's body go stiff and his eyes bulged. He writhed against his bonds and bit down hard on the gag in his mouth.

I covered my mouth and turned away.

"He's fading," Jaevid murmured. "We must hurry." Pivoting in his seat, the hero of the Gray War stretched his hand out to me, his expression firm and gaze steady. "It is not my place to deny you this. But you should know the risks. Every second you spend there will bring you closer to your own death. The spirits of the living aren't meant to linger there. You'll begin to fade, too. So, don't stop. Don't talk to anyone. Don't lose focus."

My heart kicked and pitched against my ribs, filling my face with a rush of warmth as I slid my hand into his while his other still rested on Aubren's forehead. "I'll come back."

He gave one stern nod. "I believe in you, Jenna." Then his brow twitched, mouth straightening. "I'll have to allow some of that dark power to touch you. It should pull you into the Vale, as it did Reigh." His eyes went steely. "One more thing ... should you see someone there who looks like Reigh, you must not engage with him."

"What? Why?"

"I'll explain later. Just promise me you won't speak to him. Try not to even look at him. Am I clear?"

I drew in a deep, shaking breath. My hands were clammy—something he was bound to notice. I set my jaw. Now was not the time to lose my nerve.

With one last, lingering glance toward Phillip, I let my eyes fall closed. If that was the last sight I ever saw in the mortal world, at least it would be a good one. At the last second, I decided I should tell him one more time. Phillip needed to know that I loved him.

But it was too late.

It felt like I was falling, only there was no end. No bottom. No crash. I tumbled end over end into the darkness, my head whirling with a desperate need for some fixed point to orientate by. But there was nothing—just me and a bitter cold that seeped through my skin, into my bones, and froze the air in my lungs. I kicked and flailed, groping for anything solid as my body twisted and tossed like a leaf in the wind. I tried to gasp, to scream, but the darkness swallowed everything.

A strong grip closed around my arms so suddenly, I tried to pull away. Fear tore through my body like a pang of cold lightning. Get away—whatever it was I had to get away!

Through the gloom, the hands looked like something sculpted from solid alabaster. Solid and strong, they pulled me out of the depths with one swift tug. My head broke the surface of a pool and I rattled and wheezed, drinking in frantic breaths as I was dragged the rest of the way out of the water.

I landed on my hands and knees on the bank, my clothes drenched and my body shivering. Soft grass squished between my fingers. It took me a few seconds of ragged breathing and coughing to realize the ground, my hands, and everything around me was entirely colorless. Miles upon miles of endless prairie was nothing more than a bleak grayscale. Drab stone buildings stood in the distance against a silver, featureless sky. Even my own skin and clothes had been drained of all color. Everything from my skin to my boots was the color of ash.

"W-what is this?" I yelped, glancing around for whoever had rescued me.

He stood a few feet away, eyeing me like I might be a threat. Shimmering somewhere between solid and transparent, the young man looked strangely familiar somehow. His sharp, sculpted features were undeniably human, and his appraising scowl seemed to pierce right through me. Gods, where had I seen that look before? My mind was a haze of confusion as I clambered to my feet.

"You saved me?" I guessed.

The man arched one of his brows curiously. With dark hair falling shaggily around his chiseled jawline, he stood straight and poised with his wide shoulders squared and his hands clasped behind his back. "I'm not sure that pulling someone into the Vale counts as saving them, my lady," he countered.

"It beats drowning in there," I replied, coughing again. "Who are you?"

"One of the many who linger here," he answered cryptically, his eerie, colorless eyes glinting with what I suspected was amusement—as if he knew that answer wasn't what I'd been hoping for. "I believe the more important issue is why you are here. You aren't dead, are you?"

I shook my head, wiping some of my wet hair away from my eyes. "Not yet. I was sent here. I'm looking for someone."

"Someone who has passed?"

"No. My brother. He's not dead; not yet, at least. Something terrible was done to him in the mortal world. He's been touched by foul magic. Jaevid believes he might be here."

The man's expression blanked, eyes widening as he gaped for a moment. "Jaevid sent you here?"

My eyes narrowed. Wait—was this the person I'd been warned about? No, it couldn't be. This man looked nothing like Reigh. Jaevid had been very specific about that. "Yes," I replied at last. "To find Aubren. He's trapped here. I have to find him, and help him get back to the mortal world. I won't let him perish here."

His features tightened, lips thinning as he looked me over from head to foot. It was difficult to figure out how old he might be. Surely younger than Aubren. But did spirits age in the Vale? How did that work? Before I could ask, the man gestured to a white cobblestone path leading away from the pond. "I will assist you, if I can. The city ruins would likely be the best place to begin your search."

I took a wary step toward the path. "Why help me?"

He shrugged, following along with footsteps that made no imprint on the silver grass. "Seems the proper thing to do. It's been a long time since I spoke with anyone like this, even while I was alive."

"Why not?" I tried not to look back as he walked a few paces behind me.

"I was ... ill for the latter half of my life." His tone softened, barely a whisper.

"So you remember your life before?" I couldn't help it; I stole a quick glance back at him. His handsome face was staring off into the distance, brow creased with intense focus.

"We all do. That's why some choose to stay. They know their mortal deeds will earn them condemnation," he explained. "That, or they await the arrival of loved ones to join them."

"Which is it for you?"

His brow creased, eyes going steely as they panned back to meet mine. "A little of both."

I tried to imagine a scenario that might have him both dreading divine judgment and waiting around for someone else to join him in death. "Let me guess," I thought aloud. "You betrayed your lover? Cheated on your wife? Both?"

"No, not quite." He chuckled, his tone so rich, deep, and infectious it made me glance back again. A smile spread over his face, curving across his mouth in a way that made my stomach flip wildly. Gods, he was handsome. I tripped over my own feet. Heat bloomed across my face and I quickly ducked my head, hoping he hadn't seen.

"How did Jaevid send you here if you did not die?"

I shuddered just thinking about it. "I don't know how to explain it. He goes on about gods, dark magics, and ancient powers and half the time, I've no idea what he's talking about."

"So, you know him well, then? Jaevid, that is." Something in his tone set off a warning in my head. Why was he so curious about Jaevid?

I hesitated and stole another quick look at him. "Yes. Do you?"

"No, not really," he sighed. "But I'm sure you can imagine how many of the spirits passing through here talk about him. The hero of the Gray War; chosen by a dragon and a god. It would seem he's earned many titles and no small amount of respect."

I frowned. His answer made sense, yes, but it sounded a lot like a weak attempt to dance around the truth. What was he hiding? Why wouldn't he tell me who he was?

Unfortunately, there wasn't time to sort it out now. I had to find Aubren and get out of this place before I wound up stuck here right along with him.

"Not to sound ungrateful, but really, why are you helping me?" I panted as we crested the top of a hill. There, many gray stone buildings clustered around a square with a fountain in the center. All about the square, sculptures stood tall in the shapes of faceless, winged women. Many were cracked or crumbling, and most were missing arms, wings, or even their heads. No water ran from the fountain—not that spirits needed it. Did they even get thirsty?

"A great many souls have been passing through the well lately. More than usual, anyway. I can only guess this means there is some sort of war being fought in the mortal realm again," he said evenly. "You emerged, but your spirit does not look like the others—or like mine. You are still solid, so that must mean you still live in the mortal realm. At least, that's what I guessed when I saw you floundering in there."

"What now? Hoping I will bring you back to the mortal world with me if you help me find my brother?"

"Gods, no. It's just ... nice to have a chance to help someone. I wasn't especially *helpful* during my own mortal life. I doubt anyone would celebrate my return to it."

"Ah, I see; you're hoping for some last-minute absolution?"

He laughed again. "Perhaps. Or maybe I'm just bored of standing around watching dead people crawl out of that well." That laugh, wonderful as it was, didn't do much to hide the touch of despair in his voice. "I'm not certain there is absolution for someone like me. But that's enough about my troubles. Let's find that brother of yours."

I had to stop and catch my breath for a moment as we wound deeper into the city, keeping a brisk pace. We passed more squares and courtyards that all seemed strangely empty. I only saw a few other figures lurking around, spirits with forms so translucent you barely noticed them at all. Gods, this place was enormous. How would I ever find Aubren here?

Then something on the horizon caught my eye—something standing off by itself on the wide-open grassland beyond the city.

A dark cloud, like a wisp of smoke or a lost fragment of a thunderhead, hung over some sort of small structure. It was so far away, I couldn't be sure what it was.

"What's that?" I pointed.

The man stood next to me, his presence as tall and commanding as a knight. His dark hair blew around his face as he narrowed his gaze upon the distant cloud. "I don't know. I haven't seen it here before."

A hard knot of fear twisted in my gut. "Let's go."

CHAPTER EIGHT

My mysterious guide didn't protest and followed along as I jogged headlong toward the structure. The closer I got, the more I could tell that it wasn't a building at all—it was a monument. Seven stone arches stood around a central slab of stone like a platform. There, arranged in a perfect line, were four thrones made of solid black glass. Three had been shattered into crumbled bits and shards. The one on the end, its back adorned with a halo of spines like a sunburst, was still intact, however.

And lying before it ... was my brother.

I broke into a wild sprint.

Overhead, the toiling dark cloud sizzled and popped, sending tongues of white lightning that snapped and occasionally struck one of the arches or the ground nearby. With each crack, my heart jumped, and I pushed for more speed, running to where Aubren lay.

Sprawled on his back, Aubren stared up at the thundering dark cloud with his mouth slightly open. His body wasn't translucent, just like mine, but his eyes were dark reflections of that cloud—just as they were in the mortal world.

Falling to my knees beside him, I grabbed his shoulders and began to shake him as hard as I could. "Aubren! You need to snap out it! We have to leave right now!"

He didn't move, not even to blink. I couldn't see him breathing. Was he dead? Was I too late?

Rearing back, I smacked his face as hard as I could. "Wake up!" His skin was bitter cold.

"W-what's wrong with him?" I shouted up at my strange, knightly companion as he stood nearby, watching with an apprehensive frown.

He shook his head, opening his mouth to speak.

"This is what becomes of one touched by the unbridled power of the Harbinger," a cold, menacing voice hissed suddenly.

Looking up, my whole body shivered with a rush of panic as I locked gazes with the very person Jaevid had warned me not to speak to. Gods and Fates. He'd found me.

Reigh—or some otherworldly version of him—reclined upon the only remaining dark throne. With his chin resting in his palm and a cruel smirk twisted upon his boyish face, he drummed his fingers on the glass armrest. "So, he sent my sister. Interesting."

"Reigh?" I gasped. It had to be. Every detail, even the scar across his nose, was the same.

"Hardly," he scoffed. "But don't worry, you're not the first to confuse us. I doubt you'll be the last."

"Who are you, then?"

"I have many names," he replied, his grin widening to show pointed canine teeth. "But Reigh likes to call me Noh."

My throat tightened. "You're that dark spirit, the one giving Reigh his power."

"More or less. The power belongs to both of us," he purred, leaning forward on his throne as his eyes flickered over me appraisingly. "But I doubt you came here for a speech on the specifics of divine magic."

A bolt of lightning snapped through the air, popping off the ground only feet away from us. It hit so close I could practically taste the current crackling over my tongue.

"What's happening?" I yelped, throwing myself closer to Aubren and dragging his head into my lap to try and shield him.

Noh rose from his throne, slowly descending toward us. "Using so much of *her* power without the completion of the ritual is forbidden. It's causing a rupture between Desmiol and the Vale," he said, pausing to tilt his head at us curiously. "Look at his hand."

I did, my breath catching in my chest as I spied a wide, open gash across Aubren's palm. It was as if someone had sliced a dagger deep into his flesh, but instead of bleeding, what oozed out of the wound looked like the same black, inky substance that had come from his eyes in the mortal world. It puddled on the ground and coated his arm all the way to his elbow, giving off a smell like molten tar. "W-what is that?"

"A defilement." Noh folded his arms, eyebrows drawing together into a dissatisfied frown. "This is what becomes of those who try to implant her power into a mortal vessel. Unlike Reigh, his body cannot withstand it, so it consumes him. It burns him from the inside out, searing through flesh and devouring his spirit. Soon neither will exist ... in any world."

Oh Fates. No; this couldn't happen. There had to be something; some way to fix it! "Can you stop it?" I pleaded.

Noh's frown deepened. "Perhaps," he offered. "But it would require the use of spirit energy. A vast amount, I should think. The defilement has already fractured his soul. To repair it, I would need the soul of another."

Jaevid had warned me not to even speak to this spirit. He'd insisted I should stay away from him, and I had to wonder why. Was Noh lying? Could he really help Aubren? Or was he just trying to steal my soul?

Not that I had any choice. I would not let Aubren die like this.

Combing my fingers through his shaggy, dark-gold hair, I took a deep breath. Cruelty and violence had never come easily to him. He wasn't like me. Yes, he'd made mistakes. We both had. But he was softer, kinder, and a better person than I'd ever been.

He was worth saving.

I fixed Noh with a glare. "Can you use my soul to repair his?"

He blinked, his gaze darting between us. "I could. But you do realize this would mean surrendering your spirit entirely. There would be no afterlife for you—pleasant or otherwise. You would simply cease to exist. Not even Jaevid and all the power of Paligno could undo it."

I swallowed hard. "How do I know you're even telling the truth? How do I know this isn't a trick?"

One corner of his mouth twitched at a smirk. "I suppose you'll just have to take it on faith. What other choice do you have?"

Panicked, anxious heat flushed through me. He was right. There was no other choice. With Jaevid's warning still ringing in my head, I felt the words slip out. "Please save him."

Noh crouched down before us, his eerie eyes like two bottomless pits of eternal abyss as they studied me. I expected to see evil there. But there wasn't. His boyish face stared back at me with a look of pure confusion and something that might have been sympathy. Did he truly feel bad about this? Why? He wanted to kill people, right? I was giving him permission to do that in the most extreme way imaginable. So why did he look so ... sad?

"You would truly give up your soul to save his?"

"I would." I brushed a hand over Aubren's stubbly jaw. "He'd do the same for me."

Noh's expression dimmed. "It is a shame we never met before now. Your spirit has always intrigued me. I am not pleased to see it end this way," he muttered as he began to reach out for me, as though he were going to take my face in his hands. "Close your eyes, Jenna."

I stole one last look at the mysterious stranger, who was still lurking nearby, watching us. Then I smiled down at my brother. Aubren would never understand this. He'd blame himself. But I had no other alternative. I shouldn't have left him at Northwatch. I should have made Jaevid stay or helped Reigh—anything.

"Be strong, Aubren. They're going to need you more than ever," I murmured as I kissed his forehead.

Not wanting to see it coming, I squeezed my eyes shut as Noh's frigid fingertips brushed my cheeks. My breath caught, and I trembled, resisting the instinct to cringe away. Would it hurt? Would I feel anything at all? Gods, what was I doing? I didn't want to die. I hadn't even said goodbye to Phillip!

I held my breath and waited for the end.

"STOP," A DEEP VOICE SPOKE OVER US.

My eyes flew open, staring up at the strange tall man who had followed me here. His cryptic, disapproving frown reminded me of when my father caught me doing something I wasn't supposed to—like cutting Aubren's hair with a pair of sewing scissors when we were little.

"You really intend on going through with this?" With his arms crossed and jaw set, he glared down at us as though waiting for an explanation.

"Y-yes." My voice hitched. I scrambled to keep my nerve. Every second we put this off made me question it even more. I was trusting this being, Noh, but I had no proof he could even do as he'd promised.

The man shook his head. "Then you leave me no choice."

Grabbing my arm with surprising strength, he dragged me away from Noh and Aubren and flung me aside. I clambered to my feet, shouting angry curses. What the hell was he doing? This was my decision, my responsibility to—

He seized Noh by the collar of his black robes and snarled, "You take me, not her. Understood? Use my soul to repair his. Do it now."

What? Why? Why would he do this?

"No! You can't!" I cried out.

The man shot me a silencing glare over his shoulder. "When you see Jaevid again, you must give him this message. Tell him that his father is sorry ... for everything." His face screwed up and he looked away, back toward Noh. "It won't make it right. I know that. I can't describe what it felt like, to be trapped inside my own head, to see the monster I was becoming. I couldn't do anything to stop it. But I know that doesn't make it right. He deserved so much better. They all did."

"You're ... " I gasped. "You're Jaevid's father?"

He didn't reply.

It didn't matter. He didn't have to say another word. I saw it—and it hit me like a punch to the gut. All the wind rushed out of my lungs as the realization settled in. That was why he looked so familiar. Jaevid favored him a lot, in spite of the elf ears and ash-gray hair. They had the same strong lines to their features, serious brows, and high cheekbones.

But this man was no hero, not according to Maldobar's history. He was the one who had started the Gray War, which had spanned more than twenty years and killed thousands of good people, both human and elf. He was a traitor, a thief, and, if my father's stories were true, he had been a cruel father to Jaevid, as well.

"I am truly sorry for what I did to him; for what that *thing* turned me into. Swear it to me," he rumbled under his breath. "Swear you'll tell him. You must."

My throat went dry. "I will," I promised.

Noh didn't say a word as Ulric Broadfeather surrendered. As soon as his hands brushed Ulric's face, the man stiffened and froze in place.

It only took an instant. Ulric's already translucent body shimmered, beginning to glow brightly. The light grew, shining like a white mist until his form had completely dissolved.

The light stung my eyes. It was too much. I had to look away.

The rumble of thunder and sizzle of lightning suddenly hushed. A tingling chill made every hair on my arms prickle. I held my breath and dared to look back.

Ulric was gone.

Overhead, the churning black cloud had dissipated. Now there was only more endless, bleak gray sky. Even Noh had vanished, leaving behind nothing apart from an empty throne.

But my brother—he was moving!

Noh had kept his word.

"Reigh!" Aubren shouted as he bolted up, shambling shakily to his feet. He turned in a circle, eyes wide and darting around frantically. His face blanched with panic as he seemed to notice the strangeness of the eerie, colorless world around us. "Reigh?"

Then he saw me. His mouth fell open.

Tears blurred my vision and I let out a shrill, desperate cry. "Aubren!"

"Jenna," he called back as he ran toward me. We met halfway, and I clenched my arms around his neck as tight as I could.

For a moment we stood still, holding one another. I couldn't remember the last time I'd hugged him like this. Maybe after Mother died?

"Are you all right? What happened?" He paused, looking around again. "Where are we?"

"I'm fine," I whispered, pulling back and sliding my hand into his. I didn't want to lose that contact. I didn't want to lose him again. "And there isn't time to explain now. We have to go back."

"Go back where?"

"Home." The word tasted bitter now. I couldn't understand why. I shivered, clinging to his arm as that chill lingered on my skin. My heart hardened, feeling like a heavy, cold stone in my chest. Ulric had almost destroyed Maldobar and Luntharda. I wanted to hate him. I should have—everyone else did.

But how could I?

Aubren gave my hand a firm squeeze. "Let's go then."

CHAPTER NINE

Passing back through the dark, churning waters of that well was no less terrifying than it had been the first time. It took some convincing to get Aubren to do it. But this time, the time spent whirling in that black chaos ended quickly. No sooner had I felt that constricting, crushing cold engulf me than a pair of strong hands reached out to take mine. Their warmth pulled me from the dark, and I awoke lying next to Aubren on the floor of the tent.

I was alive—I had made it back from the Vale.

The warm glow of candlelight and the gentle touch of a leathery palm against my face drew my gaze up. Jaevid and Phillip were leaning over me with similar expressions of mute astonishment. I could understand Phillip's surprise. But Jaevid? Really? Had he thought I wouldn't come back? Good to know he had no faith in me whatsoever.

"Jenna, can you hear me?" Jaevid asked quietly as he withdrew his hand.

I managed a drowsy grin. "Told you I could do it."

He cracked a smile and let out a relieved chuckle. "I'll never doubt you again."

"Good."

Phillip's eyes welled as he threw his arms around me, pulling me up into a desperate embrace. "Thank the gods!"

"Phillip! I-I can't ... you're squeezing too hard," I wheezed against his shoulder.

"Oh!" He let me go and sat back, ducking his head sheepishly. "I'm sorry. It's just ... you stopped breathing. Even your heart quit beating. But Jaevid said you weren't dead; he said he could sense you in the Vale."

I turned, my eyes tracking Jaevid as he skirted around us to kneel back down at my brother's side. Aubren had yet to stir from where he lay, eyes closed and expression now serene. His skin had regained its normal, sun-bronzed hue, but he wasn't moving. My pulse raced with worry. "Is he all right? Did it work?"

"Yes." Jaevid's shoulders sagged with relief. "The spreading of that power through his body has left him physically exhausted, but he'll be fine. He just needs to rest. He should be better by morning."

Jaevid reached for Aubren's arm, holding it up to get a better look by the light of the candle. The mark still stained my brother's palm and forearm with ominous black runes. My stomach soured. Why was the defilement still there? Hadn't Noh fixed it?

"It didn't work." My body drooped.

"No, it did," Jaevid corrected. "The mark seems to be stable now. It's no longer consuming him."

Phillip frowned. "But why isn't it gone?"

"I don't know. Think of it as a scar. Perhaps it will fade in time, or Reigh can remove it. We'll just have to wait and see. For now, let's just celebrate the fact that his life is no longer in danger. And it's all thanks to you, Jenna." He glanced up with a smile that made my insides scramble and my throat constrict like I might throw up. He looked *so* much like Ulric—the one who had *really* saved Aubren.

But how could I tell Jaevid that? I'd given my word, yes, but ... what would that news do to him? Did he even remember his father?

Thankfully, Jaevid didn't seem to notice my panic. "You should get some rest, as well. Dawn will be here soon, and then we'll have to make some decisions about what to do next. Your men will need you to be at your best."

"I'll stay with you, if you like," Phillip offered.

I nodded, easing back down onto the pallet next to Aubren's and curling up on my side so I could see him. When he did wake up, I wanted to be there. So much had happened since I last saw him. Jaevid was here, fighting with us. Reigh had been taken captive at Northwatch. Cernheist was lost. Now we had to find some way back to Halfax and pray our father would let us back into the city. Hopefully having Jaevid with us would help, but I honestly wasn't sure what to expect. There was so much I didn't know.

Suddenly, a pair of strong arms closed around my shoulders, pulling me back into a very warm and solid chest. "Jenna, it won't hurt to let it go for a few hours," Phillip's voice growled gently against my ear. His breath tickled along the side of my neck.

"How did you know I was—?"

He gave an amused snort. "We've practically known one another since birth. I can tell when you're overthinking something. Just rest, would you? The world won't fall apart in the next few hours."

"You don't know that. We have no idea what Argonox might have planned," I pointed out.

"Fair enough. But Jaevid is keeping watch. I doubt he'll sit back and spectate if that happens." His warm lips grazed the back of my ear.

Heat rose in my cheeks as he slid the collar of my tunic down to expose my neck. The sharp points of his canine teeth grazed my skin as he kissed me there, sending my pulse into a desperate flurry. Suddenly, Ulric, Argonox, and the end of the world were the last things on my mind.

"Phillip, stop, not here," I rasped. "Everyone's outside. What if Aubren wakes up? Not to mention Miri and Baroness Adeline will be back anytime."

"I thought I lost you, you know," he murmured, the words whispered softly against the nape of my neck. "Don't do that again. Don't go where I can't follow."

A hard knot caught in the back of my throat. Swallowing against it made my eyes water. I rolled over and hugged myself against him, hiding deep in his embrace. I wanted to tell him. I needed to tell *someone*. My thoughts scrambled, caught between keeping my word and the idea of what telling Jaevid about his father might do to him.

He pulled back enough to stare down at me, silver eyes shining with streaks of gold that caught in the warm light. "What's wrong?"

I ran my hands over his cheeks, caressing slate-colored skin and lightly tracing the intricate little white flecks that mottled his cheeks and forehead, as though he were freckled by stars. The switchbeast venom had changed him. It had made him into something many would fear. But I couldn't look at him without amazement. Terrifying, powerful, monstrous—he was many things now. But more than that, he was beautiful.

And he was mine.

"Jenna?" He sounded worried.

"We've never danced, have we?"

He arched an eyebrow. "What?"

"At any of the balls and parties. We've known each other for so long, but we've never danced. Right?"

Phillip's gray skin went a little rosy around his cheeks and nose as his catlike pupils widened. "I-I ... uh, no. I don't believe we have. In my defense, however, you have a habit of snarling like a cranky dragon at anyone who approaches you for a dance."

"Since when has my snarling ever discouraged you?" I sighed and burrowed in closer against him. I let my head rest on his shoulder, right against his neck. "Promise me we will."

His heart was racing. It thumped wildly against my ear as he held me tighter, his chin resting on top of my head. Was he actually nervous? Interesting. He always acted so smooth and assured; I never would have guessed that anything I said would make him anxious.

"You honestly think I'll be invited to any more balls looking like this?" he mumbled.

"Tail aside, you're still the Duke of Barrowton."

"Perhaps, if it's ever rebuilt. I'm sure the Tibrans did a fine job demolishing every square inch of it." He gave a snorting chuckle. "The entire noble court will need new underwear after I make my entrance. I suppose that might make an excellent party favor to hand out at the door."

"With Maldobar's emblem stitched on them?"

"Oh, of course."

I couldn't resist a smile. "So, does that mean you promise to dance with me?"

"Only if you can assure me there will be minimal snarling." I could hear the mischievous grin in his voice.

"I'll see what I can do."

***

MY MIND HELD ME HOSTAGE IN THE DARK, TWISTING AND TURNING THROUGH everything that could possibly go wrong. The Tibrans attacking. Beckah returning. Aubren's defilement beginning to consume him again. Halfax falling to Argonox. My kingdom burning, forced to surrender to a foreign tyrant. My people becoming slave soldiers in his legions. Me, chained to his heel like a prize.

The memory of his face, his words, were scorched into my brain as though written there in molten flame.

"You would become legendary. A queen for the ages. A goddess."

My breath caught, and my chest seized as I jolted awake, barely able to stifle my own scream. Cold sweat clung to my skin. I shivered as I sat up and curled over, hugging my knees to my chest. I wasn't back there. It was a dream, nothing more. Argonox was miles away.

Or so I prayed.

Lying next to me, Phillip was stretched out on his back with his mouth open and his clothes rumpled. He snored softly, never twitching or stirring as I slid off the pallet and began lacing up my boots. I envied that—being able to sleep like nothing was wrong and the world wasn't about to come crashing down around us. It must have been nice.

Grabbing the heavy, wool-padded tunic I wore over my thin undershirt, I slipped it over my head. Then I grabbed my cloak and blades, swiftly buckling them around me before leaving the tent. It took a moment to pick out a safe path to walk so I didn't step on anyone's fingers or toes on my way out. Miri, Baroness Adeline, Aubren, Eirik, Aedan, and even Calem had settled in and were all sleeping soundly on their pallets. It filled the interior of the tent with the peaceful sounds of deep breathing and the occasional snore.

Outside the tent, the cold mountain air chilled my skin and numbed the throbbing in my head. The smell of crisp frost and fresh pine was soothing. My boots crunched over the snowy ground as I walked to where Haldor was still sitting up, keeping watch by the fire only a short distance from the tent.

"How is everything?" I asked as I stopped across from him, stretching my fingers to the warmth of the flames.

Haldor studied me, as though silently wondering why I wasn't sleeping like the others. "Quiet," he replied at last. "Leaving on such short notice meant many of the supplies the refugees had gathered had to be left behind. There isn't much in the way of food for them, but we are making do. There are enough skilled hunters and trappers among us that no one will starve before they reach Luntharda."

"That's something, I suppose."

His mouth scrunched slightly, expression steeling into a look I knew all too well. "Permission to speak frankly, Your Highness?"

"You know you don't have to ask, Haldor," I said flatly. "Just as you know I *hate* it when people call me that, especially other dragonriders."

"In this case, I feel appropriate respect is necessary if I'm going to mention this," he muttered, his sharp features drawing into a tight, grim frown.

"Oh? So what you're saying is that this is something that will probably make me angry, right?"

His gaze met mine, eyes gleaming like warm amber in the light of the flames. "Undoubtedly. But it must be said." He paused there, combing his silky black hair out of his face as though to prepare himself for what was to come. "What happened at Cernheist was unacceptable. As a dragonrider, I am ashamed."

"Why?"

"Because we put every person in Cernheist at risk. All due respect to the one who ended the Gray War, but Jaevid Broadfeather is not fighting as a dragonrider. If we are to win this war, let alone survive, then we will have to stand together. Diving out after personal vendettas, forging alone like some sort of martyr for the cause, is not the dragonrider way. Our strength has always been in our unity. We train to fight and fly as one impenetrable force, but that is not what I saw today," he fumed quietly. "Did Jaevid come back to save Maldobar or to settle old scores?"

I crossed my arms. "You think we all should have fought her together?"

"No. The civilians did need our help. A few of us could have managed that. But Jaevid shouldn't have gone after her alone," he retorted. The faster he spoke, the more his accent slipped. It was the only time I'd heard it come out in such force—apart from a few incidents that involved a nearly lethal amount of ale. "You and I both saw what happened. You know he was not fighting to win. We've heard of his power, what he's truly capable of. He was just toying with her. Because of that, she escaped. She is still a threat, and now she is in our blind spot. The only thing more dangerous than an enemy we cannot see is one that the strongest among us doesn't have the stomach to kill."

"Point taken." I rubbed my chin, mulling it over.

"Answer me this, and think it over carefully, Jenna. The next time we meet some fragment from Jaevid's past that Argonox has dredged up from the dead and charged with foul magic, who is going to be the one to pay the price if he cannot bring himself to kill it? Innocent civilians? One of us? You?" He hung his head, turning his focus back to poking at the embers with a long stick. "I ask because I am not prepared to bear that shame. I am a dragonrider. I swore an oath, and I hold myself to it. As dragonriders, we are to leave our personal agendas at the doorpost and do what is necessary to protect Maldobar and its people. Now I must wonder if Jaevid remembers that, and if he doesn't, if he should even be called a true dragonrider anymore."

The crackling of the fire filled the heavy silence that hung between us. He was right—I didn't like hearing this. I didn't like the idea of questioning Jaevid or his intentions. But ... Haldor had a point. We had been lucky this time. But if Jaevid hesitated at the wrong moment, if he couldn't bring himself to do what was necessary, we might not be so lucky next time.

Still, I knew why Jaevid had hesitated. I'd done the same thing when faced with Aubren under the same kind of control. The sight of him like that, ready to kill me because of that defilement, had hit me in a soft spot I wasn't expecting. I doubted Jaevid had been expecting it, either.

"Where is he?" I asked at last.

Haldor gave a slight shrug and gestured over one shoulder with a thumb. "With the dragons, of course. He said something about healing Vexi. I take it he meant that wild green one." He gave the fire a forceful poke, making one of the logs collapse and sending a shower of sparks fluttering up into the night sky like fireflies. "Jenna, please don't mistake my frustration for ungratefulness. I am glad he's here to help. I just don't like seeing innocent people put in harm's way, least of all by us."

"I understand. And I appreciate your honesty, Haldor. I'm not angry. Well, not about that, at least." Taking in a little more of the fire's warmth against my backside, I strode past him—but not before giving the back of his head a substantial smack.

He cursed at me in his mother's tongue, which he knew I didn't understand. That's the funny thing about profanity; you don't have to speak the language to know when you're being insulted.

I grinned and kept walking. "That's for using my noble title, by the way."

CHAPTER TEN

I found Jaevid a not far from camp under the shelter of a cluster of sturdy pine trees. He stood in the center of all our dragons like an old man feeding very large, scaly, fire-breathing pigeons. They gathered in close to him, pushing and muscling against one another as he ran his hands over Vexi's head. Her lime green scales were easy to spot, even if she was smaller than the rest of the flock. Occasionally, one of them would hiss and snap, and there would be a spat of nipping and growling before he broke them up with a few harsh words.

The only dragon that didn't seem enamored by Jaevid's presence was his own. Mavrik lay like a mountain of royal blue scales and leathery black wings, relaxing in the snow as he watched the younger dragons squabble. His body barely fit under the cover of the trees. He'd apparently dug himself a hole in the dirt right at the base of some of them to lie in.

"Aren't you supposed to be making them behave?" I asked as I stood beside his great horned head, picking out a few patches of my own dragon's purple hide amidst the crowd.

Mavrik gave an unimpressed snort, melting some of the snow in front of his snout with his hot breath.

"He's got no place to talk," Jaevid said, emerging from the group as though he were parting a curtain of writhing scales, spines, and horns. "When he was younger, he had a knack for mischief, too."

Mavrik snorted again and closed his eyes, smacking his chops indignantly.

"Oh yes, you did," Jaevid shot him a look. "That attitude is why the dragonriders were about to clip your wing tendons, if I remember correctly."

I tapped my chin. "I've heard this story. Ironically, it's one of the few my father didn't tell. I guess he didn't know you then. But Phillip's father used to tell it all the time."

"Sile Derrick," Jaevid recalled, his tone softening. Sadness flickered across his features so quickly I almost missed it. "At the time, I couldn't decide if he was trying to make me a dragonrider or offer me to this scaly monster as an evening snack."

Seeing that sorrow on his face was like a knife twisting in my gut. Haldor was right—those memories were affecting him, and whatever made his determination waver endangered our success and Maldobar's survival. I'd promised to tell him about Ulric. But now ... Gods, was that the right thing to do? If it shook his resolve even more, if it hit the wrong chords, I'd be risking the fate of my kingdom and all its people.

"You were supposed to be resting." Jaevid spoke up again, changing the subject.

"I've never been the sit quietly and rest kind of girl," I replied.

He laughed softly. "I see. Something on your mind, then?"

A jolt of panic shot through me. My mind raced for something—anything to say. "I-I just wondered how Vexi is."

He tipped his head in a slight shrug. "Upset. Angry. Afraid. They all are, really."

"The dragons are afraid? Of what?"

His expression darkened. "Something else is coming. It's a long way off, probably in Northwatch, but I can feel it like the gathering of a distant storm. Argonox is using more of Reigh's power."

I shivered at the thought. "To revive more of our dead? Or defile the living?"

Jaevid shook his head. "It's too far away to be certain."

Well that wasn't comforting at all.

Out of the group of dragons, my handsome, purple companion lumbered toward me, lowering his head, and chirping musically. I smiled, stretching my hands out to meet him as he pushed his snout against my chest. Tracing my fingers along the horned ridges along his cheeks and the teal stripes that mottled his dark violet hide, I let my head rest against his for a moment. The air was bitter cold, but his body was warm. It felt good.

"Your bond with him is strong." Jaevid regarded us with a strange little grin on his lips. "Much stronger than any other I've ever sensed. Well, apart from mine with Mavrik. I'm glad to see Mavrik's hatchlings have chosen their riders well."

Wait, what? "Mavrik's hatchlings?"

Jaevid nodded toward the other dragons, who were still sniffing Vexi over with tense curiosity. In their midst, she sank low, her ears pinned back, and tail curled in close in submission. "She and Phevos are his direct descendants. Phevos is older, hatched from an earlier clutch, but Mavrik is their sire. I suspect Turq is a relation, as well. Distant nephew, maybe."

"Oh." I looked at Phevos again, trying to pick out similarities between my dragon and the blue king drake snoozing nearby. Apart from their eyes and spines, there wasn't much to be found. "I didn't realize."

"Felix has been busy making the world a better place for them, it seems." Jaevid's tone softened, his expression tinged with sadness as he wandered over to stand next to me.

"Because of you," I clarified. "He dedicated a lot of time restructuring the dragonrider forces. He retired the title of Lord General permanently. Now, the station is called 'High Commander,' and he oversees all the dragonrider watches and reports directly to my father."

Jaevid's smile was cryptic. "And who is it that holds that office now? You?"

"Hah!" I shot him a look. Was that an attempt at a joke? "I've only been a lieutenant for three years—and against my father's will, if you remember. He'd never consider me for that office, and I wouldn't want it even if he did. I wasn't even a seasoned rider until this mess started. I've not earned that kind of authority, and there are much more qualified riders for it."

"More qualified, perhaps," he mused. "But better? I'm not sure your companions would agree with that."

I glanced down at the tops of my boots to hide my grin. "Fair enough."

"So, who rides as High Commander?"

"His name is Ruslan Morrig. A good man, by all accounts. I understand he comes from a proud dragonrider bloodline. His father was—"

"—an instructor," Jaevid finished for me. His brow creased, and he flashed me another one of those quick, haunted looks. What was he remembering now?

"You knew him?"

He nodded. "He taught me when I was a fledgling. Combat training, I think."

"Everyone says Ruslan is doing his bloodline proud. I admit, I've only seen him a few times at court, so I can't tell you that for certain. But my father was very selective with who he put in power after the war ended. He retired out many of the old officers and brought in new blood," I recalled. "Then he started enraging noble houses and merchants all over Maldobar by passing new decrees to protect the wild dragons. It was forbidden to capture them from the wild or harvest and sell their eggs. Dragons already in captivity could remain that way, since many of them would find it hard to return to their wild kin but clipping their wing tendons will now earn you a jail cell."

Jaevid arched a brow. "And that upset the nobility and merchants?"

I smirked. "Of course. Selling and breeding dragons has lined their pockets for hundreds of years. I'd expect you to remember that, old man."

His cheeks flushed, and he rubbed the back of his neck. "I wasn't exactly a noble before, you know. But yes, I suppose I do recall many of my peers being ... more finely-dressed than I ever was."

"Except for my father, I'm sure."

"True," he added with a nervous chuckle. "I take it he still has no taste for silk or lace?"

"Gods, no." I rolled my eyes. "Not that I do, either. But he used to go straight from working with the infantry horses and dragons at the stables to court meetings without even bathing. He'd have bits of hay stuck in his beard. You could smell him from across the room."

Jaevid laughed—a real laugh this time. A deep, rich, and nearly musical sound. It made his pale eyes shine like aquamarines in the moonlight as he tilted his head back and sighed skyward. "Some things never change, I suppose."

I stared at him, studying the hard lines of his defined cheekbones and fierce brow. Hints and traces of the hero I'd seen chiseled into every fountain and marble bust throughout the kingdom were hidden there, like a ghostly whisper on his darkly tanned skin. But more than anything, I saw Ulric, and the thought turned my stomach sour.

I couldn't tell him. This resistance, our small company of mismatched warriors, was already hanging by a thread. Any tug in the wrong direction might snap it. And what then? Maldobar might fall with it. I couldn't risk that. So I swallowed that secret like a bitter pill, and promised myself I would tell him later. I would keep my word, but only when this was all over and done.

Providing we weren't all bound in Tibran chains, that is.

A deep, thrumming growl from Mavrik's throat made everyone pause—dragons included.

Jaevid and I stopped, watching as the king drake unfurled from his resting place and shook the snow from his back, snapping his jaws as his nostrils flared and sniffed the air. The other dragons did the same, clicking and chirping at one another as they bristled. Phevos lowered his head next to me, growing deep in his chest.

My body shuddered with a surge of panic. I looked at Jaevid. "Tibrans?"

His brow furrowed, jaw setting as he studied his own dragon for a moment. "No," he answered. "It seems someone has come to meet us."

"Meet us?"

His frown was as tense as it was ominous as he strode beside me back to camp. The freezing wind whipped through his shaggy ash-colored hair, and one hand rested on the pommel of the scimitar clipped to his belt. "We must gather our party. It's time to leave." I couldn't tell by his tone if this was a good or bad thing.

BACK AT OUR TENT, HALDOR WAS ALREADY ON HIS FEET, BOW AND QUIVER strung over his back as he put on his riding gauntlets. "There's a disturbance in the camp."

Jaevid nodded. "It's all right. They haven't come to fight. But we should be ready to move out as soon as possible. Go and wake the others." He waved a hand, gesturing for me to follow. "Let's go and greet our guests."

There wasn't time to ask who. Jaevid immediately turned on a boot heel and led the way down the slope. We picked our way along the steep, icy path into the camp where all the other civilian refugees and a few scattered Maldobarian soldiers from Cernheist had dug in for the night. Their tents and wagons were packed full of the young, elderly, or remaining injured. Those who couldn't find a place to sleep out of the wind had hunkered down beside one of the many campfires blazing in the weak light of dawn.

But as Jaevid and I passed by, everyone began to emerge. The camp buzzed with whispers. Children peeked out of the tent flaps. Men picked up anything they could to use as a weapon—old swords, hammers, pitchforks, and hatches—and began to follow. They weren't an army, not by a long shot, but I could only guess that seeing Jaevid made them feel the odds were in their favor if this was indeed some kind of attack.

Jaevid stopped at the edge of camp, facing the miles of frigid wilderness that stood between Luntharda and us. The terrain was thick with evergreens and the first rays of the rising sun painted the snowy slopes and mountainsides pastel shades of pink, orange, and lavender. Facing it all, Jaevid stood firm and tall, his shoulders squared and expression stony.

Whatever he sensed—I couldn't see it. Not yet.

Then the soft blast of a horn carried through the cold, morning air. My pulse raced. I *knew* that sound.

They appeared like white phantoms under the dark of the trees. Gray elves dressed in full armor, their feathered war headdresses fluttering in the wind, sat astride huge, elk-like creatures. Each one was as large as a draft horse, but their shape was far more slender and dynamic. Their shaggy hides were as white as untouched snow and shimmered like platinum in the morning light. With heads crowned with sloping white antlers boasting twenty or more lethal points, I recognized them at once.

A faundra cavalry.

The rider at the front of the formation wore a grander headdress than the rest, the mask pulled down to cover most of his face. He also carried a pair of duel scimitars belted to his hips and a long cloak of some strange, blue-tinted fur that was striped in black. I was familiar enough with Gray elf customs to know that only those of the royal bloodline would ever wear something that ornate. I'd seen this ensemble before, though only at court during formal ceremonies. He was a prince—one of King Jace and Queen Araxie's sons.

The rider stopped less than ten yards from us, throwing a hand up to the rest of his company. They all came to halt behind him, their mounts snorting, stamping, and tossing their heads. My head swam with wonder at the sight of them. I'd never seen a full cavalry like this. There must have been fifty of them at least. The sight of so many noble beasts standing in formation, their powerful bodies wearing fine leather armor and their riders stone-faced and proud, put a surge of adrenaline in my veins.

The prince dismounted, leaving his faundra stag to paw at the ground and snort as he came striding toward us with his long cloak fluttering at his heels. I knew him—even before he threw back the mask of his headdress to cast a broad smile at Jaevid and me.

His olive skin gave a rich contrast to his deeply set green eyes. They were sharp and quick as they glanced at our pitiful excuse for a camp, his long brown hair catching in the wintry air. The points of his ears were much shorter than the rest of his full-blooded company. They looked more like Jaevid's, in fact. They had the same squareness and robustness tainting their otherwise perfect elven beauty, thanks to his father's human blood.

"Greetings, cousin," he offered with a heavy elven accent. "It seems you're in need of assistance."

"Cousin?" Jaevid's bewildered gaze flickered to me.

Before I could explain, the elven prince gave a deep bow. "Forgive me, lapiloque. I am Judan, son of Queen Araxie. I believe that makes us family, doesn't it? Regardless, I watch the westward jungles. That is my charge as Second Son of Luntharda. After your tree disappeared from our horizon, many warriors began to amass in the royal city, eager to see the Tibrans undone. They rally under my mother's banner and want to join you in the fight. Our scouts have kept us well-informed of your movements." He laughed, flashing me a roguish grin and wink. "You've been very busy. Sieging Northwatch on your own with only a handful of dragons? And here I wondered if the tales of lapiloque's insane bravery were puffed up by storytellers over the years. I'm pleased to be mistaken."

"I'm afraid the siege wasn't so successful, unfortunately," Jaevid sighed. "We lost a member of our company there. He's being held captive and stands to make things ... very complicated moving forward."

"So I'm told. My scouts came with harrowing reports of a creature made of rot and bone carrying a rider in Seraph's armor." Judan's smile faded and he rubbed his chin. "When we saw smoke rise from Cernheist, we feared the worst."

"Argonox sent that thing after us," I affirmed. "The city survived, but the people could not remain there. Cernheist is not defensible, not against that manner of monster."

Judan's eyes narrowed as he looked around at our company again. Lines of worry deepened in his brow as his gaze lingered upon the tents, where dozens of children peeked out, their eyes glittering with mystification as they pointed and marveled at the Gray elf cavalry. "Where will they go?"

"To Luntharda." Jaevid's answer came firmly. It was not open for debate. "They can't stay in the wilds, and they can't go back to Cernheist. The Tibrans have all but taken the western coast. They need a safe place to wait until this has ended."

"Then we will guide them there." Judan gave a dragonrider salute, clasping his fist across his chest and bowing slightly. "It is not far to the border, but the road is steep. My scouts on shrikes can send word ahead to prepare to receive them."

Jaevid arched a brow. "I haven't seen any shrikes."

That cunning little smirk curled up Judan's lips again, making his green eyes sparkle with delighted mischief. "I should hope not. My father took great care in training all his sons in the arts of subtly and stealth, something he claims to have learned in his early life. In turn, I was permitted to construct and train a very specialized order of scouts who work exclusively at gathering information while remaining undetected. Granted, this war has been the first official test of our skills. I'm pleased to report that so far, we are yielding excellent results."

"You've managed to spy on the Tibrans?" I couldn't keep from sounding shocked.

"Oh yes," he announced with a proud flourish of his hand. "All we required was official order from the queen to begin—something she wouldn't have allowed unless there was enough support amongst the people to engage in this war. Now that we are on the move, I can supply you with information about Tibran legion positions, outposts, supply routes—you name it."

"That," I gasped. "I want all of that. Right now."

"Of course. Did you have any particular region in mind, Princess?"

"We should focus on what might stand between Halfax and us." I glanced to Jaevid, relieved to find him nodding in agreement. At least we were on the same page again.

Judan winked a gleaming emerald eye. "At your service, my lady. And might I just say, you are as fetching as ever. A shame Maldobar has still not learned to appreciate the compelling beauty of a woman who knows her way around a blade."

Heat rose in my cheeks. I wanted to say something, change the subject, but all that came out were breathy choking sounds.

"Some of us have," Phillip's voice growled at my back.

Judan's expression blanked as he gaped up at the towering figure that stepped in close to my side, arms crossed, feline tail flicking. He reached for the hilt of his blades, hands hesitating as he studied Phillip with mixture of shock and horror. "Paligno preserve us, what manner of creature is that?"

Phillip growled and put an arm around my shoulder. "The kind that can snap you in half if he suspects you're messing with *his* lady."

My neck and ears blazed with embarrassment. "N-now, Phillip, let's just—"

"Phillip?" Judan sucked in a sharp breath, his eyebrows shooting up as he glanced between the rest of us as though searching for an explanation. "*Duke Phillip Derrick?*"

"None other," Phillip rumbled.

Putting his hands up in surrender, Judan managed a nervous chuckle. "You, uh, look a bit different, my friend. I suspect there's a good story attached to this?"

"Perhaps not a good one, but a story indeed," Jaevid spoke up, motioning toward the camp. "We should meet with the rest of our company while the refugees prepare to move. Perhaps your cavalrymen can lend them a hand?"

Judan's proud grin was back full force. "It would be our honor, lapiloque."

CHAPTER ELEVEN

Men like Judan had always confounded me. They cruised the waters of the royal court like sharks in an ocean of polished marble and glittering glass. They were always on the hunt for any advantageous relationship they might kindle there. In that world, Judan's reputation painted him like an elusive stag, strutting through the ballrooms with starry-eyed noble women trailing in his wake. He was the only one of Jace's sons who had never married, although I'd heard he had no trouble lining up options. If rumors were true, then he practically had a queue outside his chamber door just in case he decided to marry, but no one at court could claim to have ever crossed that threshold. Not yet, anyway.

Once, the ladies at court had sneered at the idea of a halfbreed in their midst. Now, men like Judan were a point of intrigue. It was a ridiculous and sad spectacle, watching them all vying for his attention as though they'd lost all sense of self-respect. I'd promised myself a long time ago never to be that kind of woman. No man's attention was worth the price of my dignity—even if he was blessed with a handsome build and more than his share of that half-elven prettiness.

And Judan was *very* pretty.

Swaggering forward to take my hand and kiss my wrist seemed as natural as breathing for him—something I couldn't even begin to comprehend. Phillip seemed to grasp it well enough, though. Or at least, he was wise to Judan's game. He stood beside me like a guarding wall, planting his imposing frame directly between us as we gathered around our campfire to exchange what information we could while the refugees prepared to move out.

Judan was full of useful intelligence his scouts had collected by watching the

Tibrans. He admitted they were still receiving more as his men moved further down the western coast, but he could draw some conclusions from what they had already provided about the Tibran movements.

"They struggle with the mountain roads," he explained, gesturing to a detailed map etched into a large piece of hide he'd brought along. "It seems they cannot tunnel through the stone. And without any means of moving in the air, Argonox's forces must clear them of snow and debris before they can maneuver their war machines through. It takes time, so their progress has been slow coming in from the western coastline. Even more so, they struggle through the Marshlands. The deep mud and bogs have slowed their advance to a crawl. The soggy earth and water causes their tunnels to flood or cave in. Even the river has given them great difficulty. The spring storms have swollen its waters far beyond the established banks. The waters run fast and deep, and none of the existing bridges can bear the weight of their war machines. They are forced to wait until the water retreats." His wistful smile was filled with devious pride. "Apparently Maldobar's rugged terrain is not one the Tibrans are accustomed to. It's as though the very land itself has joined the fight to slow their advance."

"They won't stay grounded for long," Haldor murmured. "Not now that Argonox has found a way to force dragons into submission with that foul magic, I'm willing to bet good coin we can anticipate more aerial attacks."

"Then you should go quickly. Ride hard and do not stop unless you must. Here are a few places in the Marshlands where you'll be safe to camp and rest overnight." He gestured to the map, and we all leaned in to study the points. "But you should know, we are not the only ones using stealth to watch our enemy's movements. My scouts have come across many Tibran spies. We've been killing all we can without risking exposure or capture. No doubt those agents are watching the skies for dragonriders very carefully."

"Perhaps we should wait to move at nightfall?" Haldor rubbed the back of his neck, glancing worriedly up at me. "We would be harder to spot."

"Not for a spy of any skill," a deep voice spoke over us. Everyone paused, turning to watch my older brother emerge from our tent.

My heart jumped into my throat.

Dressed in bits and pieces of borrowed armor, Aubren stood with his mouth drawn into a tight, grim line and his body tense—as though he half-expected we might attack him. His shaggy dark golden hair had been brushed back away from his face, revealing deeper lines in his brow and dark, heavy circles under his eyes.

"A good point," Judan agreed quickly, not seeming to pick up on the rising tension in the air. He had no way of knowing what we'd just been through with Aubren.

My brother's fractured gaze drifted to me for a moment before he lowered his head and murmured, "You can't afford to sit here any longer. You should go now, keep above the cloud cover as much as possible."

Something in his voice made my stomach turn. What was he saying?

"You don't intend to go with us?" Jaevid guessed before I could speak.

Aubren wouldn't even look at him. "The fewer extra passengers you take, the faster you'll go. I'd be nothing but a burden to your progress now." He paused, looking past us to the refugees still breaking down camp. "Besides, someone should stay with them. Someone should warn Queen Araxie of the danger now that Reigh is ... " His voice faded, expression skewing as he looked away.

"Then we should speak alone." Jaevid stepped toward him, placing a hand on Aubren's shoulder to guide him away from the rest of our group.

My heart ached with every beat as I watched them walk away. What was this about? Was Jaevid going to ask him about what had happened while he was imprisoned at Northwatch? How that defilement had been put on him? Or what Reigh's current situation was?

Deep in my gut, another suspicion arose to gnaw away at my insides. Was it possible Jaevid knew about how Aubren had intended to betray him? If that was the case, I wanted to be there to speak up in my brother's defense. Yes, Aubren was an idiot for even imagining Argonox could be bargained with—but he wasn't a bad person. Aubren was a good man and nothing would ever persuade me otherwise.

Jaevid *needed* to know that.

I surged up to chase after them, only to be yanked to a choking halt by the neck of my own tunic. I whirled around, scowling up into Phillip's eerie feline eyes as he let go of the back of my shirt.

"You need to sit this one out," Phillip warned in a sharp whisper. "Let them handle it."

"But he's my brother!"

"Exactly. It doesn't take a divine gift to see that he's not in a good mental state right now. He's lucky to be alive. Let him have a little space." Phillip gave my cheek an affectionate stroke. "He'll come to you when he's ready to talk about it."

Phillip didn't understand—he couldn't. He didn't know what had happened in Northwatch or that Aubren had tried to betray Jaevid to the Tibrans.

Stealing a glance over my shoulder, I watched Jaevid and my brother disappear behind a clump of trees. My heart wrenched until I could hardly breathe. Whatever had happened with Argonox and Reigh, I wasn't dumb enough to assume Aubren would just brush off the last words we'd spoken to one another before this.

"We should decide now who else will go with the refugees to Luntharda," Haldor suggested, breaking the awkward tension in the air. He cleared his throat and cast me an expectant stare.

Right. I still had responsibilities here. Time to pull it together. There were still a lot of people counting on us.

"If Tibran spies are going to be tracking us, then we should use our numbers to at least cast as much confusion to their reports as possible. I suggest we split up and choose one of these places to rendezvous after nightfall." I panned a look around at our company, gauging their response.

Eirik raised his hand, and I had an immediate flashback to our fledgling training year. "Can I, uh, make a little suggestion?"

"You don't have to raise your hand. You can just say it." I tried not to laugh.

He blushed. "Right. Well, since I'm officially an unseated dragonrider, maybe it's better for me to go with Aubren and escort the refugees to Luntharda?"

That idiot. Escorting refugees? Did he honestly think I was buying that? All right, so that might have been his secondary concern, but I knew the primary reason—and she was sitting with her aunt within earshot of our war meeting, wrapped up in *his* cloak.

I couldn't resist a cattish grin. "Hmm. Well, I suppose someone should make sure the baroness and her niece arrive safely."

Eirik's flushed as red as a beet all the way to the tips of his ears. "R-right."

"That's rather mundane work for a dragonrider," Judan mused, his gaze flicking back and forth between us curiously. "Even an unseated one."

I waved a hand dismissively. "Oh, well, we must be absolutely certain that our noble families are taken care of and spare nothing but the finest of our warriors for that task. Wouldn't you agree, Phillip?"

"Absolutely." He was grinning, too.

"Then I'll, uh, go with them," Eirik croaked. "Just to make sure she—er—they get to Luntharda safely."

Phillip snickered.

I elbowed him in the ribs on my way to gesture to the map again. "In that case, I'll take a formation with Calem and Phillip. Haldor can fly wing end to Jaevid and take Aedan. We'll meet here at nightfall. Agreed?"

One by one, the rest of our company gave a nod or grunt of confirmation. We had a plan. We had a destination.

Now we just needed the tiniest bit of luck.

THE GODS WERE GRACIOUS ENOUGH TO GRANT US A BLEAK, GRAY SKY AS WE rushed through the final checks on all our saddles and gear. Another storm was approaching, bringing with it tall walls of clouds and the distant rumble of thunder over the mountain peaks. Foul weather was good—for us, anyway. In the lowlands it would muddy the roads and make the waters rise in the swamps and bogs. In the mountains, it would mean more snow, high winds, and another good freeze. Both would make things worse for our enemy, who apparently wasn't accustomed to the brutality of Maldobar's seasons.

It didn't take long to gather the dragons together. Jaevid seemed able to persuade and manipulate them without saying a word, probably because of his divine power. They gravitated to his side like eager puppies, still nipping and taunting one another. Vexi, however, was no longer among them.

When I asked about it, Jaevid confirmed that she'd vanished without a trace sometime in the night. My heart sank a bit. I didn't have to ask where she'd gone. Dragons who chose riders like she had selected Reigh were loyal to a fault. Their loyalty was relentless. He belonged to her now, and I knew better than to think she would abandon him at Northwatch—even after what she had endured already.

I just prayed that Argonox wouldn't capture her again. She seemed clever. Surely she had learned better than to get too close to the Tibrans.

At least, that's what I told myself as I tightened one of the girth straps on Phevos's saddle. I strained and pulled, struggling to wrestle the strap up one more notch. No luck. It wouldn't budge an inch.

"You!" I leaned around to glare at him. "Stop holding your breath! If this isn't tight, you'll be slinging me around all over the place."

Phevos grumbled, snapping his jaws defiantly before he went back to preening the scales on his wing arms.

"Stubborn, scaly donkey!" I cursed as I began pulling again.

Suddenly, a pair of large, gloved hands reached around me and gave the strap a stern yank. The buckle slipped into place with a *click*, and Phevos let out a cough. He swung his head around, eyes narrowed, and ears slicked back, puffing a snort of disapproval.

"Sometimes the cavalry horses do the same thing," Aubren mumbled as he stood back, putting a few feet of space between us.

I didn't know what to say. Before me, Aubren shifted his weight and refused to look me straight in the eye, keeping his right arm tucked in close against his side. The refugees were leaving. They were already setting out for Luntharda, flanked on all sides by Gray elf cavalry. I'd just assumed he had already left.

I cleared my throat. "So, you came to say goodbye?" Gods, the question sounded awkward, even to me.

"Something like that," he answered quietly, finally looking up with a despondent, fretful expression.

"Does it hurt?" I gestured to his arm, the one that still bore the defilement. He stood stiffly, still keeping his arm angled out of my direct sight even though it was covered by his clothing and gloves. "I can bear it. Jaevid insisted he would look into it again once this is all over." His voice caught, and his brow drew into a deep frown that made his jaw go rigid. "I ... I told him everything."

"You did?"

Aubren nodded slightly. "He forgave me." Looking down again, he rubbed his neck along the collar of his breastplate. "It's really him, isn't it? He's really here, fighting with us."

Somehow, it didn't seem like he wanted an answer—as though he were asking himself that question rather than me. I quirked my mouth enough to chew on the inside of my cheek and waited for him to get to the point.

"I keep expecting this to be a dream, that I'll wake up back in that *place*." He sucked in a sharp breath and shut his eyes tightly. "Jaevid knows everything I do now about Argonox and Reigh. He'll brief you when you land tonight."

"Aubren?" I dared to take a step closer, just enough that I could reach out and touch his unmarked hand. I could feel the warmth of his palm even through his leather gloves, and yet it still seemed like he was a thousand miles away.

He angled his face so I couldn't see, but I could hear the brokenness in his voice. "Jaevid might be able to excuse my betrayal, but I doubt our father will. And then trying to take your life? Dark magic or not, I don't expect anyone to forgive that easily. But Jenna, please, I am so sorry, I never meant for—"

"There is nothing to forgive!" I snatched his hand tighter, jostling him so that he would face me again. Standing on my toes, I snagged my arms around his neck, gripping him with all my strength as I hugged him tightly. "It wasn't your fault. I know you would never hurt me. Argonox poisoned your mind, and you fought it. You resisted and won. If our father can't appreciate the kind of strength that took, then I'll spit right in his face."

He bowed his head slightly, letting his chin rest on my shoulder. "Regardless, I can't face him yet. I will, when this is over. I will be the one to tell him what I've done and accept whatever punishment he orders without resistance—but not now. There are far more important things that require our whole attention."

"Gods, you stupid, stubborn man," I grumbled as I leaned back and put my hands on his face. "This discussion is *not* over. If I find out you've gone to our father without talking to me first, you will regret it. I can promise you that. You're my brother, Aubren. I love you—always."

One corner of his mouth quirked slightly, but it was only a ghost of a smile. He leaned in, looping an arm around my neck to give me one last, tight hug in return. "Thank you, Jenna. Please stay safe."

CHAPTER TWELVE

We kept the rest of our farewells brief. It was better, safer for everyone, if we moved quickly and gave the Tibrans less time to respond or catch up to us. Eirik and Aubren rode off with Judan, leading Baroness Adeline, Miri, and the rest of the refugees from Cernheist along the safest road toward the wild jungle of Luntharda.

Sitting astride Phevos, I watched the last of their company disappear along the tangled, twisting mountain pathway through the thin glass visor of my helmet. I prayed that they would make it—that Argonox wouldn't have some nasty surprise waiting for them. If they pressed on hard for the rest of the day and didn't fall prey to the encroaching storm, they might make it in less than two days.

Regardless, there was nothing more we could do for them now.

Jaevid gave the motion to take off, so Calem, Phillip, and I hunkered down to wait our turn. We watched as Mavrik and Turq took to the air first. The rapid, powerful beats of their wings stirred up the snow. I had to wipe it from my visor once they were clear.

They would be taking the western route, following the bristled spine of jagged mountain peaks down to the Marshlands. We would make a wider pass to the east, right along the foothills that sloped down into the Farchase Plains. Our goal was to meet right on the edge of the Marshlands, where the forest turned swampy, and let our mounts rest before we pressed on toward Halfax. Since our path was shorter, we were going to double back a little, just to throw off any Tibran spies that might be mapping our movements. No need to make it too easy for them, right?

If Judan's information was correct, the path would be fairly clear all the way from the Marshlands to Halfax, as long as we stayed above the marshes, where Argonox's war machines couldn't go. We'd approach from the west and pray that my father decided to let us land safely within the walls of the royal city. Jaevid hadn't really considered the possibility that he might turn us away. Maybe it seemed silly to him, considering everything else that was going on, but technically, I was still an exile from the royal city.

My last encounter with my father hadn't been a positive, heartwarming one. Not that we'd had many of those lately. Fewer and fewer after Mother passed away, in fact. That last, fiery debate had been months ago, and I'd received no word from him since. I honestly didn't know how I would be received now.

It wasn't until I felt my dragon's body flex beneath me, filling his wings with the frosty air, that I realized how much that scared me. Would he be furious? Would he banish me from my homeland altogether? Mark me as a traitor for fighting in battles and leading other dragonriders to fight without his permission? Gods, he was well within is right to demand our arrest. I might be spared a traitor's punishment, but Haldor, Calem, and Eirik didn't have the luxury of being the king's only daughter. He might put them all to the sword for taking part in my insane rebellion.

I swallowed against the hard knot of uncertainty in my throat and leaned into Phevos's motions as he pumped his wings harder, soaring toward the bleak open sky. We moved as one, rising with the winds and letting our bodies brush the heavens. Every takeoff, every flight, still gave me that rush that set my heart ablaze. This was freedom. It tasted of the wild, icy mountain air. It felt like the rolling of sturdy muscles beneath ironclad scales. It sounded like a dragon's booming roar, thundering in the deep.

It was only the strength of Phillip's arms around my middle that reminded me who I was. Everything down there, back on the ground, was complicated and painful. Part of me still wished we could just sail away on a wintry breeze and leave it all behind.

Off our right side, Perish dipped gracefully into formation with her white wings spread wide to catch the rising updrafts. Her scarlet eyes flicked around, always watching the air around us as we broke through the clouds to the clean blue sky above. Sitting astride her sleek shoulders, Calem's bronze-plated armor shone like gold. The wing-shaped details on his helm caught in the sun and his sweeping cloak fluttered behind him like a rippling banner of royal blue velvet.

Hours of daylight dragged. Beneath me, Phevos's breathing grew heavier and his wing beats more strained as the day wore on. Carrying two riders was taking its toll. It was a lot to ask of him to take us both so far. Our dragons would need to land, eat, and rest very soon.

As the sun began to dip below the clouds over the western sea, we made our last turn toward our destination and descended low enough to get a good view of the ground below. There, the dense forest flanked both sides of the Marshlands for miles, stretching along the floodplains of the river that ran all the way to the eastern coast. It made for deep, murky bogs thick with brambles and mud as thick as tar. The whole area was known for flashfloods in the spring, when the rains and snowmelt made the river swell beyond its banks.

Usually, it was a place traveled only by the dangerous and desperate. During the Gray War, it had served as a common hideout for bandits and slavers. I'd also heard of escaped slaves, elves mostly, who had tried hiding there to avoid capture. But if rumors were to be believed, there were more dangerous things lurking in that filthy mire than slavers and thieves.

A glint off Calem's armor caught my attention as he flashed his vambrace to get my attention. "*Smoke rising,*" he gestured, using our dragonrider code of hand signals. "*A Tibran attack?*"

Following the point of his finger, I narrowed my gaze upon a few plumes of dark smoke rising from the edge of the forest along the swamp. Strange. They seemed too big to be mere campfires.

"*Let's take a look,*" I gestured back. "*If it's Tibrans, I'm going in hot.*"

"*Lead on.*" Calem gave a salute.

I gave Phillip's arm, which was still wrapped around my waist, a pat before I leaned back to yell over the rush of the wind. "Hang on; we might be in for a fight!"

He didn't reply, or if he did, the wind was too loud in my ears to hear it. Still, his hold on me tightened.

With a twist of my saddle handles, I applied pressure to the underside of my dragon's saddle, letting him know when and how steeply to turn. We banked, flaring, and making a speedy descent toward the smoke curling up from four difference places just within the tree line.

There was no way of knowing what we might be diving into. A Tibran legion trying to burn their way along the swamp to make way for their war machines? That seemed the most likely at first brush.

But as we skirted in close, I could pick out more details. People were running toward the swamp, fleeing from the trees. Women carrying children tripped and staggered through the mud. Men dressed in commoner's clothes were carrying the injured, fleeing as fast as they could over the marshy ground. They were *not* Tibran.

But the soldiers chasing them most certainly were.

From the trees, lines of men dressed in that familiar bronze armor emerged with their shields interlocked. Some used crossbows to launch fire-tipped arrows at the fleeing civilians; others swung slings with miniature versions of the dragon venom-filled orbs we had seen them use in a much larger size at Barrowton. The clay orbs shattered, sending burning venom spraying in every direction. Every time one exploded, it lit up the dusk with orange flame. People screamed, some falling as they were caught in the spray.

I gripped the saddle handles so hard my fingers went numb. My jaw creaked as I ground my teeth. These were not bandits or slavers they were chasing down. These were unarmed civilians. They were butchering families with children.

I'd burn every last one of those Tibran cowards alive for it.

PHEVOS SNARLED AND BARED HIS TEETH, WINGS SNAPPING IN FOR A RAPID RUSH of the battlefield. Behind us, Perish let out a screeching roar as she followed. We took the first line of Tibrans with a long blast of burning venom, creating a barrier between them and the fleeing civilians. They wouldn't be able to pursue now.

As we swooped low over the ground, low enough I could have plucked a few blades of grass on the way, Phillip suddenly let go of my waist. I twisted around just in time to see him take one of the blades from my belt and leap from the saddle. He landed in a roll and immediately sprang up, running headlong for the nearest Tibran soldier.

Perish dipped in for another sweeping pass, lighting up a portion of the tree line. I wasn't sure why she'd bother—until I saw around a hundred more Tibran soldiers come pouring out of the thickets to escape the fire. She was flushing them out!

They ran straight for me, apparently too panicked to notice the angry purple dragon turning for a second pass. Arrows zipped past my head and glanced off my dragon's scaly hide. They pinged off my breastplate and stuck into the leather of my saddle. My pulse sped with wild fury, every muscle quivering as I leaned down against Phevos's neck. My ears rang with the screaming of men and the roar of flames in between my dragon's thundering roars.

Straight ahead, a Tibran soldier closed in on a young woman clutching a squirming bundle of muddy cloth against her breast. Sword drawn, he reared back as she stumbled and fell, covering her baby with her body as she screamed.

Heat and rage flushed through me, coursing along every nerve and setting my brain ablaze. I unbuckled from the saddle, giving Phevos a quick pat to let him know I was going in.

He chirped and ducked lower, angling himself with one wingtip barely brushing the earth.

I hopped out onto his wing, using it like a fabric slide to land in a crouch less than ten yards from the soldier. Not a second to waste.

Drawing my remaining blade, I rushed and sprang, kicking both feet hard against his back. One swing, swift and relentless, sent a spray of blood through the air. The soldier's body hit the ground with a *thud* and didn't move again.

I landed in a crouch, shaking off the pulsing rush that still hummed through every muscle as I stood. The woman let out a desperate cry as she looked up at me, tears leaving clean streaks down her mud and soot smeared face. "H-help us! Please!"

I threw back the visor of my helmet, revealing my face to her.

Her eyes went wide, mouth dropping open as she stared upward.

I assumed it was because I was a woman. It was still shocking to a lot of people, particularly the common folk who didn't get to see a lot of battle or training firsthand.

I assumed wrong.

Behind me, a resounding bellow shook the ground under my boots. I turned, catching a flash of blue scales an instant before the ground nearby exploded into flame. The blast incinerated a group of Tibran soldiers coming straight for us with crossbows at the ready. They didn't even have time to scream.

"I-is that ... ?" The woman gasped.

It was.

Mavrik descended into the thick of the fight, his leathery black wings cupping to form a shield from incoming arrows and orbs as his rider dismounted. When the huge blue dragon rose up again, his saddle was empty. He threw back his head, black horns flashing in the setting sun as he shot a plume of flame straight up into the air. His wings unfurled, and Jaevid Broadfeather strode onto the battlefield with his scimitar in hand.

CHAPTER THIRTEEN

I had to give him some credit, Jaevid knew how to make an entrance. He took to the battle not like a man or even a dragonrider. He was a vengeful god. His eyes flickered, glowing like peridot stars in the failing light of day as he flexed his divine power. A vein stood out against the side of his neck as he raised his free hand toward the line of advancing Tibran troops. His expression sharpened, lips curling in a vicious snarl. The ground shuddered, nearly knocking me off my feet. I wobbled to keep balance and threw up an arm to keep myself between the woman still carrying her infant and whatever was about to happen.

Jaevid closed his fist, sending out a sharp burst of power like a blast wave through the air. The earth flinched again. In seconds, two enormous creatures began twisting and writhing free of the swampy sludge as though they'd been buried there, right under our feet, for a thousand years. A gnarled mixture of rock, root, and dripping mud, the beasts rose up like knuckle-dragging giants. Each one was twenty feet of primal earthen power. No faces. No features. Just two bottomless, glowing green pits for eyes and *very* big fists. One hit would smash a man into jelly—armor and all. Their every step shook the ground, and their bellowing cries made many of the Tibran soldiers break ranks and flee with screams of sheer terror.

From the sky, Haldor and Calem threw down a perimeter of flame, forcing the remaining Tibran ranks into range of Jaevid's two monsters. Our makeshift meat grinders worked with brutal efficiency. While Phevos and Mavrik stood watch, crowing excitedly at the other dragons still circling, I ran the perimeter on cleanup duty. Chasing down any of the soldiers who decided to make a break for it across the swamp wasn't easy. Running through that muck and mire in armor was a challenge—but I wasn't about to let any of those cowards leave our party early.

Suddenly, a frantic scream drew my attention back toward the forest, just in time to spot a lone Tibran soldier dragging a little boy into the tree line. The child kicked and fought, screaming for help. The soldier's gaze flashed upward, meeting mine for an instant. His face paled, eyes wide in horror that reflected the flames of battle around us. Then he clenched an arm around the boy's neck and dragged him further into the tree line.

Not on my watch.

Yanking my blade free of a dead soldier's back, I started after them at a sprint. It took everything I had to keep going, fighting against the slushy mud that threatened to suck the boots right off my feet. But I couldn't stop. That boy—someone had to save him.

Suddenly, I was in the air. The battlefield whirled around me in utter chaos, and then all I could see was the ground blurring by. I was flying—no—being carried!

"Hang on!" Phillip snarled as he lugged me over his shoulder. His paw-like feet were speedy over the mud, and he carried me like I weighed nothing at all.

"There's a boy," I started to shout.

"I know! I saw," he called back. "They won't get far."

Gods, I hoped he was right.

Wrapping an arm around Phillip's neck, I sheathed my blade and quickly wriggled myself over his shoulders. No way was I going to let him tote me around like this. Clinging to his back with my legs around his middle like a child riding piggyback, I searched the edge of the forest for any sign of the boy or soldier. There was nothing.

"I smell them," Phillip said with a thrumming growl. He poured on more speed toward the forest, dropping to all fours to leap the last twenty yards in one mighty spring.

Darting through the forest, splashing through muck-filled sinkholes and leaping over fallen trees, Phillip moved like a panther on the hunt. His padded feet didn't make a sound on the soft earth, but his growling pants were hard to miss. My heart hit the back of my throat as he lurched to a halt, swinging around with his nose in the air and his pointed ears wiggling. The vertical pupils of his strange eyes widened, taking in the dim light.

Suddenly, a scream made us both jerk. It was a child's voice. And it was close.

Phillip squatted down slowly, guiding me down from his back. "Draw their attention," he whispered. "Distract that soldier. I'll move in. He'll never hear me coming."

I nodded.

My hands shook with nervous energy as I crept through the soggy undergrowth. Every step was painfully loud, squishing and splashing or crunching on twigs and fallen limbs. The warm, damp air reeked of silt and rotting leaves. Thick clouds of fog drifted aimlessly and twisted around the trunks of the trees, and the distant rumble of combat echoed through the gloom.

Then I heard it—the soft crying of a child.

Surging forward, I rounded a clump of trees and saw them at the crest of a small rise. The soldier whirled around, his whole body shaking as he gripped the little boy by his hair. He had the sharp end of a long, curved daggered pressed right up against the child's throat.

"S-stop right there," the soldier yelped. "I'll cut him open! By the gods, I swear I will!"

I slowly raised my hands, gesturing surrender. "This doesn't have to end with anyone being cut open."

He coughed out a broken, maniacal laugh. "It does! It will! You think I don't know it will? Do you take me for a fool?" His expression twisted, eyes widening as he looked all around and up toward the limbs of the trees. "We'll all die here. All of us. Cut and burned!"

Alarm bells tolled in my head. Something about this man wasn't right. He looked to be about my age, or maybe a little older—no older than thirty for sure. But his eyes were bloodshot and his cheeks sunken. His whole body twitched and tremored with more than just fear.

I'd seen the horrors of battle break men. It changed people, some more than others. But this was *not* that.

"Your accent is Maldobarian," I observed, careful to keep my tone calm. "Why are you fighting for the Tibrans?"

His gaze darted back to me. For one terrible instant, he seemed to realize what he was doing—the blade in one hand and the child in the other. His brow quivered. His eyes welled with tears.

"Please, just let the boy go. We can talk about this. It doesn't have to end with anyone dying," I coaxed.

Any sense or remorse in the man's eyes vanished, snuffed out like a candle in the night. "You don't understand," he screamed. "I didn't want this. No one wants this. They tell you to fight on. If you fight well, then you can have back everything they take. But it's a lie!" He squeezed the knife until his knuckles blanched. "Death is the only reward—the only freedom from Argonox!"

The soldier's body lurched suddenly, and he fell silent. Second by second, his expression went from crazed to blank. His arms went slack. The dagger rolled out of his hand and landed in the mud at his feet.

My heart jumped with relief. Phillip? Had he come to intervene?

As the soldier slumped forward onto the mud with a resounding *thud*, a man rose up behind him, brandishing a freshly bloodied hatchet.

It was definitely not Phillip.

He stood tall, broad shoulders not bent or bowed with age despite the silver that streaked his black hair and the deep creases in his aging skin. Dressed in a strange mixture of furs, common clothing, and bits of makeshift Maldobarian armor, the man leered at me with pale blue eyes and mouth pinched into a grim frown. "It's useless to talk to them, Your Highness," he warned in a deep, gruff voice.

My mind whirled. Who was this guy? A woodsman, maybe? Or a hunter? And how did he know who I was?

"Grandpapa!" The little boy wailed suddenly, breaking the tension as he ran for the man with arms wide open.

The burly old man slipped his hatchet back into his belt and took the child into his arms. Then he motioned to me. "Let's go. The others will need our help," he mumbled, rubbing his short white beard as his piercing gaze panned over me quickly. I could sense him sizing me up, not that I wasn't used to it. That's generally what men did when they spotted a woman carrying a blade and wearing a dragonrider's armor.

"Tell your monster to come along, too," he grumbled as he strode past.

On cue, Phillip sprang from the undergrowth and let out a disapproving snort as he stood beside me with the tip of his tail flicking. "Not sure I'd toss around names like that. I wasn't the one who just buried an axe in someone's spine."

The man gave a grunt, maybe a chuckle or a cough—I honestly couldn't tell— and kept on walking. He didn't even stop to see if we were going to follow.

Phillip and I exchanged a look and a shrug. Not like we had a lot to lose.

"Just who are you anyway?" I called as I jogged to catch up.

The old man's steely gaze never wavered as he picked his way through the underbrush, still carrying the little boy. His movements were trained and swift, and his every step smooth and calculated. I'd seen that kind of posturing before, many times in fact, but only from Maldobarian soldiers.

"One of many refugees trying to find some hole to hide in until the tide turns," he answered. "But if there are to be introductions, you can call me Roland."

Roland. Where had I heard that name before? It struck a chord in my brain right away, but the memory refused to surface, lodged somewhere just out of reach. As soon as we broke through the edge of the forest and back out onto the open marshes, however, the thought was lost.

※

THE BATTLE WAS OVER. TIBRAN SOLDIERS LAY IN BURNING PILES SCATTERED everywhere, and most of my dragonrider brothers were helping the scattered refugees regroup at the edge of the forest. By the look of things, only a few had fallen victim to the Tibran legions.

I stopped, my heart dropping to the soles of my boots as I spotted Calem struggling to pull a young woman away from one of the refugees lying in the mud. Even from a distance, it was obvious he was dead. The girl wailed and wept, fighting to stay close to the body and taking wild swings at Calem in the process. Her pale face was smeared with fresh blood and her ginger-colored hair was caked with mud.

I had almost made up my mind to try talking to her. Sometimes it helped for people to see a gentler, more feminine face in moments like this. But before I could take a step, Calem snatched off his helmet and one of his riding gauntlets and grasped her by the shoulders. He whirled the young woman around to face him. Leaning down to look directly into her eyes, he cupped her face with his bare hand. "Look me in the eye so I know you hear me. You must take a breath and listen." His voice was as calm and unfazed as ever.

She stared back at him, her chin trembling as she choked back sobs.

"Your father is dead. You, however, are very fortunate to still be alive. I'm sure he'd want it to stay that way," Calem murmured gently, withdrawing his hand slowly.

"I-I can't just leave him here to rot with them. He should be buried! He should be ..." The girl bawled. Her shoulders seized up as she leaned forward, burying her face against his breastplate to cry.

For a moment, Calem stood stiffly, his brow furrowed as he looked down at the girl as though he weren't sure what to do with her now. She couldn't have been more than sixteen, wearing what looked a lot like a long nightgown and robe. Both were coated in the same smelly swamp mud that was sloshing in her too-big boots.

When his puzzled expression finally panned to me, Calem gave me a few dragonrider signals. "*What do I do?*"

I rolled my eyes. I'd never seen Calem interact with many people outside our dragonrider circles, especially not young women. It wasn't that he didn't seem to care for them—more like, he didn't know how to relate with people in general. Battle he understood. But sentiment? Affection? That was apparently another story.

"*It's called a hug,*" I signaled in reply.

His eyes narrowed. "*That is not helpful.*"

Eh, he'd figure it out. If nothing else, this was a good learning experience. At least he was making an effort.

Continuing after Roland, I counted thirty-two more refugees huddled together like frightened sheep. Most of them were men dressed in the same sort of mismatched clothing and armor Roland was. They were carrying chipped old swords, archaic shields, work axes, or blacksmithing hammers—basically whatever they could use as a weapon. Not exactly an army prepared to rival a Tibran attack.

The women and children hiding amidst them bore haunted, empty expressions on ashen, dirty faces. Their clothes were rags, and many of them were wore nightgowns. Anger rose in my chest like a molten tide. Driving them from their homes, enslaving them, murdering helpless women and children—Argonox was doing this to *my* people.

That would not stand. I would put an end to it or die trying.

"We should move back into the cover of the forest." Roland spoke and immediately had the attention of everyone in the group. The younger men rallied to him, expressions still fierce from battle. Strange that so many of them were halfbreeds, with at least some Gray elven blood judging by their slightly pointed ears and olive skin. You didn't normally see so many this far from the border of Luntharda.

"The dragonriders have bought us some time," Roland continued. "But we need to move deeper into the marshes and make camp, tend to our wounded, and restock our supplies as best we can."

"We can help, if you like."

Jaevid's voice made everyone turn—including Roland. As the old man slowly turned to him, all the color drained from his face until his skin nearly matched his bristly white beard. "Jaevid." His eyes went round and his mouth opened slightly, just enough that the name slipped out in a breathless whisper.

Our infamous companion's mouth twitched, hinting at an apprehensive smile. He ducked his head slightly, shoulders drawing up anxiously as he flushed across the cheeks and gave a little nod. "It's been a long time, brother."

My body jolted suddenly as my heartbeat gave a frantic stammer. Gods and Fates—that's where I'd heard that name before. This man was Roland *Broadfeather*! He was Jaevid's half-brother! They'd shared the same brutal, abusive father in their childhood, but while Jaevid had been adopted into the brotherhood of dragonriders, Roland had defied their father's legacy of crafting saddlery for dragons and joined Maldobar's ground infantry.

Well, that explained the old man's finesse with a blade.

When their eyes met, Roland's entire posture gradually went slack. He bent long enough to place the little boy he'd been carrying back on the ground, then took one staggering step toward Jaevid. His breathing hitched, catching as he struggled—and failed—to choke out words.

"I know I'm a bit late," Jaevid fretted in a quiet voice. "But we are more than willing to help you in any way we can."

With a booming, rasping laugh, Roland suddenly surged forward and threw his arms around Jaevid. "It's really you!"

"Yes. It's me," Jaevid wheezed.

"I saw your dragon fly overhead, but we've heard so many stories of wild dragons taking up the fight—I didn't dare to hope!" Roland pulled back and grabbed Jaevid's shoulders to shake him.

All around us, the group of refugees pushed and shoved, ducking and standing on their toes to catch a glimpse of our fearless leader. They murmured to one another in hushed voices—right up until an older woman emerged from their midst. Though the deep bronze skin of her face was aged, she strode smoothly forward, her head held with regal poise and her multihued eyes shining bright. She was a full-blooded Gray elf, with far longer pointed ears and hair as white as morning frost woven into many complex braids down to her waist, but she wore Maldobarian clothes. There was an elven-styled bow across her back and strings of colorful clay, bone, and copper beads hung around her neck.

When she drew close, Roland reached out to take her hand and guide her closer to Jaevid. "Delphi, this is my brother."

The elven woman's lips curved into a shrewd smile. "Honestly, Rolly? You think I don't know who he is?"

"Of course, my dear." The rugged man blushed like a scolded child. "Jaevid, this is my wife."

Jaevid's eyes went wide for a blink or two. "Wife?" He blinked a few more times. "Rolly?"

Roland gave a small nod that was eerily similar to the sheepish one Jaevid had given earlier.

"You seem surprised?" Delphi arched a brow, her mouth still split with a grin.

"It's nothing against you, my lady. But the last time we spoke, Roland insisted he had no intention of taking a wife."

She giggled again. "Oh yes. He told me that too, when we first met. So naturally, I dedicated myself to convincing him otherwise. It wasn't difficult. It turns out that sulky exterior is quite thin and easily cracked. I've tamed shrikes that were far more stubborn than he is."

Roland's cheeks glowed like ripe tomatoes over his short white beard. "M-my dear, please."

"At any rate, I'm pleased to see you have returned to us, lapiloque." Delphi gave him a slight bow before gesturing to a group of refugees around her—the ones who looked distinctly half-elven. "These are our children, your nieces and nephews, as it turns out. My sons are Alani and Kaeson, and my daughters Brisa and Daeyli. And of course, their children."

Jaevid's gaze panned the crowd of curious onlookers, mouth open and brows raised. He blinked rapidly, eyes seeming a little watery as he finally stared back at his brother. "You've been ... very busy."

"Thanks to you," Roland affirmed.

He didn't reply. Instead, Jaevid bowed his head low enough that his shaggy hair hid his face. It would have been a lot for anyone to take in. I suppose he had to collect himself.

"There are rumors everywhere, lapiloque. It's hard to tell what is true and what is merely wild speculation." Delphi's tone was softer as she moved closer, grasping Jaevid's chin to gently lift his head so she could look him in the eye. "So many are living in terror, being driven from their homes and murdered in the streets, or dragged away to meet an ever-worse fate with the Tibran legions. No one has forgotten what you did for us so many years ago, but I'm afraid you are needed now more than ever."

"I made a promise," Jaevid answered, his jaw clenched and gaze steely. "I intend to keep it."

CHAPTER FOURTEEN

"We evacuated Ivangol when the Tibrans made landfall and Southwatch fell. So many good men died defending it—some I knew. But I had to take my family out of that place. We brought as many friends as we could with us, although we've lost more than half to Tibran scouting forces like you saw today. They roam the countryside looking for good roads to use to expand their reach." Sitting around the campfire, Roland's voice was heavy with exhaustion and sorrow. The light of the crackling fire turned his pale, glacier blue eyes orange as he watched the flames dancing in the dark. "We've done all right until now, keeping on the move and out of sight. But it was only a matter of time before they caught up to us."

"If it's not the soldiers, then it's the monsters," Delphi added as she sat close beside her husband with her shoulder resting against his. "Argonox set loose a hoard of strange creatures into the wild—the likes of which I have never seen, even in Luntharda. They appear as some sort of feline, but with fur as black as coal and spines along their backs."

Phillip shifted next to me.

I took his hand and squeezed it tightly.

"There were also hounds. Beastly things. Blood-hungry and wrong in the head," she continued. "I shudder to think of what that tyrant might do to dragons or shrikes. Gods help us if he were able to turn them on us."

"I can't imagine he won't try that," Haldor mumbled. "We've already seen evidence of it."

Jaevid's expression darkened and his jaw clenched.

It was time to change the subject. I cleared my throat to get their attention.

"We intend to go to Halfax as quickly as possible. We stand a good chance of making a final assault on Argonox there, if my father will listen to reason."

Roland paled. "Have you ... not heard?"

Oh no. I froze, my heart pounding in my fingers and throbbing in my toes as I held my breath. "Heard what?"

"Halfax is all but surrounded. Argonox has focused all efforts on cutting the city off from the rest of the kingdom. Word is that the people inside the walls are starving," Roland said, his tone like an apology. "They're prepared for dragonriders. You'll be hard pressed to reach it without taking heavy Tibran fire."

Jaevid sat up straighter, his face the picture of quiet ferocity. "What about demigods?"

Delphi's multihued eyes shimmered with vicious delight. "I pray not. And may you kill many Tibrans without mercy, lapiloque, for that is precisely what they deserve."

"Because of the Marshlands, their fortification of the western side of the city is very likely weaker," Roland added. "If you strike from that side, you stand a better chance of punching through their perimeter and making it to the city."

"I think I can buy you the time." From across the fire, Aedan sat forward and began drawing out a rough sketch in the dirt with the pointy end of a long twig. He marked out a rough circular shape—like that of Halfax—and began outlining it with an estimation of how the Tibran forces would be arranged. "Argonox's machines are highly specialized for sieging. His trebuchets and catapults are able to corner and turn quickly to reposition for incoming threats. But if I were to sneak back into the Tibran ranks, I might be able to disable them just before you make your assault. No doubt he has most of them focused on the city, since that's where the bulk of the remaining dragonriders are. I could make them unable to turn to face your approach. I might even be able to compromise some of the net-throwing bows, too."

"That's a lot for just one person to take on," I cautioned. "And if you get caught—"

"I'll go with him," Phillip blurted suddenly.

My mouth went dry.

Before I could even open my mouth to protest, Phillip flashed me a stern look of warning. "I hate to be the one to point out the obvious, love, but out of our group, I am most certainly the one least likely to be taken as a Maldobarian spy."

He was right. Deep in my gut, I knew that. He looked like the work of morbid Tibran engineering because, well, he was one. But that did not make it okay for him to go storming off to sacrifice himself like this. If they found out what he was doing, or even suspected he wasn't one of them ... My stomach rolled just to think of it.

"There's more than enough Tibran armor lying around out in the marshes now for us to disguise ourselves. I think we can pull this off," Phillip continued, trying to assure me—as though I would ever be okay with this plan.

"How will you get into the city after it's done?" Haldor asked.

Phillip gave a snort, waggling his claw-tipped fingers. "I think I can climb it rather easily. If we snuff a few Tibran watchmen at the right moment, we should be able to get inside without anyone being the wiser. Providing, of course, you can convince the Maldobarian guards on the ramparts not to shoot us on sight."

It was risky—beyond risky. I didn't like it one bit. But as I studied the faces of my comrades, I could see the same bitter realization rising in their faces that settled over my own heart like a cold stone. We didn't have any other choice. This was our best and only shot.

"All right," I conceded. "Let's do it."

I DIDN'T FEEL ANY BETTER ABOUT OUR PLAN THE FOLLOWING MORNING WHEN we were sitting astride our dragons awaiting Jaevid's signal to take off. Roland insisted that what Judan had told us was true—apart from a few rogue Tibran scouting legions, the western Marshlands were clear and safe to fly. The small legions moving through the area were searching for better paths to bring the larger forces through, and as far as he'd seen, none of them were equipped to deal with a dragonrider assault. They likely wouldn't even fire upon us if they saw us fly over, for fear of giving away their position.

As for how Phillip and Aedan would infiltrate the Tibran forces ... I cringed to think of it. We were putting a lot of faith in that Gray elf boy. I prayed he could manage it. We stood to lose a lot if he failed.

The tension must have been weighing on him because Aedan fidgeted and chewed on the inside of his cheek while Delphi gave him a Gray elf warrior's blessing before we departed. It had been years since I had practiced the language. Kiran tried to teach us as little children, and I'd caught onto many common phrases—particularly ones like "apologize to your brother" or "don't eat that." But I couldn't even begin to translate what Delphi said to him as she pressed the heel of her hand to his forehead and said those solemn prayers.

With his face hidden beneath a bronze Tibran helmet, I had no way of knowing if her blessing made Aedan feel any better, or at least less nervous about what we were about to do. We wouldn't be able to get close enough to drop them off without running the risk of being spotted. We agreed it would be safer to do it under the cover of darkness, and we'd have gone that night, but the dragons needed rest. Our hope was to get within range of a good drop-off point the next day, wait until nightfall, and then get in as close as we could to deliver them.

So, for the rest of the night, we'd stayed with the refugees. We passed the time helping them set up another makeshift camp. We collected as much dried wood as we could find, set up little shelters of canvas and poles, and even offered up our bedrolls for the women and young children to sleep on so they didn't have to spend another night lying in the mud. It was the least we could do, really. After everyone had settled in, I sat close to Phillip and watched them—the mothers rocking and nursing their babies and the children quietly muttering to one another as they huddled close in their beds. I wished we could do more, but our own supplies were just as limited. The best thing we could do for everyone right now was reach Halfax, convince my father to attack Argonox, and end this war before it killed more innocent people.

Morning brought the relief of sunlight and warmth, and the hunters brought a few wild hares to make into stew to fill the hungry bellies around the camp. Phillip unnerved the refugees, especially the men. I could see it in their eyes when he strode past on his paw-like feet, with skin the color of slate and black tail swishing. They had every reason to be afraid, considering what they'd been through. But he did seem to win a bit of trust when he helped the hunters by smelling out game.

But now we had to leave them behind.

I shivered, not certain if it was from the cool morning air, the hunger wrenching in my stomach, or the fact that we were about to leave all these people defenseless. Sitting astride Phevos on the edge of the forest, we waited while Jaevid said his last farewells. He'd spent most of the night talking rather than sleeping—chatting and getting to know his extended family. Not that I blamed him. It was probably nice to know he wasn't quite as alone in the world as he must have felt sometimes. He still had relatives, people that weren't just adoring fans of his past heroics. Maybe, if everyone came out of this alive, he'd even have a place to go home to and start a real life.

That was my wish for him, anyway.

As he walked amidst the small camp of clustered refugees, Jaevid led a little girl of about three years old by the hand. He was carrying another squirming infant on his hip with the other, smiling like he'd found his bliss as he laughed with Roland. They must have been a few of his great-nieces and nephews. Even dressed in full armor—most of which was borrowed off dead Tibran soldiers—Jaevid made it seem effortless and natural having both children in tow. Parenthood suited him. It was the most joyful thing that had ever broken my heart to see. He was still so young, or at least he looked it; surely there was time for him to start a family of his own. But would he ever get over Beckah? Would he get to have children? Or had that hope died with her?

Handing the infant off to Roland, Jaevid gave his brother a parting embrace, and then knelt to do the same to the little girl. She squeezed him back and patted his cheeks with her tiny hands before he stood and backed away. His brow drew up, skewed with pain he couldn't disguise. His body stiffened, and there was fresh agony in his eyes as he turned away and went to climb into Mavrik's saddle.

It tore at my chest like razors through flesh. He'd already said goodbye to his brother once. Gods, I hoped this ended differently than the last time.

Giving us all a signal, Jaevid and Haldor took off first. Calem and I followed shortly after and fell into tight formation, moving at high speed less than a hundred feet off the ground. The idea was that if we remained below the tree line, we would avoid anyone spotting us from a distance while we scooted in to drop our boys as close as possible to the Tibran lines.

Hugging the border of the forest, we skirted around and turned north at the end of the Marshlands, dropping even lower than before. Jaevid dropped in first, since out of all of us, Mavrik was the largest and the most likely to be spotted from afar. There was roughly forty miles between the royal city and the edge of the forest. A long way on foot, but that was as close as our entire group could go.

We swept in for a speedy landing, and everyone dismounted to gather quickly to go over our plan one more time ... and to say our final farewells.

At nightfall, we had to be ready to move.

"As soon as everything is in place, find an open patch of earth and bury this," Jaevid instructed, pressing an acorn the size of a thumbnail into Aedan's hand. "I'll know it, and we will begin our approach. As soon as they see us coming, I'm sure it will cause a stir. Make sure you find a spot to wait out the chaos until nightfall. With any luck, there will be enough low cloud cover to hide us, but I'm not going to bet on that. It looks like it will be a clear night."

"Can't whip up a bit of cloud for us, demigod?" Phillip teased with a nervous chuckle.

Jaevid shrugged. "I'm afraid my particular brand of miracles is restricted to earthen and living things."

Phillip leaned against me, jostling my shoulder. "We should complain. Maybe ask for a water or weather deity next time, eh?"

I couldn't join in the jest. My mind raced, searching for a good reason for me to be going in his place. Just the thought of the Tibrans having Phillip again made my insides feel like they were on fire. I couldn't handle it. I couldn't lose him again.

While everyone else confirmed our plan, I ground my jaw and dug the toe of my boot into the dirt. It should have been me. Phillip wasn't even a trained soldier. He'd never even used a blade in combat before Hilleddi tried to hack my head off. And even then, he'd barely been able to—

A warm, strong hand closed around mine. His voice spoke softly against my ear, "I'll be fine, love."

I couldn't look at him. It made my chest burn with pain, like someone was splitting it wide open. Pinching my eyes shut, I looked away. "Don't say that. Don't give me false hope."

Phillip grasped my jaw, turning my face and pressing his lips against mine. I sucked in a sharp breath through my nose. For a moment, my world stood still.

Everything was quiet. The war was a distant annoyance. Nothing but the smooth, strong mouth moving against mine mattered at all.

Then he pulled away. My tranquility shattered. As I stood staring up at him, the evening sun made those tiny flecks on his soot-colored skin shine like scattered diamonds. The switchbeast venom had changed so much about him—but the way he looked at me, as though he were seeing the sunrise for the very first time, hadn't changed in the slightest. He still touched me like I was something fragile and stared at me with admiration and awe ebbing from every corner of his face.

"If it's not too much trouble, try and persuade those soldiers guarding the ramparts not to shoot the cat demon scaling their wall, would you?" He was still teasing as he combed his fingers through my hair, tucking a few stray locks behind my ear.

"I'll try." My voice broke, and I swallowed hard.

"I love you, Jenna."

"Don't," I warned. "Don't say that now."

"Why not?"

I turned my face into his hand, kissing his palm before I pushed it away. "Because it feels like goodbye, and this is *not* goodbye."

He laughed. "Very well. I find your presence easy to tolerate, Jenna. Perhaps even somewhat enjoyable. How's that? Better?"

Despite my best efforts, a smile broke over my lips. "That will do, Phillip."

Nightfall came too soon.

Phevos was the darkest patterned of our group, apart from Mavrik, who was too large and would be easily noticed. That meant I had to send both of the boys I loved dearly toward the city. It took no small amount of bribing and sweet-talking from me to convince Phevos to let Aedan and Phillip onto his back. Until that moment, I couldn't remember anyone else ever sitting in his saddle without me in it as well. It wasn't something I cared to commemorate, though—not when every fiber of my being screamed in protest at the sight of them zipping away into the twilight. Phevos flew so low, his wingtips brushed the earth with every flap. He was going as low as possible, making a stealthy approach and drawing no attention. His job, according to Jaevid's instructions, was to get them within range of the Tibran forces, drop them off, and immediately fall back to us. No triumphant roars. No bursts of flame.

We wouldn't know he had pulled it off without being captured until he returned.

Sitting back, my heart pounded until my ribs ached. I wrenched my sweaty hands in the hem of my tunic, squinting at the horizon as more stars winked into view. Jaevid had been correct—it was a clear night. The heavens were alight with countless glittering pinpricks, so bright and perfect it was like you might be able to reach out and touch them.

"I have eight nieces and nephews," Jaevid announced as he suddenly sat down beside me and rested his elbows on his knees. "I can't even remember all their names."

I sighed and let my eyes keep wandering over the night sky. "What about the little girl? The one who held your hand?"

I could hear the smile like a warmth in his voice. "Briella. She asked a lot of questions about dragons. I promised to let her pet Mavrik the next time we meet."

"You're well on your way to becoming her favorite uncle, then, I'd say."

"Hah! I do have a few advantages working for me in that regard, I guess."

"Legendary war hero? Dragonrider? Chosen one of a god? I'd say so." I stole a peek at his face out of the corner of my eye, surprised to find him looking at the sky as well. "I'm sorry you had to leave them behind."

He sighed. "That's the soldier's lot, isn't it?"

"I guess so."

"Forty years and it still feels the same. It never gets any easier, or less painful." He looked down and rubbed his brow with both hands, massaging his fingertips along his temples. "I can feel Reigh's power growing. Whatever is happening at Northwatch, it's getting worse. We may not have much time before Argonox moves to strike."

"Perhaps he means to try and do it before we can reach Halfax?"

Jaevid gave a somber nod. "That was my suspicion, too. But the fact that Reigh hasn't completed his ritual means his power can't be forced beyond a certain point—not without killing him. That may be the only thing holding him back and buying us time."

I hated to think of that boy, supposedly my younger brother, suffering. After what Argonox had done to Phillip, I could only imagine what he might be experimenting with now—let alone what condition Reigh would be in if we saw him again.

"Have you thought any about what you'll say to Felix when we arrive?" he asked.

I mashed my lips together, resisting a few choice profanities. "No," I muttered at last. "I doubt he'll leave me much room to talk, though. What about you?"

Jaevid's mouth flattened, as well. "No."

"Maybe open with a joke. I hear he used to like that sort of thing."

"True, although usually only when I was the punchline." I caught him stealing a glance at me, then a strange squint came to his eyes. "Did he ever tell you about the ballroom dancing incident from our avian year of training?"

"Um, no. I can't say he did."

His brows shot up. "Really? And here I thought that would have been his favorite one of all."

"Perhaps you should tell it, then," I coaxed.

"Not a chance. If I had my way, I'd take that one to my grave," he said with a grin. "Besides, it would probably be much better if he told it."

CHAPTER FIFTEEN

The *thump ... thump ... thump* of wing beats jarred me from a daze. I shot to my feet, scanning the horizon in search of any spot of movement. In the distance, I saw the faintest disturbance against the canopy of stars —a dark shape eclipsing them as it moved toward us. My pulse thrashed wildly, and every muscle drew tight.

Phevos had returned and his saddle was empty.

I ran to him as he touched down, cupping his strong wings, and stretching out his hind legs like an eagle catching a perch. He snapped his jaws, still sulking as I hugged the end of his snout. I got a blast of hot, musky dragon breath right in the face when I rubbed the scales behind his ears. He made low clicking sounds and nibbled at my ponytail—something he *knew* drove me nuts. His slobber would leave my hair crusty for days.

"Rude," I scolded as I gave his nose a swat.

His clicks and chirps softened, and he nuzzled against my shoulder, casting me a pleading, round-eyed stare with his little scaly ears drooping like withered leaves. Ugh. How could I stay angry at a face like that? Not fair.

"Are they all right? Did they make it?" I whirled around, looking to Jaevid— our resident animal mind reader—for answers.

Tilting his head to the side slightly, Jaevid's brow creased as he studied my dragon. Then he breathed a sigh of relief, shoulders relaxing as he nodded. "He was able to drop them off about five miles from the nearest Tibran encampment. No alarms sounded. It seems they have every chance of making it there as planned."

"Then it's up to Aedan now," Haldor murmured, crossing his arms. "Gods, I hope he can pull this off."

"As soon as they give the signal, we have to move. Keep in close, diamond formation, and make a straight break for the castle courtyard. Don't stop or move to engage—we're not there to burn anything. Not yet anyway. We'll stay as high as we can for as long as we can, but the sound of our approach will likely give us away as we descend for landing." Jaevid turned his gaze to me, his hand resting on the pommel of his scimitar. "Once we're inside, we can assume Argonox may strike at any time. He won't want to give us time to prepare for his assault, let alone confer with your father. We need to be ready to act quickly."

I nodded. "Putting aside family sentiments in lieu of duty is practically my middle name."

Calem studied me, his frown the picture of perfect seriousness. "I thought your middle name was Evangeline?"

Haldor choked, suppressing a laugh.

There wasn't time to explain to Calem the finer points of sarcasm. Clearing his throat, Jaevid rubbed his palm along the pommel of his scimitar and shifted. He flicked me a quick look, brow tense, before he began to speak again. "While we have the time, we need to discuss what's going to happen once we reach the castle. Assuming Argonox will make his strike soon after, we may not have time go over this then."

My skin prickled, picking up on the note of reluctance in his tone. "Is this about Reigh?"

He nodded once. "Even with me fighting at your side, Reigh's destructive capability is ... extensive."

"That's putting it lightly," Haldor grunted. "We all saw what he did at Barrowton."

"If Argonox is manipulating his power, we don't know what we will be up against. I don't even know if I will be able to stop him. Our best chance will be ensuring Argonox does not find the crystal that would aid in completing Reigh's ritual." Jaevid paused, his lips thinning as he seemed to consider his next words carefully. "But I fear that might not be enough. If Roland is right, then even without Reigh, Argonox's forces have cut Halfax off from the rest of the kingdom. Meanwhile, he's destroyed every other dragonrider watch throughout Maldobar and left our forces scattered."

Heat rose in my chest, making my hands draw tightly into fists at my side. "So you're saying it's hopeless, even if we make to the city? We'd just be arriving to make a final, futile stand?" The words rolled out of me, each one sharp with anger.

Jaevid leveled a steely glare at me. "I'm saying that we are going to need *other* reinforcements if we are to win this."

"Other?" Haldor scoffed. "The Gray elves don't have a military capable of making any considerable stand against—"

"I wasn't referring to them," Jaevid cut him off. "The kind of help required doesn't exist in this world. I must go into the Vale."

Dread dropped into my gut like a stone sinking in a pond. Gods and Fates, not that awful place again. "What could possibly help us there? I saw only spirits and ... " My voice died in my throat as the memory of Noh pricked at the back of my mind like a poisonous thorn.

"I don't know if I can explain it to you in simple mortal terms," he confessed, his forehead creasing with uncertainty. "If I am unable to stop Reigh's power, then the surest bet to undo it would be to ... call out the source of it. As you know, his power is bound to a deity, just as mine is. But bringing *her* here is very risky."

"Her?" Haldor repeated, his expression sharpening. One brow slowly raised as he tilted his head to the side ever so slightly. "Surely you are not talking about the dark goddess."

"Clysiros," Jaevid affirmed.

I instantly felt sick. We'd talked about her before while we were at Cernheist, but only briefly. I knew nothing about her apart from a few old songs I'd heard bards murmuring at court. Vague references, for the most part, to the one who spun death like a spider's silk and used the dark sins of men's hearts to lure them to a premature grave. Even though that might have been nonsense, it certainly didn't paint a wonderful picture in my mind of what kind of creature we might be inviting into our midst.

"Can you even do that?" Haldor questioned. "Bring a goddess into the mortal world?"

Jaevid shook his head. "I can't risk trying it now. Using my power will certainly draw Argonox's attention. It was enough of a gamble using it in the Marshlands but doing it this close to Halfax or even to help us reach the city might push him to launch his attack. And I cannot do it alone. On my own, I can't even reach Clysiros. But there is another who can. She's living in Luntharda, and I've already prepared her in case this became ... necessary."

"Who?" I demanded.

"Princess Hecate. She is what the elves called the Akrotis—she has the gift of valewhispering. It's extremely rare. I'm not sure it's happened in this millennium."

Wait, was he talking about the same girl Aubren was engaged to? The next in line to be Queen of Luntharda? It took me a moment to wrap my head around that. Gray elf bloodlines were always traced through the mothers, so powerful titles were primarily passed to daughters or granddaughters. Since Queen Araxie had only given birth to sons, she had chosen Hecate to be next in line to take the throne of Luntharda. Years ago, Hecate had been one of several granddaughters for Araxie to choose from. But one by one, all the elder cousins had all passed away. Now I had to wonder ... could that have had something to do with this divine gift?

Before I could ask, Jaevid continued, "Hecate can channel voices and even spirits from those who have passed on. She hears them just as clearly as we hear one another now." He gestured to the rest of us. "It's a complicated talent that has a tendency to overwhelm its user if they don't learn to harness it early. With Paligno's guidance, I gave her some instruction while we were in Luntharda. If she's been practicing, then she should be able to channel Clysiros's voice while we are in the Vale. That's how we will strike our bargain."

"Hecate can walk in the Vale, too?" I asked.

"Well, it's not that simple," he replied with a nervous chuckle. "Physically, no. You'd need Reigh's power to do that. But because of her talent, she won't need to be there physically."

Haldor sank back on his heels, letting out a heavy sigh that made his cheeks puff out. "This feels desperate," he mumbled. "And insanely dangerous."

"Because it is," Jaevid agreed.

I couldn't stop myself. The words tore out of me like an insult before I could check them. "And you honestly think you can negotiate a bargain with an evil goddess of death and convince her to fight for our cause? What's to stop her from just killing everything and everyone—us included?"

"I do have one bargaining chip when it comes to Clysiros." He held up his hand, waggling his fingers. "She needs me alive. Only my blood, given as a voluntarily offering, can complete the ritual that will solidify her bond with Reigh. In short, she needs something from me, and I need something from her. I'm hoping to arrange a trade."

"That's good for you, but it doesn't exactly do much for the rest of us," I fumed. "It doesn't mean she won't butcher the rest of us on a whim."

Jaevid flashed me a sudden, somewhat menacing smirk that made me stop short. "Oh yes, it absolutely does. If she wants even a drop from me, then I'd better be satisfied with the terms—that includes Maldobar's survival, as well as yours."

"All this assuming you can even bring her here." Haldor was muttering under his breath and shaking his head as he turned away. He strolled back toward his dragon, snatching his helmet and riding gauntlets up on the way. Calem followed him silently, the wind catching through his platinum hair as he stared off into the distance. I couldn't tell if he was even listening to any of this or not.

I started to walk away, too. There wasn't much else to say. Jaevid's plan was insanity, and yet, we'd come to a point now where those kinds of solutions were our only viable options left. I didn't like it—but I didn't have a choice. It was this, or surrender.

Dragonriders did not surrender.

Suddenly, a flash of brilliant green light burst from the ground right in front of me. An explosion? A Tibran attack? I sprang back and threw up my arms to shield my face.

The dragons hissed and recoiled. Phevos sprang over, quick as a cat, and wrapped himself around me like a wall of guarding scales. His deep growl was like thunder in my ears. I had to shove one of his wings out of my way to see what was happening.

It was the seed—the one Jaevid had sent with Aedan and Phillip.

Hovering about three feet off the ground, the seed glowed like a tiny star, filling the air with its brilliant aura. Jaevid strode right toward it, purpose in every step. He stretched out a hand and plucked the seed from the air, carefully closing it tightly in his fist. The green light bled through the cracks between his fingers. It flashed brighter for several seconds before it finally went dark. When he opened his palm again, a fine white mist swirled into the air and vanished without a trace.

Jaevid looked up, fixing me with a hard stare. "They're ready."

"REMEMBER, DO NOT ENGAGE, EVEN IF YOU TAKE FIRE," JAEVID SIGNALED AS WE tucked into a tight diamond formation around him. "*We need to get to the castle as fast as possible. Lingering will draw Argonox's attention. We don't want to set off a battle we aren't ready for.*"

As tempting as it was to roast every Tibran I saw purely out of spite, he did have a point. There was no way to anticipate how my father might react to seeing us. But I sort of doubted we would be getting off on the right foot if we instigated a final battle for Halfax without giving him any warning. Still, the idea of that scenario brought a sadistic grin to my lips. What could I even say? Maybe something like, "Hi again, Dad, I know you exiled me, but I thought I'd come back, bring your revived war-buddy-demigod-savior along, and start an all-out brawl for the last standing major city in the kingdom!"

Yeah. No way that would go over well. Not without someone getting the axe, anyway.

Dipping into formation off Jaevid's left wingtip, Phevos and I locked into our positions and poured on the speed. They would hear us coming before they saw us, but there was nothing we could do about the noise of our wing beats, after all. Even from a higher altitude, they would hear our approach from five miles out. But with any luck, we'd be moving too fast and the Tibran long-range weaponry, net throwing machines, trebuchets, and orb-hurtling catapults would be disabled —thanks to Aedan and Phillip.

Across from me, Haldor and his dragon moved in flawless synchronization. He leaned with the rippling motion of Turq's spine as the bluish-green beast pumped his powerful shoulders. Haldor's legs flexed in stabilizing bursts against the boot sheaths to keep his weight centered, and his hands gripped the saddle handles with his resin-palmed riding gauntlets fitted perfectly around all but two fingers—the two on his right hand he used for firing his bow. It was the perfect union of strength and precision.

In the rear of our formation, Calem and Perish flew a few feet above us so that we could give some added cover from any arrows that might be fired at us from below. Perish's hide wasn't as thick as most dragons. Her pearlescent white scales were smaller and more delicate. A well-aimed arrow might pierce it and bring her down. Normally, her speed would make her a difficult target for all but highly proficient archers. She was forced to keep pace with us this time, however, so we would be acting as her shield until we got to the castle.

I cut my gaze forward again, watching Mavrik's majestic body gliding effortlessly through the air at the front of our formation. He was a massive creature compared to the rest of our dragons—more than twice Phevos's size. Once, he'd supposedly been the fastest dragon in all of Maldobar. But he'd grown into a size now that inevitably sacrificed some of that youthful speed. Still, he was no less impressive—or lethal. His eyes glowed like pools of molten gold, scanning the horizon with all his jagged black spines raised. The starlight glinted off his dark blue scales and each flap of his mighty wings sent a concussive boom through the air. Nothing compared to the magnificent, primal beauty of a king drake.

Ahead, the glint of a thousand lit torches caught my eye, taking a shape I knew all too well. My eyes stung and watered. My throat constricted. I bit down hard, trying to keep it all in. It had been over a year now since I'd even seen my home. As my gaze traced the grand keep, rising tall and proud at the crest of the city, I wondered if my room was still the way I'd left it. Or had Father cleaned it out when he exiled me? I hoped not. I hadn't taken Mother's letters with me when I left. Those notes were all I had left of her. If they were lost …

I shut my eyes tightly and sucked in a ragged breath. Now wasn't the time. I had to pull myself together. I could *not* be the wretched little princess who came sobbing back to her father's feet. I'd die first.

As we descended for our final approach, I finally saw them. Tibrans—more legions than I could count—surrounded my city and loomed on the northern horizon like a rising black tide. Their camps dotted the lower hills by the hundreds. The shapes of their towering war machines were easy to pick out under the wash of sterling moonlight. They almost had the city of Halfax completely surrounded. But as Roland had promised, their westward ranks were thinner. Not being able to push more of their forces up from the south and over from the west might have been the only thing still staying Argonox's hand. He didn't seem like the type of man to want to risk everything not going according to his carefully-devised plan.

Phevos snapped his jaws, body thrumming with a growl as we zipped toward the city. No sooner had we come into range then arrows began zipping past my helmet and glancing off Phevos's hide. He snarled and bared his jagged teeth, ears pinned back in anger. Mavrik did the same and, with a few angled flaps of his black wings, dropped lower to act as a living shield for the rest of us to finish our approach. Shouts and horns blared. I caught a glimpse of Tibrans scrambling, panicking as they clambered over their failing artillery devices. Relief poured over my body like cool rain—Aedan and Phillip had done it!

In their panic, the Tibrans were clumsy. Their archers kept firing, but nothing hit its mark. The only trebuchet they were able to angle toward us in time was too far away. The massive boulder hurtled through the air and landed more than two hundred yards short, crunching through a few ranks of their own men before it stopped.

Haldor let out a shout, hefting his bow in the air. I ducked back down again against Phevos's neck, unable to keep from smirking. The coming battle might not be so bad if the Tibrans kept up that sort of nonsense.

As we crossed over the high ramparts of Halfax's outermost wall, hundreds of Maldobarian soldiers poured out of the guard towers and clambered along the battlements. They whooped, waved their arms, and beat their swords against their shields in celebration. In the distance, I heard the battle horn sound, announcing our arrival to everyone in the city. By the time we circled for our final landing in the forward courtyard of the castle, bells were tolling in every corner of Halfax.

Jaevid let the rest of us land and dismount first. I hurried to unbuckle myself from Phevos's saddle and gave one of his ears a gentle tug, urging him to make room. Then, Haldor, Calem, and I stood back to make way for the king drake's arrival.

My father's elite guard, dressed in full armor with the eagle emblazoned on their breastplates and their faces covered by golden masks, gathered around us. They stood at attention, raising torches against the moonlight, and watched as the enormous blue drake descended with a *boom*. Mavrik rose up, long tail curling as he spread his wings and let out a shattering cry. My heartbeat surged and part of me prayed that, wherever he was hiding amongst his vile ranks, Argonox could hear it and would know what was coming. Jaevid Broadfeather had arrived at last, bringing hope and vengeance with him. There wasn't a soldier in Maldobar who wouldn't hear his call to arms and not a single dragonrider who would not rise up now to join him.

Argonox could still prove victorious at the end of all this—I knew that. He might still add Maldobar to his empire and butcher us all down to the very last child. But he would not take my home unfought. He would have to pry it from my cold, dead hands.

CHAPTER SIXTEEN

The instant Jaevid's boots hit the ground in the castle's grand front courtyard, one of my father's elite guards stepped away from the crowd and approached him. Through the visor of my helmet, I glanced at Haldor. His hand was clenched around his bow as he gave me a nod. This was it—the moment of truth. Would we be received as a long-awaited cavalry, or as unwelcomed vigilantes?

The guardsman offered Jaevid a deep bow and motioned to the grand arched doorway at the far end of the courtyard. "His Majesty King Felix Farrow welcomes you. Please follow me."

My shoulders sagged in relief. At least it seemed like we weren't going to be arrested right away. So far, so good.

Jaevid led the way toward the doorway, the guards falling into formation around us so that we were flanked on all sides like a parade march. Only a couple of them stayed behind, most likely to guide our dragons down into the catacombs for the night. No doubt the castle's usual dragon housing, a circular structure we called the Deck, was already at capacity with so many dragonriders called here. My desire to be anywhere other than under my father's disappointed glare was not a recent feeling, and I'd spent a lot of time at the Deck as a child, secretly tucked up alongside the snoozing dragons.

But our dragons wouldn't get to enjoy those cozy chambers. There wouldn't be room. Not that the catacombs under the castle would be terrible. I was certain my father would make sure the dragons housed down there would have every comfort. They'd get a fresh meal of raw meat, and a bed of soft hay to curl up on to sleep off the weariness of our journey. Master Godfrey had been the stablemaster in charge of looking after our horses and dragons for as long as I could remember. He ran a tight ship, and our mounts never wanted for anything.

We had almost reached the massive set of double doors leading into the castle. Every step made my heart race faster until it clashed in my ears and made my fingertips go numb. I clenched my teeth to stop them from chattering. Nearly a year's time hadn't changed this place at all—although it had changed me plenty. Too late, I realized I wasn't ready for this. I wanted to run, bolt back to Phevos, and make a break for ... anywhere else.

Suddenly, the doors before us rumbled and opened wide, groaning on their iron-wrought hinges.

Jaevid stopped. The rest of us did, too.

Felix Farrow, my father and the current King of Maldobar, came striding out into the courtyard with a flock of men in armor following close at his heels. Most of them I knew, or at least recognized the distinction of their armor. They were men of the court—High Commander Morrig, Infantry General Craig, Duke Brinton and his son, and Vaelin, who had taken over Kiran's office and now represented Luntharda as a royal ambassador.

In fact, my father was the only one not wearing his full court armor. Dressed in a simple tunic, pants, and leather jerkin underneath a black bear hide cloak, the only thing that marked him as king was the simple golden circlet nestled on his head. Even that was one of the simplest, most lackluster crowns he owned. Not that he'd ever been all that fond of courtly clothes, but we'd clearly caught him off guard.

When he saw us, my father stopped short. His light brown eyes fixed on Jaevid and went wide, white brows lifting slowly. Gods, the months had aged him. His face was creased, somber eyes now hooded, and more of his dark golden hair had turned silver. It hung to his shoulders in gentle waves, so gray now it nearly matched his neatly trimmed white beard.

My stomach fluttered as he took another step. His lips parted, and his eyes narrowed as he came closer and closer, stopping only when he was a few feet away from Jaevid. "You," my father murmured quietly, his deep voice thick with emotion. Was it anger? Sorrow? Gods, I couldn't tell.

Jaevid was motionless, standing with his entire body rigid. His fists clenched at his sides and his brow skewed into an expression of withheld panic, our resident demigod didn't say a word. He didn't even blink.

I held my breath. My mind raced, and it felt as though my heart might have stopped beating altogether.

"Forty years." My father's face twitched, scrunching violently. He squeezed his eyes shut and looked down, expression contorting and chest heaving deeply. "And now you come back."

"Felix," Jaevid rasped as he took a stumbling step forward, "I ... Gods, I am so sorry. Please, I-I ... I couldn't do anything to—"

The King of Maldobar sprang forward faster than I'd ever seen him move before. He seized Jaevid in his arms and nearly snatched the poor man right out of his boots.

Jaevid winced, going as stiff as a dried-out corpse in my father's grip at first. His eyes were as round as moons and his whole face blanched. Then, he suddenly seemed to process what was happening. His expression crumpled, and he hugged King Felix back fiercely.

My father's tearful, barking laughter echoed through the courtyard as the two men gripped one another. I swallowed against the hard knot of emotion forming in the back of my throat and was thankful to still have my helmet on so no one could see the tears welling in my eyes. I couldn't remember the last time I had heard my father laugh like that. It must have been before Mother died, years ago.

"I guess this means it really is the end of the world." My father pulled back, shaking Jaevid by the shoulders a little. "Wait—I'm forgetting something, I think." He scratched at the white beard on his chin and pursed his lips. Then, without warning, he reared back and punched Jaevid in the arm.

"Gods, Felix!" Jaevid staggered back, hissing curses under his breath as he rubbed his bicep. "Seriously?"

My father wore a cattish grin. "You have *no idea* how long I've wanted to do that."

"I'd wager about four decades or so," Haldor murmured as he slid off his helmet and slipped it under his arm. "If we're placing bets, that is."

"Hah!" My father barked another chuckle before he realized who had spoken. As soon as he spotted Haldor, his expression hardened. His brown eyes went as cold as steel and darted through the crowd gathered around him as though he were searching for someone.

Oh no.

I took a quick, careful step and dodged behind one of the elite guards.

"Wait." I could hear rising anger in my father's tone. "Do *not* tell me you came here without my daughter. Jaevid, I love you like a brother, but if you have come here to tell me she fell in battle or was taken by the Tibrans on your watch, so help me, I will—"

"Felix," Jaevid interrupted his rant.

I chanced a quick look around the guard's arm, just in time to see him point right at me. My father turned, following the line of his finger until he spotted me.

Curse it. I shouldn't have looked. Why did I have to look?

Paralyzed with fear, I swallowed over and over against the growing pain in my throat. I cringed underneath my armor and kept my gaze locked on the ground as heavy footsteps crunched across the gravel toward me. The elite guardsman stepped lightly out of the way, making way for the king, who now stood before me. I didn't want to see his face. I couldn't take that look of wrath and utter disappointment—not again.

I couldn't stop trembling as he grasped the sides of my helmet, and slowly pulled it off my head. My long hair spilled out, bolts of dark gold falling across my chest and over my shoulders. Then a warm hand touched my chin, gently bringing it up so I had to look at him.

"Jenna." There were fresh tears in my father's eyes. I saw none of the anger I'd been expecting. Only relief, joy, and ... love.

I tried to speak, but only managed to choke on a sob.

Fates, I wasn't supposed to cry. Not in front of all these men! But the more I tried to hold it in, the more the pain wrenched and tore at my heart until I had no choice. All I had ever wanted was his approval. His exciting stories of danger and adventure, his legacy in the Gray War—those things had been what lit this fire in my soul in the first place. I wanted to be like that, to walk in his footsteps, and lead our kingdom further into greatness.

Having him reject all my efforts was unbearable ... because, more than anything, I wanted to make him proud.

"Come here," he cooed gently as he reeled me in closer. He kissed my forehead and held me as though I were a little girl again. "Welcome home, love."

"LET ME SEE IF I HAVE THIS RIGHT, BECAUSE THIS IS SOUNDING SUSPICIOUSLY like one of your suicidal, save-the-world plans." King Felix leaned forward, resting his hands on the broad mapping table. "You want to go into the Vale and broker a deal with the goddess of death, all in the hope that she will honor that bargain and fight for us in the event your power isn't strong enough to stand against whatever Argonox brings onto the battlefield? That about the size of it?"

Jaevid crossed his arms. "Well, of course I'm open to suggestions."

"Oh, and let's not forget about the part where you allowed my youngest child —who I intentionally placed in the deepest, darkest corner of Luntharda where this very thing would *never* happen to him—to fall into the enemy's hands." He shook his head, rolling his eyes as he pushed away from the table to drop into his kingly chair. "Just like old times. Only now we're gambling with the lives of my children instead of just our own. Gods, I should have hit you harder. Or in the face. Maybe both."

"I am sorry about that," Jaevid confessed. "Reigh is as stubborn as any Farrow I've ever met. He wasn't going to leave without Aubren, and I wasn't about to try to convince him to leave his brother behind. There wasn't any other option."

"Of course, there was! You knock him unconscious and drag him out by the ankles," my father grumbled. "When he was born with that ... darkness in him, I knew there was no way he could ever live in Maldobar. You'd promised to return when we needed you again, and to me, that meant something was coming that would require your presence to fix. I didn't want to put any of my children in that kind of danger—least of all him. If his power turned out to be anything like yours, I worried what war might do to him."

"So you sent him away?" I heard myself ask. Shock left my skin feeling cold and tingly as I watched the realization slowly seep into my father's face. He'd just confessed! Reigh *was* his child—and he was my little brother.

"I gave him to the only man I knew I could trust to keep him safe," he confirmed, dropping his head into one of his hands. "Kiran promised to take Reigh deep into Luntharda and keep him there for as long as possible. He also knew how vital it would be for Reigh's existence to a secret kept from everyone. I couldn't allow anyone to try to abuse him for what he could do or twist him into something he wasn't meant to be." He rubbed his fingers along his forehead and sighed. "Reigh wasn't just born a prince, he was hand-chosen by a goddess. Taking that kind of power and using it in malice nearly destroyed our world once. I couldn't let that happen again. I didn't believe he'd ever be safe here."

"You mean the God Bane?" Haldor asked.

My father looked up and nodded. "Our culture has all but made him into a myth. They like to toss it around at the Dragonrider Academy like it's something to boast about, another great notch in the belt of our military. But after the Gray War ended, I was able to track down enough records of God Bane's existence to paint a good picture of what we might be up against if that threat should ever rise again. What I found was ... horrifying."

"We defeated him once, Your Majesty. We can do it again." High Commander Morrig stood on the opposite side of the war table, his sharp gaze still perusing the map of our kingdom laid out on the table.

My father glanced up, blinking in surprise as though he'd forgotten he had a room full of nobles and military officials all awaiting his decision on what to do next. With another great sigh, he waved a hand and sank back deeper into his chair. "Let's call this meeting adjourned for now, gentlemen. You all have plenty to keep you busy. In the meantime, I'd like some time alone with Jaevid and my daughter. Family business—you understand."

The High Commander gave a dragonrider salute. "Of course, Your Majesty. I'll escort Lieutenants Calem and Haldor to the barracks and have them properly outfitted immediately. We will be battle-ready and ready to mobilize on your orders."

"And I'll see that my boys on watch don't shoot your ... cat monster and his Gray elf friend when they climb over the wall," the Infantry General added with a grin. "If that elf boy is as useful as you say, he might have a lot of vital information on our enemy's positions outside the wall."

I managed a cursory smile as the general turned to depart. I'd intentionally left out the part where the "cat monster" was actually Duke Phillip Derrick.

Somehow, that seemed like one of those things they would have to see to believe. That, and I wasn't sure if Phillip would want them to know. Of course, my father would recognize him eventually—his demeanor and inflections were the same, after all. But if Phillip didn't want his condition proclaimed to every corner of Maldobar, then I'd respect that. It was his choice to make.

"Well, then. I suppose I owe you some gratitude. You saved my eldest two, after all. Returned one to me, even." King Felix pushed himself back up with a groan, stretching his neck from one side to the other before he waved for us to follow. "I've got something for you, Jae."

Jaevid flicked me an uncertain glance, as though silently asking me what this was about. Why? It wasn't like I had any special insight into their ancient friendship.

All I could do was shrug.

My father led the way from the mapping room deeper into the castle, a place I knew all too well. The fact that it hadn't changed much since I left made my heart ache for my private quarters and everything familiar I'd been missing. My bed. My clothes. The letters from my mother that I kept tucked into the drawer in my night table.

Mother must have known her pregnancy with Reigh would be too much for her to survive because she had taken the time to write me letters, arranging for them to be delivered one-by-one much later—after she was gone. I'd received one every week while I was at the academy for training. They told stories of my childhood, things she remembered and adored about me, reminded me of how much she loved my brother and me, and declared how proud she was of me. I hadn't taken those notes with me when I left, too afraid of being forced to leave them behind in the burning ruins of some battlefield. They were my most precious treasures. I couldn't bear to lose them like that.

The royal wing of the castle was off limits to anyone apart from direct family members and extremely special guests. Jaevid qualified as both, since my father had formally adopted him into our family years ago. There was even legal documentation to prove it. On paper, Jaevid was a Farrow, not a Broadfeather, although I didn't know that he'd ever used our family name. It would have certainly turned some heads.

Passing through the gilded doors flanked by more elite guards, we entered the grand foyer that boasted two elegant sloping staircases leading off in either direction. The bannisters were carved so that each one looked like a man with a sword clutched at his breast. The newel posts were engraved in the shapes of dragons raising up on their hind legs, leering down to the center of the room, where a broad blue velvet carpet covered most of the white marble floor. Overhead, an iron-wrought chandelier held three hundred lit candles that filled the room and shone off the polished mahogany walls.

To the right, my room quarters were up the stairs and down the hall—directly across from Aubren's. To the left was where my mother and father had lived in the most luxurious part of the castle. I wasn't sure if my father had slept there in years, though. At least, not after Mother passed away.

"Is that supposed to be me?" Jaevid asked suddenly, his head tilted to the side as he studied the enormous embroidered tapestry hanging on the back wall—right between where the two staircases met. It was thirty feet long at least, spanning from the ceiling all the way to the floor with an intricate design of a dragonrider seated on a snarling mount, driving the point of his scimitar at a skeletal-looking monster.

I blushed. Countless hours of my childhood had been spent sitting before that tapestry, admiring every detail of the rider's armor, his handsomely shaped features, fluttering blue cape, and compelling gaze. It was like a glimpse from a fairy tale, the glorious hero throwing down the villain in an epic battle—essentially everything an imaginative princess might dream of.

Jaevid stopped short and snapped a puzzled scowl at my father. "You hung a picture of *me* on your wall?"

"Well, if you remember, you essentially reduced this castle to rubble at the end of the war. I had to come up with some new décor. You were a popular topic of conversation at the time," King Felix wafted a hand dismissively.

"And you couldn't come up with anything else to put there? It had to be me?" Jaevid rolled his eyes. "Fates preserve us. That doesn't even look like me!"

I covered my mouth and bit down, trying not to laugh. I wondered what he'd think about being featured in every town square's fountain sculpture, as well. To be fair, he was right. The images didn't look like him all that much. They made him seem far bigger, brawnier, and older than he was.

Jaevid rubbed his brow and grumbled under his breath, "Jace hasn't seen this, has he?"

"Uhhh, well ... " My father shifted and cleared his throat.

"Great. Just great." Jaevid shot him another venomous glare as he turned away. "That thing is ridiculous, and so are you for hanging it." He thumbed back at the tapestry.

There was a glint of mischief sparkling in my father's dark eyes as he passed by, leading the way up the left staircase toward his private chambers. "*Pfft*, just wait till you see the one hanging in the throne room."

"*WHAT?*"

CHAPTER SEVENTEEN

Jaevid was still muttering like a madman when we entered my father's private study. Three entire walls of the large space were covered completely by bookshelves, crammed tight with tomes, scrolls, and ancient texts. The third was an entire wall of windows made of intricately-cut colored glass that formed the shape of Maldobar's royal seal—a golden eagle against a field of blue, gripping swords in its claws. Along the edges, green vines with vibrant red roses twisted around a golden border. It filled what would have been an otherwise dank space with radiant shafts of colored light whenever the sun struck it.

On a large, claw-footed desk right in the center of the room, papers and books were stacked around piles of parchment, and a golden inkpot held a crisp silver feather. My father wasted no time diving into the middle drawer, raking things around until he pulled out a thin wooden box. It didn't look all that special —plain and dusty, like it had been tucked away there for a long time.

Without a word, he handed it to Jaevid.

I stepped in closer, peering over his shoulder as he opened it. For a few seconds, Jaevid didn't make a sound. He didn't move. He stared down into the box with his expression blank. Then, with a trembling hand, he reached in and took out two trinkets. The first was a necklace strung on a woven cord. The teardrop-shaped pendant seemed to have been carved from bone and polished smooth before intricate, tiny elven engravings were added. The second was a very old, ragged handkerchief. By the look of it, it had seen a lot of use. Parts of it were stained with what looked like spots of blood. The edges were torn and tattered. But in the very center, stitched in blue and black thread, were the images of two dragons. They faced one another, their tails intertwined, and necks arched so that the negative space made the shape of a heart.

That was a woman's token—something usually given to a loved one before battle.

Jaevid sucked in a breath, his brow furrowing as he ran his thumb across the stitching. Pain crept into the corners of his features like an encroaching stormfront, darkening his gaze and making his mouth go tense. He was breathing heavily through his nose when he looked back up at my father.

"You know she's back," he seethed quietly, the words hissing through his teeth.

King Felix shook his head. "No. Whatever you saw was not her, Jaevid. Maybe it looked like her. Maybe it even sounded like her. But the Beckah we knew—the one you loved—would not turn against us. She would die before she joined with someone like Argonox. You know that as well as I do."

Jaevid lowered his gaze again, saying nothing as he closed his hand around the handkerchief.

My father stepped toward him and planted a hand on his shoulder to give it a firm squeeze. "He'll pay for it, Jae. Make no mistake. You and I are going to make him pay for every person he's hurt and every life he's taken. He came here looking for a fight—and by all the gods, we will give him one he'll never forget."

SERVANTS BROUGHT US A LIGHT MEAL AS WE SAT TOGETHER IN THE LOUNGE area of my father's chambers. As the crown princess, now returned to her home, I should have eaten with delicate restraint and poise while seated properly on one of the elegant, tufted chairs. Hah! As if I had patience for that after what I'd been through over the past few weeks.

I still reeked of swamp mud from the Marshlands and my hair was in a thousand knots as I stormed the table of delicacies like a barbarian. Heaping cheese-stuffed pastries, herb roasted lamb and potatoes, and a handful of my favorite candied figs on to a porcelain plate, I plopped down on the sofa and stuffed my face as fast as I could. It had been days since I'd had more than a handful of dried meat or nuts from riding rations. I couldn't remember food ever tasting so good.

I felt a little less self-conscious about it when Jaevid did the same, taking up a seat on the couch beside me. Part of me had to wonder if that was intentional, like he might be trying to ease the tension in the room. He snuck a quick glance in my direction, smiling around a cheek full of cheesy pastry goodness.

Okay, fine, so the demigod war hero was growing on me a bit. I respected him, yes. How could I not? But I also sort of ... liked him now. Not like *that*, of course. But Jaevid was steadily becoming less of the legendary figure and childhood hero I'd aspired to be like and more of a genuine friend. I understood now why my father had gotten along with him so well.

"So, Aubren has gone to Luntharda." My father exhaled deeply as he passed by all the bottles of imported wines and rich meads to pour himself a goblet of spiced apple cider. I didn't know why, but he never drank alcohol. "I suppose it's the best place for him now. Ever since he was a boy, he's always been softer and more like his mother. That strong empathy sometimes rules his head too much. I worried what war would do to him. Nothing is worse than watching the world crush your children's innocence like that, knowing there's nothing you can do to stop it. Now he's a man and I can't protect him like that anymore." The sofa lurched as he sat down on Jaevid's other side. "He's always seemed to be searching for something—himself, or meaning, or a cause, I don't know. Whatever it is, perhaps now he'll find it."

"I think we all do some of that, in our own way," Jaevid agreed. "Searching for our purpose, that is."

My father chuckled between sips of cider. "Yeah. And we generally start looking for it in all the wrong places."

The roaring of flames in the hearth filled the silence as we sat and ate. I couldn't stop thinking about Aubren as I chewed. Had he and the other refugees made it to Luntharda with Judan? Were they safe now? Trapped here in the city, with more and more Tibrans surrounding us every minute, there was no way to know.

"I'm sorry, Felix," Jaevid blurted suddenly. "I should have been here when Julianna died."

My father leaned forward with a groan, putting his empty cup onto the coffee table and letting his elbows rest on his knees. The light of the fire danced in his eyes, reflecting sparks of memory that made the wrinkles in his skin seem to deepen. "I don't blame you for her death, Jae. It wouldn't have mattered if you had been here. Her fate was my fault, not yours. Nothing you could have done would have saved her from it."

Jaevid frowned. "What do you mean?"

His lips thinned as his gaze fell to his right hand, where an old scar made a gnarled line right across his palm. "It happened here, during our battle in the throne room. You went off dealing with bigger issues, and I was ... being me. Reckless. Stupid. Anything to win." My father's eyes closed as his fingers curled in, making a fist around that scar. "I cut my hand on that black crystal, not knowing what it was. From that moment, Julianna and Reigh's fates were sealed —because of a dumb accident. There was nothing anyone could do to reverse it, not even you. I'd given the dark goddess a blood offering and I didn't even know it until years later."

I sat up straighter, forgetting about my mostly-empty plate of food. "You knew about the starium crystal? You've known all this time? And said nothing?"

My father nodded grimly. "After Reigh's birth, it was obvious he was going to be ... *different*. I'd been around Jaevid's brand of bizarre long enough to know divine power when I saw it. My only hope was that someone had left behind texts or at least documented stories about whatever was afflicting Reigh. But until I found them, I knew he could not stay here. Most of the royal archives were destroyed during the Gray War, so it took years to track them down. When I finally did, I prayed they were wrong or just making wild guesses."

"To be the Harbinger of Clysiros is a costly blessing," Jaevid muttered, his voice hardly more than a whisper.

My father gave a snort, like that was a bad joke. "Some might call it more of a curse. In fact, most of these divine gifts seem to be double-edged swords. But in Reigh's case, because of my dumb accident, he is now a part of the legacy of the most hated figure in Maldobar's history—the God Bane."

"It wasn't your fault, Felix. You didn't know. Neither of us did. How could we?" Jaevid put a hand on his shoulder.

"What does that even mean? Who was God Bane?" I had to stop and take a breath. My heart was pounding so hard it was making my eardrums sore. "I mean, we all heard the stories about the old war, about how the dragonriders were forged in the flames of that battle against God Bane, but who *was* he?"

There was a harrowing sense of hopelessness in my father's eyes as he gazed back at me. The light from the hearth cast heavy shadows, making his cheeks seem thinner, raw-boned, and deepening the puffy circles that hung under his eyes. "He was Clysiros's last Harbinger."

Panic turned my body cold. I stole a glance at Jaevid, hoping for some reassurance, but he seemed just as stunned as I was. His expression tightened, and his jaw went rigid as we sat waiting for my father to continue.

"None of the documents I found could trace his origin, only his path of destruction after his ritual with the crystal had been completed. An initial offering of blood triggers it, but the goddess chooses her Harbinger from that person's bloodline, not necessarily the one who gave it. That's why you and Aubren were spared." My father reached over, around Jaevid, and settled one of his heavy, leathery hands on my arm. "A life must also be given to bring the Harbinger into the world, because he must be able to walk here and in the realm of spirits. Two souls, one body, one shared mind. Reigh's twin was the one who paid that price."

"Twin?" I gasped.

His gaze swung back, fixing on the hearth before us once more. "Julianna—your mother—was so fragile during that pregnancy. We assumed it was because of her age. Carrying twins is difficult enough on its own, but for one of them to be the Harbinger was too much. As soon as Reigh was born, he cried out like he was in agony. He ... consumed the soul of his brother. It happened so quickly. There was nothing we could do. He'd taken his first victim and his first breath simultaneously." My father closed his eyes and bowed his head. "I was horrified. I couldn't even bear to touch him. But it was my fault, not his. I made him into this."

All the tension in Jaevid's face dissolved, gradually falling back into a look of shared sorrow. He shook his head and looked away with a heavy exhale.

"What's he like?" Father's voice was quiet, barely audible above the crackle of the flames. They danced in his eyes, reflections of some memory that seemed to carry him far away.

"Who?" I asked.

"Reigh." He stirred in his seat, brow furrowing in an uncomfortable frown. "What does he look like? Does he seem ... happy?"

I wasn't sure what to say. I'd only been around Reigh for a short time at Barrowton, and during that time I hadn't known he might be my brother. Aubren had only told me a little about him then.

"Happy and twice the fighter you ever were. He had a good life in Luntharda. Kiran raised him well." Jaevid assured him. "He's got Julianna's hair. It might even be redder than hers, if you can believe it. But he's got your eyes and—I'm sorry to say—your sense of humor."

My father gave a snort and a bemused half-grin.

"He's got the Farrow stubborn streak, for sure," I added. "He was chosen by a dragon."

Father's eyes went wide. "A wild one?"

I couldn't resist a proud smile. "One of Mavrik's hatchlings. She's as green as a tree snake and so beautiful. He named her Vexi."

There was regal pride in the way he sat up straighter, squaring his shoulders. "What did Kiran say to that? Shocked, I bet!" he asked with a laugh.

Oh, gods. He didn't know. Stealing a quick look at Jaevid, I took in a steadying breath. "Father, Kiran is gone."

His smile began to fade, draining away little by little until only a pale, hollow-eyed expression of shock remained. "What?"

"He fell at Barrowton. H-he fought well, but ... " I struggled to keep my voice steady, but the words were poison. Cringing, I turned away.

"He did not suffer," Jaevid finished for me. "And he died bravely."

My father's proud stature shrank again, seeming to wither away right before my eyes. "He was a good man, one of the best I've ever known. I hope the Gods give him rest."

"He found peace in paradise," Jaevid confirmed. "Now it is our duty to make sure that his sacrifice was not in vain."

King Felix lowered his head, as though the weight of a kingdom and the lives of thousands of people were resting on his brow.

Jaevid didn't give him a moment to dwell, though. "What else have you learned about God Bane?"

"He came here with the exact intentions of Argonox—to enslave not just every person in this world, but also all the gods. Hence the name," my father replied. "Owning the mortal world was not enough. He hungered to rule the divine one, as well. He'd spent decades scouring the earth for every trace of godly power he could, and amassed plenty. He came for Paligno's god stone but knew he would have to get through Maldobar to claim it. But we had one thing God Bane didn't."

"Dragons," I breathed, recalling the story the instructors told every new class of dragonriders when we began a new year of training at the academy.

"They are completely unique to our kingdom, apparently," my father confirmed. "They don't exist anywhere else in the world. God Bane had never seen anything like them. And they were the last thing he ever saw, as it turns out. Dragons chose human soldiers as their riders for the very first time on that battlefield. Then, as one, they tore down God Bane's ranks and sent what was left of his forces scurrying back to the shadows."

"And now they've returned," Jaevid concluded as he rubbed the back of his neck.

"I honestly don't know if Argonox is the same man as God Bane. All accounts say that man was killed. But he was a fully manifested Harbinger, able to bend the laws of death. Who's to say he isn't the same person, now stripped of his own divine power?" Father patted my arm and sat back again. "At last I had to face the reality that it doesn't matter who Argonox is—his vendetta is the same. He wants to control every source of divine power he can get his scheming hands on and I have what is quite possibly the most powerful artifact of them all. I had to do anything and everything to make sure he never got it. I can't allow him to set foot in this castle, no matter what the cost."

"So that's why you recalled all the dragonriders here," Jaevid guessed as he stood, putting his plate aside so he could pace and rub his chin thoughtfully.

"Naturally," he replied. "And I couldn't tell anyone else about it, not even the people I loved most of all. Tibran forces had already begun taking prisoners along our borders. The only advantages I had were dragonriders and the fact that Argonox didn't know the crystal's location. Based on the number of Tibran soldiers rallying outside my gates, I'd say that last one is forfeit now."

"You could have told me all of this," I scolded as I reached over Jaevid's empty seat and gripped my father's hand. "You should have trusted me. I would have understood—I would have stayed! But you exiled me like a heretic! I thought you hated me for choosing this path!"

His brows rumpled and drew up in a smile that made my heart wrench like someone was tearing it in two. "My sweet, brave girl, there is nothing you could ever do that would make me stop loving you. That's the hardest part of being a parent; realizing that your hopes for your children's futures, everything you ever wanted for them, are not within your control or right to decide."

Tears stung my eyes. I had to look away. "Well, it is *your* fault. You made me this way. All you ever talked about was the glory days and what it was like to ride on a dragon."

My father laughed loudly and gave one of my cheeks a pinch. "Oh, is that what you think? I beg to differ. You'd have heard those stories with or without my help. You can't throw a cat in this kingdom without hitting a statue of this idiot." He tipped his head toward Jaevid, who now stood staring at him with a red-faced look of horror.

"Statues?" Jaevid growled. "There are *statues*, too?"

My father ignored him, his eyes still fixed on me. "You are a dragonrider because you were chosen, not because of anything I did. That beast saw something in you, something worthy of his eternal loyalty. So don't you dare try passing credit for that off to me, understood? I may not have liked it, but only because the idea of losing yet another one of my children to a power I can't control is ... infuriating, to say the least. Regardless, embrace it, be proud of it, and never apologize for it. My daughter is a dragonrider, and I couldn't be prouder."

Heat exploded through my chest in a burst that left me breathless. It was as though all the strangling chains of shame that had held me captive my entire life snapped at once. I hadn't chosen to be the polite, dainty princess he wanted. But he was still proud of me. He still loved me.

I couldn't stop the tears. They welled up, rolled down my face, and dripped from my chin. I hid my face in my hands, too embarrassed to even look at him.

Then I felt his arms around me.

I hugged him back, burying my face against his shoulder as he petted the back of my head. "Sending you away from here was the hardest decision I've ever made, Jenna," he whispered gently. "But it was all I knew to do. I couldn't stop you from fighting, but if the hammer was destined to fall here and Argonox overwhelmed this place, I didn't want you anywhere near it."

"Gods, you're so stupid for such an old man." I sniffled.

"No argument there," Jaevid muttered. Peeking over my father's shoulder, I found him standing with his arms crossed, brow locked into a deep, bitter scowl, and lips pursed angrily. "Did you really build statues?" he demanded.

"Oh yes," Father snickered. "*Hundreds* of them."

CHAPTER EIGHTEEN

Phillip and Aedan's arrival had the castle buzzing before noon. The servants dashed about, filling the hall with anxious whispers and jittery energy as everyone gathered in the great hall to receive them. Meanwhile, the elite royal guards watched Phillip closely through the eyeholes in their golden masks, hands always hovering somewhere near their weaponry. It was clear they didn't like the look of him, not that I could blame them. He towered over everyone, a monstrous mixture of man and beast with skin the color of stone, paw-like hind feet, glowing silver eyes, and a long flicking tail. His powerful build tested all the seams of his clothes, and the claws on his feet clicked against the marble as he strode into the great hall.

Beside him, Aedan was half his height with only a little bit of short white fuzz beginning to grow back in on his shaven head. His pointed ears and multihued eyes were all that marked him as a Gray elf, and he still wore the bronze armor he'd disguised himself in. With the Argonox's brand burned into the side of his neck, he still looked like any other Tibran slave-soldier we might have plucked from their ranks.

Only, we knew better.

My father choked out loud at the sight of them, his gaze darting back and forth like he wasn't sure which one was more bizarre. Phillip won in the end, of course. He flicked a dubious glance at Jaevid before clearing his throat and attempting to compose himself. "We are, uh, pleased to have you both back safely," he said in the same kingly tone he liked to use when addressing the court. "I believe introductions are in order."

"Aedan, formerly of Brine's Hollow in the Farchase Plains." He gave a deep bow, his eyes never leaving the floor. I wondered if that was out of respect or fear. Perhaps it was a bit of both.

"He assisted in our rescue of Jenna from Northwatch," Jaevid explained. "He's proven himself to be quite the proficient spy and has certainly earned our trust."

Aedan blushed until even the tips of his long, pointed ears were as red as cherries.

"I was so injured I couldn't walk," I added. "Aedan carried me out on his back."

"I see." My father regarded him again, his expression softening. "Then I believe I am in your debt."

"Oh! N-no, Your Majesty, not at all!" Aedan stammered. "I was honored to help."

I gave one of his pointed ears a playful tug. "He's just being modest. He's quite capable with a blade, too. Perhaps you should knight him?"

Father combed his fingers along his short beard thoughtfully. "Not a bad idea. Unless, of course, he'd prefer to be a dragonrider."

Aedan didn't reply. He seemed to shrink lower and lower, cowering with the ends of his ears still glowing red.

"You should have seen him talking circles around those Tibran officers. He's a clever kid, I'll give him that," Phillip added. He patted the top of Aedan's nearly bald head with a chuckle. "He would do better in the noble court, if you ask me."

Hearing Phillip speak made my father tense and go still, staring back up at our monstrous-looking companion with a puzzled frown. He tilted his head to the side slightly, eyes narrowing as though he couldn't figure out why that voice sounded so familiar. Then his eyebrows suddenly shot up. His eyes went as wide as teacups and his mouth fell open. "Gods and Fates, is that ... Phillip?"

I immediately stepped between them. "Father, it's not his fault. Argonox took us both prisoner, and he did this to Phillip. I know he looks different now, but his mind is unchanged. He's still the same person."

A warm, heavy hand came to rest on my shoulder. I knew his touch, strong and steady, without even looking. "You don't have to explain for me, Jenna," Phillip scolded gently. "It's all right."

"H-how?" Father stopped and cleared his throat, as though he were trying to collect himself. "How did this happen? I mean, how did he do this to you?"

It took a while to explain. Jaevid had to do most of it, since he had a much more intimate understanding of how the venom worked. But the basics of it were fairly simple. The switchbeasts' bite contained a venom that slowly turned you into one of them. Most didn't survive the agonizing process, and Argonox had been experimenting with a way to make a hybrid—a person with the physical strength and abilities of the switchbeast that could still take orders like any other soldier. Phillip was the first successful subject and, as far as we knew, the only one.

"He's stable now," Jaevid assured everyone. "The venom is no longer active in his body, so he won't get any worse. But he also won't improve. What has already been changed can't be reversed."

"Well that's ... unfortunate. I'm sorry to hear about this, Phillip." My father cast him a look of earnest sympathy.

"I know I'm difficult to look at. I'm still not quite used to it, myself," he admitted with a little shrug. "Please don't worry, Your Majesty. I have every intention of resigning my noble title after the war ends. As far as anyone else knows, I perished in Barrowton. Perhaps it should stay that way."

My heart sank, disappearing beneath the depths of my silent panic as I stared up at him. Did this mean he would not return to the court at all? What about us? Would he try to leave again? He couldn't—I wouldn't allow it!

My father opened his mouth, but after a second or two, closed it again without saying a word.

"Felix, maybe it's not my place anymore to be doling out orders, but I think we should start preparing," Jaevid interjected. "I'll need a little time to get things ready on my end. I'm sure our friends would like a chance to catch their breath before we do this."

"Right, of course. I agree," my father agreed, his gaze slowly panning from Phillip to refocus on the task at hand. "Take whatever time you need to prepare. Triple the guard on the ramparts. I want all eyes on Argonox's front line. If he makes a move, I want to see it coming." He turned to begin walking away, then paused to study Aedan for a few seconds more. "And for the love of all the gods, someone get this boy some Maldobarian armor!"

Stepping into my bedroom felt like going back in time. Everything was exactly as I'd left it. The maps I'd used in dragonrider training were still spread out on my desk in the study, covered in markings to show the progression of the Tibran forces across my kingdom. All my books on aerial battle techniques were stacked on my bedside table, right beside my bottle of lavender and vanilla oil I used to help ease my restlessness and anxiety. Little dabs behind my ears or a few drops on my pillow sometimes helped.

I knew it was stupid and an inefficient use of time, but I wanted a bath. There was reeking swamp mud caked on my skin and in my hair, blood smeared and splotched all over me, and the stickiness of old sweat squished under my clothes. I was about to ride into battle, maybe for the last time in my life, and I just wanted a moment to be alone and think. My soul craved it—a few minutes of quiet, to let the world stand still. I wouldn't have long; minutes at the most.

Outside the bathroom, my chamber servants were already spreading out my armor and padding, making sure every piece was polished to perfection. My eyes lingered on it as I passed, wondering if this would be the last time. Would I die in that armor tonight?

While the servants drew the bath, I rummaged through my night table until I found all my mother's letters tucked at the back of the middle drawer. There must have been thirty of them, all neatly folded and tied into a bundle with a purple ribbon. I took the bundle into the bathroom and sat, reclining back in the steaming water, to read them all one by one.

Every tiny, carefully-printed word soaked into my mind like rain into the earth. She had been proud of me. She knew I could do anything I put my mind to. She believed I was strong enough to do anything I set my mind to. She envied my bravery. She admired my strength and hoped I would be happy.

Droplets hit the crinkled, yellowing page I held—but it wasn't from the bath. I wiped my eyes and put the letter safely on the floor outside the tub with the others. Pain ground and grated through my chest like two rough stones scraping together. I missed her. I needed her. Somehow, I had to be that person she believed I could be.

I jumped, sloshing the bathwater as someone knocked on the door. "Jenna?" His voice came softly, wrapping around my heart like an old, threadbare blanket worn by years of offering warmth and comfort.

"What is it, Phillip?" I struggled to keep my voice steady. "Is it time? Is Jaevid ready to start the ritual?"

"No, it's not that, I just ... " He paused, taking a deep breath as though steeling himself. "Can I come in?"

Oh, Fates. My pulse flourished, kicking hard against my ribs as my entire body flushed with embarrassment. This *again*?

I sank lower in the deep marble tub, barely peering over the edge. "Why?"

"I ... I just want to ... " His voice caught, and he hushed again. It was okay. I didn't need to hear the rest. He wasn't coming in for *that*. Something was wrong.

"Okay."

The knob twisted, and the door clicked open. Phillip stood in the doorway, his expression a mixture of apprehension and concern. His gaze traveled around the room, seeing the letters on the floor and me hiding, hunkered down in the water so he couldn't see anything but my face and neck. Switchbeast strength aside, I'd still punch his teeth in if he tried anything funny. Now was not the time for any of his absurd attempts at romantic gestures.

Without a word, he walked over and sat down next to the tub with his back against the side. He picked up a few of the letters and started to read, silver eyes skimming the delicately printed lines one by one.

"You miss her a lot, don't you?" he murmured at last.

I waded closer, leaning against the edge of the tub so I could peer over his shoulder at the page in his hand. "All the time," I whispered. "Somehow, whenever everything feels like it's spinning out of control, hearing her voice in my head makes it feel like I can survive."

"I understand." One corner of his mouth twitched at a smile. "That's how you've been for me."

My pulse skipped, and I forgot how to breathe. "M-me? Why?"

"You still don't understand, do you?"

"Understand what?"

Putting down the letters, Phillip turned around. His face was mere inches from mine, and his strange silver eyes searched my face for a long, quiet moment—almost like he suspected I might be making fun of him. He sighed at last and shook his head. "I've never been in love with anyone else, Jenna. It's only ever been you."

My stomach fluttered. Somehow, I knew I'd never get used to hearing him say that.

"I meant what I said," Phillip murmured as he angled his face away. His frown put little wrinkles between his brows. "I will have to resign my place as Duke of Barrowton. I can't be a noble, not like this."

There was something else—something more he wanted to say. The fact that he was holding back, biting down hard against the words as though he hated every single one, was terrifying. I swallowed hard, dangling in the gap of his silence while I waited for him to continue.

"I recommended Aedan be given the position," he continued, muttering as he turned to rest his back against the side of the tub again.

"Aedan? But he's awfully young, isn't he?"

Phillip gave a small shrug. "I wasn't much older when I took the position. He's proven himself time and again to be someone worthy of our trust. Besides, your father does owe him quite a lot now. It seems appropriate to have the first full-blooded Gray elf to take a noble title in Maldobar be at Barrowton." He bowed his head, propping his elbow on his knee as he spoke. "I offered to stay on in secret and act as his advisor—just until he's comfortable. I believe he'll do well. He's clever, humble, and seems to have more sense than most men twice his age. He'll be a hero amongst the Gray elves and humans alike after this. Well, providing we all survive the next twenty-four hours, that is."

That wasn't it. Phillip was still holding back. I could sense it, like pressure building against a dam. Drop by drop, second by second, that heaviness was mounting. It would break, and so would he.

I shrank back, using the moment of silence while his back was turned to stand up and wrap myself in a towel. I climbed out of the bathtub and sat down next to him. The marble floor was cold against my legs and my hair dripped a puddle between us.

Suddenly, Phillip's expression tensed. His jaw went rigid and his eyes squeezed shut. "Jenna, you are the Crown Princess of Maldobar. The chosen heir to the throne," he blurted at last. "You are going to be queen! And I ... "

"What?" I urged.

"The man you marry will become the next King of Maldobar." His shoulders curled forward, as though he were trying to fold into himself and hide. "How could that possibly be me?"

"Because it can't be anyone else," I said. "I love you. Only you."

"But, gods, can you imagine it? My face hanging in the hall of portraits? The looks on the faces at the coronation parade? At balls? At ceremonies? I-I can't even give you an heir anymore." His voice broke and he covered his face with his hand.

My breath caught, watching him crumble before me while those words carved fresh wounds on my heart. "You mean—?"

"I'm sterile, Jenna," he confessed, tone raw with anguish and rage. "Because of the venom and the way switchbeasts reproduce, I can never have children of my own now. Jaevid said he could sense it but there was nothing he could do. Whatever small chance there still was of your father letting me marry you won't stand, not if I can't even give Maldobar an heir."

All I could do was sit in complete shock, gaping at him. I'd never considered something like this might happen—or what it would mean for us. From where he was sitting, it must have seemed like Argonox had taken absolutely everything from him, even his hope for a family.

But that wasn't true.

"I won't consider anyone else as my husband," I announced firmly. "It's you or no one."

He shot me a dubious glare. "Have you lost your mind? That would mean—"

"Refusing the crown," I finished for him with a smile.

"Jenna, no, I can't let you do that. Not for me. It's not worth it. If Maldobar survives this war, it will need a strong figure at the helm, guiding it into restoration."

"They'll have it," I assured him. "Aubren is still alive. Reigh is also. And Jaevid is technically a member of the family. There are plenty of other heads that will fit under that crown, but mine belongs next to yours."

"But we'll never have a family," he rasped frantically. "Don't you want children?"

Taking one of his hands in mine, I scooted close enough to kiss his knuckles. "Of course I do. When the time comes, we'll figure it out." I pressed his warm, rugged palm against my cheek. "Until then, stop looking for excuses to leave me. I mean, do you even realize how horribly backward this is? I've spent the latter half of my life dodging your affection and now I'm terrified if I look away, you'll vanish."

He choked out a nervous laugh. "I suppose it is a little backward. I can't help but look back on who I was before and hate myself now. Before, I was ready to be the man I thought you would need me to be, to stand beside you and make your family proud to have me in their lineage. I believed I had enough to offer to make it worth your time. Now I have nothing. I am nothing. All I have to offer you are the broken pieces of the man I used to be. Is that really enough?"

Grabbing the sides of his face, I yanked Phillip in to press my mouth against his in answer. Of course it was enough. There was nothing Argonox could do to him that would change that. He would *always* be enough for me.

Before Jaevid could perform his ritual and cross into the Vale, we had to be absolutely sure that everything else was in place. According to him, this act would give away his position to Reigh, and by extension, Argonox. An attack would almost certainly come right after, so we had to be ready. It put thick tension in the air as we met with the rest of my father's war council in the mapping room to go over the final details one last time.

"We can't know the full extent of what Argonox has in store for us this time," Jaevid warned. "But we do know we will at least have Beckah and Icarus to contend with."

"The dragonriders stand ready," High Commander Morrig declared. "The men have been briefed on the possible threat. If any dragons, living or dead, make an appearance to fight for the Tibrans, they will have to get past us first."

"You can expect war beasts, and lots of them," Aedan said, gesturing to the map. Sporting a brand-new, navy-blue infantry uniform trimmed in gold and a broad, black leather belt with matching vambraces, he looked much more at home. If not for the brand on the side of his neck, plainly visible above the collar of his tunic, it was easy to forget he'd ever been in the Tibran ranks. "You need to find the storage wagons and take them out. That's where they'll be keeping all the dragon venom orbs until the battle begins. The wagons are ironclad and heavily guarded, but that just makes them easier to spot. If you can send a dragon or two around the perimeter and attack them, it would significantly cut down on the amount of incoming fire the walls take."

"We can handle that," the High Commander agreed.

Jaevid fidgeted with the bone-carved pendant now hanging around his neck as his gaze darted across the map. "Once Mavrik and I make our appearance, I suspect we'll have Argonox's full attention. We need to find Reigh as quickly as possible. The sooner we find him, the easier it will be to bring Clysiros forth and let her destroy whatever Reigh's been forced to create."

"Provided she keeps her word," my father pointed out. "Forgive me for my lack of enthusiasm, but a *lot* is riding on your ability to blackmail the Goddess of Death into evening this fight out for us. I've seen you do some insane things before, but this would certainly set a new bar."

"She'll do it." Jaevid ground his jaw, eyes flashing like moonlit steel.

"But in the meantime, we need to hold the Tibran lines and keep as many of them as we can from ever reaching the city," the Infantry General pointed out.

"This is going to be ugly," Jaevid warned. "I will try to bolster your advances and cover flanks with earth golems and anything else I can muster. Paligno's will is with us. But many good men are going to die in this battle."

The High Commander straightened, his expression resolute. "They know the risks—just as they know what they are fighting for."

"We will not falter," the Infantry General agreed.

"When I find Hecate in the Vale, I will send word with her to warn Araxie of what's about to happen. I can't promise Luntharda's warriors will be able to mobilize in time to help us, but it's something." Jaevid pushed back from the table, glancing around at everyone one last time. "What happens next will change everything. It isn't just Maldobar looking to us for deliverance. The eyes of the world are upon us. If Argonox falls, we stand to topple his empire. Kingdoms long subjugated under his banner will need our help in rebuilding what he has torn down. Thousands of enslaved soldiers will suddenly feel their chains break, and it's up to us to determine their fate. You see their armor, helmets, swords, and shields, but I can sense what lies beneath. Many of them are terrified. They long for their homeland and have lived in a constant state of fear and survival since they were taken from it." He paused a moment, shifting his gaze to my father. "I hope we can be merciful and not end lives unnecessarily."

King Felix gave a steady nod. "Tell our men that any Tibran who lays down his arms voluntarily will be shown mercy."

The High Commander and Infantry General saluted in unison. "Yes, Your Majesty."

There was a heavy sense of finality in the room as we all stood back, staring down at the map together. The meeting was over. Our plan was fixed. Our soldiers and dragonriders stood waiting for the order to strike. There was only one thing left to do, and only one person in the room who could manage it.

Jaevid Broadfeather wore a determined frown as his eyes narrowed upon the map, irises flickering with a hint of eerie green light. In his mind, I imagined a deity raging like a lion against a cage—pacing, restless, hungry. "Very well then," he growled through clenched teeth. "Let's end this."

PART THREE: REIGH

CHAPTER NINETEEN

Through the delirium and darkness, a face stared down at me. At least, I thought it was a face. The fresh agony thrumming through my body, slowly tearing me apart from the inside out, sort of threw everything into a haze. I couldn't tell if I was conscious or trapped in a relentless nightmare. All I knew, all I could think about, was the pain. It had to stop at some point. Either by being set free or dying—there had to be an end coming. I didn't even care which one it was anymore.

"It's gonna be okay, Reigh," a tiny female voice whispered against my ear.

"Enyo ... " Her name left my lips as a thin, rasping prayer. Was it her? I blinked, but nothing got clearer. I couldn't make out any details apart from the curve of a feminine cheek catching in the torchlight.

"No. I'm afraid not." She sounded genuinely sorry about that. "It's still Phoebe."

Involuntarily, my body seized up and cringed away. That voice—it burned in my head like the touch of a red-hot dagger point. I tried in vain to will myself to struggle, to try to get away. But it was no use. Even if she cut my bonds, I'd never be able to climb off the table on my own, let alone find my way out of ... wherever this was.

"P-please," I begged. "Kill me."

"Shhh. Don't say that. There's always hope. Always." She pressed something to my mouth and cold, wet liquid dribbled against my lips. "Here, drink this. It's only water."

Every sip burned my throat like acid. But I couldn't stop—my body lurched forward against the shackles binding my arms and neck as I gulped down as much as she would allow.

At last, Phoebe stood back and took the waterskin with her. My head slumped back down against the stone slab where I'd been chained for, well, honestly, I had no idea how long. Days? Weeks? The absence of anything but wavering torchlight made the room feel cavernous, as though we were deep underground, but I didn't know that for sure, either.

Not that it mattered. I was going to die here, in this room, strapped to this table, and there was nothing I could do to stop it. No one was coming for me. I'd given up that hope a long time ago.

"W-where's Aubren?" I managed to croak.

Phoebe bowed her head without a word, expression bleak. They'd left not long ago—my brother and that *thing*. Argonox had poured my blood and magic into them and sent them on their way. How long had they been gone? Were they coming back? Was Aubren going to be okay? Would he ever be the same again?

Or had my power destroyed him forever?

With her ginger hair pulled into two chaotic-looking ponytails right behind her ears, Phoebe glanced up at me. Wide, frightened eyes the color of sunlight through raindrops met mine. I wasn't a good judge of character, but it didn't seem like she was enjoying this any more than I was. Granted, she wasn't the one chained to a table and being tortured. But still, she didn't seem to get any pleasure out of it.

Or so I wanted to believe.

"He wants me to try again," Phoebe murmured, brushing some of her tightly curled bangs away from her face.

My throat constricted. On impulse, I pitched against the bonds and shrieked. No—gods, please, not again. I yelled and fought, begging her not to go through with it. I couldn't do this again!

I couldn't hold back my desperate sobs and screams as Phoebe came back to the tableside holding a mask made of cold, dark metal. The inside was coated in something like black glass with little panes of it set into the eyes. I didn't know what it was, or where it had come from. Argonox had called it the Thieving Mask, and when she buckled it around my head, I couldn't see anything through the black glass eyeholes. The instant the cold mask touched my skin, my body started to tremble. I sucked in frantic, shallow breaths and tried to pray. *Let it kill me this time. Anything to make it stop. Please, Paligno—Clysiros—anyone! I can't do this anymore! Jaevid, help me!*

Then it didn't matter ... because I was drowning in the dark again.

Everything came into focus as I crawled out of the Well of Souls, my lungs stretching as I sucked in gulps of the stale air. Around me, the familiar grayscale of the Vale made my heart sink. I was back. But why? Why would Argonox or Phoebe want to send me here?

I wanted to look for Noh or call out for him. He had to be here somewhere, right? If anyone could help me get out of this, it was him.

As soon as I thought to move, my body jerked a different way—totally out of my control. My body got up, standing shakily, and turning in a slow circle. I wiped my hair from my eyes and glanced back at the well behind me, its dark waters deceptively serene on the surface.

Then I saw it.

The reflection in the water wasn't mine—it was Jaevid's.

It only lasted a second, a single glance. That was all it took, though. Somehow, the Thieving Mask had put my consciousness inside Jaevid's body. I could see through his eyes, see and hear everything he did, but I had no control over him.

I was a spy in his head.

"You," a familiar voice hissed suddenly.

Jaevid whirled around, staggering a bit when he found himself nearly nose-to-nose with Noh.

"You are not supposed to be here. The Vale is *my* domain," Noh seethed quietly. Standing motionless, Noh had his arms folded into the sleeves of his long silver and black robes.

"I didn't come here for a holiday," Jaevid snapped back. "I came because your other half is in trouble. I would think you'd be aware of that."

Noh's eyes narrowed, and his nose scrunched as he curled his lip. "Am I to believe Paligno's champion has come to offer me help? Hah!"

"Believe whatever you like; it makes no difference to me."

"How? How did you manage pass through the well? It should be forbidden to you," Noh interrogated, eyes glittering with distrust.

"Unless it is *her* power that brings me here," Jaevid countered. "I have the crystal in my possession. I used its power to bring me here, just as I used the defilement's pull to send Jenna through before."

Noh's expression went slack. His eyes popped open wide and his lips parted just enough for a few breathless words to hiss out. "You ... you have it?"

"Yes. It's safe—for now. But if you want it to remain that way, then I'm going to need your help." Jaevid took a step away from the well, water sloshing in his boots. "Reigh is running out of time. He won't last much longer."

Well, at least someone else agreed with me on that point.

"What can you possibly do for him? He is beyond even my reach now."

I wished I could have control of Jaevid's body just long enough to sock Noh across the jaw. *Stop mouthing off and help him, moron!*

"Mine as well. But not hers." Jaevid marched forward, scaling the grassy knoll that overlooked the bleak stone city.

Hers? Wait a second, he wasn't seriously thinking about asking ...

"Clysiros?" Noh gasped the name as he trotted to catch up. "Are you mad? You cannot speak with her! She is imprisoned in Desmiol! Not even I can hear her speak. Reigh is one of the few who can."

"One of the few, yes," Jaevid countered. "But not the only one. Now, if you're finished with your interrogation, take me to the Sivanth. We need to do this quickly." He gestured to the city and waited.

Noh studied him with a sulky scowl, his mouth pursed as he licked the front of his teeth. "Fine. Have it your way. But I do not think you'll find Clysiros eager to help your cause."

"We'll just have to see, won't we?"

"Indeed." Noh snorted as he led the way down the hill. "We shall see if life can bargain with death."

THE NEARER WE DREW TO THE SIVANTH, THE MORE SPIRITS APPEARED AROUND us like shimmering, translucent figures. Some whispered and stared. Others seemed totally oblivious to our presence. Noh could pass through their crowds like a ghost. His body became a fine black mist instead of crashing into them, and effortlessly reappeared as solid on the other side. Jaevid didn't seem to have that same ability. He dodged and ducked through the huddled crowds of spirits, jogging to keep up.

Overhead, a dark cloud gathered on the horizon. The encroaching thunderhead, massive and snapping with bolts of lightning, rolled in slowly. Every time a bolt would pop nearby, zapping a rooftop, the spirits would wail and huddle in closer with their forms quivering in fear.

"What is that?" Jaevid asked.

"As you said, Reigh is running out of time," Noh replied dryly. "Whenever the power of the Harbinger is used to a great extent in the mortal realm without the completion of the ritual, it threatens to tear the Vale apart. Desmiol will inevitably consume it, and soon after, the mortal realm as well. With no means of passing into the afterlife, spirits will roam wild in the mortal world unchecked. The dead will walk. The ancient evils Clysiros bound within the earth in the first age will break free." He paused long enough to flash Jaevid a cold glare over his shoulder. "In short, the world will end."

"I see." Jaevid sounded unfazed, which I had hard time believing. Maybe he was just keeping his responses in check, fortifying his reactions for what was to come. "Then it sounds like fixing this as soon as possible is in *everyone's* best interest."

Noh didn't reply. In fact, he seemed to get more anxious the closer they moved to the swelling storm cloud in the sky. Weaving through the streets and around clumped crowds of spirits, Jaevid's gaze flashed back and forth between Noh's back and the sky, as though he wasn't sure which one was more unsettling.

It was a toss-up for me, too.

Darting around a corner, Noh came to a halt in the middle of a long, straight avenue. Enormous statues of white stone, more than twenty feet tall, flanked each side of the road like pillars. Each one was identical, appearing like a woman garbed in a flowing white robe. The figures stood with heads bowed toward the road between them and hands covering their eyes.

Noh walked down the center of the street, passing between the statues without giving them a second look. Jaevid seemed more impressed, or maybe unnerved, because his gaze continually turned up to study them as they passed.

Not a single spirit stood in this road. If anything, it almost seemed abandoned. Weird. Didn't some spirits want to seek the afterlife? Surely some did. Then again, the huge dark cloud hanging over the street was probably a deterrent. It rumbled and buzzed with chaotic energy, lashing out with tongues of lightning that snapped off the tops of some of the statues.

At the far end of the avenue, an even larger pair of statues stood on either side of a raised stone pedestal. A graceful, arching stairway led up to it, and walking there would inevitably leave a person standing right between those two figures. At first glance, it was hard to see. The farther we went down the street, the more the air seemed to grow dim and suffocating, as though we were sinking gradually into a bank of fog. It was so subtle, I hardly noticed at first. Then Jaevid started jogging faster and squinting to try and keep Noh in sight ahead of us.

When we caught up to him at last, we were standing at the base of the staircase. The statues on either side of it were monstrous—towering like silent giants. One was made of stone as dark as onyx. The other was a pearly, milky white. But apart from that, both were identical.

And both were dragons.

With their necks arched and wings folded close, the pair of dragons gazed down at the pedestal between them with tranquil indifference. Nothing about them seemed threatening, apart from their size and the fact that, you know, a dragon that size could eat a person in one bite.

Jaevid regarded them for a moment, and then stared back at Noh. "The Fates are dragons?"

"That is the mortal word for them," he replied with a shrug. "Here, they are called Viepol—*those who see all.*"

"Are they any relation to the dragons in Maldobar?"

The corners of Noh's mouth curled slowly into a secretive little grin. "We're all related in one way or another, lapiloque. But it does make you wonder, doesn't it? Do the dragons who choose riders do so by random chance? Or is it because they can actually *see* something in that person no one else can?"

Jaevid muttered an elvish curse under his breath. I guess he wasn't a fan of Noh's mind games, either.

"At any rate, this is the Sivanth," Noh gestured up to the stairs and pedestal. "Souls come here to face the judgment of the Viepol and accept whatever reward they've earned, be it paradise in the kingdom of the gods or banishment to the prison of stars. This is as close to Desmiol as anyone can get without actually passing into it."

"Good," Jaevid muttered under his breath as he began up the stairs. "Let's hope it's close enough."

CHAPTER TWENTY

Lightning sizzled through the air, popping off the ground mere feet away as Jaevid ascended the staircase. The two dragon sculptures never moved, and yet it felt as though their eyes were following him the entire time. At the last step, he hesitated. The wind from the storm churning and boiling overhead teased through his gray hair. I couldn't fathom what he must be thinking. This was madness. He had no way of knowing what was about to happen. The Fates—Viepol—whatever they were called, might send him into the afterlife. And what then? Who would be left to help Maldobar? Who would stand against Argonox?

And me ... who would prevent me from destroying everything I'd ever loved?

There was nothing I could do to stop it, though. With one final step, Jaevid stood on the circular pedestal between the dragons, his gaze flicking back and forth between their monstrous heads. Thunder cracked and shook the ground.

"All right, Hecate," Jaevid whispered. "You can do this. I know you can."

Hecate? Wait, was she coming here, too? How? That didn't make any sense; how could she get into the Vale without Noh or me helping her? Was it even safe for someone with her abilities?

No time to hash it out now—not that I could. I got the impression Jaevid had no idea I was watching, seeing everything through his eyes as it was happening. The Thieving Mask had that effect, although the first four times Phoebe had tried putting it on me, Noh had been adamant in resisting it. The result? Pure agony—like my head was a melon being squeezed in a vice while both Noh and the mask battled for control.

This time, Noh hadn't even put up a fight when Phoebe put the mask on me.

Had using so much of our power weakened him? Or was he just giving up? Either way, I doubted that was a good sign. Jaevid was right; I was running out of time.

Raising his gaze to the cloud overhead, Jaevid stretched his arms wide and closed his eyes. Everything went dark. And then there was light—blinding, searing, white-hot light that sent a jolt of pain and panic through my body like I was being lit on fire. I couldn't move, couldn't resist, or pull away from it. The heat tingled through every part of me, rising like a mug filled with boiling water. I tried to stop it, tried to break the mask's hold, but nothing worked. I was stuck in Jaevid's head. Death or unconsciousness were the only ways out of this, and I couldn't force either.

Jaevid opened his eyes, looking to the sky again. Suddenly, a giant head eclipsed his view. On either side of the pedestal, the dragon statues quivered and twisted, writhing free of their spots to spread their wings and stretch their legs and long tails. The black one craned its neck to stare right at him with eyes of bottomless, blinding light.

Pain roared through me again, more intense than before. Could it see me? Sense my presence somehow?

The creature blinked owlishly, stone nostrils flaring as the flashes of lightning sparkled over its onyx scales. Then the other dragon moved in to inspect Jaevid, as well. Except for their differing colors, they were perfect mirror images of one another down to the very last detail.

"*Who is it?*" a voice asked, its tone piercing through me like a molten spear. I wanted to scream, to get away, but there was nothing I could do.

"*Alive,*" another voice grumbled. "*Not for judgment. He does not belong here. We must send him back.*"

"Wait!" Jaevid protested, throwing his hands up toward the dragons. "I am the chosen of Paligno. I carry his essence, and I have come here to seek council with Clysiros!"

The dragons blinked, their stone faces eerily indifferent and unchanging as they loomed over him. At last, one of the voices confirmed. "*The lapiloque.*"

Jaevid nodded. "Yes."

"*No one can speak to Clysiros,*" the other voice snapped. "*She must never pass beyond Desmiol.*"

"I don't need to bring her here," he clarified. "There is another way to speak with her. The Akrotis can help me, if you allow her consciousness to enter the Vale. Surely you can sense it. She's looking for a way in and a willing host to lend their voice. Please, allow her to speak through you."

Once again, the dragons fell silent. After several grueling seconds, the black one recoiled and snapped his mighty jaws. "*We cannot allow it. No one else may enter the mind of the Viepol, for therein hides secrets that surpass the ages, the lies of a thousand kingdoms and the truths of the ancients.*"

"Then she can use me," Noh spoke up suddenly. "All we will require of you is to bring forth the gateway to Desmiol, so the goddess can reply. Is that something you'd allow?"

Turning, Jaevid watched in silence as Noh ascended the staircase to stand right next to him. With his arms still folded beneath his robes, Noh kept a sharp scowl focused on the Viepol. I couldn't believe it. He was *helping*? Things must have been bad if Noh was volunteering to do something useful that didn't involve killing anyone.

The two dragons considered in tense silence, and I got the creepy feeling that they were somehow able to debate with one another without having to say a word. At least, not one that we were able to hear. Finally, the white one let out a blasting snort that blew Jaevid's hair back and turned away.

"*We will allow it.*"

Jaevid's shoulders dropped in relief. "I am grateful."

"I would suggest saving the gratitude until you are standing safely back in the mortal realm," Noh snorted.

Jaevid didn't even look at him. "I am. That's why I didn't thank *you*, yet."

Ouch. I felt that burn from worlds away. Noh didn't retort, though his lips thinned, and he shot Jaevid a brief, scathing glare. I wondered if wrinkling my nose made my scar crinkle like that, too. Probably, since Noh and I were identical.

"*Mortal eyes must turn away*," the dragons warned in unison as they stirred, snouts turning to the empty air behind the pedestal. "*None but the dead may gaze upon the maw of Desmiol or risk being pulled to it.*"

"That would be you, lapiloque," Noh added.

Jaevid was already turning around. "I gathered that."

An instant before his back was turned and my view was lost, the two dragons opened their jaws wide and drew back, blasting the air with a sudden burst of power like a plume of white fire. It made a huge circular portal appear. Then I couldn't see anything. Overhead, the cloud rumbled louder. Searing pressure rose in my body, squeezing harder and harder at my already frazzled mind. My vision spotted and dimmed—or was it Jaevid's? No, it had to be mine. Something about that portal was putting a strain on the mask. It was too much. Already, I could feel its hold beginning to slip like sand through a sieve.

I was going to lose it, or die, or maybe both.

"*Jaevid Broadfeather. I've been expecting you. A shame it's always the handsome ones who dare to keep a lady waiting,*" a woman's voice whispered, purring like a lover in his ear.

It was Clysiros—her voice was coming from Noh's mouth!

Her voice hit me like a knockout punch straight to the nose. My vision flashed, going dark for a few seconds. For an instant, I was back in hell, with cold chains biting into my skin and dry screams in my throat. Phoebe must have been somewhere close because she was whispering to me frantically, assuring me it was going to be okay. It was almost over. Just a few seconds more.

"Unfortunately, this isn't a social call," Jaevid replied, keeping his gaze trained upon Noh.

"It never is," she replied. "*You've been so very busy, just like before. Not that I'm complaining; I always did enjoy watching you work. And to find the Akrotis, too? I am thoroughly impressed.*"

"Then you know why I've come," he guessed. "Things cannot remain the way they are."

"*Naturally,*" she snickered. "*But then, they were never meant to be this way in the first place. Stones and nonsense running about, bathed in blood. This reckless chaos was inevitable. I tried to warn them. It's far too clumsy. You mortals are a clever lot. But reason and truth become lies if spoken from an unpopular throat.*"

Jaevid took a deep breath. "Well, I'm not here for popularity. There is more at stake than Maldobar's future if Argonox remains unchecked and Reigh's power is twisted until it destroys the Vale. The balance must be reset, and that can't be done without your help."

Clysiros laughed again, which was especially creepy since Noh's expression never changed from a blank stare. "*Of course.*"

Every word grated on my brain, adding just a little more pressure. More heat. More pain. I couldn't take it much longer. I was going to break.

"I have the crystal, and I'm willing to help, to give you what you need to see this done," Jaevid declared as he held up one of his hands, staring down at his open palm. "But Paligno and I have terms."

"*Oh, I'm sure you do. My brother always did love a good bargain,*" she purred excitedly. "*Every drop of sweat and blood has a price. So, what is yours, lapiloque? What will it cost to free me from this starry cage?*"

THE CONNECTION BROKE SO SUDDENLY; I DIDN'T UNDERSTAND WHAT HAD happened at first. Darkness swallowed me, snatching my consciousness from the Vale and dragging me back into Argonox's torture chamber. I thrashed against the chains, my cries muffled by the mask until Phoebe began unbuckling it.

"Shh, it's okay. It's over now," she cooed as she pulled the mask away. "You did so good, Reigh. I think that will make him happy this time."

My body throbbed; every muscle fiber was raw as I went slack on the table. The cold sweat beading on my skin made me shiver. But it was no relief to the searing heat in my mind. It felt like my eyeballs might melt right out of their sockets. Something warm oozed from my nose and eyes, dribbling down the sides of my face. Blood?

"P-please," I begged hoarsely. "You h-have to make it stop. K-kill me."

Her cheeks flushed until all the hundreds of little freckles along her cheeks, nose, and forehead became invisible. Her delicate features drew into a shattered look of regret. Tears welled in her eyes as she stood over the table, looking childish and tiny in a leather apron that was far too big for her. "Don't say that. There is hope. There *has* to be hope," she said. "Someone will stop him. I think maybe Jaevid can. I know Lord Argonox has never faced anyone like him before."

"R-right," I growled, letting my eyes fall closed. It hurt too much to keep them open, and I couldn't stand to look at her for another second. "Cause you'd want that, right? Y-you're helping him destroy the world, making all these things for him, torturing people. You're just as bad as he is!"

I couldn't see her face. I didn't want to. And yet I could hear the brokenness in her voice as her footsteps began to retreat. "Not all chains are made of iron."

I knew what she meant. Phoebe was as much a prisoner here as I was. Sure, Argonox hadn't bound her to a table, but she had to do his bidding. There was no telling what he'd threatened her with, or what he'd done to her already. The Tibran soldiers called her "Miss Artificer" like it was something precious, but they always locked the doors behind them whenever they came and went from this place. She was not free to leave.

Remembering that while she was experimenting on me with various artifacts was difficult, though. She could kill me. I wanted it. Anything was better than spending what was left of my days in chains being stretched and drained until my power or my captor killed me. She could do it now and make it quick and painless. Maybe then I could forgive her for what she'd done to Aubren, Vexi, me, and so many others.

"D-don't you get it? If you l-let me live, everyone will die. N-not just me, or the people h-here in Maldobar," I fought to growl through ragged breaths. "Argonox d-doesn't want me—he wants the world, and the l-lives of everyone in it. Whatever d-deal you struck with him only lasts until he d-doesn't need you anymore."

The lurch and clank of the door lock made my eyes fly open again. Someone was coming in. In an instant, Phoebe reappeared at my side and stashed the water skin under her apron. Her face was pale, and I could see her trembling as she stood close by, eyes like two big raindrops watching the door.

"Miss Artificer," the voice of a man addressed her from the doorway—a soldier, judging by the faint clinking of his armor. "Lord Argonox would like your report on the most recent test."

Phoebe's smile was as haunted as it was forced. "Oh, yes. I've only just finished. I'll just need some time to write up the results."

"That won't be necessary." The soldier's footsteps came closer. "He wants you to deliver the report personally. He's already on his way."

"Lord Argonox is coming here?" she squeaked like someone had stepped on a baby rabbit.

"He will arrive momentarily. I was sent to give you notice and to assist in moving the prisoner to the bleeding stocks."

Horror gripped me like a snagwolf to the throat. I couldn't move—couldn't speak or even breathe.

"Oh, but I'm afraid he's much too weak to withstand that procedure right now." Phoebe's voice trembled. "Perhaps if we waited a day or two—"

"I'm afraid that won't be possible," the soldier interrupted. "Orders have already been passed down. The legions are mobilizing. Lord Argonox intends to strike tonight, as soon as the final bleeding is complete."

"F-final ... ?" The question died in her throat and she swallowed hard.

"Don't fret, my little bird," another deep, masculine voice spoke over them. It echoed from the direction of the doorway, smooth and even, with a calculating edge I'd come to recognize. Just the sound made my pulse thrash in my ears.

It was Argonox.

The last time he'd come to pay me a visit, the result had come the closest of any of Phoebe's experiments to successfully killing me in the most painful way imaginable. It had also resulted in reanimating yet another deceased war hero—only this one was not a demigod or supposed to be alive again. Well, if you could even call *that* being alive.

There was no mistaking who she was. I'd never seen her in person, but Kiran had told many stories about the bravery and grit of Beckah Derrick, the first woman to ever ride on a dragon. Defiling her grave and reanimating her remains ... I didn't want to think about what kind of punishment that might earn me in the Vale. But Argonox wanted his own champion in a dragonrider's saddle. And now, thanks to me, he had one.

The state she'd been in reminded me more of a whirling tornado—destructive, powerful, and directionless if left to her own devices. She was beyond dangerous and without any sense of her spirit to guide her, she couldn't be reasoned with by anyone except the one holding her leash—which was Argonox.

What my power had done to that girl was wrong on too many levels to count. Noh had resisted reanimating her remains every inch of the way, and the process had almost ended my suffering. But I wasn't that lucky. Argonox understood a lot more about Noh's power and how to manipulate our bond than I'd expected. He'd used it to corrupt Aubren, bind my dragon, and so much more. I doubted even Jaevid knew the extent of it. He'd find out soon enough, though.

I just prayed I didn't live to see it.

"How did the session go? Were you able to learn anything more?" Argonox asked evenly, as though he might as well have been asking about the weather. The metallic tinge of old blood and sweat in the air paired with the musk of scorched metal and ash from Phoebe's crafting didn't seem to bother him at all.

"Yes, My Lord." Phoebe was still shivering as she stood by the table right next to my head. She blinked rapidly, chin quivering as her eyes followed his movements. "The one who serves Paligno has reached Halfax, just as your agents reported. The conversation indicated that he ... " Her voice caught, and her eyes darted down to me for the briefest instant. "He doesn't have the crystal. It must be at Halfax, still guarded by the king, and most likely somewhere in the castle."

My heart thumped so hard I could feel it in my throat. That wasn't what Jaevid said—Phoebe was lying. But why?

"Excellent. Then our timing is perfect. Perhaps they still do not know how to complete the ritual or hope to rescue their friend before they do. They may not even know what it is they harbor there at all." A strong hand grabbed my jaw suddenly, turning my head so that I was looking squarely into Argonox's piercing gaze. He studied me like a tigrex considering an injured fawn, dark eyes glinting with delighted malice. "I must apologize to you, Phoebe. I did have some doubts that your skills would be enough to salvage this situation. He's not been as useful as he might have been with the crystal's ritual already completed. Even so, you've proven yourself once again to be the finest artificer in the world."

Phoebe didn't reply, shying away from the table when he came close. She nibbled on her bottom lip, wringing her hands against her apron as her gaze darted back and forth between him and the direction of the door—as though she were contemplating trying to flee.

"One final bleeding should be enough to secure the dragons and shrikes we've acquired," Argonox went on. He let go of my face and wiped his hand on the front of his jerkin. "Then I want my armor prepped."

"My Lord, I, uh, I should mention that it is very unlikely he will survive another bleeding right after the Thieving Mask session," Phoebe whimpered. "Perhaps we should let him rest a moment, even a few hours might—"

Only Argonox's eyes moved, flicking immediately up to her. She made a panicked squeak and went silent, cringing as she ducked her head. "Phoebe, my bird, I realize this must be ... *difficult* for you, but we cannot lose focus now. Surely you haven't forgotten the terms of your role here?"

"N-no, My Lord."

"Good girl. It's extremely important that you remember what we've discussed." He pointed down to me. "*This* is not a person. Anyone chosen by these so-called gods are not people anymore. They're only vessels, like clay pots. You're simply finding the best way to crack them open and draw out the treasure inside."

She bobbed her head frantically. "Only pots. Yes, My Lord. I remember."

His expression slid smoothly into a venomous smile before he turned away, walking out of view. "I knew I could count on you. Hurry now. There isn't much time. Take whatever you can from him and send it with the Captain."

"Yes, My Lord." Her brows crinkled upward as she glanced down at me. "And if he survives the bleeding?"

Argonox's footsteps halted, as though he'd stopped to consider that for a moment. "Then chain him for relocation," he decided. "He'll make a fine adornment for my chariot."

PART FOUR: JENNA

CHAPTER TWENTY-ONE

The battle horn sounded, rumbling in the deep and sending pangs of adrenaline like cold fire through my veins. It echoed through the granite halls and corridors of the castle, resounding through the throne room, and wailing against the gathering dusk. That sound could only mean one thing: our enemy was stirring at last. The time had come. Tonight, Maldobar's fate would be decided, written upon the pages of history in the blood of its fallen soldiers.

Jaevid's ritual was complete. He'd walked in the Vale, counseled with death itself, and now all our hopes hung on those negotiations. All that remained was to strap our boots on, don our helmets, and heft the blade of war one last time.

I stood alone on a long carpet of deep blue that spanned the length of the floor of the dimly lit hall. Overhead, the vaulted ceilings were all but invisible without the chandeliers lit. In fact, the only light came from two ornate braziers burning on either side of the alabaster platform where the figures of three golden dragons made up my father's throne. With two of the beasts forming the arms and legs on either side of the seat, the third rose up right at the center. The dragon's wings were spread wide and its head craned down to watch the long room with ruby eyes.

But that wasn't what caught my interest now.

I studied the glittering dark crystal set in the center of that middle dragon's head. I must have seen it more than a hundred times growing up here. That crystal, as black as obsidian, had never meant anything to me until now. I'd seen it as some frivolous adornment. A strange design choice—but nothing more. Now the sight of the brazier light wavering over its glossy surface made my body tense under my dragonrider armor. It made my blood run cold and my hands clench inside my riding gauntlets. How long had it sat there, watching kings come and go? Whoever had placed it there must have known what it was, or at least had some idea. Was it meant to send a message, like some trophy of war?

I suppose it didn't matter now. The only message it sent to me was one of impending doom. Argonox was coming for it, and the fate of our world depended on keeping it from his grasp.

"I remember the last time I was here." Jaevid seemed to appear out of nowhere, standing beside me with a distant expression as he considered the crystal, too. "I stood right here in this same spot and your father was, well, right about where you are now, actually."

"You killed Hovrid, the imposter king, and stole back the god stone," I recalled. "That story is one of my father's favorites, I think. He likes the part where he single-handedly killed a company of elite guards *and* a giant boar. Interesting that he left out the bit about cutting his hand on a cursed divine artifact, though."

We stood together in the light of the braziers, not saying a word as we stared up at the throne while the war horn continued to wail in the night. For a moment, it felt like the world stood still. Then I felt his gaze turn to me like sunlight breaking through a storm. "Are you ready for this, Jenna?" he asked.

I smiled. "Is anyone?"

He chuckled. "Probably not."

"I am ready." The words broke out of me with a force that quaked my soul to its foundations—as though they'd been trapped there, caged, and confined, since the day I was born. Now they were free, and so was I. Unashamed, no longer an exile, I could ride into battle without an ounce of regret.

"Good." Jaevid stepped past me, ascending to the throne with confidence in every step. I watched, half in dread, half in hope, as he reached up and plucked the black crystal from its resting place on the golden dragon's head. It wasn't much larger than an apple, resting innocently in his hands as he stepped back down from the throne. His pale blue eyes studied it, defined brow furrowing and mouth tensing into a straight line. The different jagged edges, jutting in all directions, showed tiny reflections of his face. With a heavy sigh, Jaevid tucked it away into the leather satchel strung over his shoulders.

My father had obviously provided him something else to wear, which was good. Dressed in full dragonrider armor, he looked much more the hero our soldiers were undoubtedly expecting. The silver breastplate, helm, gauntlets, and greaves were adorned with intricate details of various animals. The creatures wound all over the metal, flowing with the shape of each piece, and were inlaid with gold.

Most complex of all was the dragon on his helmet. It had been carefully crafted to look like Jaevid's face emerged from the dragon's open maw, with a ridge of spines and horns sweeping back regally along the top and sides. When he slid the visor down, slits of green glass that made the dragon's eyes allowed him to see. I'd never seen a helmet quite like it.

We wore the same dragonriders' cloak buckled to our shoulder pauldrons, lengths of vibrant blue cloth sweeping behind us as we walked out of the throne room. But where mine was lined with the traditional white fox fur around the neck, Jaevid's had been crafted from the silvery pelt of a faundra stag. Hints of his Gray elven heritage were sprinkled throughout his armor—a faundra stag's head on the center of his breastplate and the pommel of his scimitar, curled elven writing scrolling along the edges of his gorget, vambrances, and gauntlets.

Father had really outdone himself this time. No doubt he'd paid some lucky blacksmith a fortune for its commission. I had to wonder how long he'd had it stowed away, just waiting for Jaevid to return. Years?

We passed groups of servants and elite guards rushing through the castle halls. Most of the staff had already taken cover in the undercrofts beneath the castle. Those that remained were barricading doors, dousing candelabras, and pulling curtains and draperies over the windows. If the castle was sieged, we didn't want to make things too easy for our enemy. They'd have to find their way around in the dark, through barred doors, all while meeting hidden groups of elite guards and soldiers at every turn.

We took the tunnels from the castle's central keep into the narrow passes of the north wall. There, the infantry forces usually housed within the city had been forced to make room when the dragonriders arrived. Quarters were cramped and, according to my father, supplies were beginning to run scarce since the Tibrans were cutting off all attempts to deliver more by encircling the city's outer walls. Things were not ideal for the soldiers here, but I had to give them credit. As we walked the narrow hallways, weaving our way upward toward the nearest turret, everything was spotless. Bedrolls were neatly folded into corners or stacked out of the way, the floors were clean, and the armories were organized. They were making the most of a bad situation.

When we passed, the line of infantrymen waiting to receive their freshly-sharpened swords from the armor masters stood straighter. They watched us with wide eyes, never saying a word. A few of the younger recruits scrambled to salute, and Jaevid gave them a small nod.

"They look scared," I whispered as we passed through a pair of large, iron-reinforced doors that led into the northernmost turret.

"They have good reason." Jaevid's expression darkened as his gaze grew distant.

I was getting familiar with that particular look. It meant something bad was likely coming our way. "What is it? What do you feel? Is it Reigh?"

He flashed me a troubled glance. "Yes. They're moving this way."

"Who?"

He let out a shuddering breath, cringing and setting his jaw as though something was causing him pain. "I'm not sure. It's hard to put into words," he said, his deep voice going quiet so only I could hear. "I feel Reigh's power growing, as though it has been used to infect a great many things. It's hard to determine what they are from this distance, but it feels similar to Aubren's defilement." He shook his head. "Everything is so frenzied. I should be able to sense more when we get closer."

"He's still alive?" I heard myself ask, although the question left me so numb, I couldn't bear to look at him while he answered.

"Yes," Jaevid murmured. "At least, I think so. Jenna, please understand; I can't promise anything at this point."

My gut soured at those words, and I bit back hard against the taste of bile in my throat. What, by all the Fates, was Argonox doing to *my* little brother?

THE TURRET WAS PACKED THICK WITH INFANTRY ARCHERS. THEY CLUSTERED around their sergeants, gripping their bows tightly as they listened to their final orders. Elves and humans, men and women, stood together with mixed expressions of pasty horror and stony determination. While it was still frowned upon in Maldobar for women to join the ranks, that hadn't kept a few from choosing that path. And with Gray elven culture blending gradually into ours, ladies learning the craft of archery and swordplay was no longer unheard of—especially if you happened to have pointed ears. Ironically, the rumor floating around the barracks was that Gray elf women were far better archers than any human man could ever dream of being.

The air grew colder with every step as we made our way to the second highest floor of the turret. There, more infantrymen stood guard at the iron-wrought doors that led out onto the ramparts. They saluted when they saw us and hurried to open one of the doors, so we could pass through. A blast of bitter night air hit my face, catching in the loose locks of my hair that had already slipped free of my braid.

Two steps out the door, I stopped short. My breath caught in my chest, held in suspense by the company that was waiting for us just outside. Four hundred dragonriders in complete battle dress stood at attention in two long rows on either side of the passage. They stretched from one turret to another, packed in tightly without so much as a foot of space between them. With helmets under one arm and the other clasped in salute over their breastplate, each one stood before a snarling dragon bearing a saddle. Some of them had been painted for battle with swirls of blue over their scales, and others had battle notches carved along their horns—a mark for every kill.

I spotted Perish first. Her white scales stood out against the rest, like a glowing cross between angel and monster. Before her, Calem was watching us with his handsome features as sharp and bare of emotion as ever. Haldor and Turq were right next to them, ready to receive orders.

The sight of those men, two riders who'd become like family to me, filled my heart with blooming heat and the gnawing desire to be right there beside them. Rank and status separated us now, and that left a sour taste in my mouth. I was supposed to be Jaevid's wing end in this fight, so all I could do was wait, hope, and pray that I would see Haldor and Calem again when it was over.

When we appeared upon the rampart passageway, every dragonrider turned at once to face us. My heart thumped wildly against my ribs, and I chanced a look at Jaevid. His pale eyes were round, face flushed except for that faint scar over his cheek. A vein stood out against the olive skin on his neck and his jaw was tense, although I couldn't tell if it was from embarrassment or the overwhelming sight before us. Maybe a bit of both.

"My Lord Jaevid Broadfeather," High Commander Morrig called out to us as he strode up, passing between the two lines of dragonriders. His own silver armor was polished to perfection, reflecting the night sky like mirrors. "Four hundred and seven of the finest Dragonriders of Maldobar stand with you tonight. We are honored to have you in our company. Is there anything you would like to say to the men?" The Commander paused a moment and flashed me a quick, approving smile. "And women, of course."

"I'm not much of a speechmaker." Jaevid was certainly blushing now.

"Nor am I," the Commander laughed. "But I'm sure they'd rather hear you stammer through one than me."

He did have a point there. The heroic tales of the little halfbreed who was chosen by a wild dragon and rose to become Maldobar's greatest hero in the Gray War were known by everyone who set foot in the academy. I had no doubt every man standing before us had heard them all at least twice. Now he was here, fighting alongside them, in a battle that would decide the fate of our kingdom. Speechmaker or not, we were all looking to him now.

This moment was his.

I stood back, watching alongside the High Commander as Jaevid Broadfeather faced the assembled dragonriders. He was taller than most of them, and there was no disguising those sharp elven features even with his helmet covering his ears. With his visor pulled back, it was easy to pick out the hints of uncertainty that crinkled his brow. Then all at once, that apprehension disappeared behind a stern look of fierce resolve.

"Dragonriders of Maldobar, tonight we stand on the edge of the abyss." He squared his shoulders, eyes the color of glacier water scanning the crowd. "At this very moment, the eyes of the world are upon us. Every man, woman, and child left stamped into the mud, crushed beneath the wheels of the Tibran Empire, waits to see if we will suffer the same fate." He paused, taking a breath.

"We stood against this evil once. We knew it by a different name then, and just like now, victory seemed impossible. But we knew we had to try. *Someone* had to try. And the ferocity of our spirit, our determination to stand unshaken in the face of that evil, shone so brightly that not even the wild dragons could look away. They were drawn to it—drawn to us—and joined us not as servants, but allies. Now we stand together, unified, forged as one by the bonds of blood and duty to oppose anyone who would dare threaten us with the chains of bondage!"

A cry like the thrumming boom of thunder roared overhead, accompanied by the burst of giant wing beats. Mavrik rose up, blue scales flashing and yellow eyes glowing in the night. He landed atop the turret behind us with a *boom* that shook the wall and made the rest of the dragons growl and stir with excitement. They flapped and chirped, trumpeting at their king.

"That is why, tonight, we don't fight for Maldobar. We don't fight for kings or crowns, for borders or blood," Jaevid snarled over the noise. "We fight for our brothers and sisters, to resist the chains of bondage, and to set our people and many others free. We will send Argonox, and every other tyrant who would dare to set foot on our shores, a message that will echo through the ages." Jaevid widened his stance, drawing his scimitar to raise the point to the night sky. The length of his cloak caught in the wind, rolling at his heels and billowing around his armored form just as it did in those countless sculptures and draperies. "If there is even one dragonrider left to carry the flame, we will *never* submit! Ours is a spirit that will *never* be broken! Ours is the spirit of the dragon!"

A chorus of cries, yells, and cheers went up through the ranks as the Dragonriders of Maldobar drew their blades and raised them to the night sky. Behind every one of them, a dragon joined in with a trumpeting roar and burst of flame. I couldn't resist. Before I knew it, my own blades were in my hands and I was screaming my war cry along with the rest of them, my heart thrashing in my ears and dragon fire blazing through my veins.

Jaevid didn't say another word as he turned away, sheathing his blade and giving me a distinct nod to follow. I did, but not before stealing one last look at Calem and Haldor. I had to believe they would be safe, and I would see them again. To think anything else was ... unbearable.

Jaevid led the way back into the turret, up the last flight of stairs, and onto the rooftop, where archers and spotters for the catapults were already in place. Granted, they were all making a wide berth around a certain king drake, who snarled and snapped his jaws at the sight below.

Our enemy was moving closer. As far as my eyes could see, an endless ocean of torches, armor, and bronze shields were gathered. They moved closer and closer, like an encroaching tide, pushing their war machines into range to the deep booming of war drums.

We only had minutes left.

"Here we are again, my old friend." Jaevid greeted his dragon with a broad smile, wrapping his arms around the creature's head.

Mavrik closed his eyes and made low chirping sounds, his ears perking toward the sound of his rider's voice.

"Do you remember our bargain? The one we made when we first met?" Jaevid closed his eyes as well, resting his forehead against the dragon's. "I promised I'd never make you do anything you didn't want to do, and that when our war was over, you would be free to return to the wild place they took you from." He pulled back slowly, a sad smile touching his lips as he scratched Mavrik behind the ears. "It's still your choice. If you want to ride with me again, let's make this a fight to remember."

The king drake gave a snort and growl, lifting his head and pointing a savage snarl at the encroaching Tibran army. At least—I thought it was the army.

I was mistaken.

The shape of a monstrous black dragon, silhouetted against the starry sky, landed atop a rocky hill amidst the Tibran ranks. With scales glittering in the torchlight like polished obsidian, the beast let out a roar that vibrated my breastplate and made my insides flutter. Icarus had returned.

From high atop the turret, the rider seated in his saddle was plainly visible, bathed in the glow of torches and ambient starlight. Her black armor was still adorned in golden painted wings, and a long red cloak swept from her shoulder pauldrons to flutter in the night wind. Though her face was hidden beneath a golden-painted helmet, I knew who she was ... and what she meant to the young man standing next to me.

Beckah Derrick was the only person I suspected might make Jaevid falter. He would have to face her again. But this time, if he hesitated to do what was necessary, it wouldn't be Cernheist at risk of burning. If Jaevid could not make that killing blow, then Maldobar would fall, and with it, every person I had ever loved.

Mavrik unfurled to face the imposter king drake, his teeth bared and black spines bristling along his back and head. His tail whipped, and his plated chest heaved with furious breaths. Burning venom drizzled from his open maw, hissing as it hit the stone. Feral wrath blazed in his yellow eyes as he looked back to us, as though silently demanding we hurry up.

Jaevid's expression twitched. He turned slightly, glancing over one shoulder as two more dragons circled and landed next to us. Phevos and Vexi crawled in closer, dipping their heads in respect and chirping at us anxiously. I hesitated, studying the pair. That couldn't be right. Vexi was wearing a saddle—and there was someone sitting in it!

Gods, had she done it? Had Vexi rescued Reigh already?

My heart leapt, swelling with hope. But when the man threw back the visor of his helmet to grin down at us, it wasn't Reigh. My father, King Felix Farrow, was sitting casually astride the green dragoness in an ensemble of dragonrider armor I'd never seen him wear before. It was old, tarnished in places, and a little too small for him around the middle.

Oh no. Surely that wasn't his old dragonrider armor from the Gray War. He hadn't worn it in ... well, probably sometime before I was born. That must have been well over twenty years ago!

"You didn't honestly think I'd let you run off to have all the fun without me, did you?" He chuckled when he caught me gaping.

I blinked, just to make sure I wasn't hallucinating. I sort of hoped I was. "But, I thought Vexi chose Reigh to be her rider? H-how did you manage to convince her to let you ... ?"

"I can be very persuasive," he said, puffing his chest out proudly.

Jaevid rolled his eyes. "Felix, you had nothing to do with it. I, on the other hand, spent two hours talking her into this. And she only agreed to do it if we made rescuing Reigh our first priority."

My father wafted a hand. "Details, details. The important part is, we're back in the sky causing trouble again. Just like old times, eh? You and I, impossible odds, the fate of the world, and nothing but a bit of dumb luck on our side."

"Just try and keep up," Jaevid taunted, a little smirk playing on his lips as he grabbed ahold of Mavrik's saddle and climbed into place. "I did warn her to take it easy on you. Being forty years out of the saddle, I'm sure you'll appreciate a *gentle* reintroduction."

Father's lips pursed with any annoyed scowl. "If I'm not mistaken, you've been out of the saddle a while, too. Only difference I see is that you still can't grow a beard. Just try me, Jae. We'll see who's really out of practice."

Jaevid was laughing as he slid the visor of his helmet down, covering his face. That was my cue to get ready.

Gripping the saddle handles, I hauled myself onto Phevos's back with one swift motion. My legs slipped comfortably into the boot sheaths on either side of his strong neck, and my fingers flew over the buckles as I strapped myself in. My hands shook with nervous energy, teeth rattling as I fumbled with my helmet. In my rush, my sweaty fingers slipped over the slick, polished metal. My helmet went tumbling. I flailed to catch it, but it was too late.

A swift, slate-colored hand, glinting with tiny white specks along the wrist and fingers, appeared out of nowhere, snagging my helmet out of the air before it could hit the ground.

Phillip stood right beside us, staring up at me with his silver eyes shining in the starlight. His wavy black hair blew around his face, nearly hiding the smile that showed the points of his incisors. He stepped in closer and handed the helmet back up to me. "Nervous?"

"No," I lied.

"I thought I should come see you off," Phillip said, glancing around at Jaevid and my father. Both were watching us. "I'll be helping hold the wall. The men are terrified. We're outnumbered twenty to one. But I won't let them falter—not when your life depends on it."

My heart hit the back of my throat. Suddenly, I wished I wasn't already buckled into my saddle. I wanted to hug him, to kiss him one last time. Gods, if this was the last time we ever saw one another, I had to tell him, to make sure he knew how much he meant to me.

"Phillip, I—"

He shook his head, pressing a finger to his lips as he backed away. "No goodbyes. Not tonight. Go on, love. When it's over, you know where to find me."

CHAPTER TWENTY-TWO

The Tibran ranks advanced, marching with a pace that resounded like thunder, with hundreds upon thousands of soldiers carrying their crimson banner ever closer to our city walls. Every block of troops stood beneath the golden eagle standard, bronze shields interlocked, and bloodshot eyes fixed upon us. What came next was inevitable. Like the calm before the rush and chaos of a storm, a moment of silence hung in the air as though the whole world had stopped to hold its breath.

Only one question lingered, caught in the mind of every man and woman on the battlefield: who would draw first blood tonight?

The answer came in a cacophony of shrieks and bellowing roars. Like ghosts from the moonless night, the shapes of creatures sailing through the air toward Halfax took form. They came at varying speeds, some as fast as a shrike, others more steadily like dragons—because that's precisely what they were.

I recognized a few of the dragons right away. Once, they were proud and honorable beasts. They'd fallen in battle at Northwatch, defending it to their last breath, only to be left upon that battlefield with their deceased riders still belted into the saddles. There was no way to go back for the bodies so that they could receive the proper burial rites. Argonox did not honor ancient battle customs. He chose to use the corpses for fouler things.

Like this.

The creatures were in the same state as Icarus—reanimated, rotting corpses brought back to some semblance of life by Reigh's divine power. Whatever honor they had possessed before was gone. Tonight, they were our enemies.

Biting back my revulsion, I steeled myself as best I could. This was only the first of Argonox's horrors. No doubt he had many more in store for us.

As the flock of monsters soared past, Icarus let out a rumbling cry, spitting a plume of white-hot flame into the night. The monstrous black drake reared onto his haunches, sweeping tattered wings open and diving forward into the air to lead the charge. That was all the motivation they needed. The Tibran army shuddered into motion, advancing straight toward us.

On our left, Mavrik stirred and hissed, ears slicked back, and jagged teeth bared at his imposing rival. Jaevid barely had time to signal to us, "*You two find Reigh. The dragonriders will hold their sky assault. Mavrik and I will deal with Icarus.*"

My stomach dropped. He was going after them alone? Oh no—not this again.

There was no time to reply or argue as Mavrik kicked off the turret and surged forward, aimed directly to intercept Icarus and Beckah's path. With Haldor's words of warning still ringing in my ears, I had no choice but to signal to my father and take off. Phevos and I took point, taking to the air and immediately bolting upward to get out of range of the Tibran ground fire and net-throwers.

From the air, it was easier to map out the true immensity of the Tibran forces. Blocks of legions moved as one, responding to the cadence of drummers to tell them where to go. Lines of cavalrymen came after, their steeds straining to haul the first of their war machines, huge metal ladders, toward the city walls. Each one was tall enough to reach the ramparts and armed with grasping hooks to anchor them in place. It took no less than four horses to haul them forward, and the beasts were well-guarded by the soldiers clustered around them.

Behind them came more legions, different blocks brandishing different styles of weaponry—some of which I'd never seen before. Masses from around the world, enslaved and spurred to fight for this madman, carried all manner of devices and dressed in strange styles of armor. Some rode on the backs of beasts, creatures like giant boars as big as bulls, and hefting double-headed axes. Others were dressed in gleaming silks, brandishing curved scimitars as they rode in chariots hauled by stallions with pelts that shone like scales and cloven hooves.

An entire line of war beasts like the one Hilleddi had ridden into Barrowton stomped and bayed, swaying beneath platforms of bone and steel. Moving slow, twelve of the beasts tromped across the earth behind a leader whose scaly hide was as red as ruby. Its body was studded with spines and horns, like a cross between lizard and porcupine. Seated on one of those raised platforms, snapping the long chains anchored to the creature's stocky forelegs, was a figure I could have sworn I recognized. No—that was impossible. It couldn't be.

I steered Phevos a bit lower, doing a swift pass just to be sure.

Gods and Fates and all things holy ... it was *her*!

Hilleddi stood atop the platform of that spiny creature, her eyes milky and skin as pale as a corpse. Some sort of iron collar had been fixed around her neck, most likely to put her head back where it was supposed to be, and she looked out across the battlefield with her mouth drawn into a sneer.

A thousand questions ran roared through my brain like a surge of electrical current. Had Reigh's power been used to revive her corpse, as well? When? How? Why would Argonox defile the body of his own sister that way? Did he have no sense of morality or honor at all? If not even his sister's body was sacred, then what else had he revived to send against us?

A sudden shriek from Vexi drew my focus away. The green dragon pitched her head, snapping and yelping as we passed the army below. She fought my father's directions, flapping and snarling as she tore away from our formation and past the line of war beasts Hilleddi was leading.

Suddenly, I saw why.

Behind them, flanked by legions pushing countless trebuchets and catapults into range, was a grand chariot. Lord Argonox himself stood at the front of the carriage, draped in a long dark cloak that looked as though it had been cut right from a dragon's scaly hide. Clever, if not completely barbaric. A dragon's own hide was the only thing that couldn't be melted or burnt by their venom.

Bound to a long draft pole by iron-wrought chains were two dragons, each harnessed by the same cruel muzzle device that had been used on Vexi. From where I sat, it looked as though their wings had been cut—leathery membranes sliced away entirely so they stood no chance of ever flying again. The sight made my eyes well and anger burned in my chest as hot as hellfire. My vision swerved with fury. Beneath me, Phevos let out a roar of disgust. How *dare* he disfigure them that way!

But that was not what had Vexi pitching wildly in the air like an unbroken horse, trying to buck my father out of her saddle.

Tethered between the two dragons, his arms held wide by shackles bound to the muzzle of each of the beasts, was Reigh. The sight of him, slumped and nearly naked, his limp body dragging over the ground between the dragons like a prize, was too much. I couldn't bear it.

A scream tore out of me, so primal I didn't even recognize it. Rage and grief boiled up from my soul. With all the gods as my witness, Argonox would *pay* for this.

Vexi cried out again, shaking her head and spinning wildly as my father fought to keep her at bay. Now it all made sense. She wanted to go to him—her rider. She wanted to set him free.

"*Let her go*," I signaled to my father, who was struggling just to stay in the saddle. "*That's him! That's Reigh!*"

Father immediately released the saddle handles and leaned down, pressing his body flat against her neck for stability. The young dragoness dove straight for Argonox like a tongue of lime green lightning. I urged Phevos to take up the chase, and he bellowed in agreement. There was no way we would let her do this alone.

⚜

THE BATTLE BEGAN LIKE A MIGHTY WAVE BREAKING UPON AN ANCIENT SEASIDE fortress.

Dragons and shrikes collided in the air above countless Tibran soldiers, plumes of flame flashing in the night as dragons spat their burning venom and catapults launched orbs that smashed against the city walls. Mavrik and Icarus collided in midair like two eagles, rear legs and talons extended and jaws snapping. The night was a riot of men shouting, swords clashing, bowstrings snapping, and the *swoosh—boom* of trebuchet fire. The acrid smell of dragon venom mingled with the metallic stench of fresh blood.

Before they could reach the outer wall of the city, Argonox's cavalries were interrupted by the sudden appearance of a hundred enormous earthen golems. They writhed free of the ground, resembling the ones Jaevid had summoned out of the Marshlands before. Only these were larger—*much* larger. Their bodies were crafted of stone and root rather than mud and rot. They lumbered forward, smashing through enemy lines with boulder-fists flying.

Enemy fire from the ground howled past me in barely discernable blurs. Arrows glanced off my armor. Spears zoomed passed my head, missing by inches. A net snagged at the edge of one of Phevos's wings, but he was able to shake it off and continue his rapid dive toward the ground.

We'd trained for years on how to make an assault like this. It was our primary mission—to lay down fire and clear the way for ground infantry. Vexi, however, had never seen a single day of official training. She was still wild and didn't know how to work with a rider in battle. So, the instant the young dragoness touched down, Phevos and I moved as one to hold the perimeter so that my father could dismount. It was safer for him to get as far away from her as possible. His life wasn't the one she was interested in saving, after all.

He unbuckled quickly and kicked free of the saddle, hitting the ground in a roll before springing up to run headlong toward Reigh with his sword drawn.

Argonox saw him coming. He unfurled a long, nine-tailed whip and drew it back to strike, snapping the tip off the rumps of the grounded dragons hauling his chariot. The beasts screeched in pain and bucked as Argonox pulled back on the reins, undoubtedly wrenching those pinch bits into their soft tongues. The dragons responded with a spew of burning venom aimed right for my father.

Fire exploded into the night. I had to look away, shielding my eyes from the bloom of intense light. When I looked back, there were only flames. I couldn't see anything—no sign of my father.

"No!" I shrieked and whipped the saddle handles, giving the command to pursue. There was still time. I could make it! I would not let my father die this way!

A figure unfurled from the flames. Two broad, birdlike wings spread wide, their feathers as bright and colorful as gemstones as they beat once. The flames instantly died out, snuffed by the rush of wind off those feathers.

How was that possible? Nothing could douse dragon fire!

I gaped, barely able to keep myself upright in the saddle as a creature rose from where it had wrapped itself protectively around my father. It had appeared out of nowhere, but now it stood like a riot of color amidst the churning darkness of battle. It was a bizarre mixture of bird and fox, with feathers as bright as a jungle parrot's and eyes that glowed like fiery emeralds in the night. It was almost as big as a dragon, although far stranger than anything I'd seen before— outside of paintings and tapestries from the Gray War, anyway.

I gasped. It was a foundling spirit.

On slender birdlike feet, the creature crept around my father, its large pointed ears perked forward, and vulpine snout wrinkled in a snarl. Throwing off his helmet, my father stood and aimed a broad grin up toward Argonox. He was alive! And without so much as a singe mark anywhere that I could see.

As Vexi sailed in from the sky, her sides swelling with the distinct deep breath that preceded a spray of fire, King Felix drew his sword. He rushed for the chariot, swinging wide with a furious shout I heard clearly over the roar of battle. "*Give me back my son!*"

PART FIVE: REIGH

CHAPTER TWENTY-THREE

My body was so numb I couldn't feel my own breathing anymore. Everything was cold, as though I were suspended under ice water, drifting while my last few seconds of consciousness slipped away. Was my heart still beating? Was I even alive?

No—I had to be alive.

I could still feel the dull sensation of iron shackles biting in to my wrists and the scrape of the earth under my legs and knees as I was dragged forward and across the ground. Phoebe had tried to bandage my arms after the bleeding. I didn't understand why. And it didn't matter now. The shackles reopened the wounds, and that small amount of discomfort somehow made it through the haze of raw power humming through my body—just enough to keep me conscious. But where were they taking me? What was happening? I was slipping, falling into the cold darkness again. This time, I didn't resist. I couldn't. My strength was gone.

I just wanted it to be over.

The muffled roar of beasts—dragons and Tibran monsters—spun through my frayed mind like echoes of an invisible nightmare. The rumble of explosions, blasts of fire, and cries of men came from every direction. The world seemed to shake around me, smelling strongly of ash and brimstone. But I was too far gone to be afraid. Why? What was the point? Death was the only way I would ever escape. Argonox would never let me go.

A voice boomed over the noise, so loud I could feel it rattling in my skull. "GIVE ME BACK MY SON!"

My arms went slack as though someone had cut the chains bound to my wrists, and suddenly there was nothing there to force me upright. My legs buckled. I fell, too weak to even try to catch myself, and hit the ground face-first.

What was happening? Who was that? My ears rang, and I strained to hear that voice again.

Bellowing howls and thunderous booms shook the ground under me. The sound of snarls, snapping teeth against scales, and shrieks of pain seemed to come from every direction. I recognized the deep inhale and throaty hiss, followed by the roar of flames. A dragon was spitting its fiery venom so close by I could smell the acidic tinge of it lingering in the air. The low hum of something huge swooshed right over me, probably missing me by inches. A tail? Wings? Gods only knew. But I couldn't even lift my head to see.

The brawl seemed to end as abruptly as it had begun. No more roars. No more flame. A break in the commotion with only the distant sound of the battle to fill the silence.

A soft whine and series of pops, clicks, and chirps resonated against my ear and a hot blast of musky breath blasted over my cheek. I felt it. Something huge was looming over me. But I couldn't move or open my eyes.

A rough shove rocked my senses, rolling me over so that I flopped onto my back. More hot breaths blasted against my face. I didn't have to see her. I knew it was Vexi.

It took every ounce of strength left in my body to will my eyes open. The end of her big green nose was right in my face, smelling me and whining. She licked at my forehead, one big swipe of sticky dragon spit up the bridge of my nose all the way to my hairline.

"H-hey there," I managed to rasp weakly.

She chirped, huge blue eyes blinking down at me with concern. Curling her scaly body around me like a protective living barrier, she laid her head on the ground right next to mine. Her ears perked toward me and nostrils puffed in deep, as though she could sense I was in bad shape.

Too late, I realized that leaving her, trying to send her away, was by far the stupidest thing I'd ever done. That's saying something, I know. Doing stupid stuff was basically my life's hobby. But Kiran had told me about the loyalty of dragons many times. And right after Vexi chose me, Jenna had said something about it, too. She'd said that our bond was special—that Vexi would stick by me no matter what, even in death. At the time, I hadn't understood what that meant.

Now I did.

"I-I'm sorry, Vexi," I croaked, not sure if she'd even understand. I'd have given anything just to touch her, maybe pet her head a little or give her ears one last good scratch.

My dragon tucked herself in tighter around me, sniffing through my hair and wrapping her wings around us. It muffled the chaos. It made me feel safe. Nuzzling her big head under my arm, she lay still and stared at me, the deep rhythm of her heartbeat right in my ear. I'd never heard anything so soothing in my entire life.

"I found him! He's here!" a woman shouted nearby, her voice familiar even muffled by Vexi's body around me. That was ... I mean it sounded like ... Jenna.

"Where?" a man yelled back. It wasn't Argonox, Jaevid, Aubren, or Phillip. No, this was someone else—a voice I didn't recognize.

Vexi's body tensed around me. She hissed, unfurling somewhat to lift her head and growl.

"Easy there, girl. I know he's hurt. He needs our help. Let me see him, all right? I'll be careful," the man crooned. "Just let me take a look."

Vexi hissed louder, snapping her jaws, and gave a strong blast through her nose as one last threat. Then she leaned away.

And I saw him.

A human man bent over me, his light brown eyes the same color as mine. They seemed kind; gentle, somehow. Staring into them was bizarre, and the more I studied him, the stranger I felt. Why was his face so familiar? His stony, rugged features were crinkled with age, and his wavy, dark golden hair was streaked with gray that was the same color as his short beard. At the sight of me, his thick brows lifted, and his mouth opened. Only one word escaped. "Reigh."

He knew me? How? I didn't recognize him at all. Was he Tibran? Surely not. His armor looked like a dragonrider's ensemble.

Before I could muster a reply, the man was ripping off his riding gauntlets and rushing toward me. He fell to his knees and gathered me into his arms, squeezing me tight. His breathing hitched. Was he crying? Why?

"You've got to get him out of here," Jenna spoke over us suddenly, appearing like an armored angel of vengeance. "Phevos and I can't stay here. Argonox abandoned the chariot and we lost him in the ranks. I don't know what he's up to, but he's on the move and the war beasts are advancing this way. They will be upon us in minutes! I can't cover you any longer; we have to rejoin our formation."

The man didn't respond.

She growled louder. "Father! Did you hear me? You have to get out of here now!"

Wait—*Father*? This man was ... ? So that meant he was my ... ?

I wanted to look at him again, to check his features over for any more traces of a resemblance. But the next thing I knew, the man was hefting me into a dragon's saddle and climbing on behind me. It was only after he'd started buckling us together that I realized this saddle was on Vexi. Since when did she wear a saddle? Was this Jaevid's doing?

With one arm wrapped around me and the other gripping a saddle handle, he gave her a nudge and Vexi spread her wings. She bounded skyward with a shrill cry and a wild rush of wind. The earth fell away. My head lulled, and for an instant all I could see were the stars overhead. Countless. Brilliant. Only now when I looked at them, all I could think about was the dark goddess taunting me from behind that glittering barrier. The cold of her power had all but consumed me. I was hanging by a thread, waiting for the snap and fall into a restful abyss.

Vexi leveled off with a few hard beats of her wings and I slumped forward, resting against her neck with my cheek against the warm, smooth surface of her scales.

Through the haze and delirium, something else caught my eye. Far below, there was more light, but no stars. No, this was something far worse. A scene of unspeakable horror spread out below us. Halfax was under siege. And from where I sat, it was as though the entire world was burning in the night.

There were Tibrans on the ramparts. They'd pushed their metal ladders to the wall and were climbing, one right after another, to clash against the Maldobarian infantry waiting there. The land all around the city was boiling with the motion of thousands of soldiers—all converging upon the city walls. Swords flashed. Shields bashed. In the air, dragons and shrikes collided in aerial combat with plumes of burning venom. Trebuchets hurled orbs that smashed against the walls and turrets, exploding with a force that blew soldiers to their doom far below. It was like watching burning oil being poured over an anthill.

And in the thick of it all, I saw Jaevid.

GRANTED, WHEN IT CAME TO PICKING PEOPLE OUT IN THE THICK OF A BATTLE, Jaevid Broadfeather was easy to spot. Mavrik was one of the two largest dragons on the field. The other—well—I knew that monster far too well. It was the one Argonox had forced me to reanimate. The first experiment. Now that abomination was writhing on the ground, white bone peeking through its rotting hide. The two king drakes kicked and rolled, snarling and snapping like two enormous feral cats. They crunched over any soldier who was stupid enough to get too close.

Nearby, Jaevid had his blade drawn, locked in combat with *her*.

Beckah Derrick.

My brain throbbed at the sight of that black and gold armor, and acid burned at the back of my throat. Even from a distance, her presence made my head swim and my body quiver with a rising swell of cold. So much power had been poured into her, but in the end, it had only brought back her body and maybe a few fragments of her muscle memory—enough to make her a contender in a fight. But there was nothing else inside her except raw, crackling dark energy. No spirit. No soul. No essence of who she'd been before.

I just hoped Jaevid realized that.

From where I was sitting, it didn't look good. Beckah had him on the defensive, bearing in hard with a pair of strange white blades that looked familiar. Crap

—those were my kafki! I was sure of it; those were the same white elven blades Hilleddi had taken off me when Aubren and I were captured on our way to Barrowton! Argonox had given her *my* weapons? And now she was using them against Jaevid? Of all the sick, twisted—

Beckah suddenly lunged in with a brutal assault, swirling the white blades with an effortless grace. Every movement was precise, steps in a deadly dance, as she swung wide. Dipping and feinting, she darted around him in complex strikes that would have forced even a seasoned fighter to put up their guard.

Jaevid, however, was just as fast. He had size and reach on her but didn't seem to need to use either as he met every strike like they'd rehearsed this beforehand. They dueled like demons, their armor reflecting the glow of dragon fire and exploding orbs, and their faces twisted with similar expressions of rage. But where Beckah's seemed more disconnected and violent, Jaevid's was riddled with grief.

With an abrupt surge of energy, Beckah rushed him with a swing of those white, scythe-shaped blades and sent him reeling backward. The slice missed his neck by centimeters. He rocked back, off balance for less than a second. But that was all the time she needed. Faster than a viper's strike, Beckah planted a boot right in the center of his chest. The kick sent him flying with a burst of dark power. He skidded over the ground, losing his grip on his scimitar, and rolled to a halt flat on his back.

I felt my pulse return with a vengeance, thrashing in my ears with a rush of adrenaline and fear. Jaevid couldn't lose. Not now—not like this.

Beckah spun the blades over in her hands as she prowled forward, her spine rippling with confidence in every swaggering step. Jaevid sat up on his elbows, staring at her with brows crinkled upward as he shouted at her. Whatever he said, I never heard it. The words were lost to the rumble of the battlefield.

She stopped over him. I cringed, every muscle instinctively drawn tight with dread as she brandished my razor-sharp kafki. This was it.

All of a sudden, Jaevid's eyes began glowing like two emerald stars. He snapped a hand forward, clenching a fist in the air. At the same instant, three huge vines burst out of the ground and snaked around Beckah's body, pinning her arms to her sides and anchoring her to the earth. They held her fast, suspended so that she was eye-level with Jaevid when he got to his feet.

His eyes still shone through the night as he approached her cautiously, his mouth moving. What was he doing? Reasoning with her? Couldn't he tell there was no trace of her spirit in that monster Argonox had forced me to create? That was *not* the real Beckah!

Jaevid bent down, fingers wrapping around the grip of his scimitar. When he straightened, his eyes were pinched shut and his mouth screwed up as though he were in pain. He didn't look at her again, even when he rammed his scimitar to the hilt into her chest.

Beckah's milky, lifeless eyes went wide. Her jaw went slack, and then so did the rest of her. My blades slipped out of her hands.

It was over.

Jaevid slid his scimitar back, head hung to his chest as he turned away. I couldn't see his face until he slowly turned back to her. With broad shoulders curled forward, his expression shattered into anguish. His eyes welled, and his chin quivered, hand shaking as he grasped the back of her head and let his forehead rest against hers. He stood like that for a second or two, and then brushed his fingers over her face to gently shut her eyes.

Jaevid stumbled back away from her, his whole face twitching and expression skewing. He let out a horrible, broken cry as he crumpled to his knees before her and buried his face in his hands. He couldn't see the figure in spiny black armor approaching through the ranks of soldiers.

Oh no.

Clenching my teeth, I gave Vexi's neck a pat to get her attention. "T-there. We h-have to warn him," I rasped. "Hurry!"

She chirped and flashed me a disapproving glare. Fine, so she had a point. I wasn't exactly in prime shape for a fight. This probably looked a lot like a grand gesture of suicide. But my focus was on warning Jaevid. I had to. This was a fight he couldn't win.

"Trust me, okay?" I forced a weak smile.

She snorted, looked away, and made a swift, spiraling descent toward Jaevid.

The dark figure was getting closer. Twenty yards away. Through the toiling hordes of soldiers, no one else seemed to notice him. But I couldn't look away. I had to stop this. Jaevid didn't know!

"What are you doing?" The old man sitting behind me protested. Father or not, he didn't seem to like what was going on and pulled me back from Vexi's neck, restraining me against his chest.

I didn't have the strength or time to explain. I was already on borrowed time. That dark figure in armor was drawing closer, and as far as I could tell, Jaevid still hadn't seen him. He didn't know what was coming—what I had been forced to create.

Vexi laid down a broad perimeter of her burning venom to clear a landing path. She hit the ground at a trot and loped in as close as she could without getting caught in the fray of the dueling king drakes. With a gale-force rush of wind, the two beasts kicked off the earth and took their fight back into the sky. With the undead drake making speed toward the city, Mavrik took up the chase with a shriek of wrath.

Vexi ducked as they howled past, her emerald hide shivering. She chittered anxiously and looked all around as the Tibran ranks began to converge on us from all sides, armed with net-throwers and spears. I guess they'd been instructed to stay clear of Beckah and Jaevid—but we were fair game.

I had to hurry.

Shoving away from the man, my father, I hurled myself off Vexi's back and hit the ground like a dead fish. I lay there for a moment, mustering the will to crawl across the dirt as far away from them as I could.

With a desperate, final breath I yelled back at my dragon, "GO!"

She screeched in dismay, and the man on her back shouted at me again. There was no time to debate it. Jaevid was in trouble. I had to stop it. He had to know—that man, the armor—whatever happened, Jaevid could *not* attack him!

CHAPTER TWENTY-FOUR

"Jaevid!" The cry left my lips a second too late.

A deep laugh resonated over us like the rumble of thunder.

Jaevid and I looked, moving in unison, just in time to see the figure of a man clad in black armor step forward out of the line of awestruck Tibran soldiers. With a black cloak of dragon hide draped over his shoulders, every inch of his body was fortified behind armor that made my mind scream in panic and protest. I felt its presence like a white-hot brand pressing at the base of my skull. It pierced the numbness, the cold, and threatened to burn me alive from the inside out.

I opened my mouth to scream, but nothing would come out. My breath—my voice—hung in my throat as my body convulsed on the ground.

That armor was more than a defilement or abomination. Every inch of that dark armor had been crafted especially for this moment, etched in runes and forged with *my* blood infused in the metal. Basically, if evil had a garment of choice, Argonox was currently wearing it.

Jaevid was already staggering to his feet. His nostrils flared with deep, enraged breaths as he fixed Argonox with a focused stare. With his hands curled into fists at his side, he strode forward to meet him. Emerald light bloomed from his eyes once again, sparking to life at the same instant two white feathery wings unfurled from his back. Each feather seemed to be crafted from shining mist, piercing through the haze of combat like guiding starlight. Sweeping white horns like those of a faundra stag grew from Jaevid's head right above his pointed ears. His skin shimmered with a pearlescent hue like scales along his cheekbones and brow.

With lips curled back into a snarl, he flared his white wings and drew back a hand.

NO!

I dug my hands into the dirt, trying to claw my way in closer. I had to warn him! *Stop! Don't do it, you idiot!*

Jaevid launched his assault with a thrust of his hand. The ground shuddered, cracking open like an eggshell along the path of a bolt of green power that hurtled toward Argonox. The green comet collided full force against his breastplate with a flash of blinding light and a gusting blast wave.

My spine went rigid. Pain coursed through my body, setting every nerve on fire. I could feel it in my bones, the electrifying power like acid in my marrow. It rattled in my teeth and sizzled over my skin.

"Reigh!" Jaevid called out to me.

I couldn't reply or do anything at all except lie there, my vision tunneling in and out, until the pain passed.

As the light faded and the dust began to clear, Argonox let out a booming laugh. "Hah! It seems that didn't quite kill him. Care to try again?" He stepped from the swirling smoke, sliding off his helmet and tossing it onto the ground between them. He prowled closer, a satisfied grin curled across his face. "Perhaps your next strike will save me the trouble. Did you really think I'd bring him here if he could be so easily rescued? His power—his very essence—is tied to me now. Every strike you make will seal his fate."

Jaevid stared at me, his glowing eyes wide and expression devoid of any emotion. Not exactly the most hope-inspiring look, considering the circumstances. Didn't he have a plan for all this?

"It's pathetic, really," Argonox sneered as he stepped in closer, tipping his chin up in confidence. "I mean, him, I get. He's a sniveling child, too stupid and naïve to know his place in this grand symphony. But I expected more from you. Not that it matters. You'll both die on this battlefield, mired in your own blood and filth, while I claim every prize this kingdom has to offer. There's a far more powerful artifact to be had and I won't have to worry about keeping some sniveling whelp alive to use it. This power, this divine rite, after centuries of waiting and searching ... I am finally *myself* again." Argonox's laugh crackled in the cold air. "I am the only Harbinger this world deserves."

Jaevid bowed his head to his chest, obscuring his face behind clumps of sweaty ash gray hair as he turned to face me. His arms moved, and I sucked in a sharp breath.

I was the problem. If he killed me, it would be merciful. Then he could deal with Argonox without having to listen to me scream the entire time until one of his powerful blasts finally finished me off. He could end my suffering now.

He moved like a blur, so fast I didn't even have time to brace myself.

Throwing back his dragonrider cloak, Jaevid grabbed a small leather satchel that was strung across his back and reached inside.

The ambient glow of torch and starlight made the dark crystal sparkle in his hand. As he drew it free of the satchel, my mind erupted with a chorus of whispers that sent cold shivers through my body. I couldn't look away. Every jagged point and glittering inch of that crystal made my body tremble and quake with power, bubbling up from somewhere deep inside.

What ... what was that thing?

"Is this the artifact you had in mind?" Jaevid asked, his voice laced with spite as he kept his face hidden.

Argonox's eyes grew wide and desperate. "It's mine! Give it to me!" He roared and surged in for a charging assault.

Jaevid snapped his gaze to meet mine, and I saw a tiny hint of hesitation quirk across his brow. His hand flourished over the crystal, jerking strangely. I could have sworn I saw blood drizzling over one of the jagged points of the crystal.

IN A SINGLE HEARTBEAT, EVERYTHING AROUND ME STOPPED. EVERY SECOND became a decade. I was suspended, weightless, ... free. My mind was as quiet as the stillness of the deepest winter freeze. There was no more pain as I pushed myself up to my knees, staring around at the eerily silent and frozen chaos around me.

Everywhere I looked, Tibran soldiers stood like statues, caught in the middle of their strikes and parries with Maldobarian infantry. Overhead, dragons were suspended in the air, locked in combat with shrikes or others of their kind. Everything was frozen in time.

In fact, the only one still moving besides me was Jaevid and ...

"*Hello, Reigh. About time we met face-to-face, isn't it, my pet?*" The woman before me loomed like a giant, eight feet tall at least. She was like a living statue, larger than life and bathed in ageless beauty. With skin as white as milk and lips of ruby red, she studied me with eyes that glittered the same way that dark crystal had— black, bottomless, and eternal. "*A gift of pure blood is a difficult thing to come by. But the blood of the lapiloque? Well, there's nothing purer unless it came from the veins of the foregods. But I doubt they'd be so accommodating. After all, they were the ones who built my starry prison. Lovely, isn't it?*" Her laughter crackled in the air as she gestured upward, to where the stars shone more brightly than ever, seeming to flicker and pulse.

I staggered to my feet as she began to come closer, bolts of her wavy black hair flowing down to brush the ground at her bare feet. The length of her black robe slid off one creamy-white shoulder and didn't seem to be made of any kind of earthly material. Every movement made the bolt of fabric ripple and shimmer, as though millions of tiny dark crystals were embedded into it.

"*Don't be afraid, my darling,*" she crooned in her smooth, breathy tone as she stopped before me and bent down, crouching so that we were looking eye-to-eye. "*I've waited a long time for this moment.*"

"Clysiros," I managed to croak her name.

Her smile was electric and staggeringly beautiful. It pulled me in like a single candle burning in a dark cave. I wanted to go closer. To hear her speak. To know her. Something told me being in her embrace would be peaceful—restful, even.

She stretched out a hand and brushed her fingers along my cheek, each one so big she could have mashed my head like a grape. "*An eternity trapped in a cage, imprisoned with the damned and despised, with only my trusted Harbinger to be my eyes and hands in this world. And then the lapiloque comes to me with a bargain. So many favors in exchange for a fresh start.*"

"Favors?" I glanced back over to where Jaevid was watching, his expression fixed in a tense frown.

"Terms," he clarified, his expression sharp and ominous. "We spoke of this before. Paligno and Clysiros require some form of manifestation on earth for their powers to remain effective. Formerly, that was the stones. I shattered Paligno's and became a vessel for his essence instead. But your crystal remains." He paused, emerald eyes flickering to Clysiros and narrowing. "It must also be destroyed. A new balance must be struck—a new way for the gods to manifest."

Right. I did remember that discussion, although at the time I hadn't envisioned we'd be reopening the topic in front of an actual deity. "You have an idea?"

Clysiros's pouty red lips curved into another alluring smile. "*He proposes we resume our presence on earth as it was in the old times. No more silly stones in need of mortal speakers. But with the added agreement that should either of us seek to dominate the other, a most terrible punishment would befall.*"

"What kind of punishment would a god fear?" I almost didn't want to know.

"*The thing all gods fear, my darling.*" She traced a cold fingertip down the bridge of my nose. "*Mortality.*"

"The god found guilty of overstepping his or her bounds would suffer a lifetime of mortality—devoid of any divine power," Jaevid concurred. "Hopefully such an existence would be as educational as it would be humbling."

"*I doubt if anything could humble my brother,*" Clysiros scoffed with a taunting grin.

Jaevid gave a snort. "I pray we never find out."

"*At any rate, these terms are agreeable to the three of us. But we need an accord of all parties for this to work. As long as this agreement is acceptable to you, as well, then we have only one small matter to attend to.*" She drew back slightly, licking her lips as she stared at me like a hungry she-wolf eyeing a meal. "You must complete the ritual and become my Harbinger."

My mind raced. Standing in that frozen eternity, my gaze darted from the Tibran soldiers, Maldobarian infantry, dragons, and war beasts to the blood-caked mud under my feet, the vines Jaevid had summoned, and the men who had already fallen to a blade, arrow, spear, or flame.

Then, of course, there was Argonox. My lip curled. Anger swelled in my already frazzled brain, making a coppery taste rise in my throat.

I set my jaw and looked back to the goddess. "What about all things he did with my—er—your power? Can it be undone?"

She grinned. "*Of course. He was such an unruly child. It was never enough, all the power I gave him. He always wanted more.*"

"And my abilities? Those will be gone, too?"

"*Don't look so disappointed, darling,*" she crooned again. "*What we had was beautiful while it lasted.*"

My stomach tensed. "What about Noh?"

Tilting her head to the side made Clysiros's hair brush against her porcelain-hued cheek. "*Is that a hint of concern I hear? Are you worried for your dear brother?*"

"I think he deserves better than dying alone in the Vale. I don't understand him, but he was dragged into this mess because of me. I can't just turn my back on him."

She studied me with those bottomless black eyes. Something about them reminded me of the Well of Souls—as though they were churning with the same chaotic force and I might drown in them if I stared for too long.

"*I will still need a faithful guardian to guide the spirits there and shepherd them on to their final rewards. He may remain, if he chooses, and hold that position. You have my assurance that he will be well taken care of,*" she agreed. "*Is that your only request? Lapiloque has already demanded much of us.*"

I looked past her to where Jaevid stood, silently observing our debate. What else would he have possibly asked for? At that moment, I was doing good just to comprehend what was happening. I didn't keep a wish list of potential favors to ask from deities tucked into my back pocket.

"I-I, uh, I suppose it is." I glanced back to Clysiros. "I just want this to end, for all our sakes."

Her silky, coy laugh hung in the air. "*You mortals are all the same! Always fretting over the present, barely able to perceive all that's come before you and all that will come after.*" Combing her fingers through my filthy, tangled hair, she took a lock of it and teased it with her thumb. "*Everything ends, my love. Then it begins again. Cycles upon cycles, the spheres of time are endlessly turning. Not even the gods can stop it. So, try to appreciate the now. Nothing else is guaranteed, my love.*"

"Then let's end it. How ... how can we complete my ritual?" I almost didn't want to know. Somehow, I doubted it would be anything pleasant.

Her face drew in closer, only a breath away as she stroked a single, cold fingertip from my forehead, down the bridge of my nose, to my lips. *"With the kiss of death. Come now. It's rude to keep a girl waiting. And we have left much to do."*

PART SIX: JENNA

CHAPTER TWENTY-FIVE

It took less than two minutes to join in with another dragonrider formation. They were already preparing to intercept Hilleddi's company of monstrous war beasts, something I had a little experience with. Irony like ash soured on my tongue as Phevos and I fell into position. Ahead, I spotted the glimmer of Perish's white scales shining like a pearl against the night. Calem was in this formation. Perhaps Haldor was, too, although I couldn't see him anywhere.

We made four clean passes and broke the enemy line, bathing the battlefield in waves of burning dragon venom to stop the war beasts' advance. Separated and dazed by the fire, they would be far easier for our troops on the ground to contend with.

Three of the creatures fell, overwhelmed by the flames. Four more began bucking and swinging their massive heads, pitching against their chains and trying to flee. A portion of our dragonrider company immediately split off in pursuit, while the rest of us stayed the course and prepared for another pass on the remaining line.

Gritting my teeth, I steered Phevos into position at the point of one of the formations. My pulse clashed in my ears, and my palms sweated under my thick leather gauntlets as I gripped the saddle handles so tightly my knuckles ached. I'd already seen what one of those beasts was capable of at Barrowton. Halfax was far less fortified, even with the dragonriders to guard it. We could not allow them to reach the outer wall.

We banked in hard for our approach, lining up through the hailstorm of assaults coming from the ground. We veered and weaved sharply, dodging hurling nets and flying orbs of venom. Arrows pinged and clanged as they glanced off my armor. A few passed so close to my head I heard the scrape of the metal arrowheads against my helmet.

A dragon's panicked cry screamed out over the roar of battle. I turned just in time to see the dragonrider off my left wingtip begin to fall, his mount's body hopelessly tangled in one of the Tibran nets. Both dragon and rider plummeted, pitching and whirling toward the ground. My heart hit the back of my throat, and before I could think, I signaled to the rider on my right to take over point.

Then Phevos and I dove after our fallen comrade.

With his wings snapped in tight, Phevos zoomed toward the ground. We only had seconds. We were body lengths away. Then yards. Then feet. The ground rushed up, beckoning death on impact.

No—not if I could help it.

Phevos let out a hiss and stretched his hind legs out at the same moment he spread his wings wide. He caught the falling dragon by the tangled net with his claws. His powerful wings filled like ship sails, braced in the wind to break the force of the impact.

We hit hard—but not as hard as it would have been in free-fall. My brain rattled against my skull and my vision spotted. I wheezed, my chest so tight I couldn't breathe as I hit the saddle and Phevos's neck. It took a second or two to shake it off, peel myself back upright again, and figure out who had survived.

The snared dragon wriggled out from under us. Already his rider was cutting away the net and signaling me his gratitude. They were both alive. Thank the gods for that.

Phevos shook himself and snapped his jaws. He craned his big head around to glance at me, as though checking to make sure I was still okay. I gave his neck a pat. "Still here, big boy! Let's get off the ground!"

He chirped his agreement and crouched, prepped for takeoff.

Light exploded in my vision.

In an instant, I was flying again, my saddle straps snapping like threads. Flung free of my saddle, my body pitched wildly, skidding over the ground like a stone over water. Phevos gave a sharp cry—a noise I'd never heard him make before.

I landed in a heap, dazed and breathless. Heat and agony bloomed through one of my shoulders. Sitting up, I threw off my helmet and sucked in a desperate breath of the cold wind. Without that metal bucket to buffer the sound, the rumble of battle was nearly paralyzing. I blinked through the bright spots still flashing in my vision.

Gods—I was sitting in the middle of a cauldron of pure pandemonium. The sky was alive with fire and the screech of dragons locked in combat. The ground around me boiled with soldiers, both Tibran and Maldobarian, and the air rang with the metallic *clang, smash,* and *scrape* of blades upon shields.

Phevos? Where was my dragon?

The sight of purple scales drew me to my feet, cradling my left arm. It was dislocated, maybe worse. With my armor on, I couldn't tell exactly. Regardless, it was useless now. I couldn't even hold a blade with it.

"Phevos!" I screamed for him as I staggered toward him.

No reply.

Faster—I had to go faster. I had to reach him. He needed me!

Yards away, Phevos lay motionless while a Tibran soldier approached his head with sword in hand.

Rage blazed through my body like hellfire. I ran, screaming as I drew my blade with my only usable arm. He would *not* touch Phevos.

I launched for him, leaping the last few feet to kick the Tibran soldier's knees out. He fell, too stunned to retaliate, and I landed on him in a rabid frenzy. Before the soldier could even move, I sank the point of my sword into the chink between his pauldron and breastplate. He shrieked under his helm and went still.

"Phevos!" I screamed again.

He still hadn't moved, lying on his side in a motionless heap. But his sides—they were moving. He was breathing!

As soon as I got to my feet, my legs threatened to buckle. I wobbled, barely able to stand, as my body flashed hot and cold. My head spun as I looked up, setting my jaw to begin a desperate stagger toward my fallen dragon.

Behind me, a monstrous roar shook the ground. It knocked me back onto my rear, and I gaped up in horror at the war beast tromping toward me. Its every step made the earth flinch, and its bellowing cry sent the soldiers around us scattering in terror.

That's what had hit us—a blast of electric energy from that creature's maw. It was the same stunt that had almost killed us at Barrowton. Now the beast loomed over me, a behemoth ready to crush me underfoot.

From the iron and bone-wrought platform on its back, Hilleddi's ashen face was twisted into a sneer. Her milky, glazed eyes stared right at me as she snapped the chains, ordering the monster to run me over. With another booming cry, the beast obliged. It reared, pawing the air, and came down with one foot aimed right for me—howling through the air like the fist of the sky god.

There was no escape. I couldn't run. I couldn't even stand.

Death bore down, and I closed my eyes to meet it.

But death never came.

Over the constant storm of battle, a familiar shout found my ears. I opened my eyes and gasped, heartbeat stalling at the sight of a man standing over me. With legs braced and arms locked overhead, Phillip had a grip on the war beast's enormous foot and refused to let it fall. His body shook, back and arms bulging against the crushing force that bore down from above.

"Get out of the way!" He snarled through fanged teeth.

I tried to breathe and choked. Where had he come from? How, by all the gods, had he found me in this ocean of chaos?

"*Now!*"

I snapped free of my daze, seized my sword, and immediately kicked into an evasive, sideways roll. I clenched my jaw as the pressure of the maneuver set my injured arm and shoulder ablaze with pain again. No time to fret over it now.

Back on my feet, I ran, tripping and stumbling, to get out of the way.

The second I was out of range, Phillip let out another primal cry. I whipped around just in time to see him give the giant's foot one violent shove before he ran after me. He ran like an animal, leaping and bounding, and snatched the blade of the Tibran soldier I'd killed. His fangs flashed, eyes glowing like platinum fires as he charged for the war beast at full sprint.

And he wasn't alone.

Overhead, the rush of wind off the wings of a dozen dragons hummed like thunder. They bathed the creature in flame while Phillip, dodging and dancing to avoid the spray, used his clawed hands and feet to climb the creature's hide. Reaching the platform, I glimpsed his silhouette through the flashing flames as he drew back and made a vengeful strike right at Hilleddi's neck. She fell one way and her head rolled the other, separated once again.

Phillip tossed the blade aside and sprang skyward with his arms outstretched, burning venom licking at his heels. Right on cue, Turq and Haldor made a low pass right over him. The dragon caught him by the arms and broke skyward. He might have a little singed fur on that tail of his, but Phillip was alive.

Alive—and more incredible than I ever could have imagined. I'd never seen anyone fight like that.

Hilleddi's war beast fell as the flames rose higher, so intense I had to shield my face from the heat. It hit the ground with a deafening *boom*, and the impact blew me backward and knocked my sword out of my hand. I landed on my rear again, spitting out rubble and wondering which deity I'd pleased enough to help me dodge certain death so many times in one day.

Whoever it was, I prayed they'd grant me one last favor as I limped toward my fallen dragon as fast as I could. Phevos stirred the instant I touched his snout, rubbing my hands along his cheek and neck. His big yellow eyes opened, blinking and rolling until his pupils narrowed with focus.

Tears sprang to my eyes as I pressed my lips against his scaly nose. He gave a snort of disapproval. Now wasn't the time for that. We had to move. There were still more of those war beasts to contend with, and while Phillip had a head start, I wasn't about to let him drop another one without me.

I couldn't see any visible injuries or wounds as Phevos gathered his legs beneath him and shook the rubble from his back. My saddle, however, was in shambles. Being torn out of it like that had compromised the seat. The girth straps were in shreds.

Dread sank to the pit of my stomach like a cold stone. My saddle was useless.

And with my left arm injured, unable to grip onto his scales and spines in flight, so was I. I couldn't ride him bareback—not in this state. If the tingling and pain in my shoulder was any indication, I could only guess it was dislocated. It might have even be broken.

I took a deep, steadying breath, and made a decision. Drawing a dagger from the side of my boot, I cut the remaining straps and let the saddle slide off. It landed with a thud on the ground beside me. It was nothing but dead weight now, anyway.

Phevos growled and blasted my face with furious puffs of hot breath as I quickly cut some of the leather straps off. "Oh, stop fussing, you big baby. I'm fine," I said as I pushed his head away.

It only took a minute or two and a few strong leather straps to secure my wounded arm against my body. Phillip and Turq had given me an idea. If I couldn't ride, then Phevos was going to have to carry me.

Suddenly, we were out of time.

Tibran soldiers surrounded us—too many for me to even bother counting. Despite their numbers, they advanced slowly, uncertainty in every step. Their hands shook on their weapons and their eyes flashed to my dragon. They were right to fear him.

Phevos curled himself around me with a growl, shielding my body with his. He bristled his spines and opened his jaws, showing rows of jagged teeth that dripped with burning venom.

Carrying me this way would slow us down. We would be easy prey for the net throwers and archers. It was the only way, though. I knew better than to hope I could talk Phevos into leaving me behind.

"We must fall back to the wall," I murmured against his ear as I stepped back, close against his side. "You have to carry me."

Phevos gave a snort of confirmation.

I took a deep breath, never taking my eyes off the Tibran soldiers encircling us. "Go!"

CHAPTER TWENTY-SIX

With a spray of flame and a rush of wings, Phevos launched off the ground. He showered the Tibrans with a long blast of burning venom, blinding them long enough to snatch me up in his clawed hind legs and hoist us both skyward. Our flight was awkward and off balance. I dangled like a dead sheep in his grasp, gripping onto his eagle-like toes as tightly as I could.

In a rush of wind and heat, the ground fell away. The battlefield spread out before me, a tapestry of anarchy mottled with fire, blood, smoke, and steel. Hanging from my dragon's grasp, it was nearly impossible to make out anything specific as we rose beyond firing range of anything from the ground. Phevos wasn't taking any chances.

The roar of another dragon nearby drew my gaze. I still couldn't see much, but a flash of white scales was all it took. Calem and Perish were with us. From his saddle, Calem's gauntlets flashed as he waved his hands. He was trying to signal to me. In my current state, however, there was nothing I could do to answer.

Phevos landed carefully, releasing me less than two feet off the ground as he touched down on a secure area of the ramparts. I lay on my back, arms still crossed over my breast, breathing in the smoke and acrid smell of venom. The pain in my shoulder made it hard to move. I couldn't sit up.

A pair of familiar, worried yellow eyes appeared over me. Phevos sniffed at my face, sucking my hair into his nostrils and smacking his lips against my cheek like a curious horse.

"Jenna!" Calem appeared over me suddenly, ripping off his helmet and shoving

Phevos's head out of the way. Maybe it was just delirium from the pain, but I could have sworn I saw relief in his eyes. "I thought—gods, woman—I thought you were dead!"

"Sorry to disappoint you," I rasped as he helped me sit up. "My arm is ... " Pain throttled the words out of my throat before I could finish.

Calem moved quickly, dismantling my crude attempt to secure it against my body. He untied the straps and unbuckled my breastplate and shoulder pauldron, never looking away even as Maldobarian infantrymen rushed all around us. They were shouting orders, lugging shields and extra quivers packed full of arrows, and rolling carts loaded with heavy stones—ammunition for the catapults.

"The shoulder is dislocated, and your collarbone might be broken," Calem pronounced as he fastened my armor back in place. "We need to get you to the medics. You're done."

I cursed under my breath. This is not how I wanted my fight to end.

An earsplitting *whoosh* sent Calem diving over me, shielding my body with his as something enormous sailed overhead. Incoming fire from a Tibran trebuchet? It had to be.

The boulder passed like a moon overhead, missing us by mere feet as it hurtled by and smashed into ramparts. Men screamed. Shards of stone, ash, and twisted bits of metal flew in every direction.

"Calem!" I choked, struggling to wheeze through the dust. "We have to move! We need to get off the ramparts!"

No reply.

I jostled him as best I could with my one working arm. Shakily, he pushed himself off me, and sat back onto his knees. His movements lurched, unsteady as he struggled to get to his feet. Something wasn't right. His face was blanched, stark and pasty against the blood beginning to seep through his lips. He fixed me with a stare—and I knew.

"C-come on." He grabbed me under my good shoulder and hoisted me up. Together, we shambled across the crumbling ramparts toward the nearest turret. Our dragons circled, chirping their concern, but unable to land again. It was too risky. All the enemy's fire was focused upon these walls—on us.

"Almost there," I wheezed with every step. "Just a little farther. Almost there."

He didn't answer. His breathing rattled through clenched teeth as he staggered beside me, gaze focused on the turret's open door.

We were going to make it.

Calem fell just inside the threshold. He crumpled forward, taking me with him. We landed in a tangled heap of armor not far from the doorway. Wrestling myself free, I whipped back to try to get him up again. We weren't safe—not yet. Another one of those hurtling stones could easily smash right through this tower. The only difference was now we wouldn't see it coming.

"Get up!" I shouted as I crawled to him.

Lying on his front, I could see three, no, four coin-sized holes in the back of his plackart—the portion of his armor that was supposed to shield his torso from harm. The jagged tip of a metal shard stuck out of one of the holes, glittering wickedly in the gloom.

Fear tore through me like a mountain wind.

I fought to roll him over, heaving his heavy, armored body onto its back. One glimpse of his face stole the breath from my chest.

Blood oozed from the corners of his mouth, staining his cheeks and sticking in his corn silk hair. His eyes were wide, fixed straight ahead, and as empty as a starless night.

A cry tore out of me—half sob, half scream. My body shook as I gripped him fiercely. It wasn't real. It couldn't be. It wasn't supposed to be this way. If he hadn't thrown himself on top of me, if he hadn't been so stupid, then it would have been me lying there.

It *should* have been me!

His skin was still warm when I pressed my forehead against his, cupping the sides of his face. I kissed his brow and closed his eyelids, my tears peppering his blood-smeared cheeks. There was nothing more I could do. Over the boiling rumble of battle, I heard Perish roar as though she were looking for him.

But Calem was gone.

My ears were still ringing as I sat on the edge of an examination table, staring out across the white canvas tent. Medics and healers rushed around me, calling to one another as they raced to treat the injured brought in from the battlefront. I couldn't remember how I'd gotten here exactly. A medic team sweeping the ramparts for the wounded had found me, but after that ... everything was a haze of shouts and the distant roar of combat.

Sitting with most of my armor stripped away to the padded garments I wore underneath, my body felt cold and exposed. How long had I been here? Minutes? Hours? What about Calem? Had they left him behind?

A thunderous boom shuddered the ground, so loud and close I could feel it echo in my chest. Everyone stopped. All eyes turned upward and for a few seconds, no one made a sound. Gods and Fates, what was happening outside?

"It's going to hurt, Your Highness," the young medic warned as she prepped to wrench my shoulder back into place. She couldn't have been more than fifteen, and her hands trembled as she probed around my shoulder.

"Just do it," I growled.

A twist, pop, and release of pressure brought tingling feeling back to my fingertips. I let out a shuddering sigh of relief. Flexing my arm, I tested squeezing my fist and wiggling my fingers. Every movement still sent a sharp bolt of pain across my chest, but it was bearable. At least I could move now.

Good enough.

"Wait a moment! Please, my lady, you're not fit to fight," the medic protested as I stood and gathered my gear. "Your collarbone is most certainly fractured, possibly broken. You should not be lifting anything—"

I spun on her with a frown. "Who is in charge here?"

"Medic Captain Evined," the young woman sputtered, paling as she pointed across the room full of groaning, wailing patients. Most were far worse off than I was and far more deserving of her attention.

I thanked her and left, buckling my sword belt back around my hips as I stepped through the maze of bedrolls on the floor. The air was thick with the smell of blood and medicinal herbs. In a far corner, body-shaped lumps covered in white sheets were piled out of the way. I grimaced and looked away.

Medic Captain Evined was in an absolute frenzy. The plump woman rushed about, sleeves rolled to her elbows and sweat dotting her forehead as she doled out medicines and materials. With just a glance, it was easy to tell she was at her wit's end, with far more patients pouring in than one official could manage. Fresh blood speckled her white robes and apron from wrist to elbow. It was caked in the creases of her hands and smudged across her face. She gaped at me for a second, her warm, hazel eyes wide and frantic, when I asked where I could find the nearest officer's post. Of course, she didn't know. And in this mess, who could blame her?

I was on my own.

Somehow, I had to find my way back to the battle. With my arm mobile again, I would be able to hang onto Phevos. We could resume the fight, even without a saddle. Providing I could find him, that is.

I left the surgical tent at a jog and was immediately surprised—I recognized this place. I was deep in the undercrofts of the royal castle; possibly the only safe place left in the city now. It was an excellent place for the medics to work without fear of being crushed by incoming fire from the trebuchets. But, gods, it was a long way to get back to the city walls. Dangerous as the ramparts were, that would undoubtedly be the best place to spot Phevos.

Setting my jaw against the sharp pain in my collarbone, I sprinted along the corridors and dashed up flights of stairs. Maldobarian soldiers rushed by me in groups, their armor and swords spattered with blood, as I wound my way higher and higher in the castle. The fastest path I knew to get to the ramparts meant crossing the main courtyard. Risky, considering it was out in the open and where my father had positioned several of his largest catapults to return fire over the wall.

I was running low on choices, however.

Darting through one of the narrow servants' passages, I burst through a small door hidden behind a line of prickly shrubs. Before me, the courtyard burned and boiled. An exploding orb of dragon venom hurled from Tibran lines had already smashed one of the great machines and left it in cinders. Soldiers surrounded the two that remained operational, working the cranks that aimed the arm and coiled rope along the winch. More soldiers rolled massive stones from the backs of wagons into the firing bucket.

I crossed the courtyard in a mad dash, seizing the arm of the first soldier I could reach. "What's happening out there?"

The man turned to me, multihued eyes betraying his elven heritage even behind his helmet. "We're supposed to keep firing!" he shouted back over the *whoosh—snap—boom* of the catapult fire. "They say reinforcements from the north have broken the Tibran lines; a cavalry of faundra led by Prince Aubren!"

My brother was out there? Riding with the Gray elves?

I clapped a hand on his shoulder as a gesture of thanks and kept running. There was an entrance to the wall passageways at the far side of the courtyard. Providing no one had barricaded it before the battle, that would be my fastest way up onto the ramparts. From there, I prayed I could find Phevos. Surely, he was nearby, looking for me. I had to believe that he was still—

I skidded, tripping and nearly falling as a sudden surge of wind and a flash of gleaming white and purple scales dropped from the sky before me. Perish and Phevos landed side by side, craning their huge horned heads to peer at me expectantly. The soldiers manning the catapults panicked. They called out to me, waving their arms, and ordering me to run. I couldn't blame them. Without my dragonrider armor, I looked like a common infantry foot soldier at best.

Not the sort to be wrangling a pair of dragons.

Phevos chirped insistently, snapping his jaws, and swiveling his ears. Perish responded with a hiss, lashing her tail and leering at me with eyes like pale rubies. She crawled closer, her tapered snout wrinkled with a twitching snarl as she flattened herself before me.

Was that ... an invitation?

Phevos gave a grunt of approval.

Knees shaking, I edged toward her. Before Calem, it was common knowledge that she'd killed riders for doing this very thing. Why now? Why me?

Perish answered with a look, her scarlet eyes steely and brimming with intelligence. The anger and anguish in her gaze mingled with my own. This wasn't a choosing. I wouldn't be permitted to do it again. But for the honor of her fallen rider, for vengeance, she would allow it.

I climbed into Calem's saddle with my eyes tearing and my chest burning with agony-driven rage. His secondary weapon was still buckled to the back, and I quickly clipped the short sword to my belt before securing the straps that would hold me in place. Phevos watched with his golden gaze ardent. He prowled around us, bristled and anxious, as Perish stood and coiled for takeoff.

Maybe he didn't quite trust her not to kill me. Honestly, I wasn't sure I did, either.

It was far too late to second-guess things now, though.

Perish coiled her legs and sprang skyward with a graceful leap, arching her back and flapping her white wings swiftly. I gripped the saddle handles, my pulse throbbing in my palms and clashing in my ears as I leaned into her movements. Her flight was as fast and brutal as it was effortlessly smooth—much different from what I'd gotten used to with Phevos over the years. She moved with exacting speed and sharp precision, conquering the dark, war-torn skies with a challenging roar.

Phevos flew close behind, his eyes never leaving me as we surged above the city walls and spiraled higher. I squinted through the wind, scanning the battlefield for some idea of what was happening. In the distance, the low tone of Gray elven war horns helped me to spot their advance.

The line of mounted cavalry moved like a wave of silvery white, smashing into the bronze shore of Tibran shields. Each of the monstrous faundra stags was the size of a draft horse, sixteen hands to the withers, and around a thousand pounds. That, paired with the crown of razor-sharp white horns on their heads, made for a formidable beast when it was charging at full speed. Many of the Tibran soldiers broke and ran. The ones who stood firm were easily trampled or impaled on those brutal horns—if they survived the flawless aim of the elf archer on its back, that is.

At the front of the line, Aubren's physique was easy to pick out even from a distance. He wasn't as slight or petite as the elves, and he wore human armor beneath a rippling cape of gold and blue—Maldobar's colors. Hefting his sword high with one hand, he gripped the reins of his stag in the other as he led the charge. My heart raced at the sight, and I steered Perish toward them. Perhaps we could offer some help clearing the path for their advance.

Suddenly, a sharp explosion like the crack of a whip burst through the air directly below us. Perish shrieked in dismay and behind us, Phevos gave a cry of warning. Was it another one of those Tibran orbs exploding? Or a dragon crashing to the ground? I leaned to get a look.

My eyes went wide. A panicked breath caught in my throat, lodging before I could make a sound. My blood seemed to freeze solid in my veins.

Gods and Fates … what had Jaevid Broadfeather done?

PART SEVEN: REIGH

CHAPTER TWENTY-SEVEN

The wheels of reality ground back into motion with the sounds of war raging like a dark symphony in the night. I staggered back, putting some distance between the goddess and myself as she rose back to her full height. From a few yards away, Jaevid sent me one final, earnest look before he raised the black crystal above his head.

This was it. I knew it. He knew it.

There was no turning back.

I held my breath.

At the last second, Argonox seemed to catch on. His eyes darted between the three of us before he pitched forward wildly, his expression twisted with frantic rage. "NO!"

A horrible *crack* pierced the air. It bored into my ears and rattled my bones.

Jaevid smashed the crystal against the ground at his feet. It fractured on impact, splitting in half, and sending black shards, like slivers of obsidian, flying in every direction.

I fell to one knee, wheezing and gripping my chest. Heat blazed through me, prickling and spreading with every heartbeat, until it raged from my ears all the way to my toes. My lungs expanded, stretching to their fullest as I sucked in a deep breath of the cold night air. Warm serenity washed over me—a soul-deep calm and strange emptiness I could barely comprehend. It tingled through every finger and shivered down my spine. I could feel it with every thundering thump of my heart.

The chains of death and divine power I'd toiled under for so long had finally been broken. Life rushed back in to breathe new energy into every weary muscle, filling me up like a wild spring wind. I wasn't the Harbinger anymore.

I was ... free.

Too bad there wasn't much time to savor it.

Clysiros let out a shrill laugh of pure delight and spread her arms wide, body arching as three sets of black-feathered wings unfurled from her back. Each one was mottled in intricate designs of silver in flecks like tiny diamonds, and horns of spiked black crystals crowned her head like a tiara. With one beat of those six wings, she hovered over the battlefield, robes and hair floating as though she were weightless.

Argonox skidded to a halt right before her, eyes wide and mouth agape. Even dressed out in his wicked armor, the goddess towered over him. I guess he hadn't planned on meeting an actual deity today. Bathed in ambient starlight, her skin glowed and the silver designs on her wings sparkled as she regarded him with a bemused grin.

The battlefield around us fell silent. The lines of Tibran soldiers all around stood frozen, their faces pasty at the sight of Clysiros and their reigning tyrant facing off. It was as though they were all waiting to see who would prevail before they decided whether to strike or flee.

With a sharp scrape and ring of metal on metal, Argonox drew a straight-bladed sword from his belt.

Clysiros moved like a blur, vanishing like a wisp of smoke and suddenly reappearing mere inches from Argonox's nose. He flinched, shrinking back, but much too late. Her fingertips traced the sharp edge of his sword—totally unfazed by it. Mortal weapons were useless here. She studied him, her bottomless dark eyes gleaming with pleasure as the metal began to rust and decay, rotting away to ash in his hands until he was left with nothing except an empty hilt.

I had to give him some credit; he was a sick, deranged, tyrannical maniac, but Argonox was as fearless as anyone I'd ever seen. That, or I'd just never encountered the level of stupidity it took to attack the Goddess of Death. Maybe he was still assuming that armor would protect him?

I gaped as he threw down the useless hilt and snatched the morning star—a club with a spiked ball on one end—that was hanging from the other side of his belt. He reared back to swing, and Clysiros vanished again. His club howled through the air and hit nothing but empty air.

Stumbling forward with surprise, he whirled in a frantic circle, his gaze darting all around for some sign of the goddess. Argonox's bloodshot eyes searched the crowd of soldiers and the skies in vain before finally settling on Jaevid. His jaw set, expression sharpening and lips drawing back over his teeth in a snarl, as though he'd found an acceptable substitute.

But Jaevid didn't move. He didn't even blink.

The fight wasn't over.

Before Argonox could take a single step, a huge, pale hand reached from behind and grasped his throat. His whole body went rigid and all the color drained from his face.

Clysiros reappeared behind him, her chin on his shoulder so that her red lips brushed his ear with every word. "*Tsk tsk tsk. You've made quite the mess, haven't you, little man? You smeared my magic on the unworthy. You defiled my name.*" She stretched one finger up to stroke along his jaw. "*Whatever shall I do with you?*"

"Your time in the mortal realm is over," he growled through clenched teeth. "I am the only true Harbinger. Your power is mine. This world belongs to me."

"*Oh my darling,*" she purred. "*My time has only just begun.*"

Her pale fingers tightened upon his throat as her eyes fluttered closed. One euphoric smile from those scarlet lips sent a shudder through the air like a burst of frigid wind. It radiated out from her, expanding and touching every soul standing on that battlefield.

I reeled, thrown back on my heels as it tore through me. Jaevid braced, leaning into it with jaw tight, hands clenched, and eyes still burning like fiery emeralds.

Overhead, a sharp screech came from Beckah's reanimated king drake. Mavrik hesitated, instinctively drawing back. The massive creature twisted, howling and spitting erratic plumes of burning venom before it froze, hovering in the air directly over us as motionless as a statue.

Suddenly, its glowing red eyes went dark. Rotting flesh and naked bone melted into the air, turning into flecks of ash, and curling black smoke. In seconds, it was completely gone.

One by one, the rest of Argonox's monstrous creations—soldiers, dragons, shrikes, and other creatures he'd forced me to drag back from the abyss—began to dissolve, as well. Empty suits of armor hit the ground with a *thunk* and clatter. War machines groaned to a halt. Ash from a hundred undead dragons fell from the sky like snow.

Clysiros's laugh tolled over the masses, as harrowing as the bells of doomsday. She stood, Argonox writhing in her grip as she snatched him off the ground like someone picking a carrot. He pitched and kicked, screaming as she held him at arm's length, her huge fist still closed around his neck.

"*There is nothing you own I cannot destroy, nowhere you can hide to escape my kiss. I curse you, Argonox, God Bane, and every firstborn of your bloodline.*" She giggled, her tone dripping with delight. Her dark eyes flashed, glinting with pleasure, as the wicked armor on his body began to dissolve, too. "*A life to repay each one you took while defiling my name.*"

With his armor gone, Clysiros dropped Argonox into a heap at her feet.

My breath caught. Was that it? She wasn't going to end it? End *him*? Why? Why would she possibly let him go after—

Argonox sprang to his feet and tripped all over himself as he backed away from her, trembling with terror. He spun, turning to bolt. He didn't make it two steps.

Argonox ran straight into the point of Jaevid's scimitar.

ARGONOX CHOKED, EYES WIDE AS JAEVID BORE IN, DRIVING THE BLADE INTO his body all the way to the hilt.

"Never again," Jaevid growled. His lip twitched back in a snarl, expression caught between disgust and wrath as he gave the blade a brutal twist before yanking it free. He planted one swift kick to Argonox's torso and laid him flat. His body hit the ground with a *thud*.

It was over.

Clysiros looked on, swiping her tongue hungrily across her bottom lip, as Jaevid stepped back. The end of his blade dripped red and his body heaved with deep, swift breaths as he stared up at her. I held my breath, too afraid to move, as the goddess gave him a final, coy smile. She blew a kiss in my direction. Then she vanished without a sound.

The living Tibran soldiers stood still, staring at their dead ruler in horror, their faces smudged with the ash of their fallen monsters. Some of them cried out and immediately threw down their weapons as they dropped to their knees in surrender. Others began to flee. They wouldn't get far, though. Seeing the sudden change in the tide, the Dragonriders of Maldobar were already throwing down perimeters of flame in an attempt to hem in the deserters.

Plenty more Tibran soldiers, however, were either too determined or too far gone to realize what was happening. They charged.

Sucking in a ragged breath, I glanced back to meet Vexi's worried stare. She gave a whine as King Felix climbed down off her back. He forged toward me, sword drawn and shield at the ready.

Jaevid stepped forward to meet him, and they took up the fight, standing back-to-back, their movements a perfect balance of lethal speed and brutal force.

I darted across the ground in a mad sprint, seizing my kafki blades and spinning into position to fight alongside them. No sooner had I fallen into rhythm, dealing blow after blow to the onslaught of crazed Tibran soldiers, then a dragon with scales as white as fresh snow dropped from the sky. I'd seen that dragon somewhere before—Barrowton, maybe?

Suddenly, it didn't matter. The dragon crouched long enough for a familiar female figure to climb off her back, sword in hand. Princess Jenna had blood spattered on her face and a storm in her eyes as she whipped in to join the fight.

The ground quaked as Mavrik let out a booming roar. Every dragon on the battlefield answered in a united call like a roll of thunder—a cry that shook the very foundations of my soul. Vexi and the white dragon joined their king in the air, soaring with a group of dragons to deliver blasts of flame on every Tibran war machine still standing.

My ears rang with the clash of blades and cries of the men who fell to my blades. Sweat soaked through my clothes and streaked down my face. But I wouldn't stop. This was it—the moment Enyo and Kiran believed would come. I was not a monster. I wasn't a beast or a demon. I was no longer the Harbinger of Clysiros.

I was Reigh Farrow, Prince of Maldobar, and I would not fail.

CHAPTER TWENTY-EIGHT

The end of the battle came as the sun began to rise. The red horizon revealed a canopy of black smoke curling up from the cinders of Tibran war machines, fallen dragons, and more dead men than anyone could have counted. But the city of Halfax still stood, the tattered blue and gold banners of Maldobar waving in triumph from the castle spires. Horns sounded from every corner of the ramparts, declaring our victory.

The Maldobarian soldiers, dragonriders, and cavalry raised their blades high and shouted in triumph. But as I stood amidst the bodies of slave soldiers and smoldering dragon venom, I couldn't join in. The smell, that horrible acrid stench of death, burned my eyes and caught in my throat. I gagged.

This victory tasted like ash.

I leaned over, hands aching as I let go of my kafki blades and struggled to catch my breath.

"Reigh! Are you okay?" Jenna called out as she jogged toward me. "Are you injured?"

I shook my head. A few nicks, cuts, and shallow sword slices didn't count. "All good," I panted. "Where's—?"

Jenna hugged me before I could get the words out, gripping me so hard it was as though she was afraid I might disappear. "Gods, you stupid ... reckless ... "

"Farrow," someone finished for her.

Pulling back, Jenna and I stared together as the King of Maldobar approached, the length of his cloak rippling behind him. In the light of the rising sun, I got my first good look at his face. His light, amber-colored eyes studied me, too. The more I looked, however, the harder it was to see because my eyes welled with tears. I could see *myself* in him. His eyes, the shape of his jaw, the crooked way he smirked as he brushed his hand through my hair.

It wasn't a trick. This wasn't my imagination. He really was ... my father.

"Reigh," he spoke softly.

I cringed. He knew my name? How? Had Jaevid told him?

"I suppose I have a lot of explaining to do," he murmured with a sad smile.

No kidding. Emotions like a tangled briar patch writhed in my chest, pricking and stabbing with every breath I took. He'd thrown me away like I was garbage, hadn't he? Why? I deserved an explanation—and yet, I was terrified that if he gave me a good one, I would be obligated to forgive him, and move on like nothing had happened. My mouth screwed up, chin trembling. I clenched my teeth and looked away, fighting to keep it in. I couldn't do this, not yet.

"When you're ready, we'll talk about it," he said. "For now, just know that you are my son, and I love you."

I swallowed hard, and held my tongue.

"Father, look!" Jenna broke in suddenly, seizing him by the arm.

Not far away, Jaevid was picking a careful path across the battlefield toward the mass of vines he'd summoned to ensnare Beckah. It had continued to grow, weaving and twining together like reeds in a basket, to form a huge sphere. My heart thumped against my ribs as he stopped before it, hand clenched around the hilt of his scimitar.

What was he thinking? Would he hack his way through them? Surely, after what Clysiros had done to the other reanimated monsters and soldiers, there wouldn't be anything left of her now.

Jaevid's blade hit the ground with a clatter.

"You promised," he begged, his mouth locked into a desperate, shaking frown. "You gave me your word."

Jenna and I exchanged a confused glance. Who was he talking to?

Suddenly, warm, golden light blazed from inside the sphere. It shone through the cracks between the interwoven vines, glowing like a netted star. I shielded my eyes, struggling to squint through my fingers to catch a glimpse of what was happening.

The vines moved, twisting and curling away, as a single, slender hand emerged. It reached out from within the light, and Jaevid stepped closer without hesitation. He seized the hand, lacing his fingers through those delicate digits.

With a sudden powerful flash, the sphere of vines burst, shattering into fragments that instantly dissolved into mist. It was so bright, I couldn't bear it. The instant before my vision blanked, I could have sworn I saw the shape of a creature rising from the light. A stag, maybe? It was too brilliant to be sure.

Then, as I blinked away the glare, I saw *her*.

THE YOUNG WOMAN STANDING WHERE THE SPHERE HAD BEEN, LIFTED HER head slowly. She still held onto Jaevid's hand, staring at him with eyes the color of evergreen needles. Her fair skin was freckled over her cheeks and nose, and her dark hair was pulled back into a loose braid that hung down to her waist. The cool wind teased through the length of her pale blue gown, billowing over her lean frame and bare, freckled shoulders.

No one said a word as she and Jaevid stared at one another in total silence.

Then, as softly as a spring rain, the girl breathed his name. "Jaevid?"

His voice cracked and halted, as though he could hardly get the word out. "Beckah."

She blinked, a crinkle of confusion on her brow as she took a tiny, shaking step toward him. "I-I don't understand. I was ... gone. I lost you. How did you bring me back?"

"There is nowhere, mortal or divine, I would not go to find you," he said. "I love you, Beckah Derrick. In that life, in this one, and until the end of our days."

With a yelp of joy, Beckah leapt at him. Jaevid snagged her in his arms and lifted her off her feet. He planted his lips firmly against hers in an earnest kiss.

Beside me, King Felix gave a chuckle and smacked a hand on my back so hard I almost fell forward. Jenna chocked back a sob, covering her mouth with her hand as she watched them embrace. Other Maldobarian soldiers who had gathered around to watch began to applaud.

How he'd done it, I'd never understand. During our brief exchange, I recalled Clysiros mentioning that Jaevid had demanded a few favors in exchange for his help. Be that as it may, I felt certain that gleaming white stag I'd spotted rising out of the light wasn't anything sent by Clysiros.

It was something else—something greater.

"This is going to call for some new tapestries, I think," King Felix mused with a mischievous grin. "Perhaps a few statues, too."

Jenna flashed him a teary-eyed glance and gave his arm a playful shove. "Oh, stop it. You're terrible."

"No worse than you," a deep voice interrupted.

Wait—I knew that voice!

King Felix, Jenna, and I turned at once. We gasped in unison. From the back of a proud faundra stag, Aubren led a group of Gray elf cavalry in full battle dress. The brightly colored feathers of their war headdresses fluttered in the wind and their mounts stamped and bleated, still riled from battle. Right behind Aubren's mount, however, was a creature I knew all too well—and it was no faundra. A foundling spirit with colors as vibrant and vivid as a parrot stood, tall ears swiveling and bushy tail swishing. Seated on the spirit's back, her fingers clenching earnestly to its silky fur, Hecate panned a teary-eyed smile in my direction.

"I suppose it runs in the family. Bad luck for you, Reigh. You had your fun frolicking around in Luntharda, but now you're stuck with this sorry lot." Aubren smiled, giving me a wink before he passed his shield off to the nearest soldier and climbed down to meet us on foot.

Jenna hit him like a charging bull, knocking him flat on his back in a frantic hug. He wheezed and laughed as she yelled at him for making her worry. A few of the soldiers around us started laughing, too.

"He's right, you know," King Felix murmured as he stood close at my side. With his arms folded over his ornate breastplate and his fingers stroking at his short beard thoughtfully, he cast me a curious sideways glance. "This is your home. I won't force you to stay, but you are welcome—and wanted—right here."

I swallowed hard and took a deep, steadying breath. "I'll consider it. But only on one condition."

He lifted a brow. "Yes?"

"I get to call you Father."

King Felix laughed and grabbed me by the shoulder, wrenching me into a gruff hug. "Don't you dare ever call me anything else, boy."

CHAPTER TWENTY-NINE

The war was over. Argonox was gone. And as word spread from Saltmarsh to the boundary like wildfire, cities and villages throughout Maldobar celebrated with tolling bells and parades through the streets. They were already toasting to our names and telling our stories. Once again, Jaevid Broadfeather was a hero and a legend for the ages.

But this time, so was I.

I tried not to think about that as I lay in a soft, lavish, four-poster bed in Aubren's wing of the royal castle. I didn't feel much like a hero at the moment. Being kept as a Tibran prisoner for so long had left me badly injured, dehydrated, and so weak I could barely stand. Not being the Harbinger anymore helped, of course, but it didn't do much to speed the healing of my physical body.

Aubren had lent me a room in his quarters to rest and recover. Not that I wasn't grateful, but it was weird and a little uncomfortable to hear the servants and healers calling me "Your Highness" every time they came in to bring me a meal, draw a bath, or change my bandages. That would take some getting used to.

After a week, I was well enough to get up and walk around without help, although the medics and healers still warned me not to do any heavy lifting or dragon riding just yet. It was good timing, because I wanted to attend the funeral ceremony for several of the dragonriders that had died in the battle for Halfax.

One of them, I'd learned, was a close friend to Jenna and had even been her wing end. I couldn't imagine not being there for her during that event. She'd been through a lot, and while she did a good job of not to letting it show, I could tell watching the procession as they carried his body to the pyre was almost more than she could take. Her whole body remained stiff and rigid, dressed in formal battle armor and scalemail that gleamed like gold in the light of the setting sun. Her expression stayed locked into a somber frown that didn't waver the entire time. After it was over and his ashes had been locked away in a majestic granite vault alongside many other fallen dragonriders, I watched from a distance while she and the rest of her comrades gave him one final salute.

That image stayed burned into my brain as I made my way back to my room in Aubren's wing. Every step ached as I hobbled through his private library, lounges, and parlors. I could walk without limping too much, but it still hurt. Walking this far always left me sweaty, sore, and exhausted by the time I flopped back down onto the bed.

"Have a nice stroll?" A familiar voice snickered from the chair at my bedside.

I floundered upright, gaping at the dark, ominous figure who sat there casually, his arms crossed under black, silken robes. "Y-you!" I rasped.

One corner of Noh's mouth curved into a half-smirk. "Relax, brother. I'm not here to cause you any trouble. Not today, anyway."

I eyed him over, body tense and hands shaking as I clenched the sheets with trembling hands. "Why are you here?"

His expression smoothed, and he flicked his gaze away. "I came to thank you," he answered simply. "And ... to say goodbye."

"Goodbye?" I didn't understand.

He nodded slightly. "I am to remain in the Vale as its guardian. It is unlikely I will ever return to the mortal world again."

"Oh." A hard knot formed in the back of my throat. For some reason, hearing that made my chest feel tight. He was leaving. We'd never speak again—after having his haunting presence living in my head literally since birth.

"You asked Clysiros to spare me." He stared at me again, with eyes the color of rubies catching in the candlelight. "I thought you should know that, regardless of how we began and what transpired, I have never thought badly of you. I've never blamed you for what happened."

I opened my mouth to reply, but nothing except for a few choking sounds would come out.

"I did envy you, though. I still do, in fact. You will go on to share your life with your family—*our* family. And I find myself wishing I could do the same." His brow creased slightly, as though he were uncertain. "Please do not take it the wrong way when I say I look forward to their deaths. I ... I look forward to meeting them."

With a heavy sigh, I sat forward on the edge of the bed and let my elbows rest on my knees. "Well, as it turns out, our father is *really* old, so you'll probably get to meet him soon. Maybe even sooner, if he keeps commissioning statues of Jaevid."

Noh's expression split with a mischievous grin that made his scarlet eyes shimmer. "I will miss you, brother," he added with a chuckle. "Though I realize the sentiment may not be mutual. I know our encounters were never easy for you."

"No, they weren't," I agreed. "But that doesn't mean I won't miss you, too."

His face went blank, mouth opening slightly for a moment as his brows lifted in surprise.

"Take care of yourself, okay? And if you do get a chance to come back here to the mortal realm, don't be a stranger." I managed an unsteady smile, gritting my teeth against the stiffness in my throat.

Crap. I was really going to miss him.

Noh rose from his chair and regarded me with a smile that seemed almost as unsteady and forced as mine. His brow and chin trembled a bit as he stretched out a hand to shake mine. "Until death reunites us again."

I took it and clasped firmly. "Until then, brother."

He dipped his head in a small nod and winked one of his crimson eyes. Then his shape quickly dissolved into a fine black mist that dissipated without a single sound.

I REALIZED ABOUT TWO SECONDS BEFORE MY GIANT, GREEN, SCALY, overexcited dragoness landed on top of me that I was probably about to die. Crushed to death by my own mount. Great.

I threw up my hands, yelling at the top of my lungs.

She didn't listen.

Vexi smacked into me like a charging faundra—a huge wall of muscle and scales that sent me flying like a ragdoll across the grass. I wheezed for breath as I hit the ground under her massive body. Thankfully, she didn't squish me for long. Wrapping her tail around me like a giant python, Vexi swiped her long, sticky tongue up the side of my head. She chirped and squawked with delight, purring as she rubbed her horned head against mine.

"Y-you're crushing me!" I managed to rasp as she blasted my face with a puff from her huge nostrils.

She loosened the grip of her long tail and I slumped to my knees to gasp and cough for breath. I'd almost recovered when my face and hair got a second coating of gooey dragon spit.

I gagged. "For crying out loud, would you stop that?"

"Aw, look. She loves you!" Jenna giggled as she stood back at the far corner of the courtyard, watching and making no attempts to rescue me. "How sweet."

After another week of rest and rehabilitation, I was almost back to my old self again. The pain in my muscles was nothing more than a dull soreness now. I could manage walking the castle on my own without having to stop to catch my breath. My wounds were well on their way to healing, and I was able to get by without needing any sort of pain medicine. Although, after this, I'd probably need something for bruising.

"Maybe she needs to love me a little less," I grumbled as I tried wiping my face on my sleeve.

Now that I was able to walk the castle grounds, I usually wound up with company for my afternoon strolls. Jenna and Aubren seemed to be taking turns, alternating days to follow me along the white stone paths through the gardens or through the cavernous castle halls while we talked. I'd be lying if I said it wasn't a little awkward. They were my siblings—my older brother and sister—and I knew almost nothing about them. Most of the time, I had no idea what to say because there was so much I wanted to know. What had our mother been like? Did we have anything in common? Did I have grandparents? Aunts? Uncles? Cousins? Would I get to meet any of them, too?

Jenna was a little easier to talk to than Aubren, if only because of what had happened in Northwatch. He'd begun wearing long, black leather gloves all the time, and while it usually suited the rest of his princely attire, I knew the real reason he wore those gloves. He didn't want anyone to see the marks *my* power had left on his hand.

Guilt soured in my gut like poison every time I saw him. Would that feeling ever go away? Or would there always be this weird tension between us? As much as I wanted to apologize to him for basically ruining his life, every time I tried, the words lodged in my throat and I couldn't even look him in the eye. Anything I said sounded pathetic whenever I rehearsed it in my head.

Thankfully, today was Jenna's turn. Besides being more affable, she was almost as socially awkward as I was. Maybe that was a family trait, too.

"It's interesting, isn't it?" She mused as she walked over to run a hand across Vexi's lime green scales. "Jaevid said the Fates look like dragons. I've never heard of such a thing. But it makes me wonder if our dragons really are descended from them somehow."

I shifted, lowering my gaze and avoiding her eyes. Thinking about that moment dredged up painful memories of being forced into the Thieving Mask. "I'm kind of hoping I can just forget about everything I ever saw or heard in the Vale, to be honest."

Her expression dimmed as she nibbled on her bottom lip. "If only it were that easy."

No kidding. Jenna and I had shared a lot about our experiences during the war. She'd mentioned going into the Vale to rescue Aubren, although she'd been very careful to dance around the details of exactly what happened there. Not that I blamed her. I'd kept my own recounting of my experiences there brief, too. Eventually, I might be up to having that discussion. Not yet, though.

"Reigh, can I ask you something in confidence?" Jenna's hushed tone caught me off guard.

I leaned around Vexi's neck to get a better look at my older sister. She was still nibbling away at her lip and staring down at the tops of her boots with a fretful frown crinkling her brow. "Sure. Of course."

"If you knew something—a secret that you promised to tell someone—but you knew telling might cause that person a lot of pain and sadness, would you still do it?" Her keen blue eyes darted up to search my face for a second or two. "Would you still share that secret, knowing the hurt it might cause?"

I had to think about that. She was being awfully vague. But if talking about the Vale had somehow brought this question up from the depths of her heart, then I could guess what this might be about. "It's Jaevid, right?"

Jenna drew back slightly, her jaw tensing. She wouldn't look me in the eye.

"You can trust me," I assured her. "I won't say anything to him."

She stood rigid for a moment. Then, little by little, her shoulders sagged. Jenna let out a small, defeated sigh. "I met someone in the Vale when I went there to rescue Aubren. I met ... Ulric Broadfeather, Jaevid's father."

My mind blanked. "The traitor? The one who started the Gray War?"

She nodded. "He ... he wasn't at all like I thought he would be. He was nothing like the stories said. And the way he talked—" She stopped short, quirking her mouth as she chewed on the inside of her cheek. "He said he was waiting there for Jae so he could apologize because he'd never meant for any of that to happen."

"And that's the secret?"

Jenna nodded again. "He wanted me to tell Jaevid that he was sorry for all of it. I ... I promised that I would. But I can't seem to find the right time to tell him. I don't even know if I should."

I rubbed the back of my neck. "Well, maybe Ulric should just tell Jae himself."

Jenna's expression crumpled, collapsing into a grimace before she turned her back. Her shoulders shook some as she sucked in a trembling breath as though she were trying not to cry.

"Jenna? What's wrong?" Pushing Vexi's neck out of the way, I stepped over to take my sister gently by the arm. "What happened?"

"He's gone, Reigh. Ulric sacrificed himself; he gave up his spirit to save Aubren." She bit the words through clenched teeth. "That's why he made me promise—because he won't be there now to tell Jae himself."

The wind rushed out of me like I'd been punched in the gut. No wonder she was struggling with this. Ulric probably hadn't considered what that kind of promise would do to her. She probably felt like it was her fault somehow, even if it wasn't.

"Does Aubren know?" I kept my voice quiet.

"No."

"Good. Don't tell him. He can never know." Jenna looked up, meeting my stare through tear-filled eyes. With her lips pressed into a tense line, I saw agreement slide over her features like a stony mask of resolve.

"He's been through a lot already. Knowing he's only alive right now because someone gave up their entire spiritual existence would destroy him." I put an arm around Jenna's shoulders and drew her in, hugging her tight. Despite being a few inches taller, she still felt fragile as she gripped me back. "It wasn't your fault, you know."

"I keep thinking if I'd done something different, if Jaevid had gone into the Vale instead of me, then he would have been able to say goodbye," she sobbed against my shoulder. "How can I tell him? What do I say?"

"You don't have to say anything," a deep voice interrupted suddenly.

Jenna and I turned, gaping, to where our father, King Felix, stood nearby. I had no idea how long he'd been there, watching us and listening in. The wind caught in his gray-gold hair and snagged in the lengths of his long, dark blue cloak as he strode closer. I spotted my reflection in his light amber eyes as he stood over us, considering Jenna and me for a moment before he spoke again. "I'll tell him."

Jenna protested, "But, Father, I was the one who—"

He raised a hand to silence her. "It doesn't matter. Ulric has always been a difficult topic for him to talk to anyone about. He should hear it from me." King Felix's expression softened, the hard lines around his mouth, eyes, and along his forehead smoothing slightly as he smiled down at us. "Besides, soon I'll be passing the crown to you and all the many burdens that come along with it. It would be my honor to carry this burden for you."

I swallowed hard. I'd had a lot of visits from Jenna and Aubren while I was recovering. But King Felix, my father, had only come to see me once. I was pretty sure it wasn't because he didn't care about me, though. It seemed more like ... he didn't know where to begin. I didn't either. We were strangers. And even as he'd sat at my bedside and told me about my birth and how he'd voluntarily given me over to Kiran for safekeeping because of my dark birthright, I could hear the guilt and sadness in his voice.

I could see it in the depths of his eyes now, too.

My father hadn't thrown me away like garbage. He'd given me away to the only person he believed he could trust to watch over me because he hadn't believed he could keep me safe. As much as I wanted to be angry and hold a grudge for being passed off like that ... I had to admit, it was probably the right thing to do.

The only issue now was figuring out how to pick up the pieces of our shattered lives and use them to patch together something good. I had to figure out how to be a Prince of Maldobar. And he had to figure out how to be my father. Easier said than done. I'd yet to really talk to him about how I felt. We still didn't know each other, and every encounter seemed more painfully awkward than the last.

"It'll be dark soon." King Felix cleared his throat and flicked a quick glance between us. "I ... thought maybe we could have a meal together. All of us. Like a proper family. Seems long overdue, doesn't it?"

Jenna and I exchanged a look. She let out a breathless laugh, tears still in her eyes as she smiled. My heart thumped sloppily as I tried to find the words. That sounded ... amazing.

"I think that would be wonderful." Jenna smirked as she brushed past our father, grinning at him tauntingly on her way back toward the castle. "Will dear Uncle Jae be joining us, as well?"

King Felix let out a deep, cackling laugh that almost made me jump out of my boots. "Of course! How else am I going to show off the newly-embroidered table runner and matching painted plate chargers? I'm sure he's going to *love* the designs I chose."

Jenna joined in, giggling all the way back into the castle. I gave Vexi a parting scratch under her chin and followed along behind her. King Felix fell in step right beside me, planting one of his large hands on my shoulder. My heart wrenched deep in my chest, torn somewhere between a nervous breakdown and pure, unbridled joy. I stole a glance up at my father's face, jolting a little when I found him staring right at me again.

"Everything all right?" he asked.

"I was just thinking," I murmured in reply, half hoping Jenna wouldn't hear. "I'm ready to have that talk you mentioned."

His heavy brows rose. "Oh?"

"Yeah, well, if I'm going to hang around here, then I should probably get to know you better." I shrugged, trying to play it off like I was indifferent. I guess he knew better. Maybe an inability to make a convincing bluff was one of the things I'd inherited from him.

"Very well, Son," he chuckled as he ruffled my hair. "We'll talk after dinner."

I couldn't resist a smirk. "Sounds good, Father."

CHAPTER THIRTY

"I-I can't breathe," Jaevid wheezed as he paced back and forth, tromping through the sand. "What if she doesn't come? What if she changes her mind? It's been a long time, hasn't it? Things are so different now. I-I'm not even sure I'm the same. If she changes her mind, then—"

"Calm down," King Felix sighed as he drummed his fingers and leaned against the wooden podium set up right in front of the shoreline. "She loves you. Of course she's coming; don't be ridiculous. And stop pacing like that. You'll wear a trench in the aisle."

Jaevid stopped next to me but didn't stay still. Dressed in a formal dragonrider uniform, complete with a silver ornamental breastplate and matching vambraces polished to sparkling perfection, Jaevid shifted his weight from one foot to another. He fidgeted with the embroidered collar of his tunic and the fingers of his black velvet gloves, occasionally flashing me a wild-eyed look like he might run screaming down the beach at any moment.

"Maybe three months wasn't enough time," he muttered under his breath. "I should have given her longer to adjust. There's so much she—we—don't know. The house isn't even finished yet. I should have insisted on waiting until after Jenna's coronation."

My father groaned and rolled his eyes. "You're hopeless."

I couldn't dispute that, although Jaevid was right on a few counts, too. The past three months had flown by, packed with a mixture of memorials and celebrations that made everything sort of run together. Jenna was set to take the throne as Queen of Maldobar soon, although she had our father's assurance she wouldn't be tossed to the wolves and left to scramble on her own. He was still going to help and advise. Well, as much as she allowed him to, anyway.

Even with extra help, I didn't envy her whatsoever. The idea of wearing the crown was terrifying on its own. Pair that with the prospect of trying to put all the broken pieces back together—not only of our kingdom, but also the dozens of others that were now in shambles thanks to the conquest of the Tibran Empire—and you were left with a mountain of problems and responsibilities that looked insurmountable. Jenna had her work cut out for her. But if I had to bet on who could pull it off, I would have put all my money on her.

For now, we had a small break in our chaotic schedule—a quick moment to breathe. Standing on the beaches of Saltmarsh, I watched the dragons chasing one another through the waves and wondered if this was the first time so many had been welcomed in attendance to a wedding—as guests instead of an accessory or honor guard. Vexi and Phevos yipped and chattered, darting over the surface of the rolling ocean. Nearby, Turq and Perish dove down to snag fish from the sandy bottom.

Only Mavrik was lounging on the beach, a mountain of blue and black scales, sleeping while he basked in the sun. Next to him, a foundling spirit named Pasci was also reclining in the warm sand, preening her brightly colored feathers. She seemed particularly fond of my father, who confessed he'd taken a liking to her after the Gray War. She came and went as she pleased but could usually be found snoozing in the rose bushes outside his private courtyard. She'd made a few trips back to the wild jungle of Luntharda, of course—most recently to answer Princess Hecate's call to arms.

According to Aubren, Hecate's role as the Akrotis had allowed her the ability to speak to foundling spirits. She'd rallied many of them to join the fight, including Pasci. But now, thanks to Jaevid's bargain, none of us had to worry about divine gifts any more. Hecate was free, too.

The dragons and spirits weren't Jaevid's strangest guests, though, just the largest. Phillip towered over everyone by at least a foot. He looked ... a little *different* from the last time I'd seen him at Barrowton. Jaevid had explained the basics of what had happened to me, and while Phillip was terrifying to look at, with his beastly features and eerie silver eyes, his personality seemed pretty much the same. It still spooked a lot of the servants and staff around the castle. Fortunately, his bizarre appearance hadn't done anything to slow him down in the romance department because he and Jenna were practically inseparable. I wasn't sure how that had happened. The last time I'd heard anything about them was at Barrowton before the siege and from what Phillip had said, it sounded hopeless for him.

Now, the only thing hopeless about that situation was the hopelessly mushy way they looked at one another while they walked the halls holding hands. Our father had already given his blessing for Phillip to officially court her, but I had a feeling it was going to be the world's shortest courtship ever. He'd probably already acquired a ring and was just waiting for the right moment to propose.

Phillip stood alongside Haldor, Roland, and me at the front of the gathering as part of Jaevid's patron court, waiting for the ceremony to begin. Human weddings were already proving to be a much more complicated and formal affair than Gray elf ones. Jaevid had insisted on keeping it "small," which wound up being around two hundred and fifty guests. I guess it added up quickly with so many extended relatives and new friends to account for. I was still struggling to learn all their names, but a few were easy to pick out.

King Jace and Queen Araxie stood alongside Hecate, beaming with pride. They'd also brought along their own sons, the three princes of Luntharda, with their spouses. Aubren and Jenna stood together, each holding a squirming baby—some of Jaevid's great-nieces and great-nephews, most likely, since Roland had brought his *entire* family. Next to them, Miri and Eirik were a couple I'd only met a few weeks ago, although Eirik looked somewhat familiar. Maybe I'd seen him in passing at Barrowton? I couldn't remember. Aedan was next to them, and he gave me a broad smile and nod when our eyes met. I still owed him one for getting us into Northwatch to save Jenna.

There might have been more people I knew, but before I could scour the audience for more familiar faces, King Felix straightened and cleared his throat, nodding further up the beach. Right away, Phillip bowed to the crowd and stepped away with a secretive smile, his strange feet leaving paw-like impressions in the sand. When he returned, he was leading Beckah by the arm.

The sight of her made Jaevid suck in a sharp breath. He stood stiff, eyes as wide as saucers, while his face and pointed ears blushed bright red. I was a little concerned he might've stopped breathing until I saw him let out a long, shaky exhale of relief. He blinked rapidly, eyes watering and hands shaking at his sides as he watched her approach as though he were counting down every step that brought them closer.

Beckah was radiant in a simple white gown that dragged along the sand behind her. The corset bodice fit her slender frame elegantly, and her dark hair had been woven into an intricate crown of braids dotted with pearls and tiny white flowers. Behind her, two older ladies wore crowns of flowers and carried baskets of flower petals, sprinkling them in her wake. Judging by their dark hair and green eyes, I decided they must be her sisters. It was beyond strange to think that they were actually her *little* sisters, even though they looked about forty years older—chalk that up to divine happenstance.

Phillip escorted Beckah to Jaevid's side, passing her arm over to him with a quick kiss on her cheek. He looked a little misty-eyed too when he came back to stand next to me. I bit back a smile and passed him the handkerchief from my pocket. He immediately wiped his eyes and blew his nose into it. Gross. He could keep it.

"As many of you know, the ceremony of marriage is one held in highest esteem among dragonriders," my father began to speak over the rush and roar of the surf. "Today, I'm honored to be performing this sacred rite, not only because it will be one of the final acts of my reign as King of Maldobar, but because, as many of you know, these two have ... incredible significance to me. They're more than friends. They're more than legends. They're family."

In the crowd, Araxie was already crying against her husband's shoulder, and the pudgy little baby squirming in Jenna's arms let out a coo of delight. They were wonderful sounds, though. Those were the sounds of family—of the people that loved them.

My heart ached, carried far away for a moment as I thought about Enyo. She was doing an excellent job looking after my clinic in Mau Kakuri, working her fingers to the bone so I could be here. I'd written her dozens of letters but had yet to actually steal enough time to fly back and visit. The distance put a knot in my chest I knew wouldn't go away until I was back on that doorstep, gazing into her beautiful, multihued eyes.

"When a Dragonrider of Maldobar marries, he offers his chosen bride a token—a gesture of his eternal vow. We call it a square-cloth, and it is a tradition passed down in our brotherhood since its founding," King Felix continued. "He cuts a small piece of the cloth from his cloak, the very same cloak given to him when he took his oath at the feet of the king and became a true dragonrider. He gives that square of cloth to his bride because it represents the piece of himself that stays behind with her whenever he must leave for battle."

Pausing, my father's expression tensed for a moment as he gripped the sides of the podium where he stood. Half a minute passed before he seemed able to go on, his tone heavy. "When she dies, that piece is placed in her hand and buried with her. Jaevid, I know your original cloak is lost. Gods only know where it wound up. But I still have mine. Hopefully you won't mind that's already missing one piece."

Reaching under the podium, my father took out a long, royal blue cloak. The length unfurled smoothly, brushing the ground as he tied it around Jaevid's shoulders. The neck had a plush mane of soft white fur, and a diamond-shaped hole was cut right below the neck on the left side. Drawing an ornamental dagger from his belt, King Felix cut another diamond of cloth out directly beneath it, and then placed it in Jaevid's hand with a smile.

Only when he stepped back behind the podium again, dabbing at his eyes and clearing his throat, did I realize why that was so significant. The other hole in that cloak, the one my father had mentioned, must have been from the square-cloth he'd given to my mother.

And she had been buried with it.

The rest of the ceremony went smoothly. They repeated a few vows, swearing by the Gods to remain faithful and to cherish one another until death. Jaevid placed the square-cloth on Beckah's palm, closing her fingers around it and pressing his lips to her knuckles. By the time they finally embraced for a kiss, there weren't many dry eyes left in the audience.

Everyone cheered and threw petals in the air, thronging around them with congratulations and well wishes. I found myself squished between a bunch of Jaevid's relatives as they rushed in from every side. It took some wrenching and squeezing before I managed to squeeze free of the crowd. My heels sank in the sand and I wobbled backward, tripping and smacking against someone's chest.

"Easy, there." Aubren grinned as he steadied me. "And here I thought a boy raised by elves would be used to a lively gathering."

I dusted off my tunic, and straightened my collar. "I am. But there's a lot more smooching and hugging going on around here than I'm used to. I gotta get out of here before anyone else tries to—"

He ruffled my hair. Ugh. I'd almost killed myself and helped save Maldobar, and still people kept petting me like I was a puppy. Aubren laughed off my scowl and nodded toward the beach. "You're not the only one plotting a stealthy escape." Somehow, Jaevid and Beckah had managed to slip away. They were walking the shoreline together, hand in hand, the waves lapping at their feet.

Once again, I found myself envying him and wishing I were somewhere else. "You think they'll be upset if I don't stick around for the reception?" I asked.

Aubren rubbed the back of his neck as he studied me out of the corner of his eye. "Got somewhere else to be?"

I chewed the inside of my cheek and looked down at the sand clumped on my boots. There was a fair amount scraping around inside them, as well. "More like someone else I'd rather have doing all the kissing and hugging," I admitted quietly. "Not the petting, though. That's got to stop. Seriously, I'm gonna start biting people."

He smiled and gave me a nudge with his elbow. "Give it the rest of the night. It's a long journey back to Luntharda from here. No sense in making it on no sleep and an empty stomach."

"True," I conceded and nudged him back. "It would be a shame to miss out on free cake."

"Not to mention the gifts," he added, his tone ominous. "Just wait until you see what Father has done."

CHAPTER THIRTY-ONE

King Felix gave them a house.

I should say a chateau, I suppose, because the drawing of it he presented to the happy couple was extravagant to say the least. It was one of the few that had survived Tibran occupation and only needed minor repairs.

"It's been in the family for years," he explained as he passed Jaevid the document bearing the official royal seal. "My mother used it as a summer home. It's been empty for so long—seems only fitting someone make some good memories there. And since I did legally adopt you into the family all those years ago, no one can argue that it isn't staying under the Farrow name."

Jaevid was frozen, his mouth hanging open in shock, while everyone gathered around to get a good look. It was no secret Jaevid had been working on his own "house" the past few weeks—a small cottage somewhere in Mithangol. This was about fifty times bigger and came with tracts of wide-open land that bordered the coast just outside Eastwatch, deep in wild dragon territory.

"Felix, this is too much," he managed hoarsely.

Father waved a hand and snorted. "Don't start with that nonsense. You've saved Maldobar twice. You're just lucky I don't wrestle you onto the throne to take my place."

"You can thank me for talking him out of that." Jenna leaned over to nudge him with her elbow. "No way was I going to let him pass this mess off to you."

Jaevid's shoulders sagged, his expression drooping with genuine relief. "T-thank you."

"Oh, don't thank me yet," Jenna added with a laugh. "I plan on enlisting your *veteran* expertise for advice whenever I need it, Commander. There is a lot of work to be done fixing what Argonox destroyed."

Everyone got a good chuckle out of that. Well, except for Jaevid. He was scowling at her with his mouth scrunched and his face flushed several shades of red. He'd dodged the crown, yes, but my father wasn't going to let him sail into the sunset worry-free. The title of Academy Commander might take him some time to get used to, though.

While Jaevid and Beckah stood close together, taking well wishes and compliments from their guests, the great hall filled with the sounds of laughter, music, and excited conversation. According to Jenna, Haldor's family had insisted on hosting the reception banquet at their home. They were renowned merchants who owned a fleet of trading ships that came in and out of the port at Saltmarsh. Their home wasn't enormous, and it had suffered some Tibran abuse, but it was packed full of exotic curiosities from all over the world. Their great hall was large enough to host a great, albeit cozy, reception, and had been decorated with wreaths of flowers and colorful ribbons.

Inviting aromas floated from long buffet tables lined with fancy cakes, pastries, and pies of every flavor imaginable. I guess Jaevid had a special passion for pie, because every time I spotted him through the crowd ,he had a new piece on his plate. Not that I was going to judge. I couldn't resist stealing a slice of flaky, buttery, peach-and-cinnamon-packed goodness, either.

I was still licking the sugary juices off my fingers as I wandered through the hall. Servants stood by the corners of the room offering refills from bottles of bubbling ginger and fruit ciders. Queen Araxie had also brought along quite a few bottles of sweet wine—a Gray elf delicacy—for everyone to share.

After the feasting came the dancing, and I drifted to the back of the room close to the door. I still hadn't quite gotten the knack of human-styled dancing, but it was still fun to watch. Couples twirled under the warm candlelight, clapping and dancing to the rhythm of the music. Girls dashed by in groups, giggling and tying ribbons around their wrists and in their hair. Every now and then, one would stop to ask me if I wanted to dance and I stumbled through an awkward explanation of why I didn't know how. That wasn't the *real* reason, of course. There was only one person I wanted to dance with ... and she was miles away from here.

Everyone cleared the dance floor when Jaevid and Beckah began to waltz to a gentle tune. From where I lurked the doorway, I watched them glide past with their expressions the picture of total infatuation. It was the kind of happiness you could almost taste, like the subtle hint of honeysuckle floating on the summer breeze outside.

Jealousy twisted in my chest, squeezing at my heart. I had to look away. My mind knew three months wasn't that long, but my heart begged to differ. I wanted to go home.

I wanted to see Enyo.

While everyone was still transfixed by Jaevid and Beckah's wedding dance, I slipped out the door and into the night. The night wind carried the stalky, fishy scent of the harbor nearby. The tall masts of the ships groaning and swaying at their moorings barely peeked over the rooftops as I made the short walk back out to the beach.

Vexi was waiting there, preening her bright green scales, and nuzzling along Mavrik's side like a kitten craving attention from an older, much more dangerous cat. As soon as I called her name, she perked up. Little ears swiveled in my direction and she let out a screech, swooping over the sand and landing so close it sent a spray of sand all over me.

Great.

"Are you kidding me? Now I'll be itching all the way back to Luntharda," I grumbled as I tried to shake the sand out of my hair and blow it out of my nose.

"Leaving so soon?" someone asked. I tensed and slowly turned around. Jaevid stood behind me with his arms crossed and a strange, almost wistful smile on his face. "Still not an animal fan, I take it?"

Vexi lowered her head right next to mine and puffed heavy dragon-breaths right in my ear. "Not really. This one is growing on me, though." I gave her chin a scratch and she purred.

"They do that." His smile widened. "So, you were planning on running away? Without even saying goodbye?"

"I, uh, well, um ... " I couldn't come up with a good excuse—other than the truth, anyway. "So much has happened. I need to go back. I need to see her again."

The wind tousled his ash-colored hair as Jaevid gazed out at the ocean.

"I will come back," I clarified quickly. "I know I've got responsibilities here."

"Like attending dragonrider training at Blybrig Academy?"

I hesitated as my thoughts blurred through the realization of what that meant. Now that I'd seen first-hand what it truly meant to be counted as one of them, and what that might mean for me in the future, I could appreciate what that meant. Jenna had been right—being a dragonrider wasn't something to take lightly. It wasn't just zipping around in flashy armor, drinking in the envy and admiration of everyone in the kingdom. There was a legacy in their name, a tapestry stitched by the lives of hundreds of men who had taken that oath.

But was I ready to be a part of that?

The answer rose up in my chest, blazing like a raging firestorm. "Yes."

"I won't go easy on you," Jaevid warned with a smirk. "Prince, Harbinger, and all that aside—you'll be just another fledgling."

I shot him my best challenging grin. "I wouldn't have it any other way, Commander."

"Good."

"Still friends though, right?" I just had to check.

"Of course."

The rumble, boom, and hiss of the surf filled the silence as Jaevid and I stared at one another. The light of the moon glinted over his polished breastplate, putting shadows of bold relief over the design engraved across his chest: the head of a stag. An interesting choice for dragonrider armor, considering that was the symbol of Gray elf royalty. But then again, he was an interesting guy. And, hey, it did match his scimitar.

"So, it's really over? No more lurking dead twins or whispering goddesses for me?" I rubbed the back of my neck and found a few more bits of sand stuck inside my shirt collar.

He glanced toward the heavens and the millions of twinkling stars. "That was the agreement. They get to walk the mortal realm again, and we don't have to carry their essence as our burden anymore. No more harbingers, lapiloques, akrotis, or otherwise will be necessary."

I couldn't resist a smile. "That's good news."

"Hopefully," he agreed.

"I never thanked you for helping with Noh—and, well, for everything else."

Jaevid tensed and met my gaze with his brows knitted. "Reigh, you should know, I ... when you get back to Luntharda you might ... " His mouth hung open, as though he were going to finish that thought, and then suddenly snapped shut. He shook his head. "Never mind."

I raised an eyebrow. "Isn't there a big party you're supposed to be at? Something to do with a pretty girl in a white dress?"

He laughed and waved a hand. "Have a good trip, Reigh. We'll see each other again soon."

I stood alone on the sand, watching Jaevid disappear back into the dark city streets with his long blue cloak fluttering at his boot heels. Beside me, Vexi let out an anxious chirp. I couldn't agree more—it was time to get going.

My chest tingled with excitement as I climbed into the brand-new saddle fixed to her back. The dark chestnut leather was oiled to perfection and the brass saddle handles shone like gold in the moonlight. Slipping my feet down into the deep, boot-shaped compartments on either side, I strapped the securing harness around my waist and gave her neck a pat. More and more, we'd been practicing learning how to fly together and to communicate in the air. Now, sitting in that saddle while she flared her wings for takeoff felt as natural as breathing.

I loved every second of it.

We charged skyward as one, veering over the city and harbor before we set our noses to the wind. Luntharda was a long flight away. We'd probably have to stop to rest somewhere in the Farchase Plains. But every long hour in the cold wind with my rear end sore from the saddle would be worth it. Luntharda was home—and half my heart was already there.

VEXI TOUCHED DOWN AT THE BOUNDARY LINE BETWEEN MALDOBAR AND Luntharda in a few graceful wing beats. Tired, hungry, and sore from flight, we both groaned in unison as I climbed out of the saddle. I stretched my back and shoulders while she did the same. My knees creaked and ached as I walked around her, unloading the rest of my gear from the saddle. There wasn't much, just my kafki and a bag of supplies and personal items. I didn't need much else.

Now came the hard part.

"Okay, Vexi, we went over this. Jaevid went over it. Mavrik, too. So, no fits this time, all right?" I warned as ran a hand down her snout. "I'm coming back, I promise."

She narrowed her sky-blue eyes, nostrils puffing in an irritated snort.

"Think of this as a vacation for you, too. Go back home and visit the family. Tell them all about the scrawny kid you're about to drag through the most brutal training in the kingdom."

Vexi swiped the side of my head with her tongue, leaving a foul-smelling, sticky trail behind.

"Yuck! Come on!" I wiped the side of my head, only to wind up having to peel my sleeve off my face when it stuck to her spit.

Lowering her head again, my green dragoness bumped her nose against my chest. I ran my fingers along the horns on her head, scratching behind her ears, and brushing over the places where the muzzle Argonox had put on her left scars in her hide. The sight of them threatened to take me back there, a flash of dark memory that could yank me under at any moment.

I clenched my teeth and looked away, but not before giving her chin one last scratch. "I'll see you soon, pretty lady," I promised.

She yipped and sprang backward, leaping into the sky with a rush of wind that nearly knocked me on my back. With a flash of green scales, Vexi spiraled out of sight, heading straight for the eastern coastline where her wild kin lived. After watching her at Saltmarsh, it was easy to imagine her there, dancing over the waves and grooming herself on the ledges of the steep cliffs. She'd get to enjoy a few weeks of freedom before we had to return to Halfax for Jenna's coronation.

Right now, however, all I could think about was making it to Mau Kakuri. There was still at least a two-day journey for me to reach it through the jungle. I wasn't about to wait a single minute to start.

I found an encampment of scouts less than a mile inside the jungle boundary.

Fighting in the Tibran War and being the Harbinger of Clysiros had earned me a little distinction amongst the Gray elves—or at least, enough that they let me borrow a shrike, so I could make good time getting back to Mau Kakuri. Zipping through the vivid green maze of the jungle, past the towering giant trees with their interwoven branches, massive fern fronds, vibrant flowers, and wandering banks of fog, I drank in all the familiar smells of home. Every breath of the moist, cool air felt like taking in a healing elixir. And yet, the closer I got to the city, the faster my heart raced. I couldn't sit still. My sweaty hands squeezed and wrenched on the saddle.

Suddenly, the thick jungle greenery opened to a rocky, moss-covered valley, where towering waterfalls spilled down the side of a steep cliff, pooling and filling the narrow canals that flowed all through the city. The falls filled the air with fine mist that hung and sparkled like diamonds. It was like I'd never left.

I urged the shrike to land, touching down right at the city gates. All around the square, shopkeepers were just beginning to open for the day. Merchants unfurled their carpets and opened their stands. Bakers and blacksmiths lit their fires. Shepherds and faundra breeders guided herds along the cobblestone streets.

As much as I would have enjoyed standing there to drink in every detail of this place I had missed, there was somewhere I had to be.

I coaxed the shrike onward at a casual speed, buzzing down the market district where the clinic stood. We landed at the base of the front steps, and for a moment, all I could do was sit there with my heart hammering in the back of my throat. I was home.

I tripped twice scrambling down from the saddle and totally forgot to tie the shrike, so he didn't wander off. It didn't matter. I had to get to that door. *Now.*

Running up the steps, I screeched to a halt with my hand hovering over the knob. My heart hammered in my ears like war drums. Wait—should I knock? It was my house, right? But I'd been gone for so long. Maybe I should, just in case Enyo—

The door swung open.

The old, stiff-looking Gray elf man standing on the other side didn't say a word at first. His multihued eyes studied me from head to foot, mouth set in a hard line, as though he were looking for obvious signs of damage. His brow furrowed deeply in parental disapproval.

I couldn't take offense, though.

Kiran looked at everyone that way.

My heart stopped. All the wind rushed out of my lungs as I trembled in front of him, too stunned to make a sound. Tears welled in my eyes until I couldn't see him anymore. My chest heaved, bursting with emotion I barely understood. A strangled sound tore out of my chest—something between a scream and a sob.

It wasn't possible. It couldn't be. How? When?

"Enyo," Kiran called back over his shoulder. "He's here. Better draw a bath. He smells awful."

"K-Kiran," I managed to croak through wheezing gasps.

A corner of his mouth lifted, curling into a familiar half-smile. "Jaevid sends his regards."

That sneaky ... secret keeping ... JERK!

I lunged forward, grabbing Kiran and squeezing my arms around his neck in a rough hug. I half expected to find nothing but empty air—that this entire moment was nothing but a hopeful dream. But it wasn't.

Kiran put his arms around me and laughed, holding me tight as he patted the back of my head. "It's all right, Reigh."

Behind him, I spotted Enyo leaning around the corner from the sitting room. Her eyes crinkled with a broad smile as she wiped a tear from her cheek. She'd been keeping this from me, too. I'd have to think of a good way to get revenge later. For now, I burned my face in his shoulder and tried to catch my breath. Every inhale filled my nose with his smell—the scent of the herbs he used for medicines and damp jungle soil. It was the same smell I'd known since childhood.

"I'm so sorry," I blurted. "Kiran, I-I—"

"There's nothing to be sorry for," he said as he stepped back, motioning for me to come inside. "But I wasn't joking about the bath. Don't sit on anything until you've washed." He leaned in to give my head a sniff, then cringed back and made a face. "Is that ... dragon spit?"

I flushed. "I-it's a long story."

He and Enyo exchanged a knowing smile. "I look forward to hearing it, then. Welcome home, Reigh."

WANT MORE DRAGONRIDERS?

Continue the adventure with the
#1 international bestselling series:

THE DRAGONRIDER HERITAGE

Available in ebook, paperback, and audiobook from Amazon.com

ABOUT THE AUTHOR

Nicole Conway is a graduate of Auburn University with a lifelong passion for writing teen and children's literature. With over 100,000 books sold in her DRAGONRIDER CHRONICLES series, Nicole has been ranked one of Amazon's Top 100 Teen Authors. A coffee and Netflix addict, she also enjoys spending time with her family, rock climbing, and traveling.

Nicole is represented by Frances Black of Literary Counsel.